Praise for these nationally bestselling authors:

Jayne Ann Krentz

"A master of the genre..."
—*Romantic Times*

"Who writes the best romance fiction today?
No doubt it's Jayne Ann Krentz."
—*Affaire de Coeur*

Diana Palmer

"Nobody does it better!"
—*New York Times* bestselling author
Linda Howard

"No one, absolutely no one,
beats this author for sensual anticipation."
—*Rave Reviews*

Debbie Macomber

"Debbie Macomber can always be counted on
for first-class entertainment..."
—*Affaire de Coeur*

"I've never met a Macomber book I didn't love!"
—Linda Lael Miller

Author Bio

Jayne Ann Krentz

One of today's top contemporary romance writers, Jayne Ann Krentz has an astounding twelve million copies of her books in print. Her novels regularly appear on the *New York Times,* Waldenbooks and B. Dalton bestseller lists. First published in 1979, Jayne quickly established herself as a prolific and innovative writer. She has delved into psychic elements, intrigue, fantasy, historicals and even futuristic romances. Jayne lives in Seattle with her husband, Frank, an engineer, and her bird, Ferd, whom she modestly refers to as "a truly brilliant budgie."

Diana Palmer

A prolific writer of women's fiction, Diana Palmer got her start as a newspaper reporter. As one of the top-ten romance writers in America, she has a gift for telling the most sensual tales with charm and humor. Her readers have grown to treasure her emotional style. This popular author has over ten million copies of her books in print, and is the recipient of eleven national bestseller awards and numerous readers' choice awards.

Debbie Macomber

Debbie Macomber has always enjoyed telling stories— first to her baby-sitting clients and then to her own four children. As a full-time wife and mother and an avid romance reader, she dreamed of one day sharing her stories with a wider audience. In the autumn of 1982, she sold her first book, and that was only the beginning. Debbie has been making regular appearances on the *USA Today* bestseller list—not surprising, considering that there are over forty million copies of her books in print worldwide!

Jayne Ann Krentz

Diana Palmer

Debbie Macomber

The Power of Love

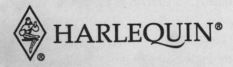

HARLEQUIN®

TORONTO • NEW YORK • LONDON
AMSTERDAM • PARIS • SYDNEY • HAMBURG
STOCKHOLM • ATHENS • TOKYO • MILAN • MADRID
PRAGUE • WARSAW • BUDAPEST • AUCKLAND

HARLEQUIN BOOKS
225 Duncan Mill Road, Don Mills,
Ontario, Canada M3B 3K9

ISBN 0-373-83399-7

THE POWER OF LOVE

Printed in U.S.A.

The Waiting Game
by Jayne Ann Krentz

For Ann Maxwell,
who understands the fantasy

Chapter One

Sara Frazer paused in the act of searching Adrian Saville's desk and told herself for the hundredth time that what she was doing was illegal and potentially dangerous. And while she had her faults, as her family had only recently pointed out to her in some detail, she had never, until that moment, sunk to the level of doing something of this nature.

But Sara was concerned, worried, anxious and more than a little suspicious of the stranger whose study she was going through with such haste. Besides, she told herself with her customary impulsive enthusiasm, the opportunity had been too good to let pass. The door to Saville's isolated home had not been locked when she had arrived twenty minutes earlier. And she had, after all, no intention of stealing anything. She just needed some answers.

Impatiently Sara scanned the room as she closed the drawer of the desk. The study was a clean-lined, orderly room. It was a quiet, solid, masculine room, and she couldn't help wondering how accurately it reflected its owner. Hardwood floors, simple, substantial furniture and a great deal of shelving were the main features. If the den did mirror its owner with any degree of accuracy, she would be in trouble should Saville happen to walk in the door. Something about the place seemed to resist and resent her intrusion.

A greenhouse window that overlooked the cold, dark water of Puget Sound provided the main source of light. Dusk was settling in on Bainbridge Island, where Adrian Saville made his home, and across the expanse of water the lights of Seattle began sinking into life. Sara didn't dare turn on a lamp for fear of alerting a neighbor to her presence. The house was tucked away by itself amid a stand of fir and pine, but one never knew who might pass by on the road outside. It was late summer and she ought to have enough fading twilight to get her through the rest of the search.

She was turning away from the desk, intent on exploring the bookshelves, when she noticed the apple. Startled, Sara reached out to pick it up. In that moment she was forced to acknowledge that she might have been mistaken in her suspicions of Adrian Saville. After all, she had an apple just like this one and there was only one person who could have given it to Saville.

Sara held the object up to the fading light and studied it intently. It was not just any apple, of course. It was fashioned of heavy crystal, and the stem with its leaf was of intricately worked gold. The person who had made a gift of the apple believed in substantial things such as gold, Sara knew. Small bubbles had been captured inside the apple by the artist. They reflected the light in an intriguing manner, making anyone who held the object want to examine it more intently.

All in all, it was a very attractive paperweight, and the fact that it sat on Adrian Saville's desk put a whole new light on the situation. Sara stood still, turning the apple so that the crystal caught the light, and wondered what she was going to do next.

"Offer me a bite."

The deep, graveled voice came from the doorway. Sara chilled for an instant as fear and embarrassment washed through her. She nearly dropped the crystal apple as she spun around to face the man who was lounging calmly against the doorjamb. Frantically she struggled for self-control and a reasonable explanation of her presence in his study. Unfortunately the situation did not do wonders for her presence of mind. Sara found herself wishing very badly that she had never succumbed to the temptation his empty house had provided.

"I'm sorry," she managed, stumbling over the words. Vaguely she realized that her hands were trembling. "I didn't hear anyone. I mean, there was no one at home when I arrived, and the door was unlocked. I had no business wandering in to wait for you, but it seemed pointless to sit outside in the car and I—" She broke off abruptly as something occurred to her. "You are Adrian Saville, aren't you?"

Eyes that were either unusually colorless or else were washed of color by a trick of the dim light swept curiously over her. Sara had the feeling that the stranger had taken in every detail in that brief glance.

"If I'm not Adrian Saville, this situation is going to get even more complicated, isn't it?" he noted softly.

Sara's fingers tightened on the paperweight as she forced herself to sound reasonably cool and collected. "It would mean that there are two intruders in Mr. Saville's home instead of just one. Yes, I would say that would complicate things. But I don't think that's the case. You are Adrian Saville."

Arms folded across his chest, the man regarded her with mild interest. "What makes you so sure?"

"You're leaning much too casually in that doorway, for one thing," Sara retorted. Whatever he was thinking, he didn't seem intent on doing her any immediate harm. Actually, he really didn't look like the sort of man who would harm someone unless greatly provoked. The fear died away, leaving only the embarrassment. "Look, I can explain this, Mr. Saville."

"I can't wait to hear the explanation."

Sara felt the warm flush paint the line of her cheekbones. Carefully she set the crystal apple back down on his desk. It was a relief to have an excuse to look away from that strangely colorless gaze. "Then you're going to acknowledge your name, at least?"

"Why not? This is my home. I might as well use my name," he murmured easily.

"I'm Sara Frazer," she said quietly, turning her head to meet his eyes once more. "Lowell Kincaid's niece. I have a paperweight just like this one at home."

"I see."

She hadn't expected the silence that followed. It made her feel uneasy and awkward. Hurriedly she tried to fill it with further explanations. "I came looking for you because I couldn't locate Uncle Lowell. I just arrived from his place in the mountains late this afternoon. I caught the ferry here to the island and by the time I found your house it was getting quite late. There was no answer when I knocked on your door, and when I tried it, it was unlocked. I'm afraid I just came on in to wait for you," she concluded with a tentative smile.

"And wound up searching my study as a means of passing the time?" He didn't return her smile but he didn't seem unduly upset.

Sara took a deep breath. "I happened to notice the paperweight," she lied politely. "It really is just like the one I have. Uncle Lowell gave it to me a few months ago. I assume he gave you this one?"

"Umm."

Sara decided the noncommittal sound was an affirmative. "They're quite beautiful, aren't they? I have mine on my desk at home."

He ignored her determined chattiness. "What were you looking for, Sara?"

Something about the calm manner in which he asked the question convinced her that Adrian Saville wasn't going to accept her explanation of why she happened to be in his study. Sara exhaled slowly, considering her options. This might be a clear-cut case of honesty being the best policy, she decided ruefully. Folding her arms across her small breasts in a subtle mockery of his own stance, she leaned back and propped herself against the edge of the desk. She met his gaze with a level one of her own.

"I was looking for something."

He nodded as if it were the most natural thing in the world. "For what?"

She shrugged. "That's the problem. I don't know. Anything that might give me a clue about where my uncle is."

Adrian continued to regard her with solemn interest for another long moment. This time Sara resisted the impulse to fill the silent void with attempts at explanations. She could be just as remote and laconic as Adrian Saville could, she promised herself.

"What makes you think I might have some answers for you?"

"I'm not sure you do. But Uncle Lowell once told me that if anything ever happened to him, I was to notify you. He gave me your address several months ago, shortly before he sent the apple, in fact."

"And you think something has happened to Lowell?"

"I don't know," Sara admitted. "I only know that he's not at his home up in the mountains."

"Perhaps he's taken a short trip. Was he expecting you?"

Sara swallowed uneasily. "Well, no. I just showed up on his doorstep unannounced, I'm afraid. I did try to call but all I got was his answering machine."

"Then why the concern?" Adrian pressed quietly.

Sara looked at him searchingly. "How well do you know my uncle?"

"Well enough."

Not much to go on, but she might as well see what happened when she told him the reason for her concern. "His neighbor said he went hunting."

Adrian Saville greeted that bit of information with more silence. Then he straightened away from the door. "Have you had dinner, Sara?"

Sara frowned as he turned away and started down the hall. "Wait a minute! Don't you understand?" she demanded, hurrying after him. She caught up with him just as he rounded the corner and walked into the small, rather old-fashioned kitchen. "They said he went *hunting*."

"And Lowell Kincaid doesn't go in for blood sports. Yes, I understand." Adrian opened the refrigerator door, examining the contents with a wary eye.

"It's because of his old job," Sara said quickly. "Before he retired he worked in a rather violent world, you see."

"He worked for the government, you mean." Adrian finally decided on a plastic-wrapped chunk of cheese. He removed it from the refrigerator and set it on the counter. Then he opened a cupboard and reached for a box of crackers. "I know what your uncle used to do for a living, Sara."

She blinked, watching him carefully. "Oh."

"You didn't answer my question. Did you have any dinner?" Adrian began slicing cheese with smooth, methodical strokes of a knife.

"Uh, no, I haven't had time," Sara said vaguely. Her mind was on other things and had been all afternoon.

"Neither have I. Cheese and crackers and some vegetables okay?"

"Look, Adrian...Mr. Saville...I'm really not very hungry. I just came here to see if you knew anything about Uncle Lowell."

"And stayed to rifle my study." He nodded. "Sorry I can't offer anything more interesting. But it's kind of late in the evening to start something more elaborate. And I'm really not that good a cook in the first place."

"I didn't rifle your study!" Sara exploded, beginning to lose her patience. She didn't have a great deal of that commodity in the first place. Life was short enough as it was, she felt. What good was an excess of patience? "Now, about Uncle Lowell..."

"There's some wine in that cupboard next to the sink. Why don't you open a bottle while I slice up a few carrots and some broccoli?"

"But I don't want any wine!"

"I do." He glanced back at her over his shoulder, a faint smile playing at the corner of his mouth. "I'm celebrating, you see."

That stopped her. "Celebrating what?"

"The sale of my first novel."

Sara stared at him, astonished. "Are you really?"

"Umm."

Again she assumed the noncommittal sound was a yes answer. Her enthusiasm sprang up, as usual, out of nowhere and rushed into her voice. "Adrian, that's fantastic! Absolutely fantastic! A once-in-a-lifetime event. I can't believe it. I've never even met an author before."

"Neither have I," Adrian said dryly. He finished slicing the cheese and opened the refrigerator to pull out a handful of carrots. "Choose whichever bottle of wine you want."

A little bemused, Sara found herself obediently reaching into the cupboard and selecting a bottle of Oregon Pinot Noir. She'd heard the Northwest wine industry was starting to flourish but she hadn't yet had much experience with the products. They hadn't yet become chic in California. "You must be very excited."

He thought about that. "Well, it was a relief to make the sale," he began consideringly.

"A relief! Why, it's marvellous! Terrific! Thrilling! What's the matter with you? I should think you'd be doing handsprings or something."

"I imagine it's easier to get excited when there's someone else around to get excited with you," he murmured, arranging raw vegetables on a platter and putting a dollop of mayonnaise in the center. "I did go out and have a beer down at a local tavern. That's where I was when you arrived, in fact."

Sara poured the wine and handed him a glass. With a smile she raised her own glass in a grand salute. "Congratulations! And here's to nice, fat royalty checks." She sipped her Pinot Noir with attention. It was good. She made a mental note of the fact. There appeared to be a future in Northwest wines. Then she remembered belatedly that she didn't have to worry so much anymore about being on top of the latest culinary trends. "Too bad you can't tell Uncle Lowell. I'm sure he'd be very happy for you."

Adrian regarded her over the rim of his glass as he took a deep swallow. "Yes, I think he would be quite satisfied."

Sara smiled at him quizzically. "Did he know you were writing a book?"

"He knew."

"Then you really are a close friend of his?" she went on doggedly.

"Umm."

Sara shot him a narrow glance. "Can't you just say yes or no?"

"Sorry. Yes."

"Then you do realize that it was odd he would tell his neighbor he was going hunting?" she continued more seriously.

"Is that exactly what his neighbor said? That Lowell said he was going hunting?" Adrian picked up the platter of vegetables and led the way into the rustic living-room. He set the plate down on a low wood-and-brass table in front of the couch and went over to the old stone fireplace. Going down on one knee, he reached for a handful of kindling. Although it was still technically summer and the day had been sunny and warm, the first hint of the coming fall was in the air tonight.

Sara sat down in the corner of the worn black leather couch, studying the man in front of her. "That's what the woman who had the cabin near his said. Her exact words."

Adrian didn't respond, his attention on constructing the fire. Sara sipped her wine and continued to watch him. There was a certain fluidity to his movements that intrigued her. There was also a definite logical precision to the way he built the fire. A coordinated, controlled man. He was dressed in a pair of faded jeans and a black denim workshirt. The clothing molded a lean, tautly built body that seemed totally balanced. On his feet he wore a pair of dusty, soft-soled canvas sport shoes. Now that she had a moment to think about it, she decided the strange eyes were really a shade between blue and gray. In the right light they might appear as silver.

He was a friend of her uncle's and that took the nervousness out of contacting him, even if he had caught her going through the contents of his desk. Although he gave the impression of being easy-going and very friendly, Lowell Kincaid was actually quite cautious in his friendships. He had worked too long in a world where few people could be trusted. If he liked Adrian Saville, then Sara knew she, in turn, could trust the stranger in front of her. Her uncle had always been an excellent judge of people. Sometimes his life had depended on those judgments. The fact that he had survived and been able to retire at the normal age was evidence of just how accurate his analyses of other people had been over the years.

Adrian set a match to the kindling and the yellow flames leaped to life. He crouched for a moment in front of the fire, making certain it had caught properly, and the flickering light illuminated the hard line of his profile.

He was far from being a handsome man, Sara reflected. The planes and angles of his face had been carved with a dull knife, not finely chiseled. But there was a primitive strength in the aggressive nose and the austere cheekbones. He wasn't the kind of man who would smile easily; the grim set of his mouth wasn't shaped for such expressions. Sara guessed his age at somewhere between thirty-five and forty; probably closer to forty. She thought she saw something of the fundamental sureness and strength in him that her uncle must have seen before he decided to make Adrian a friend. Lowell Kincaid was sure of this man and therefore Sara knew she could be sure of him, too. She relaxed even more and took another sip of her wine. She sensed she had done the right thing by seeking out Adrian Saville.

She just wished he'd show a little more interest in her concern for her uncle. But then, a man who had just sold his first book probably had a right to be thinking of other things at the moment.

"What's it called?" she asked as he got to his feet and paced back to the couch.

"My novel?" He seemed to have no trouble following her abrupt shift in the conversation. Adrian picked up a cracker with cheese on it and downed the whole thing in one gulp. *"Phantom."*

"Is it a horror tale?"

He shook his head slowly, his eyes on the fire. "Not in the sense you mean. It's what's called a thriller."

"Ah, secret things, espionage, plots and counterplots. That sort of thing. I read a lot of thrillers." She smiled. "Are you writing under your own name?"

"I'm writing under the name Adrian Saville."

"Good, then I won't have to jot down your pseudonym. You'll have to autograph a copy of your book for me when it's published. I'm sure Uncle Lowell will want one, too."

"Lowell's already seen the manuscript," Adrian said quietly. "Because of his, uh, background, I thought he might be able to give me a few ideas that would make *Phantom* sound more authentic."

"Did he?"

"Umm." Adrian stared into the fire. "He was very helpful. You're really worried about him, aren't you?"

Sara resisted the temptation to say "umm." "Yes. My uncle doesn't hunt. He doesn't even like to fish. Why would he tell his neighbor he was going hunting and then drop out of sight?"

"Beats me." Adrian swirled the wine in his glass. "But don't you think you may be overreacting? You should know your uncle can take care of himself."

"He's in his late sixties now, Adrian. And he's been out of the industry a long time."

Something close to amusement gleamed briefly in Adrian's eyes. "The industry? You sound like an insider. Lowell uses words like that."

Mildly embarrassed, Sara's mouth turned down wryly. "That's how he always referred to his government work. I guess I picked up the term."

"And some of the skills?" he asked too blandly.

She looked away, reaching for a carrot. Sara knew he was referring to the fact that he had found her prowling around his study. "Obviously I didn't pick up the skills. If I had, you would never have caught me the way you did this evening. How did you sneak up on me so quietly, anyway? Must be those sneakers you're wearing. But I was certain I'd hear any car pulling into the drive."

"I walked back from the tavern. The car is still in the garage behind the house."

"Oh." Chagrined, Sara chewed industriously on her carrot.

"You'd better practice checking out those sorts of details if you plan to follow in your uncle's footsteps."

"Don't worry, as much as I like my uncle, and in spite of the fact that I happen to be in the market for a new career, I do not intend to go into intelligence work. I can't think of anything more depressing and grim. Imagine living a life in which you couldn't trust anyone or anything. Besides, I like to limit my close association with violence to reading thrillers," she added with a small smile. "It's okay on a fantasy level but I certainly wouldn't want to make a career out of it."

"If you feel that strongly about it, you'd better give up the habit of going through other people's desks. You could have just as easily turned around and found yourself facing an irate homeowner holding a gun as a friendly, trusting soul such as myself."

She eyed him thoughtfully for a moment. "Actually, you did take the whole thing quite calmly."

"You didn't look that dangerous," he informed her gently. "In fact, you appeared rather inviting standing there in the twilight, gazing into the apple. Besides, as soon as you said you had one just like it, I knew who you were."

"You were certain I was Uncle Lowell's niece?"

"When he gave me the crystal apple he told me he'd given a second one to you. He had them made up specially for us, you know."

"No, I didn't know. That is, I didn't realize he'd had a second one made until I saw it sitting on your desk. When I spotted it, I decided I probably didn't have any reason to go on being suspicious of you," she added apologetically. "Unfortunately, I came to that brilliant conclusion a bit late. You'd already snuck up and found me in what I guess qualifies as a compromising situation. You really don't know where Uncle Lowell might have gone or why he would say he was off hunting?"

"No. But I do think Lowell can take care of himself. My guess is he'd want you to stay out of the way until he's handled whatever needs handling."

"Then you do believe something's happened to him!" she pounced.

"I didn't say that," Adrian protested mildly. "I only meant that he probably had his reasons for disappearing. Maybe he just wanted to take off by himself for a while. Maybe he's got a woman friend and didn't feel like explaining all that to his neighbor. There could be a hundred different reasons why he's not at home, none of them particularly sinister.''

"I don't like it,'' Sara muttered, feeling pressured by the logic.

"Obviously, or you wouldn't have taken the trouble to find me. So Lowell told you to look me up if you were ever worried about something having happened to him?''

"He said you'd want to know, or something like that. I wasn't exactly certain what he meant. He doesn't have a lot of close friends. I assumed you might be one of them.''

"But you weren't sure where I fit in so you decided to take a quick look around my desk drawers while you waited for me to return. Are you always that impulsive?''

"It seemed prudent, not impulsive, to take the opportunity to find out what I could about you before I confronted you,'' she said cautiously. "Some of my uncle's old acquaintances aren't the sort with whom you want to get involved on a first-name basis.''

"You've met a lot of them?'' Adrian inquired politely.

"Well, no. But Uncle Lowell has told me about a few of them.'' Sara shuddered delicately, remembering one particular tale. "He's got a great collection of stories and personal recollections, although he always changes names and locations to protect the guilty. I suppose he's mentioned a few of the more colorful characters to you if you used him as resource material for *Phantom*.''

"We've shared a few beers and talked on occasion,'' Adrian admitted.

"You see a lot of my uncle?''

Adrian moved his hand in a vague gesture. "He doesn't live that far away. I get out to his place once in a while and sometimes he makes it over here. What about you? See a lot of him?''

Sara grinned. "Not as much as I would have liked over the years. I'm afraid Uncle Lowell has always been considered the black sheep of the family. As you can imagine, though, I found him quite fascinating. He was the unconventional relative, the one who had the mysterious career, the one who showed up when you least expected him. He was unpredictable, and kids like that, I suppose. The rest of the family thought he was a bad influence on me and, of course, that made him all the more interesting.''

Adrian leaned back against the sofa, slanting her a glance. "Why did they think he was a bad influence?''

"Because he always encouraged me to do what I wanted to do, not what my family wanted. And he had a way of understanding me, of knowing what I was thinking. He told me two years ago, for instance, that I wasn't going to be happy for long as a mid-level manager in a large corporation. Said I didn't have the proper corporate personality. He was right. I think I knew it at the time but everything seemed to be on track and running smoothly in my life. I was living the perfect yuppie life-style, and to be honest, it had its moments.''

"Yuppie? Oh, yes—" Adrian nodded. "—Young Urban Professional.''

Sara gave him another laughing smile. "I was into the whole scene down in California. I had a lifetime membership in the right athletic club, dressed for success, had my apartment done in the high-tech look and kept up with the trends in food. I ground my own coffee beans for my very own imported Italian espresso machine, and I can tell you the precise moment when pasta went out and Creole cooking came in, if you're interested.''

"No, thanks. I eat a lot of macaroni and cheese. I don't want to hear that it's 'out.' So Lowell advised you to dump the yuppie life?''

"Macaroni and cheese does not count as real pasta," she told him forcefully. "Yuppie pasta is stuff such as linguini and calamari or fettuccini Alfredo. And, yes, Uncle Lowell did advise me to dump the yuppie life. Along with the yuppie males I was dating at the time," Sara confided cheerfully. "I think he thought they were all wimps. He said none of the ones I introduced him to would be of any use in a crunch. I explained I didn't plan to get into any crunches but he just shook his head and told me to come visit him when I came to my senses.''

Adrian regarded her assessingly. "And that's why you went to his place today? To tell Lowell you'd come to your senses?''

Sara stirred a little restlessly on the couch, tucking one jeaned leg under her as she shifted her focus back to the fire. "Something like that. I quit my job last week. I think I'm going through a mid-life crisis.''

"You're a little young for that, aren't you?''

Sara ignored the underlying trace of humor in his question. "Don't patronize me. I just turned thirty. As it happens, I've been through several mid-life crises and I know them when I see them. I'm ready to make some changes in my life again.''

"You're sure that change is what you want?" Adrian got to his feet to throw a bigger log on the fire.

"Oh, yes," she whispered with great certainty, "I'm sure.''

She sounded quite resolute, Adrian decided as he fed the flames. He'd heard that quiet certainty in Lowell's voice from time to time. Must be a family characteristic.

For some reason, Sara Frazer wasn't quite what he'd expected, though, even if she did have some of Lowell's iron-hard determination. Adrian toyed with the flames a moment longer, considering the female who was curled on the couch behind him. When a man had waited nearly a year to meet a woman, it was perfectly natural that he would have developed a few preconceptions.

The few expectations he had, however, had never been fully formed. Lowell had given him some vague, odd bits of information about his niece but little that was concrete enough to build a picture in his mind. Just like Lowell to deliberately leave a great deal to the imagination. He was, after all, a man, and he knew what a man's mind could do when it went to work on a mysterious woman.

Adrian realized that he hadn't expected Sara Frazer to be a flaming beauty and in that regard he'd been correct. Taken individually, her features didn't add up to those of a beautiful woman. What surprised him was that the hazel eyes, long light-brown hair and slender figure somehow went together to create a subtly appealing combination.

On second thought, it wasn't the collection of physical characteristics that made for that appeal. There simply wasn't anything that unique about eyes that hovered between green and brown or about hair that was worn parted in the middle and clipped casually behind her ears. The red knit top she was wearing emphasized small, pert breasts rather than lush voluptuousness.

Adrian turned the matter over in his mind for an instant longer before he decided that Sara was somehow more than the sum of her parts. There was intelligence, ready laughter and more than a dash of impulsiveness in those hazel eyes. And when she had learned of the sale of his first book, her spontaneous enthusiasm had been very real even though he was a stranger to her. It was her inner animation that somehow pulled the ordinary together and made the total package strangely intriguing.

He'd been consciously and unconsciously anticipating her arrival for several months but the end result had still taken him by surprise. He simply hadn't expected to feel such an immediate and compelling attraction. He hadn't thought he'd react to the reality of Sara with such intensity. It was unsettling but he'd lay odds that Lowell would probably say "I told you so" the next time he saw him.

Satisfied with his analysis, Adrian turned and moved back toward the couch. He'd long ago accepted the fact that for some things there were no answers, but he still preferred situations that could be taken apart, analyzed and understood. He liked to have a handle on things, Adrian told himself. No, it was more than that. He liked to know he was in control of his environment. Having everything accurately assessed and properly analyzed gave him the only real sense of security one could have in this world. Sara Frazer was a new and disturbing element in his environment and it was good to know he was already beginning to comprehend her. More importantly, he was comprehending and accepting his reaction to her. He rather thought Lowell Kincaid would be pleased at the progress of the situation.

"It's getting late," Sara mused as she munched the last cracker. "I suppose I'd better be on my way. If you really don't have any idea of where Uncle Lowell is, there's no point imposing on you any longer."

"Where were you planning on going tonight?" Adrian sank back down on the couch, aware of an unexpected and totally irrational sense of disappointment. She had just arrived. It didn't seem right that she should already be planning to leave. That wasn't the way it was supposed to be. A part of him was disturbed that she seemed oblivious to the fact that things were different now. Clearly Kincaid had not given her any idea of what he'd had in mind when he'd set about engineering a meeting between Adrian and his niece.

He wondered how much to tell her about her Uncle Lowell's plans for her. He wondered how she would take the news. She might be furious or she might treat the whole thing as a joke. Women were tricky. It occurred to Adrian that in spite of being nearly forty years old he didn't know nearly as much about them as he should. It would probably be better not to bring up the subject of Lowell's plans this evening. On the other hand, Adrian found himself fiercely reluctant to let Sara go without putting the first delicate tendrils of a claim on her. Something elemental had come alive deep within him, something hard to deny.

"There's an inn on the outskirts of Winslow. It's only about a mile from here. I'll stay there tonight and be on my way tomorrow."

Adrian frowned. "You're planning on returning to California?"

Sara shook her head vigorously. "Not until I satisfy myself about Uncle Lowell. I'm worried, Adrian, even if nobody else is."

Adrian rolled his empty wineglass between his palms. "I don't think you have anything to be concerned about."

"Maybe I've got an overactive imagination. People are always accusing me of it." She lifted one shoulder in careless disregard for the fact. "But Uncle Lowell's former career must have contained some loose ends. And I know that at times he was involved with some dangerous people. There was one in particular he once told me about—" She broke off abruptly, eyes narrowing.

"What do you think you can do about the fact that he's not available at the moment?" Adrian asked reasonably.

Sara gave the matter some thought. "I think I'll go back to his cottage in the morning and break in. Maybe he left some notes or something on his desk." Her eyes grew pensive with the plans running through her head.

Adrian looked down at the glass in his hands. "The last time you tried that trick you got caught."

She laughed. "Well, no harm done if Uncle Lowell comes home unexpectedly and catches me in his house. In fact, it will be a great relief. The mystery will be solved, won't it?"

Adrian experienced a flash of amused amazement. "You're going to do it, aren't you?"

"Why not? Maybe I'll get some answers."

"I think you'll be wasting your time."

Sara grimaced. "At the moment I have time to waste. As I explained earlier, I'm unemployed."

"There are probably more productive things you could do with your newfound time," Adrian suggested dryly.

"I know. Such as look for another job. But I think I'll see what I can find out about Uncle Lowell first."

"Are you always this impulsive and stubborn?"

"Just since I turned thirty," she told him with benign menace, her eyes mirroring an amused challenge.

Adrian found himself smiling back at her. Her gaze went to his mouth, and he realized she was very interested in his expression. Did the smile look that odd on his face? "Well, if you're intent on another act of breaking and entering, I suppose I'd better go along with you."

She was startled. "Why? There's absolutely no need for you to come with me."

"You're wrong," Adrian said gently. "There are several good reasons why I'd better tag along, not the least of which is that Lowell Kincaid would probably nail my hide to the wall if I didn't."

"Why on earth should Uncle Lowell care?"

"You're worried about him to the point where you're willing to break into not one but two private homes. Lowell would expect me to take your concerns seriously, I think. He'd also want me to make sure you didn't get into trouble. What if a neighbor saw you going through a back window and called the law? You'd have some difficult explanations to make. Messy. Lowell likes things neat and tidy." Adrian paused a moment. "So do I."

"Well, I still don't see why Uncle Lowell would expect you to take the responsibility of keeping me out of trouble," Sara declared firmly.

Adrian deliberately kept his voice casual even though he was oddly aware of the strong, steady beat of his own pulse. "Don't you? The explanation's simple enough. Lowell Kincaid has plans for you, Sara. You've arrived a little ahead of schedule. I think he was planning on you coming to visit him in a couple of months, but the timing doesn't change things."

For the first time since he had caught her in his study, a degree of genuine wariness flared in Sara's gaze. Adrian immediately wished he'd kept his mouth shut. But the strangely primitive desire to let her know she wasn't quite as free as she assumed was pushing him.

"What plans?" she demanded suspiciously.

He'd already said too much, Adrian decided. In a way it was alarming. He'd allowed his unaccustomed emotional response to push him in a direction he'd guessed would be awkward. Odd. He usually had a much better sense of discretion. Having gone this far, however, he was committed to finishing the business. He couldn't take back the words he'd already spoken. The next best thing he could do was concentrate on keeping his tone light and whimsical.

"Didn't your uncle tell you that he has decided to give you to me? You're my reward, Sara. My gift for finishing *Phantom* and a couple of other things that were hanging fire in my life."

Chapter Two

"Uncle Lowell has always had an odd sense of humor. If you're really a close friend of his, I imagine you know that by now. I've always thought he would have made a good cartoonist. Between his constant doodling and his offbeat notion of what's funny, he'd have been very successful."

An hour later Sara lay in the unfamiliar inn-room bed rerunning her response to Adrian Saville's casually outrageous remarks. She decided she'd handled the scene reasonably well. She would have suspected Saville of having a warped sense of humor except for the fact that she knew her uncle. It was entirely possible that Lowell Kincaid had "given" her to his friend. He'd told her more than once that she didn't know how to pick her men. It was Lowell who had the fractured sense of humor, Sara decided grimly. What worried her was that under that trace of whimsy, she sensed Adrian might have taken him seriously.

She turned onto her side, bunching the flat pillow into a more supportive shape, and thought about what her uncle had done. It was annoying, irritating and totally in keeping with Lowell Kincaid's somewhat bizarre way of arranging things. His affinity for the unexpected was probably some sort of survival trait. A good secret agent couldn't afford to be too predictable, Sara thought with a sigh. Normally, however, Lowell didn't allow his penchant for the unique approach to infringe too much on the lives of friends and family. He knew intuitively where to stop.

But he'd let himself go overboard this time, and Sara found herself wondering why. Couldn't he see that Saville was a man who took life seriously? You didn't play jokes on people like that. They either got mad or hurt. There was always the possibility that Lowell was deadly serious about handing her over to a man of whom he approved, of course. He'd made it clear often enough he didn't think much of her own choices in male companions. Yes, Lowell might have been very serious in his intent. In which case she would be sure to give him a piece of her mind when he showed up again.

Sara watched the shadows behind the gently blowing curtains. The window was open a few inches, allowing the fresh, crisp night air into the room. She knew a lot about her uncle's sense of humor. Over the years she'd seen enough examples of it. Strange that he was such good friends with Saville. No one would ever accuse him of having much sense of humor, warped or otherwise. The faint flashes of amusement she had seen in him that evening disappeared so quickly she might have imagined them. She had the impression that when they did appear they surprised him as much as her. Saville was a controlled, quiet man who not only seemed quite different from her uncle but who was also a perfect opposite to the kind of men who circulated in her world.

Her ex-world, Sara reminded herself. Yuppiedom was another ex-world to add to the pile of such interesting experiments. It had been fun, but she had known when she'd gone into it that it wouldn't be permanent. Sara knew she would recognize the life she wanted to live on a permanent basis when she found it. Until then she played games with the world. She wondered if she was getting a little too old for games.

Restlessly she switched to her other side and plumped the pillow again. Still, she had learned some useful skills during the past few years. For example, she knew how to slide out of a socially awkward situation such as the one that had occurred tonight. A light laugh, a wry expression and an easy comment.

Adrian had accepted her withdrawal from the topic, although he had insisted on accompanying her to the inn in her car. He'd offered her a bed at his house but had not seemed surprised when she politely declined. There was no sense complicating an already complex situation, Sara had told herself. As much as she had been intrigued by Adrian, she had been a little wary of him toward the end of the evening.

She was accustomed to men who didn't take anything except their careers, their running and their new Porsches seriously, men who knew the socially acceptable vocabulary of the new male sensitivity by heart but who didn't really know how to make commitments. Sara knew how to handle men such as that. She wasn't so sure about Adrian Saville. She sensed he took a great deal in life very seriously.

There was more age in his eyes than on his face, she thought. And there was quiet, implacable strength in that pale gray gaze. She thought she understood why her uncle liked him. But she could also picture her unpredictable uncle trying to lighten the somberness that surrounded the younger man like an aura. She could just see Lowell Kincaid laughing and telling Adrian that his niece would be good for him and that he could have her when he'd finished his novel.

Sara made a rueful face. Perhaps her easygoing uncle hadn't realized just how seriously a man like Adrian Saville would take such an outrageous comment. Ah, well. She would do her best to keep things light and easy between herself and the budding author on the drive back into the mountains tomorrow. And when this was all over she would give Lowell a lecture on interfering in the private lives and fantasies of his friends. Assuring herself of that, Sara finally drifted off to sleep.

It was sunny and warm the next morning as Sara showered and dressed for breakfast. Accustomed to that kind of weather in San Diego, she didn't think much about it. She buttoned the wide cuffs of the oversized men's-style shirt she had chosen to wear and fastened the yellow belt that clasped the tapered olive-green trousers. Hastily she clipped her bluntly cut hair with two clips and wondered if Adrian Saville would be on time for breakfast as he'd promised. She decided he would be. Authors were entitled to be erratic in their habits, Sara felt, but Adrian was the kind of man who would be exactly where he said he would be at the specified time. Dependable.

She hurried downstairs and across the street. The coffee shop Adrian had pointed out last night when he'd escorted her back to the inn was full of people who weren't nearly so inclined as she was to take the local weather for granted. There seemed to be a kind of desperation in the air, as if everyone was determined to grab the last of summer before the Northwest winter took hold. Everyone from the hostess to the busboy commented in a dazed fashion on the fact that the Seattle area was getting another day of sunshine.

"Yes, it certainly is marvelous weather," Sara agreed politely as she was seated. Privately she thought that no one in San Diego would have even bothered to comment on it. "By the way, I'm waiting for someone." Something made her glance back toward the doorway. "Oh, there he is now. Would you show him to my table?"

The gray-haired, middle-aged hostess chuckled. "Sure." She waved energetically at the man who stood in the doorway surveying the room. "Hey, Adrian. Over here."

Not just Adrian but everyone else in the room looked around. Sara experienced an acute twinge of embarrassment. She should have guessed that in a small community like this everyone knew one another. Determinedly she smiled as Saville walked toward her.

Striving for a casual pose of polite welcome, Sara was astonished to realize that she was actually mildly fascinated with Adrian's approach. His stride was a deceptively easy, flowing movement that covered the distance between the doorway and her table very quickly. He had a coordinated, masculine grace that went beyond the kind of athletic motion her male friends developed by running or working out. Sara had a feeling Adrian's physical control and smoothness had probably been born in him, the way a cat's coordination was.

The pelt of dark hair that he obviously kept disciplined with a scissor was still damp from his shower and combed severely into place. He wore jeans and a cream-colored button-down shirt. On his feet were the usual sneakers, Sara noted in amusement. The shoes made his progress across the coffee shop quite soundless. If Sara hadn't been watching him, she would never have heard him approach the table. Just as she had never heard him come down the hall to the study last night, she reflected as he greeted the hostess.

"Good morning, Angie. How's it going today? Looks like a full house this morning."

The hostess nodded, pleased. "Give these Northwest folks a little sunny weather and they crawl out of the woodwork in droves. We've been doing real good this past week. Real good. Have a seat with your lady friend here and I'll send Liz on over for your order." Beaming impartially down at Sara and Adrian, the hostess bustled off to find the waitress.

"Lady friend!" Sara winced. "I've always heard that in small towns people pay a lot of attention to what their neighbors are doing but I hadn't realized they were so quick to jump to conclusions! Better be careful, Adrian. When everyone finds out you've gone off to the mountains with me for the day, you'll be a compromised man."

"I can live with it." He appeared unconcerned, turning his head to greet the teenage waitress as she hurried over to the table.

"Morning, Adrian. Coffee for both of you?" Liz began filling Adrian's cup without waiting for confirmation and then glanced inquiringly at Sara.

"Please." Sara smiled.

"Ready to order?" Briskly Liz whipped out her pad.

"Try the scones," Adrian suggested before Sara could speak.

"Scones?"

"Ummm. Homemade. They're great," he assured her.

"Well, I usually just have a croissant and coffee," Sara began uncertainly.

"You're leaving that yuppie life-style behind, remember?" Adrian pointed out seriously.

Sara felt a wave of humor. "All right. An order of scones and a poached egg," she said to the waitress.

"Got it," Liz responded. She glanced at Adrian. "The usual for you? The number-three breakfast without the bacon?"

"Fine, Liz."

Liz giggled and hurried off toward the kitchen.

Sara stirred cream into her coffee and slanted a glance at Adrian. "Okay, I give up. Why the giggle over your order of a number-three breakfast?"

Adrian's mouth twisted wryly. "Because a number three without bacon is really a number one. The first time I ate here I didn't notice the difference on the menu and just told Liz I wanted the number three minus the bacon. For some reason she's made it into a standing joke between us."

"I see. You don't like bacon?"

"I don't eat meat," he explained gently.

Sara was instantly intrigued. "Somehow you don't look like a vegetarian."

He leaned back against the cushion of the booth and picked up his coffee cup. "What do vegetarians look like?"

"Oh, I don't know. Maybe like leftovers from a sixties' commune or like a member of some exotic religious cult. Do you avoid meat for health or moral reasons?"

"I avoid it because I don't like it," Adrian said too quietly.

Feeling very much put in her place, Sara managed a faintly polite smile. She knew when she was being told to shut up. "I guess that's as good a reason as any other. So much for that topic. Let's try another one. When will you be able to leave for the mountains? I'd like to start as soon as possible, if you don't mind."

Adrian's dark lashes lowered in a thoughtful manner and then his steady gaze met Sara's. "Was I rude?"

"Of course not," she assured him lightly. "I should never have pried. What you eat is entirely your own business."

"I didn't meant to be rude," Adrian insisted.

"You weren't. Forget it. Here come the scones and they do look good." Sara flashed her best and most charming smile. The one she reserved for cocktail parties and management types.

"Don't."

She blinked and arched a brow in cool question. "I beg your pardon?"

"I said don't," Adrian muttered as his plate was set in front of him.

"Don't what?"

"Smile at me like that."

"Sorry," Sara said rather grimly. Perhaps she would go to the mountains without him.

"It looks like something left over from your yuppie days," Adrian explained carefully. "Kind of upwardly mobile. A little too flashy and not quite real. I'd rather have the real thing."

Sara couldn't resist. "Choosy, aren't you?"

"About some things. I can leave right after breakfast if you like."

"Actually," she began forbiddingly, "I'm on the verge of changing my mind."

"About breaking into your uncle's cottage?" Adrian slid a piece of egg onto a piece of toast.

"About taking you with me," Sara said sweetly.

He glanced up, surprised. "Just because I was a little short with you a few minutes ago?"

Put like that, it did sound rather trite. Sara was at a loss to explain exactly why she was vaguely reluctant to have him accompany her, but the feeling had been growing since she'd awakened that morning. She didn't really have a valid excuse for refusing his companionship, however. After all, she was the one who had sought him out and she had done so precisely because Lowell Kincaid had advised it several months ago. The sense of ambivalence she was feeling for Adrian was a new emotion for her. Sara drummed her berry-tinted nails on the table and decided to lay down a few ground rules. Normally she didn't think too highly of rules, but there were times when they represented a certain safety.

"I suppose I can't stop you from coming with me, although I'm not at all sure it's necessary. But I would appreciate it if you would keep in mind that this whole plan to get into the cottage is my idea."

"Meaning you're in charge?" Adrian munched his toast, watching her with intent eyes.

"Something like that. Forgive me if I'm jumping to conclusions, Adrian, but I have this odd feeling that you might be the type to take over and run the show." Even as she said the words, Sara realized the truth of them. Perhaps this was the source of her vague wariness regarding this man.

"Think of how nice it will be to have someone else along to share the blame in the event you get caught breaking and entering."

Sara's eyes widened. "Not a bad point," she conceded. Then her sense of humor caught up with her. "What did you do before you became a writer, Adrian? You seem to have a knack for getting what you want. Were you a businessman?"

He considered the question. "I guess you could say I was sort of a consultant."

"A consultant?"

"Umm. Someone you call in when things go wrong and have to be fixed in a hurry. You know the type."

"Sure. We used a lot of consultants in the corporation where I recently worked. What's your area of expertise? Engineering? Design? Management?"

"Management."

Sara nodded, familiar with the field. "Get tired of it?"

"More than that. I got what is casually known as burned out."

"I can understand that. I think that in a way that's what happened to me. Uncle Lowell is right. It takes a certain type of personality to be really happy in corporate management. I guess neither you nor I is the type."

A slight smile edged Adrian's hard mouth. "Maybe we have more in common than you thought. We're both in the process of changing careers and we both like Lowell Kincaid."

Sara laughed. "Do you think we can keep each other company on a long drive given those two limited things in common?"

"I think we'll make it without boring or strangling each other."

An hour and a half later Sara was inclined to agree with Adrian. The drive east of Seattle into the Cascades had passed with amazing swiftness. There had been stretches of silence, but the quiet times had not been uncomfortable. Adrian was the kind of man a woman didn't feel she had to keep entertained with bright conversation. In fact, Sara was privately convinced that Adrian would be disgusted if he thought someone was deliberately trying to entertain him with meaningless chatter. It was rather a relief to feel so at ease with him in this area, she realized. Her early-morning tinglings of ambivalence faded as Adrian guided the car deeper into the forest-darkened mountains.

When they did talk, the topics varied from the spectacular scenery to speculation on Lowell Kincaid's whereabouts. In between they discussed Adrian's fledgling career as a writer and the turning point Sara had reached in her own life.

"Are you in a hurry to find a new job?" Adrian asked at one point.

He had calmly assumed the role of driver and Sara had acquiesced primarily because she suspected he would be excellent behind the wheel. She was right. His natural coordination and skill made her feel comfortable at once. He had insisted on using his car and Sara couldn't complain about that, either. The BMW hugged the curving highway with a mechanical grace and power. Normally Sara wasn't particularly enthusiastic about being a passenger in a car being driven by someone whose driving techniques she didn't know well.

"I've got enough of a financial cushion that I can afford to take my time," she told him, her eyes on the majestic mountains that rose straight up from the edge of the highway. Small waterfalls spilled over outcroppings of granite. A crystal-clear stream followed the path of the highway on one side. Heavily timbered terrain stretched endlessly in front of the car. It was hard to believe such mountain grandeur lay so close to the heart of a cosmopolitan city. "But I'll get restless if I sit around too long trying to make up my mind about what I really want to do with my life."

"Any ideas?"

"Well…" She hesitated realizing that she hadn't discussed her tentative plans with anyone else, not even her family. "I've been thinking of going into your old line of work."

Adrian's head came around in a sudden, unexpected movement. "My old line?"

She nodded, smiling. "That probably seems odd to you, but to tell you the truth, I think I'd be a fairly good management consultant. I'd like the opportunity to be my own boss, though. I wouldn't want to work for a firm of consultants. And I'd pick and choose my contracts. I know it sounds like a contradiction in terms, Adrian, but even though I don't like working within an organization, I do have a flair for management techniques that work in an organization. It's one of the reasons I hesitated so long about quitting my last job. I was good at it in a lot of ways."

Adrian's attention was back on the road ahead. "I don't think it sounds like a contradiction. A lot of people can give objective advice about things they wouldn't want to make a living doing."

"It would take a long time to build a clientele," Sara said slowly.

"I know the feeling. It will take a long time to build a writing career."

"But I do have some good contacts who would be glad to recommend me to companies looking for a consultant," Sara went on more enthusiastically.

"And I've sold my first book. Sounds like we both have a toehold on the future," Adrian said with the first hint of a smile that day.

Sara grinned. "Assuming we both don't wind up in jail because one of Uncle Lowell's neighbors sees us breaking into his cottage!"

It was shortly after noon by the time Adrian pulled into the drive of Lowell Kincaid's mountain cabin. They had stopped for lunch at a small roadside café en route.

The weatherworn house was one of a number of such cottages scattered about the forested landscape. Many were filled with summer visitors but a few, such as the one just over the next rise, were owned by permanent residents. Lowell Kincaid liked his privacy, however, and had purchased a cottage that was not within sight of the next house. Unless his nearest neighbor happened by on a casual walk, no one would notice two people jimmying the back window, Sara told herself.

"Have you ever done this before?" Adrian asked blandly as he climbed out of the BMW and stood surveying the cottage.

"I got into your place, didn't I?" Sara reminded him.

"The front door was unlocked, remember?"

"You should probably start locking it," she told him seriously. "You can't be too careful these days."

"I'll try to remember to do it," he said dryly. "Now, about this little business…"

"Well, I'll admit I have no direct experience of prying open a window, but how hard can it be? People break into houses all the time."

"And occasionally get shot doing so."

Sara gave him a bright smile. "Maybe we should knock on the front door first, just to make certain no one's home."

"Good idea."

Adrian strode to the front door of the cottage and pounded loudly. There was no response. There was also no sign of Lowell's car.

"Looks like we'll have to do this the hard way," Adrian observed morosely. "We'll probably wreck the window and Lowell will send me the bill."

Sara started around the corner of the house looking for a window at the right height and of the right size. "Don't be so pessimistic. I brought you along to help and to lend moral support, not to paint a picture of doom and gloom."

"It's just that I have this image of Lowell coming home and finding his window broken. He won't be pleased."

"I'll leave a note," Sara offered as she stopped in front of an appropriate window. "What do you think about this one?"

Adrian frowned and stepped forward to examine it more closely. "I guess it's as good as any of the others. We'll need something to jimmy it with. Maybe the jack handle in the car. I'll go see what I can find." He swung around and then halted abruptly, staring at the next window on the side of the cottage. "Well, hell."

"What's wrong?" Sara turned to follow his gaze. "I don't…"

"Looks like someone else has been here ahead of us," Adrian said softly.

Sara peered more intently. "Do you really think...oh." For the first time she felt a distinct chill of unease. It was obvious the window had been crudely but effectively forced open. The frame was badly marked from whatever instrument had been used, and the window itself was still half raised. "Vandals?"

Adrian was examining the damage. He didn't look around. "Surely you're not going to be satisfied with the notion that a couple of young punks broke into your uncle's house. Not after all the exotic mischief and mayhem you've been imagining."

"Don't be sarcastic. What are you doing?"

"I'm going inside to have a look." Adrian shoved the window completely open and casually swung a leg over the sill.

"Wait!" Sara grabbed for his arm. "What if someone's still in there?" she hissed.

He glanced inside the house and shook his head. "The place is empty."

"You can't be sure. It's very dangerous to corner burglars in a house. You're supposed to go call the cops before going inside."

"Is that right?" Adrian said vaguely. Then he swung his other leg over the sill and dropped lightly to the floor inside.

Annoyed, Sara leaned through the window to lecture him further. But the words caught in her throat as she took in the chaos of the room. "Oh, my God."

"Umm." Adrian walked past a bookcase that had been ransacked and came to a halt in front of the old roll-top desk.

Feeling stunned, Sara followed him through the window. Inside the house she stood staring in speechless dismay as Adrian examined the desk. She remembered the desk well. She had helped Lowell select it at a junk shop in Seattle. Her uncle had spent hours refinishing it.

Now the surface was a jumble of strewn papers, books and magazines. The drawers had been unceremoniously hauled open and emptied. Folders of personal business papers had been tossed on the floor along with a notebook of Lowell Kincaid's sketches.

Infuriated more than anything else by the way the sketchbook had been dumped on the well-worn Oriental rug, Sara bent down to retrieve it. "Stupid bastards," she muttered as she tried to smooth the pages and close the cover. "Whoever it was just wanted to make a mess. I thought we had all the mental flakes down in California."

"We have a few up here in the Northwest." Adrian walked slowly through the living room into the adjoining kitchen. "Looks like someone really enjoyed himself."

"It's sick." Sara wrinkled her nose at the smell of decaying food. The contents of the refrigerator had been thrown against the walls. "Absolutely sick."

"Or else someone wanted it to look that way," Adrian murmured slowly.

Sara swung around to stare at him wide-eyed. "Good heavens, I hadn't thought of that. That's a possibility, isn't it? Whoever broke in might have deliberately tried to make it look like the work of vandals. That way no one would be able to figure out what he or she had been looking for."

"On the other hand, it might have really been a couple of genuine vandals." Adrian shrugged, moving on into the single bedroom.

"Make up your mind!" Sara hurried after him.

"How can I? I don't know what's going on here any more than you do."

"Good point." Sara couldn't keep the sarcasm out of her voice. "Given that basic fact, I guess we'd better go find the local police or sheriff or whatever passes for the law here."

Adrian paid no attention to her. He was looking at the phone-answering machine that still sat on the table beside the bed. Whoever had gone through the room yanking open drawers and closet doors had ignored the telephone. The red light was gleaming, indicating a message had been recorded.

"The message on there is probably from me," Sara said quietly. "The one I left when I called him a couple of days ago to let him know I would be arriving. There was no answer, so I just kept driving."

Adrian pressed the button that rewound the tape. The first voice on the machine was Sara's, as she had predicted.

"Uncle Lowell? I'm driving up from California to see you. Just wanted you to know I took your advice. Mom and Dad are in a deep depression over the whole thing but I think they'll survive. Maybe they're getting used to my life-style changes. Personally, I feel great. You were right. See you tomorrow."

Sara caught her breath when she heard the next voice on the tape. Her uncle's easy growl was as unconcerned and laconic as ever.

"Adrian, if you and Sara are the ones listening to this, then you'll have realized I have a small problem on my hands. I can't explain everything just now but don't worry. We'll talk later. Pay attention to me. This isn't anything I can't handle but I need a little time and privacy. Some unfinished business regarding your wedding present,

I'm afraid. It's tough enough to find just the right gift for a special couple like you and Sara. I didn't realize it would be even harder to protect it. Do me a favor and don't bother the local cops. This is a personal matter. Oh, and Adrian, Sara tends to have a rather vivid imagination and she doesn't handle waiting very well. A distinct lack of patience in that woman at times. I heard her message on the tape when I phoned to leave my own. I know she's on her way here and when she doesn't find me she'll probably look you up. Which, of course, explains why you're standing there listening to this tape. Aren't you impressed with my wondrous logic?'' There was a rough chuckle. ''Take care of her for me and keep her out of trouble until I get back. I'll see you as soon as I can.''

The tape wound on into silence while Sara stood utterly still, staring at the machine in astonishment and dread. ''Wedding gift?'' she finally got out very weakly.

Adrian punched the stop button. ''I told you Lowell had plans for us,'' he reminded her dryly.

''Adrian, none of this makes any sense!''

''Yes, it does.'' Adrian turned to look at her. His light eyes were unreadable, but the set of his harsh features was intently serious. ''Lowell says that whatever's going on is private business. He'll take care of it. He doesn't want any help or he'd ask for it. And he wants me to keep you from getting involved. I'm supposed to take care of you. It all seems clear enough to me.''

''Don't be ridiculous. There is nothing clear about this mess.'' Sara spun around and stalked back into the living room. ''Damn Uncle Lowell anyway. Why couldn't he have left a simple straightforward message or called you and told you exactly what was going on?'' She headed toward the rifled desk. ''Just like him to leave a lot of questions lying around for us to try to answer.''

''He says it's a private matter. He doesn't want us involved. He probably didn't call because he didn't want to alarm us unnecessarily. On the other hand, he figured if we got this far he'd better leave some sort of message.'' Adrian followed her on silent feet, stopping to examine the stack of books that had been stripped from the bookcase.

''If it's such a personal matter, what was that business about protecting our wedding present?'' Sara shot him a scathing glance as she began picking up the scattered magazines that had been spilled from an end table. Lowell Kincaid was an inveterate magazine reader. Sara had frequently teased him about the number of subscriptions he maintained.

"You know your uncle. There are times when he simply can't resist throwing out a teaser." Adrian seemed unconcerned.

"It's his unfortunate sense of humor, I suppose." Sara sighed and shuffled a stack of insurance papers. "Adrian, this whole thing is going to drive me crazy. How are we going to know he's all right?"

"We won't until he gets back. But I've told you before, Sara. Your uncle can take care of himself."

"I don't like that comment about 'unfinished business,'" she went on unhappily. "It sounds dangerous. Like something from his past coming back to haunt him."

"Lowell was right. You do have an active imagination."

"Well?" she challenged. "How would you interpret that message?"

"Like something from his past that has come back to haunt him," Adrian admitted in resigned tones. He picked up a stack of books and put them back on the shelf. "The real problem is that food on the walls in the kitchen. That's going to be a mess to clean. It's going to take quite a while, too."

"Stop changing the subject! This is important. We have to figure out what's going on." Sara frowned intently down at the papers in her hand. Predictably enough, many of them, even the most important-looking ones, contained small sketches and doodles. Lowell Kincaid was forever covering books, papers and notepads with his drawings. He did them almost unconsciously, Sara knew. He could be talking about one thing and sketching a totally unrelated subject. She remembered once having coffee with him in a restaurant and discussing her growing dissatisfaction with her latest job. Lowell had carried on a detailed and logical conversation while making comical character sketches on a napkin of the people in the next booth. "What do you suppose whoever did this was looking for?"

"That's something we can't even guess until Lowell shows up."

"Except that we know it has something to do with our so-called wedding gift," Sara muttered in growing annoyance. "What in the world could Uncle Lowell have been talking about?"

"If he'd wanted us to know, he would have told us."

"You're awfully casual about this, Adrian." Sara glared at him over her shoulder.

"I know your uncle very well, Sara," Adrian said. "He doesn't want us getting involved."

She ignored that, her sandaled foot tapping impatiently under the desk. Thoughtfully Sara stared out the window toward a stand of fir. "He said he'd already gotten the gift. Now he has to protect it."

"Something like that." Adrian reshelved another batch of books.

"So whoever did this must have been looking for whatever Uncle Lowell calls our wedding present."

"Are you going to give me a hand cleaning up the kitchen?"

"You know, Uncle Lowell once told me he believed in the old theory that the best hiding place was the one that was in full view. People really do tend to overlook the obvious. He says answers are always quite clear when you know where to look." She glanced around the room with narrowed eyes. "He'd had some experience along those lines. He ought to know what he's talking about."

Adrian went into the kitchen. "If whoever made this mess didn't find what he was looking for, the odds are you won't find it, either. It may not even be here. Or Lowell might have removed it and hidden it somewhere else. Or this chaos might really be the work of casual vandals who happened on an empty cabin. A coincidence. Sara, we don't have a clue. There's no point beating our heads against a stone wall. Let your uncle take care of his own business."

Sara heard water running in the kitchen sink. Reluctantly she put down the stack of insurance papers and got to her feet. Adrian was right. They should clean up the kitchen first.

"Uncle Lowell said he was thinking of putting in a fancy alarm system. Too bad he didn't get around to it in time to prevent this," she commented.

"I know. I was going to help him install it," Adrian said from the kitchen.

Sara took a step forward and her toe brushed a thick sheaf of papers that had been lying on the floor beside the chair. The pile of neatly typed pages was still bound with a rubber band. Automatically she leaned down to pick it up. Halfway down the first page a single word, underlined, leaped out at her. *Phantom.*

"Adrian! Here's a copy of your manuscript," she called, aware of a surging sense of interest in what she held. Curiously she flipped through a handful of pages.

"I think I mentioned that I had given a copy to Lowell," Adrian said softly from the doorway of the kitchen.

"Would you mind if I...?" Sara's request to read the manuscript died on her lips as she looked at the penciled sketch in the right-hand corner of the first page. There were other doodles at the bottom of the page, but it was the one at the top that made her grow cold.

The drawing had been done hurriedly, but Lowell Kincaid's talent lay in the quick character sketch. Strong, simple lines defined the figure in only a few brief strokes. It was the head of a wolf.

"No," Sara whispered as she stared at the drawing. "Oh, no."

"Sara? What's wrong?" Adrian tossed aside the sponge he had

been holding and came toward her, his expression one of grave concern.

Feeling decidedly unnerved, Sara sank back down into the desk chair and looked up at him. "See that drawing on your manuscript?"

Adrian glanced at the page and then back at her strained face. "What about it? Your uncle is always doodling and sketching. You know that." He leaned down to flip through the rubber-band-bound stack. "Look. There are little drawings on nearly all the pages."

"I know. But this is more than just an idle sketch." She swallowed, struggling to remember details. "There was a real wolf in his past, you see. A renegade killer. Never mind, it's a long story. Uncle Lowell told me about him one night over a few drinks." Dazedly she stared down at the drawing. "Adrian, if this is the 'unfinished business' my uncle is taking care of, he's in real trouble. We've got to do something."

Adrian's mouth tightened. He reached down and picked up the manuscript. "We are going to do something. We're going to stay out of Lowell's way and let him handle his unfinished business."

"Adrian, we have a responsibility!"

"My responsibility is to take care of you. Very clear—very simple. That's what your uncle wants and that's what I'm going to do. Now, if you really want to do something useful for Lowell, come on into the kitchen and help me clean up the mess. If we don't take care of it, some helpful, foraging skunks or worse will take care of it for us."

Chapter Three

She was genuinely scared, Adrian reflected a few hours later. Tense, nervous, restless and scared. He had spent the past three hours alternately trying to reassure her that Lowell Kincaid could handle his own problems and trying to convince her that she was letting her imagination play havoc with her common sense. Neither attempt had been particularly successful. But then, he hadn't had a lot of experience attempting to soothe the fears of others.

It had been late by the time they'd finished cleaning up Lowell's cabin, and when Adrian had suggested they spend the night at a motel instead of driving all the way back to Seattle, Sara hadn't argued. He'd scrupulously booked two rooms at a charmingly rustic little lodge located just off the main highway.

Now, as he studied her across the restaurant table, it occurred to Adrian that he was going to have his hands full trying to carry out the task Kincaid had assigned him in that damned recorded phone message.

Nothing was going the way he had thought it would, and the knowledge irritated him. For the better part of the past year the unknown Sara had been hovering in the back of his mind, her nebulous image planted there by Lowell Kincaid.

"The two of you are going to be great together," Lowell had told him with vast assurance. "But you both need a little time. You've got to get *Phantom* out of your system and she has to reach a few conclusions on her own. I figure in another few months—"

"Lowell, you may be my best friend but I don't want you playing matchmaker. Understand?" Adrian had been very firm even though he'd already downed a great deal of beer before the conversation had gotten around to the subject of Kincaid's niece.

"You're going to love her, pal. Trust me. The two of you have a lot in common."

"That's rather doubtful, isn't it?"

"I know people, Adrian. You should realize that by now. She's perfect for you. She's intelligent and full of life. She's also fundamentally genuine and honest. She'll help you keep your life in balance. You need a dose of enthusiasm and optimism. You're too cautious. Furthermore, she's capable of making a commitment to the right man. Luckily for you, she hasn't found him yet. And she won't as long as she hangs around those wimps she's been dating for the past few years. She's smart enough to play with the dross but wait for the real gold.'' Lowell had grinned. "She's really very good at playing with life. In college she played at being pseudo-intellectual. She used to spend hours arguing about philosophical treatises. A lot of people thought she was serious, including her teachers. Got good grades. When she graduated she decided to play at being an artist for a while. Rented a genuine garret, wore her hair long and went around in paint-stained jeans. She actually sold a couple of paintings through a gallery that made the mistake of taking her seriously. Then she went through an activist phase during which she went around protesting against environmental polluters. Eventually she wound up as the epitome of the young, upwardly mobile urban professional. She always did have a good sense of timing. She also has a real flair for management. She enjoys life the way some people enjoy a game.''

"And just what am I going to be offering her in return?'' Adrian had asked roughly as he popped the top on another can of beer. The discussion was outrageous, but such conversations were allowable when you were sharing several beers with your only real friend. Besides, there was something about the unknown Sara that intrigued him more than he wanted to admit. He found himself wondering what she would think of him if Lowell ever got around to introductions.

"She needs someone strong, someone who can appreciate what she has to offer. She also needs a counterfoil for her natural enthusiasm and impulsiveness. Someone stable and steady. When she does give her heart for real, it will be completely. She'll need someone who will make the same commitment to her that she'll be making to him. A lot of men aren't capable of that. They might know several fancy names for spaghetti or how to select the right brand of running shorts but that's about the extent of their sensitivity.''

"Been reading those articles on the 'new male,' I see. I warned you about that. You should cancel some of those magazine subscriptions. Bunch of garbage and you know it.''

"Is that so? Well, how many men would you trust with your life or your wallet or your woman these days?'' Lowell had countered.

That had struck a chord, Adrian remembered. "Not many. Maybe you. That's about it."

"And you're the only one I would trust with anything I value. I value my niece, Adrian. Perhaps because there's something in her that reminds me of myself."

"So you're going to give her to me? I'm not sure that you're taking your responsibilities as her uncle seriously enough."

"I know what I'm doing. You should be thanking me. You need a woman who can give herself completely. You also need someone who has a real understanding of loyalty. You could also use someone who occasionally shakes you up a bit. You're so damned controlled, son, that it worries me at times. It's as though you've built a carefully organized, well-defined little world for yourself and nothing gets in unless you've fully analyzed and comprehended it first."

"I like to be sure of things, Lowell. You know that."

The older man had grinned complacently. "Once you get to know Sara you'll realize you can be sure of her in all the ways that count. There's a lot of love and loyalty in that woman, and the man who taps it is going to be very rich. You'll see."

The conversation, as Adrian recalled, had gone downhill from there. The beer had flowed freely, and mercifully it had inspired Lowell Kincaid to bring up other topics for discussion. Adrian couldn't remember too many of them the next morning, but he definitely recalled the little matter of Kincaid's niece.

Phantom had absorbed most of his time and energy in the ensuing months. He hadn't seen a great deal of anyone, not even Lowell Kincaid, but the older man had known what he was doing. As usual.

The seed had been planted, and as he'd worked steadily, often painfully, on the novel, Adrian had found the presence of the mysterious Sara hovering in the corners of his mind. Sometimes late at night after he'd put in hours on the manuscript he'd dosed himself with brandy and gone to bed thinking about what he would do if he had Sara there. He'd let himself fantasize about having a woman who loved him, a woman who knew what loyalty meant. And then he'd gone to sleep with a body that still ached from the stirrings of an irrational passion.

On the rare occasions when he did talk to Kincaid, Adrian had heard himself ask after the woman with what he hoped was deceptive casualness. Lowell had supplied information readily enough, telling him about her success in her job or the latest "wimp" she was seeing.

When he'd begun to realize he didn't like hearing about the newest males in Sara's life, Adrian had finally acknowledged to himself that he might have a problem. It was ridiculous and quite asinine to start wanting a woman you'd never met, but the sense of anticipation had taken firm root. That anticipation had been followed by a curious sensation of possessiveness that was even more perplexing than the fantasy-induced desire.

Her undefined image had remained on the borders of his mind, always waiting for him. She was there when he took a break during the day from *Phantom*. She emerged to haunt him before he went to sleep at night. And she casually made herself felt when he sat by himself in front of the fire in the evenings sipping a lonely glass of wine.

Lowell had said he'd see about introducing Sara to Adrian when the book was finished. Over a period of months she had begun to seem like the prize at the end of a quest.

Last night when he'd returned from his small celebration of the sale of *Phantom* and walked home to find the lady in his study, Adrian had experienced the disorienting sensation of having met his destiny. The quest had been completed and now his gift was within reach. The fantasy hadn't diminished since the previous evening.

It should have, Adrian thought objectively as he watched Sara prod a sun-dried tomato in her pasta salad. Fantasies were supposed to die quick deaths when reality took over. But reality was proving very interesting in this case, far more gripping than fantasy.

"So what are we going to do?" Across the table Sara finally gave up on her salad and set down her fork. Challengingly she waited for Adrian to say something brilliant.

Adrian realized he couldn't rise to the challenge. "Nothing."

"As an answer, that lacks a certain something," she muttered. "In management training I learned that you're always supposed to sound confident and in charge."

"Maybe I should take the course."

"This is not a joke, Adrian. We can't just sit around and wait."

"Why not? It's what your uncle wants us to do. We'll drive back to Seattle in the morning. You can stay with me on the island until Lowell returns."

She eyed him with abrupt wariness. "I don't think that's such a good idea."

"It sounds perfectly reasonable to me. You're certainly not going to spend the time waiting in Lowell's cottage. If you think I'd leave you there knowing that whoever went through that place once might return, you're out of your little ex-corporate skull."

He hadn't raised his voice, but Sara felt the diamond-hard determination in him more clearly than if he'd shouted the words.

"Don't worry," she said bluntly, "I'm not particularly eager to stay alone at Uncle Lowell's cottage. Not after seeing that sketch of the wolf."

Adrian glared at her and picked up his wineglass. "What the devil is all this nonsense about the wolf, anyway? You've been acting as if you'd seen a ghost ever since you saw Lowell's dumb doodle on my manuscript."

"I did. In a way." Moodily Sara stared at the tablecloth in front of her, remembering. "It's a long story, Adrian."

"We've got a long evening ahead of us," he noted grimly. "You might as well tell me the tale."

"I only know bits and pieces of it." Sara sighed and pushed aside her half-eaten meal. "Uncle Lowell never told me all the details. He probably couldn't because of security reasons, although lately my uncle has begun to demonstrate an amazing disgust for all the bureaucratic paranoia that generally controls matters of security." A brief flicker of amusement lit her eyes for a few seconds as she thought about that. She heartily approved of the trend.

"So what did he tell you about this wolf business that has you so upset tonight?"

"There was a man," she began slowly, recalling the conversation with her uncle that had taken place nearly a year ago. "A man who carried the code name of Wolf. Uncle Lowell said it suited him." Sara gave Adrian a level glance, willing him to understand the importance of what she was trying to say. "Lowell said he was so good at what he did, so dangerous, that when he walked into a room the temperature seemed to drop by twenty degrees."

Adrian considered that in silence for a moment and then murmured very distinctly, "Bull."

Sara scowled at him. "It's true."

"Your uncle's right. You do have an overactive imagination."

"It was Uncle Lowell who told me about the guy. That business of the room going cold was his description, not mine. He meant that the man could literally chill your blood. Even Uncle Lowell's blood, apparently. Now do you want to hear the rest of the story or not?"

Adrian shrugged and buttered a roll. "Go ahead."

"All right. But only if you're going to listen seriously to what I'm saying. This is not a wild tale, Adrian. Uncle Lowell meant every word the night he told me the story. He was...upset."

"Lowell was upset?"

"Yes. You see, he knew the man they called Wolf. The guy was supposed to be his replacement. Uncle Lowell had the job of grooming him to step into his shoes when he retired."

"Lowell officially retired five years ago."

Sara nodded. "But my uncle kept tabs on his replacement, I guess. He must have been very uneasy about him right from the beginning. He said this Wolf was almost frighteningly ruthless. He seemed to have no emotions, no human sensitivity. Sending him on a mission was like aiming a gun and pulling the trigger. From what Uncle Lowell said, the man would probably qualify as a sociopath. You know, someone who doesn't really function in society. No emotional equipment. Sick. Working for the intelligence group Uncle Lowell was in gave him an outlet for his antisocial tendencies and his ruthlessness. If he hadn't gotten that kind of job, he probably would have ended up as a first-class criminal."

"Lowell said all this?" Adrian seemed both skeptical and reluctantly fascinated.

"Some of it I've inferred from his description that night. My uncle was very restless about something that evening. He wanted to talk to someone, I think. I've never seen him in quite that mood. And he'd certainly never made a habit before of talking about his, uh, former business associates. Sometimes he'd tell me stories and tales but they were always deliberately vague on details. I could tell that the story wasn't being embroidered or altered for security reasons this time. Anyhow, he'd come down to spend a weekend with my family in San Diego. We had all gone out to dinner, and when we were finished he drove me over to my apartment. I knew something was bothering him, and when he started talking, I just let him go on until he'd gotten it all out of his system."

"Did he give you any specific details on this character he calls Wolf?" Adrian asked softly.

"You mean like a description or his real name? Of course not." Sara smiled wryly. "Even when Uncle Lowell's in a chatty mood, he knows how to watch his tongue. I guess he spent too many years being cautious. All I know about Wolf is that Lowell was worried. I think he believed his protégé might be slipping over the edge. Wolf was dangerous enough when he could still be aimed by his superiors and fired like a weapon, but if he could no longer be at least minimally controlled... If he decided to go into business for himself, for example..."

"You're saying Lowell thought the guy might have gone renegade?" Adrian demanded.

Sara took a breath. "That's the impression I got that night. I only know that Uncle Lowell was tense and worried about what he had helped create."

Adrian chewed meditatively on another chunk of his roll. "Dr. Frankenstein and his monster."

"I know it sounds melodramatic," Sara admitted, "and if I hadn't seen that little drawing of a wolf's head on your manuscript, I wouldn't have thought twice about that conversation with my uncle. But after hearing the message on the telephone-answering machine and seeing the mess that cottage was in and then finding the drawing—" She broke off, her anxiety clear in her eyes.

"Why do you suppose your uncle happened to make that little doodle on the front page of my manuscript?" Adrian asked reflectively.

Sara lifted one shoulder negligently. "You know him. He's constantly sketching and doodling. He uses whatever's handy. I've seen him make the most intricate little drawings on cocktail napkins or paper towels or the back of his income-tax forms. Your manuscript probably happened to be nearby when he was thinking of this Wolf person. Or..." Sara's eyes widened as a thought caught her attention. "Maybe something in your manuscript reminded him of the wolf."

"Not likely. Not from the way you've described the guy," Adrian said flatly.

Sara thought about that. "Then he must have been thinking of the wolf at a time when your manuscript was lying nearby. Which means that something was making him uneasy. He tells us in that recorded message that he's going to take care of unfinished business. I think...I think Uncle Lowell always considered Wolf unfinished business."

"Because he'd trained him and then turned him loose?"

"Something like that. How would you feel if you'd been assigned to train someone and had him turn into a...a criminal or worse. Perhaps a renegade killer. Wouldn't you feel you had to do something about it?"

"Not a pleasant thought," Adrian said slowly.

"But wouldn't you feel responsible?"

"I might."

"Then maybe—"

Adrian interrupted abruptly. "But, Sara, that doesn't explain Lowell's message completely. Remember, he said he was out to protect our, er, wedding present."

"I know. I can't figure out that part," she admitted morosely.

"Face it. We don't stand a chance in hell of figuring any of this out until your uncle gets back and tells us just what was going on. The only thing we can do is wait." Adrian's rare smile flickered briefly at the corners of his mouth. "At least I got assigned a task to keep my mind off Lowell's problems."

"What task?" She frowned at him across the table.

"Taking care of you. I'm supposed to keep you out of mischief, remember?"

"Oh, that." She waved the entire matter aside. "That was just a casual comment on my uncle's part."

"Nevertheless, I feel obliged to take it seriously. After all, you're worried, and if someone doesn't keep an eye on you, I can envision you getting into all sorts of trouble."

"Don't be ridiculous."

"You might," Adrian concluded without any trace of amusement at all, "even manage to make some trouble for your uncle."

That caught her attention. "What on earth do you mean?"

"I think that, left to your own devices, you'll convince yourself that Lowell really is in trouble. You'll start poking around, perhaps asking questions. There's no telling what small waves you might set in motion that could ripple back to Lowell."

Sara studied him, stricken. "You're serious, aren't you? I wouldn't do anything to jeopardize my uncle."

"I know you wouldn't do anything deliberately, but how could you even begin to guess what might or might not have an effect?"

"Oh, come off it, Adrian, I'm hardly in a position to do anything dramatic one way or the other," she protested.

"No?" He pushed aside his plate and leaned forward, his arms folded on the table in front of him. "What if you go back to talk to that neighbor of his? What if you decide to do a little investigating on your own? Find out if anyone noticed someone hanging around your uncle's cottage recently, for example. And what if someone notices you and takes exception to your involvement? I can see you doing all sorts of little things that could blow up in Lowell's face. Or worse yet, your own face."

"That's ridiculous and you know it. Now you're the one whose imagination is running wild," she scoffed. But deep down she felt a prickle of guilt. It had occurred to her only a few minutes earlier that it might be interesting to talk to her uncle's neighbors. A vague plan to talk to some of them had been formulating in the back of her mind. She knew her flushed cheeks betrayed her.

Adrian gave her a very deliberate look. "Going to deny you were making a few plans?"

"Well, no, but I certainly don't think..." She trailed off, flustered.

"Umm. I think my little assignment is going to be the tough one," Adrian groaned. "I have a hunch Lowell knew exactly what he was doing when he asked me to keep an eye on you. If you're finished playing with your food, let's head back to the rooms. It's getting late.'' He stood up without bothering to wait for her agreement. The waiter hurried over with the check.

Disgruntled at the abrupt termination of the meal and the conversation, Sara got to her feet more slowly and allowed Adrian to walk her out of the small restaurant. Her head was spinning with worry, speculation and half-formed plans. In fact, her attention was focused so completely on her thoughts that she didn't notice where Adrian was guiding her until she suddenly became aware of flagstone under her strappy little sandals. He was leading her along a path that wound around the motel.

"A little late for a walk, isn't it?" she asked, glancing into the shadows of darkened stands of trees. Behind them the lights of the motel flared in the night.

"I thought a walk before turning in might calm you down a bit." Adrian took a firmer grip on her arm as she stumbled lightly on a cluster of pebbles. "Watch your step."

"That's tough to do since I don't see well in the dark," she complained.

"I'll guide you."

"You can see in the dark?" she asked very politely.

"Umm. I've always had good night vision."

"That must come in handy for this sort of thing," she allowed still more politely.

"What sort of thing?"

"Enforced midnight marches with unsuspecting females," she drawled.

"It's only nine-thirty and believe it or not I can't even remember the last time I went for an evening walk with a female, unsuspecting or otherwise." He hesitated, mulling that over. "It's very pleasant."

"Even though I'm having trouble walking in a straight line?"

"That's the best part."

"Oh." Her brief amusement vanished as suddenly as it had appeared, and Sara went back to thinking about her missing uncle.

"It won't do you any good, you know," Adrian said after a moment.

"What won't do any good?"

"Worrying."

"But I'm so good at it." She sighed.

"What you need is something to take your mind off your problems." Adrian came to an unexpected halt, catching hold of her with both hands as she stumbled into him. "And I think I need the same thing," he added almost under his breath as he stood very close in the darkness and ran his palms down her arms.

Sara felt the strength in his hands as he pulled her close. She looked up, aware of a fierce surge of sudden awareness as she realized he was going to kiss her. For an instant she tried to read his shadowed gaze, seeking answers to questions she couldn't formulate. But in the almost nonexistent light his eyes were colorless and infinitely unintelligible. She was enthralled by her own reaction to that gaze. It lured her, promising something she wasn't sure she wanted. Before she could fathom the strange sensation, Sara felt herself pressed against him, and in the next moment Adrian's mouth was on hers.

What startled her most about his kiss was the urgency in it. It seemed to wash over her, a combination of male curiosity, hunger and carefully restrained desire. The first kiss from a man was usually tentative, polite and as practiced as he could make it. This was something else again. There was nothing tentative or polite about it. Nor was there any element of practiced seduction in the damp heat of his kiss.

Sara was tinglingly aware that it was the most honest kiss she had ever received. She wasn't sure how she knew that with such certainty but there was absolutely no doubt in her mind. It was like finding gold after years of sorting through scrap metal. The vivid realization brought forth a response from her that she'd had no intention of indulging until it flared into life. Then it could hardly be denied.

Slowly, savoring the moment of unexpected awareness, she slid her arms around his neck and found the dark pelt of his hair with questing fingertips. She was thirty years old, she thought, and not given to such episodes of instant attraction. This was something unique and she was wise enough to know it.

"Sara?"

Slowly, reluctantly, Adrian lifted his mouth from hers. He raised one hand to tangle in her hair while with the other he stroked the length of her back. She could feel the intensity in him as he urged her soft thighs against the hard planes of his lower body.

"I believe you said this was supposed to give me something else to think about?" she murmured gently.

"I don't know about you, but I may have given myself a little too much to think about tonight. Forgive me, honey, but I've been wondering what you would taste like for a long time." Once again he lowered his mouth to hers.

Sara felt her lips being parted and then he was deep in her unresisting mouth exploring her with such intimacy that she trembled.

For countless moments time stood still for her there on the narrow path. She gave herself up to the intriguing, captivating touch of a man who qualified as a near-stranger and wondered why he seemed so right to all her senses.

She offered no resistance as Adrian drew her deeper and deeper into the embrace. When his palms slipped down to cup the contours of her derriere, she stood on tiptoe, nestling closer. His leaping desire made itself felt through the fabric of his jeans and her own body struggled to answer the ancient call. Sara had never known such driving urgency. When Adrian freed her mouth to seek out the sensitive place behind her ear, she heard herself murmur a throaty response. His breath was exciting and warm in her hair.

Then, slowly at first but with gathering strength the night breeze began to make itself felt. Sara became vaguely aware of the gathering chill as it swirled and eddied around her. The warmth of Adrian's body warded off some of it but not all. He seemed to realize what was happening at about the same moment and slowly lifted his head.

"I think it's time to go back," he said huskily.

"Yes." She didn't argue. He was right. It was time to go safely back to her own bed. But she felt unexpectedly weak and she found herself holding on to his arm.

For a moment longer Adrian's palms framed her upturned face. She sensed the hesitation in him and was warmed by it. He was reluctant to break the spell and that pleased her. She didn't want to be the only one caught up in the magic, Sara realized.

"If it weren't so cold out here and if you'd had a little more time to get used to the idea..." Adrian let the rest of the sentence trail off as he took her hand and started back toward the lights of the motel.

"Get used to what idea?"

"Never mind," he told her laconically. "My imagination is proving to be as vivid as yours, although it seems to be running along different lines."

Sara smiled serenely to herself in the shadows, knowing exactly what was going through his head. He wanted her, and the knowledge sent a primitive thrill through her veins. Adrian wouldn't do anything about it tonight, of course. It was much too soon. They barely knew each other and there were a great many factors that might get in the way of a relationship between them. Still, tonight she would go to sleep with a sense of anticipation that was entirely new to her.

But an hour later as she lay in bed in the room next to Adrian's Sara realized that, anticipation or not, sleep was not going to come easily that night. Adrian had succeeded in distracting her for a while, she decided ruefully, but now that she was alone again, too many jumbled thoughts were swirling in her head. Her mind skipped around from worries about her uncle and his "unfinished business" to memories of Adrian's urgent kiss. She needed something to relax her.

"Like a good book," she decided aloud, pushing back the covers. And she knew just where to get one.

Padding barefoot across the carpet, her long cotton nightgown trailing behind her, Sara went to the suitcase in the corner. Opening it, she reached inside and removed the manuscript of *Phantom* that she had picked up off her uncle's desk. For a moment her gaze rested thoughtfully on the sketch of the wolf in the upper corner, and then she told herself to ignore it. She was after relaxation, not added worry.

A deep curiosity filled her as she climbed back into bed and started *Phantom.* Silently she admitted to herself that it was the desire to learn something more about the man she had spent the day with rather than a wish to see how the story ended that prompted the feeling. How much could you tell about a man by his writing, she wondered.

On the surface, *Phantom* was high adventure. It involved the perilous race to retrieve a cache of gold that had been smuggled out of South Vietnam during the last, chaotic days of the war. The treasure had been hidden near the Cambodian border and had been inaccessible for years because it was simply too dangerous to go after it. Only a handful of men knew the location.

As the story opened, it was learned that more than a treasure had been hidden. Secret documents that could destroy the career of a powerful government official had been buried along with the gold. Suddenly any risk was worth taking to retrieve the cache.

The action was well plotted and moved with the swiftness of an avalanche, but what held Sara's attention until nearly two in the morning was the inner conflict of the protagonist, the man called Phantom.

He was portrayed as a man who had clearly reached the limits of his emotional and physical endurance. Too many years of tension and violence had taken a savage toll. Now he had been assigned one last job by the government agency for which he worked. He was told to retrieve the gold and the documents hidden with it. At any price.

In the end the man called Phantom did the job he had been assigned to do, but it had nearly destroyed him. Then he had accidentally discovered that the incriminating documents buried with the gold constituted a shattering indictment of the man who ran the very agency for which he himself worked. The secret papers pointed at treason at the highest levels. Phantom had learned far too much. He had not been expected to survive his mission, but now that he had, his life was in jeopardy.

By the time Sara finished the harrowing and emotionally gripping tale, she felt exhausted but not at all relaxed. The writing had been lean and stark, which didn't surprise her. Adrian Saville struck her as the kind of man who wouldn't use one more word than necessary to tell his story. But she was left with the same question she'd had when she'd begun reading. How much insight could you gain into a man by reading his fiction?

Restlessly she restacked the manuscript pages and climbed back out of bed. She put *Phantom* back in the suitcase and turned to eye the rumpled sheets. She really didn't feel like climbing back into bed just yet. The book had left her far too keyed up and strangely tense.

On impulse she walked over to the sliding-glass door that opened onto the balcony and unlocked it. Taking a deep breath of the chilled mountain air, she stepped outside.

"You should have been asleep hours ago."

Sara jumped at the sound of Adrian's voice. Whirling, she saw him lounging against the railing of the balcony next to hers. He had one foot propped on the lowest rung and his elbows planted on the top one. The shadows hid the expression on his face, but she was aware of a strange tension in the atmosphere between them.

"I couldn't sleep," Sara whispered. "I've been reading."

"Phantom?"

"Yes."

"Learn anything?" he inquired sardonically.

Sara half smiled. "Only that I think you're going to have a very successful career as a writer of suspense novels. I couldn't put it down, Adrian."

"But did you learn anything?" he pressed softly.

She wished she could see his face. "You know I started it out of curiosity, don't you?"

"Umm."

"Well, I finished it because it was a very gripping tale. But I don't think I learned much about you in the process." She paused, thinking. "No, that's not true. I guess I did pick up a few things along the way."

"Such as?"

"You have a set of rather fundamental values, don't you? You believe in integrity and justice. Things like honor and loyalty are important to you. If they weren't you wouldn't have been able to portray the hero's emotional turmoil so well. You tore that poor man apart, Adrian. Halfway through the book I almost hated the writer for doing that to his protagonist. And then in the end, even though you pull together all the strands of the story and see that justice is done, you leave us wondering a little whether or not Phantom will survive emotionally.''

Even as she spoke Sara realized the truth of her own words. She had learned something about Adrian Saville by reading his manuscript, and what she had learned was disturbing on some levels. This was not a man who would ever understand games, let alone a light-hearted approach to life. On other levels Sara was aware of a strong feeling of respect. There were so few men who knew what it meant to have a personal code of honor and integrity. Adrian must know or he would never have been able to create Phantom. On still another level of awareness Sara experienced a sensation of compassion. Adrian must have known what it felt like to hold yourself together by sheer willpower. She wondered what he'd gone through in order to comprehend the depths of that kind of struggle.

"You wanted a miracle cure?" Adrian turned his head to look out toward the night-shrouded forest.

"I like happy endings," Sara admitted with a soft smile.

"I'm not sure there are any."

Sara leaned sideways against the rail, the chilly breeze whipping the hem of her nightgown around her ankles. "Adrian, I swear, if you turn into one of those cynical New York-style writers I won't read your next book."

He looked at her then and she saw the flash of a genuine grin. "Maybe the trick is not to write endings. Just cut the story off after the main issues have been resolved and let everyone go their own way. Readers like you can assume it all ends happily."

"You won't be able to fool me," she warned. "I know a real happy ending when I see one."

"I'll work on it," he promised so quietly she could barely hear him.

"Adrian?"

"What is it, Sara?"

"About the basic story line of *Phantom*..."

"What about it?"

"Where did you get the idea of the gold being hidden during the last days of the Vietnam war? It was very ingenious. And you made all the action so realistic."

"I got the idea from your uncle. He told me the tale of the gold."

"Really? It's a true story?"

"It's just a legend, of course. There are always a lot of tales and legends that come out of a situation like the last days of South Vietnam. Lowell told me the story one night about a year ago. Supposedly the gold was used by U.S. intelligence to buy information and finance certain clandestine operations. Your uncle told me privately that it's far more likely the gold was a payoff from some big drug deals that were going on in the south. Vietnam was a hotbed for that kind of thing toward the end of the war. At any rate the last man to actually see the gold was a U.S. agent. He arrived at his rendezvous point minus the treasure. No one really knows what happened." Adrian shrugged. "And thus are legends born."

"You added the bit about the secret incriminating documents?" Sara hazarded.

"It's called literary license. I needed an extra fillip to make the tale more than just a treasure hunt."

"You certainly accomplished that." Sara shuddered. "I really empathized with your hero. I think I fell a little in love with him."

There was a moment of silence from the other balcony and then Adrian said very calmly, "I'd much rather you fell in love with me."

Chapter Four

Perhaps it was the knowledge that she was concealed in the shadows of her balcony and that Adrian was isolated, in turn, on his own little island that made Sara feel safe enough to indulge the dangerous curiosity. Or perhaps she was still wondering just how much she had learned about him from reading his book. Then again, it might have been simply a woman's endless need to probe a man's words, searching for the real meaning. Whatever the cause, she couldn't resist asking the question.

"Why?"

"Because I think it might be very pleasant to have you fall in love with me."

The answer was straight enough, Sara had to admit to herself. Straightforward and honest. Just like the man. The bluntness of it served to wilt the small blossom of excitement within her before she'd even had a chance to fully analyze it. She stifled a small sigh of regret.

"Pleasant," she mused. "That sounds a little insipid."

He seemed surprised at her interpretation. "No. Not at all. I've learned to value the pleasant things in life," he continued slowly. "Pleasant things are civilized. They bring an element of grace and gentleness and peace into our lives. A glass of wine before dinner or a can of beer on a hot afternoon, a late-night walk on a beach, a friend you can trust with your life, a woman whose love is unshakable even if she knows you've been to hell and back. A wise man values such things."

"It must be the writer in you that can put the love of a woman in the same category of pleasantness as a glass of wine. Don't expect a woman to be impressed, however. We like to think we're special," Sara said with a degree of lightness she wasn't feeling.

"You're not going to take me seriously, are you?"

"Not tonight. It's two o'clock in the morning and we've had a disturbing day. I feel a little strange after reading *Phantom;* restless in some way. And as for you, you're a man whose understanding of life's pleasures seems to be different from the way other men view them. I'm not sure I understand you. All in all, I think there are too many jumbled emotions and unknown factors hanging around tonight for me to risk taking you seriously." She said it all very easily but Sara believed every word she was uttering.

"You may be right," Adrian agreed. He paused before asking, "Are you always this cautious with a man?"

She laughed in spite of herself. "It's the only area of my life in which I am careful. Or at least that's what my family would tell you. A woman can get burned falling in love with a man who's only interested in the superficial pleasures and pleasantries life has to offer. And there are so many men out there who are only interested in the superficial things. Uncle Lowell is right. But then, he usually is when it comes to judging people."

"I'm different, Sara," Adrian told her as he faced the sea. "I'm not one of your superficial wimps."

"No, I don't think you are. But I'm a long way from figuring out just exactly what category of male to put you in, Adrian Saville. And until I do…"

"You'll be cautious?"

"I think so. Good night, Adrian." Deliberately breaking the spell, Sara turned and stepped back into her room. Resolutely she closed the sliding-glass door and pulled the curtain. She stopped for a moment, listening to the silence, trying to examine the strange emotions swirling within her. Perhaps she was only feeling the remnants of the passion Adrian had ignited with his kiss.

But that kiss had ended hours ago. Perhaps she was simply disquieted by the tale of Phantom, she thought. No, there was far more to it than the restlessness left by the powerfully told story of a man on the brink. She had to face the fact that her suspicions concerning Adrian's serious approach to life were true. In all probability he really did look upon her as the prize he'd been promised by Lowell Kincaid.

What made her deeply uneasy was that she wasn't resisting the idea of being handed over to Adrian nearly as much as she ought to. Was it because she couldn't bring herself to take the notion seriously? Or was it because she was finding herself attracted to this stranger in a way that she'd never experienced with any other man?

Pleasant! Adrian thought it would be *pleasant* to be loved completely by a woman he could trust. Sara gritted her teeth. The man had a lot to learn emotionally. Either that or he needed a new vocabulary! After having read *Phantom,* though, she couldn't believe he lacked emotions.

But after having read his novel she could believe he was the kind of man who was determined to stay in control of the emotional side of his nature. The story of Phantom told her that on some level Adrian viewed the emotional side of life as full of risk. He would want to be very certain of a woman's love before he could allow himself to trust it, Sara realized.

It was all too complicated to figure out tonight and there were so many other things to worry about. Sara took a deep breath and went back to bed.

It was the kind of conversation that neither of them would want to mention the next morning. She felt certain of that. The late hour and the inherent safety of being on separate balconies with the soft rustle of the wind in the trees as background had combined to create a strange mood that had infected both of them. The mood would be gone by morning, and she had a hunch Adrian was wise enough to let it go.

Besides, she didn't really care to be lumped into the same category as a glass of wine or a can of beer.

Out on his balcony Adrian watched the shadowy sway of a tall pine and decided that, as a writer, he really ought to pay more attention to his choice of words.

Obviously words such as "pleasant" and "pleasure" were not the right ones to use around Sara Frazer. To her they were part of the games one enjoyed in life. Not matters of seriousness. She just didn't realize how much he valued the softer things in this world, or how seriously he took everything. Well, he'd try to watch it in the future.

After all, he sure as hell didn't want to fall into the same category as all those lightweight males Kincaid claimed she dated.

Straightening away from the railing, Adrian paced back into his room and closed the door. He had been unable to sleep earlier, his body far too aware of the fact that Sara was awake next door. The glow from her room while she read had lit her balcony and had been plainly visible from his own room. Now that she'd finally turned out her light perhaps he'd be able to get some rest.

THE NEXT MORNING Sara decided to take the initiative. She would put the mood and the conversation back onto a safe track. Setting an assured, easygoing tone was second nature for her. It was a skill she'd picked up early on in the world of corporate management and perfected even more in the world of casual dating.

"I've been thinking," she said as Adrian held the car door for her the next morning, "that you never really got a chance to properly celebrate the sale of *Phantom*. You had a beer by yourself and a glass of wine with me later, and that was it. Since then, I've had you running around helping me break into a private house, clean up a nasty mess and calm my fears. This evening I think we should celebrate properly."

"How?" Adrian turned the key in the ignition.

"I'll cook dinner for you. How does that sound?" She smiled.

"It sounds very pleasant." His mouth twisted. "I mean it sounds very nice." He cleared his throat and tried again. "It sounds great." He appeared pleased with his final choice of words. "Can you cook?"

"A good yuppie can fix the current gourmet fad food at the drop of a hat," she assured him.

"How about an ex-fad food like pasta?"

"No problem, as long as it's not macaroni and cheese. Imbedded in my brain cells is a recipe for a wonderful pasta and vegetable dish that will knock your socks off."

"No meat?"

"Absolutely not. Meat would ruin the delicate flavor of the dish, anyway. We'll need a nice Chardonnay to go with it."

He nodded. "Sounds like we'd better make a stop at the Pike Place Market before we board the ferry home."

"Terrific. I'd love to see the market. I've heard about it for years. I keep meaning to go whenever I visit Uncle Lowell, but somehow we've never had the time." Her sudden enthusiasm bubbled over.

"It's one of Seattle's main attractions. The only problem is finding a place to park. The place is usually crawling with tourists on a day like this."

They followed the highway down out of the mountains, crossed the bridge that connected Bellevue and Mercer Island to Seattle and then descended the steep streets downtown to First Avenue. Seattle's aggressive new skyline faced Elliott Bay, hugging the western coast of the continent and waiting eagerly for the daily traffic of cargo ships from around the world. The Pike Place Market, an old and honored institution, occupied prime territory a block from the waterfront. But if anyone had dared to suggest that it be razed and replaced by a high rise, he would have been lynched by the local citizens, Adrian told Sara. Seattle loved its market, with its blocks of vegetable stands, craft shops, bakeries and restaurants.

Adrian pulled off the neat coup of finding a parking space not more than a block from the busy outdoor market. He seemed quite proud of himself for being able to avoid one of the expensive parking garages. Men always seemed to see it as a challenge to find street parking, Sara realized with an inner grin. She congratulated him as he reached for her hand and led her up a flight of steps into the bustling atmosphere.

"I got lucky," he acknowledged modestly. "Stay close. I don't want to lose you."

Street musicians, a mime, a puppeteer, craftspeople and various and assorted panhandlers added noise and interest to the basic color of a working public market. Sara was fascinated by the array of intricately arranged vegetables in the produce stalls. The fish vendors hawked their wares in loud voices, waving live lobsters around to attract attention. Meat vendors offered every cut imaginable. Tourists and locals thronged the crowded aisles and spilled out onto the cobbled street that ran down the center of the market. Sara noticed that Adrian did not glance at either the fish or meat stalls.

"There's a shop where we can get the pasta at the far end of the market," Adrian advised as Sara halted to study an artistically arranged pyramid of red peppers. "And there's a wine store across the street."

"Why don't you go select the wine and pick up the pasta while I choose the vegetables?" Sara suggested. "I'll meet you back at the flower stall on the corner. That way we can save a little time. It's getting late."

Adrian hesitated. "Sure you won't get lost?"

"I'll be fine. The flower stall in fifteen minutes." She smiled up at him.

"Well, all right. You said you wanted a Chardonnay?"

"Right." Sara turned to plow through a gaggle of tourists who were trying to photograph the red peppers forming a pyramid. She was intent on finding the perfect broccoli. And she mustn't forget some Parmesan cheese, she reminded herself. There was a cheese vendor up ahead.

Somewhere between selecting the broccoli and choosing the fresh peas Sara began to lose track of time. Fifteen minutes went by very quickly and she was in the process of ordering the grated Parmesan when she happened to glance at her watch and realized she was going to be late meeting Adrian back at the flower stall. But surely he wouldn't hold her to the exact minute, she decided. He'd realize she was bound to be a little late what with all the hustle and bustle and the endless distractions around her. On the other hand, she had a hunch Adrian Saville was a man who valued punctuality. No sense kidding herself, she thought wryly. He would insist that she be where she said she would be when she said she would be there. Demanding punctuality was an element of control one could exert, and Adrian liked exerting control.

She thought about that as she ordered the cheese, realizing she had just had a strong insight into Adrian's personality. He needed to be in control of his environment. He needed to be sure of things. Maybe she'd better hurry.

She handed her money to the cheese vendor and accepted the package of Parmesan. It was as she turned away to plunge back into the stream of foot traffic that a large, male tourist careered into her.

"Excuse me," Sara said hastily, hanging on to her armful of packages. "It's so crowded here, I—" She broke off as the man gripped her arm.

"Your uncle wants to see you," the stranger grated. His fingers tightened, digging into her skin through the fabric of her shirt. He began pushing her deeply into the passing crowd.

Sara nearly dropped her parcels. Her mouth fell open in shock. "My uncle!"

"Come on, lady, we don't have time to waste."

She looked up at him, taking in the narrowed dark eyes, the gray-streaked black hair and the aquiline cast of his features. She was suddenly very scared.

"Who are you?" she managed, aware that she was being pushed toward the far end of the cobbled street. Around her the crowd ebbed and flowed. A string of cars vainly searching for the few parking spaces right next to the market stalls inched through the crowds. The flower stall was in the opposite direction. "What do you know about my uncle? And let go of my arm!"

The man didn't answer, intent on making progress through a cluster of tourists wearing name tags that declared they were all from New York. They seemed to resent his insistence.

"Hey, watch it, buddy," one of the group snapped.

"I thought folks out here were supposed to be laid back, not pushy. I coulda stayed home if I wanted this kinda treatment," muttered a heavyset woman with a huge camera strung around her neck.

The man with the face of an eagle didn't bother to respond. He simply forced his way through the grumbling tourists, pushing Sara ahead of him.

"Wait a minute," Sara gasped, beginning to panic. "I'm not going with you until you tell me who you are and what you know about my uncle! Now, unless you want me to start screaming—"

"Sara!"

She turned her head at the sound of Adrian's voice. "Adrian! Over here."

With a savage oath the man holding her arm released her. Sara spun around to watch him as he melted into the crowd. He disappeared in an instant.

"Sara, what the hell is going on?" Adrian came up beside her, pushing aside a few more New Yorkers in the process. He paid no attention to their enraged lectures on manners. "When you didn't show up at the flower stall on time, I figured you'd gotten lost. You're just lucky I spotted you when you stepped out into the street a minute ago. Who was that guy?"

"He said my uncle wanted me," she gasped. "He grabbed my arm and started pushing me along as though I were a sack of potatoes or something. Adrian, he knew who I was! How could he possibly know me? I've never seen him before in my life. And how could he know about Uncle Lowell?" She felt a wave of relief as she huddled against Adrian's side. His arm wrapped around her waist, fastening her securely as he began propelling her back toward the car.

"What did he look like? Tell me his exact words, Sara," Adrian ordered.

Sara clutched her packages and tried to think. "He looked very vicious. Sort of like a hawk, and his eyes were mean."

"Sara, that's not exactly a description, that's an emotional reaction, for heaven's sake."

"Well, I can't help it. I didn't have a lot of time," she defended herself. "He—he had dark eyes and dark hair that was turning gray. I'd say he was probably in his mid-forties. He was wearing very nondescript clothes. I can't even remember what color his jacket was. He said my uncle wanted to see me and that we didn't have a lot of time to waste."

"Those were his only words?"

"I think so. He was quite rude. Just ask those New Yorkers."

"He simply walked up to you and said that?" Adrian demanded. "Nothing else?"

She shook her head, trying to think. "No, I don't think so. I asked him who he was and what he knew about Uncle Lowell, but he didn't answer me. I was getting ready to start screaming when you showed up, Adrian, I have to tell you, I was very glad to see you! In fact I was never so happy to see anyone in my life as I was to see you a few minutes ago!" It was the truth, she realized. The sight of Adrian had meant safety.

They reached Adrian's car and he unlocked the door. His eyes narrowed as he took her arm to settle her in the front seat. "You're trembling."

"That man scared me," she said evenly. "There was something very frightening about him."

"Given the fact that it looks like he was trying to abduct you, I imagine he was somewhat scary," Adrian growled as he slipped into the seat beside her and started the car. "The bastard. I should never have left you alone."

"You know, I said he had hawklike features but you could describe them another way," she noted thoughtfully.

He slanted her a sharp glance. "How?"

"You could say that with those dark eyes and those strict features he looked a little like a wolf. Ruthless and potentially violent."

Adrian froze, his hand resting on the steering wheel. "You're letting your imagination get carried away again, Sara."

"I don't think so," she whispered, staring out the window. Behind them an impatient driver who wanted the parking space honked loudly.

With an oath Adrian put the car in gear and pulled away from the curb. He headed down toward the wharf and the ferry docks. "Sara, listen to me. I'm the writer in the crowd, remember? Leave the melodramatic touches to me."

"But I didn't get a really *cold* feeling," Sara went on, remembering her reaction. "I was scared and my palms got damp, but it wasn't like the temperature dropped twenty degrees or anything."

"For pete's sake, it's eighty-three degrees today! The meanest-looking guy in the world is hardly likely to make you feel as though the temperature dropped into the low sixties."

"True," she admitted dryly. "And I suppose Uncle Lowell only used that bit about the temperature drop for effect."

"Your uncle likes to tell a good tale and he's quite happy to embellish it for a willing audience."

Sara's mouth curved upward. "I know. I've been a willing audience since I was five years old." But there had been something different about the way her uncle had described the man called Wolf. Sara hadn't had the impression that her uncle was embroidering a story for her benefit. He had been in an oddly reflective mood the night he'd told her about the man he'd trained. Lowell Kincaid had been uncharacteristically quiet that evening. Almost morose.

"Forget your uncle's descriptive turn of phrase," Adrian said grimly as he guided the car into the line of traffic waiting for the white ferryboat. "We've got more important problems on our hands, thanks to him."

Sara shivered. "You mean the fact that someone knows who I am and managed to find me in the crowd at the market?"

"Exactly. We have to assume someone followed us. Probably from your uncle's cabin. Must have been watching it. The freeway was busy coming into Seattle today. It would have been hard to spot a tail if I'd had the sense to be looking for one."

Adrian's self-disgust was plain in his voice and it bothered Sara. "It's certainly not your fault that man found me in the market. For heaven's sake, don't blame yourself, Adrian."

"Well, he's not going to find you alone again."

"What are you talking about?"

"I'm going to start doing my job," he stated resolutely.

She smiled. "You mean keep an eye on me?"

"Umm. You'll stay at my place, not the inn, while we wait for Lowell to get in touch. I don't want you out of my sight again."

Sara absorbed the deep determination in his voice and knew he meant every word. Adrian had decided he had a job to do, so he was going to do it properly. That meant in his mind that he had to be in complete control of the situation. She would be spending the next few days with him. On the whole, she wasn't inclined to object at the moment. The man in the market had scared her. The relief of having Adrian appear at the critical moment was still with her. She wouldn't forget that sensation soon. The instinctive knowledge that he offered safety and protection was one more element to add to her growing list of things that seemed to fascinate her about Adrian Saville.

"What do we do about him?" she asked after a moment.

"The man you think is Wolf?" Adrian shrugged negligently. "Nothing right now. There isn't anything we can do except take care to keep him away from you."

"But we have no idea when Uncle Lowell will get back from wherever it is he's gone. We can't just wait indefinitely," she protested.

"Sara, honey, a long time ago I learned the value of patience. We'll wait."

"I think we ought to do something, Adrian."

"We'll wait," he repeated stonily.

"But that man seemed to know where Uncle Lowell was," she pointed out.

"If that character knew where your uncle was, why would he need you?" Adrian asked simply.

"Good point. Why *would* he need me?"

"Possibly because he intended to use you to lure your uncle out into the open."

Sara swallowed uneasily. "You have a devious turn of mind, Adrian."

"Umm. Probably an occupational hazard of being a writer of thrillers."

"So we wait?"

"It's either that or try the police—and your uncle specifically asked us not to do that."

"I doubt there's much they could do anyway," Sara said unhappily.

"No, I don't think there is."

"I guess we'll have to start locking your front door, won't we?" she offered, trying to keep her tone light.

"Lock the front door?" He glanced at her quizzically. "Oh, you mean the door you walked through so easily the other night."

"No offense, Adrian, but I got the distinct impression you haven't had to be too security conscious on your island," she said gently.

"Don't worry about it. You'll be safe. There's an alarm system installed. Lowell helped me install it a year ago."

"It wasn't on the night I walked in the front door?"

"It was on."

"But I never heard an alarm and no police came," she protested.

"My system works on a slightly different principle from most alarm setups."

"What principle?" She was deeply curious now.

Adrian parked the car inside the ferry and reached for the door handle. "The idea that it's sometimes simpler and more effective to trap an intruder inside the house than attempt to keep him out. I can set it in reverse mode, however, and keep intruders out just as easily as I can let them in. When I'm inside the house I set it that way. But when I'm gone, I use the first setting."

She blinked, not finding the idea either simple or effective sounding. But what did she know about alarm detection systems, Sara asked herself. "I see," she responded vaguely. "If I had tried to get back out of the house the other night, would I have found myself trapped?"

His mouth picked up at the corners in one of his brief flashes of humor as he helped her out of the car. "Weren't you?"

"Hardly. I mean, you just walked in and happened to find me in your study," she grumbled. He was leading her up to the passenger deck and it was hard to hear him distinctly in the noisy stairwell.

"I knew where you were in the house before I came through my own front door, Sara. I carry an electronic device that warns me when the system's been activated. The device starts working within a mile of the house."

"Really?" She was impressed.

"You never had a chance," he drawled.

She laughed. "Is that supposed to reassure me?"

"If you don't like my alarm system, blame your uncle. He's the one who helped design it."

"It sounds like something he'd come up with," Sara admitted. "It's that sense of humor of his. It would be just like him to design a system that can reverse the general principles of burglar detection. It fits in with some of his other theories, such as hiding something right out in the open where the whole world will see and overlook it. Well, if you're convinced it's safe, I'll trust your judgment."

"I'll take care of you, Sara," he said very seriously.

He meant it, Sara realized. The knowledge touched her on a very deep, perhaps primitive level. She hadn't met a lot of men who would say that sort of thing these days. And if they did say it, a woman couldn't risk believing it completely. Adrian Saville, Sara decided, meant it. And she could trust him.

She thought of something as they took a seat in the passenger section where they could watch the Seattle skyline recede into the distance. "Did you remember the pasta?"

"How could I forget the featured item in my celebration dinner?" he asked whimsically.

In spite of the unnerving scene at the public market, Sara found herself enthusiastically preparing her specialty pasta and vegetable dish later that evening. Adrian poured each of them a glass of wine and lounged in the kitchen, watching as she put the finishing touches on his dinner. He seemed to be fascinated with her every move. The kitchen took on a cozy feeling that made Sara almost forget her fear that afternoon.

"I can see you're going to expand my culinary horizons," Adrian noted as he sat down at the kitchen table he had set while Sara had fixed the Parmesan-flavored sauce for the pasta. "This sure beats macaroni and cheese."

"When did you stop eating meat?" she asked casually. Too late she remembered the last time she had asked him a question on the subject he had cut her off rather quickly.

"A little over a year ago," he answered calmly.

Relieved that he didn't seem to be taking offense over the issue, she decided to risk another question. She couldn't seem to stop wondering about every aspect of this man, Sara realized. "You don't miss it?"

"No." He plucked up a spinach leaf from the salad bowl. "Great dressing on the salad."

"Thank you." She hesitated and then tried again, delicately. "Did you just suddenly lose your taste for meat?"

"In a way." He eyed her silently as she sat down. "I was going through my mid-life crisis at the time. When I emerged, a lot of things in my life had changed. I quit my job, moved to a new state, started a book and decided I really preferred being a vegetarian."

"All those changes sound wonderful." She smiled. "I'm in the mood for some massive changes myself. Have you ever married?"

He arched his eyebrows as he forked up a mouthful of pasta.

"Sorry. I didn't mean to pry," Sara mumbled, lowering her eyes to her plate. It was difficult to know just how far she could push with this man.

"It's all right," he surprised her by saying after a moment. "I'm just not used to personal questions. No, I've never married. There's never been time. What about you?"

"No. I always seem to be changing careers and that tends to keep the available pool of men changing, too. The right one never seemed to come along."

"You'll know him when you find him?"

"Definitely." Sara laughed softly. "Uncle Lowell has been telling me for two years that the right man never was going to come along in the world in which I was living. He's always been a bad influence on me. Just ask my parents. They think I get my occasional bursts of unpredictability and unconventional behavior from his side of the family."

Adrian nodded. "He can be unpredictable and unconventional but he has a way of getting things done. He really did give you to me, Sara. I'm not making that up."

The camaraderie she had been feeling faded into a new kind of uneasiness. "It was a joke, Adrian. I'm sure of it. Even Uncle Lowell wouldn't go that far."

"Then why the matching gifts?"

"The crystal apples? They probably just took his fancy in some shop and he decided to buy a couple."

"He told me he had them specially made by a craftsman on the coast who works in glass," Adrian said.

"Adrian, I really don't know why he would give us a matching set of crystal apples, but I don't see that it matters one way or the other!"

"And what about that message on the tape at his cottage? The bit about protecting our wedding gift?"

"Now that," she admitted dryly, "was fairly bizarre. Your guess is as good as mine. But knowing Uncle Lowell, he was probably referring to something obvious."

"It would be just like him," Adrian agreed thoughtfully.

"When he shows up," Sara went on forcefully, "I'm going to have a few pointed remarks to make to him."

It was after dinner that Sara began to experience a strange nervousness. She knew the focus of it was the inevitable approach of bedtime and the necessity of making a dignified exit that was neither provocative nor rude. You learned to distinguish such subtle variations of behavior when you'd been through as many different careers as she had, she decided ruefully.

It wasn't that she was expecting a heavy-handed pass from Adrian. He didn't seem to do things heavy-handedly as far as she could tell. Just very deliberately. He certainly wouldn't pressure her into bed. But there was no denying the sexual tension that now existed between them, and if he alluded to it, she would find it difficult to deny.

The graceful approach was to keep things light and casual, she decided. That's the tone she would strive to maintain. After this first night it would be easier. Tonight would set the tone for the rest of her stay under his roof. She sensed it instinctively.

"Ah, a checkerboard," she exclaimed as she followed him into the living room after dinner. It struck her as the perfect answer to the question of how to spend the rest of the evening. "Are you any good?"

"At checkers? Fair, I guess. I'll give you a couple of games." Adrian poured two brandies and carried them across the room to the table where Sara was busily setting up the game. "I've played your uncle a few times."

"He prefers chess."

"So do I, usually."

"I only played it during my college years," she confided cheerfully. "It seemed to fit the academic image. Haven't played it since. I didn't really like it." She lined up the checkers in their little squares. "All that business about strategy and having to think several moves ahead was far too much like work to me. When I play games, I like to *play*."

"I see." He gave her a half-questioning, half-amused glance. "Checkers may be simpler but it's a game of strategy, too."

"You play it your way and I'll play it mine," she ordered, reaching out to make the first move.

Four games later they faced each other across the width of the table. Adrian's expression was one of wry wariness. Sara was feeling quite cheerful.

"That's two wins apiece," she pointed out. "One more game to settle the matter."

"Who the hell taught you to play?" he grumbled as he set out his pieces.

"I'm strictly self-taught," she acknowledged brightly. In truth, she was secretly pleased with her two victories. They had been achieved with wild, haphazard moves that clearly offended her opponent, who had won his two games with careful, precise strategy.

"It shows. You didn't win those two games with hard work. You got lucky on some wild moves. You have an extremely off-the-wall manner of playing, if you don't mind my saying so."

"You're just envious of my inborn talent. The way you play, a person would think the fate of the nation hinged on your next move. You're much too serious about the game, Adrian. You'd have more fun if you'd just loosen up a bit."

He looked at her, light eyes intent. "I'm afraid I tend to be a serious sort of man."

"Not given to fun and games?"

"No."

Sara caught her breath as she realized that they were suddenly inexplicably discussing more than a game of checkers. For reasons she didn't want to analyze she was afraid of the new direction. Desperately she tried to find a casual way of turning the conversation around before it strayed into the realm of the personal again. "Well, we'll see whose approach works best with this next game. I warn you, I'm going to be at my most off-the-wall!"

"In the long run, strategy and planning always succeed more often than wild luck, Sara."

"Prove it," she challenged rashly.

He shrugged and proceeded to do so. Fifteen minutes later Sara was left staring in vast annoyance at the board. She didn't have one single playing piece left on it. Adrian had beaten her with cool, deliberate ease, never relenting for a moment. Every move from first to last had been plotted and carried out with ruthless intent. Her cheerfully haphazard approach had netted her only a few of his playing pieces. Even those, she was convinced, he had deliberately sacrificed at various points to lure her into traps he had set.

"I demand a replay! You don't play fair. You play exactly like my uncle."

"What's unfair about it?" he asked, tossing the checkers back into the box.

"I don't know, but there must be something sneaky and underhanded about all that strategy," she complained. "It must be quite terrifying when you and Uncle Lowell play together."

"The games tend to last a long time," Adrian said with a faint smile.

"Who wins?"

"We're fairly evenly matched."

"You mean you win frequently?" she asked curiously.

"Umm."

"That's interesting. I don't know of anyone who can consistently beat Uncle Lowell at checkers or any other game. But sometimes I can take him," she added proudly.

"With one of your wild moves?"

"Yes." She grinned. "The thing about people who always use intense strategy is that you can occasionally upset them with my technique."

"Only occasionally. Not consistently," Adrian informed her politely. "You got lucky twice tonight, but that was about the best you could do, playing with your style."

"Something tells me that people who play with your style will never appreciate people who play my way."

And on that note, Sara decided suddenly, she had probably better make her gracious, unprovocative exit to the bedroom he had given her earlier.

Chapter Five

Adrian watched moodily as Sara went off to bed and wondered how he was going to get to sleep himself. When she had disappeared into the bedroom, he sprawled in an armchair and considered having another brandy. He needed something to squelch the restlessness that seemed to be thrumming through his veins.

This sensation was far worse than the disoriented feeling he'd had when he'd finally finished the book and put it in the mail. Then he'd felt suddenly at loose ends, as if everything had ended too quickly. But tonight's uneasiness was multiplied a hundred times by the dull ache of desire.

He could not remember the last time he'd desired a woman as intensely as he wanted Sara.

Adrian stared across the room at the waiting brandy bottle and decided against pouring himself another glass. He needed it, but this was not the night to indulge. Not when he was standing guard over a lady who had no real conception of the kind of trouble that might be waiting outside the door.

"Kincaid, you old devil, you really pulled out all the stops this time, didn't you?" he muttered, leaning his head back against the chair. "Who or what are you hunting?"

Whoever Kincaid's quarry was, Adrian didn't have any doubts about the outcome. Lowell had been out of the business for a long time, but he'd once been the best there was at what he did. He'd get his man. In the meantime, Adrian knew exactly what was required of himself. Kincaid had assigned him the task in that phone message. His responsibility was to take care of Sara.

"We also serve who only sit and wait," he paraphrased, mockingly solemn.

The fact that someone had actually approached Sara that afternoon was eating at him, fueling his unease and gnawing at his mind. His instincts were to run with her, take her as far away as he could, and hide her well. But when he left emotion out of the process and concentrated on logic, he knew she was safest here in the house. The alarm system Kincaid had helped him install was good. The best. The place was a walled fortress. Actually, when he thought about it, most of his life had become a walled fortress. Strong, secure, protected, with everything under control.

Until he'd walked into his den the other evening and found the lady with the crystal apple standing in the filtered gold of a setting sun.

He really should be trying to get some sleep, Adrian thought. He wasn't doing himself any good sitting here fantasizing about a woman with an apple. And there was no need to stay on guard all night in this chair. There would be ample warning if anyone tried to get to Sara while she was here. But somehow the thought of going off to a lonely bed was depressing. It didn't make any sense, because he was used to a lonely bed. But tonight the prospect bothered him.

Forcing his mind away from the tantalizing image of Sara undressing for bed down the hall, Adrian wondered just where Lowell Kincaid was at the moment. The older man had dropped out of sight and would probably stay out of sight until it was all over. Good, logical strategy. In the meantime all Adrian could do was wait and keep watch over the woman in his care.

Patience, he had told her that afternoon, was of great value. He wasn't sure she had believed him. The thought edged his mouth with a wry flicker of amusement. The lady did things with a certain impulsive flair. He could see why she probably wasn't cut out for the corporate world in the long run. She didn't have the patience for elaborate strategy and she didn't show any interest in restraining her impetuousness. In the short time he'd known her she'd enthusiastically broken into two private houses, comprehended and been a little shaken by the gut-level action of *Phantom,* nearly gotten herself abducted, and fixed him a celebration dinner with all the excitement of a woman who genuinely cared about his success. She'd topped that off by serenely taking herself off to bed as though she were simply a visiting relative rather than a woman who'd been subtly tantalizing him all evening.

Yes, he could see why she probably couldn't have gotten too much further in the corporate world. They liked flair in that world, it was true, but they liked it coupled with a certain amount of predictability and internalized respect for the corporate image. Adrian had a strong hunch Sara didn't have any such thing as an internalized respect for that type of image. Just as she probably hadn't had any for the academic image or the artistic image. She would play at maintaining the corporate facade the same way she played at being a yuppie.

After a while, upper management would probably have figured out that she wasn't one hundred percent committed to their world. Apparently she had figured it out first and decided to make a graceful exit.

The same kind of exit she'd made tonight, Adrian concluded grimly. Did she know he was sitting here, his body in a state of semiarousal while his mind tried to anticipate the next move the guy outside in the shadows might make? He wished to hell Kincaid would call and provide some clue as to what was happening. In the meantime all he could do was sit tight and practice the virtue of patience. It was a virtue he'd learned well.

Two hours later Sara came drowsily awake and lay still in the wide bed wondering what had brought her up out of a light sleep. It had been hard enough to get to sleep in the first place. She was momentarily annoyed at the intrusion.

Then the reality of where she was and why came back and she sat up, absently rubbing her eyes. She listened for a moment but heard nothing. A wary glance at the curtained window showed no menacing shadows. Why on earth was she awake? Perhaps it was simply nerves. She certainly had a right to a severe bout of nervous tension, she assured herself. Patting a yawn, she thought about getting up for a drink of water or a glass of milk. Then she noticed that light was seeping under her bedroom door from the hall. Adrian must still be up, she realized in concern.

If he wasn't able to sleep, it was because of her. He was sitting out there in the living room, worrying. Sara was certain of it. The man took his responsibilities too much to heart. She didn't want him staying up all night to stand guard over her.

Pushing aside the covers, she climbed out of bed, found her robe and went to the door. The hall outside her room was empty and the light left on in it seemed to be the only light in the house. Perhaps she was wrong. Maybe Adrian had gone to bed after all. She would feel much better if he had.

As long as she was up she might as well see if there was any milk in the refrigerator. Stepping out into the hall, Sara walked toward the living room, intent on reaching the kitchen. It was as she left the lighted hall and moved into the shadows en route to her goal that she saw him.

"Adrian?"

He was standing near a window, his lean frame a dark silhouette amid the various dark shapes of the living room. She knew he was watching her, although the silvered eyes were lost in pools of shadow.

"Do you make a habit of running around a lot at night?" he asked gently. "This is the second evening in a row that I've found you out and about instead of tucked into bed."

She smiled. "The fact that you've been awake to observe my nocturnal habits means yours are a little odd, too. Why aren't you in bed, Adrian?"

"I wasn't sleepy," he said simply.

"I don't believe you." She took a few steps forward, her bare feet silent on the wooden floor. "You're worried, aren't you? I thought you said the house was safe."

"It is."

"Then you should be in bed, not prowling around out here."

"Is that what I was doing?" He seemed vaguely amused. "Prowling?"

Sara moved still closer. She came to a halt a foot away from him and lightly touched his arm. "I don't think I'm going to be able to sleep unless you do. I'm not used to someone fretting over me like this. It makes me feel strange, Adrian. You don't need to assume this kind of responsibility toward me."

"I don't have any choice." His tone was suddenly grim.

"You mean because of that message my uncle left on the tape?" She groaned. Her fingers tightened urgently on his arm. "Adrian, you mustn't take that too seriously. I'm not really your responsibility. There's absolutely no need to feel that you have to play bodyguard."

"After what happened this afternoon?" he asked dryly.

She shook her head resolutely. "When it comes right down to it, Adrian, that was my problem, not yours. I mean, I certainly appreciate your interest in my welfare, but I don't want you to feel you have to get so involved."

"I've already told you; I don't have any choice." He lifted his hand to touch her cheek. "And I think you know it."

Belatedly she remembered that he could see much better in the dark than she could. Sara was very much afraid he might be able to read the uncertainty in her eyes as she looked up at him. "Adrian, please..."

"What are you afraid of, Sara? That you might come to rely on me? Your uncle says you move in a world where you can't count on a man when the chips are down."

"Sometimes my uncle exaggerates," she said huskily, acutely conscious of the roughness of his fingertips. She wanted to move away from his touch and couldn't.

"Your uncle knows a lot about human nature. He learned it the hard way."

"But he's prone to sweeping generalizations," she protested. "He met a couple of the men I've dated and decided everyone in my world was like them. I don't think he approves of the 'new male,'" she added, trying for a spark of humor.

Adrian didn't respond. His hand slid down the side of her throat, resting just above the collar of her robe. "I don't think you approve of the 'new male' either, Sara, or you would have been married by now."

"It sounds as though you're prone to sweeping generalizations, too! Actually, there's a lot to be said for the new breed of male. He acts as if he's sensitive, communicates his thoughts and feelings with all the right words; he's into things like art and gourmet cooking and he's able to handle the idea of a woman in the professional world, or says he is..."

"And he thinks in terms of relationships instead of commitments. But a woman like you needs commitment, according to your uncle. That says it all, Sara. Your uncle is right. You would never have found what you were looking for in your old world."

"How can you know so much about me?" she whispered, feeling confused and unsure.

"Your uncle has told me a lot about you. For nearly a year he's been feeding me bits and pieces of information about you. Enough to torment me and bait me and tease me. I've remembered everything he said. And now that I've had you with me for a couple of days I've had a chance to learn a few things on my own."

"You're an expert on human nature, too?"

"Umm." The hand on her throat was warm and compelling. He traced the curve of her shoulder as if deeply intrigued by it.

"And did you gain your knowledge the hard way, also?" she demanded, striving to maintain her sense of balance, both emotional and physical.

"There is no easy way."

"Adrian..."

"There's nothing else to say, Sara. We're together in this. I'm going to look after you, whether you think I have the right to do so or not."

She moved her head in a slow negative. "Because my uncle 'gave' me to you?"

"Perhaps. I haven't had a lot of gifts in my life. I've learned to take care of the ones I do get."

"Just as you've learned to value life's little pleasures?"

He muttered something under his breath, something that sounded disgusted. "You misinterpreted what I meant last night."

"Did I?"

"And now you're using that misinterpretation as an excuse to withdraw from me tonight, aren't you?"

"Yes," she acknowledged, aware of an ache of pain and regret because of her own defensive behavior. She wanted to toss it aside and give into the promise of the moment. Feeling torn in a way she had never known before, she couldn't bring herself to release her grip on his arm and walk back to the bedroom. It should have been a simple enough action. She knew it would certainly be the wisest thing to do under the circumstances.

"Sara, you don't have to be afraid of me," he said so softly she almost didn't hear him. It was the urgent need in his voice that got through to her.

"I know that." The bluntly honest words were out before she could halt them, a response to the urgency in him. Hastily she tried to retreat. "It's not that I'm afraid of you, I simply don't want you assuming so much responsibility toward me."

"I know. Because you're afraid that if you give me that right, you'll come to rely on me and at some point in the future that could be dangerous, couldn't it?"

"Dangerous?"

"You're afraid that one day you'll turn around and I won't be there or I won't be the man you think I am at the moment you need me most."

Sara took a deep breath and tried to control the trembling in her fingers where they rested on his sleeve. "That's quite an analysis."

"I told you; I've been studying you. Between your uncle's observations and my own, I've got a fair amount of data," he murmured.

"So you think you know a great deal about me now, is that it? What about you, Adrian? What do you need?"

"You."

The single word was a monolith between them. Sara knew there was no way around or over the starkness of his answer. She could only retreat or accept it. It was not possible to ignore it.

Intellectually she knew she should retreat. But her intense emotional reaction anchored her to the spot. She could not move. In that moment she knew she wanted him, too. The one element of caution that she had always practiced in an otherwise playful approach to life seemed to be disintegrating. The strange swirl of emotions she experienced around this man was blowing into a full-scale storm. Sara was no longer certain she could resist the impact.

"Adrian," she heard herself whisper, "are you sure?"

"Do you have to ask?"

"No." She looked up at him wonderingly. "No, I don't think I do. I've never met anyone like you."

"I know. I've never met anyone like you, either." The hand on her throat held her very still as he brought his mouth down to hers.

Sara trembled a little beneath the warm onslaught of his kiss, and there was a soft sound far back in her throat that was lost against his lips. She felt the need in him and the leashed hunger and knew that the honesty of his desire was going to be overwhelming.

Slowly her palms lifted to rest against his strong shoulders as her mouth flowered open.

"Sara..."

Her name was a husky groan uttered deep in his chest and then he was tasting the damp warmth behind her lips. The aggressive intimacy of the kiss seemed to swamp her, making her sway against him. Adrian steadied her, holding her with a kind of fierce gentleness that provided all the strength she needed.

Slowly he lifted his head until he could look questioningly down into her face. His eyes gleamed with a silvery brilliance that captivated her, and she knew in that moment that she was lost. Or found. She couldn't be sure which. Nothing seemed normal or totally rational. But one fact seemed to emerge from the shimmering world of her emotions. If Adrian wanted her tonight, she was his.

He must have read the vulnerable response behind her lowered lashes because he let out a long sigh and lifted her into his arms.

"It's all right, Sara." His voice was a dark and passionate stroke along her nerves. "It's all right, honey. I'll take care of you. I'll take care of everything. I've waited and wondered so long. I didn't even realize how much I needed you until you finally walked into my life."

Sara felt the easy power in him and rested her head against his shoulder. Unconsciously she surrendered the last remnants of her caution. She didn't care where he was taking her or what would happen when they arrived. Never had she been so certain that it was safe to abandon the future for the moment. There was no longer a distinction between the two in her mind. In fact, it seemed to her that there could be no real future without this timeless interlude. Adrian needed her and she needed him.

She was vaguely aware that he carried her into his own bedroom, not hers. Carefully he stood her on her feet while he turned back the covers. His eyes never left her face. When he'd finished the small task, he stood in front of her and put his hands at the base of her throat. There was more than passion in his touch, Sara realized. There was that sense of need and urgency she had responded to last night on the balcony of her motel room. Once more it enthralled her and this time there was no barrier to keep her from tumbling into the glittering net.

"Don't think about anything else except us," he whispered as he slowly slid his hands inside the robe and pushed it off her shoulders. "Please, Sara. Just us."

"I don't think I could concentrate on anything else even if I wanted to," she said truthfully. Again she shivered. The light robe fell to the floor at her feet.

"Are you afraid of me?"

Sara shook her head. "No."

"You're trembling." He seemed incredibly concerned over the fact. His fingertips stroked her bare arms and then he touched the rising swell of her breast just above the edge of the nightgown.

"I know, but not because I'm afraid." She smiled a little as she covered one of his hands with her own. "You're trembling a bit, too."

"I'm shaking like a leaf. I want you, Sara. I've been wanting you all evening. No, longer than that. I've been wanting you for months." The words were raw with honesty.

"Adrian, it's probably much too soon—"

"No," he interrupted roughly. "It couldn't possibly be too soon. Not for us."

His hands moved down over her breasts and she felt the tantalizing heat of his palms through the thin material of the nightgown. She knew he must realize that her body was already responding. Sara could feel the tautness of her nipples as they came tinglingly alive. She caught her breath and began to fumble with the buttons of his shirt.

"Please, Sara," he breathed into her hair. "Yes, please."

His need filled her with a longing to satisfy and comfort him. Slowly she made her way down the front of his shirt until it parted, exposing the dark hair on his chest. So entranced with the vivid sensuality of the moment was she that Sara was hardly even aware of her nightgown floating to the floor.

But when Adrian's hands slid down her back to the full curve of her hips, she moaned softly and stumbled a little against him. She glanced up into his face and read the masculine anticipation there.

"You're so soft," he murmured in tones of wonder. His fingers sank luxuriously into the flesh of her derriere and he pulled her tightly against him.

"You're not soft at all," Sara said unthinkingly and then buried her flushed face against his chest as he growled his amused response.

"No, I don't suppose I am. I feel as though I'm made up of angles and rough edges. You, on the other hand, are composed of curves and gentle valleys. Places where a man can lose himself."

He let his fingers trail into the cleft between her buttocks and Sara's nails dug lightly into his skin as he followed the path to the dampening juncture of her thighs.

"Adrian..."

"Say my name like that again," he demanded hoarsely as he picked her up and settled her on the bed. "It sounds different when you say it."

"Does it?" She lay watching as he yanked off his shirt, stepped out of his shoes and unclasped his jeans. A moment later he stood nude beside the bed, the light from the hall emphasizing his lean, hard body. He was wonderful, she thought dazedly. Everything she could ever want in a man. It was strange to be so certain of that, because until now she hadn't been quite sure just what she had wanted in a man. She had only known that she hadn't found it.

"Oh, Adrian," she whispered as he came down beside her. "Adrian, I didn't know..."

"Didn't know what?" He flattened his palm on her stomach and smoothed her skin down to the curling hair that veiled the heart of her femininity.

"Never mind. I don't think I can explain it just now." She curled into him, shifting languidly under his touch. "I can't even think right now."

"There's nothing to think about." He leaned down to kiss the peak of her breast. His tongue teased the firm bud of her nipple until she cried out and pulled him closer. "That's all you have to do right now," he told her approvingly, the words heavy with desire. "Just give yourself to me. Let me open my present. I've been waiting so long for you, sweetheart."

She obeyed, wrapping her arms around his neck as he touched her with growing intimacy. When his prowling fingers found the hot damp center of her need she said his name again, this time with an urgency that matched his own.

"Sara, my sweet, Sara." He pinned one of her legs with his strong thigh and probed her deeply with a deliciously questing touch. When she shuddered, he muttered hot, dark words of encouragement into her ear.

She lifted herself against his hand, unable to resist the caress. Never had she responded so completely and so readily. Her senses seemed inflamed, thoroughly alive and aware in a way that was new to her. Fascinated by the world of sensation that was beginning to spin around her, she stroked his smoothly muscled frame. Her palms slipped over the sleek contours of his back, down to the hard planes of his thigh. Then, with gentle boldness she moved her fingertips around to find the flat terrain of his stomach. For an instant longer she hesitated. Then her hand went lower.

"Yes," he grated with harsh need when she dared to tease his male hardness. "Take me inside, sweetheart. Let me have all of you. I need you so."

She couldn't find words but he seemed to know she was ready. With passionate aggression Adrian pushed her into the pillows and lowered himself down along the length of her.

"Put your arms around me, Sara, and never let go," he commanded. "Never let go...."

She did as he instructed, pulling him to her until she felt the blunt hardness of him waiting at the gate. The knowledge that he was on the verge of entering her fully and completely brought a brief, startling flicker of alarm. For an instant Sara had a vision of the reality that lay beyond tonight. *This man was unique. After tonight nothing would ever be the same.*

The fleeting glimpse of the future was gone an instant later as Adrian moved heavily against her. All of Sara's senses returned to the moment, lost once more in the pulsating excitement.

"Oh, *Adrian*..." The words were torn from her as she felt the full impact of his body taking possession of hers.

"Hold me, Sara."

Instinctively she obeyed as she adjusted to his sensual invasion. Then he began to move within her, slow, tantalizing strokes that pushed her senses into tighter and tighter bundles of energy that strove for release.

The end was a revelation to Sara, a new understanding of her body and its responses. She found herself clinging to the man above her with an abandon that she would never have believed if she hadn't experienced it firsthand.

"That's it, honey," he rasped as she cried out his name once more. "Let go. Just let go. I'll take you with me all the way."

Willingly, unable to do anything else, Sara gave herself to him completely and gloried in the knowledge that he was returning the gift in full measure. She heard the sound of her name as it was wrenched from him and then he was pushing deeply into her one last time. His hard body shuddered for a long moment and then collapsed. Outside the window the night breeze briefly stirred a stand of fir and then all was silent.

It was a long while before Sara became aware of the sprawled weight that still trapped her in the depths of the bedding. She opened her eyes to find Adrian lying on top of her, his head on the pillow beside hers. He was watching her from behind half-closed lashes.

"Am I too heavy for you?" he asked lazily.

"Umm."

His mouth flickered in brief amusement as he recognized her deliberate imitation of his characteristic response. "What does 'umm' mean?"

"I don't know. You're the expert. You tell me."

"It means 'uh-huh.'" He sighed regretfully and slowly rolled onto his side. Then he gathered her close. "Too bad. You're very comfortable."

"Am I?"

His head inclined downward once in a short nod. "Incredibly comfortable. I can't recall when I've been this comfortable. Or this relaxed. Or this content."

"Neither can I," she said honestly. It was the truth. Tonight there were no pretenses or games or caution. Her fingertips worked small, idle patterns on his chest. "Adrian, I've never felt quite like this before in my life."

"You don't sound as if you're sure you like feeling this way." He touched her cheek.

Nothing will ever be the same. "It feels strange."

"We'll get used to it," he assured her.

"Will we?"

"You're nervous all of a sudden, aren't you?"

"No," she denied quickly.

"Sara, honey, don't try to fool me now. You can't do it," he told her gently.

"Well, maybe I am a little nervous. It was too soon, Adrian."

"It was inevitable, so the timing doesn't really matter."

"We hardly know each other."

"You were a gift to me, remember? I was bound to open you as soon as I could."

She flushed. "I thought you were a great believer in patience."

"Only when it's the best option."

"You don't think we should have waited awhile longer? Made certain of our feelings?" she asked anxiously.

"I am certain of my feelings," he told her roughly.

"I don't want you confusing your feelings of responsibility for me with...with your, uh, more personal feelings."

He looked down at her in mocking pity. "Believe me, I'm not mistaking a sense of responsibility for raw passion. From my point of view the two are quite distinct. You're the one who sounds confused."

"You're not?"

"Not at all, Sara. If anything, tonight just makes everything even simpler and more straightforward."

She eyed him curiously. "What does that mean?"

"It means we don't have to have any more arguments about my right to take care of you, for one thing." He brushed her parted lips and then drew back to study her expression. "You belong to me now. That gives me all the rights I need."

"I've never met a man so anxious to assume responsibility," she tried to say lightly. But she was very much afraid her voice cracked a little on the last word.

"I've never been particularly anxious to assume responsibility for anyone else," he told her seriously. "With you, it's different."

"And what do you want from me in return?" she asked carefully.

"I've already told you, remember?" He pushed a strand of hair back behind her ear. "I want you to love me. I like the idea of having you love me. I like it very much."

"You think it would be 'pleasant,'" she couldn't resist saying somewhat tartly.

"You said you fell a little in love with the hero in *Phantom*."

"So?" she challenged softly.

"How do you think he would treat a woman whose love he wanted?"

The question startled her. She frowned. "I think he would take care of her. She could trust him."

"I want you to trust me the same way."

She half smiled. "You're not Phantom."

"I created him. There must be something of me in him and vice versa."

Sara studied his intent features. She had asked herself so many questions about the similarities between Adrian and his hero the previous night when she'd read the manuscript. "Yes, I think there might be."

"Trust me, sweet Sara," he grated, rolling onto his back and pulling her down on top of him. "Trust me with your love. Like your uncle, I know what has value in life. I'll take good care of you."

"Aren't you worried about how well I'll take care of you?" she parried, aware of the renewing tautness in body.

"You won't play games with me."

"What makes you so sure?" she demanded, rather irritated with the certainty in his voice.

"Because it would tear me apart if you did," he said simply. "You wouldn't do that to me, would you, Sara?"

Horrified at the thought, Sara cradled his face between her palms. "No, Adrian. Never that," she vowed.

Unaware of how deeply she had just committed herself, Sara kissed him, translating the verbal promise into a physical one. His hands came up to wrap around her waist and he arched his lower body demandingly into hers.

"Adrian?"

"Umm."

She didn't bother to ask him what he meant. It was becoming very obvious. Sara parted her legs for him and her mouth locked with his as he began the spiraling climb to passion.

THE FIRST HINT OF DAWN was in the sky the next time Sara came awake. There was a moment of lazy curiosity as she opened her eyes and absorbed her surroundings. Adrian's room was a thoroughly masculine affair, with its warm cedar walls and heavy, clean-lined furniture. It was as orderly and controlled-looking as the rest of his house. She was finding it interesting until she became aware of the weight of his arm across her stomach. Then she awoke completely.

Memories of the night filtered back in a haze of lingering passion and midnight promises. She turned to look at Adrian and was grateful to discover he was still sound asleep. What exactly had she agreed to last night, she wondered with a sudden feeling of panic.

There had been talk of love and responsibility and a promise not to play games. But it seemed to her that most of the dangerous, reckless promises had come from her. The only thing he had vowed in return was to take care of her.

It was crazy, Sara chided herself as she cautiously slipped out from under his arm. She hadn't intended to let things go so far. She had never meant to wind up in bed with him, at least not so soon. She had barely met the man. This was exactly the sort of behavior she had instinctively avoided in the world she had just left. What on earth was the matter with her?

Adrian stirred restlessly when she slid off the bed but he didn't awaken. On silent feet Sara fled down the hall to her own room and scrambled about for her jeans and a shirt. She badly needed to get out of the house for a while. She needed time to think and reevaluate the whole situation. Her family had often warned her that her periodic bouts of impulsiveness would land her in real trouble someday. Even Uncle Lowell had felt obliged to point out that there were some risks involved in playing games with life.

But last night had been no game. Last night had been for real. Twenty-four-karat real.

Shoving her feet into a pair of sandals, Sara yanked a lightweight Windbreaker out of her suitcase and hurried down the hall to the living room. She let herself out the front door and stood on the porch, inhaling deeply of the sea-sharpened morning air.

For a moment she hesitated, unable to think clearly enough to decide on a destination. Then she remembered the car she had left parked in the inn parking lot. With a small sigh of relief at having provided herself with a focus for the morning walk, she hurried down the steps and out to the road. She would walk back toward town and pick up her car. Wonderful. It would give her something useful to do while she tried to sort out her future, she thought. Sara patted her jeans pocket to make certain she had the keys.

Behind her she was unaware of the house purring to life with news of the unauthorized exit. Adrian came instantly awake as the nearly silent vibration in the headboard jolted him. The alarm-clock radio beside the bed was blinking in a fashion that had nothing to do with its normal function. The message was quiet but clear.

The house was doing its duty. Faithfully it undertook to warn its owner that Sara was gone.

With an oath that was half rage and half pain, Adrian threw off the covers and reached for his clothes.

Chapter Six

The flash of rage and pain gave way to another emotion even as Adrian slipped out the front door. Fear began to claw at his insides, and in that moment he could not have said whether it was fear for Sara's safety or fear that she was leaving him. The two seemed to combine in the bottom of his stomach, forming a knot of tension that increased as he realized she was already out of sight. He was at a loss to explain how he could have been so sound asleep that he hadn't even felt her leave the bed. Normally he never slept that deeply. Last night had altered something as fundamental as his sleeping patterns and that was unnerving in some ways.

The truth was he hadn't handled last night all that well. He'd practically pushed her into bed, Adrian berated himself. He should have waited. He'd known it was much too soon. She hadn't spent nearly a year with a fantasy nibbling at the edge of her mind the way he had. She couldn't know what it was like to have a fantasy become reality. As far as Sara was concerned she'd only known him a couple of days. She must have awakened this morning with a head full of doubts and anger aimed at him.

So she'd taken off without bothering to say good-bye.

Damn it, he thought furiously, where the hell could she have gone? There had been no sound of a car. She must be on foot and that meant she couldn't have gone far.

The car. Hers was still at the inn and it probably represented escape to her. The road would seem the fastest way into town to her, Adrian decided. Without hesitating a second longer, he loped down the steps and started up the drive toward the winding road that led into the Winslow.

He saw her just as he reached the pavement. She was walking briskly along, her light-brown hair catching a sheen of gold from the dawn light. It complemented the faint gleam of gold from the little chain on her wrist. He remembered the way the tiny little bracelet had glittered last night against her skin. She had told him that her uncle had given it to her a long time ago. Her slender, soft body moved with an ease that seemed to emphasize the intriguing round-ness of her hips and the subtle, feminine strength he recalled so vividly that morning. Adrian watched her in silence, remembering the sweet passion he had tapped during the night.

The year's wait had been worth it, he acknowledged to himself as he began to pace silently a few yards behind her. He had not set himself up for disappointment by allowing Lowell to build an image in his head. In his wildest imaginings, though, he could not have envisioned that she would wrap her arms around him with such aban-doned demand. Nor could he have dreamed up the clean, womanly scent of the real Sara Frazer. It was unique to her and he would never forget it. There was no way his fantasies could have created the exact feel of her soft thighs as she opened herself to him and there was nothing in fantasy that approached the real-life sensation of sinking himself deep into her soft, clinging warmth.

But it was the words he remembered with such stark clarity that morning. Her soft words of need and the promises he had coaxed from her lips. He had thought the words would hold her even if the lovemaking could not. She had told him she would not play games with him and she had said she wanted him.

But this morning she was running from him.

It would be easy enough to catch her. She wasn't even aware of him prowling along behind her on the empty road. Her mind seemed focused on her destination, whatever that was. Was she planning to take the car and head back to San Diego? Or would she go to Kin-caid's house and wait there for her uncle?

Not that it mattered, Adrian thought grimly. His hand curled and uncurled briefly in a subtle act of tension. He couldn't let her leave.

He ought to just catch up with her and explain very succinctly why he couldn't let her off the island. Perhaps she would be rational about the matter. Or he could simply overtake her, scoop her up and carry her back to the house. She'd probably start screaming. Then again maybe it would be simplest if he caught her and swore never to touch her again as long as she did as she was told. And just how would he manage to keep a promise like that?

None of the alternatives seemed viable. With a savagely stifled oath, Adrian continued to trail her along the narrow road. It was ridiculous following her like this, unable to make up his mind about how to handle her. Kincaid would collapse in laughter if he could see him now. The Adrian Saville he knew had never been prone to indecision or uncertainty.

Several yards ahead Sara walked toward town with an energy that was fueled by a sense of impending fate. She couldn't explain the feeling of being caught in a trap, but the sensation was strong in her mind. A part of her could not regret last night no matter how hard she tried. But another side of her warned that everything had happened much too quickly. It was so completely alien for her to catapult herself into a situation like that. She shook her head morosely, unable to comprehend her own emotions. Throwing herself into bed with a virtual stranger was one game she had never played.

There was no denying that the unfamiliar blend of emotions she had experienced around Adrian had taken her by surprise. In a way, it seemed almost logical, almost inevitable that they had culminated in last night's sensual conclusion. That sense of inevitability, however, was new and disturbing. What irony that Adrian had been worried about her playing games with him! Nothing had ever seemed less like a game than her own fierce response in his arms. Perhaps if it had seemed more like a game, she would be feeling far more comfortable this morning.

Of course, Sara decided caustically, she could always reassure herself that Adrian wasn't exactly a stranger. Hadn't Uncle Lowell apparently chosen him for her? Dear outrageous, unpredictable and not infrequently brilliant Uncle Lowell. The man should be dangled over hot coals for creating this mess.

Uncle Lowell.

Her uncle's name brought a dose of common sense. This whole mess had been precipitated by Lowell Kincaid. Where was he and when would he return?

Sara's brows were shaping a thoughtful line above her hazel eyes when she finally reached the inn on the outskirts of the small town. Her car was still waiting patiently for her in the parking lot. She hoped the inn management wasn't upset about her tardiness in picking up the vehicle. Digging into her pockets for the keys, Sara started forward.

She had her hand on the door handle, absently trying to identify the slip of paper she noticed resting on the front seat when the shock of Adrian's voice behind her spun her around.

"You can't just disappear into the mists, you know. Only fantasies can evaporate like that and you're not a fantasy any longer." The remark was made in a cool, conversational tone that completely belied the shimmering intensity of his gaze. He stood a few steps behind her, his hands thrust into the back pockets of his jeans. The familiar canvas shoes were on his feet and Sara dimly realized that he must have followed her for nearly a mile without making a sound in those shoes.

For an instant the unlikely combination of the easy tone and the fierce demand of the silver eyes caused Sara to feel as though she had somehow lost her balance. Her hand closed tightly around the door handle behind her as she steadied herself.

"I didn't realize you were behind me," she finally managed, pulling herself together quickly. It was ridiculous to let him throw her like this. "You should have said something."

"If you'd wanted company, you probably would have mentioned it before you decided to sneak out of the house."

She was taken aback by the tightly reined emotion she sensed in his voice. Was it anger or pain? In that moment she couldn't be certain. But she knew she'd prefer that it was anger. Even in her uncertain state of mind this morning she realized that the last thing she wanted to do was hurt Adrian Saville. On the other hand there was such a thing as self-preservation. Sara acknowledged that she felt more than a little on the defensive.

"I didn't sneak out of the house. I simply went for a walk and decided to pick up my car while I was out. You're the one who was sneaking around! You and those sneaky shoes you wear!"

"The last time I let you go off by yourself you nearly disappeared, remember? It's my job to keep you out of trouble until your uncle gets back."

"Is that what you were doing last night?" she challenged, goaded by the accusing tone of his voice. "Keeping me out of trouble?"

"If we're going to talk about last night, let's do it somewhere else besides this damn parking lot," he growled. He stepped forward and closed his fingers around her upper arm. "We can get a cup of coffee down at the wharf."

"Adrian," she began firmly, and then decided against an argument. Uneasily Sara acknowledged that she couldn't tell what he was thinking this morning. Nor could she be sure of the state of his emotions. Given the uncertainty in his mood and her own odd feelings, it seemed wisest to avoid an outright confrontation.

He led her down the hill from the inn to a pier that thrust out into the beautiful, sheltered cove that was called Eagle Harbor. A marina full of peacefully tethered boats of all shapes and sizes extended out from the pier. On the other side of the cove Sara could see private homes tucked away above the water's edge. At this early hour there were several people lounging on the rail, or working on their boats. Fishing rods and tackle were in evidence as folks came and went from the marina to the small wharf buildings. Near the entrance to the short pier a small shop featured coffee and fresh pastries. Adrian bought two containers of coffee to go and wordlessly handed one to Sara.

"Thank you," she murmured with exaggerated politeness.

He didn't bother to respond to her comment. Instead he seemed to be deep in thought as though he were struggling to find the right words. The idea that he was having trouble made Sara relax a bit. She had the impression Adrian was not accustomed to dealing with this morning's sort of situation. She was glad.

"I wasn't exactly going to disappear into the mists," she tried tentatively.

"No?" He sounded skeptical.

She shook her head, sipping at her coffee as they walked out onto the pier. "No. I only intended to pick up my car and drive it back to the house. If I'd been planning to duck out, I would have taken my suitcase. Or at the very least, my purse."

"Umm."

She slanted him a glance. "What is that supposed to mean?"

"That you've got a point," he said grudgingly. "I should have thought of it. I just figured you were so upset about last night that you raced out of the house without bothering to pack or say goodbye."

Sara focused on the far end of the pier. "I was upset about last night." She felt him examine her profile but she didn't turn her head to look at him.

"I rushed you into bed," he said finally.

"*We* rushed into bed," she corrected firmly.

"You're not going to let me take all the blame?"

"Do you want all the blame?"

Adrian took another sip of coffee. "No. I'd like to think you had a hand in the final decision. I don't have much interest in playing the role of seducer of unwilling females."

The response that came to Sara's lips was cut off abruptly as a fisherman who had been unloading his morning's catch walked past with a bucket of water in which two fish swam lethargically. The man turned to wave to a comrade who hailed him from a nearby yacht. Quite suddenly he stumbled over a fishing-tackle box that someone had left on the pier. In the next instant the bucket of fish tilted precariously and one of the silvery, wriggling creatures fell out. It landed right in front of Adrian's foot and lay shuddering as it began to die.

"Whoooeee, look at that sucker!" a young boy exclaimed excitedly.

"Must be six pounds if it's an ounce," another man said approvingly. "Nice catch, Fred."

The man named Fred grinned proudly as he caught his balance. "Thanks, Sam. Thought I'd do 'er over a mesquite fire tonight. The wife's having the neighbors in for cards."

Sara was aware of a familiar pang of regret at the sight of life going out of the fish. She understood about the food chain and that humans were inclined to be carnivores but she preferred her fish neatly filleted and packaged in plastic in a supermarket.

She glanced away from the fish before realizing that Adrian had come to a halt and was staring down at the creature that lay dying at his feet. There was no expression on his face. He simply stood silently watching the wriggling, flopping fish. The man who had caught it leaned forward to retrieve it.

Without stopping to think, Sara reached out and grabbed Adrian's wrist. He glanced up as she pulled him firmly around and led him toward the pier entrance. He followed her lead, not saying anything as they walked away from the sight of the now-dead fish.

"That sort of thing is hard enough on us supermarket carnivores," Sara heard herself say casually. "I imagine it's rather sickening for a vegetarian."

"Don't worry, I'm not going to be sick out here in public," he said dryly.

She cast him a quick, assessing glance. "No, you're not, are you?"

"I'm a realist, Sara. I don't eat meat but I understand how the world works," he said quietly.

"Yes, I suppose you do." She dropped his hand, feeling foolish at having made the vain effort to protect him.

"That doesn't mean I don't appreciate the thought," he told her softly.

"What thought?"

His mouth was edged with quiet amusement and a hint of satisfaction. "You were trying to shield me from a bit of reality back there. It was very—" he hesitated, hunting the word "—very compassionate of you."

"Forget it," she said sturdily. "Now about our plans for the immediate future..."

"Does this mean we've finished our discussion of the immediate past?" he inquired politely.

"There's nothing to talk about. We've both agreed that we were equally to blame for rushing into the situation." She straightened her shoulders. "We're adults and we should be able to analyze our actions and learn from our mistakes. We are stuck here together until my crazy uncle sees fit to get in touch, so we will have to conduct ourselves in an intelligent manner. Now, I suggest we both put last night behind us instead of trying to rehash it.''

Adrian shrugged. "Suits me."

"I'm so glad," she muttered too sweetly.

"You weren't running away this morning?" he confirmed quietly.

"No, I was not running away. I just wanted a little time by myself. I felt as if I needed some fresh air.''

He nodded and then said calmly, "I think I can understand that."

"Kind of you," she drawled.

"Just make damn sure you don't do it again."

A faint trickle of unease went through her at the cool way he spoke. "I beg your pardon?"

"I said, don't do it again."

They were back in the inn parking lot, approaching Sara's car. She had the keys in her hand but her mind was on his quiet command. "Adrian, one of the reasons I decided to get out of the corporate world is that I don't take orders well. We'll get along much better if you don't get carried away with your sense of responsibility.''

"I hear you," he said agreeably.

"Good." She reached down to open the car door and slid into the front seat.

"Just don't go running off again without me," he concluded as he settled smoothly on the seat beside her. He held out his hand for the keys.

Sara felt goaded. "The next time I try it I'll be sure to look back over my shoulder to see if I'm being followed.''

He lounged into the corner of the seat, never taking his eyes from her stormy gaze. "I thought we were going to act like adults about this.''

She drew a deep breath, aware of feeling extremely childish. "Sorry," she mumbled. "You're right, of course. I should never have left the house alone this morning. I wasn't thinking. I was feeling rather, er, emotional. I assume you don't have that problem frequently yourself?''

He didn't smile at her sarcasm. "Wasn't I emotional enough for you last night?''

Sara felt a flush suffuse her face. "What you appeared to be feeling last night is often referred to by an entirely different name.''

"Passion?"

"Try lust," she bit out.

"I thought we just got through agreeing that we're adults. If that's the case, then I think it's safe to say both of us know the difference between lust and..." He hesitated. "And other feelings."

She stared at him in silence for a long, troubled moment. She knew the difference, she thought. She just wasn't quite ready to admit that what she had felt last night went by a very dangerous name of its own. It was called love.

Instinctively Sara moved a bit farther over in her seat, seeking to put some distance between herself and Adrian. The car seemed filled with him, she thought. As she slid across the upholstery something crackled beneath her thigh. Belatedly she remembered the slip of paper she had noticed earlier on the car seat. Grateful for the minor distraction, she reached for it.

"You'll give me your word you won't take off alone again?" Adrian asked in a neutral tone as he switched on the ignition. He glanced at the paper in her hand as she unfolded it.

"Oh, I'm nothing if not cooperative."

"I appreciate it. What's that?" He put the car in gear, ignoring her sharp tone.

"I don't know. Just a piece of paper that was lying on the seat. I don't remember..." Sara's voice trailed off in stunned amazement as she read the short message she held.

Adrian frowned at her, his foot on the brake. "I said, what is it, Sara?"

"A problem. A very big problem." Mutely she held the typed message out to him.

Adrian stared at her wide eyes for a second longer before switching off the ignition again and reaching out to take the note from her hand.

It wasn't a long note. Sara had it memorized after reading it through twice.

The one-fifteen ferry to Seattle. Come alone.
You'll be safe.

"Well, hell," Adrian said thoughtfully.

TWO HOURS LATER he was still acting and sounding very thoughtful. It infuriated Sara because she had argued herself hoarse in the meantime. She no longer felt in the least thoughtful. She felt quite desperate in fact. For the hundredth time she paced to the far end of the living room and whipped around to glare at Adrian, who was lounging quietly on the sofa. He had one foot on the coffee table in front of him and was flipping through a magazine with absent attention.

"Listen to me, damn it!" Sara was sure her voice would give out at any moment. It seemed to her she had been yelling at him for hours. "I haven't got any choice! I have to be on board that ferry at one."

"You don't have to be anywhere at one." Adrian's responses had been quiet and reasonable for two solid hours. They were driving Sara up a wall. How could anyone remain quiet and reasonable and totally inflexible for two solid hours?

"How else are we going to discover what this is all about?"

"People who leave notes in cars are no doubt creative enough to think of alternatives when Plan A doesn't work." Adrian turned the page of his magazine. "Under the circumstances I think it would be better to make them resort to whatever it is they didn't want to do first. No sense letting them have the easiest option. Gives them an advantage."

"Adrian, I don't want to wait around for Plan B!"

"That's what the guy is probably counting on. Be patient, Sara."

Sara swung away, striding restlessly back to the other end of the room. Anger and nervous dread alternated relentlessly in her head. She was furious at Adrian's refusal to even consider letting her go alone on board the one-fifteen ferry. The nervousness was a growing fear that whatever her uncle was involved in was proving to be more than he would be able to handle. She braced a hand against the window frame and stared out at the stand of trees that guarded the drive.

"Uncle Lowell must be in very big trouble," she forced herself to say carefully.

"Or someone wants you to think he is."

"Since when are you the expert on how people such as that man Wolf think and operate?" she snapped. "You've only written one thriller, for heaven's sake. That hardly qualifies you as an authority on the real thing."

Adrian put down the magazine. "Sara, I'm only doing what your uncle asked me to do."

"I understand," she said, trying to be patient. "But you're taking his instructions much too literally. The situation calls for a little improvising. Something's gone wrong, don't you see?"

"No."

Her fingers closed into a futile fist and she leaned her forehead against the window. She was rigid with exasperation. "Adrian, please listen to me."

He came up behind her, moving soundlessly across the floor to rest his hands on her shoulders. "Honey, if I let you go on board that ferry by yourself, we wouldn't be exactly improvising. We'd be following someone else's plan. Surely you spent enough time playing corporate manager to know that following the opposition's game plan is usually not to your advantage."

"We've got to find out what he wants!"

"What he wants," Adrian said distinctly, "is to use you."

"We don't know that. Maybe he has news. Maybe he wants to give us some information. For heaven's sake, Adrian, whoever left that note might not even be what you call the 'opposition.' He might be a friend of my uncle's trying to get a message to me."

"Sara, your uncle has a strange sense of humor but I don't see him pulling a stunt like this."

"Whoever is going to be on that ferry is someone who knows something about Uncle Lowell. I'm going to find out who it is and what he knows." Sara lifted her head away from the window, aware of Adrian's fingers sinking heavily into her shoulders.

"Sara..."

She shook her head, tired of arguing, her mind made up. "No, Adrian. I'm through discussing the matter. I'm going to be on the ferry. Be reasonable. What can happen to me on the boat? It will be full of people commuting to Seattle. Whoever is going to meet me will be trapped on there, just as I will be until the ferry docks. He can hardly pull a gun and shoot me, can he? After all, he'd be stuck with the body until he gets to Seattle."

He turned her around beneath his hands, his face drawn and grim. "Sara, this isn't a game like corporate management or checkers. You can't handle it with your casual off-the-wall style. You don't know what you're getting into."

"I'm already into it," she pointed out stiffly. "And I can't stand the waiting, Adrian."

He searched her face. "I can force you to stay here."

"Not unless you tie me up and throw me in a closet," she retorted.

"That's a possibility."

"Don't be ridiculous!"

He dropped his hands to his sides and turned to walk back toward the sofa. "You can't go alone," he finally said flatly.

She frowned, trying to decide if she'd just won part of the battle. "But the note said—"

"Damn the note!" He glanced at her over his shoulder. "You can't go alone."

"Are you saying you're going to come with me?"

"If you're refusing to listen to my advice, then I don't have much choice, do I?" he asked, sounding bleakly resigned.

"Not unless you really do tie me up and throw me in a closet." Sara tried for a tremulous smile, hoping to lighten his mood now that she appeared to have won the confrontation.

Adrian just looked at her. "The temptation is almost overwhelming."

Sara let the smile fade abruptly. "You're not a good loser, Adrian."

"No. I never was."

She'd won half of the concessions she needed, Sara realized. It shouldn't be tough to get him to agree to the rest. The note had specified that she be on the ferry alone.

"I'm glad you've decided to be logical about this, Adrian," she began cautiously.

"I generally am logical and reasonable."

"Then you can understand why I have to go alone today."

"Forget it, Sara. I'm not that logical and reasonable. Try to get out of this house alone and you'll find me standing in the way. Think you can walk over me?"

At ten minutes to one, Sara was sitting beside Adrian as he drove down the ramp onto the ferry. The crowd was a small one for the afternoon crossing and they easily found seats in the main lounge. Scanning every face that went past her, Sara suddenly realized that her palms had grown damp around the strap of her shoulder bag. She wasn't accustomed to this kind of tension, she decided unhappily. Her body felt unnaturally alert, poised for the unknown. There had been no sign of the wolf-faced man in the ferry terminal.

"It's very stressful, isn't it?" she muttered to Adrian, who was sitting across from her in the booth they had chosen by a wide window.

"Very," he agreed wryly.

"You can jot down your feelings and put them in your next book," she suggested with false lightness. "It'll add a note of realism."

"I'll do that."

Sara twisted the shoulder strap. "What if he doesn't show because you're with me?"

"Frankly, I'll be relieved."

She glowered at him. "Are you going to drag this little incident out every time we quarrel in the future? Throw it at me and use it to illustrate how headstrong and foolish I am?"

"I doubt I'll need any additional evidence. You seem to provide enough on a day-to-day basis." He paused, thinking, and then asked interestedly, "Will we be doing it a lot?"

"Doing what?" she grumbled, watching people as they filed past to the snack counter.

"Quarreling."

"I hope not," she said feelingly. "It's wearing. I feel as though I've been through the wringer today and the main event hasn't even taken place."

"Umm."

The ferry moved out of its slip, beginning its crossing to Seattle. In the distance a giant freighter loaded with containers of cargo headed toward the bustling port of Seattle. Sea gulls hoping for tidbits kept pace with the ferry, wheeling and gliding alongside.

"You know, Adrian, there's something to be said for living in this area," Sara remarked wistfully. "It's beautiful country."

"Umm."

Sara was about to demand an explanation of his monosyllable response when she caught sight of the man who was walking into the lounge from the outside deck. She went very still as she recognized the grimly handsome aquiline features. He looked at her down the length of the passenger lounge.

"Adrian," Sara whispered tightly, "it's him. The man who tried to grab me in the market."

With a casual movement that Sara couldn't help but admire, Adrian turned calmly to stare at the hawk-faced man. He examined him in silence for a moment and then swung his gaze back to Sara. "Looks like he's going to go ahead with Plan A, even though some of the details have been changed."

"You mean the fact that you're with me?" She watched the stranger make his decision and walk firmly down the aisle of window seats. "If you want to know the truth, Adrian, I've changed my mind. I'm glad you're here. Very glad."

"It's always nice to be appreciated," he muttered just as the other man came to a halt beside Sara.

"Miss Frazer?" His voice was quiet and unruffled.

Sara swallowed, trying to keep her face unemotional. "Yes."

"I'm Brady Vaughn. I'd like to talk to you."

"We assumed that from the rather melodramatic note you left in her car," Adrian said before Sara could respond. "Why don't you sit down and tell us what this is all about."

Brady Vaughn coolly examined Adrian and then appeared to dismiss him. He returned his attention to Sara. "This concerns your uncle, Miss Frazer. It's a very private matter."

Sara stared up into the darkest eyes she had ever seen. The man was towering over her, and if Adrian hadn't been sitting quietly across from her, she would have felt terribly vulnerable. As it was she instinctively took her cue from Adrian and gestured at the seat beside her. "Whatever you have to say can be said in front of my friend. He is as concerned about my uncle as I am. Please sit down, Mr. Vaughn."

"For your own sake, Miss Frazer, I think the fewer people involved in this, the better."

"I'm already involved," Adrian growled softly. "Sit down, Vaughn, or leave us alone."

Sara held her breath as the tall man flicked another assessing glance at Adrian, who returned the look expressionlessly. Then the aquiline-faced Vaughn shrugged and sat down beside Sara. When he spoke he ignored Adrian.

"This is rather a long story, Miss Frazer."

"Perhaps you could summarize?" Adrian suggested easily. "We've got short attention spans."

Sara saw the flare of impatience in Vaughn's eyes. "Please, Mr. Vaughn. Tell us what's going on."

Vaughn rubbed the side of his jaw with an air of contemplation. Then he nodded slowly. "To put it simply, Lowell Kincaid is in trouble."

Sara caught her breath. "Do you know where my uncle is at the moment?"

"We think he's in Southeast Asia."

"Southeast Asia!" Sara glanced in astonishment at Adrian, who kept his gaze on Brady Vaughn. "What on earth would he be doing there?"

Vaughn sighed. "I told you this was a long story. The truth is it goes all the way back to the last days of the Vietnam war."

Sara went still. "Go on."

"Your uncle was working for the government in those days, Miss Frazer. He was assigned to the embassy in Saigon but he spent a lot of time in the countryside. He knew his way around South Vietnam as very few Americans did. He had friends in the oddest places.'' Vaughn looked a little pained. ''If you remember the news reports, you'll recall that things were very chaotic toward the end. Panicked crowds from the city tried to overrun the embassy walls in Saigon. Everyone wanted a seat on one of the evacuation helicopters. Things were in turmoil. A lot of men such as your uncle had to play it by ear when some of the normal chains of command broke down.''

With a disturbing sense of déjà vu, Sara listened to the tale. She never once looked at Adrian to see how he was reacting. Something told her she should respond to Brady Vaughn as though she were hearing the story for the first time. Not as if she had read the nucleus of it in a manuscript called *Phantom.*

''There was a lot of valuable material that had to be salvaged during the U.S. evacuation of the country,'' Vaughn was saying quietly. ''Some of it was taken out by helicopter but some of it was sent out through less obvious routes. Your uncle was in charge of handling a particularly valuable shipment. He was to take it across a border. To be blunt, Kincaid reached his rendezvous point in Cambodia but the shipment he was assigned to safeguard never made it.''

''I see.'' Sara's throat felt constricted.

Vaughn looked at her with a cold, even glance. ''We think he's decided to go back and bring out the shipment he left behind, Miss Frazer.''

''Who's 'we'?'' Adrian inquired politely.

Vaughn frowned. ''The people for whom Kincaid used to work.''

''The government?'' Sara pressed.

Vaughn inhaled slowly. ''Yes and no.''

''That's a little vague, isn't it?'' Sara asked tartly.

Vaughn's handsome features twisted ruefully. ''I should make it clear, Miss Frazer, that while I have ties to the same agency for which your uncle worked, this is something of a personal matter for me. I am not representing the government in this.''

''You want that shipment for yourself?'' Adrian drawled.

Vaughn shook his head tiredly. ''There's no chance of getting that shipment out of Southeast Asia. Kincaid will only get himself killed trying. I'd like to prevent that. Your uncle and I go back a long way together, Miss Frazer. I owe him. He was my friend.''

"Who would kill him if he went back?" Sara whispered.

"The story of that lost shipment of, uh, material, is not exactly a secret, Miss Frazer. There have been rumors and speculation for years. A couple of very dangerous people are aware of its existence and of the fact that only your uncle knows where it is. They've dropped out of sight since Lowell Kincaid did. I have reason to believe they've gone after him. I want to get to Kincaid before those others do."

"And just where do I fit into all this?" Sara demanded urgently.

"Your uncle is a very independent man. Especially now when he no longer has any ties to his former employers. He probably won't listen to me but I think he might listen to you. I want you to come with me, Miss Frazer."

"Come with you where?" she asked dazedly.

Vaughn slid a speculative glance at Adrian and then refocused intently on Sara. "I'd rather not say our destination. But it will be in Southeast Asia. There are ways of getting a message to your uncle once we're in contact with certain local people."

"I don't have a passport," she heard herself say.

"That detail can be handled. Leave it to me."

Adrian stepped in, his voice remote and restrained. "She needs time to think it over, Vaughn."

"How much time?" Vaughn kept his gaze on Sara. "We haven't got a lot to spare."

"Forty-eight hours," Adrian answered for her.

Sara glanced at him and once again instinct made her follow his lead. "Forty-eight hours, Mr. Vaughn. Please. I have to think about this."

Brady Vaughn got to his feet. The Seattle waterfront was rapidly filling the horizon. He touched Sara lightly on the shoulder. "Forty-eight hours, Miss Frazer. For Kincaid's sake, please don't take any longer." He turned and walked away.

Sara sat staring at Adrian as the ferry bumped gently into the dock. She ran her damp palm over her shoulder where Brady Vaughn had touched her. "Does it feel as if it's gotten colder in here?" she asked vaguely.

Chapter Seven

Sara concentrated on another bite of the chocolate-chip ice cream she was eating as she strolled along the Seattle waterfront. Beside her Adrian neatly devoured the pecan-flavored cone he had chosen. The ferry wouldn't be leaving for another half hour. It had been Adrian who had suggested they take a walk on the picturesque wharf before they caught the boat. Neither had said much until after they bought the ice cream at one of the many fast-food stalls that dotted the wharf.

Sara knew the reason for her silence was probably the same as Adrian's. They were both lost in contemplation of the scene on the ferry with the man who called himself Brady Vaughn. Finally Sara polished off the last of her cone and flipped the napkin into a trash container outside the entrance to the aquarium.

"You know what I think?" she announced, thrusting her hands into her pockets.

"What?" Adrian seemed fascinated with his disappearing ice cream.

"I think that legend Uncle Lowell told you about the gold is not pure fiction."

"Brilliant deduction."

She slanted him a disgusted glance. "Either it's for real or else—"

"Or else other people such as Brady Vaughn believe it's for real, which amounts to the same thing," he concluded grimly.

"Know what else I think?" Sara went on determinedly.

"Let me guess. Your uncle's idea of the perfect wedding gift is a cache of gold buried somewhere in Southeast Asia." Adrian swore softly.

Sara sighed. "He always did like gold. Said it was the only real hedge against an uncertain world. I can imagine him thinking gold would be the perfect present for me. Whenever he's given me a gift, it's usually been made out of gold." She extended her wrist briefly, displaying the thin gold chain. "And he did say something about going off to protect our, uh, wedding gift."

"Does chronic idiocy run in your family?"

"My uncle is not an idiot!"

"I know," Adrian agreed derisively. "He just has a bizarre sense of humor. You'd think I'd realize that by now."

Aware of Adrian's irritation, Sara felt obliged to turn the conversation away from a defense of Lowell Kincaid's odd actions. There would be time enough to defend her uncle later. With any luck he would return to take up his own defense. Heaven knew it had always been a little tricky making excuses for him. Sara decided to go on the offensive.

"Are you quite certain that Uncle Lowell didn't say anything about the legend being for real when he told you the story?" she demanded.

"He told me it was only a tale. There are others like it that came out of the war, you know. I turned up a lot of them while doing research for *Phantom*. It certainly isn't unique."

"Really?" Momentarily distracted, Sara stared up at him, her eyes widening. "Tell me some of them."

Adrian lifted one shoulder in a heedless shrug and tossed away the end of his cone. A trolley car designed to carry tourists from one end of the waterfront to the other clanged past along tracks that paralleled the street. Adrian didn't speak until the sound of the whistle had faded. "Well, there's a story about the CIA agent assigned to destroy vital documents in the hours before the embassy was overrun."

"And?" Sara prompted.

"According to the legend he kept some of the more interesting ones, such as a list of agents and their covers operating in Asia. Then he tried to hold an auction."

"He was going to sell the list to the highest bidder?"

"That was the plan, I gather."

"Did he?" she demanded interestedly. "Hold the auction, I mean?"

"Sara, it's just a legend. How should I know what happened?"

"Oh." Disappointed, Sara pushed for more information. "What other tales did you hear?"

"Leftover legends from that particular war?" Adrian's heavy brows came together in thought. "I think there was a story or two about businessmen who were supposedly hired by the U.S. government to supervise construction projects in Saigon and the surrounding area. Apparently they used their visits to South Vietnam to establish heroin connections that continued long after the war ended, making them very rich men. Then there are the tales of gold deals made in the north. The list of such stories is endless, Sara. Wars breed them. Just think of all the stories and legends that came out of World War II. People still write novels based on them.''

"I see what you mean. So when Uncle Lowell told you the story of the gold, you assumed it was just that: a story.''

"Umm.'' Adrian appeared lost in thought. "It still might be just that.''

"I don't know,'' Sara mused. "I can see Uncle Lowell doing something like this—hiding a cache of gold in a bizarre location and then telling me it's supposed to be my wedding gift.''

"*Our* wedding gift,'' Adrian corrected. "Don't forget he gave me the story first.''

Sara ignored that. "What I can't see is him stealing the gold in the first place.''

"We don't know that he did. At this point all we've got is Vaughn's version of things.''

Sara shivered. "Creepy guy, isn't he?''

Adrian looked at her with a wry expression. "That's one way of putting it.''

Sara came to a halt and leaned over the railing to stare out across Elliott Bay. Several long piers on either side of her, many full of import shops and souvenir stands, poked fingerlike out into the water. Around her, children ate popcorn and other assorted goodies while their parents browsed around the shops and enjoyed the sun. Another large ship was making its way into port flanked by tugs. Its deck was stacked high with containerized cargo. The ship carried a strange name and a foreign flag. A sailing yacht skirted the tip of a pier, seeking a place to tie up so that its passengers could come ashore for a meal at one of the many restaurants featuring fish. The sight of all the seagoing traffic made Sara think of places she had never been to and which, under normal circumstances, she would probably never go to, places that had bloody histories stretching back a thousand years.

"Have you ever been to Southeast Asia, Adrian?''

There was silence for a moment and then Adrian moved to lounge against the rail beside her, his eyes following her gaze. "Why do you ask?''

"Just curious. I was wondering what it's like.''

"You're not going to find out in the company of Brady Vaughn,'' he told her roughly.

Her head came around, her face mirroring her serious mood. "I may not have a choice, Adrian."

His fingers tightened on the railing. "You think I'm going to let you get on a plane with him forty-eight hours from now?"

Sara moved restlessly, not quite certain how to handle the harshness in him. "That reminds me," she said, not answering his question. "What made you think of asking for a couple of days' leeway?"

"I didn't ask."

"That's right." She nodded, remembering. "You just told him that we were going to take that much time, didn't you? That was very quick thinking, Adrian."

"I try," he murmured sardonically.

She frowned. "Maybe writing thrillers helps you think fast on your feet in situations such as this."

"I was sitting down at the time."

She peered suspiciously at his profile, wondering if he'd actually attempted a small joke. "Well, I'm just glad you were there. I'm not sure that he wouldn't have been able to pressure me into going with him if I'd been alone."

"You're not accustomed to dealing with people like him. They can be very convincing, especially when they're using the fate of someone you love as bait."

"You really think Vaughn is lying?"

"There's a hell of a lot we don't know about this mess, Sara."

She was silent for another moment or two as she turned things over in her mind. "He must be who he says he is, Adrian."

"Who? Vaughn? What makes you think he's telling the truth?"

"Well, there was that business about being able to get me a passport on two days' notice, for one thing. I mean, no one but a real government agent could accomplish that."

"Money and the right connections can buy just about anything in this world."

"Oh, yeah?" She was beginning to resent his calm, cynical superiority. "And just where would someone like Vaughn go to buy a fake passport?"

There was a slight pause and then Adrian said quietly, "He might try Mexico City."

"Mexico City!"

"Umm. It's huge, Sara. One of the largest metropolitan areas in the world. Here in the western hemisphere it's one of the places frequented by a certain kind of 'in crowd.' A man can shop for anything, including a fake passport. He can also get lost there and reappear on the other side of the globe without bothering to answer a lot of inconvenient questions.''

She stared at him. ''More lore you've picked up from writing thrillers?''

Adrian watched the sailing yacht make another pass along the piers. ''Legends and tales, honey. A writer of thrillers collects them.''

''Which is probably why Uncle Lowell couldn't resist feeding you that story of the gold.''

''Probably. Lowell knows a sucker when he sees one.''

''Well, we'll deal with him later,'' Sara vowed. ''In the meantime, we have to deal with Vaughn.''

''Sara, we can't trust that guy one quarter of an inch,'' Adrian said evenly. ''You said yourself he's a, uh, creep.''

''But he knows where Uncle Lowell is,'' she protested.

''He *says* he knows where he is. But if we go on the assumption that we can't trust Vaughn, we have to assume we can't trust anything he tells us, right?''

''It's very confusing, isn't it?'' she groaned. ''And in the meantime Uncle Lowell could be in real trouble.''

''I think we're the ones in real trouble, thanks to good old Uncle Lowell,'' Adrian said, pushing himself away from the rail. ''Come on, honey. The ferry will be leaving soon. We'd better get going.''

''Forty-eight hours isn't a very long time, Adrian.''

''I know.''

''What if my uncle doesn't get in touch before the deadline?''

''I didn't set the deadline because I hoped Lowell would have sense enough to contact us. I set it to give myself some time.''

Sara glanced at him in astonishment. ''Time to do what?''

Adrian wasn't looking at her. He appeared to be concentrating on the brightly dressed crowds of casual strollers who were ambling along the waterfront. ''Sara, I'm going to leave you alone for a while tomorrow.'' He spoke slowly, as though measuring each word.

''Why?'' she demanded, utterly startled.

He hesitated. ''There's something I want to check out. A man I want to see.''

''Are you going to try contacting that government agency my uncle used to work for?'' she demanded.

''No. I'm not sure we could trust any answers we got from that source,'' he told her honestly. ''Look who we're dealing with from that department now.''

She wrinkled her nose. ''Vaughn. I see what you mean. So who are you going to contact?''

"Somebody who may know for certain whether or not Lowell really is in Southeast Asia."

"But if we don't know it for certain, who would?"

"Sara..." Adrian reached out and threaded his fingers through hers. His tone was low and urgent. "Sara, would you please not ask any more questions? Your uncle and I have talked a great deal during the past year. He's told me things I don't think he's told anyone else."

"But, Adrian..."

"Please, Sara. Just trust me, okay?"

She wanted to scream that no, it was not okay. She wanted to tell him it had nothing to do with trust, that she simply deserved some explanations. Sara was infuriated and frightened and she felt like lashing out but she realized with an instinct that went to the bone that it wouldn't do any good. Her uncle had apparently shared some confidence with Adrian that neither of them had seen fit to share with her. Adrian would not tell her anything else at this point. She was certain of it.

"If you've known someone we could contact all along, why haven't you already done it?" she asked in a carefully controlled voice.

"Because your uncle wouldn't want me doing it unless I thought we had a full-fledged crisis on our hands. Up until now I've been going by what he said in that taped message."

"You've been assuming he could handle his 'old business.'"

"Yes."

Sara pulled her hand free from his, putting a small distance between them. "All right. There's not much I can say if you won't tell me what's going on. Go ahead and contact whoever it is you think can give us some information."

"You're angry, aren't you?"

"I'm feeling a little annoyed at the moment, yes," she bit out. "I don't like being kept in the dark."

"I'm sorry, Sara," he began but she cut him off.

"Forget it. Just don't ever again accuse me of playing games. You're turning out to be a real pro at the art."

That stilled him for a moment. He said nothing until they were back at the ferry terminal and walking on board the boat. Then Adrian told her the rest of his decision. "It will take me most of tomorrow to do what I have to do. You'll be alone at the house."

Sara threw herself down on a seat, her arms folded across her breasts in cool disgust. "Why? Or is that part of the game?"

He sat down beside her, his hands clasped loosely in front of him. He studied his linked fingers. "I'm not playing games, Sara. I have to leave you alone because I wouldn't dare risk using the phone to contact your uncle's friend, even if I thought I could get through to him.''

She watched his profile through suddenly narrowed eyes. "You think the phone's tapped?"

"After meeting Vaughn, I'd say we have to assume the worst, wouldn't you?"

"Probably. What do you mean, you aren't sure you could reach this man on the phone even if you did dare use it?"

"From what your uncle says, this guy isn't the sort who trusts people over the phone. I'll have to see him in person."

"Where is he?"

"Not far," Adrian answered evasively. "I can catch a plane and reach him in a few hours. I'll leave as soon as I can book a flight in the morning. I should be home by late tomorrow afternoon."

"And in the meantime I just sit patiently waiting, is that it?" Sara muttered.

"Sara, you'll be safe in the house," he told her quietly.

"I'd rather go with you."

He shook his head, staring down at his clasped hands.

"Can't you at least tell me why I can't accompany you?"

"Sara, please—"

She interrupted whatever it was he intended to say with an exclamation of impatience. "Forget I asked."

They were politely remote with each other for the rest of the day. They walked up the street from the ferry docks and into Winslow so that Adrian could make his plane reservations at a pay phone. Sara was too proud even to attempt to overhear his conversation with the airline clerk. Later she berated herself for not having tried to eavesdrop. At least she could have found out where he was going. When he rejoined her to walk back to the cottage, she asked only if everything was settled.

"I can't get a flight out until nearly seven tomorrow morning."

"I see."

"That means I'll have to take the first morning ferry to Seattle."

"Yes."

His mouth thinned as he listened to her aloof responses. "Sara, there's one thing I want to make very clear."

"That would be a change."

He ignored that. "You're not to leave the house for any reason after I've gone."

"I understand." She didn't look at him, her gaze fixed stonily ahead.

"Good. You're safe in the house after I've set the alarms. No one can get in unless he decides to use explosives."

"What a pleasant thought."

"Don't worry about it," Adrian said dryly. "Just give me your word of honor you won't leave the house until I get back."

"Or until Uncle Lowell gets back," she amended smoothly.

He nodded. "Promise?"

She wondered briefly what would happen if she didn't promise and decided not to push the matter. "All right. Word of honor."

"I swear I'll return within a few hours, Sara. I'll be back on the five-fifty-five ferry."

"I believe you."

"Then can't you stop giving me the ice treatment for a while?" he asked gently.

"Speaking of cold," she drawled slowly.

He gave her a sharp glance as they walked down the drive and opened the door of the house. "Is that your imagination I hear cranking up again?"

"I think Vaughn might really be the one they called Wolf," Sara told him in a low voice. "It would make sense, wouldn't it? He was once very close to my uncle, so he might know about the gold."

"There's no sense speculating about it, Sara."

"Why not? Maybe if we speculate long enough and hard enough, we'll come up with some answers."

"Not on that subject." He stood in the hall for a moment, listening. Then he ushered her inside.

"Just think, Adrian. That creep is probably the renegade. Uncle Lowell might have gone to Southeast Asia thinking he could hunt him down and remove him before he got the gold."

"Sara, all we've got at the moment are a lot of questions. Not answers."

"But why would Vaughn be hanging around here if he was after Uncle Lowell's gold?"

"How the hell should I know?" Adrian stalked into the kitchen and put a kettle of water on the stove.

Sara trailed after him. "Adrian, I think we're missing something. Something crucial."

"Like your uncle?" he suggested bluntly.

"I mean a clue!" she gritted. "Listen to me, Adrian. Let's assume Uncle Lowell really does have some connection with that gold and that he had some fantastic notion of giving it to us as a...a wedding gift."

Adrian leaned against the stove waiting for the water to boil. He crossed his arms on his chest and eyed Sara deliberately. "All right, for the sake of argument, let's assume it. Now what?"

Sara tried to construct her thoughts into a logical sequence. Frowning intently, she began to pace the kitchen. "Okay, he knows where that gold is but he hasn't made any attempt to date to retrieve it. At least no attempt that we know of. In that taped message he didn't say he was going to *fetch* our wedding gift. He only said he was going to *protect* it."

"True." Adrian watched her closely.

"Now if he suddenly decided he had to protect it for us, it must be because he got word that someone was out to steal it. We have to assume that very few people would even know for certain that the tale was anything more than a legend. The most logical person my uncle might have confided in besides you or me is his ex-protégé."

"We're back to Wolfie?"

"This is not a joke!" she hissed.

Adrian exhaled heavily and turned around to pour the boiling water into two cups. "I know. Go on."

She glared at his broad shoulders. "Not only is Wolf or Vaughn or whoever he is the one man who might know about the gold and might even know its approximate location but we have the evidence that Uncle Lowell was definitely thinking about him before he left for parts unknown."

"You mean that sketch on my manuscript. Sara, that's pretty damn slim evidence."

She shook her head. "I don't think so. I think it means that the man called Wolf was on Uncle Lowell's mind recently and that could easily be because he had reason to fear the guy was going to make a move on the gold. Something or someone we don't even know might have tipped him off. Who knows how many mysterious contacts my uncle has left around the world? You yourself are going to try to find one of them tomorrow!" She flung her hands outward in a sweeping gesture. "Don't you see? Uncle Lowell is trying to protect our so-called wedding gift from the one man who might be able to steal it."

"Then what's Vaughn doing hanging around the Northwest?" Adrian asked logically. "Why isn't he in Southeast Asia?"

"Because he doesn't know where exactly in Southeast Asia the gold is hidden. No one knows except Uncle Lowell. Vaughn is probably looking for my uncle. Maybe he thinks he can use me somehow." Sara nibbled on her lower lip while she considered that. "My uncle has dropped out of sight. He told the neighbor he'd gone hunting. Guess who the quarry is?''

"Wolfman?" Adrian asked mockingly.

"Go ahead and laugh if you want, but I think I'm getting a handle on this."

"I'm not laughing at you, Sara." Adrian handed her a cup of tea. "You may be right for all I know. But I think the first thing to establish is whether or not your uncle is where Vaughn says he is. And I only know one way to do that."

"Find that man whom Uncle Lowell mentioned. I know. I'm not going to argue with you any more on that score, Adrian. I can see your mind is made up," she said wearily.

It was over a rather strained dinner a couple of hours later that Adrian brought up the subject again. Sara was poking idly at the roasted red pepper salad she had made when, after a long silence, Adrian spoke.

"There's one other thing," he began thoughtfully.

She glanced up. "What's that?"

"Lowell told me the story of the gold for a reason. He knows it forms the kernel of the plot in *Phantom*."

"That's right." Sara set down her fork.

"If you're right about the wedding gift being that cache of gold, then what he was really doing was—"

"Giving you the first clues about what your wedding gift actually was and where it was located," Sara finished on a note of excitement. "I can see him doing something like that."

"So can I. Damn it, I may pound the man into the ground if and when he finally does show up," Adrian growled. "He knows I don't like games."

THE SPARSE CONVERSATION at dinner faded into a very long silence by mid-evening. The strain in the atmosphere grew stronger as bedtime approached. Adrian watched the clock move slowly toward ten and knew from the remote expression in Sara's eyes that he would be sleeping alone tonight.

He'd been expecting to find himself in a cold bed, of course, ever since he'd awakened that morning and realized that for Sara everything was happening much too quickly. She had a right to some time to adjust to the idea of having him as a lover. After all, she didn't have all those months of fleshing out a fantasy that he'd had. He was too much of a stranger yet, too much of an unknown quantity.

Adrian inclined his head politely when she excused herself and disappeared down the hall to her own room shortly after ten. He sat in his chair, legs stretched out in front of him, and repeated the admonitions he'd been giving himself all evening.

Not enough time.

Too much of a stranger.

Too many other problems at the moment. Big problems.

And she was mad as hell because he wouldn't take her with him tomorrow.

All in all, a formidable list, he thought wryly. But the logic and the rationalizations didn't seem to be making much of an impact on the pulsing desire that was going to keep him awake tonight.

He thought about what he had to do in the morning and told himself that he needed sleep, not a night spent brooding in an armchair. He'd already had enough of those during the past year.

No doubt about it. He needed sleep; he could do without the brooding and he had no right at all to go to Sara's room. All three things were perfectly clear and logical in his head. But, as he'd learned the hard way, clear logic didn't always chase away the shadows of emotions. Adrian wondered briefly at that. Emotions were odd things. There had been a time when others had sworn he didn't have any. Adrian knew better.

Slowly he got to his feet and began a silent tour of the house. Sara would be safe here. The house could keep out intruders. And he would be back for her as soon as possible. Quietly he checked and double-checked the hidden alarms and the exotic barriers Kincaid had helped him install. Lowell, with his skillful hands and his crafty, convoluted mind. *Where are you tonight, my friend?*

His soft-soled shoes making no sound on the hardwood floor, Adrian walked from one checkpoint to another, reassuring himself that the gift from Lowell Kincaid would be safe. Keeping Sara secure was the most important priority in his world, Adrian realized. It was a strange feeling to accept such total responsibility for another human being. Almost primitive in a way. He considered just how completely she had infiltrated his thoughts and then he headed down the hall toward his bedroom.

He would not pause in front of Sara's door. He would not listen for a moment to see if she was restless in her bed. He would not stand in the hall and let himself think about what she would do if he opened her door. He was a disciplined man and he could deal with his body's hungers.

It was the hunger in his mind he wasn't sure about, Adrian admitted as he approached Sara's closed door. How did you discipline the need for another person? Especially when you'd spent a lifetime not really needing anyone?

His steps slowed in spite of all the logic and discipline, and Adrian was vaguely aware of his hand curling tightly against his thigh. She would be asleep by now.

Sara lay very still in the wide bed, her hair fanned out on the pillow, and watched the shifting light under her door. She couldn't hear him but she knew he was standing there. She sensed the tension in her body and realized she was waiting for the door to open. She'd been lying there waiting for it since the moment she'd turned out the light and climbed into bed.

Because, Sara thought grimly, there was no way she could allow him to leave in the morning without letting him know that he had a right to be in her bed tonight.

The knowledge was sure and complete in her mind. She couldn't account for the certainty, but it was there.

Sara threw back the covers and sat up on the edge of the bed. She was reaching for her robe when the door of her room opened soundlessly. Adrian stood framed in the doorway, his face in deep shadow. Sara's fingers froze around the fabric of the robe as she looked up at him.

"You're not asleep." His voice was low and gritty; the words a statement, not a question.

"Neither are you." Sara let the robe drop from her hand. The wave of longing that swept through her was startling in its intensity. She was afraid that if she tried to stand up she wouldn't have the strength.

"You should have been asleep," he told her very seriously.

"Should I?"

"It would have made things...easier." He didn't move in the doorway.

"Easier for whom?"

"For me."

Sara drew a deep breath. "But not for me," she whispered, and held out her hand in an ancient gesture of feminine invitation.

"Sara?" Adrian's voice was raw with the question.

"Come to bed, Adrian. Please."

He hesitated for a timeless moment. Then he moved forward in a dark, silent glide that swept her up and bore her back onto the bed.

"Adrian..."

"Hush, Sara. There's no way on earth I could let you change your mind now." He was sprawling heavily on top of her, his hands pinning her passionately against the pillows as he sought her mouth with his own.

She wanted to tell him that she had no intention of changing her mind, that she wanted him, needed him, that she had never felt like this about a man before in her life. But the words seemed to be locked in her throat as he began to make love to her.

Adrian pushed the canvas shoes off his feet without even bothering to sit up on the bed. Sara heard them thud softly to the floor. She felt him fumble with the fastening of his jeans and then the buttons of his shirt. And all the while he kept her achingly close to him, deliciously trapped under his strength.

"I told myself I shouldn't stop at your door," he grated as he kicked his clothing to the floor.

Sara's head moved from one side to the other on the pillow. "No, this is where you belong." She circled his neck with her arms, pulling him close.

"Sara, my sweet Sara." He tugged at the nightgown, pushing it off her shoulders and down to her waist. Flattening the palms of his hands across her breasts, he grazed her nipples with a rasping, tantalizing touch that brought them to taut peaks.

Sara uttered a soft sigh into his mouth and dared him with the tip of her tongue. He responded instantly, thrusting deeply behind her teeth. She traced the contours of his sleek back with her fingertips until he groaned heavily.

Lifting himself for an instant, Adrian pulled the nightgown down over her hips and let the garment fall to the floor beside his jeans. Then he came back down beside her and Sara felt the demanding hardness of him against her thigh. She could feel the almost violently taut need in him and her own body reacted to it with fierce awareness.

Slowly, with deliberate provocative strokes, Adrian caressed her. His fingers played an enticing game on the inside of her leg until Sara thought she would go out of her mind with excitement. When he moved his hand upward, she cried out against his mouth.

Then she was struggling passionately to return the heady thrill and the throbbing anticipation. She slid her hand down his back to the slope of his thigh, feeling the crisp curling hair. Then she explored him more and more intimately until she cupped the heavy evidence of his desire.

"Sara, you're driving me wild," he groaned out.

"Yes, please," she whispered breathlessly.

"Sara, are you sure?"

"I've never been more certain of anything in my life." She used her nails with excruciating delicacy, and he muttered something soft and savage against her throat.

"Adrian?"

"I couldn't stop now if all the forces in hell got in the way," he said, and then he was parting her legs with his own, sliding toward her warmth until he was only a pulse beat away from possessing her completely.

Sara whispered his name again and again, lifting herself with undisguised longing.

"That's it, sweetheart. Give yourself to me. Just give yourself to me. I need you so."

She gasped as he entered her, the shock of his passionate invasion ricocheting through her whole system. Then she tightened her arms and legs around him, wrapping him as close as possible.

Lost in the embrace, Adrian knew only that he wanted Sara to cling to him forever. There was nothing else besides this shattering moment and Adrian seized it with all of his strength. There would be time enough tomorrow to wonder at the intensity of her need, time enough to worry that she was only reacting to the drama of the situation, time enough to reconsider the wisdom of letting himself be swept up in her hot, damp warmth. There was always time enough to regret the past. But he was living for the moment tonight, he told himself, and for this hour he would revel in it. He would allow himself to believe it was all for real.

When he felt the telltale tightening of her body, it precipitated an echo in his own. For an instant he forced himself to raise his head so that he could watch her face during the fiery release. He had a few seconds to wonder at the compelling possessiveness he felt for the woman in his arms and then he was trapped in the vortex of their combined desire. It swept them both to a violent, throbbing climax, left them hanging for a sweet moment and then slowly, slowly ebbed.

The moment in which he had been living was already becoming the past, Adrian thought distantly as he lay beside Sara. Soon the morning would arrive and with it another slice of the past. Perhaps there was some sense of balance in nature. Perhaps one piece of the past could offset another. He would have the memory of Sara's warmth tonight to carry with him as a talisman against the chill of tomorrow.

She stirred in his arms. "Adrian?"

"I'm here, Sara."

"Good," she murmured drowsily. "See that you're here tomorrow night, too."

When tomorrow night comes will you really want me here, my darling Sara, he wondered silently.

HE LEFT AT DAWN and Sara was at the door to watch him go. She had awakened the instant he did, her senses aware of his every movement. He'd lain quietly for a long moment looking down into her face and then he'd brushed his lips lightly against hers. Words flooded his head but he couldn't find a way to say them aloud. There wasn't time now to say the things that should be said. Perhaps it was better this way.

Pushing aside the covers, he'd climbed out of bed and headed for the bath. Without a word she'd fixed coffee for him while he dressed and then she'd stood on tiptoe to kiss him good-bye.

"Be careful, Adrian. Please be careful."

"Hey, I'm only going to talk to a friend of your uncle's," he protested gently. He was afraid of the intensity he saw in her gaze. He liked it better when she was laughing up at him with her eyes or watching him with passion. Adrian realized just how much he had come to value the impulsive warmth that was so much a part of Sara. Life would be very cold without it. "I'll be home by sundown."

"Yes." She didn't argue.

"You won't leave the house," he said again, making it an order.

She shook her head. "Not unless you or Uncle Lowell tell me to leave the house," she answered obediently.

"Sara..." He hesitated on the porch, turning back to her one last time.

"Just hurry, Adrian. I'll be here when you return."

He looked at her, nodded once and left without glancing back again.

Chapter Eight

The house seemed incredibly lonely after Adrian left. Sara wandered around from room to room, wondering if doing a little housekeeping might help her deal with the strange mood in which she found herself. The thought brought to mind the question of who actually did Adrian's housecleaning. Something told her he probably took care of the chores himself. Certainly no one had been in during the few days she had known him to sweep the hardwood floors or dust. But everything seemed orderly and reasonably clean. Keeping his environment neat and precise was undoubtedly a part of his nature. It fit with what she knew of his preference for being in control of his world.

Sara wondered if Adrian had ever felt out of control. When had the need to be in command of everything around him come into existence? Perhaps he had been born that way. Or perhaps something in his past had made him so cautious and controlled. Surely the average person didn't install the kind of sophisticated electronic gadgetry that protected this house unless some event had instilled a raging desire for security. Adrian was definitely not the type of man to let his imagination make him paranoid. He must have his reasons for his self-control and the controls he had imposed on his surroundings. The only time she sensed that he slipped his own leash was when he made love to her.

The images engraved on her mind from the previous night rose to warm her now. She remembered the passion and intensity of the man who had held her. And she recalled her own ungoverned responses.

She drifted into the library and drew a finger along the top shelf of the bookcase. There was a smudge on her hand afterward but nothing really terrible. Just a normal amount of dust. The kind she herself collected on the top shelf of her bookcase. The kind people living alone tended to collect. She wondered how long Adrian had lived alone. Most of his life, apparently.

Finding the thought depressing, she turned away from the bookcase and walked over to his desk. Having been through it once, she felt there was no point amusing herself by browsing through it again. She sat down in the swivel chair and remembered the way Adrian had caught her here a few nights ago. She hadn't heard his approach, she recalled. You hardly ever heard the man. He moved very quietly in those well-worn sneakers.

A shaft of morning light caught the crystal-and-gold apple, making the trapped bubbles come alive for a moment. Sara leaned forward and studied the shimmering effect. She liked the notion of Adrian having sat here at his desk for months, the apple in front of him, while he worked. How many times had he glanced up idly and found himself studying the apple? Perhaps as many times as she had.

But she hadn't known there was a duplicate crystal apple in existence, Sara reminded herself. While Adrian had known all along that there was another apple and that someday he would encounter its owner. She wondered what he had expected her to be like. What picture had her uncle sketched for him? It was suddenly very important to Sara that Adrian had found his gift satisfactory. She wanted to be sure he would return to collect it this evening.

"Adrian," she whispered aloud, "remember what I said about taking care of yourself. I don't think I should have let you go alone." As if she'd had a choice.

Uneasily Sara stood up and walked slowly back out of the study. She'd make herself another cup of coffee and see if she couldn't find something to read. It was going to be a very long day.

She was pouring the coffee when she realized that what she wanted to read was *Phantom.* Perhaps if she went through it a second time, this time knowing her uncle had deliberately been planting information, she might pick up something useful. Digging the manuscript out of her suitcase, she carried it back to Adrian's study and sat down to read it with the cup of coffee at her elbow.

She wrinkled her nose at the sketch of the wolf on the first page and then deliberately set herself to go through the manuscript with an alert eye. There must be something in it. Didn't Lowell believe in hiding things in plain view? He certainly had doodled a great deal on the pages. But then, that was standard operating procedure for Lowell Kincaid whenever he found himself with a pencil in hand and a sheet of paper nearby. The man should have been an artist instead of a secret agent.

Just as had happened the first time through *Phantom,* Sara once again found herself caught up not in the intricacies of the plot but in the hero's pain and savage determination to survive. The feelings of protectiveness she had experienced the first time she read it returned anew. She longed to comfort the hero even as she told herself that only he could endure his own survival both emotionally and physically. In the end she knew she would again be left wanting to know for certain that there really was going to be a happy ending. And once more the question of how much of Adrian existed in the guise of *Phantom* returned to haunt her. This was a first novel. Somewhere she had read that they tended to be the most autobiographical.

Sara was into chapter three when the phone on the desk rang shrilly. The unexpected sound startled her. In the time she had been staying at Adrian's home, the thing had never rung. She hesitated a few seconds before reaching out to pick up the receiver. Then the thought that it might be Adrian calling for some reason made her fumble with the instrument.

''Hello?''

''Sara.''

''Uncle Lowell!'' Sara sat stunned as she heard her uncle's distinctive growl of a voice. ''Uncle Lowell, where are you? I've been absolutely frantic. This whole thing is—''

''Sara, don't talk, just listen to me,'' Lowell Kincaid said quickly. ''Come back to my place as soon as you can.''

''But Uncle Lowell—''

''As soon as you can, Sara. I can't explain. I'll be waiting.''

He hung the phone up in her ear before she could get in another question.

Her first instinct, Sara realized, was to panic. She had no way to reach Adrian to tell him what was happening, no way to find out if her uncle needed immediate help such as an ambulance, no way even to begin to figure out what might be wrong. All she could do was obey Lowell Kincaid's summons as swiftly as possible. Desperately she tried to reassure herself with Adrian's words about her uncle's competence. *He can take care of himself.*

Whatever else was happening, at least she knew he wasn't in Southeast Asia! If only she could get in touch with Adrian to call him off that wild-goose chase. Frantically Sara tried to think. It took her a moment to break through the paralysis engendered by her uncle's phone call. Then she was on her feet and running toward the bedroom. Her purse was where she had left it, slung on the bed. She grabbed it and scrabbled around inside for her car keys.

Sara was almost to the front door when she remembered the elaborate warning devices built into Adrian's house. Forcing herself to slow down and concentrate, she went into Adrian's bedroom and programmed the alarms as he had taught her so that she could leave without causing a disturbance. Almost as an afterthought she pushed the reset button so that the house would be able to detect intruders. Adrian wouldn't thank her for leaving the exotic alarm system completely turned off. She was afraid to set it to keep out intruders because Adrian hadn't told her now to bypass the alarms if she were to leave and then try to reenter. There was always the chance that she might be coming back here this evening with her uncle. This way the house would recognize that it had been entered, but she would be able to get back inside if she wished. When she was finished, the alarms were set just as they had been the night she'd walked so easily into Adrian's study to search it. She'd better leave a note, too, just in case Adrian returned before she got back.

She dashed back down the hall to the study and found a pen and a piece of paper. Hastily she jotted down the facts about the phone call and Lowell's summons. Then she glanced around for a means of anchoring the slip of paper. The crystal apple caught her eye. She picked it up and a shaft of morning light broke into a rainbow as it passed through the apple and touched the frozen bubbles inside. Sara found herself staring into the depths of the crystal for a split second. The apple had been the start of this whole mess, she realized. And it had provided the first link between herself and Adrian.

Shaking off the momentary sense of distraction, she plunked the crystal apple down on top of her note. Time enough later to figure out whether the apple was more significant than it seemed.

Finished with the task, she flung herself out the door and down the steps to where her car was parked in the drive. She was furious with her own nervous tension and her anger just served to make her more nervous. It seemed an incredible chore to get the key into the ignition. The wait at the ferry dock was interminable. The Interstate was jammed through the heart of Seattle and over the bridge to Mercer Island. Everything seemed to be conspiring to keep her from making good time out of town.

When at last she was free of the city's congestion, she found it difficult to keep within shouting distance of the speed limit. Every instinct was to hurry. Uncle Lowell's words had sounded extremely urgent. But there had been an oddly flat quality to his voice, she thought as she drove. She'd never heard him sound quite that way.

On the other hand, she had never been around him when he was "working." For her he had always been the laughing, witty man who had seemed to understand her even when the rest of the family hadn't. There had been an affinity between her and her uncle since she was a small girl. Her parents tolerated it good-naturedly most of the time. But there had been occasions when she had been warned that it wasn't right to play games with life. The black sheep of the family might be a lot of fun but he didn't set a responsible example for a young person.

With every passing mile Sara wondered what had gone wrong with Lowell Kincaid's latest game.

It wasn't until nearly two hours later when she was turning off onto the narrow road that led toward the cottage that Sara remembered to wonder why her uncle hadn't mentioned Adrian. If there was anything really wrong, would Lowell have asked her to come alone?

Impatiently she slowed to take the twists and turns of the old road. Quite suddenly she was furious with both her uncle and Adrian. Men and their little macho schemes. And they had the nerve to say she played games! When this was all over, Sara decided as she braked for a sharp curve, she would give them both a piece of her mind. More than that. She'd tear a wide strip off each of them.

The car that blocked the road on the far side of the curve came as a distinct shock. It was sitting across both lanes, making it utterly impossible to get past. Sara, who had her foot on the accelerator again as she came out of the curve, hurriedly slammed on the brakes.

"Damn it to hell!" It was the last straw, Sara told herself as she came to a halt. Well, at least she could walk to the cottage from here. Angrily, her mood fueled by a firestorm of mounting concern, she pulled over to the side of the road, pushed open the door and climbed out. There was no one in the other car as far as she could tell. Who on earth would be stupid enough to leave a vehicle in the middle of the road? Probably some drunk driver who hadn't made it home from a local tavern.

Leaning down, Sara reached inside her own car to yank her purse off the front seat and remove the keys from the ignition. It couldn't be more than a mile now to her uncle's house. Luckily she'd worn comfortable sandals. She straightened up, stepped back to slam the car door, spun around and found herself staring straight into Brady Vaughn's hawklike face.

"Congratulations, Miss Frazer. You made excellent time." He motioned almost negligently with the compact, snub-nosed gun he held in his right hand. "I just put the car across the road fifteen minutes ago. Thought you'd take a little longer to get here."

"I shouldn't have hurried, apparently," Sara managed in a tight little voice. She couldn't take her eyes off the gun. The casually efficient way Vaughn held it seemed as frightening as anything else that was happening. A man who held a gun that coolly must have had plenty of practice. "Who are you, Mr. Vaughn?"

"Let's just say I'm an old acquaintance of your uncle's." He nodded toward his vehicle as he spoke. "Now I think we'd better get these cars off the road. This isn't a well-traveled area but I wouldn't want some stranger coming along and starting to ask silly questions."

"Such as why you're holding a gun on a woman?" Sara didn't move. She wasn't certain she could.

Vaughn's smile was an odd travesty of humor. "Take it as a compliment, Miss Frazer. I learned long ago that the female of the species can be just as dangerous as the male. I don't take chances. Get in the car. You'll drive."

When he stepped toward her, Sara discovered that she could, indeed, move. She edged back toward the nondescript compact that was lodged across the road. "Drive where?"

"To your uncle's cabin, of course. That's as good a place to wait for him as any."

"I thought you said he was in Southeast Asia!"

"I lied. I do that quite well. You should start getting used to it. A lot of men in your life lie to you. Now move, Miss Frazer. And please, for both our sakes, don't try anything too tricky, okay?"

There was no opportunity to try anything clever even if she had been able to think of something truly brilliant, Sara discovered. At the point of the gun she slid into the driver's seat. Her fingers trembled as she took the wheel. Her red shirt was turning dark under her arms from nervous perspiration. Vaughn got in beside her, his eyes never leaving her for an instant.

The drive to Lowell Kincaid's cabin was a short one. Sara fantasized briefly about stomping down on the accelerator and trying some wild maneuver that might dislodge the weapon from Vaughn's hand but common sense warned her it wouldn't work. There was no way she could get the car up to a fast rate of speed before he could put a bullet in her. There would be plenty of time for him to kill her and grab the wheel.

The cottage appeared exactly as she and Adrian had left it. When Sara obediently switched off the ignition, Vaughn ordered her out of the car.

"Now we'll walk back and get the other one." He stood aside and waited for her to start back down the road ahead of him.

"Why the stunt with the car across the road? Why didn't you simply wait for me in the cabin?"

"I was afraid you might be suspicious about entering the house when you noticed the strange car in the drive. And there wasn't any convenient place to hide it and still have it readily available." He indicated the clear area that extended from the drive to the front of the house. "I also didn't know if you and your uncle might have some particular signal."

"You're giving me a lot more credit for caution and observation than I deserve," Sara told him dryly. "I doubt that I would have thought twice about the car. I would have assumed it was my uncle's. And we don't have any special greeting signal! Good grief, I'm his niece, not a secret agent."

"Oh, I'm aware of who you are, Sara Frazer. Very much aware. I'm counting on your identity to lure your uncle out into the open, you see."

She turned to glance back at him over her shoulder. The gun was still pointed unwaveringly at her back. "But that was my uncle's voice on the phone. I don't understand. Where is he?"

Vaughn arched an eyebrow. "It was your uncle's voice, all right. Right off the tape on his answering machine."

"His answering machine! But he didn't say those things on the machine," Sara gasped, startled.

"Sure he did," Vaughn told her with a soft chuckle. "He just didn't say them in quite that order."

"You mixed his words from the tape into different sentences?"

"And recorded them onto another tape. It takes a little work and the right equipment, but it can be done. I had both his recorded message to callers and the message to your friend Adrian with which to work. Plenty of material from which to get a few simple sentences."

Sara stared unseeingly at her car as she rounded the bend. "You appear to be very professional at this sort of thing, Mr. Vaughn," she whispered dully.

"Very," he assured her. "It would be best if you didn't forget it."

She drove the second car back to the cottage under the same circumstances as she had driven the first. When she finally parked it beside Vaughn's compact, he motioned her into the house.

"What now?" she asked quietly as she stepped inside.

"Now we wait. Make some coffee if you like. It's probably going to take a while." Vaughn appeared unconcerned.

"But what exactly are we going to wait for?"

"Your uncle should be contacting us in the near future."

"But why would he do that? How would he even know where I am or that I'm with you?" The shock of the situation was affecting her mind, Sara thought vaguely. She couldn't seem to think properly. Perhaps she ought to take Vaughn's advice and make some coffee. At least it would give her something to do. She was very much afraid that if she sat down or stood still she would begin to tremble uncontrollably.

"Your uncle is looking for me. It's only a matter of time before he figures out I'm waiting patiently right here on his home stomping grounds. And when he does, he'll discover I have you with me."

Sara turned on the tap in the kitchen sink, aware of Vaughn watching her from the doorway. "You're going to use me?"

"I'm going to trade you to your uncle for the information I want," Vaughn confirmed. "I see it all as a business deal."

"And what information is it that you want, Mr. Vaughn?" she demanded softly.

"Don't you think you should start calling me Brady?"

"I don't see us ever getting together on a social basis," she gritted out as she set the pot into place in the drip machine.

"But we are together, Sara," he drawled smoothly. "Perhaps for some time. You made it very easy, really. I was a little worried about how to get rid of the boyfriend. I wasn't sure until yesterday where he fit into the scene. I had a couple of plans I thought would work but he simplified matters considerably when he obligingly left on the morning plane to Mexico City. His leaving for Mexico also confirmed his part in all this."

"Mexico City!"

"I got the clerk at the airline counter to verify that he bought a one-way ticked to Mexico. What's the matter, Sara? Didn't he tell you where he was going?"

"Yes, but I...I just don't see how you could find out that sort of information." Sara was surprised that she could get the lie fairly glibly past her lips. Mexico City! It didn't make any sense. You didn't pop down to Mexico City for the day and return by early evening. And just yesterday Adrian had been telling her tales of how a man could disappear into Mexico City and reappear on the other side of the world.

"You can get all sorts of information out of people if you flash the right badges at them," Vaughn informed her. "Poor little Sara. You still don't realize what he's done, do you? You've been had, lady. In more ways than one."

"He's a writer," she explained, struggling for something logical to say. "He does a lot of research and he's had this trip planned for some time. My showing up got in the way of his schedule, I'm afraid. He's setting the next book in Mexico." Did that sound reasonable? "I didn't have the time to go with him."

"Is that a fact?" Vaughn said musingly. "So he just left you up here all by yourself to worry about your uncle? After asking for forty-eight hours to think over your problem?''

"I...yes." It was probably better not to weave any more strands into the story. She wouldn't be able to keep it straight in her own head.

"Not terribly gallant of him, was it?"

Sara said nothing. She focused on the pot filling with coffee.

"You're a fool, Sara," Vaughn finally said calmly. "You've been dumped. As long as Saville figured you were the easiest way to get at the gold, he was willing to play lover. But yesterday when I let him know that others were getting close to the prize, he panicked and decided you were no longer the quickest or safest means to an end. I know better. I know that you still are the best means to this particular end. I'm a patient man, Sara."

She cast him a quick, frightened glance. He smiled again. "Want me to tell you the real reason he's gone south?"

"What's your explanation, Mr. Vaughn?"

"Oh, it's simple enough. Mexico City is a wide-open town. It has a certain reputation in the industry. Among other things it's a jumping-off point for people who want to head for such places as Cambodia without letting the U.S. government know where they're going. You can buy anything in Mexico City, including alterations on your passport. Your boyfriend has skipped out on you. He's probably heading for Southeast Asia."

"I thought," she said weakly, "that the stories about Mexico City were just the product of espionage fiction. Legends and tales."

"Fact, I'm afraid. Your lover has skipped." Vaughn seemed amused.

Sara lowered her lashes. "Why would he do that?"

"Because he's decided to risk going after the gold on his own instead of waiting for your uncle to return. As I said, he got nervous yesterday when he realized others were closing in on it. He's obviously a friend of your uncle's and Kincaid made the mistake of trusting him, both with his niece and with the information about the gold. Kincaid never used to make mistakes like that, but he's getting old. He's trusted the wrong man with the details of what was probably intended to be your dowry. The race is on, Sara, but I'm the one with the inside track. I've got you. I'm not worried that Saville tried to buy himself forty-eight hours for a head start. It won't do him any good because he's obviously an amateur. A greedy amateur, but an amateur nonetheless."

"Why do you say he's an amateur?"

"Because a professional would have realized that you're the most useful key around. And that I'm the biggest threat. A professional would have made a try for me before leaving town, if for no other reason than to find out just how much I know. Southeast Asia is a big and dangerous place to go hunting without specific directions and a few contacts. Saville will probably just succeed in getting himself killed trying for your uncle's gold. And it does nothing to change my plans. One way or another I wound up with you, and ever since you appeared on the scene so conveniently, that's been my goal. I'm a highly adaptable man. Before you came along I was using a different approach. I'd been through this cabin with a fine-tooth comb. I was just realizing how useless that method was going to be when you showed up out of the blue. Couldn't figure out who you were at first, but after you'd left the first time I remembered seeing the phone-answering machine. I played it back to see if I could pick up any information about Kincaid's unexpected female guest, and sure enough, all the news I needed was on that tape. That's how I found out you're Kincaid's niece.''

"You want that gold, don't you?'' Sara reached for a cup and poured coffee with exaggerated care. She was afraid that if she wasn't extremely cautious she would spill the hot liquid all over her feet. "The gold you said my uncle left behind in Southeast Asia.''

"Yes, Sara. I want the gold. Pour me a cup, too. Just set it on the counter. I'll get it. Wouldn't want you trying to throw it in my face with a grand, heroic gesture.''

"So you're going to use me to force my uncle to tell you exactly where he hid the stuff?'' Sara persisted, standing back so that Vaughn could pick up his coffee.

"Precisely.''

"You said Uncle Lowell thinks you're in Hawaii,'' she began with a frown as she tried frantically to put the pieces of the puzzle together.

"I made certain he got information to that effect. Rumors are very effective in our crowd, even among the, uh, golden-agers. I wanted him sidetracked for a while so that I could try getting the data I needed the easy way.''

"You searched this place,'' she whispered, remembering the chaos she and Adrian had discovered.

"Unfortunately, as I said, my search didn't turn up anything so convenient as a map or a set of coordinates that would have made my task a straightforward one. I really thought I'd have a chance of finding what I wanted because I knew your uncle rather well at one time, Sara. I know his theories on hiding important data, for example. He always got a kick out of concealing things right in front of someone's nose. Kincaid had a sense of humor, you can say that for the man. When I didn't turn up anything, I realized matters were going to get complicated. I made the search look like the work of punks and decided to keep watch on the cabin for a while. It paid off. You happened along and greatly simplified my life.''

Sara leaned back against the counter, her hands braced against the cool ties. ''Why would my uncle go tearing off to Hawaii just because he thought you were there, Mr. Vaughn?''

''He thinks that after all these years I've decided to go after the gold. He's got a couple of other reasons for following my trail, too. He and a few others, I believe, have some private suspicions about me.'' Vaughn sipped tentatively at his coffee. ''Not bad,'' he declared. ''I enjoy good coffee.''

Sara took a deep breath before plunging in with the next question. ''My uncle has other reasons for hunting you down?''

''''Hunting' sounds a bit melodramatic, don't you think? Let's just say he couldn't resist the hint that I might have surfaced and that he might be able to find me.''

Sara met his gaze unflinchingly. ''Do you by any chance go under the code name of...of Wolf?''

Vaughn went still, the coffee halfway to his mouth. Slowly he lowered the cup, his dark eyes narrowing speculatively. ''Now what would you know about the man called Wolf?''

Her fingers tightened around the counter's edge. Sara was beginning to wish she hadn't brought up the subject. ''Not much. My uncle mentioned him once. That's all.''

''And you've been assuming I might be...Wolf?''

She didn't like the cold amusement that was suddenly in his eyes. ''The thought occurred to me.''

''Fascinating.''

''Well?'' she challenged bravely.

Vaughn's mouth drew back in a humorless smile. ''Your uncle always could tell a good story.''

''Is that all Wolf is? A Lowell Kincaid tale?'' she breathed. It was getting difficult to tell legends from reality, she realized.

Vaughn chuckled, shaking his head. ''No. As usual with your uncle, there's a germ of truth in the story. There really was a man called Wolf. I never met him. Few people did and survived to tell about it. His cover was very deep and he protected it. They said he had a thing about maintaining his cover.''

A man who liked to be in total control of his surroundings. Sara shivered. ''What do you mean his cover *was* deep?''

''He's a legend, Sara. Just like the gold that never made it out of

Vietnam. But he was real like the gold, too. Lethally real, from what I understand. In my business legends can be real.'' His mouth twisted ironically.

"But you're not him?''

"Hell, no.'' Vaughn grimaced. "Give me some credit. The guy cracked up completely, according to the old gossip. Went bonkers on his last mission. He never returned.''

Sara was very still. "What do you mean, he cracked up?''

"Just what I said. The story goes that he broke like a fine-tuned violin string. Came apart. Went crazy. Cracked. Couldn't handle what he was paid to handle. Got himself killed on his last assignment. Why the interest? Because you've been assuming I'm him?''

"The thought had crossed my mind,'' she admitted softly.

"I'm not especially flattered. The guy may once have been good, the best there was, in fact, but I sure as hell don't intend to lose my nerve the way he did.''

"What are you going to do with the gold if you get it?'' she pressed, desperate to keep the conversation moving. She had no particular wish to chat the afternoon away with Brady Vaughn, but she somehow felt safer when he was talking.

"I'm going to retire, Sara. Somewhere far, far away. Some nice island, perhaps where a lot of gold will buy a lot of silence and a lot of what I want out of life. I've been living under a great deal of tension for the past couple of years. And you know what they say about the dangers of too much tension. I've done well financially, but as the magazines say, stress takes its toll.''

"Like it did on the man called Wolf?'' she flung back.

Vaughn shook his head. "That was an entirely different sort of situation. According to the story, he simply broke. With me, dropping out is more of a reasonable, strictly pragmatic business decision. You see, I've been working very hard lately. And I'm a little tired. Holding down two jobs will do that to a man.''

"Two jobs?'' she questioned, confused.

"Never mind.'' Vaughn shifted his position in the doorway. "I really don't feel like discussing it any further at the moment. Let's go into the living room and sit down. We might have a long wait ahead of us. But have no fear. Sooner or later your uncle will figure out that he's been sent on a wild-goose chase. When he does he'll rush back here. We'll be waiting for him. I bought some food. Enough to last us a couple of days, if necessary. But I doubt we'll have to put up with each other's company for that long. Your uncle is a smart man.''

What did you talk about when you found yourself whiling away the hours with a man who kept a gun in his hand while he conversed with you?

Sara was still asking herself that sometime later as she sat almost immobile on the sofa in front of the cold fireplace. She hadn't moved in so long that she was afraid her foot might have grown numb. When she did move it cautiously, Vaughn glanced at her sharply.

"Going somewhere, Sara?"

"The bathroom, unless you have any objections," she muttered, rising slowly to her feet. There was a tingling sensation in her left foot but it wasn't completely numb.

Vaughn eyed her thoughtfully. "None. There's no way out of that room. I've checked. Try to resist the temptation to forage for a pair of scissors or a razor blade. You'd only wind up cutting yourself."

Sara didn't respond. She turned away and went down the hall to the bathroom. When the door closed behind her, she sagged against the sink and stared at her drawn face in the mirror.

She had to do something. She couldn't bear this endless waiting. What was it Adrian had said about the value of patience? In her case it bought nothing but anxiety. It didn't seem to bother Vaughn particularly, she reflected. He was very professional about the whole thing. Or at least he seemed professional. Hard to judge, given her limited experience in this kind of business. Sara winced.

Vaughn had the ability to wait but would he bother with that route if he thought there might be a shortcut to his goal, she asked herself as she splashed her face with cold water. He'd tried a shortcut once before when he created the diversion that had sent her uncle off to Hawaii. If she could make him think there was an alternative to this interminable waiting, perhaps he would go for it. She dried her flushed face and thought of Adrian's promise to return by early evening.

There was no way he could make it back tonight if he'd actually gone to Mexico and Vaughn seemed convinced he'd gone.

But Adrian had promised her he'd be back. And the house was set on its alarm status. If she were inside the house with Vaughn, Adrian would know as soon as he returned that there was trouble. His small signaling device would warn him there had been an unauthorized intrusion when he came within a couple of blocks of his home.

That scenario would only work if Adrian really was planning to return tonight. If he was even now en route to Mexico City, she was in very bad trouble. Heaven only knew where her uncle was.

Sara wrenched herself away from the mirror. It was an incredible disaster, and if she didn't act, it was going to get worse. She didn't have any illusions about the man in the next room. He was quite capable of casually raping her tonight and killing her later after he had what he wanted from her uncle.

Her only real chance was to bank on the fact that Adrian had told her the truth about returning this evening.

Legends and reality. How could a woman be sure of the difference, she asked herself.

A few minutes later Sara opened the bathroom door and went down the hall to the living room. She saw the fleeting spark of interest in Vaughn's eyes as she resumed her seat on the couch. No, the last thing she wanted to risk was spending the night here with him.

"In another couple of hours we'll have to discuss the sleeping arrangements, Sara," Vaughn mused, tossing a magazine into the bin beside the chair. "I think that could be interesting."

"Really? Do you sleep with your gun in your hand, Mr. Vaughn?"

He chuckled. "I think I can dispense with the gun once I've tied you up for the night. You'd look interesting spread-eagled on a bed."

Sara shuddered and nerved herself for the next bit. "I'm not interested in sharing a bed with you."

"Perhaps I will find it a challenge to see if I can create a little interest," he suggested coolly.

"I doubt it. I'm going to be married soon."

"Are you?" he murmured blandly. "To the boyfriend who just skipped town? You'll have to catch him first, won't you?"

Sara chose her next words carefully. "That gold you're after is supposed to be my wedding gift from my uncle."

Vaughn's eyes narrowed thoughtfully. "Just how much do you know about your uncle's little social-security cache?"

She tried for a mild shrug, her arms wrapped around her drawn-up knees as she sat on the couch. "About as much as you do. You know my uncle. He's fond of dropping little, uh, hints."

"Kincaid never does anything without a reason. And in spite of that easygoing facade, I worked with him long enough to know he's a shrewd and careful man. If he was dropping hints to you about the gold, then he must have truly believed it was safe for you to know about it. No reason he shouldn't think it was safe after all these years, I suppose."

"In addition to being shrewd and careful, my uncle also likes to plan for the future," she added deliberately. "He wanted Adrian and me to know enough about the gold to be able to find it someday in the event something happened to him."

Vaughn leaned forward on his chair, the gun cradled loosely in his fist. "That's very interesting, Sara. Very interesting. It puts a whole new light on the situation. Up until now I've assumed that no one except Kincaid knew the truth about the gold. It's a fact that your uncle tries not to leave much to chance, though. Tell me more, little Sara. Tell me what made Saville think he's got a shot at the gold. I've been wondering who he plans to contact after Mexico City."

She caught her lower lip between her teeth, watching him the way a small mouse probably watched a hovering eagle. *Adrian, where are you?* "Mr. Vaughn, I'll make a deal with you."

He smiled and she could almost hear the way he must be laughing inwardly at her naiveté. The knowledge made her grit her teeth.

"I'm listening, little Sara."

"If I...if I show you where I think the information is hidden, will you take it and go away?"

"I'd have no reason to hang around any longer if I had a map showing the location of the gold," he murmured.

Sara wanted to cringe, but she managed to project a hopeful expression. "It's at Adrian's."

"Your boyfriend's house?"

"He's the man I'm going to marry. Uncle Lowell gave us each a copy of the map. If what you say is true about Adrian being in Mexico, then he must have taken his copy with him. But I have my own. Or at least I have information that will lead me to the gold. I'm not sure that it's exactly a map."

"I can't quite decide whether or not to believe you, little Sara," Vaughn finally said.

She clenched her fingers tightly together. "I can show you."

"But first we have to drive all the way back to that damn island? I don't like islands, Sara. A man can get trapped on islands. So few ways off, you see."

"I thought you were going to retire to an island," she shot back.

"Ah, but that will be different. Much different. There I will have my own means of transportation."

She let out her breath. "Then you're not interested in getting your hands on the information my uncle gave to me?"

Vaughn was quiet for a long while and then he suddenly seemed to come to a decision. "It would make things much simpler if it turned out that you're telling the truth, although I have a few doubts. Still, your boyfriend is several thousand miles away by now following some lead. I'd give a lot to know exactly what kind of lead he thinks he has. Who knows when your uncle will show up." He drummed his fingers on the arm of the chair, his eyes hooded and speculative. "I suppose there's no harm in checking out your story. We could be into the city and over to that damn island within a couple of hours."

"Yes." She could hardly breathe as she waited for the final decision. Was greed finally going to swamp this man's patience?

He nodded once. "All right, Sara. We'll go. But I warn you that if you've lied to me, I will make things most unpleasant for both you and your uncle. And probably your boyfriend, too."

"I'm not lying," she said with great conviction. "I know where my copy of the information is hidden. I had finally realized it just before you made that fake phone call this morning."

"I do believe you're telling the truth," Vaughn mused as he studied the certainty in her expression. "Fascinating. Remind me to thank you later."

Sure, thought Sara as she got to her feet. *I'll remind you. Just before you pull that trigger.*

Chapter Nine

The drive back into Seattle was the longest and most exhausting traveling Sara had ever done in her life. She decided that the normal stresses and strains of rush-hour traffic are not enhanced by the fact that your passenger is casually holding a gun in his lap.

Brady Vaughn didn't say much during the drive. He was undoubtedly contemplating his imminent retirement, Sara thought as she navigated the off ramp from the interstate and found the street that led down to the ferry docks. He kept the gun discreetly shielded under a jacket but he kept it aimed in her direction. She had a hunch that once she had parked her car on the ferry Vaughn wouldn't allow her to go up onto the passenger decks. The thought of sitting on the car deck for the entire length of the ferry ride was depressing.

She was right, of course. Vaughn simply lounged in his corner of the car and watched her speculatively. Unobtrusively Sara glanced at her watch. Her timing, at least, was good. If Adrian had told the truth this morning, he would be catching the ferry that would be leaving Seattle forty minutes from now. She would have forty minutes to entertain Brady Vaughn. Her fingers flexed uneasily on the wheel.

The whole exercise would be extremely pointless if Adrian didn't show up on the right ferry. Halfway across the bay Sara had a wild thought or two about flinging herself from the car and making a dash to the passenger decks. It would be a futile move and she knew it. Even if he chose not to use the gun, Vaughn could probably run her down easily in the close confines of the parked cars. Besides, she reminded herself, that wasn't the plan. She had a much better one in mind.

If it worked. *Legends and reality.* Where did the truth stop and the legend begin? Perhaps in some cases there was no difference. Perhaps a woman just had to make the leap to faith.

"You look nervous, Sara," Vaughn observed politely. "I trust you're not wasting my time with this little chase? It won't do any good, if you are. I know what I'm doing."

She shook her head. "All I want is for you to take the information about the gold and leave."

"Sounds simple enough. I do like simple plans; don't you?"

"Yes." How simple was hers?

"Will you dream about the gold you could have had, Sara? Will you think about it occasionally in the future? Wonder what it might have been like to have your hands on your uncle's cache?"

Again she shook her head. "Even if the gold is still there, I don't see how I could get it out. How are you going to accomplish that little feat, Vaughn? Just walk into that part of the world and tell the current government officials you'd like to do a little digging on their borders?"

He chuckled. She was learning to hate that poor excuse of a laugh. "Nothing that obvious. I prefer quieter techniques. I have contacts and I'll have cash with which to grease the way. I'll be going in through Cambodia. That gold must be somewhere near the Cambodia-Vietnam border."

"Gold is heavy. You won't be able to simply hoist it over your shoulder and hike out of the country with it. Not if there's as much there as you seem to think."

"I'll have help," he explained absently.

Sara slanted him a curious glance. "Help?"

"There are men who will undertake a great many risks for a promise of a split of the profits." He shrugged.

"You'll find some mercenaries to help you get the gold out?"

"They undoubtedly think of themselves as entrepreneurs," Vaughn murmured.

Sara closed her eyes and willed the ferry to a faster speed. She couldn't take much more of this unremitting tension. Whether her scheme worked or not, all she wanted to do at the moment was get it over and done with. She didn't see how anyone could live constantly under the stress of genuine danger. It was easy to see how a man or a woman might crack.

The ferry docked eventually and Sara turned the key in the ignition with a sense of fatalism. Forty minutes from now, if she was very, very lucky, Adrian would be driving off a similar ferry. If she was not so fortunate… Sara pushed the thought aside. There wasn't much point dwelling on that possibility. She would deal with it when the time came.

She drove slowly along the narrow road that wound around the island's perimeter, more slowly than was really necessary. Any time she could eat up this way was that much less that had to be used up at the house waiting for Adrian.

For the first time since she had arrived in the Seattle area the weather was finally beginning to live up to its reputation. The day was rapidly turning gray and overcast. A light mist began to fall.

"Come on, let's get going." With one of his first hints of impatience Vaughn moved the gun in an ugly gesture.

Sara tried to think of something calming to say. "You don't have to use the ferry to get back off the island, you know. You can drive across a bridge on the far side. It's the long way around if you're trying to get back to the airport or Seattle, but—"

"Just shut up. I know my way around."

Of course he did. He was, after all, a *professional*. He wouldn't trap himself on an island. Sara pulled into the driveway in front of Adrian's house. The windows were still dark, so that removed the possibility that by some miracle Adrian had actually arrived home ahead of her. *Forty minutes.*

"Is it true?" she began tentatively as she slowly opened her car door.

"Is what true?" Vaughn reached out and snapped the keys from her hand. He pocketed them.

"That you really have a chance of getting that gold out of Southeast Asia?"

"Believe me, I wouldn't be going to all this trouble if I didn't think it was possible." Vaughn made a careful outside inspection of the house, reassuring himself that no one was around. Then he cast an amused glance at Sara. "What's the matter, honey? Having second thoughts about giving me that map?"

She stopped at the top of the steps and looked back at him. "I admit that until now I assumed the gold was completely inaccessible."

He chuckled. "For years I believed it probably didn't exist at all! Kincaid hid the truth well behind the legend. He made everyone think it really was just one more wild tale set in the last days of the war. There were a hundred other similar stories and there was no real reason to think this one was for real. But a year ago I came across an old file that had been sealed since shortly after Saigon fell. The one thing that damned war generated was paperwork. Files and memos and reports will probably still be turning up twenty years from now. At any rate this one contained some notes by a journalist who claimed he'd interviewed some villagers in the south. He said they told him a story about an American agent who had worked with them toward the end of the war. They described him as a man who knew how to laugh and how to hold his whiskey. A man who was always telling stories. A man who could sketch your face before you even realized he was holding a pencil.''

Sara caught her breath.

"Exactly.'' Vaughn nodded grimly. "A perfect description of Lowell Kincaid. The reporter's notes went on to tell a fascinating story. It culminated in Kincaid's departure for the Cambodian border with a jeep full of gold. The villagers didn't actually see the gold in Kincaid's jeep but they did see the share of it he left for them. He apparently stashed it in the village well and told the elders to wait until the North Vietnamese had passed through before digging it back out. Just like Kincaid to make a grand gesture like that. He was a brilliant agent, but he had some definite weaknesses. When I put that report together with the legend I'd first heard back in 1972, I began to believe I might be dealing with more than just another war tale. It's taken me months to piece together some idea of what might have happened and where. The file with the journalist's notes led to other files. Eventually I knew I was onto the real thing.''

"What happened to the journalist?'' Sara heard herself ask.

"He died,'' Vaughn said carelessly. "An accident down in South America earlier this year, I believe.''

"I see.'' She wondered how much Vaughn had had to do with the "accident.''

His mouth twisted wryly. "I do believe I recognize that look in your eyes, little Sara.''

"What look?''

"Greed, love. Pure unadulterated greed. I saw it in your boy-friend's eyes yesterday and it's in yours today.''

She feigned a nonchalant movement of her shoulders and turned to open the front door. There was no sound from within. The house was as quiet and innocent-looking as it had been that first night when she'd arrived and searched Adrian's study.

"Doesn't your boyfriend believe in locking his front door?'' Vaughn drawled as he followed Sara into the house. He held the gun at the ready while he verified that the place was empty.

"He says there's virtually no crime around here.''

"A trusting soul.'' Vaughn smirked. He took in his surroundings with a quick, professional eye. "I take it back. It goes beyond trust-ing. I think we can safely say your friend Saville is probably a fool.''

"And what about me?'' She slung her purse down on the sofa and turned to face him.

"Oh, you're very smart, Sara. Very smart indeed, if you're telling the truth.'' Vaughn's eyes hardened. "Where's the map?''

She grabbed for her courage, using all of her willpower to keep her expression cool. "I've tried to tell you, it's not exactly a map," she began carefully.

"What the hell are you talking about?" The violence in Vaughn was very close to the surface.

"My uncle has his own unique way of doing things. You know that. He made sure I'd have the information I needed but he hid it in an unique manner. I don't know how he gave Adrian his information, but I think I know where my copy is." Her fingernails dug into her palms. She wondered if Vaughn realized just how scared she was.

"Sara, let's not play any games. You'll lose, believe me. Where's the map?"

"It's not a map. I'm trying to explain. It's a sort of...of code."

Vaughn stared at her. "A code? You told me you and your uncle didn't go in for codes."

"I said we didn't have any prearranged greeting signals."

"Then what are you saying?"

"I'll show you." Moving cautiously so as not to alarm him, Sara turned and started down the hall toward the study. This business of trying to think two steps ahead of a man with a gun was tricky. The ferry that might or might not be bringing Adrian to the rescue had left Seattle by now. Her fate was in the hands of the Washington state ferry system. They claimed to have an excellent safety record.

Vaughn was close behind her as she stepped into the study. The crystal apple gleamed on Adrian's desk, still pinning her note. Beyond it the manuscript of *Phantom* waited.

"There," she whispered, indicating the pile of typed pages. "Everything you want to know about that gold is in that manuscript. My uncle has jotted down little doodles and notes all over the margins, you see."

Vaughn stared first at the stack of papers and then gestured viciously at her with the nose of the gun. "You little bitch. What kind of game do you think you're playing?"

She hugged herself, trying to master the faint trembling that threatened to weaken her limbs. Her head bent forward and a sweep of her hair hid her expression. "It's there. I promise you. And I know how to get at the information you want. It's in code and my uncle once taught me the code. It will take a while, but I can do it."

"Why you little fool!" he snarled. "Stalling isn't going to get you anywhere. There's no one around to come to your rescue. If there was any likelihood of that, I'd never have agreed to let you drag me here."

"No." She shook her head and lifted her chin defiantly. "I'm not trying to stall. I'm...I'm trying to make a deal. You said you were going to be hiring professional help to assist you in getting the gold out of Southeast Asia. Well, I want you to consider me as hired help, too. I can decode Uncle Lowell's doodles on that manuscript. I can do it here and now, in fact, and prove that what I'm saying is true. In return, I want you to cut me in for a piece of the action."

He studied her derisively. "You've got your uncle's nerve, little Sara, I'll say that for you. Decode the manuscript. What a crock of—"

"It's true," she insisted. "You know Uncle Lowell. It would be just like him to hide the information so I would be sitting right on top of it all the time. That manuscript was waiting for me at his cabin the other day. It was right out in the open. You'd overlooked it, naturally. He says people always overlook the obvious. But I recognized the doodles on the margins. It's the code he taught me when I was a little girl. It was a game we used to play together. Give me half an hour and I'll have the information you need to find that gold."

Vaughn was clearly and dangerously undecided. His eyes slid from the manuscript to her face and back again. "Half an hour?"

She nodded quickly. "Is it a deal?"

"I can afford half an hour's wait. I was prepared to wait for much longer than that for Kincaid to return. And your boyfriend is no doubt getting ready to land in Mexico City so there's plenty of time on that end. All right, my greedy little Sara. You've got yourself a deal."

"You'll cut me in for a slice of the profit?" She had to make it sound real, Sara told herself. She tried to inject just the right note of hopeful greed.

"Sure. Why not?" He threw himself down into a chair in the corner. "Half an hour. And if it turns out that you're lying, little Sara—"

"I'm not lying." She sat down slowly behind the desk. From there she was looking through the study door and into the hall beyond. Brady Vaughn would be able to see anyone who came through the door but from his seat in the corner he could not see into the hall as she could. Sara figured she would have a couple of seconds' advance notice if and when Adrian arrived. Nervously she reached out and pulled the manuscript toward her.

She found herself staring down at the sketch of the wolf. For an instant it almost paralyzed her. Then, with excessive care, she turned over the first page of *Phantom* and picked up a pencil.

Time ticked past with a slowness that made Sara think she was waiting for eternity to end. She would have no way of knowing until the last moment whether or not Adrian would arrive. He would have the warning about the invasion of his house shortly after he drove off the ferry. He would probably leave the car down the road and walk the final few yards, she decided. Neither she nor Vaughn would have the sound of a vehicle to alert them.

Carefully she went through the manuscript, occasionally stopping to jot down a meaningless number or word on the notepad beside her. It would be particularly ironic if there really was a code imbedded in her uncle's margin doodles, Sara decided at one point. A real joke on her. As far as she knew she was looking at nothing more than meaningless notes and drawings.

Time crept past. Outside the window the mist turned to rain. Sara turned on the desk lamp. Vaughn's eyes never left her as she went page by page through the manuscript. His patience was as amazing to her as Adrian's had been. Where did they learn that kind of skill? Perhaps some people were just born with it. It was a cinch she wasn't one of those lucky souls. She shuddered and turned over another page. She would force herself not to sneak another glance at the clock or her watch for at least ten minutes, Sara decided resolutely at one point. The last thing she wanted to do was give Vaughn the idea that she was waiting for someone. She kept her head bent over the manuscript for what she estimated must surely be at least ten minutes if not more and then, unable to resist, she slid her gaze upward to the clock on the wall near the door.

She almost didn't see Adrian standing in the shadows of the hall. When she did, she thought her breath had stopped permanently. He was simply waiting there, watching her in absolute silence. It was as if a ghost had materialized out of thin air and in her odd, light-headed state of mind she might have believed just that if it hadn't been for the rain-dampened Windbreaker he wore. It took her another instant to see the gun in his hand.

"Something wrong, Sara?" Vaughn asked conversationally from the corner. He lifted his gun in an easy threat. "You seem a little tense."

Sara swallowed and dropped her eyes from Adrian's still, shadowed figure to the crystal apple in front of her. "I've just realized that I made a mistake."

"Did you?" Vaughn seemed only politely interested. "Just what kind of mistake would that be, little Sara?"

She picked up the apple and held it so that it caught the light from the desk lamp. "The information you want isn't in the manuscript."

"Then you have a problem, don't you, Sara," he said with brutal emphasis.

She shook her head. "No. I don't think so. Not anymore." She tossed the apple up in the air and caught it again. "Here's what you want, Mr. Vaughn." She tossed the crystal object once more and caught it easily. Beyond the door Adrian did not move. He was as still as midnight waiting to descend. She couldn't see his eyes but she knew they would be quite colorless.

"I think," Vaughn said abruptly, "that I've had enough of your games, bitch."

"Ah, but I'm so good at them," she protested gently. "What you want is right out here in front of your very eyes, Mr. Vaughn. As clear as crystal. Just the sort of trick my uncle would pull, don't you think?" With sudden decision she hurled the apple toward the window.

"What the hell...I've had it with you, lady. I'm going to kill you for this!" Without warning, Vaughn's patience snapped. He surged out of the chair, his gun trained on Sara but his eyes following the apple as it crashed against the tempered glass.

The sound of the crystal striking the window and falling to the floor was lost beneath Brady Vaughn's scream of pain and rage as Adrian floated through the doorway and brought the base of the gun down in the direction of the other man's skull. In the split second before the butt of the gun would have made contact with his head, however, some instinct must have warned Vaughn. He threw himself to one side, tumbling across the desk. Adrian's gun struck him violently on the shoulder but it didn't stun him. The weapon Vaughn had been holding, however, fell to the floor and skidded along the hardwood surface until it struck the edge of a rug.

On the other side of the desk, Sara screamed. She was trapped against the wall as the momentum of Vaughn's panicked, sliding rush across the desk threw him toward her. An instant later he seized her even as he stumbled wildly to his feet. Sharp steel blossomed in his hand. He held the knife to Sara's throat, his arm locking her against his body.

"Hold it right there, Saville. Come one step closer and I swear I'll kill her."

Sara couldn't take her eyes off Adrian. The temperature in the study seemed to have suddenly dropped by about twenty degrees.

His face was utterly without emotion. It reminded her of the way he had watched the fish dying at his feet the other morning on the pier but it was a thousand times more remote. He didn't look at Sara.

His whole attention was on the heavily breathing man who was holding the knife to her throat.

"Let her go, Vaughn."

"You think I'm crazy? She's my ticket out of here. Drop the gun." He jerked his arm more tightly around Sara's neck. "I said, drop it, damn you! Think I'm playing games?"

"No, I don't think you're playing games." Moving slowly and deliberately, Adrian took a step forward and set his handgun down on the floor at his feet. The blue steel gleamed savagely in the light of the desk lamp.

"Come on, you bitch." Vaughn tugged Sara around the edge of the desk, clearly heading toward the spot where his own weapon had landed when it had been jolted from his hand. "Move, damn you!"

Sara tried to make her body as limp and heavy as possible but the feel of the steel at the base of her throat kept her from refusing to cooperate entirely. Vaughn would use that knife, she knew. Just as he would use the gun when he got his hands on it.

Across the room Adrian stood balanced a step away from his own weapon. If push came to shove, Sara didn't doubt but that he'd make a grab for it. He watched Vaughn the way a wolf might watch a circling hyena.

"Your best bet is to make a run for it, Vaughn. Hanging on to Sara will only slow you down."

Sara felt the tension in her captor's body as he pulled her toward his gun. "I've come too far in search of that gold, Saville. I'm not leaving without getting what I want."

"Sara doesn't know where it is."

"Maybe. Maybe not. I can't quite figure sweet Sara. But Kincaid knows where it is, and when he finds out I've got his niece, he'll bargain."

"You think so? I've never known Kincaid to bargain for anything without coming out on top," Adrian said thoughtfully.

"You don't know him as well as I do," Vaughn assured the other man. He stopped beside the gun on the floor and his fingers bit abruptly into Sara's shoulder. "Bend down very slowly, Sara, and pick up the gun, muzzle first. And keep in mind that I'll have this knife at the nape of your neck."

Sara realized that it would be dangerously awkward for him to try scooping up the gun while still retaining a stranglehold on her. The action might give Adrian the opening for which he was clearly waiting. So Vaughn was going to make her pick up the lethal chunk of steel and hand it over politely to replace the knife.

Sara glanced down at the gun and then up at Adrian's still, unreadable face. If she gave the gun to Vaughn, he would surely use it against the one thing that stood between him and the door: Adrian.

"Do as I say!"

Slowly Sara knelt, aware of the tip of the knife following her nape. Adrian didn't move, his eyes never leaving Vaughn's face. She went all the way down on her knees and reached out reluctantly for the muzzle of the gun.

"Hurry up," Vaughn snarled, forced to bend over slightly in order to keep the knife within striking distance of her neck. "Pick it up and give it to me!"

She wasn't going to get a better opportunity, Sara realized. It was now or never. Handing the gun to Vaughn was the equivalent of signing Adrian's death warrant. She took a deep breath.

Then she threw herself full-length on the floor and rolled to one side, straight into Vaughn's legs. Her falling body covered the gun.

"Damn you!"

The knife flashed as Vaughn was forced to step backward in order to regain his balance. The blade arced downward, scoring Sara's shoulder. She felt the icy sting of the steel even as she struck his left leg. The pain brought a startled cry to her lips.

"Sara!"

Her name was the only sound Adrian made. In the next instant he launched himself across the room in a deadly rush.

But Vaughn was already moving. He hurled the blade straight at Adrian, who must have guessed what was going to happen next. Sara opened her eyes in time to see Adrian throw himself to one side. The blade whipped harmlessly past and imbedded itself deep into the far wall. The rushing assault had served to draw the snake's fangs.

In the small space of time he had bought for himself, Vaughn glanced down and seemed to realize he didn't stand a chance if he took another moment to push Sara off his gun. He raced for the door even as Adrian dived for his own gun.

Sara gasped in pain, her fingers going to the wound on her shoulder just as Adrian leaped for the door. Her cry of anguish stopped him as effectively as a steel cable. He whirled and came back to her even as the sound of Vaughn's running footsteps disappeared down the hall.

"My God, Sara." Adrian went down on his knees beside her. "How bad is it? Let me see." Carefully he guided her to a sitting position, pulling her face into his shoulder as he pushed aside her shirt.

"I...I don't think it's all that bad," she managed, inhaling sharply as she leaned into him. She was trembling. "It just hurts."

"I know, Sara," he soothed in a soft growl as he examined the shoulder. "I know. But you're right. It isn't very deep. Do you think you can handle it yourself?"

"Myself?" She lifted her head in astonishment and then realized what he meant. "Adrian, you're not going after him!"

"I've got to, Sara. You know that."

"No, I do *not* know that," she retorted. "Let the police worry about him. It's not your job—"

"Sara, it is my job." Adrian's face was a cold mask, his light eyes frozen, crystal pools. "After what he's done to you, I don't have any choice."

"No, damn it!" she raged, grabbing at him as he rose to his feet. "You'll never catch him, anyway. He'll take my car. He's got the keys." But even as she argued she realized there was no sound of a car leaving the drive.

"I took care of the car before I came into the house. A precaution." Adrian moved away from her, scooping up the gun and started for the door. "He'll be on foot and unarmed. This is easy hunting, Sara. Don't worry about it."

"I don't want you going hunting! Please, Adrian, wait...."

But she was calling to no one. Adrian had already disappeared down the hall after his quarry.

Easy hunting. Sara's eyes filled with tears. She didn't want Adrian going hunting. In that moment she would have given her soul to keep him from pursuing Vaughn.

Once again she remembered the way Adrian had watched the fish dying on the pier.

Outside the house Adrian paused briefly on the porch, listening. He shoved the gun back into the leather holster he wore at the base of his spine. The rain was coming down heavily now, obscuring visibility. Sara's car stood silently in the drive, unable to function since he'd clipped two strategic wires.

He'd really made a mess of this, Adrian told himself grimly as he started down the porch steps at a long, loping run. Everything was coming apart in his hands, and to top it all off, he'd nearly gotten Sara killed. The fury and fear he had felt when he'd realized what was happening inside the study were unlike anything he'd ever experienced in his life. The combination of the two had risen up to choke him, causing him to mishandle the situation badly.

But Sara was safe now. The knife had drawn blood but it hadn't gone deep. She had been too close to the floor, depriving Vaughn of an easy target.

Vaughn. Adrian shook his head as his sense of logic returned. There were only two ways off the island, the ferry from Winslow and the bridge at the far end of Bainbridge. Vaughn would head for the highway and try to commandeer a car to go for the bridge. The ferry was already pulling out of its slip on the return run to Seattle. There would be no chance for Vaughn to catch it.

His hunting instincts told Adrian that Vaughn would stick as much as possible to the wooded terrain until he spotted a car that could be hailed. And he would want to keep moving in the general direction of his goal, the bridge. Panicked quarry didn't think to backtrack or race off along a route that would seem to be in the opposite direction. When you were trying to escape, the sense of urgency effectively destroyed a good portion of natural logic.

With grave certainty, Adrian started toward the woods that bounded the road. He moved silently on the wet ground, oblivious to the rain that was soaking his hair and clothing. He knew he was heading in the right direction when he found the scrap of cloth Vaughn had apparently lost when he'd blundered into a thick cluster of blackberry bushes. After that, the trail became increasingly easy to follow.

Just like old times, Adrian thought with a chill that did not come from the rain. Maybe you could never really leave the past behind. Maybe it stayed with you forever.

He had told himself a year ago that a good, solid, iron-tight cover was the answer. A good cover had saved his life often enough in the past. Logically it should be able to provide him with a new life in the future. He'd had it all worked out, every detail in place, every aspect of his new world under control. He was a writer now, a slightly eccentric vegetarian, a man who could fall in love and marry just as other men did. If asked, he could have supplied a complete life history that would have satisfied any inquiring reporter.

The cover had been letter perfect until this afternoon when he'd walked into his study and seen the truth in Sara's eyes. That's when Adrian had learned that there was no such thing as a perfect cover.

She knew who he was. He'd blown it all when he'd stood in the hall with a gun in his hand.

A good cover, it seemed, couldn't quite cover up the past.

Vaughn was moving with increasing carelessness. Probably because there hadn't been any traffic on the quiet road. Maybe he was beginning to realize that making his way to the other end of the island was going to be very difficult.

Not difficult, Adrian thought savagely. Impossible. Vaughn wasn't going to drive, walk or fly off Bainbridge Island. At least not under his own power. Adrian quickened his pace, gliding silently through the rain-wet trees, skirting the berry bushes and listening with every nerve in his body.

In another couple of minutes he heard the first faint sounds of his quarry. Vaughn might be good but he obviously didn't know much about this kind of fieldwork. He was probably more accustomed to the streets of foreign cities. Most likely he'd never done a lot of real fieldwork in Vietnam or South America. An office spy. A man who worked embassies and cocktail parties.

Easy hunting.

Adrian could hear him clearly now. Vaughn wasn't far ahead of him. What lead he'd had had been chewed into by berry bushes, a driving rain and a woodsy terrain with which he wasn't familiar.

Adrian, on the other hand, knew every inch of the woods around his house. He'd walked them often enough, head bent against a cold drizzle, hands stuffed into his jacket. He'd thought about *Phantom* during those long walks. And he'd thought about the mysterious Sara.

Sara. My passionate, impulsive, loving Sara. Sara, from whom he would have done anything to keep the truth. Too late now. The cover was blown.

A rough, hastily bitten-off oath from the man ahead blended with the steady beat of the rain but Adrian heard it. He slipped forward, starting to reach for the gun in his holster at his back. And then he caught sight of the muted, striped shirt Vaughn was wearing. Vaughn was having to swerve in order to go around another thicket of blackberry bushes. Adrian changed his mind about the gun. *Easy hunting. Easy prey.*

You should never have touched her, Vaughn. You should never have gone near Sara. It's going to cost you everything.

Vaughn trotted to the left, searching for a way around the thorny bushes. He heard nothing as Adrian made his silent rush through the trees. In the last second, though, Vaughn felt the movement behind him. He whirled, clawing at his pocket to withdraw a switchblade.

But he was too late. Adrian's body catapulted into his quarry's, bearing both men to the soggy ground. Adrian had his hands locked around the fist that held the knife. He crushed with all his strength, hearing something snap. Vaughn yelled. The knife fell into a pile of leaves.

It was all over in less than a minute. Adrian had the advantage and he used it. With brutal efficiency he used his hands to stun his opponent. In a startlingly short period of time Vaughn lay limp and dazed beneath his attacker.

Chapter Ten

Sara adjusted the bandage on her shoulder for the twentieth time, using the bathroom mirror to guide her. It had been exceedingly awkward trying to bandage the wound without help but at last she'd gotten the bleeding stopped. She had been right. It hurt like hell, but the slicing cut wasn't all that deep. Her gaze went to the watch on her wrist. It had been over two hours since Adrian had left the house in pursuit of Vaughn.

Too much time. She was growing increasingly frightened as the minutes ticked past. But she felt incredibly helpless. Not because she thought for a moment that Vaughn would succeed in ambushing Adrian, though. Her mouth twisted in response to another stab of pain from her shoulder. No, Adrian would get his man. The wolf was on the hunt and he always did what had to be done.

Just as Phantom always did what must be done.

What truly frightened her was the thought of Adrian being thrown back into the life he had left behind. She would have given anything to keep him from having to resurrect the past. Because now she knew just how hard he had worked to put it behind him. But there was nothing she could do.

Adrian was the man they had once called Wolf, the legend who had been only too real. She had been coming slowly to that conclusion all day as bits and pieces of evidence came together in her mind.

When she had realized that her only hope of escaping Vaughn lay with Adrian, Sara had acknowledged the truth. Her life had depended on the man code-named Wolf, the man she had once imagined was a renegade killer.

And she had known on some instinctive level that Adrian would save her. That was why she had lured Vaughn back to the island house.

It was her love for Adrian that had enabled her to view the evidence of his past with different eyes. That love had begun from almost the first moment she had turned to find him watching her going through his study. She had known in that first glimpse that this man was different. He was her uncle's friend. The kind of man you could count on when the chips were down.

She had known for certain she was in love last night when she'd lain in Adrian's arms and prayed he wouldn't leave in the morning.

It was all so clear now. Crystal-clear, in fact. She probably should have been suspicious from the start about his identity. He was a man who needed to control his environment, to maintain a cover. It was the way he had built a new life.

Sara shuddered and tears filmed her eyes as she wondered how Adrian had felt when he'd realized his carefully structured world was crumbling around him. She ached to be able to comfort him but she was terribly afraid he wouldn't want the comfort. He had depended on no one but himself for too long.

The knock on the door shocked her into dropping the roll of tape she had been using. Sara frowned into the mirror. Adrian wouldn't knock on his own door, surely. Nervously she held a square of gauze to her shoulder and adjusted her shirt as best she could. Then she went cautiously down the hall to the front door. Standing on tiptoe, she peered through the tiny viewing port.

A man dressed in a wildly patterned aloha shirt and holding a festive-striped umbrella stood on the porch.

"Uncle Lowell!" Sara flung open the door and rushed into his arms. "My God, Uncle Lowell, are you all right? We've been so worried. Adrian's gone after Vaughn and it's been over two hours! I've been going out of my mind. How did you get here? Where have you been?"

"Easy, Sara," Kincaid said, smiling down at her. "One question at a time. Where did you say Adrian was?"

Sara stepped back into the house and held the door. "He's gone after Vaughn." She shook her head, trying to sort it all out for him. "Vaughn was holding me prisoner. He was going to trade me to you for information about that damned gold. Adrian rescued me but in the process Vaughn got away."

Kincaid arched shaggy eyebrows. "He did?" He followed his niece through the door, shaking out the umbrella as he did so. "That doesn't sound like Adrian."

"Well, it was all very chaotic, believe me." Sara sighed. "Vaughn was holding a knife at my throat and he'd made Adrian throw down his gun. Oh, it's a long story. But the end result is that Vaughn got clear and Adrian went after him. I've been worrying myself sick, Uncle Lowell."

"What's wrong with your shoulder?" Kincaid leaned forward, thick brows drawing into a solid line.

"Vaughn scratched it with the knife." She turned her head, trying to look at the gauze-covered wound. "It's not really that bad but it hurts so."

"Knife wounds generally feel like fire. Here, let me see if you've got it properly bandaged."

"The wound is all right, Uncle Lowell. It's Adrian I'm getting frantic about." But she stood still while Lowell glanced at the slice in her shoulder and then taped down the gauze.

"Adrian can take care of himself."

"You two keep saying that about each other but, personally, I'm having severe doubts! And I didn't want Adrian having to...to go back to his old business!"

Lowell tilted his head to one side, studying her speculatively. "So you've figured out what the old business was?"

Sara nodded grimly. "And I mean to have a heart-to-heart chat with you about that. But we can do it later. I've got other things on my mind just now."

"So have I. Got any coffee? After a few days in sunny Hawaii, it's a bit of a shock to come back to Seattle." Lowell started in the direction of the kitchen.

"But what about Adrian?" Helplessly Sara followed in her uncle's wake.

Lowell Kincaid was the same as ever, she decided. You'd never know that behind the laughing blue eyes was a brain that could function in the most convoluted patterns. He was nearing seventy now and had gone quite bald except for a fringe of well-trimmed gray hair. Kincaid had never gone to fat; his body was still whipcord lean. In addition to the aloha shirt, he was wearing sandals and a pair of white cotton slacks that were spotted with rain. On his wrist was a gold watch. It went nicely with the thin gold chain around his neck. Sara knew the gold was real. Her uncle never wore fake gold.

"Adrian will be back when he's taken care of things." With the familiarity of a man who has frequently been a guest in the house, Lowell began making coffee. "Damn sorry he had to clean up my mess, though."

"Uncle Lowell," Sara said with forced patience. "Why don't you tell me what the hell has been happening?"

Lowell stretched and lifted a hand to rub the point between his shoulder blades. "Well, to put it in simple terms, I've just spent the last few days following a false trail in Hawaii. Came back today when I realized it was a dead end. Vaughn really had me running around the countryside,'' he added ruefully. "I feel like an idiot."

"Who is Vaughn, anyway?"

"Old business."

"Oh, yes." She nodded, remembering the taped message. "You said something about taking care of old business."

"Look, when Adrian gets back, he's going to want some explanations, too. Why don't we wait until we're all sitting cozily around a nice warm fire. And what about dinner?"

"Dinner," Sara said vengefully, "is the last thing on my mind at the moment. What are we going to do about Adrian?"

"Absolutely nothing. Never was much anyone could do about Adrian,'' her uncle said reflectively as he poured boiling water over instant coffee. "Just aim him and pull the trigger."

Sara felt sick to her stomach.

SARA KNEW who he was. *She knew who he was.* Adrian couldn't forget the memory of her description of the man she knew as Wolf. Her words still rang in his head. A renegade killer or something equally picturesque. A man who, when he walked into a room, chilled everything and everyone. He'd seen the expression in her eyes when he'd stood in the hall just outside the study early this evening. She had looked up from the manuscript and he'd known that for her the room had grown very cold.

It was all over.

He drove back to the cabin with a sense of deep foreboding. There was a good chance she wouldn't even be there. Then what? When he pulled into the drive and saw the familiar green Toyota, he felt some sense of relief. Lowell was back. And that meant Sara was probably still around. Her car was still there but that didn't mean much since he'd disabled it earlier.

It was nice that Kincaid was home safe and sound, of course, Adrian told himself as he opened the car door. But the real benefit to his return was that it meant Adrian wouldn't have to face Sara alone. He still hadn't figured out what to say to her and he was beginning to accept the fact that he might never figure it out. He'd never been very good with words around Sara. In any event, she would probably be gone from his life soon, anyway.

She wouldn't want to hang around a wolf.

He walked slowly up the porch steps. The wet night had descended completely now and the warm lights of the house beckoned. But Adrian wasn't fooled. He knew the warmth was an illusion. Without Sara, there could be no real warmth in his life. He tried to dredge up some polite greetings, the sort of thing a man might say in this situation. He should be a gentleman about it. Give her an out. But deep inside he wasn't sure he could do it. He wanted her so and he'd begun to believe lately that he could have her. The thought of letting her walk out now filled him with a tight, gnawing tension.

There were a lot of things a man could take in this world but a woman's love was not among them. It had to be given willingly and it had to be for real. He had spent the last few days realizing the truth of that. The wonder of having Sara for himself couldn't be pushed back into the corners of his mind where he now kept other things that were better forgotten. He couldn't give her up.

But she hated and feared the man called Wolf.

The mechanical-sounding words Adrian had been practicing as he climbed the steps were wiped out of his head as the front door was thrown open.

"It's about time you got back!" Sara cried as she flew across the porch. "Adrian, it's been hours!"

He felt the soft impact as she hurled herself against him. Automatically his arms went around her. He was dazed by the greeting.

"Sara?"

"You said you'd be back on the five-fifty-five ferry," she whispered into his wet shirt. "I knew you'd get back on time. I knew all I had to do was have Vaughn here and you'd take care of everything."

He held her fiercely, absorbing the warmth of her. "Yes." He stroked her hair wonderingly. "I got the readout from the house alarm system right after I drove off the ferry." His fingers tightened abruptly in her hair. "I've never been so scared in my life, Sara."

"Hi, Adrian, sorry about all this. Everything okay?"

Adrian gazed over Sara's head, his eyes meeting those of his friend. "Everything's taken care of." He felt Sara shiver in his arms.

Kincaid nodded. "Figured it would be."

"You may have a few questions to answer from your old pals at the agency in the morning, though."

Kincaid's eyes gleamed. "How's that?"

"I left Vaughn tied up in a neat package a few yards off I-90. Then I called the West Coast agency office and left a message telling them where they could find him. When the guy who took the call demanded to know who was leaving the message—"

"You gave him my name." Kincaid grinned ruefully. "Thanks a lot, pal. Well, I guess I can't complain. I deserved it. Lord knows I owe you for taking care of Sara. Besides, maybe Gilkirk and his boys will be so delighted to have their hands on Vaughn they won't want to ask too many questions."

Sara lifted her head, her hands moving upward to frame Adrian's face. "You didn't kill him."

"No."

She smiled. "Of course not. Supper's ready. Go and take a hot shower. I'll pour you a glass of wine." She pulled free and disappeared back into the house.

Adrian stared after her, aware of a gnawing uncertainty. The uncertainty was painful but it was better than the cold, dead certainty of loss he'd been feeling earlier. Uncertainty contained hope. He followed Lowell into the house and headed for the bathroom, stripping off the wet Windbreaker as he moved.

ADRIAN HAD BEEN WATCHING Sara since he'd emerged from the shower, trying to second-guess her thoughts. She'd chattered about the gold while she'd prepared a hearty rice and vegetable salad, making a joke out of her uncle's idea of a wedding gift. She'd poured him and Lowell a glass of wine and put the sourdough rolls in the oven while discussing Lowell's unplanned vacation in Hawaii. Then she'd kept up a running monologue on Kincaid's new aloha shirt and how typical it was of him to bring something like that back from Hawaii.

Lowell had talked easily, too, leaning against the kitchen counter while responding to her teasing about his new shirt.

"Glad you like it. Got three more in the suitcase. Picked 'em up while I waited for the flight back this morning." He'd glanced down at the front of the splashy shirt with obvious pleasure.

Adrian had felt left out of the conversation but he hadn't known how to get into it. Sara and her uncle kept up a bright dialogue that covered everything under the sun except the subject of the man called Wolf. Adrian told himself morosely that it was probably because they were both too polite to talk about someone when the object of the conversation was within hearing distance brooding over a glass of wine.

During dinner Sara finally pounced on her uncle, demanding answers. Adrian surreptitiously kept an eye on her lively hazel eyes while she quizzed Lowell Kincaid. He searched for signs of disgust or fear or rejection in her expressive features. The stranger inner anxiety was eating him alive, demanding assurances and explanations and at the same time preparing him for the worst. Surely, after everything she had believed about the man named Wolf, she couldn't possibly be this warm and nonchalant now.

Adrian's fingers crumpled the napkin in his lap and he glanced down, vaguely astonished at the outward show of tension.

"All right, Uncle Lowell, let's have it," Sara demanded as the meal came to a close. She leaned back in her chair, her fingertips steepled beneath her chin as she regarded Kincaid with a gleaming gaze.

"Well," Lowell began with an easy grin, "I had to go to about three shops before I found just the right selection of shirts but when I saw this one with the pineapples on it, I knew—"

"Lowell Kincaid, I am not talking about the aloha shirts and you know it. I want to know about the gold."

"Ah, the gold," he echoed softly. "I figure that you may not be able to get at it until sometime around your twenty-fifth wedding anniversary, or you may have let your children inherit the treasure map, but either way it makes an interesting wedding present, don't you think? Even if you never actually see the gold itself, you'll have it to talk about and laugh about and tell stories about. I can just hear the tales you'll be telling your kids."

"I think," Sara interrupted firmly, "that we're getting a little ahead of ourselves. I'm not interested in what I may be telling my kids, especially since I don't have any."

"Yet," Lowell interjected wisely.

Sara raised her eyebrows but Adrian noticed she didn't look at him. She kept her attention on Kincaid. "I'm more concerned with the past at the moment. Did you or did you not steal CIA gold and stash it near the Cambodian border?"

Kincaid grinned at Adrian. "She's rather aggressively direct when she wants an answer."

"Umm." Adrian sipped the last of his wine and wondered why Sara hadn't been aggressively direct in pinning him down about Wolf. Maybe she didn't want to know the full truth. He set down the wineglass with grim care.

"Okay, Sara, here's the story," Kincaid began. "For starters, it wasn't CIA gold. It wasn't U.S. gold in any sense of the word, really. It belonged to some very astute gentlemen who were doing an active drug business under the guise of working in a civilian capacity for the U.S. government. I accidentally stumbled across them while working with some friends of mine."

"Friends?"

Lowell nodded. "I had spent a lot of time with the people of a particular village. They had been very useful during the war, supplying information and some very brave young men and women. At any rate, I was in the village when rumors came of the two drug runners being killed. The business career of a drug runner is precarious, to say the least. I was near the scene of the killing and, through a series of, uh, arranged coincidences, managed to get my hands on the gold.''

"Uh-huh." Sara sounded distinctly skeptical. "'Arranged' being the operative word, I imagine."

"I then had myself a problem. I knew things were deteriorating rapidly. Saigon was about to go under, and everyone who had any sense was aware of it. I was several miles away and there was no way I could make it back to the embassy with the gold. I would have been lucky to make it back with my life. So I decided on another route out of the situation."

"A route that would allow you to take some of the gold with you?"

Kincaid chuckled. "You know me and gold, Sara. I couldn't bring myself to just toss it away."

"Vaughn said he uncovered a file that indicated you left some of it behind with your friends in that village."

Kincaid's shaggy brows lifted. "A file, hmm? I wondered how he got curious enough about the gold after all these years to make a try for it. Well, Sara, let me tell you a fact of life. There's nothing quite as useful as gold when you're trying to survive in a country that's recently been overrun by a conquering army. And I owed those villagers. As for myself, I'd been making some friends near the Cambodian border and decided to call in a few favors. I loaded my share of the gold on a jeep and drove to the border. There was no way I could get it out of the country, so I buried it, made a map and then rendezvoused with my contacts. They got me out of the country."

"Where does Brady Vaughn fit into all this?" Sara demanded.

"Vaughn has been a thorn in the agency's side for some time. We all knew he was working both sides of the street."

"He said something about working two jobs," Sara said dryly. "Was that what he meant? He was selling information to the other side?"

"Information we wanted him to sell, although he didn't know it. We used him after we'd learned he'd been turned." Lowell smiled. "But his usefulness was becoming limited from what my former associates have told me. Apparently the other side felt the same. Vaughn was smart enough to sense that something was going wrong and wisely decided to disappear. Apparently he wanted a little nest egg to cushion his sudden retirement."

"And he chose your cache of gold."

"He'd been assigned to Saigon during that last six months. We'd worked together on a couple of jobs. But I never did fully trust the man. I tried to plant my own rumors about the gold whenever I heard it mentioned after the war. I knew it would be almost impossible to keep the whole thing absolutely secret. There were all those villagers who knew about it, for one thing. And Lord knows who the drug dealers knew. But I made sure most of the gossip about the missing gold implied the stuff was government material kept at the embassy and used for clandestine operations. I sort of left the impression that the two drug dealers were really agents. And of course I kept my own name out of it. You never know. I didn't want to implicate myself. If someone knew the drug story or got too friendly with the villagers, he might be able to track down more of the tale.''

"Apparently some journalist did get friendly with the villagers," Sara said. "And his notes somehow ended up in an old file that Vaughn came across.''

Lowell sighed. "I thought after all these years the story of the gold really had become nothing more than a legend.''

"Vaughn said he deliberately planted a rumor about him being in Hawaii recruiting mercenaries to help him get your treasure," Sara said.

Kincaid shook his head. "I'm embarrassed to admit it worked. I got wind of the plan and did exactly as he anticipated. I took off for Hawaii." He glanced at Adrian. "I honestly thought I'd have everything taken care of within forty-eight hours or so. Didn't think you'd be bothered with cleaning up my mess.''

Adrian couldn't think of anything to say. He just nodded austerely and continued to watch Sara's face through narrowed eyes. Why didn't she say something about what had happened that afternoon. The suspense was going to shred him. A part of him wanted to get the confrontation over and done with. Another part wanted to pretend nothing devastating had occurred. Abruptly he pushed his chair away from the table and went over to where he kept the brandy.

"Can I pour you some, Lowell?" His voice felt thick and scratchy in his throat.

"Sounds great." The older man beamed.

Sara focused on her uncle again. "Vaughn is definitely out of the way? He won't be bothering us again?''

Lowell Kincaid smiled. "You don't have to worry about him. I'll talk to Gilkirk in the morning. But from what I hear the agency's tired of using him, anyway. Even if he got turned loose tomorrow, he realizes everyone knows who he is and what he's been doing. He'd disappear in a hurry.''

"He had plans, you know," Sara mused.

Adrian could feel her watching him as he poured the brandy. "What plans?" he managed to ask, although he couldn't have cared less. Vaughn, as Kincaid had just said, was no longer an issue. He'd made sure of that when he'd left the sullen man bound and gagged in the rain beside the freeway. Vaughn was smart enough to know that everything had fallen apart. Vaughn, too, knew what it meant to have his cover completely blown.

"He thought that, given the map and a few carefully selected mercenaries, he could get into Cambodia and get at the gold. He told me all about his scheme," she finished blithely. "Aren't you going to pour me some brandy, too?"

Adrian turned back to the counter and poured another glass. "Sorry," he muttered shortly. When he handed it to her, she raised it cheerfully.

"Here's to finally getting some answers." She downed a healthy swallow.

Lowell grinned. "Haven't I always told you that answers are always crystal-clear once you know where to look?"

With a snap, Sara set down the brandy snifter. "Speaking of crystal-clear answers," she began. And then she was on her feet, hurrying down the hall toward the study.

Kincaid traded glances with Adrian. It was the first time they'd been alone together without Sara in the room. "Everything's under control?"

Adrian nodded. "Yeah. The agency will handle it. I really did lead them to believe you were the one who'd wrapped Vaughn up for Christmas. I guess if Vaughn says too much, though, Gilkirk may figure out I'm still around."

Kincaid chuckled. "Even if he does, you'll be all right. You're old news now, I'm afraid. The last time I talked to Gilkirk I casually brought up your name just to see what he'd say. He wasn't terribly interested, frankly. You'd be a minor curiosity and that's it. Gilkirk won't push it. He owes you and he knows it. He's a good man. Pays his debts."

"I like being old news." Adrian thought about that. "But Sara..."

"Don't worry about Sara," Kincaid said softly. "She's my niece. I know her."

"She's a woman," Adrian countered. "And she had a wild image of Wolf built up in her mind. What did you tell her about me, Kincaid?"

"Only bits and pieces. I was very concerned about you a year ago, my friend. I wasn't sure if this book was going to be the therapy you needed. I guess I had a few drinks with Sara one evening and talked. More than I should have, probably. She took the information and embroidered it a bit with her rather active imagination.''

"Did you really give her some idiotic story about the temperature, uh, dropping in a room when I walked in?'' Adrian demanded.

Kincaid blinked. "I suppose I did. There are times when it's perfectly true.''

Adrian winced. "No wonder I don't get many invitations to cocktail parties.''

Lowell Kincaid howled with laughter. "Don't worry. The description only applies when you're working. If you're not getting party invitations, it's because people suspect you're not the party type. Not because they don't need an extra ice bucket.''

"What about telling her I was a...a renegade?''

Kincaid looked surprised. "I never said that. I'm afraid she came to that conclusion on her own. I told her that I had trained a man who wound up with the code name of Wolf and that I was now worried about him. I guess she assumed—'' He was about to say something else and stopped as Sara trotted back down the hall, tossing the crystal apple in her hands. "Ah, the apple.''

"Yes, the apple.'' She pinned him with a mock-ferocious glance. "This is where the answer is, right Uncle Lowell? Clear as crystal?''

He nodded genially. "It's a microdot masquerading as one of the bubbles captured in the crystal. Pretty little apple, isn't it? I had one made especially for both you and Adrian. You each have half of the map. That's the wedding present, you see. Not the gold itself but the adventure of having a treasure map of your very own. And someday, someone in your family will be able to go after the gold. Maybe twenty years from now, when the politics and violence in that part of the world have changed. Maybe the next generation will get it. Who knows? In the meantime you'll have the fantasy.''

"It was a brilliant gift idea,'' Sara said with a warm smile.

"I thought so. Just the thing for a woman with an overactive imagination. When did you figure out that the apple was the key?''

"While I was talking to Vaughn. I knew the answer wasn't in the manuscript.'' She slid a quick glance at Adrian. "*Phantom* answers some other questions, but it doesn't tell where the gold is hidden. I just used that as an excuse to get Vaughn back here to the house. I figured out the role of the apple, though, when I put everything I knew together. The gold, you implied, was a wedding gift. Something to be shared. And you had given both Adrian and me an apple. It was a link between us. The key. Then there was your penchant for hiding things out in the open, the way you always say answers are crystal-clear. The apple itself has a gold stem and leaf and that was another clue. The gold on the apple was meant to be a connection to the gold in Southeast Asia, right? And you'd given us the basic clue when you told Adrian the legend. Last but not least, I knew you always like to cover your bases. You would have wanted the information available to both Adrian and me just in case something ever happened to you. It made sense that you had given us the answers. And you would have given them to us jointly. All we had to do was look around."

"And you realized that the only thing I had given both of you was the apple." Kincaid nodded. "Not bad, Sara. Not bad at all."

"Games," Adrian heard himself mutter.

"Better get used to them if you're going to marry into the family," Lowell advised lightly.

"I've played enough for one day. If you both will excuse me, I'm going to go to bed. Lowell, you can have the couch. Your niece has the spare bedroom." Adrian got to his feet.

Sara's head came up quickly. "Adrian..."

He stood still, looking down at her. "What is it, Sara?"

"I...I just wondered about your trip this morning." She chewed on her lower lip, obviously searching for the right words. "I mean, Vaughn seemed to think you'd gone to Mexico."

"That's what I wanted him to think."

"But..."

"I bought the ticket. But the plane made a few stops between here and Mexico City. I got off in L.A."

"I see," she said quietly. "You planned it that way to make Vaughn think you'd left the country to go after the gold yourself."

"I thought my leaving would draw him out into the open," Adrian explained very patiently. "I figured he'd make his try at night, thinking you'd be alone. I'd planned to circle back and be waiting for him. I had it all worked out. But you rewrote the rules."

"He tricked me," she protested. "I had a phone call from Uncle Lowell. Or at least I thought it was from him. Vaughn made a tape from the answering-machine recordings in Lowell's cottage and mixed up the words into whole new sentences."

"I know," Adrian said. "Vaughn told me."

Sara eyed him curiously. "Did he?"

"He told me a great many things," Adrian said. "Good night, Lowell. Sara." He left the room.

Sara watched him go, the smile fading from her eyes and being replaced by a wistful yearning. Slowly she lowered the apple into her lap as she sat down beside her uncle.

"He has a nerve accusing us of playing games," she whispered.

"What does he think he was doing today when he fed me that song and dance about going off to find a mysterious contact who might know where you were?"

Kincaid swirled the brandy in his glass. "He wasn't playing games. Adrian never plays games. He simply didn't want you to know the truth."

"What truth?"

"That he didn't have any magic man to contact. The only one around he could depend on to protect you was himself. He had to make Vaughn believe he had really left town and the only way to do that was to actually get on the plane. Mexico City was the logical choice because it has a reputation in the industry. Vaughn made all the assumptions he was supposed to make when he discovered that was Adrian's destination."

"But why didn't Adrian tell me?" She sighed.

"He wanted to keep you from finding out the truth about him. In the end there was no way he could accomplish that. Not and save your life, too."

"What did you mean about Adrian never playing games?"

"Just that." Lowell took a long swallow of brandy and gazed up at the beamed ceiling for a moment. "You and I, Sara, we have a capacity for stepping back emotionally from a situation we don't like. You did it all the time in the corporate world. You treated it as a game when it threatened to get too serious or intense. I saw you do it in the academic world and when you played at being an artist. It was a survival mechanism for you. It works very well. I should know. I've used it myself. I could frequently put my work into that kind of perspective when things got too grim. I would detach myself and instinctively try to see all the moves and countermoves as just part of a great big chess game."

"And Adrian couldn't do that?"

"No. For him it was very real. He gave everything he had to his work and it finally took its toll."

"*Phantom.*" Sara stared down at the crystal-and-gold apple. "The real truth in the manuscript isn't the hint about the gold that you put in, is it? It's the part Adrian put into the story. The reality of what he faced."

"When he finally realized the job would eventually break him, he turned in his resignation. It wasn't accepted. They told him there was one last mission."

"And he went on it." Sara shuddered. "I think he just barely survived, Uncle Lowell."

"He did what he had to do. Adrian always does what has to be done. He was quite lethally serious about his work and that attitude made him the best there was in the industry.''

"Better than you, Uncle Lowell?"

"Better than me. But the violence and the frustration of that last job were the end for him. When it was over he simply disappeared. He showed up on my doorstep three months later, calling himself Adrian Saville.''

"That's not his real name?" Sara asked in astonishment.

Lowell Kincaid smiled. "It is now. I told you, Adrian doesn't play games. Everything is for real. He took another name and started a new life. He would have done anything to keep it real.''

"Well, it is real," Sara protested. "Nothing's changed.''

"Now you know the truth about him," her uncle pointed out quietly.

"But I don't feel any differently about him," she breathed. "How could he think—''

"Apparently you gave him quite a horror story about Wolf.''

"That was all your fault. You're the one who told me the tale!''

"I was a little drunk that night as I recall. And I was genuinely worried about Adrian. I wasn't certain writing the book was going to work for him.''

"That's no excuse. You told me things—''

"They were all true," Lowell Kincaid said, giving her a level glance. "But I will not assume responsibility for what you did to the facts with your imagination.''

Sara grimaced. "When I found myself realizing this afternoon that my only chance for surviving lay with Adrian, I knew who he was. I also knew that whatever he had been, he was now the man I loved. You were right about him. He's the kind of man you can count on when the chips are down. Why did you sketch that wolf's head on the manuscript?''

"I was just doodling. It was natural that I'd be thinking about Wolf when I read the tale of Phantom.''

"I suppose so. It put me on the wrong track altogether, though. I thought it was Wolf you had gone after." Sara fell silent for a moment. "I guess I'll go to bed, too.''

"You do that," her uncle murmured blandly.

She shot him a half-humorous, half-rueful glance. "Going to throw your favorite niece to the wolf?''

"Wolves take care of their own." Lowell got up and headed across the room to the brandy bottle. "Good night, Sara.''

She went over to him and hugged him affectionately. "Good night, Uncle Lowell. I'm so glad you're safe.''

"Not half as glad as I am that you're okay. Guess I owe Adrian for that."

Sara said nothing. She merely smiled and walked down the hall toward Adrian's bedroom with a deep sense of certainty.

Lying in bed, his arms folded behind his head, Adrian stared into the darkness and listened to the sound of Sara's footsteps. He waited for them to stop outside her bedroom door, and when she didn't even pause he tensed.

It would be best if she stayed in her own room, he told himself. Quickly, silently, he ran down a list of why she shouldn't open his door tonight. Too much had happened today and she was inclined to be emotional. She was also inclined to be impulsive. She needed time to sort out her feelings. He didn't want her coming to him without having had time to absorb the full implications of what she had learned about him today. She might be feeling sorry for him. She might have convinced herself he needed her and she was too compassionate to deny him comfort. He didn't want her pity.

So many reasons, he thought savagely. So many excellent reasons why he should send her back to her own room if she dared to open the door.

She turned the doorknob and stepped inside. Adrian looked at her as she stood silhouetted against the light and knew that he could never find the willpower to send her back. He needed her warmth too badly tonight. It had been so cold today.

"Asleep, Adrian?" she asked softly, shutting the door and coming forward into the shadowed room.

"No."

"You must be exhausted."

"Umm."

There was a rustle of clothing as she undressed. He saw the pale gleam of her bare shoulder and then the lighter area of her hip as she stepped out of the jeans.

"I'm a little tired myself," she admitted softly as she walked naked to the bed.

"Sara..." He tried to say the words that should be said, tried to explain why she shouldn't be there. But she was pulling back the comforter and slipping in beside him and the logical phrases disintegrated in his throat. The warmth and softness of her as she reached out to hold him were a temptation and that was far more difficult to resist than all the gold in Southeast Asia.

"Don't worry," she whispered huskily. "I won't be making any demands on you tonight. We've both had a hard day." She stroked her fingers through his hair, soothing the nape of his neck.

"Sara, it's not that, it's just... Oh, Sara, hold me. Put your arms around me and hold me."

She did, cradling him even as he pulled her tightly into the curve of his body. Adrian inhaled the familiar, enticing scent that was uniquely hers, knew the incredible comfort of her touch, felt the shape of her locked securely in his arms and relaxed for the first time since the day had dawned. Now he would be able to sleep.

Hours later he awoke to the light of dawn and the knowledge of what he must do. A part of him resisted the knowledge even though another side of him realized it was the only sure way. It was best to do things the sure way, he reminded himself. Careful, cautious, certain. He had spent the past year carefully, cautiously, certainly pulling himself back together. He knew about patience. He knew about being sure.

It would be tricky trying to teach those skills to the warm, frequently impulsive woman who lay curled so contentedly in his arms. But it was the only way. Above all else he wanted her to know exactly how she felt about him.

No games. Not even the kind played out of pity or compassion. Especially not those.

Adrian didn't move as he lay beside Sara. He was almost afraid of disturbing her because once she came awake he would have to explain his decision. He preferred to steal these last few minutes of closeness and warmth, make them last as long as possible. A wolf, he thought wryly, took whatever he could get.

Sara opened her eyes slowly, aware of Adrian's arm around her, his hand resting possessively on her breast. She lay still for a moment, letting herself realize fully just how good it felt to lie next to him. It felt right. A sense of deep certainty settled on her. It was unlike any emotion she had ever known. She was in love with Adrian Saville. She had known it since yesterday.

It didn't surprise her that love would arrive like this. Such an emotion, when it finally came into her life, was bound to happen in just this manner. For someone like her there was no other way. Quick, impulsive, but absolutely right. She knew real gold when she found it. Lazily she stretched, a serene, confident expression in her eyes as she turned to meet Adrian's steady gaze.

"Good morning," she murmured, touching her mouth lightly to his. "How did you sleep?"

He blinked, his features holding a trace of surprise as he thought about the question. "Solidly." His hand moved on her, following the curve of her thigh. "Thanks to you."

"Good." Feeling vastly pleased with herself, Sara stretched again, this time bringing her body quite deliberately against his. "I'm glad I'm useful for something. I felt like such a fool yesterday when I walked straight into Vaughn's hands."

Adrian didn't respond to the invitation of her languid stretch. In fact, she decided, he seemed almost tense. Not at all like a man who'd had a good night's sleep.

"It wasn't your fault," he told her. "Anyone would have been fooled by the recording. I've heard tapes scrambled from other tapes. They can sound very real. But you kept your head. You got him back here."

"I knew you would be coming back and that you could handle everything," she said.

"How long have you known?" He watched her with cool eyes.

Sara knew the coolness was deceptive. She also knew the real question he was asking. She knew him very well now, Sara decided. Reading *Phantom* had filled in many of the blanks a person normally encountered when learning about another human being. Her heart ached to replace what had originally occupied those blanks in his life.

"How long have I known that you were the man they used to call Wolf?" There was no point in not being totally honest. "Since yesterday for certain. When Vaughn told me that Wolf had been a legend at one time but had not made it back from his last assignment—"

"Because I'd cracked," Adrian put in bluntly.

Sara refused to acknowledge his interruption. "I began to think about Phantom. About a man who had been to the brink and hung on instead of going completely over the edge. A man who had forced himself to survive when by all logic he should have been crushed. And then I thought about the way I feel safe around you..."

"Safe?"

She nodded. "I realized it that day at the Pike Place Market when you showed up just as Vaughn was about to coerce me into his car. And yesterday when I found myself trying to think of a way to deal with Vaughn. Something told me I only had to get him back here. When you arrived I knew I would be safe again. There were lots of other little clues, of course. Your concern with the security of this house. The way you move. That sketch of my uncle's. Even the way you play checkers. So intense and cool. Then there was your recent conversion to vegetarianism. Somehow that seemed symbolic. Something a carnivore might do if he were trying to put aside that aspect of his life. It all fit. Especially once I knew for certain that Vaughn wasn't Wolf."

"You had such a terrible image of Wolf," Adrian began heavily.

"By the time I realized you had once been Wolf, I was ready to throw the image out the window. I knew the real you by then." She smiled dreamily, loving him with her eyes.

Adrian's face became remote. "I'm not so sure, Sara."

"Not so sure of what?"

"That you know the real me." He stilled the protest that rose instantly to her lips by putting his fingers against her mouth. "Listen to me, Sara. I rushed you into bed that first time. The second time was too intense, too emotional because you knew I was leaving and you weren't sure what was going to happen. We've been living in the eye of a storm ever since I walked into this house and found you in my study. There's been no chance for you to get to know me in a normal fashion."

Alarm flickered into life. Sara watched him intently. "Are you trying to tell me you aren't sure how you feel about me, after all?"

He shook his head once, a quick, violent negative movement. "I know how I feel about you. I've been wanting you for months. You've been growing in my mind every day, taking shape, tantalizing me, until I knew I had to have you. But your uncle was right. There was something else I needed to do first."

"Write *Phantom*."

"That book was a final step in freeing myself, Sara."

"I understand." And she did. Completely now.

"You were a goal, a treasure waiting for me after I had put the past behind me. I feel as though I've been getting to know you for months. Your uncle saw to that. But it didn't work that way for you. You've only known me a few days and that time has been too intense, too dangerous and too emotional."

"Falling in love is bound to be emotional!" she put in quickly.

"Are you saying you think you're in love with me?" He searched her face.

"Yes." She spoke the single word with gentle assurance.

"Sara, you can't know that!"

"You told me once that you would like me to love you," she reminded him.

His fingers tightened on her. "I want that very badly. But you have to be certain. You have to be sure. No games, Sara."

"I've never played games with you."

"How about with your own mind? Honey, it's just too soon. You can't possibly know how you feel. Not yet. Hell, up until yesterday, you've been thinking of Wolf as some kind of psychotic killer. Now you've learned that Wolf and I are one and the same. You can't tell me you've managed to adjust to that kind of news overnight!''

"I get the feeling I can't tell you much of anything," she tossed back. "You're not ready to listen to me. You've already decided the way things have to be, haven't you?" The alarm was coiling tightly in her as she began to see where his words were leading.

"Sara, I want you to have time to get to know me," he told her urgently. "This time around we'll do it right."

"I don't understand!" But she did and the realization panicked her.

Adrian continued forcefully, his certainty clear in every word. "Yes, you do, honey. We're going to do it right. I want you to have a chance to make absolutely certain of your feelings. The next time you tell me you love me I want you to have had plenty of opportunity to think through just what you're saying."

Sara pulled free of him, sitting up with the sheet held to her breast. Her hair swung in a soft tangle around her shoulders as she stared at him. "Are you sending me away?" Her voice sounded odd. She was clinging to more than the sheet. She was hanging on to her control with both hands.

Slowly Adrian sat up beside her, his eyes almost colorless. He was committed to finishing what he had started, Sara realized. She would not be able to reason with him this morning.

"We're going to start a normal relationship," he said.

"What's normal? Adrian, you of all people should know by now that life is short and highly uncertain. We've found something wonderful together. Why should we waste time? Please don't do this." The plea was all wrong, she thought. She was letting her emotions rule her tongue. Adrian wouldn't trust her to know her own feelings if she did that. He didn't trust emotions.

"I'm not sending you to Outer Mongolia," he said.

"No? Then where are you sending me?"

"I think it would be best if you went back to San Diego."

"San Diego! But I don't even have a job there!"

"You've got your apartment, don't you? It's still your home."

She groped for an argument. "What about you? Are you just going to sit around here until you figure I've had enough time to know my own mind? Adrian, that doesn't make any sense. I'm an adult. I already know how I feel."

"I'm going to come and see you. Call you. Sara, I'm going to court you, don't you understand? I'm going to give you plenty of time—"

"How much?" she challenged.

He looked blank. "How much what?"

"How much time, damn it!"

"I don't know." He frowned. "However long it takes, I suppose."

"That's not fair, Adrian. If you're going to sentence me to exile, you have to at least put a time limit on it. Give me a date. One week? One year? I want a date."

"Sara, you're getting hysterical."

The worst part was that she knew he was right. She was losing her self-control. It was the shock, Sara decided. The shock of waking up in love and being told by Adrian that he wasn't ready for her love. Sara gulped air, swallowing sobs of anger and panic. The more emotional she became, the less Adrian would trust her to know what she really wanted. For the sake of their future, she had to get hold of herself.

"Yes," she whispered, sliding off the edge of the bed. She looked around a little frantically for something to wear and finally saw her shirt on the floor where she had left it last night. "Yes, you're quite right. I'm getting emotional." Her fingers fumbled with the buttons but she managed to get the shirt on. Then she picked up her jeans with hands that still trembled. Adrian never took his eyes off of her.

"Sara, honey, listen to me."

She shook her head. "No, no, I'm all right. I understand. You don't fully trust intense emotions because you learned once that they can take you to the edge of the disaster. I should have realized that after reading *Phantom*. That was the lesson you learned when you went through with that last mission and then disappeared, wasn't it? Your emotional response to your work nearly got you killed. You kept yourself so tightly leashed and under such control for so long that in the end you almost came apart when the explosion occurred. That's why you talk in terms of appreciating life's pleasures. Anything stronger than pleasure might be dangerous."

Adrian got slowly to his feet, completely unconcerned with his nakedness. "I just want you to be sure of how you feel," he repeated stubbornly.

She got her jeans zipped and lifted her head to meet his eyes. "You want to be sure of everything. Sure of the security of your house, sure of me, sure of your own self-control. Well, go ahead and make sure, Adrian. Being absolutely sure of things seems to be one of the few *pleasures* you get out of life. Who am I to deny you?"

Whirling, Sara fled from the room.

Chapter Eleven

Adrian's version of a courtship, Sara decided a month later, was going to drive her slowly insane.

Over and over again she told herself that he was the one who needed the time. Time to be sure of her. She would give him that. After all, she loved him; she would give him anything he asked. But how long would the farce continue, she wondered dismally.

"Farce" was hardly the most respectful term for Adrian's courtship, but it was the one that came to Sara's mind most often during the torturous, contrived, carefully choreographed weekends. True to his word Adrian flew down to San Diego every Friday evening. He spent Saturday and Sunday with her and then flew home to his island.

Sara's hopes for the first weekend were dashed when he checked into a motel near her apartment and continued to retreat to it every evening of his stay. The other weekends were no different. He took her to dinner, shows, the zoo and the beach. But he never took her to bed.

In fact, he rarely touched her with any intimacy at all. That was the part that was beginning to drive her out of her mind, Sara realized. She was left with a feeling of genuine panic every Sunday evening when she saw him off at the airport. Perhaps he wasn't capable of making the final step of total commitment. She knew he wanted her, knew he took pleasure in her company but he had convinced himself that she didn't understand her own feelings.

What she really feared, Sara decided, was that he didn't understand the depths of his own feelings for her. He was afraid to surrender completely to the force of his emotions.

They would be fierce and intense, the emotions of a strong man who had much to give once he had accepted the power of his own nature. But he had learned the hard way that there was a risk in losing some of his self-control. She yearned to set him completely free, to urge him to take a risk both on her and on himself but there was no way to break through the controlled facade. On Monday morning after the fourth weekend Sara acknowledged that Adrian had established the rules and he was going to force her to play by them.

Bad analogy, she told herself wryly as she fixed coffee with her imported Italian espresso machine. Adrian didn't like anything that smacked of game playing. She stared morosely out at the palm tree in front of her kitchen window and thought of the carefully restrained kiss she had received at the airport the previous evening.

Uneasily she tried to brush aside the worry that perhaps Adrian would never be able to relax and let himself trust both of them completely.

He did love her, she told herself with some violence. He hadn't said the words but that was all right. She knew him, understood him. She had complete confidence in his love. Her only fear was that he would never have the same confidence.

Somehow he had to learn that the iron control he held over himself wasn't necessary any longer. He was a whole human being now. He'd healed himself. He must learn to have faith in the health of his emotions and in those of the woman who loved him. He could live safely now without a perfect cover.

And she did love him, Sara knew. With every fiber of her being. One month of the stilted courtship hadn't changed that. Nothing on earth could change it. She had never been so certain of anything in her life.

She was at home that evening when he called. She was always at home these days. Not because she didn't have friends or invitations but because she was terrified that Adrian might phone and find her out. She wanted nothing to upset him or alarm him. She wanted him to know that she was simply waiting for him.

The conversation followed by its now predictable path.

"How was the flight back to Seattle?" she asked politely.

"Fine." He hesitated. "Have you eaten?"

"Oh, yes. I fixed myself a salad." Sara searched mentally for something to add to the careful conversation. "And I had a glass of wine."

"I went down to the tavern and had a beer."

At least you got to get out of the house, Sara thought irritably. *I'm forced to sit here from five o'clock on because I can't be sure when you'll call. And I'm terrified you'd use the evidence of my not being at home as an indication that you were right not to trust me.* "Sounds good," she said brightly. "How's the plotting going on the new book?"

"Okay. I'm trying to figure out how to untwist some things in chapter four without giving away too much information. This book is going to be a lot easier to write, though, than *Phantom* was."

Not surprising, Sara thought. This second book wouldn't be nearly so autobiographical. *Phantom* had been a form of catharsis. The next book would truly be fiction. She didn't have any doubt that it would be as good in its own way as its predecessor, however. The bottom line was that Adrian really could write. "Speaking of giving away information, Adrian," Sara heard herself begin quite firmly.

He paused before inquiring cautiously, "Yes?"

She floundered. "Well, I was wondering. I mean, it's been a month now and I was just thinking that you might have come to some, er, decision."

"About what?"

Sara very nearly lost her temper. "About us!"

"Oh. You still want a date when everything's going to be settled, don't you?"

"Adrian," she tried reasonably, "this is getting us nowhere. I've tried to be patient—"

"You don't know much about patience, honey."

"Don't be condescending. Just because people like you know all about patience, doesn't meant the rest of us—"

"What do you mean, people like me?"

Sara wanted to cry for having used all the wrong words. The forbidding cold was back in his voice. "I just meant that you seem to have developed a great deal of patience during your life. I, uh, I haven't been quite that fortunate, Adrian, I'm trying to give you the time you need, but—"

"I'm not the one who needs the time," he interrupted quietly.

"Well, I sure as hell don't need it! I know what I want. I'm in love with you, and this past month has been awful. I feel like I've been in exile. You don't touch me, you're so polite I could spit, and you won't tell me how long it's going to go on. There are times when I really begin to wonder if you—" She halted the flow of words abruptly.

True to form, Adrian refused to be left hanging. "You wonder if I what?"

"Nothing," she mumbled.

"Sara, tell me what you were about to say."

She sighed. "I wonder if you will ever really trust yourself or me enough to love me." There. It was said. She hadn't dared anything that intimate before and she wasn't at all certain how he would react. She had been assuming a great deal, Sara thought bleakly.

Silence on the other end of the line greeted her statement. Then Adrian's voice came with rock-hard certainty.

"I love you, Sara."

She caught her breath, her fingers clutching the receiver. "You do?"

"You've been a part of me for months. I can't imagine life without you."

The simple words were devastating to her. "You never said anything quite that explicit before," she finally got out rather weakly.

"I don't think I've thought it out quite that explicitly until now," he admitted slowly. "You've just been there, a part of me."

She closed her eyes in relief. It was finally over. It must be over. "Oh, Adrian, Adrian, thank you. I love you so much and I've been going crazy down here waiting for you to be sure."

"I've been sure all along." He sounded vaguely surprised. "It's you who needed the time."

Sara's eyes narrowed as she picked up the first inkling that her waiting might not be ended after all. "I don't need any more time, Adrian. Please. I've been very patient. I could wait forever if there was a real need, but there isn't. There's no need for us to be apart."

His voice hardened. "I want you to have more time."

She heard the finality in his words and fury mingled with despair. "You think I'm playing a game with you."

"No, Sara, it's not that. I just—"

She didn't let him finish. "Adrian Saville, you don't know what real game playing is!" Quite precisely and quite definitely, Sara hung up the phone. Then she walked to the hall closet and found her shoulder bag. There was a chic, cheerful little tavern down the street and around the corner. If Adrian could have a beer in the evenings, so could she. Come to think of it, she needed it a lot more than he did tonight.

The phone rang insistently behind her but Sara ignored it. She walked to the door, opened it as the phone continued to ring, and then she stepped outside. It was a wonderful, balmy Southern California evening. The scent of the sea hovered in the air and the row of palm trees lining her street rustled lazily in the evening breeze. Sara walked briskly down the sidewalk, wondering what the trees looked like in Southeast Asia.

The tavern was only half full, with a crowd of people in their late twenties and early thirties. The women, with their cleverly casual hairstyles, their silk shirts and jeans, chatted vivaciously with men in equally expensive hairstyles and designer jeans. Several heads nodded familiarly as Sara took a lone seat in the shadows at the back of the room. She ordered an imported beer and sipped it thoughtfully when it arrived.

The trees in Southeast Asia. Images of menacing jungles and treacherous swamps came to mind. Not really her kind of place. Adrian had learned caution the hard way in such places around the world. Caution and patience.

But there was a time and place for caution and patience. Surely they shouldn't be allowed to stand in the way of a loving commitment. Love was so rare and so valuable it was a shame to make it wait on caution and patience. Sara took another taste of the expensive import and thought about Adrian's reluctance to release himself completely from the reins of his self-control.

He had let those reins slip on a couple of occasions, she reminded herself. The first time he had made love to her, for example. The second time as well. Of course, on those occasions he had been assuming that he could keep his past hidden from her. He'd had no need to fear her reactions to learning his full identity because he'd assumed she never would know of it.

But even that last night at his home he had been unable to send her away although he had already made up his mind to give her time. He had needed her that night, not in a sexual way, but in the way a man sometimes needs comfort from a woman. He'd let her comfort him to some extent, she reminded herself on a note of hope. He'd held her very tightly that night, even in his sleep. She'd been aware of the tension gradually leaving him. She seriously doubted that Adrian had ever risked taking much comfort from others.

Sara turned the matter over in her mind. He loved her and she loved him. And as she had told him, life could be short and precarious. Love was too important to risk losing because of too much caution and patience. She needed to find a way to make Adrian understand that. She needed to yank him out of his cautious, patient, controlled world.

An hour later she walked home alone, opened the door and saw the gleam of the crystal apple as it sat reflecting the light of her desk lamp. She stared at it for a long moment, thinking of Vaughn's plans to retrieve the gold. Then, very slowly and very thoughtfully, she closed her door.

The phone rang just as she was about to get into bed an hour later.

"Hello, Adrian."

"Have you calmed down?"

"I've calmed down."

"I love you," he said quietly.

"I know. I love you."

"Just give it a little more time, sweetheart," he urged. "The waiting isn't easy for me, either."

"I think it's easier for you than it is for me," she told him.

"No," he said in a raw tone. "It isn't. Good night, Sara. Sleep well."

"Good night, Adrian."

She hung up the phone and trailed slowly out into the living room. Once more her eyes fell on the crystal apple. There must be a way to break the impasse. The apple held the key to the gold. Perhaps it held the key to unlocking Adrian's emotions.

Again she wondered what the trees looked like in Southeast Asia.

ADRIAN ANSWERED his phone on Friday morning with a sense of anticipation that he couldn't deny. Very few people in the world had his unlisted number. Sara was one of those people.

"Hello?"

"She's gone crazy, Adrian. I warned you this would happen. Don't say I didn't warn you!" Lowell Kincaid was one of the few other people who had the number.

"You didn't warn me," Adrian said patiently. Determinedly he squelched his disappointment that the caller wasn't Sara. After all, he would be seeing her this evening. He could wait. "Calm down and tell me what you're talking about, Lowell."

"You think it's a joke, but I can tell you from past experience, it isn't."

"Okay, it's not a joke. Now tell me what it is that isn't a joke."

Kincaid spoke grimly. "She's applied for a passport."

Adrian paused, absorbing that. "A passport?"

"And she called me up to see what I knew about getting in and out of Cambodia."

"That is a joke, right? You and she both have a very strange sense of humor, Kincaid. I've told you that on previous occasions." But Adrian's hand was like a vise on the telephone receiver.

"Believe me, I'm not finding this funny. Applying for a passport isn't the end of it, either."

Adrian sucked in his breath. "All right. Let me have it."

"She asked me for a second copy of your half of the map and she's put an ad in the L.A. *Times.* Want to hear it?"

"No. But I think I'd better."

"Listen to this." There was a rustle of newspaper on the other end of the line and then Lowell began to read: "'Danger, adventure, financial reward for the right person. Applicant must be willing to travel out of the country, able to take care of himself and willing to follow employer's orders. Personal interviews only, no phone. Three o'clock on Friday.' That's today, Adrian.''

"I know it's today."

"She goes on to name the hotel down in San Diego where she'll be interviewing applicants. You know as well as I do that every California bozo who's into fantasy violence is likely to show up. Adrian, this is all your fault. I'm holding you personally responsible.''

"My fault? You're the one who gave her half a map and a legend, for pete's sake!''

"And then I gave her and the map to you, damn it! I thought you would now how to take care of both!'' Lowell hung up the phone with a crashing noise that made his listener's ear hurt.

Adrian stood silently staring at the receiver for a very long moment. The lady was playing games again. In her usual impulsive, off-the-wall style she was issuing a full-blown challenge.

She appeared to have absolutely no fear of him. Sara must know that he would be furious when he found out what she had planned. Everything she had done was quite deliberate, of course. She'd notified her uncle just to make certain Adrian would find out immediately what was happening.

A challenge, Adrian thought as he yanked his canvas overnight bag down from the closet shelf. She had one hell of a nerve. He recalled the way he had walked into his home that first night and found her casually searching his study. She'd had no fear of him then, not after she'd found the apple. And she obviously had no fear of him now.

But she had shuddered and gone cold whenever she had mentioned the man called Wolf. And she knew he had been Wolf.

He had wanted to give her plenty of time to accept him completely once she'd learned the whole truth. He'd wanted to be certain she could handle the idea of what he had once been. He loved her. It would tear him apart if deep down she was unable to accept him and his past. A few more weeks or months and he would have been more certain she knew what she was doing.

But Sara had no patience for strategy. She had applied for a passport and put an ad in the papers. She was going to force his hand.

Adrian zipped the bag closed, checked for his keys and set the house alarms. It would take him several hours to get to San Diego and he didn't want to waste any time. There was a midmorning flight that he just might make if he moved quickly.

He was astonished to find himself suddenly very impatient.

THE LINE BEGAN FORMING outside the hotel room at two o'clock. Sara watched in growing trepidation from the lobby, trying not to be obvious. If any of the wildly varied assortment of men in the line realized that the potential employer was the lady in jeans who was hanging around the front desk, she would be mobbed.

She had never dreamed so many people would show up in response to that ad. What really alarmed her was that Adrian was not among the thirty-plus males lounging in line. Nervously Sara wiped her hands on her denim pants. In a few minutes she was going to have to start dealing with that motley crew. Several of them looked rather tough. One or two appeared to be ex-bikers. A few were probably ex-military and some appeared merely curious. None of them was an ex-wolf.

Reaching for a pad of hotel paper and a pen Sara tried to jot down a few interview-type questions. What did one ask a mercenary? Especially when one had absolutely no intention of hiring him? She needed a question or two that would definitely exclude everyone in that line. Desperately she searched her brain for something that would make each of the waiting men ineligible.

At five minutes to three Sara steeled herself for the task ahead. Adrian was nowhere in sight. She was going to have to start the interviews or risk a very discontented line of applicants. The hotel management would not thank her for starting a riot.

Chin high, she took hold of her jangled nerves and swept down the line of rather scrungy-looking males. Without glancing at any of them she opened the hotel-room door and said over her shoulder, "I'll see the first man in line now."

Five seconds later she found herself alone in the room with a swaggering young man who was wearing a much-abused military fatigue shirt. He took one look at her and grinned arrogantly.

"You the lady who wants to hire me?"

"I'm the lady who is looking for the right man," Sara said coolly. "Now, if you don't mind, I'm going to ask you a few pertinent questions."

"Go right ahead, ma'am," he retorted with mock courtesy. "I'm at your service."

The swaggering young man's grin was gone when he stomped out of the room five minutes later. He was grumbling fiercely under his breath. Sara beckoned for the next applicant.

She had sent fifteen of the men packing when there was a loud commotion in the hallway outside the room. Angry voices rose in protest and a second later the door was shoved violently open. Sara looked up from interviewing candidate number sixteen and saw

Adrian filling the doorway. Anger, a seething impatience and a vast masculine annoyance burned in his eyes when he looked at her.

But the room didn't go cold.

Adrian pinned her for an instant, then his gaze flicked to candidate number sixteen, a middle-aged ex-military type running to fat.

"Out."

The ex-military type examined the newcomer for a few taut seconds, then shrugged and got to his feet. "I was just leaving. Seems I don't fit the profile of the successful applicant," he drawled. He used the words Sara had just spoken a second before the door had been flung open. He sauntered past Adrian, a flicker of amusement in his expression. "A very interesting lady. Good luck, buddy. I think you're going to have your hands full."

Adrian ignored him and turned to confront the remaining candidates. "Everyone can go home. Interview time is over. The lady has already hired a man. Me."

"Now wait just a damn minute, pal...."

Adrian glanced over his shoulder at Sara. "Tell them, Sara."

She got to her feet and realized her knees were slightly shaky. She had seen Adrian in a lot of different moods, including the one that could chill a room. She had never seen him thoroughly annoyed. She summoned a polite smile as she nodded at the men in the hall.

"I'm afraid he's right. Mr. Saville is the perfect candidate. Thank you all for showing up today."

There were a few growls of protest but the cluster of men dissolved. A moment later the hall was empty and Sara was left to face Adrian alone.

He leaned back against the doorjamb, his arms folded across his chest. "What the hell kind of game do you think you're playing, Sara Frazer?"

She sighed and sat down again. It was easier than standing. "I didn't know so many people would actually answer an ad like that."

"This is California, remember? Put an ad like that in the paper and you're bound to lure a lot of nuts out into the open." He came away from the wall and stalked over to the desk, flattening his palms on its surface as he leaned down to glare at her. "Did you think I'd let you get away with a stunt like this?"

She smiled tremulously. "No."

He narrowed his eyes. "I'd have been here earlier but the flight was delayed. I've been amusing myself for the past several hours thinking of what I was going to do to you when I finally did get to San Diego."

"I can imagine."

"I ought to take a belt to your sweet backside."

"Sounds kinky."

"Damn it, Sara, what the devil do you think you're doing?" He straightened away from the desk and paced to the window. "I'm furious with you."

"Yes. I'm sorry about that part, but I—"

"Sorry about it!" He whipped around to stare at her. "Sorry about it!"

"I couldn't think of any other way to force you into realizing that this stupid courtship has to end. It's driving me crazy, Adrian." She sprang to her feet to confront him. "We're wasting time and love, and everyone knows those are commodities that are too valuable to waste."

"What makes you think you've achieved anything other than annoying the hell out of me?"

She faced him determinedly. "There's only one way you can keep me from going to Southeast Asia."

"Really?" he asked with soft menace. "And what's that?"

"You're going to have to marry me. If you don't, I'll be on my way as soon as my passport arrives."

He looked dumbfounded. "Marry you!"

"This is blackmail, Adrian. Pure and simple. I'm giving you an ultimatum. Marry me or I'll go off on my own in search of that gold."

Adrian continued to stare at her as if she'd taken leave of her senses. "You're serious, aren't you?"

"I'm serious. This isn't a game, Adrian. I don't play games with the really important things in life."

"And I'm one of those things?"

"Adrian, you are the most important thing in my life," she said with simple honesty.

There was a moment of profound tension as he regarded her with an unwavering gaze. Sara had the impression he was seeking the proper words to express his feelings. She waited in an agony of suspense.

"Sara," he finally said carefully, "I'm very angry. I can't ever remember being quite this angry."

"I know," she whispered. "And I regret that, but—"

"But you're not afraid of me, are you?" he finished.

"Are you kidding? I've crossed all my fingers and toes." Her mouth curved in wry humor.

"But you're not terrified, are you?" he pressed.

"Not the way you mean, Adrian. The room hasn't gone cold. The only time it ever did was the time you rescued me from Vaughn. And I knew at the time that the chill was my protection, not something I had to fear. I love you and you love me. How could I be truly terrified of you?''

He ran a hand through his hair and turned back to the window. ''I've been scared to death,'' Adrian admitted starkly.

''Of loving me?''

He shook his head. ''Of worrying that you couldn't really love me knowing who I am.''

Sara stepped around the desk and walked slowly toward him. ''I love you, Adrian. I love you so much that I'll do whatever I have to do to stay with you. I know all the important things about you. I read *Phantom,* remember? I told you after I read it that I'd fallen in love with the hero.''

''And I told you that I'd rather you fell in love with me.''

''You thought it would be pleasant.'' She nodded.

''I think,'' Adrian said huskily as he turned toward her, ''that it would be more than pleasant. I think it's absolutely essential.''

''Oh, Adrian,'' she breathed, throwing herself into his arms. ''I love you so much. Don't send me away again. I couldn't bear it.'' She buried her face against his shirt, clinging to him.

''You do tend to dramatize, don't you? I never sent you away. This past month was supposed to be a courtship.''

''It was a test and I hate tests. I trust you, Adrian. All I want is for you to trust me.''

''Or else you'll blackmail me into marriage?''

Her nails bit into the muscled back beneath his shirt. ''I've told you, I'll do whatever I have to do in order to keep you.''

He stroked her hair, tangling his fingers possessively in the golden-brown strands. ''I believe you, honey. After this fiasco today, how could I not believe you? I have to admit you're not exactly looking for a way out of our relationship. But I thought I had to offer you that escape if you wanted it.''

''So that you could be sure of me. Well, I'm not looking for an escape, Adrian Saville.''

''I love you, Sara.''

She lifted her head, eyes shimmering with emotion. ''I love you.''

He smiled and wrapped her close. ''Can we go home now?'' Adrian asked.

''Yes.''

''We can stop in Vegas on the way back to Washington,'' he went on thoughtfully.

''You really are going to marry me?''

"I thought I didn't have a choice."

"You don't," she assured him.

Adrian thought about being wanted so badly by Sara that she'd do anything to keep him. It was a novel idea. He discovered he liked it. He was suddenly very sure she wasn't playing games.

The phone was ringing in Sara's apartment when they walked in the door a few minutes later. Adrian reached for it.

"It'll be your uncle," he explained as Sara glanced at him in surprise. Then he spoke into the receiver. "Hello, Lowell. You can stop panicking."

"I knew you'd handle things once you got there," Lowell said in tones of great satisfaction. "What happens now?"

"We're going to get married in Vegas on the way up to Washington."

"The hell you are! Whose idea was that?"

"Sara is blackmailing me into it," Adrian explained, watching her as he talked.

"Blackmail, hmm? I always knew the two of you had a lot in common. You both know what's important in life and you'll both do whatever it takes to get the job done. You just approach things in a slightly different style, that's all."

"Umm."

"But that doesn't mean I'm going to let you two get away with a Las Vegas wedding. I've been waiting for years for Sara to find the right man. I demand a real wedding. With me there." Lowell paused and then said in tones of satisfaction. "I won't have to worry about shopping, will I? I've already given you your gift. That reminds me, I'll be expecting a thank-you note." Lowell Kincaid hung up the phone.

Adrian stood looking at Sara. "Your uncle wants a thank-you note."

"Don't worry, I'll write one."

"He's also demanding what he calls a real wedding. He doesn't approve of the Vegas idea."

Sara grinned. "He just wants an excuse to wear one of those dumb aloha shirts."

"Lowell always did like parties."

Sara smiled. "Well, much as I hate to admit it, we may have to accommodate him. I'm extremely grateful to him. But not for the map."

"I know what you mean. I feel the same way." Adrian moved, sweeping her up into his arms. "You're the real treasure. I will take very good care of you, my sweet Sara."

She nestled trustingly against him. "I know. And I will take very, very good care of you."

It was a long time later that Adrian stirred in the depths of the tangled sheets of Sara's bed and remembered the question he had wanted to ask earlier. He drew a hand playfully down her spine until he arrived at her derriere.

"Sara?"

"Umm?" She was rapidly adopting his characteristic response.

"What did you tell all those candidates before I arrived at the hotel? How did you get rid of them?"

"I told them that there was one important requirement the successful candidate had to meet."

"What requirement?"

"The successful applicant had to be a vegetarian."

There were a few seconds of startled silence. Sara turned over onto her back in time to see the laughter dawn in Adrian's eyes. A moment later it consumed him completely and she was left to marvel at the first full-throated laugh she had ever heard from him.

She decided that a laughing wolf was a very enthralling sight. She would make certain Adrian laughed a lot more in the years ahead.

THE WEDDING RECEPTION, held on the ocean-front terrace of the home of Sara's parents, was a loud and exuberant success. Mr. and Mrs. Frazer were pleased with their new son-in-law. For them, Adrian's cover was still nicely intact. They thought he would have a steadying influence on their beloved but often unpredictable daughter. They had several qualms about allowing Lowell Kincaid to act as best man, however.

"I knew he'd wear something ridiculous," Mrs. Frazer said with a resigned groan as she stood with her daughter near the punch bowl. "Just look at him in that silly shirt. Everyone else is in formal wear! I should have put my foot down right at the beginning and made it clear he would not be allowed to participate in this wedding unless he was willing to conform!"

"You wouldn't have had much to say about it, Mom." Sara laughed at her attractive, worried mother. "The best man was the groom's choice, not yours."

"It's not that I don't love my brother dearly, it's just that he's so...so..." Mrs. Frazer waved her hand helplessly.

"Have some more punch, Mother." Sara leaned over to pick up a fresh glass of the frothy red concoction.

"And that's another thing," her mother went on a little grimly. "Does this punch taste funny to you?"

"Spiked to the hilt, I'm afraid," Sara admitted cheerfully. She was watching her new husband as he stood talking to her father. The two men appeared to be involved in a very serious discussion.

"I knew it," Mrs. Frazer exclaimed. "I thought I saw Lowell fooling around near the punch bowl an hour ago! The champagne wasn't enough for him, I suppose!"

"Excuse me, Mom, I think I'd better go rescue Adrian before Dad sells him on the idea of investing all his royalties in long-term certificates of deposit."

"Adrian is a very stable, very intelligent man, dear. I'm sure he'll want to hear your father's advice. He's a man who will want to plan for the future."

"Adrian has me to help him plan his future." Sara swept up another glass of punch for herself and went off to join her husband.

The look in Adrian's eyes as she went to stand beside him warmed her from head to toe. He loved her. Above all else, he loved her. His was a total commitment. Just as hers was to him.

"Your father's been telling me about the advantages of long-term investments," Adrian said, putting his arm around his wife's waist.

"I'll just bet he has." Sara smiled at her father.

"I'll go over some more details with you later, Adrian. So glad Sara found herself a man who has his feet on the ground," Frazer said easily. He nodded in a friendly fashion, leaned down to kiss his daughter and went off to have some more of the heavily spiked punch.

"Feet on the ground, hmm?" Sara tipped her head up so that Adrian could brush his mouth against hers.

"That's not where they're going to be in a couple of hours," he warned.

"No?"

"Nope. Unless we decide to try something really unusual in the way of wedding nights, I plan to spend the evening horizontally."

"Adrian, I must tell you that lately you've begun to develop an odd sense of humor."

"Any sense of humor is better than none," Lowell Kincaid declared jovially as he sauntered up to join them. He was holding a glass of champagne in one hand and a glass of punch in the other. "Nice party, Sara. Your mother can throw a decent bash when she sets her mind to it." He took a sip out of each glass.

"Glad you're enjoying yourself, Uncle Lowell."

"I always enjoy parties. Say, I'm glad I finally caught the two of you alone. I've been wanting to talk to you all day."

Adrian looked at him warily. "Is that right?"

"Yeah, you know, I've been thinking."

"I'm getting nervous already."

Lowell shook his head. "No, no, this is serious. I've been giving some thought to Vaughn's little plan for getting the gold out through Cambodia. After Sara put that ad in the paper—"

"Don't remind me of that ad," Adrian warned.

"I'm telling you, Adrian, it's given me pause. There just might be a way to do it." Lowell leaned forward conspiratorially. "If we put together the right team—and you know we've got some good contacts—we could slip in and out of the country without anyone even knowing we were there."

"Uncle Lowell!" Sara's eyes widened excitedly. "Do you really think so?"

"Well, it would be risky, of course. But it just might be feasible."

Adrian's gaze narrowed. "The only reason it sounds feasible to you, Kincaid, is because you've been drinking too much of that damn punch. Forget it."

Sara turned to him eagerly. "But, Adrian, just think. What an adventure it would be!"

"I said forget it and I meant it." Adrian lifted his champagne glass and swallowed deeply.

"But, Adrian, darling..."

"Don't 'Adrian, darling' me. I said no. That's the end of it."

Lowell chuckled. "How about this. Your first marital quarrel."

"And you started it," Adrian shot back.

"You know what I think?" Sara demanded, glaring up at her husband. "I think Adrian is taking his new sense of husbandly duties a little too seriously. He's starting to lay down the law and we haven't even left the reception."

"Start as you mean to go on," Adrian quoted blandly. "And speaking of going on, I think it's time we said good-bye to all these nice folks. We've got a wedding night waiting for us. Are you ready to leave, Mrs. Saville?"

"Yes, Adrian."

"I've never seen her quite so amenable," Lowell marveled.

Adrian grinned suddenly. "It won't last. I intend to take advantage of it while I can. Let's go, honey."

Sara caught her uncle's eye as she obediently turned to leave on her husband's arm. Kincaid winked. Sara laughed silently back at him. The gold could wait for a while. After all, legends lasted a long time.

Lowell Kincaid's sister drifted up to stand beside him. She smiled maternally after her daughter. "Well, Lowell, in spite of that idiotic shirt you're wearing, I have to admit that this time you really came through. I was beginning to wonder if my daughter was ever going to fall in love. But you seem to have found just the right man for her.''

Kincaid raised one of the glasses he was holding and grinned. "The best. A legend in his own time.''

Diamond Girl
by Diana Palmer

To Jeanette,
and the girls at Carwood

Chapter One

It was raining in chilly gray torrents, and Kenna Dean made puddles on the floor beside her desk as she shed her beige raincoat and its matching hat. Even her long, wavy dark hair was soaked, and she pushed it angrily out of her bespectacled eyes. She was already ten minutes late because she'd missed the bus, and now her suede boots were drenched along with the hem of her new blue ruffled frontier skirt. She sighed wearily. What was the use? She had just bought the new frontier skirt and a matching high-necked ruffled blouse on Saturday, and this morning she walked out of her small apartment with confidence. Today she was going to make Denny Cole look at her and see a woman, not just an efficient secretary who made good coffee. But then it rained and she'd missed the bus and had to walk four blocks to the downtown Atlanta law office where she worked. It was starting out to be a typical Monday.

Denny Cole's office door opened just as she had known it would, and her tall, boyishly attractive boss walked into the outer office. One fair eyebrow rose expressively as he looked across at her, and she could see that he was struggling not to laugh. She could imagine how she looked: tall, gangly, and small-breasted, wearing clothes that suddenly seemed to emphasize all the faults in her figure. To complete the image of disaster, her mascara was running down her cheeks. She looked like an ideal applicant for the Ringling Brothers & Barnum and Bailey Circus.

"Go ahead, say it," she dared him, pursing her full lips, which were ineffectually painted with thick, pink lipstick. "I'm off to join the clowns."

"I'm a gentleman, or I might," he admitted, letting his white teeth show in a smile as he jammed his hands into his pockets and moved closer. "What's on the agenda today, Kenna?"

Just like that. No notice of anything except the job, even when she looked horrible. She should have known better than to try to dress up for him.

She reached into the top drawer and pulled out the appointment book. "You've got Mrs. Baker about the property suite at nine, you're due in court at ten-thirty on the James case, and you've got a meeting in chambers with Judge Monroe at two-thirty. Isn't he sitting on the James case?"

He nodded.

"Then if you don't finish by two-thirty, you can forget the meeting in chambers, I suppose."

"Are you kidding?" he chuckled. "Henry will recess until we talk over that continuance. How about the rest of the afternoon?"

"You're free."

"Thank God," he sighed. He winked at her. "I've got a heavy date with Margo tonight. I don't know how I live from evening to evening!"

She tried to smile and look unconcerned, while her heart was being slowly strangled by the thought of the dark-haired, dark-eyed beauty he'd been dating for the past two months. It was beginning to look serious, and she was really scared. How would she live if Denny married someone else? She seemed to have loved him forever—at least for the past year. And all he ever noticed was her typing speed.

"Has Regan come in yet?" he asked.

She felt herself tense at the thought of Denny's older stepbrother. He frightened her with his hard, dark face and his huge physique. He was the most abrasively masculine man she'd ever known, and the six months he'd been in partnership with Denny had been the most trying of her work history. She still couldn't understand why Regan had left a lucrative law practice in New York to come down to Atlanta and join Denny's, when Regan already had a national reputation as a trial lawyer and Denny was just out of law school.

"I don't think so," she murmured after a minute. "I just walked in the door, and I haven't looked."

"You won't, either, unless I insist, will you?" he asked curiously. "It amazes me how nervous you are around my brother. The other day he told me that you seem to go into hiding when he's here. He has to hunt for you to give dictation."

She shifted restlessly. She wasn't a timid person. She had a temper and on occasion she showed it even to Denny. But Regan made her bristle. She couldn't be in the same room with him for five minutes without wanting to take his trash can and dump it over his shaggy dark head of hair. And that wouldn't do at all because Denny worshipped his brother. So she tried to avoid trouble by avoiding Regan Cole. In her mind they were one and the same.

"I'm busy most of the time," she reminded him. "There are those files in the storeroom that I'm trying to alphabetize when I'm not typing petitions for you or entertaining nervous clients...."

"I know, I know," he sighed. He cocked his head at her, and his fair hair, so unlike Regan's, glinted gold in the fluorescent light. "You don't like Regan, do you?" he asked bluntly.

She shrugged her thin shoulders. "I suppose I'm a little in awe of him," she said after a minute, searching for a tactful way to admit that she hated his guts and finding none.

"Because he's famous?" Denny chuckled. "His name always makes the gossip column when he goes to Hollywood or the Big Apple, all right. Regan attracts women the way honey attracts bees. He's not a bad-looking devil, and, God knows, he's not poor.

"Come to think of it, I'm surprised he didn't bring his own secretary when we began the partnership," Denny murmured, smiling. "Sandy was quite a dish. Uh, not that you aren't..."

She managed a faint smile, to show him that she didn't mind being thought of as drab and uninteresting by the man she worshipped.

"Maybe Sandy didn't want to leave New York," she suggested.

"Maybe." He turned. "Well, send Mrs. Baker in as soon as she gets here. I'm not snowed under with mail yet, am I?"

"I'll run down to the mail room and get it," she said.

"Made coffee?" he called over his shoulder.

Sure, she muttered to herself, and swept the floors and decobwebbed the corners and reupholstered the chairs and the sofa and patched the carpet and painted the door facings, all in the past three minutes since I walked in the door.

"Not yet," she replied sweetly. "As soon as I get back, okay?"

He sighed. "I guess it will have to be," he mumbled, closing his door behind him.

"Oh, damn men everywhere," she muttered as she opened the outer door, and came face to face with Regan Cole.

She had to force herself not to start at the unexpected sight of him. He was intimidating—not only his superior height, but the sheer size of him, and not an ounce of that physique was flab. He could back down most opponents just by standing up. His eyes were brown with amber specks, and they were hard and cold as ice when he was angry. His face was broad, his mouth chiseled and faintly sensuous, his nose was too big and had been broken at least twice; it matched his hands and feet, which were equally oversized. But somehow they all suited him.

She moved quickly aside to let him enter the office, and felt herself bristle as he came by her. He had a frightening vitality, an aura of pure menace when he was out of sorts. And he was always out of sorts with Kenna.

"I'm expecting a letter from a colleague in New York," he said without preamble and without a trace of good humor. "Bring the mail in as soon as you get it."

His broad back disappeared into his office and the door closed behind it. She glared at it and, giving in to a sudden whim, went down on her knees and salaamed in front of his closed door. Just as she was giving her best to the effort, the door suddenly opened again.

Regan's thick eyebrows rose while Kenna struggled to regain both her feet and her forgotten dignity.

"I'll need you for some dictation when you get the mail, so bring your pad in with it," he said curtly.

"And if you're auditioning for the stage, don't practice on my time."

He turned back into his office and slammed the door.

There was a muffled laugh from behind her, and she turned to see Denny struggling to keep a straight face. They looked at each other and burst into laughter, rushing out into the hall together to keep from exploding where Regan could hear them.

This was Denny at his best, a co-conspirator with a sense of humor that she loved. Regan's exact opposite, in every way.

"I thought you were going to faint when he opened the door," Denny chuckled, leaning back against the wall in the deserted corridor as the laughter passed. "That made my morning."

"I wasn't expecting him to open the door," she confessed. "I couldn't help it, he throws orders around like a conquering army."

"He always has. I've learned to nod my head and listen and then go do what I please. It works half the time," he added with a rueful smile. "Poor kid, he's rough on you, I know. I truly didn't realize he was going to leave his own secretary behind in New York and then want to share mine."

She flushed at that unexpected sympathy and smiled up at him. "It's okay," she murmured, ready to wade through crocodile infested waters for him. "I'd better get the mail before his lordship comes out with battle axe in hand. Then I'll get your coffee."

"No rush, I'll survive," he said with a wink. "Don't let him intimidate you, Kenna. He's not what he seems. In a lot of ways, Regan's had a hard life." He straightened away from the wall. "Chin up, and all that rot," he said in his best fake British accent. "Right, troops?"

She saluted. "Aye, sir!" She turned and rushed down to the elevator.

A little over an hour later, she was sitting at her desk when Denny came out, shrugging into his trench coat on the way.

"I'm late again," he sighed and smiled at her. "I should be back by three-thirty. You can call the courthouse if you need me before then."

"Will do," she promised. "Have a nice day."

"I'll do my best. Oh, pull out the Myers file and photostat those deeds for me, will you? And do a cover letter, along the lines of, 'Dear Mr. Anderson, enclosed please find copies of the deeds for the Myers land dispute. When you have looked them over, see if you concur with our client's contention that the new survey confirms his ownership of land his neighbor has deeded for an industrial park. I will wait to hear from you, etc.' Okay?"

She was scribbling on the back of an envelope, because, as usual, he wasn't waiting for her to open her pad. "Got it," she agreed.

"Hold the fort, honey," he called over his shoulder. He stopped with his hand on the doorknob. "Oh, if Margo calls, tell her I'll pick her up at six for the ballet, okay? That's my girl."

And he was gone. She glared at the door, feeling vaguely betrayed. She hated Margo, because Margo was beautiful. The Argentinian woman was black-haired and black-eyed, with a complexion like ivory and the most sensuous figure Kenna had ever seen. She ached to look like that, to have that slinky walk and that air of unshakable confidence that drew men like flies. She got out her compact and stared at the plain little face in the mirror with a rueful smile. She wasn't going to set any men on fire with desire, that was for sure. With a sigh she put away the compact and rolled a sheet of letterhead into the electronic typewriter.

The morning went quickly, and pleasantly. Regan stayed in his office. His clients came and went, and the telephone lines stayed busy, but Kenna didn't have to see him. She liked days like this, when confrontations could be avoided. She didn't like Regan. She didn't exactly know why, but compared to his stepbrother, he was like winter to spring. Denny was so personable and pleasant, such a charming man. The only thing Regan might appear charming to would be something as dangerous as he was—maybe a rattlesnake.

She was grinning wickedly at that thought when Regan's office door opened and he came out into the office with curt, deliberate steps.

"Get me the Myers file," he said curtly.

She had it on the desk, having just photocopied the deeds. He rattled her, though, when he used his courtroom tone on her, and she jumped up and started looking through the filing cabinet for it.

His dark eyes went over her with distaste before they fell to the desk. His big hand moved, lifting the edge of the file folder. "Isn't this it?" he asked, his voice sharp.

She turned, flushing as she realized it was. "Yes, sir," she said for lack of anything more original.

He opened it, thumbing through it. His eyes shot up, pinning hers. "What are you doing with it?"

"Denny dictated a cover letter on his way out," she explained coldly, "and said to copy the deeds and send them along."

He tossed the file back onto her desk with a scowl. "I wish to God he'd take time to tell me when he's already done something he's asked me to do."

"He was in a hurry," she said defensively. "He had to be in court by nine-thirty."

He rammed his hands in his pockets and studied her. She wished she hadn't been standing up; that derisive going-over was embarrassing.

"Seen enough?" she asked, angry at his bold inspection.

"I saw enough the day I walked in the door," he said, turning. "Is he taking that Margo woman out again tonight?"

She felt a surge of pleasure at the disapproval in his voice. He didn't care for Denny going out with Margo either, by the sound of it. "You'll have to ask him that, Mr. Cole," she said demurely.

He gave her a sideways glance. "So protective, Miss Dean," he growled. "Denny's a grown man, he doesn't need a bodyguard."

"Most secretaries are protective of their bosses," she parried.

"You carry it to new heights." His glittering eyes narrowed. "How long have you been here?"

"Almost two years," she said.

"How long have you been in love with my brother?" he continued, and she didn't like the mocking smile that held no trace of amusement.

She felt her muscles contract, every one of them, and her eyes glittered behind the big frames of her glasses. "It's hard to work that long around a man without being fond of him," she countered.

He stuck his big hands in his pockets, obviously enjoying himself. "Are you fond of me?" he returned.

"Oh, just burning up with fondness for you, sir," she replied, and grinned wickedly.

"Is that why you were salaaming at my office door when I came in this morning?" he asked politely.

She felt the flush coming again and averted her face before it showed, pretending to gather up the photostated documents on her desk. "I dropped a pencil. I was picking it up," she informed him.

"The hell you were."

She glanced up at him. "Was there something else, Mr. Cole?" she asked.

"Eager to get rid of me?" he questioned, arching his thick eyebrows. "I wouldn't think a woman of your attributes would turn away male attention."

She was doing a slow burn, but perhaps she was getting angry without reason. "My attributes?"

His dark eyes narrowed as they appraised all of her that was visible over the desk. "Small though they are," he added with pursed lips. "Was that outfit supposed to catch Denny's eye?"

She clenched her jaw. "I beg your pardon?"

"That outfit," he repeated, pulling a hand from his pocket to gesture toward her blouse. "You'd look better in a pair of overalls."

She stood up, seething. "Mr. Cole, you may be one of my employers," she began coldly, "but that gives you no right to criticize the way I dress."

"I have to look at you," he replied. "Surely I have a say in the decor of my own office?"

"This," she indicated her clothing, "is the latest style. Pioneers wore clothes like this," she added with pointed sarcasm.

"No wonder the Indians attacked them," he remarked.

Her fingers clenched. Her lips compressed. She wanted nothing more than to attack *him*.

"If you want to take my brother's eyes away from his Latin acquisition, you'll have to do better than that," he persisted. "You look about twelve in that getup. And what do you do to your hair to make it stand on end like that—watch horror movies before you come to work?"

Her fingers curled around the file folder viciously.

"Are you such a prize, Mr. Cole?" she asked coldly. "Your nose is too big and so are your feet and you're nobody's idea of Mr. Beautiful!"

His eyebrows arched. "This, from a woman who could qualify for the Frump of the Year nomination?"

"Oh!" she burst out, and before she had time to think, she had flung the file folder at him, scattering paper all over the desk and the floor.

He cocked his head at her, a peculiar smile momentarily softening his hard features. "How fortunate for you that it didn't connect," he murmured. "I hit back, honey."

"You started it!" she accused, her eyes flaming green and brilliant, changing her face so that despite the inadequacy of her makeup, she was almost pretty.

"A matter of opinion." He pulled out a cigarette and lit it calmly, watching her hesitate before she reluctantly bent to pick up the scattered papers.

Her fingers were trembling; her body was trembling. She wanted nothing more than to hurt him, to wound him. She couldn't remember ever feeling such rage at any man.

And especially her boss. She colored, remembering that. He'd be within his rights to fire her, and that would take her right out of Denny's life, because Denny wouldn't go against Regan. She'd seen proof of that often enough.

She glanced up at him apprehensively as she clutched the disordered sheets of paper to her bosom and stood up.

"Feeling apologetic?" he asked, and the cold smile told her he understood exactly why she was regretting her temper.

She swallowed her pride. Any sacrifice, to be near Denny. "I'm very sorry, Mr. Cole," she choked. "It won't happen again."

"Poor little Cinderella," he murmured mockingly, and took a draw from his cigarette while she blushed again. "Sitting among the ashes while the wicked stepsister makes away with the handsome prince."

"Yes, indeed," she returned curtly, "almost as bad as having to kiss the frog." She smiled meaningfully at him.

He turned away. "I wouldn't hold my breath, if I were you," he murmured. "I'm damned particular about who kisses me."

"I'm amazed," she muttered. "You probably have to pay women to do that."

"What was that?" he asked, turning.

In enough trouble already, she controlled her temper. "Not a thing, sir," she replied with a theatrical smile. "Just commenting on the weather."

"It would break your heart if I fired you, wouldn't it?" he asked suddenly, looking disgustingly smug. "Because Denny wouldn't lift a finger to bring you back, and you know it."

"That would be hitting below the belt, counselor," she said quietly.

"Yes, it would. I might remind you," he added with a flash of a mocking smile, "that I'm a criminal lawyer. I don't mind hitting where it hurts the most. Do we understand each other, Miss Dean?"

She swallowed. "Yes, sir, we understand each other."

"One more thing," he said, as he took a step into his office and turned with cold brown eyes to look back at her. "The next time you throw anything at me, you'd better be wearing your track shoes."

And he closed the door behind him.

She spent the rest of the day avoiding him, finding excuse after excuse not to go near his office. She didn't like Regan Cole, but it was even more apparent that he disliked her. He always had, since the day he walked into the office for the first time and saw her. She didn't think she'd ever forget the coldness in his eyes, the instant hostility that had met her tentative greeting. He couldn't have made his dislike more obvious if he'd shouted at her. Not that he minded allowing her to take his dictation and his phone calls and type his briefs, she thought angrily. Oh, no, he didn't mind letting her work herself into a frenzy trying to cope with his impatience and his black temper.

When Denny walked back into the office at three-thirty, she was still simmering.

"Hi, girl." Denny grinned, whistling a gay tune as he sauntered in and perched himself on her desk. "How's it going?"

"You had four calls. I put the messages on your desk. And I've got the letter on the Myers file in there for your signature, complete with copies," she said, warming to his charm. He was like a breath of spring compared to his wintery stepbrother.

"Is Regan in?"

She felt her face go rigid. "He left about a half hour ago."

He cocked his head at her. "You say that with such relish," he murmured, grinning.

"For my part, I wish he was in darkest Africa, being slowly cooked in somebody's stew pot, pith helmet and all," she said, visualizing the scene with glee. "Of course, he'd poison whoever ate him...."

"How savage," he remarked. "Might I ask why you have this sudden compulsion to feed my stepbrother to strangers?"

"He called me a frump," she returned with glittering eyes. "Not only that, he hinted that I was a public eyesore and should be under Indian attack...."

His eyebrows arched toward the ceiling. "He what?"

She cleared her throat. "Well, never mind, it's too complicated," she murmured.

"He doesn't like you, does he, little one?" he asked quietly. "I've noticed how hostile he is toward you. It's not like Regan; he's usually the soul of courtesy with women.''

"Ah, but that's the problem,'' she explained, grinning. "He doesn't think I qualify for the status of a woman. I look about twelve in this rig, he said.''

Denny didn't say a word, but his eyes revealed that his own opinion matched his brother's. "Might I ask what you were doing while all this commentary was going on?''

"Flinging file folders at his shaggy head, that's what,'' she returned. "And if you want to fire me, go ahead.''

He chuckled softly, his eyes gleaming with delight.

"Oh, no, lady, not me. If you're brave enough to throw things at Regan, you've got a job for life.''

She smiled sheepishly. "Old dragonslayer, that's my name,'' she murmured. "Not that the dragon didn't flame up,'' she added with a sigh. "He said if I threw anything else at him, I'd better be good at track.''

"I don't doubt it. Take my word for it, Regan in a temper is something to be avoided at all costs.''

"I'll keep that in mind as I sharpen my trusty saber.''

"Better not rattle it too loudly, either. Want me to talk to him about you?'' he asked with genuine concern.

She sighed. "He'd probably chew it up, too,'' she replied. "Don't talk to him, please. He'll just accuse me of crying on your shoulder and it will only make things worse. I can take care of myself.''

"If worse comes to worse, I'll insist that he bring in his own secretary,'' Denny promised. "Maybe he misses New York after being away six months. I can't imagine why he gave up that practice to come south, although it's sure been great for me. I never would have gotten such a big start without his help.''

"He asked me if you were seeing Margo,'' she confided.

He frowned. "And what did you tell him?'' he asked, his voice cool.

"Nothing,'' she said quickly. "I told him that if he wanted to know, he ought to ask you.''

His face relaxed. "Good girl. Margo is none of his business.'' His eyes warmed, softened. "Isn't she a beauty, Kenna? All fire and determination. A very strong woman with great business sense. I've never known anyone like her.''

His voice had gone as soft as his eyes, and Kenna wanted to scream with jealousy. She couldn't remember ever hurting so much in her life. Oh, Denny, look at me, she pleaded silently. Look at me and love me for what I am, for what I could be....

But he only smiled that friendly charming smile that he always had ready. "How about making me a cup of coffee? And then we'll get the rest of the dictation out of the way. I might let you go home early. I need a little extra time by myself."

Yes, because he was taking Margo to the ballet and wanted to look his best, she thought miserably. So she'd go home early, back to her lonely apartment, and stare at the television set. Because she didn't date. No one ever asked her out, and she was far too shy to go to one of the singles bars or invite men to her apartment.

"I'll get my pad and pen and be right there," she said after a minute's hesitation, and sighed as she followed him into his office.

When she got home she put on her jeans and T-shirt and glared at herself in the mirror. The jeans were too big and the shirt was too big and she looked older than she was with her hair hanging down around her face. Her eyes weren't bad, though, and her mouth had a full, nice shape. If only she could get rid of the rest of her and just be eyes and a mouth, she might catch Denny's eye. The thought amused her and she grinned, turning away before the mirror could tell her how different she looked with her face and eyes animated by laughter.

She turned on the television before she went into the small kitchen to fix herself a sandwich for supper. She'd never had much appetite, but she seemed to have even less lately. Well, she wouldn't have to worry about getting fat, she told herself.

She walked around the dining room with her sandwich and cup of coffee in hand, smiling at the modest furniture. She enjoyed this apartment where she'd lived for the past two years. It wasn't expensive, but it was cozy and the green flowered sofa and matching chair looked friendly in the gray-carpeted room with its pale gray drapes. She'd splurged a month ago to redecorate the living room in a burst of early spring fever. Now it was really beginning to be spring, and she liked the new look. It made her feel brighter inside just looking at the furniture.

She watched television until bedtime, trying not to think about Denny out with Margo. She'd seen him in evening clothes before and remembered miserably how gorgeous he was in black. It emphasized his blond good looks. He was so handsome. A prince if there ever was one. Prince. That brought back Regan's horrible remark and she bristled again. Wasn't it bad enough that she had to listen to Denny moon over Margo without having to put up with Regan's evident dislike as well? She stormed off into the bedroom and went to bed before the memory had time to work her into a rage and keep her awake half the night thinking up horrible things to do to him.

The next morning she wore a beige sheath dress that clung lovingly to the curves of her slender body. The color did nothing for her, although the fit wasn't bad. She left her hair long, hating its frizzled look, but she didn't suppose it made that much difference. Denny never noticed the way she looked, anyway.

He was whistling when she got to the office, already pouring himself a cup of coffee and looking like a man on top of the world.

He turned when Kenna walked in and grinned. "There you are," he said. "Regan made coffee."

She flinched at the sound of his name and bit her tongue before she could say something foolish. "Did he?" she asked. "How nice."

"He's an early bird, all right."

She hung up her coat and uncovered the typewriter, then turned the appointment calendar to the right page and sat down.

"You're cheerful this morning," she said with a careful smile.

"I feel cheerful. I'm off to the lake Friday for a long weekend. Come to think of it, you might as well take Friday off, too, if Regan doesn't need you," he added.

For one wild, beautiful moment, she thought he might be going to ask her to go to the lake with him, and she beamed. The sudden radiance of her face captured his attention, and he frowned slightly.

"I'd like that," she told him.

"Got a date?" he asked.

"No," she said quickly, just in case.

"Too bad," he remarked, smiling dreamily as he stared at the other wall. "I'm taking Margo up to Lake Lanier with me for some fishing. Can you imagine, she likes to fish?"

Somewhere in Kenna's heart, a candle went out. "Oh, really?" she murmured calmly.

"I'm looking forward to the relaxation," he confessed. "I've been putting in twenty-four-hour days lately."

That was true, he did need the rest, but why did he have to take Margo, she wondered miserably.

"Well, we'd better get to it," he sighed. "The sooner we finish, the sooner we can leave. Grab your pad and come on..."

"Kenna!" came a muffled roar from Regan's office.

She gritted her teeth, casting a helpless glance in Denny's direction.

"Better go," he chuckled. "I'll wait my turn."

"Thanks, I'll do you a favor someday," she muttered, tossing him a dark look as she grabbed her pad and deliberately took her time going into Regan's office.

He knew she'd delayed on purpose, it was in his glittering dark eyes when she opened the door after a perfunctory knock and walked in. He was leaning back in his swivel chair, his jacket off, his broad chest rippling with muscles as he clasped his hands behind his head. Under the white shirt, she could see the thick shadow of dark hair, and the woman in her involuntarily appreciated the sheer masculinity of him.

"Yes, sir?" she asked sweetly.

He looked her up and down, and something in his eyes made her knees go weak. He was always appraising her, as if she were for sale, and it disturbed her more than she liked to admit. She tingled when those cold, dark eyes traced her body, feeling things she'd never experienced until he walked into her life. She didn't know why she felt that way, and she didn't like it. As a result, her hostility toward him grew by leaps and bounds.

"The color stinks, but it's an improvement," he murmured.

She flushed, clenching the pad in her fingers. "You wanted something, Mr. Cole?"

He leaned forward. "I need to dictate a couple of letters. Have a seat."

She started toward the chair, aware of his eyes assessing her coldly.

"Have you been crying on my brother's shoulder?" he asked suddenly.

She sat down heavily, gaping at him. "Sir?"

"You heard me. He asked me this morning if I minded letting up on you."

Her chin came up. "I slay my own dragons," she returned. "I don't need help."

He raised an eyebrow. "Should I be flattered? Yesterday I was a frog, today I'm a dragon..."

"I didn't call you a frog, Mr. Cole," she reminded him.

"At any rate, that's the wrong fairy tale. I've got something in mind for you, Cinderella," he murmured.

Her eyes widened, and he made an impatient sound. "Good God, I'm not that desperate for a woman," he growled, and she flushed angrily. "At any rate, this isn't the time to discuss it. Take a letter, Miss Dean..."

It only took fifteen minutes to finish the dictation, but she was almost shaking when she started out the door.

"Just a minute," Regan said behind her, his voice curt to the point of rudeness. "Denny's taking Friday off; did he mention it to you?"

She swallowed. "Yes, he did."

"Then presumably he told you why?" he added with narrowed eyes.

She only nodded.

"I'll be out of the office for a couple of days. But I'll expect you here Friday morning at 8:30 a.m. sharp. We're going to talk."

"About what?" she asked curtly.

"Well, Miss Dean," he said, leaning back again with his lips pursed, "you'll just have to wait and see, won't you? I'd like those letters as soon as they're typed. I have a case this morning."

"Yes, sir," she said, and forced herself to walk out without asking any more questions.

Denny was sympathetic when she told him that Regan wouldn't let her off.

"I guess it's that criminal case he's handling," he sighed. "Well, that's the breaks," he added with a sheepish grin. "We tried."

"We tried," she agreed, and her eyes clung lovingly to his handsome face. It was so pleasant to sit and look at him, to be with him. Oh, if only she were beautiful like Margo.

"By the way," he said, "would you call the florist and have them send Margo a dozen red roses?"

She jotted it down, keeping her eyes lowered so he wouldn't see the sudden pain in them. "Red, hmmm?" she teased, putting up a brave front.

"Red, for love," he laughed. "She's a tiger, my Margo. Spicy and passionate, every man's dream."

"Do I hear wedding bells in the distance?" she murmured, and stiffened as she waited for the answer.

He sighed, toying with a pencil on the desk blotter. "That would depend on the lady," he murmured. "She's not much for cages. But speaking for myself, I'm more than ready to put a ring on her finger. I've never known anyone like her."

She wanted to scream and throw things. Instead, she smiled and reminded him about a letter they needed to get out on a case that they'd just won. He grinned and started dictating. And if his secretary's face was strained and paler than usual, he didn't notice.

Chapter Two

She wore the frontier outfit deliberately Friday morning just to irritate Regan, because she knew he didn't like it. If he thought he was going to dominate her like he dominated everything and everybody else around him, he had another think coming.

She hung up her light coat and uncovered her typewriter, grumbling steadily. Since Denny was out of the office—she didn't want to think about where—she'd only have to get the mail for Regan. But he'd want it yesterday, so she headed for the door and in her haste almost collided with Regan, who was coming through it.

He lifted a bushy eyebrow at the quick rush of color that tinted her high cheekbones.

"Do you do it deliberately?" he asked her, unblinking, unsmiling, blocking her path with his cowhide attaché case.

"Do what...deliberately?" she asked.

"Make yourself as unattractive as possible."

It was the first time she'd ever raised her hand to a man in her life. But she took a swing at him with all her frustration and wounded pride behind it.

He caught her wrist before she connected, jerking her back into the office and booting the door closed with his foot. Without breaking stride, ignoring her faint struggles, he half-dragged her into his own office and slammed the door behind them.

She felt the clasp of his fingers with a sense of wonder at the new, unfamiliar sensations his touch was causing. She'd never tingled like that. Perhaps it was temper, but then why was her breathing so shallow? She disliked the surge of emotion, and her eyes narrowed angrily as she glared up at him.

He dropped the attaché case on the floor and caught her other wrist as well, just holding her there in front of him until she stopped struggling and stood still, panting with smothered rage.

When he saw that she was through swinging, he dropped her wrists and glared down his formidable nose at her.

"If you ever lift your hand to me again, it'll be the last time," he warned in his courtroom voice, deep and cold.

Her lower lip trembled briefly with the suppressed hatred that filled her stiff body. "If you ever insult me like that again, it'll be the last time, too, counselor," she tossed back, her voice choked with emotion. "I'll walk out the door, and you can find some stacked blonde with knee-deep cleavage to replace me, and see if she can type your contracts and your briefs and your petitions in between polishing her nails!"

"Calm down, Kenna," he said after a minute. "Sit down, honey."

He pushed her gently down into a big, leather armchair and perched himself on the edge of the huge polished wood desk. He gave her time to gather herself together, lighting a cigarette and taking a deep draw before he spoke.

"Don't call me *honey*," she bit off.

"Denny does. So do half the attorneys who walk in that door. Why not me?"

"Because..." She stared up at him, her lips parting as she tried to picture Regan ever saying the word and meaning it, with his dark eyes blazing with passion. Her own thoughts embarrassed her and she caught a deep breath, looking at his black leather shoes instead. "Oh, never mind."

"He's getting involved with Margo," he said quietly. "And I don't just mean involved in bed. It looks as if he's thinking about marriage, and I don't want him married to her."

She felt sick all over again as he confirmed what Denny had already admitted. Denny, married! The thought was more than she could bear.

"Stop looking like the heroine of a Victorian melodrama, for God's sake." He spoke so sharply that she sat straight up. "He isn't married yet!"

"How are you going to stop him?" she asked miserably.

"I'm not. You are."

She blinked. "Excuse me, I'm always dim before I've had my morning coffee and my supply of razor blades."

His mouth tugged up, a rare show of amusement that made her feel strange when she saw it. "You're going to save him from Margo."

She cocked her head and studied him blatantly. "You don't look like the fairy godmother to me, Mr. Internationally Famous Trial Lawyer. And I don't have a pumpkin to my name. And if you'll take a good, long look at me several things will immediately occur to you. The first is that I'm drab," she admitted painfully, "the second is that I have no looks to speak of, and the third is that I've been here almost two years and the most intimate thing your brother has ever said to me is, 'Kenna, how about a cup of coffee?'"

He didn't laugh. He took another draw from the cigarette, and his eyes were busy, bold, and slow as they took her apart from the face down.

"Taking inventory?" she muttered.

"In a manner of speaking." His eyes fell on the too-ruffled blouse. "Do you wear a bra?"

She caught her breath at the sheer impudence of the question.

"And do, please, try not to faint while you're thinking up an answer, Cinders," he said with a mocking smile. "I'm trying to find out if you're naturally flat-chested, or if you simply overlook the fact that breasts need support to be noticed."

Her face was bloodred and she stood up. "Mr. Cole..."

"My housekeeper calls me that." He caught her shoulder and jerked her against him, bending her arm back so that she was helpless. "Tell me, or I'll find out for myself," he threatened, and his free hand came up to hover over her blouse.

"Oh, for God's sake!" she squeaked. "All right, I don't wear one!"

He let her go, watching with amusement as she hid behind the chair and then gaped at him over it.

"Are you crazy?" she burst out.

"No, but you sure as hell are repressed," he replied. "Twenty-five, isn't it?"

"We aren't all wildly permissive," she said, choking.

"I begin to get the picture," he nodded. "Not much of a social life, I'll bet."

"I date!" she threw back.

He blinked. "Date what? You don't look as if you've ever been kissed...or did you think that would get you pregnant?" he asked with an outrageous smile.

She glanced at the trash can, measuring it for his head. He followed her gaze and chuckled softly.

"Go ahead, honey," he dared her in a soft voice. "Try it."

"I wish I were a man; I'd cream you!" she burst out.

"Haven't you ever heard of women's lib?" he asked casually.

"Men aren't supposed to be superior anymore. Come on, honey, throw a punch at me."

"Do I look stupid?" she asked, taking in the sheer size of the man. "On second thought, if I were a man, I wouldn't come at you with anything less than a bazooka!"

"That might be wise," he agreed. He leaned back against the desk, unusually attractive in his navy blue pin-striped suit. She always noticed his clothes; he had a flair for picking styles and colors that gave him a towering elegance.

"Anyway," he continued, bending to crush out his cigarette, an action that strained the material across his muscular arms and his broad back, "what I have in mind is transforming you."

She stared at him warily. "I'm not sure I want to be transformed."

"Don't be ridiculous, of course you do." He glanced up and down at what he could see of her figure behind the tall chair. "First order of business is going to be a haircut. I know long hair is supposed to be sexy, but yours looks like barbed wire most of the time."

"Oh, you're just great for my ego," she ground out.

"And the second order of business is a bra," he continued, unabashed, his eyes narrowing. "Don't you know that the worst thing you can do is sag?"

"There's not enough of me to sag," she said miserably, avoiding his eyes.

"I'd bet there is," he returned, not unkindly. "You're tall, and you have nice legs. You have a natural elegance of carriage that could work well for you. And with the right makeup, the right clothes..." He pursed his lips, nodding. "I think you might be more than enough to catch my brother's wandering eye."

"You've forgotten something," she advised.

He cocked a bushy eyebrow. "What? Your teeth are all right," he began.

"Oh, thanks, and they're all my own too!"

He chuckled softly. "You'll do. Well? Do you want to be alone for the rest of your life, or do you want to take a chance?"

"I can't," she said, exasperated, as she came reluctantly around the chair. "What you're talking about costs money, and I'm not independently wealthy. All I have is my salary, and out of it has to come my rent, utilities, groceries, clothes..."

"I'll take care of it," he told her.

"Like fun you will," she tossed back, her eyes flaring up.

"I said I'll take care of it," he replied. "It was my idea, and it's my brother I'm trying to save from that Latin temptress. I don't want a money-hungry tramp in my family."

"No, you'd rather have a secretary with no money, no connections, no social position..."

"Do I look like a snob?" he asked incredulously.

"I didn't mean it like that," she confessed. She drew in a deep, steadying breath. "Anyway, what's Denny going to think if he knows you're footing the bill?"

"He won't know," he promised, "because we're not going to tell him. I'll pick you up Saturday morning at your apartment, and we'll get started. Make yourself an appointment with Frederickson's downtown."

"But they're horribly expensive!" she protested.

"Make the appointment early," he continued, "because when we finish there, we're going to Almon's to have you outfitted."

Almon's was a charming boutique with a resident designer and some of the trendiest new styles in the country. She stared at him as if she couldn't believe her eyes.

"You'll go to the ball, Cinderella," he promised. "Even if you have to ride in a Mercedes instead of a coach drawn by white horses."

"There isn't a ball..."

"There most certainly is, next Saturday night at the Biltmore, and I'm taking you." He shot back his white cuff and looked at his watch. "And that's all the time we have this morning. Get back to your ashes, and don't breathe a word to Denny next week. I'm going to have a photographer along just to capture his expression when he sees the new you."

"Could he get my expression while he's at it?" she asked hopefully. "I'll need something to convince me I'm not dreaming."

He looked at her for a long, long time before he spoke, unsmiling. "Have you ever had an expensive gown?"

She avoided his eyes and walked toward the door. "The only way I'm going to have one now is if I get to pay you back, counselor. I mean that," she added, looking over her shoulder. "I pay my own way, frugal though it may be."

"All right, we'll deduct a little from your check each week," he agreed, moving around behind his desk. "When you make the coffee, how about bringing me a cup?"

She nodded and closed the door quietly behind her. She went down to get the mail in a daze and wondered if her unfulfilled longing for Denny had finally pushed her over the brink into insanity. The morning had been unreal.

Chapter Three

Kenna hadn't given Regan directions to her apartment, but he seemed to know the way. She had just finished dressing in slacks and a long-sleeved blouse and sweater when the doorbell rang at eight-thirty sharp the next morning.

Regan spared her a brief glance from hooded eyes. "Ready?" he asked carelessly, looking as if he were regretting the whole thing already. "Let's go, I'm double parked."

She followed him into the elevator, approving of his casual slacks, deep burgundy-colored velour shirt, and tweed jacket. The shirt was open at the throat, and she saw a glimpse of darkly tanned skin and thick, very thick hair in the opening. It made him look even more masculine, more threatening, and she wished she'd never agreed to this. Being around him at the office was bad enough, but this was…unnerving.

"I won't rape you, I promise," he said out of the blue, cocking an eyebrow at her as she retreated to the other side of the elevator.

"If you did, you'd be disappointed," she sighed, not rising to the bait. "Twenty-five-year-old virgins aren't much in demand these days."

He seemed shocked at the comeback, and she grinned at him.

"I'm not a Victorian miss, as you reminded me the other day," she said with a sheepish grin. "but you knocked me off balance. I had you pictured as a very staid type who wouldn't even suggest anything remotely sexual around a woman."

"My God, were you off base," he remarked.

"So were you." She sighed. "I may not be a stacked blonde, and I may look like a frump, but I don't faint at the thought of a man's bedroom. It's just that I've never wanted to occupy one." She glared at him. "And the reason I don't wear a bra is because it's the mark of a liberated woman!"

The elevator door had just opened, and a little old lady with blue-tinted hair actually gasped as she heard that last impassioned statement.

Kenna stared at the elderly woman and slowly went beet-red. "Oh, my gosh," she groaned.

Regan, trying to keep a straight face, caught Kenna by the arm and half-dragged her out of the elevator and through the lobby.

"Liberated woman," he scoffed, giving her a mocking glance. "You might as well give up the act; I know pure bravado when I see it."

She sighed. "I can't even act like a normal woman," she grumbled, jamming her hands in her pockets. "No wonder Denny doesn't notice me."

"I notice you."

She didn't even look up. "When you want a cup of coffee or a letter typed, you do."

He stopped and turned to face her, and she looked up to find his dark, steady eyes holding her own.

"I know what it is to be lonely, Kenna," he said quietly. "I know how it feels to look around and wonder if the world would ever miss you if you died."

"You've got all kinds of women," she faltered.

"I've got money. Of course I can have women," he said with a cynical smile. "I've even been married, did you know?"

That was faintly shocking. Denny never talked about Regan's private life. "No," she admitted.

"Jessica was twenty-six. Blond and blue-eyed and as perfect as a dream. The marriage lasted exactly a year."

She saw a flash of raw emotion in his face. "Were you divorced?" she asked.

"No," he replied curtly. "She died."

"Oh. I'm sorry," she said gently, and meant it.

His hands idly moved up and down on her arms. "It's been almost three years. I'm older and wiser. But there are nights when..." He let go of her and moved away to light a cigarette, and she realized for the first time that he was, indeed, a lonely man. It was a shock to realize that she cared that he was lonely.

"Life is too short to try living it in the past," he remarked after a minute. He turned. "And far too short to long for things and not try to go and get them. Isn't Denny worth a few changes in your life?"

She had always thought so. "Yes," she said, giving herself a mental shake. "Of course he is."

"Then let's see what we can do to get his attention."

The first stop was the beauty salon. She watched her long, dark hair fall in strands onto the spotless floor while Mr. Andrew snipped and discussed the latest styles and called back and forth to other patrons. Kenna found herself caught up in the cheerful surroundings and the excitement of doing herself over. Perhaps Regan was right. She was twenty-five, and it was time she took herself in hand. It was time she started to live.

When her hair was washed and blow-dried, she stared blankly at the girl in the mirror. She'd forgone makeup that morning, and now she was glad. With her rosy cheeks and full, soft mouth and unadorned eyes, she looked fresh and natural. And the short, beautifully-shaped hair framed her face in darkness, making her look like a pixie with her slightly slanted eyes, thin brows, and high cheekbones. She grinned at herself wonderingly.

"Is nice, no?" Mr. Andrew chuckled. "Now, miss, you go to makeup counter and have face done and see difference. I promise, you like."

She did that, finding herself with an extra half hour before she was to meet Regan in the couture department. She watched, fascinated, as the makeup expert did her face like a canvas, outlining her lips in plum and filling them with a deep, rich magenta, then delicately tinting her cheeks and eyebrows, lengthening her lashes, shadowing her eyes and finally enhancing her lovely complexion with the faintest touch of powder.

"Is that me?" she asked after a minute, captivated by the difference, wondering at the girl with the small, straight nose and big, shimmering green eyes and soft oval of a face with its bee-stung mouth.

"Quite a difference," the makeup expert agreed with a smile. She sold Kenna the right cosmetics to keep the new look daily and waved her off.

Regan was wandering around the mannequins with a dark scowl, sizing up each dress, while the saleslady darted curious glances his way.

"Waiting for me?" Kenna asked from behind him.

He turned, still scowling, and his eyes widened suddenly as he recognized her. "My God." It was all he said, but the inflection was enough to convey his meaning. He walked around her, staring. "Well, well, Cinderella, you do have something."

"While you're trying to figure out what," she said, "couldn't we go into the budget shop and look for clothes? I'm going to owe you my soul if we have to buy anything in here. They don't even have price tags on most of these things!''

"You're going to a ball, not a beach party," he said curtly. "I'm not taking you to the Biltmore in a dress off the rack."

"But..."

"Oh, shut up," he said impatiently, and taking her arm, he led her to the saleslady. While she stood rigidly, Regan told the tall, thin elderly woman exactly what he wanted for Kenna and then waited impatiently while the saleslady went off to search through her stock.

She came back in a minute with a long, sensuous confection of green-, gold-, and aqua-patterned Quiana with a low criss-cross neckline.

"This is one of our designer models," the woman said with a smile. "And perfect for a figure like yours, my dear," she added to Kenna.

"Well, try it on," Regan said. "Then come out here and let me see it."

The saleslady sent Kenna into the back, where she tried on the dress in front of the long mirror in the plush dressing room. She stared at herself as if entranced.

"How does it fit, my dear...oh, my," the saleslady murmured approvingly as Kenna walked out of the fitting room.

"It fits like a dream," she said sheepishly, almost afraid to touch the silky material for fear of running it. "Like gossamer..."

"The color is perfect," the older woman agreed. "Just perfect, with that light tan of yours."

She led Kenna back out into the showroom and stood with hands folded, while her client moved forward toward the tall dark man who was waiting for her. Regan was idly watching passersby when he heard Kenna's step and turned.

He didn't say anything. His eyes went up and down and up again, and his face hardened.

"Is—is it all right?" she asked, desperately wanting to be told that she looked stunning, that Denny would fall at her feet...anything.

He nodded. "Yes," he said in a strange, husky tone, "it's all right. Now see what you can find for the office. A tailored suit, some skirts and blouses that don't look frumpy, and a couple of ensembles for leisure."

"But...but what for?" she asked.

"Going out with me one time isn't going to give Denny any

hints," he said curtly. "Or did you expect him to take one look at you and drop to his knees to propose?"

She hated that cynical question. The dress had made her feel like a princess, and now he had spoiled it all. "No," she admitted. "I didn't expect that." She turned, but he caught her bare arm and held her back, out of earshot of the saleslady.

"You look enchanting, is that what you want to hear?" he asked at her ear, his voice husky, his breath warm against her neck. "That dress makes a man want to smooth it away from your body and see what's underneath."

She caught her breath at the blatant seduction of his voice.

"Embarrassed?" he chuckled as he let her go. "Well, you wanted to know, didn't you?"

She rushed off before he could manage anything worse and was surprised at the furious beat of her heart when she went to take off the dress.

It was the most wonderful shopping trip she'd ever been on. She bought a two-piece suit, pink with a plum feather pattern; it had a straight skirt and a long-sleeved V-neck jacket secured by a plum-colored rose at the peplum waist. She bought several skirts and revealing blouses that she wouldn't have looked at if Regan hadn't been with her, forcing her to buy them despite her own misgivings. She bought an expensive bra that added at least one size to her small breasts and some lacy lingerie. And as she mentally calculated the cost on the way out of the store, she sighed.

"I'll be working for you for the rest of my life," she murmured.

He glanced down at her from his superior height and smiled. "Would you mind? As long as I made the coffee once in a while?"

The tone of his deep voice surprised her into looking up. And when she did, she felt a warm surge of sensation that rippled down to her feet. His eyes, dark and quiet and intense, held hers until the jostling of passersby broke their strange exchanged look and brought them back to reality.

"Thank you for going with me," she murmured, following him out to his gray Porsche.

"I didn't have a choice," he said, glancing sharply at her as he unlocked the door and helped her inside. "Left on your own, you'd have come back with the same clothes you thought looked great on you before." He went around the car and eased his formidable bulk in beside her. She glared for all she was worth.

"I am not stupid about clothes," she informed him.

"Your idea of fashion is a gunny sack with arm and neck holes," he replied as he started the sleek car.

"Well, it's better than looking like a prostitute," she tossed back, "and that's what I'll look like in some of those things you made me buy! The neckline on one of those blouses is halfway to my knees!"

"Don't exaggerate," he said shortly. His dark eyes dropped to her T-shirt. "How many of those damned things do you have, anyway?"

"What things?" she demanded.

"Those shapeless things you hide your body in."

"I like loose clothing," she retorted.

"Obviously." He threw a careless arm over the back of the seat as he turned to back the car out of the parking space. His face was much too close to hers. Involuntarily, her eyes went to his wide, chiseled mouth, and she wondered what it would feel like to kiss him.

He stopped the car to put it in gear, but he didn't move. She sensed the sudden heavy beat of his heart, the warmth of his body.

"Look at me," he growled.

She looked up and her eyes were held by his, possessed by his, so that the world was suddenly contained in a pair of intense brown eyes under thick, short lashes.

His gaze dropped to her soft, parted lips, and he moved fractionally, his own lips parting. She waited, and wanted, hardly breathing, and her eyes narrowed to slits as he came closer. She drank in the scent of his cologne, the warmth of his big body, the faintly smoky scent of his breath as she felt it against her lips. And she wanted to kiss him with a longing that had her spinning. She wanted to kiss him hungrily and hard and see if the touch of that chiseled mouth would be as maddening as she was imagining it would...

"Get going, will you!" The loud voice was followed by the equally loud blaring of a car horn.

The dark brown eyes blinked and Regan looked into the rear-view mirror with vague curiosity, while Kenna felt herself trembling with hunger for a kiss she wouldn't get. She wanted to jump out of the car and kick the driver behind them for interrupting. Why she should feel that way when she loved Denny was something she didn't dare question. She cleared her throat.

Abruptly Regan put the car into forward and eased down on the accelerator, glancing toward her as he left the irate driver behind them. "Would you mind telling me what that long, soulful look was all about?" he asked, a bite in his deep voice.

She swallowed. "I wasn't looking at you. I was thinking," she countered weakly.

"About what?" he asked as he pulled into traffic.

"You mentioned that taking me out one time wouldn't be

enough," she murmured, nervous with him all of a sudden. "What did you mean? You said we were just going to transform me..."

"It's going to take more than a haircut and new clothes to do that," he said flatly. He lit a cigarette while they stopped at a red light. "And going out with me is the best way I know to catch Denny's attention. Or haven't you noticed how competitive he is with me?"

"I don't know if my ego can take more than one date with you," she said matter-of-factly, glaring at him.

"It will have to, if you really want Denny," he told her. "And I'm not going to pull my punches. I'm going to teach you how to dress, how to walk, how to flirt, the works. Because what you need most is confidence, and you're sadly lacking in that commodity."

"And you think having my appearance torn to pieces is going to give it to me," she mused ironically.

"Ultimately," he agreed. His eyes scanned her briefly. "I'd bet good money that you spent every high-school dance standing with your back to the wall, slouched, your arms folded across what bosom you've got, praying for some boy to ask you to dance."

She gasped and blushed all at once, because he was dead right. She couldn't even manage to look at him, and involuntarily her arms folded defensively across her breasts.

"How did you manage to get so repressed?" he asked. "Didn't your mother spend any time showing you all those little tricks women use to hook men?"

"I didn't have a mother," she replied. "She and Dad were divorced when I was young. I lived with him and my stepmother until I grew up and went out on my own. My stepmother let me stay on sufferance, but we avoided each other whenever possible. Does that answer your question?"

Her tone would have cut a lesser man dead, but Regan only lifted an eyebrow. "Have you seen your mother since?"

She shook her head. "She died a few years ago. Look, can we talk about something else?"

He took a long draw from the cigarette. "Have you ever been serious about a man?"

She laughed shortly, bitterly. "I've never had the chance," she confessed coldly. "Men these days are only interested in sex. If you say no on the first date, they don't come back."

"And that's a lot of bull," he shot back. "You aren't going to convince me that every man you dated tried to rape you the minute you climbed in a car with him."

Startled, she glanced at him. "I didn't mean it that way," she said. "I only meant..." She drew in a slow breath. "Oh, what's the use? I've only been out with four men in my life, and two of them were blind dates. And of course they didn't try to rape me, they couldn't get me home fast enough."

"Did it hurt to admit that to me?"

"Yes, if you want to know," she said curtly. She fumbled in her pocketbook and fished out her glasses, unfolding them to perch them on her nose. "And I'm tired of seeing blurs instead of people, I'm half blind without these."

He laughed softly. "Then why weren't you wearing them this morning?"

"I figured that if I could see how I looked in those things you made me buy, I wouldn't buy them," she grumbled.

"Ostrich," he accused.

"That's me. You were right about the dances, you know," she added miserably. "I've always slouched because I hate being so tall. And now I'll slouch because of those incredible necklines."

"No, you won't. Not when I get through with you."

"I'm not at all sure I want to be what you're going to make me into," she murmured. "Denny may not like me that way."

"He likes Margo that way," he said with cruel emphasis and a cold smile. "And I hope you're not naive enough to think they're up at Lake Lanier playing checkers?"

She flushed to the roots of her dark hair. "Margo has a lot going for her."

"So I hear," he replied flatly. "But I'd guess it's not so much what she's got as what she does with it, honey. Like all attractive women, she probably makes the most of her assets."

"How is it that you know so much about fashion and flair?" she asked curtly, glancing toward him.

He stared straight ahead with eyes that were momentarily blank. "Jessica was a top fashion model," he said, his voice quiet and soft in memory.

"Oh." She looked away from him, embarrassed by the emotion in his deep voice.

He crushed out the cigarette with faint violence. "Denny will notice you before we're through, I promise you that."

"I know why I don't like Margo, but why don't you? You haven't even met her," she noted when he was pulling up in front of her apartment.

He cut off the engine and leaned back against his door, studying her. "Because I sense that she's more woman than Denny's going to be able to handle. She'll have him standing in the corner like a coatrack before she's through. Besides that," he added darkly, "I don't know beans about her background, and that bothers me. Denny could be getting into something over his head."

"You mean, she could be a secret agent or something?"

"My, what wide eyes," he murmured. "I mean, Denny is wealthy and stands to be a lot wealthier. From what he's told me, she's the type of lady who wants to be well-kept. It isn't hard for a woman to want a rich man, Kenna," he said with bitter humor. "Denny deserves more than that."

She stared down at her folded hands. Yes, he did. She herself loved him, after all. She could give him love, if nothing else.

"I'll pick you up at two tomorrow afternoon," he said. "And we'll start the lessons. You can wear one of your new outfits."

She lifted her head and blinked, staring at him. "Tomorrow?"

"I assume you don't have a heavy date lined up?"

She glowered. "Wouldn't it shock you if I did?"

"The way you dress," he said derisively, "it would."

"If you have your way, I'll be walking the streets naked," she burst out.

"That," he returned shortly, "would be worse than what you're wearing."

She could have thrown her purse at him. She couldn't remember ever in her life feeling this kind of maniacal rage toward a man— the same rage that had made her fling that file folder at his proud head. But it seemed to get worse every time she was with him.

He was already out of the car with the shopping bags before she could find her voice, and she led him stoically up to her small apartment.

"How did you find my apartment building?" she asked, as he opened the door and let her go in first.

"I asked Denny where you lived. He looked it up." He glanced at her as he dumped the packages on her colorful sofa. "Obviously, he's never been here."

She shook her head sadly, and then she laughed. "Nobody's been here, except family and an occasional girl friend."

He jammed his hands in his pockets and looked around him. "Too bad you don't dress like you decorate," he said finally. "The room has personality."

"And I haven't?" she murmured defensively, bristling again.

"I don't know," he replied. His dark eyes went over her withdrawn face. "I've never paid much attention to you."

"That's not surprising," she sighed. "I've seen photographs of the women you go around with."

His eyebrows went straight up. "Meaning?"

She laughed self-consciously. "Some of them make even Margo look ugly by comparison."

He pulled out a cigarette and lit it, studying her curiously. "I get lonely. Don't you?"

Her eyes widened with something like shock. She was beginning to realize that he was human after all, not the ogre of her imagination. Perhaps he missed his late wife. It didn't make her like him any better, but it helped her to understand him better.

"Everyone gets lonely, I expect," she hedged, turning away. Some more than others, she added silently, like me, wanting a man I can't have.

"And that's your whole problem, Kenna," he growled. "You walk around hunched over with your head hanging, feeling sorry for yourself. My God, no wonder you're twenty-five and living alone!"

She whirled gracefully, like a ballerina, her eyes reckless with challenge. Anger made her whole face come alive.

"I like living alone!" she tossed back.

"Like hell you do," he countered. "How much television can you watch before you get sick of it and your own company?"

She felt her lower lip trembling with indignation. He was hitting too close to home. "Don't you have someplace to go?" she asked coldly.

"As a matter of fact, I have a date tonight," he said cruelly, smiling at her involuntary grimace. "I won't be sitting home alone hoping for the phone to ring."

Her eyes clouded with mingled fury and hurt. "She must have been desperate, to go out with you!" she flung at him, even though she was positive it was the other way around.

He only smiled with quiet confidence. He had the look of a man who knew everything there was to know about women, and his gaze was so frankly sensual that she was shocked. She hadn't realized before just how sexy he was. She didn't want to think about it now, either; it disturbed her.

She turned away. "I have things to do."

"So have I. I'll pick you up at two tomorrow." He opened the door and went out without a backward glance, leaving her to fume silently and alone.

Chapter Four

Kenna spent a sleepless night, full of dreams in which she took Denny away from Margo and he carried her off to a castle to live happily ever after. But she woke up to a lonely apartment and a day she dreaded. It was hard enough putting up with Regan Cole at the office. How in the world was she going to stand hours of forced companionship with the man without murdering him?

She got dressed an hour before he came to pick her up, defiantly choosing a pair of designer jeans and a white turtleneck. That ought to burn him up, she thought, grinning at her reflection in the mirror. She'd done her face as the cosmetics expert had taught her, and the difference, even with her glasses on, was something to write home about. She couldn't wait for Denny to see her tomorrow.

The doorbell rang at two-thirty sharp, and she opened the door reluctantly.

Regan, dressed in tan slacks and an open-throated black and tan shirt, glared at her. "Why didn't you just wear the sack you brought that home in?" he demanded.

She glared up at him. It was a long way, because this afternoon she was wearing ballerina shoes with flat heels. She'd never been more conscious of the sheer size of him.

"I'm only spending the afternoon with *you*," she tossed back. "I didn't see any reason to try looking seductive."

His eyebrows arched. "I thought the whole idea of this exercise was to teach you to be exactly that—seductive. Not," he added coldly, "for my benefit, you needn't worry about that. We've already agreed that you're not my type."

"Thank goodness," she sighed with a sarcastic smile. She turned. "In that case, I'll put on one of those slit-to-the-navel numbers you made me buy."

"Don't wear longjohns under it," he called after her. "And put on a bra!"

She slammed her bedroom door as hard as she could.

Ten minutes later, she slunk back into the living room, feeling self-conscious and about as seductive as a hunk of cheese.

He turned from a brooding contemplation of the photos she kept on her coffee table and stared at her. The new blouse was a pale olive. It had cap sleeves and a neckline that ended just between her breasts, hinting at their soft curves. The bra she'd bought to wear with it gave her the appearance of grander assets than she possessed, and the color of the blouse brought out the deep green of her eyes.

"Stand up straight, for God's sake," he growled, rising from the couch.

She did, but her eyes told him what she thought of the comment.

"You walk like a mortician," he remarked, leading the way to the door.

"At least I don't look like one," she said, staring pointedly at his grim face.

"That's debatable," he said imperturbably. "Let's go."

"Why can't we stay here?" she asked curtly.

"Afraid to be alone in your apartment with me?" he asked with a malicious smile.

"I'm hardly in a position to worry about my honor," she reminded him sweetly as they walked to the elevator, "if I have to be taught how to seduce a man." She glared up at him as the elevator stopped and the door began to slide open. "Aren't we lucky that I don't have to lure *you* into my bed?"

The same elderly lady who'd listened to her opinions on bras the day before stood stock-still in the elevator, staring at the red-faced girl and the tall man. She seemed to be debating whether or not to get out.

"My, my, what a lovely day...isn't it?" The sweet little lady faltered and muttered an apology as she rushed out of the elevator and down the hall.

Regan was trying to keep a straight face as he held the elevator door for Kenna. He pushed the ground floor button and glanced at her.

"Does she lie in wait for you?" he asked.

She sighed. "Up until this weekend, she thought I was a nice, retiring young lady with admirable moral principles."

"Do you mind what people think?" he asked suddenly.

She glanced up at him, wondering at the sudden shock that went through her when she met his unblinking gaze. She looked away quickly, oddly disturbed. "No, I don't think so," she replied.

"Then why lock yourself in that apartment like a hermit and deliberately dress yourself into the woodwork?" he asked.

She stared at the floor of the elevator. "Because I don't drink or do drugs," she said quietly. "I don't believe in free sex, and I'd rather be walking in the woods than dancing to a disco beat."

He didn't say a word, but his eyes didn't move away from her bent head until the elevator stopped.

"Come on, diamond girl," he murmured, letting her precede him out of the elevator.

"What?" she asked, surprised into looking up.

"Diamond in the rough," he murmured. "All you need is a little polishing."

"That could be painful," she said, trying to make light of it.

"Cinderella didn't get the prince without a little suffering, honey," he reminded her.

She sighed. "I feel more like the pumpkin than Cinderella right now, thanks."

"That's what we're going to work on."

She followed him out to his car, apprehensive and not a little nervous. Regan bothered her; being with him made her feel shaky. If only she'd never agreed to this! But if there was a chance in a million that he could make her noticeable to Denny, she'd take it, and gladly. No sacrifice was too great to catch Denny's eye, not even spending time with a man she disliked intensely.

Regan lived in a luxurious apartment in downtown Atlanta, overlooking the Regency Hyatt House's distinctive saucer and the night lights that made Atlanta look like a many-colored jewel. The whole apartment was carpeted in thick gray pile and decorated with Mediterranean furniture and bold gray-and beige-striped curtains at the windows. There were a lot of carved wooden sculptures and animals that had a distinctively African flavor, including the masks on the wall. An antique table held a single photograph in a small, ornate frame. She knew without being told who it was, that beautiful blonde with the long, windblown hair. It was Jessica.

"Don't stand on ceremony," he growled from behind her. "You might as well ask me about it."

She flushed, embarrassed at being caught in her scrutiny. She turned, looking up with apologetic eyes. "I'm sorry," she said quietly. "She was very lovely."

His eyes clouded and he turned away, his hands jammed deep in his pockets. "Sit down."

She moved toward the sofa and sank into it ungracefully.

"That's where we start," he said, surveying her narrowly. "You don't even sit like a woman, you attack chairs as if you were afraid they might leap up and bite."

She clamped her teeth together. It was going to be a long session, and she could see that holding her temper was going to cause her some problems.

But somehow she managed to make it through the long afternoon, while she was told everything that she did wrong and how to correct it, right down to picking up cups and holding them gracefully in her hand.

"I can't imagine how I lived to be this old all by myself," she said sweetly when he called it a day.

"Neither can I," he agreed infuriatingly. "One more thing, think feline. Be conscious of your body as an expression of grace in movement. Walk seductively."

"Maybe you could take me down on the streets, and I could watch the experts...?"

He glowered at her. "There's a difference between seductiveness and blatant sexuality. Haven't you ever noticed models move down the runway in fashion shows?"

"I never really paid that much attention," she confessed.

"There are fashion shows telecast over the cable network," he told her. "Start watching them. It wouldn't hurt to enroll in a ballet class."

"That's where I draw the line," she told him shortly. "I don't have time to prance around with preteens in a tutu."

His eyes went down her body slowly, appraisingly. "Let's see you walk, Cinderella," he said.

She took a deep breath and tried to remember everything he'd drummed into her reeling mind. She moved with conscious grace, her body gently swaying like a windblown reed, her face held high, her steps easy, and the lines of her body straight and tall.

His dark eyes flashed and narrowed as she approached him. His gaze dropped pointedly to the thrust of her small breasts.

She flushed at the intimacy of the look, and her jaw tightened.

"Not bad," he murmured curtly. "For a rank beginner," he added, lifting his eyes to hers. "But you've got a hell of a long way to go, and not a lot of time. Margo's got the jump on you, honey."

"I know that," she muttered miserably. "And the body to go with it."

"There isn't a damned thing wrong with yours," he said, his eyes leaving her in no doubt that he meant it. "All you need to do is to learn how to use it."

She felt her toes tingle. "If you mean what I think you do, you can just forget it! I don't have any intention of trying to get Denny into my bed!"

His mouth curled up at one corner. "Don't you want him?"

"Of course I do, but not...well, not like that...I mean," she faltered, avoiding his probing stare. What did she mean? She loved Denny, of course she wanted him...she guessed. How could she know, though? He'd never tried to touch her that way in all the two years she'd known him.

"Do you know what you mean?" he asked. He moved closer, and the sheer size of him was intimidating. He smelled of spice and tobacco, and he was warm....

"Look at me. Flirt with your eyes," he murmured, watching her. "Let's see what you've learned."

She managed to meet his dark gaze. She smiled shyly and dropped her own, to raise them again and let them glance off his, and treat him to a gentle flutter of her long lashes.

"Better?" she murmured, raising her face.

His eyes were unusually dark and he didn't answer for a minute. "You've got possibilities," he said finally. "Are your lashes real?"

"Of course," she said. She blinked, surprised at the question. Then she noticed his own lashes, thick and dark, making a perfect frame for his very dark eyes. They were nearly black, and his complexion was olive, darker than she'd realized before.

His eyes caught hers and held them, and a long, searching exchange built the tension until she felt her knees tremble at the intensity of it. It was like touching a live wire, and she had to tear her eyes from his.

Her lips parted on a nervous breath. She moved away from him, away from the sudden magnetism of his big body. "I guess I'd better get home," she said in a voice that sounded oddly strange.

"I guess you had," he agreed. "By the way, I've arranged for Denny to be out of town all next week. The first time he'll see your new look will be Saturday night at the ball."

"Where is he?" she asked, suddenly miserable. She'd looked forward to Denny seeing her tomorrow and now he wouldn't be there.

"Don't look so tragic," he chided. He lit a cigarette and turned. "He's in New York, doing some leg work for me. Or so he believes. He grumbled too. Margo's still here," he added with a wicked smile.

Her heart leaped. "Putting some breathing space between them, huh, fairy godfather?" she murmured with a grin.

He turned, catching the amused light in her eyes. He stopped, just looking at her until she flushed and lowered her gaze to his broad chest. That was even worse. She could see the thick mat of hair that obviously covered his muscular body, and it had a strange effect on her.

"That was the idea, all right," he said tautly. "Not that I expect it to do much good. We'll have to wait and see how he reacts to your new image."

"I'll cross my fingers," she murmured.

"So will I. You'll need all the help you can get," he said flatly. "Let's go. I want to take you home and get back to work."

"Do you have to work all the time?" she asked involuntarily as they went out the door.

His jaw was taut, his eyes suddenly haunted. "If I want to stay sane, I do," he said curtly.

She stopped at the elevator and stared up at him. It was only because he was Denny's brother—stepbrother—that she was curious about him, she told herself.

"Because you miss her?" she asked softly, nodding toward the apartment.

He seemed to know immediately what she meant, but his face tightened dangerously. "I don't discuss Jessica," he said harshly. "Not even with family, and you're damned sure not that. Not yet."

Her face flamed at the rebuff. She hadn't expected the sheer savagery of it, and it almost brought tears to her eyes. She went into the elevator and not another word passed between them all the way back to her apartment.

The next week went by with merciful swiftness. Kenna spent it missing Denny and doing her best to avoid Regan. That wasn't possible. He spent his free time schooling her, tutoring her in the cold voice that she'd learned to hate. She resented him fiercely, and let him know it with every look, every word. The tension between them was almost visible, and she knew without words that he felt the same hostility she did. Their animosity was feeding on itself, and she found herself living for Denny's return.

Friday came finally, and Kenna breathed a sigh of relief as she gathered up her purse and coat to leave the office.

The door to Regan's office opened before she escaped, and he stood there with his jacket off, his shirt carelessly unbuttoned at the throat, his sleeves rolled up and his tie off, staring at her.

She didn't speak. She was trapped in that all-encompassing glance that took in her low-cut beige blouse with the pleated tan skirt and flashy polka-dotted scarf. Her makeup was perfect, and even with her glasses on, she was becoming enough to draw attention.

"Come here," he murmured, watching her.

She went to him involuntarily, her body swaying seductively, her eyes holding his, her steps sure and graceful. She stopped just in front of him, and watched the slow, sensuous smile that tugged at his chiseled, sensuous mouth.

"Nice," he murmured under his breath. "Very nice. I think you'll pass muster, Miss Dean. Which dress were you planning to wear tomorrow night—that sea-colored bit of witchery?"

"Yes," she agreed, her voice sounding breathless. She wondered why he was having this effect on her.

He nodded. "I'll pick you up at six-thirty. Denny's going to have a surprise and a half, isn't he?" he mused.

"He probably won't know me," she agreed, smiling.

"Just remember that you're supposed to belong to me," he reminded her curtly. "And don't fling yourself at his head at the first opportunity or you'll ruin everything."

She glared furiously. "I remember the game plan, counselor, I don't need constant reminding."

"You'll get it, nevertheless. I want this to work as much as you do," he reminded her. "The whole idea is to make Denny jealous. You'll only manage that if he thinks we're getting involved."

"Does that mean I have to look at you adoringly and bat my eyelashes in public?" she asked, her expression conveying distaste.

"That's exactly what it means," he agreed. "We'll have to put on a show in the office as well, if we're going to make him believe it."

"I will not sit on your lap to take dictation," she said shortly.

"What the hell makes you think I'd let you?" he asked, his eyes hard.

She turned around, clutching her purse in a stranglehold and made for the door just as it swung open and Denny came in, grinning.

He stopped short at the sight of Kenna, both eyebrows going up. "Well, well," he murmured, stunned.

Regan went up behind her, one arm sliding around her shoulders with seeming affection, and Kenna almost flinched at the unfamiliar touch of his warm, hard fingers.

"I wasn't expecting you until tomorrow," Regan told the younger man pleasantly. "You're taking Margo to the ball, I presume?"

"Uh-uh-uh—yes," Denny stammered, taking in the sight of his stepbrother apparently being affectionate with his secretary.

"Kenna was just going home," Regan continued. "You didn't plan to work this afternoon?"

"No," Denny managed.

"I'll see Kenna out, and then I'll fill you in on what's been happening while you were away. And you can tell me what you found out in New York." He tightened his grasp on Kenna, as if he were afraid she was going to make a grab for Denny. "I'll walk you out, love," he said.

She managed a wan smile in Denny's direction.

"Welcome home, boss," she called over her shoulder.

"Yes," he said in an odd voice. "Welcome home."

Regan purposely left the door ajar, aware of Denny's following gaze. He caught Kenna by the shoulders.

"I'll see you tomorrow at six-thirty," he told her, his deep voice sensuous, full of velvet. "Wear that sexy dress for me, baby," he added, and his eyes warned her to go along with him. He bent to her mouth and she let her eyes close, hating what was coming but powerless to move away. After all, the whole purpose of the exercise was to catch Denny's attention, to make him jealous.

Regan's mouth was hard and warm, and she barely felt its rough crush before he drew back and let her go. "I'll call you later," he told her, his eyes as cold as stone despite the deliberate warmth of his voice.

"Don't work too hard," she said, trying to infuse that same warmth in her own voice. She smiled half-heartedly and turned, walking quickly to the elevator.

Once she was inside it, she half-collapsed against the railing.

She felt strangely weak. It was seeing Denny again, she imagined, the sudden shock of seeing him when she hadn't expected to. Her fingers touched her mouth. She still felt the quick, hard pressure of Regan's lips, like a wound.

What if he were wrong? What if Denny didn't get jealous, what if he were too wrapped up in his precious Margo to care that Kenna was supposedly involving herself with Regan? She sighed. It would be just her luck to have the whole thing backfire. And if it did, she'd never forgive Regan.

Saturday night she dressed with special care, taking longer than usual with her makeup and leaving off her glasses. Who cared if she was half blind; Regan could just lead her around by the hand. That might be more convincing anyway, and he could describe Denny's expression to her.

He was on time, as usual, and she opened the door to find him in very conservative black evening clothes, with a white silk shirt emphasizing his darkness.

She squinted up at him. "Mr. Cole, I presume?" she asked.

"Can't you tell?" he asked, and she felt the impact of his eyes on her slender body. The dress left very little to the imagination.

"I don't need my glasses as long as I'm with someone," she returned, leaving him standing there while she went to find her purse and the black shawl she planned to wear with the dress. "All you have to do is steer me around open manholes."

"Your glasses look fine," he growled.

"That's tough, counselor, because I'm not wearing them tonight," she said antagonistically, whirling with skirts flying to confront him.

His face was only a pale blur, but she sensed his anger. "Let's go," he said shortly.

She followed him out the door without a word. She felt strangely vulnerable without her glasses, unprotected. But his bulk was reassuring, and she knew instinctively that she couldn't be more secure than in his company. He might not like her, but he'd take care of her.

He was quiet all the way to the hotel, and she didn't speak either. Strangely enough, her mind kept going back to the quick, hard kiss he'd crushed against her surprised lips outside the office. It wasn't the first time a man had kissed her, but it had made her feel odd. She didn't even like Regan, for heaven's sake, and she was in love with Denny, so why should that kiss have had such an impact on her? She forced herself not to think about it.

The ballroom boasted a live orchestra, and the colors of the women's gowns made a bright kaleidoscope. All Kenna saw were shapes and swirls of color, not individual faces, but it was enchanting and when she squinted she could recognize people. She found Denny and Margo immediately. They were standing by the punch bowl, smiling at each other, and she felt the color drain out of her face.

"Stop that," Regan said curtly. "You look like somebody's grandmother when you squint."

"Thank you, fairy godfather, for the coach and glass slippers," she returned, glaring in his general direction, "but now could you wave your magic wand and disappear?"

"Sorry, honey," he murmured, "there's nothing I'd like better, but circumstances dictate a different course. Act loving, you sweet little prude, and smile!"

She did, sickeningly, and clung to his hard arm as she caught a glimpse of Denny and Margo heading toward them. "My, my, how you do go on," she drawled. "And how I wish you would—go on, that is."

"Shut up, they're coming." He slid his arm around her waist. "Hello, Denny."

"Hi, big brother," came the pleasant reply. A thrill of pleasure went through Kenna at the sound of Denny's voice. "Who's this dishy thing with you?"

"As if you didn't know," Regan chuckled, hugging her close. "Kenna and I just got here."

Denny was close enough now that Kenna could see his shocked features as he studied her. "What happened to you?" he mumbled "You look...different."

"I happened to her," Regan said, his tone threatening enough to catch his brother's attention.

"Well, well," Denny muttered, "and I thought you two were likely to kill each other if I left you alone for a week."

"May I be introduced?" the dark-eyed, raven-haired woman at Denny's side asked gently.

"Oh, excuse me, of course! Margo de la Vera, this is my stepbrother, Regan Cole, and my secretary, Kenna Dean."

Regan caught the woman's hand and raised it to his lips with devastating finesse. *"Señorita, mucho gusto en conocerla,"* he said in perfect Spanish.

Taken aback, the full-lipped woman smiled widely. *"Con mucho gusto, señor. Habla usted español?"*

"Un poco," he agreed, smiling back. "Denny has good taste."

"No, *señor*, it is I who have that," Margo said softly, and her eyes openly worshipped Denny. She was unexpectedly gracious, smiling even at Kenna, her eyes gentle, friendly.

Kenna, who had seen Margo in the office several times but had never spoken to her, had expected a cold, icy veneer with a money-hungry heart under it. This woman was totally unexpected.

"I'm very pleased to meet you," Kenna managed with a wan smile. Margo was only a year or so older than she was, but possessed far more maturity and poise.

"And I, you," Margo replied, nodding. "Denny says that the office would surely fall apart without you."

"How kind of him," Kenna mumbled.

"How honest of him," Regan chuckled, drawing her closer. "She keeps our noses to the grindstone, don't you, honey?"

Denny was frowning now, puzzled. "Would you like to dance, Kenna?" he asked suddenly.

Kenna's heart leapt up and she was opening her lips to accept when Regan shook his head and his fingers bit into her waist. "Sorry," he told his stepbrother with dangerously glittering eyes. "She's booked for the night, I'm afraid."

Denny looked uncomfortable, but he quickly erased the expression from his face and caught Margo's hand. "I don't blame you, the way she looks," he told Regan. "Well, we'll go sway to the beat some more. See you later."

"Come by my place about midnight and we'll have a nightcap," Regan told them.

"We'd like that," Denny said, drawing Margo along with him.

"Oh, damn you," Kenna spat at Regan the first chance she got, as he was pushing her around the ballroom to a waltz.

"Your one chance to be in Denny's arms," he laughed mockingly, "and I cheated you out of it, is that what you're thinking? Well, honey, no man wants what's openly on offer. The harder it is to come by, the more he wants it."

Her face closed up and she dropped her gaze to his shirt-front, fixing it involuntarily on Denny and Margo as they waltzed past. Margo, in her peach-colored gown, with her dark coloring was strikingly beautiful. It wasn't hard to see why Denny was so attracted to her. Even with her new trappings, Kenna felt inferior to her.

"She's beautiful, isn't she?" she asked Regan. "And not the cold, mercenary woman you assumed."

"Appearances can be deceiving, honey," he reminded her. "I've seen innocent little things who were as cold as cash registers in bed."

"Do you have to buy your women, counselor?" she asked with an oversweet smile.

His eyes glittered down at her. "You'll pay for that one," he said quietly.

"I'm shaking in my size eight shoes," she assured him. "Isn't it lucky for me that we're in this crowd?"

"Enjoy it while you can."

"I would, if you'd let me dance with Denny," she grumbled.

"I know what I'm doing, even if you don't," he said, whirling her around. His arm suddenly drew her tight against him, and she started at the close contact with his long, powerful legs.

The involuntary little gasp was something she couldn't help. The feel of him was like a brand, and she tried to draw back.

His arm only tightened until her breasts were crushed softly against his jacket. "Will you relax?" he growled. "Denny's glaring in this direction; I'd like to give him something to think about."

"Oh!" she exclaimed, and let him fold her closer. The feel of his big, hard body at close quarters was doing strange things to her equilibrium. She felt light-headed, shaky. She must be tired, she told herself.

"That's it," he murmured over her head, "just let go, let your body rest against mine. Dancing is like making love, you have to let the man lead."

She flushed to the roots of her hair and stiffened, until the caressing movements of his hand made her give in again.

"You haven't danced much, have you?" he asked quietly. "You flinch every time your thighs brush mine, as if even this kind of intimacy is new to you."

It was, but she wouldn't admit it to her worst enemy. Her fingers clutched at his lapels, and they felt like ice, numb with nervousness. She didn't dare look up. It was bad enough that his cologne was invading her senses, that the warm maleness of him was wrapping around her and sapping her strength. She couldn't risk meeting his eyes at point-blank range. He frightened her too much.

"Don't stiffen up, darling," he whispered, and his fingers curled into hers seductively. "Let go. Let me feel you."

He was drowning her in new sensations. She knew what he was doing, he was using his expertise to seduce her so that Denny would think there was something between them. But her body was being tricked into responding to his, and her mind couldn't protect it anymore. Her thighs, when they met his, trembled wildly, and she caught her breath when his hand slid down low on her back to bring her hips completely against his.

"Oh, no, don't!" she whispered shakenly, tugging against his hand.

His head bent so that his breath was on her ear, and he nipped the lobe with his teeth. His own breath was strangely harsh, quick. "Don't you know what I'm doing?" he asked.

"Yes," she agreed in a stranger's voice. "But..."

"Don't read anything personal into it," he murmured gruffly. "We're putting on a show, that's all. You're vulnerable to this kind of intimacy because you're a virgin. It would be the same with any experienced man."

Would it? She almost voiced the question, and her own thoughts shocked her. The way she was reacting to him was dangerous, but she couldn't help it. Her senses were screaming for something she'd never experienced, wanting a closer contact than this, wanting something...more.

"Regan?" she whispered shakily.

His breath seemed to catch at the unfamiliar sound of his name on her lips. "What?"

"Please...don't hold me like this," she pleaded. Her fingers crushed the lapel of his jacket. "It frightens me."

He drew in a slow, deep breath and loosened his tight hold. "Why?" he asked.

She couldn't tell him that. She didn't know herself. But she sighed with relief when he let her move slightly away. Something had been happening to him, too, something she wasn't familiar with, a rigidity that was unmistakable.

"Isn't the music lovely?" she asked nervously.

His fingers moved caressingly on hers. "A man's body can play tricks on him," he whispered at her ear. "It doesn't necessarily take the feel of a woman against him to trigger it, either."

She flushed wildly and wondered if she could pull loose and run without attracting too much attention.

"It wasn't that," she choked.

"Wasn't it?" He drew back and looked down into her stunned eyes. "If you could see your face," he murmured with a strange smile. "Did it shock you?"

She tore her eyes from his with a tiny cry. "Don't," she whispered.

"Virgin," he murmured quietly. His fingers contracted violently around hers for an instant, and she thought she felt his cheek brush softly against her hair.

She swallowed down her nervousness and managed a shaky laugh. "Don't get any ideas about offering me up as a sacrifice, will you?"

He laughed softly beside her forehead. "Those cultures died out years ago. Have you ever seen the pyramids in Mexico and Central America?"

That brought her eyes up quickly. "And in Peru? Oh, I'd give anything to climb all over them," she said without reservation. "I wanted to go into archaeology, but I didn't have the money to pursue graduate courses...."

Something had shadowed his eyes for an instant as he stared down at her. "I'll have to show you my collection of photos one of these days," he murmured. "I took an archaeology tour a couple of years back and saw all those places."

Her face brightened with mingled pleasure and surprise. "Well, well, who'd have thought it?" she murmured. "I didn't think you old fossils liked other old fossils."

His eyebrows went straight up. "Flirting with me, Miss Dean?" he asked in an odd tone.

She'd forgotten for an instant that he was the enemy. She turned her eyes to Denny, and a pang of regret went through her as she saw him bend his blond head to listen to Margo's animated chatter. The sadness showed in her face and Regan reacted to it violently, his arm crushing her against him for an instant.

"Stop it," he growled. "Must you wear your heart on your sleeve?"

"It's not working," she muttered miserably, staring at his shirt front, at the quick rise and fall of it. "He wouldn't notice me if I danced a flamenco nude."

"Give it time, honey," he said. "You can't expect everything at once."

"So they say." She was glad when the music ended. Dancing with Regan was disturbing, and she was relieved to break contact with his hard body.

As it turned out, she didn't manage even one dance with Denny, although the hope of it kept her beaming all evening. But at eleven thirty, when Regan gestured for her to join him, she was forced to give up. Apparently, what Regan had said to him at the beginning of the ball had kept Denny from even asking her to dance. Head down, she went to the door, her evening bag clutched in her hand, and let Regan lead her out into the night.

Chapter Five

Regan seemed preoccupied with his own thoughts and hardly said a word on the way back. Kenna sat rigidly beside him, feeling odd and unfamiliar sensations and disliking them and him acutely.

Why hadn't he let her dance with Denny just once? It wouldn't have mattered so much, and she would have lived on it all her life. Her eyes closed on a wave of pain. Denny was so obviously wrapped up in his South American paramour. How did a plain little country girl go about fighting that kind of beauty and sophistication? Oh, she'd drawn his eye, thanks to Regan's coaching. But it took more than physical attraction to make a relationship work. She wanted more than that from Denny. So much more!

"Take off the glass slippers, honey," Regan said with a bite in his voice as he parked the car in the garage beneath his apartment building. "It's almost midnight."

She opened her eyes with a sigh. "Are we here?" she murmured, glancing around at the dark blurs of other cars.

"You little bat," he grumbled. "If you'd wear your glasses, you could see for yourself."

"This is much nicer," she countered, opening the door for herself before he could do it for her. "I don't have to see you, do I?" she added with a cold smile.

She caught the flash of his eyes before he slammed the car door behind her and locked it. "Don't push your luck, Kenna," he said curtly.

It was one of the few times he'd ever used her name, and the sound rippled through her like tumbling water. She tossed her head, and suddenly she missed the former length of her hair. Her hand went to it, rumpling the waves.

"I miss my hair," she murmured, following him into the elevator.

"Well, I don't," he growled, and lit another cigarette. He was setting new records tonight, he'd smoked so many. He glanced at her head. "At least it doesn't look like barbed wire now."

"Do, please, say what you think," she said with biting sarcasm, glaring up at the hazy features of his hard face. Her wide, bright eyes searched his in the silence; she could hardly make them out without squinting. But she wasn't going to squint. She looked away.

"I always do," he returned coldly. The elevator door opened and he led the way to his apartment, unlocking it with a minimum of motion and then standing aside so she could enter first.

He turned on the lights and went straight to the bar. He poured himself a whiskey, a big one, and took a long sip before he glanced her way.

"Would you like sherry or a brandy?" he asked curtly.

"I am allowed to drink hard liquor," she said, her eyes flashing. "Or do I look like a milk fanatic?"

"Whiskey would go to your head," he replied. He poured an inch of brandy into a snifter and set it on the coffee table in front of the sofa, where she was perched on the very edge of the seat. "Can you see it?" he asked with a mocking smile, "or would you like me to shove it under your nose?"

"I'd like to tell you where to shove it," she flashed back at him, feeling herself bristling, sparring with him, wanting to fight. Needing it.

"Go ahead," he invited, draining his glass. He set it roughly on the coffee table in front of her.

"You are so smug," she accused. She took a sip of the brandy, grimaced, and put it back down. Her indulgence in alcohol was limited to wine on special occasions, and, blissfully unaware of its age and excellence, she didn't appreciate the fiery taste of the brandy. "Rearranging people's lives for them, deciding whom they should marry," she continued, her face livid with anger and wounded pride and disappointment. "Who pulls your strings, Mr. Famous Attorney, the ghost you live with?"

He went rigid. Absolutely rigid, and it was as well that she couldn't see the dangerous glitter in his eyes. It probably wouldn't have stopped her, anyway.

"It's all right for you to pull my appearance to pieces and order Denny's life for him, but nobody discusses your life, do they?" she continued, rising from the sofa. "What's so secretive about your late wife that you can't even discuss her without exploding, Mr. Cole? Was she trying to get away from you when she died...oh!"

The sheer fury of his sudden movement cut her off in midsentence. She felt his hands grasping, hurting, as he slammed her down onto the sofa and pinned her there with the impact of his big, warm body.

"Damn you," he growled as he took her mouth, hurting her, grinding his lips into it until she felt his teeth cutting her lower lip. "Damn you to hell..."

She could hardly breathe for the weight of him, and she was afraid of a man for the first time in her life, physically afraid. His hands were inhumanly strong as they pinned her wrists into the cushions above her head, his chest hurt as it ground down against her soft breasts. There was a tautness to his powerful body that threatened, and his physical superiority was both evident and terrifying.

Tears were stinging her eyes as his mouth bit hers, twisting angrily, hurting and meaning to hurt, as if he were taking out his anguish on her defenseless body.

She had no idea how far he might go, and she knew that she couldn't stop him. She stiffened, closing her eyes against the fleeting glimpse of his furious scowl, the dark passion in his face. She moaned piteously against his rough mouth, breathing in its smoky warmth as she tried to get enough air to breathe.

The sound seemed to get through to him, along with the tears he could taste on her face.

He lifted his dark head, breathing roughly and much too fast, and looked into her frightened eyes. His mouth made a straight line when he saw her pale face, her swollen lips, her tear-reddened eyes.

"My wife," he breathed unsteadily, "was six months pregnant with our baby when she died. She was flying to meet me in Charleston when the plane went down."

She felt her eyes burn with new tears. She ached for him, for the hurt she read in his steady gaze, for the pain he must have suffered. It would have been bad enough to lose a woman he loved. But to lose her like that, to lose his child with her....

Her body relaxed all at once. She searched his face. "I'm sorry," she said softly, and all the anger and fear and pain went out of her with the words. "I'm so very sorry, Regan."

His face contorted. "I loved her," he breathed roughly, the words torn from him. "Three years, three long, lonely years."

His body relaxed, too, although he didn't move. He looked down at her steadily, curiously. "I hurt you," he murmured, as if he was only just realizing it.

Her tongue touched the place his teeth had damaged. "It's all right," she whispered. "I deserved that, and you know it. I never dreamed I could hurt anyone deliberately...."

His eyes dropped to the swollen lip. "We're even, then," he said quietly. "Because I've never been that rough with a woman in my life."

Her breath was still coming far too quickly, and she was becoming slowly aware of new sensations in her slender body. Her breasts were tautening, swelling, and the dress had slid away until one of them was all but bare to the sudden interest in his dark eyes.

She felt her body tremble suddenly, knowing that he could feel it, too, couldn't help but feel it. His eyes slid back up to search hers before they fell to her soft, trembling mouth.

His head bent again, wordlessly, and his mouth brushed softly against hers. His tongue drew a slow pattern over her swollen lower lip, healing, tantalizing, his breath smoky and faintly unsteady.

He stretched her, his hands tugging gently at hers to draw her body to its full length even as he covered it fully with his own. She felt his hips pressing firmly over hers, and the same thing that had happened to him while they danced was happening again.

She stiffened under him, and his lips poised just above hers.

"No, don't do that," he said softly, his voice almost unrecognizable, because it was tender. "I won't hurt you." His hands, where they held hers, became slowly caressing. His mouth brushed down over hers in a tingling parody of a kiss. "Lie still," he breathed against her lips. "Despite what you've heard about men, most of us aren't that dangerous when we're hungry."

The very calmness of his tone eased the tension out of her. She didn't understand why she wasn't fighting, or demanding to be let loose. The feel of his body was intoxicating, all warm muscle and strength. He was bigger than she'd realized, her arms would barely have reached around that broad chest. She shifted involuntarily, and he eased his hips to one side, so that only his chest was pinning her to the soft cushions.

Her eyes looked straight up into his, curious and searching. He returned the frank stare, without blinking. "You're very soft," he breathed.

Her lips parted. "You're...enormous," she managed. She studied the broad, quiet face poised over her own, fascinated by its hard lines. It was as if she'd never really looked at him.

"What are you staring at so hard?" he murmured.

"Your nose," she confessed. "It's been broken."

"Twice," he agreed, and smiled faintly. "I served in Nam, in the Marines."

She wanted to touch that formidable nose, his mouth. "Would you let go of my hands?" she asked.

He released them, to slide his own hands under her back, where the dress left it bare. Her fingers moved up to his face, hesitating.

"It's all right," he said softly. "I don't mind being touched."

Her fingers ran over his nose, where the break had been, and over his cheeks. He was clean-shaven, but there was already a trace of stubble. His chin was square and his heavy brows jutted over his deep-set eyes. There were faint lines at the corners of his eyes, and he had traces of silver tangling in the hair at his temples.

He bent, nuzzling her nose with his, so close now that her eyes could hardly see him. "Your eyes have gold flecks in them," he murmured.

"Yours don't," she whispered back, framing his face with her hands to hold it away. "They're very nearly black."

"My French ancestry," he said. His eyes narrowed. "Still afraid of me, Kenna?"

Her lips parted. "No," she said, and her own reply shocked her. But she wasn't afraid of him. Not anymore.

His finger touched her lips and his eyes fell to it. "That's interesting," he said, "because I think I'm afraid of you."

"Why?" she asked involuntarily.

"Virgins make me nervous," he murmured, with a wicked smile. "I suppose you'd faint if I eased that witchy gown down around your waist and looked at you, wouldn't you?"

She felt her cheeks catch fire. "Yes, I probably would," she admitted.

He frowned slightly. "You're damned inexperienced, do you know that?"

"Yes," she said, grimacing. "Well, the way I look... looked...who'd want to teach me anything?" she added bitterly.

"The way you look right now, who wouldn't?" he mused. He propped himself over her so that his breath was warm on her lips. "You need a little educating, Miss Dean," he breathed, "for your own sake. It takes experience to make a woman seductive."

She swallowed, once again shockingly aware of the message his body was sending out. "That depends on what kind of education you have in mind."

He smiled wickedly as his mouth brushed over her eyelids, closing them. "Nothing traumatic, little nun," he murmured. "Just some remedial lovemaking."

Before she could find an answer to that blatant observation, his mouth was on hers. She stiffened for an instant at the intimacy. It wasn't unpleasant now; he wasn't trying to hurt. His lips were patient and very gentle. She barely felt them. But as the pressure began to deepen and the pleasant brushing turned to hunger, her eyes opened and looked up. His own eyes were closed, his brows drawn together in something like pain. His lashes were thick as brushes, and dark as night where they lay on his cheek. She closed her own eyes again, strangely touched.

One arm slid under her, and she felt his fingers just at the outer edge of her breast, lightly brushing. Not intimate, but oddly arousing, causing sensations she'd never felt.

His mouth lifted for an instant. "How sore is that lip?" he asked in a deep whisper.

Her eyes lazily came open. "What?" she murmured, drunk on pleasure.

He laughed softly. "Never mind." He bent again, lifting a hand to catch her jaw and open her mouth gently. "Now leave it like this," he breathed as his own mouth opened and fitted itself to hers exactly.

She caught her breath at the new intimacy. She felt his tongue exploring her inner lip, darting into her mouth, and she gasped at the sensual feel of it. Her fingers bit into his arms and trembled.

He raised his head, scowling. "You are a little nun, aren't you?" he asked under his breath. "It's called a French kiss," he told her, searching her wide eyes. "Men like it."

Her eyes went to her own fingers, digging into his hard, muscled arms. "I...I think I like it too," she admitted, meeting his eyes again. "No one ever kissed me like that, Regan."

"I'm beginning to realize that no one ever did much of anything to you," he replied. His eyes searched hers quietly. "Have you been lonely for a long time, Cinderella?" he asked suddenly.

The question startled her, because it was so close to the truth, and tears stung her eyes.

"Don't," he said softly, and bent to brush the tears away with his mouth. "Don't. I know what loneliness is. I know how it feels."

Yes, he knew, probably better than she ever would, and she ached to take that horrible pain out of his eyes. Her fingers moved up to smooth away the hair at his temples.

He kissed her face tenderly, touching every soft inch of it. "The nights are the worst, aren't they?" he breathed. "Going to a movie and watching couples hold hands, seeing families grouped together in restaurants—oh, yes, I know what it's like."

"There's a difference," she murmured, feeling so safe with him, now, so strangely in tune with him. "Men can ask women out."

He lifted his free hand to touch her face. "And you can't?" He smiled gently at the expression on her delicate features. "It's allowed these days."

She shifted restlessly. "And men get the wrong idea, don't they? Or rather, the right idea, because most girls don't care."

"That," he sighed, "is a fact. I'm pretty old-fashioned myself, Cinders. I don't like being chased."

"Are you...chased?" she asked.

He nodded. "I'm rich, haven't you noticed?"

She shook her head and smiled. "I was too busy noticing your big feet and your broken nose...oh, no fair!" she gasped when he dug her in the ribs.

He chuckled down at her. "Salaaming at my door...I was in a rotten mood that morning, I felt like sitting on you."

She smiled back. "I'm glad you didn't, my hospitalization policy doesn't cover damage done by irate bosses."

"What a sharp little tongue." He moved down, and something new and exciting glittered in his dark eyes as they studied her mouth. "Do you know what to do with it now?" he asked.

Even as he spoke, he touched his mouth to hers, and smiled as it opened and her tongue repeated the wild little caress his had taught her.

His breath came quick and rough, and his free hand moved to her throat. "Again," he whispered against her lips. "Don't stop just when you're getting the hang of it."

She lifted her arms around his neck and gave in to him, sharing a kiss that made her toes curl with pure pleasure as her tongue met his and fenced with it. Seconds later, she felt his hand easing down to brush lightly at the soft curve of her breast. The other hand was under her arm, lightly teasing, and between the two of them, she felt her body go taut with something strained and threatening.

She caught her breath and he lifted his dark head to watch her.

I should stop you, she told herself as she drowned in those dark eyes and reveled in the tantalizing seduction of his hands as they played around the edges of her breast. But she was curious and blazing with unexpected hungers. Involuntarily her body arched and twisted to invite his hands inside the thin dress.

"Your eyes are the shade of budding leaves," he whispered, looking into them, "in a spring mist. I could get lost in them. That's it, honey, lift up for me."

"Please," she whispered, shaken.

"Not yet," he replied, his voice, his eyes, tender, his hands tormenting, until what she felt bordered on anguish. "Not until you want it more than breath."

"Do you want me...to beg?" she moaned.

"No," he whispered. "I want you to need it. I want you to need me. I want to make it the sweetest pleasure you've ever known."

She arched again, dragging at breath, staring straight into his dark eyes the whole time while her body caught fire and burned. "What are you doing to me?" she moaned helplessly.

"Taking possession," he breathed, and even as he spoke, his hand slowly moved, moving inside the bodice to cup her, to press against taut, swelling flesh.

It was so sweet that she cried out, tears swimming in her eyes, brimming, as she bit her lip at the tiny, delicious consummation and clung to him, burying her face against his shoulder.

"You see?" he whispered, cradling her small breast gently. "You can't rush it. It has to be slow to be good."

She trembled in his embrace, feeling him turn so that she was lying beside him, against him, without the enforced intimacy of his body.

Without knowing why, she began to cry. His arms swallowed her, meeting behind her back, and he held her, rocking her softly, his cheek on her dark hair.

"I'm sorry," she whispered, shaken, "I don't know what's the matter with me."

His hand smoothed her hair, gentling her. "I'm the one who should be apologizing," he murmured. "I didn't mean to hurt you, Kenna."

"I know that," she whispered into his shoulder. "I don't know why I said those horrible things to you...."

"Probably for the same reason I've been saying them to you, but this isn't the time or the place to hash it out." He sighed and stretched lazily. "Feel better?"

"That's a leading question," she replied, sitting up. She glanced down at him and blushed.

He chuckled at the expression on her face. "What a revealing color. Scarlet, isn't it?"

She made a harsh sound and scrambled over his long legs to get to her feet. She grabbed up the brandy snifter and drained it, hardly aware of the taste.

"Kenna..." he began.

She put the snifter down. "Uh, Denny and Margo should be here soon, shouldn't they?" she asked, suddenly nervous and uncertain.

He got up, too, and moved in front of her to take her gently but firmly by the shoulders. He tilted her face up to his searching eyes.

"I'll never hurt you again," he said quietly. "That's a promise.

Don't start getting self-conscious with me because I lost my head for a minute.''

"I'm self-conscious because I lost mine," she confessed, avoiding his gaze.

"That should have happened to you years ago," he said quietly. "Some very lucky man should have shown you what it was all about.''

Her eyes fell to his chest. "No one ever wanted to," she admitted miserably. She glanced up at him, aching. "Was it pity tonight?"

"My God, no!" he burst out. His hands tightened on her arms. "If you want the truth, I suppose I wanted to make amends for hurting you. But it wasn't out of pity, or misplaced compassion."

Her eyes searched his. "Were you pretending that I was her?" she asked, nodding toward the small framed photo.

He scowled darkly. "I don't play that kind of game," he replied coldly. "I loved my wife, but I didn't climb in the grave with her, and I don't need substitutes. Does that answer your question?" He released her all at once and moved away to light a cigarette.

She stared at his broad back, remembering how the warm muscles had felt against her hands. It mattered, that he hadn't pretended she was Jessica while he was kissing her. She didn't understand why, but it mattered very much.

"I'm sorry," she said helplessly. "I seem to make a habit of sticking my foot in my mouth lately."

He turned, his eyes holding hers. "Don't you know why we strike sparks off each other? Aren't you even mature enough to understand that?''

Her tongue touched the small bruise on her lower lip, and he followed the movement with his eyes. "Yes," she admitted, feeling raw. "I understand why."

He took a long drag on the cigarette, but he didn't look away. "In that case, you'll also understand if I tell you that we're going to have to tone it down and start getting along with each other. Denny's the object of the chase, not me.''

She blushed red. "I hadn't forgotten," she replied with equal coldness.

His eyes went up and down her body, lingering on her bodice, and she knew that he was remembering, as she was, the feel of skin against skin.

"It should have been Denny, shouldn't it?" he asked bitterly. He laughed mirthlessly as he lifted the cigarette to his chiseled mouth. "Well, there'll be other firsts for him." His head jerked as the sound of the doorbell suddenly exploded into the strained silence. "Just in time."

He went to open the door, leaving Kenna to stare blankly after him.

It wasn't until Denny and Margo walked in the door that Kenna realized how she must look. Denny was close enough that she could make out his expression, and there was open curiosity in it as he added her ruffled hair and swollen lips to Regan's equally ruffled hair and lipstick-smeared mouth.

"Had you forgotten you invited us?" Denny asked Regan, and there was a note in his voice that Kenna had never heard him use with the older man.

"Not at all," Regan said smoothly. "What can I get you to drink?"

"Bourbon, straight, for me," Denny said coolly. "Margo, what would you like?"

"I prefer cognac, if you have it," the other woman replied, studying Denny with eyes that suddenly went from affectionate to angry.

"Kenna?" Regan asked, barely glancing her way as he went to the bar.

"Another brandy, please," she murmured, handing him her snifter.

"Well, how did you like the ball, Kenna?" Denny asked, moving close to study her small, wounded face.

"It was very nice," she managed.

"I also enjoyed it," Margo said, moving to Denny's side to grasp his arm possessively. She hugged him close, her eyes warning Kenna off.

"What happened to your lip?" Denny asked curtly, glancing toward Regan.

"None of your damned business," Regan said in a dangerously soft tone as he handed the drinks around.

Denny's eyes narrowed as he grasped the glass in one hand. "That could change very easily," he replied.

Regan lifted his own glass in a mock toast. "*Nolo contendere,* counselor," he said.

Kenna watched Denny's face flush angrily as he recognized the legal phrase which meant *no contest.*

Denny finished his drink and Margo sipped at hers, while Regan sidetracked his stepbrother into a discussion of a case they were working on. But the tension was still there fifteen minutes later, when Denny suddenly announced that he and Margo had to leave.

Margo had said hardly two words to Kenna, her whole posture

defensive and jealous. Kenna disliked her possessive attitude, but wasn't as upset by it as she would have expected. And that was puzzling, too. She felt confused.

Kenna escaped to the powder room to get away from the emotional undercurrents, and when she came back, Denny and Margo were gone.

Regan stood quietly in the center of the living room, turning as Kenna joined him.

"You'll be delighted to hear that Denny was prepared to commit mayhem on your behalf," he said pleasantly, raising his glass in a salute.

She blinked. "Why?"

He moved close and touched her lower lip with his forefinger. "Because of that," he said. "He thinks I was manhandling you."

"With reason, I'm afraid," she reminded him. "Did you tell Denny why...?"

"And spoil his disgusting suspicions? I did not." He drained the glass and set it down on the bar. "I'd sleep with my doors locked, if I were you. Margo's sweet disposition went into eclipse."

"I noticed that," she said with a faint smile. "Denny was really worried?" she persisted, brightening.

"He was worried," he said, his tone harsh. "I'd better get you home. It's late."

"You could call a cab," she suggested, moving to pick up her shawl and purse from the sofa.

"You're not going home alone," he said firmly. "No city is that safe."

She took one look at his set features and decided not to argue. He was quite capable of carrying her down to the lobby.

He drove her home without speaking, keeping the radio on to fill the silence. Her eyes darted to his grim face, as she tried to reconcile the hostile, taciturn man she worked for with the ardent, expert lover who could have carried her unprotesting to his bed less than an hour before. She could still taste him on her lips, feel the tender brush of his fingers on her bare skin. The sensations memory aroused shocked her. She hardly recognized the passionate woman who'd begged for his hands on her untouched body. So much for her fine principles. They'd collapsed at the first temptation. All at once, she wondered how it would have been with Denny and was surprised to find that she couldn't imagine being touched that way by the man she was supposedly in love with.

They stood apart on the elevator, and he glared at the closed doors as if they stood between him and salvation. Not one word passed his lips all the way to the door of her apartment.

She was bending down to the doorknob trying to see where to put the key when he took it away from her with a disgusted sound.

"If you'd wear your damned glasses, you'd be able to see where to put the key, you blind little bat," he growled.

"I could tell you where to put the key," she returned hotly, straightening to glare up in his general direction.

"Go ahead," he invited.

She drew in a steadying breath. "Good night, counselor," she said.

"Good? Not very, Cinderella." he replied shortly. "You lost Prince Charming somewhere along the way."

"And ended up with the beast," she shot back.

He stared down at her, and she caught a glimpse of aching loneliness in his hard face before he quickly erased it. "Story of my life," he murmured half-humorously. "Good night, Cinders."

He turned and walked away, and tears burned her eyes. She started to call to him, just as the elderly little woman down the hall opened her door and came out to take her garbage to the chute. Kenna sighed and turned back into her lonely apartment.

She made herself a cup of hot cocoa and paced the living room while she drank it. What was the matter with her, for heaven's sake? Why should she feel so miserable about calling Regan a beast? He was a beast!

A beast. She sighed. Sure, a beast who'd bent over backwards to help her improve her appearance, to act slinky and seductive and sophisticated so that she could attract Denny. And tonight she'd attracted Denny, and that didn't matter nearly so much as the fact that she'd deliberately gone out of her way to hurt Regan. That crack about his late wife had been utterly horrible. No wonder he couldn't bear to talk about it.

She moved toward the phone and stared angrily down at it. He was probably asleep already, this was insane! But all the same, her fingers searched through the telephone directory for his number and dialed it.

Her hand clenched around the still warm mug of hot cocoa while the phone rang once, twice, three times....

"Hello?" came a familiar, gruff voice over the line.

She opened her mouth and tried to speak, failed, and cleared her throat. "Regan?" she murmured.

There was a pause. "Kenna?" he asked softly.

"I don't think you're a beast at all," she said with equal softness and put the receiver down.

She stared at it for a long moment before she put down the mug, turned out the lights and went to bed.

Chapter Six

Sunday promised to be an ordeal. Kenna came home from church in no particular hurry, with nothing more to look forward to than more of her own company. She wandered down the street, staring up at the tall skyscrapers, her eyes drifting to the occasional oasis of trees that graced downtown Atlanta. It was odd how the downtown area had a suburban feeling to it. She constantly ran into people she knew, like the secretaries in the offices below hers and the owner of the small grocery store on the ground floor of her apartment building and the manager of the small boutique which was also among the businesses located there. It wasn't as lonely an existence as she'd once thought it might be when she moved to Atlanta from the small town where she'd grown up.

She dragged her feet, drinking in the sweet spring air, watching buds just beginning to pop out on the tall oak and maple trees, and the smaller dogwoods. The dogwoods would be in full blossom before too long, just in time for the city festival that bore their name.

With a final wistful sigh at the sight of a couple holding hands and sitting on a stretch of concrete bench along the street, she went into her apartment building. At least she felt good today, in her new lavender and white patterned dress, with its full skirt and neatly ruffled little neckline and puffy sleeves. She felt young and womanly all at once, gorgeous, a model. She made a leap into the elevator, whirling to push the button for her floor. She leaned dreamily back against the rail. Glasses or no glasses, old girl, you have got something, she told herself. She grinned. Confidence, perhaps. Maybe that accounted for this buoyant feeling. When she got to her apartment, she'd clean out her closet and get rid of those dowdy old clothes she'd been wearing for the past two years. That ought to keep her occupied.

The elevator stopped and she danced off it, her skirts flying against her long, lovely legs as she turned toward her apartment. She stopped so suddenly that she almost fell forward, and her heart jumped into her throat.

Regan was leaning back against the wall, brooding again, his eyes staring straight ahead at her door. One hand was in the pocket of his gray slacks, the other was holding a smoking cigarette. He was wearing a blue blazer with an open-necked white shirt, and his hair was rumpled…and it suddenly occurred to Kenna that she was falling in love with him. The discovery froze her where she stood. That notion had to go, and quickly, she told her heart. No mutinies around here, not when she was about to catch Denny's eye and live happily ever after. Cinderella didn't fall in love with the fairy godfather, it wasn't allowed.

As if he sensed her uneasy scrutiny, Regan's head turned and he stared at her. He was a good three doors away from where she was standing, but he might have been beside her. Her heart ran wild.

He straightened up as she forced her legs to carry her to him, and he smiled. And all at once, the sun came out and everything burst into glorious bloom.

"Hi," he murmured, giving her the once-over.

"Hi," she replied, sounding breathless.

"I thought you might be at loose ends. I'm driving down to see my parents. I thought you might like to come with me. Denny and Margo are going to be there," he added with a careless smile.

Something froze in blossom, but she erased the coldness from her eyes and smiled. "I'd like that very much. Should I change?"

"That's up to you. Personally," he murmured, studying her closely, "I like you this way."

"I might need a sweater," she said, unlocking her door. "I won't be a minute. Want to come in?"

He shook his head, disappointing her. "I'll wait out here. I don't expect it's going to take that long, is it?"

"No, of course not," she said quickly, and rushed in to get her sweater. Apparently he didn't want to be alone with her for any length of time unless they were in a car, and that suited her fine. Why should she want to risk a repeat of last night, after all? And Denny was the quarry, not Regan. She repeated that to herself as she tugged a white sweater from her closet, ran a comb through her hair, and hurried back to him.

"Does Denny know we're coming?" she asked Regan when they were inside the Porsche and speeding north toward Gainesville, where his father and stepmother lived.

He laughed softly. "Yes, he knows we're coming," he murmured, glancing toward her. "So does Margo, worse luck. I hope you're up to it, darling; you'll need your wits around that lady."

Darling! Why did the sound of that casual endearment on his lips make her heart run double-time? She shifted restlessly in the seat.

"What would you have done if I hadn't been home?" she asked.

"Checked the hospitals," he murmured, tongue-in-cheek.

"Thanks so much, you do wonders for my self-esteem," she grumbled, and her lips pouted.

He cocked an eyebrow. "Broke the truce, did I? All right, I'll reform. You look lovely, Miss Dean, and if you weren't hot and bothered by my stepbrother, I think I'd park this car and kiss you until you couldn't think straight."

She found it extremely hard to breathe after that rash admission. In her lap, she had a stranglehold on her purse. "Would you?" she asked in a high-pitched tone.

"Yes," he said shortly, "I would. And you'd let me."

Her eyes darted out the window to escape his. She didn't say anything because she couldn't.

"Why did you call me last night?" he asked harshly.

"Because I felt ashamed of myself," she ground out. "I always seem to say the wrong thing to you, at the wrong time. You've gone out of your way to help me, and I've done nothing but fight you."

He crushed out the cigarette he'd been smoking. "I've made you fight me," he said after a minute. "I put your back up the day I walked into the office, and I've done my damnedest to keep it that way."

The confession startled her. She half turned in her seat and stared at him across the console. "Why?"

He met her gaze levelly as he stopped at an intersection. "You know why," he said coldly.

Her face flamed as he said the words, and she couldn't have looked away from him to save her life. It was the most curious sensation, like being shocked. A jolt of electricity seemed to have surged from his vibrant body to hers.

"Kenna," he growled. They were on a county road, with no traffic anywhere around them. All at once he reached out, catching her by the back of the head, and pulled her mouth under his. "Come here, damn it," he muttered. The kiss was a wild sharing of mouths and tongues that blazed up like a forest fire in the sudden stillness.

His hand released the steering wheel to catch her under the arms and lift her as close as he could get her, despite the bucket seats and the confined space. Her breasts were crushed against his blue blazer, and his mouth hurt, a sweet, aching hurt that she wanted more than air.

He drew away a minute later, his breath shuddering against her lips. His eyes were glazed with desire, as she knew her own must be, because she wanted him suddenly, shockingly.

His nostrils flared as he searched her face, blind to the pickup truck crossing the intersection to the right of them, its occupants openly curious.

"I want you," he said curtly, putting it into words.

"I know," she whispered, her voice breathless and soft.

His hands contracted around her for an instant before he eased her back into her seat and took a deep breath, gripping the steering wheel hard. He lifted his head, glancing behind them at an approaching car.

He took another breath and put the car in gear, easing across the intersection and then speeding up again, changing gears with smooth ease. He pulled a cigarette from his pocket and handed it to her.

"How about lighting that for me?" he asked quietly.

"May I...have one, too?"

He handed her another one, with a curious glance. "Do you smoke?"

"No," she confessed. "I just need something."

"Am I that potent?" he murmured with a forced laugh.

"Don't joke about it, please," she murmured as she lit his cigarette and handed it to him, turning back to light her own.

"I have to," he said. "Physical attraction is a damned poor basis for a relationship. I don't want involvement. I've had all I can stand of it for one lifetime."

She sat back against the seat, tempted to deny what she was feeling. But she couldn't. Having it out in the open was the best way to cope with it, after all.

"And you're not the type for an affair," he added curtly, his eyes pinning hers for an instant. "There's no way I'm going to take a virgin into my bed just to satisfy a temporary hunger."

She dropped her eyes to the heavy rise and fall of his chest. Where the shirt was open, thick black hair showed, and she remembered desperately wanting to open his shirt and touch him there the night before. She hadn't, though, and probably it was just as well. Her eyes turned away from his sensuous masculinity.

"Thank you for that," she said quietly. She took a careful draw from the cigarette and blew out a cloud of smoke without inhaling. "I feel very vulnerable with you. I didn't expect it to be like that...."

"Neither did I," he said. He turned onto another country road and they passed through miles of open country with only an occasional house or service station or country store. He laughed shortly. "You were a new experience for me. I can't remember a woman ever crying when I made love to her."

She stared out at the passing landscape, the cigarette hanging forgotten between her fingers. "You're very experienced," she murmured.

"And you're very inexperienced. My God, it was sweet," he said half under his breath, glancing toward her. "Something I'll remember all my life."

Her eyes lifted to his and moved quickly away. "So will I," she confessed.

He drew in a slow breath and stared straight ahead at the road. "I'm so damned noble," he muttered. "All I need is a white horse and a halo."

She managed a smile. "Or a unicorn," she suggested.

"They were rumored to be fond of virgins, weren't they?" he asked, smiling back. "Why aren't you one of those modern women who take the pill and notch their bedposts? It would make my life so much easier right now."

Mine, too, she thought, but she wouldn't admit it. He didn't want an answer anyway, so she said nothing.

"Come on, talk," he said after a minute, his cigarette sending up curls of smoke. "Are you afraid of sex?"

She curled up in her seat as far as the shoulder harness would allow and shrugged. "I don't know. I don't think so. I just don't like temporary things. I want a home and children..." She glanced at him apprehensively.

"Don't pull your punches," he said quietly, meeting her apologetic gaze. "I did my grieving when it happened. It still hurts, but not as much, and I'm not that sensitive about chance remarks. Except," he added with a rueful smile, "deliberately cutting ones. As you found out."

"I understand now why it hurts to talk about her," she said gently. "I won't ever ask again."

He crushed out the cigarette and laid his hand on the console, palm up. "Give me your hand."

Without thinking, she laid her free one in that warm, callused grasp, and felt his fingers close snugly around hers. Tingles of pleasure worked their way through her body, and involuntarily, she increased the pressure.

"I'll tell you all about Jessica one day," he said quietly. "We'll get together one New Year's Eve and share a bottle of Irish whiskey and cry on each other's shoulders.''

"I can just picture that," she murmured drily. "You, crying on anybody's shoulder."

"Being a man doesn't make me superhuman, honey," he reminded her. "I did my share of crying after the crash. I'm not ashamed of it, either."

"I didn't think you would be. It takes a strong man to cry," she said. Her fingers tangled in his.

"We can't be lovers," he said quietly.

"No," she agreed in a whisper.

His fingers contracted. "Then be my friend, Kenna."

She smiled, feeling a sudden urge to burst into tears, because she wanted more than that lukewarm arrangement. But if it was all that was available, it would have to do. After all, she wanted Denny...didn't she?

"How about your sister-in-law?" she teased.

His face hardened, darkened. He let her hand go.

"That reminds me, we'd better come up with some plans for next weekend."

"Why?"

"Because Margo's going to be in Argentina for the next two weeks, and Dad's having an anniversary party for my stepmother. You're sure to be invited, and I don't want Denny having it too easy." He glanced at her with a cool smile. "He likes competing with me, you see. Anything I want, he wants."

"Is that why he took up law?" she asked.

He nodded. "He's very competitive. I've got a long jump on him. That rankles. Especially now, when Dad's thinking of retiring from the computer corporation he owns."

She studied his broad face. "He'll expect one of you to take it over, won't he?" she asked, suddenly understanding.

He nodded and turned onto the highway that led to his parents' home.

"Would you like that?" she asked.

He frowned thoughtfully. "I don't know. I like what I do. I'm not sure I could make the transition from attorney to businessman, Or that I'd want to."

"But Denny would." She was sounding him out.

He glanced at her. "Yes, he would."

"Then, where's the problem?"

"My father is the problem. He doesn't think Denny's mature enough to assume that much responsibility.

"Denny's very capable at law," she remarked.

His eyes darkened. "Yes," he agreed curtly. "But corporate administration is a far cry from running a one-man law office."

He was right, much as she hated admitting it. It was hard enough for Denny to say no to potential clients. And, unlike Regan, he didn't practice criminal law, confining himself instead to divorces and property settlements and business law. He didn't have the killer instinct. But Regan did. He could hire and fire and assume responsibility for his mistakes, if there were any, without looking for scapegoats. He was strong enough to take criticism, and that was what the job called for. She could see very well why Mr. Cole would want his eldest to take over his corporation when he stepped down.

"What are you thinking about?" he asked finally.

"How you'd look in a tutu with a magic wand," she murmured wickedly.

He glared at her. "Wait until I stop this car, and then say that again."

"Do I look stupid?" She sighed, unable to take her eyes from him. "For a fairly ugly man, you're not bad."

He burst out laughing. "Does that mean you're ready to take back your apology for calling me a beast?"

"No," she told him. "If you remember, that particular beast changed into a handsome prince."

"He didn't have a nose that was broken in two places and big feet," he reminded her.

"Stop making fun of my friend," she chided gently.

He smiled at that, and reached out to ruffle her hair as he pulled the car into the long, paved driveway that led up to the two-story brick home where his parents lived on Lake Lanier.

Kenna had been there many times for business meetings and had always loved the house. It was gray brick, built on the order of an English Tudor home, but with unique variations, like the Victorian turret at one end, and the stained-glass skylight above the front door. All around it were trimmed boxwood, azaleas, camellias, and dogwood trees, along with a glorious profusion of blooming bulbs. A white latticework gazebo stood in the middle of the rose garden.

"I don't think I'll ever see another place on earth as beautiful as this," she remarked.

"It was my grandfather's home," he said. "He had it built to his own specifications. The gardens were my mother's idea," he added. "And Dad's kept them just as they were when I was a boy."

"How old were you when you lost your mother?" she asked.

"Eight," he said. He smiled. "I gave my stepmother hell for two years. After that, she began to grow on me."

"I know exactly what you mean," she murmured. Over the years Kenna had become very fond of Abbie Cole.

He parked the car in the big garage behind the house, and opened her door for her. When she was outside, he pulled her against him and walked her toward the house with his big arm around her shoulders.

"For appearances," he reminded her with a grin. "You're not supposed to enjoy it."

Her own arm snaked around his waist. "Heaven forbid that I should enjoy it," she said demurely, flirting with her eyes.

"Watch yourself," he muttered, pinching her arm and making her jump. "I've always wondered how it would feel to make love to a woman on the floor of the gazebo...."

"I'll behave," she promised him, "with utmost decorum. I won't even try to rip open your shirt."

"You'd better not," he warned as they started toward the back door, which was just opening. "My chest is an erogenous zone. And I know just where yours is, too, baby," he added outrageously.

Before she had time to gasp, blush, or snap at him, his tall, gray-headed father was striding toward them, wearing a dark gray business suit and carrying a briefcase. Behind him was his small, very pretty wife, her platinum hair curling softly around her delicate face. She was smiling as usual.

"Hello and goodbye," Angus Cole said, shaking his son's hand and grinning at Kenna. "I'm off to Seattle for a conference. Don't eat up all my cheese crackers and keep your hands off my Napoleon brandy," he added with a scowl in Regan's direction. "Watch him, Abbie," he called to his wife.

"Yes, darling," the older woman promised. "I'll only let him drink your thirty-year-old Scotch, is that all right?"

Angus muttered something as he climbed into his black Mercedes and roared off, tooting the horn abrasively.

"Hello, dear," Mrs. Cole laughed, hugging Regan. "Hi, Kenna, welcome back, where have you been for the past two months, and what in the world have you done to yourself, you're gorgeous!" she said all in one breath.

"I've been busy," Kenna managed, as she hugged the shorter woman back. "How are you? You look gorgeous yourself."

"In jeans and a sweatshirt?" she laughed, indicating her clothes. "I've been digging in the rose garden."

"I told you about that buried treasure," Regan said drily. "The pirates buried it on the coast, not here."

"Spoilsport," his stepmother grumbled darkly. "Anyway, I'm digging up worms, not gold. A good worm is the best fertilizer God ever made. I'm transplanting them from your father's fish-bait bed into my petunias."

"God help you if he catches you," Regan replied.

"Tell him," Mrs. Cole challenged, "and I'll tell him what really happened to the Mercedes the night you took that Olson girl to the senior prom."

He sighed. "I'll keep your dark secret if you'll keep mine, Abbie," he promised.

"Fair enough. Denny and Margo are down by the lake feeding the swans," she said. "Want to come in and have coffee?"

Regan shook his head. "We'll bring them back with us and have it then."

Abbie Cole was watching the two of them with sharp, interested eyes. She smiled. "Is there something in the air?"

"Spring," Regan told her.

"Is that so? Well, mind the dog, he's loose out there somewhere," she added, waving them off.

"Pooch?" Kenna asked, scanning the landscape for the familiar toy collie.

"Pooch. And he'll be one long furry clump of mud and leaves, as usual." He glanced at her. "I'll shave his fur if he gets one speck of mud on that dress. It suits you."

She beamed. "Thank you, fairy godfather," she murmured.

"Stop that. Uh-oh, watch out!"

The warning almost came too late. Pooch came flying up from the vicinity of the lake, his fur as sleek as a seal's from swimming and as muddy as a rain-swollen river. He headed straight for Kenna, who always played with him despite his antisocial tendencies.

She was looking for a tree to climb when Regan swooped and lifted her like a child in his big arms. "Down, Pooch," he said in his courtroom voice, and the dog immediately sat down and whined at him, looking so impish he might have been a furry human.

"You do that very well," Kenna remarked, reveling in the pleasure of being held so close to him, in the sheer male strength of the big body supporting hers.

"I practice on hostile witnesses," he informed her. His eyes searched hers.

"You're so strong," she murmured, letting her hands rest around his shoulders. Her voice sounded girlish, and she flushed at the inane remark.

"Sorry," she added demurely, "I didn't mean to sound star-struck. Of course you're strong, you're as big as a tree."

"Not quite." He swung her around, laughing at the way she clung to him, her face flushed and radiant, her eyes laughing back.

He buried his face in her soft hair and deliberately crushed her close. "You smell delicious, woman," he growled in her ear. "I'd like to take several bites of you."

"You'd poison yourself," she assured him.

"That's not likely, or I'd have died last night." He lifted his head and looked into her wide, misty eyes. "Why did you cry while I was loving you?" he whispered.

Shudders of wild pleasure rippled through her at his wording, and her lips parted on a trembling breath. "Because it was so beautiful," she managed unsteadily.

His eyes dropped to her parted lips. "We'd burn each other alive if we made love completely," he said, and his deep voice sounded as unsteady as her own. There was a tremor in the arms that held her. He moved, brushing her lips with his own, creating a shiver of sensation that made her gasp. "All I have to do is touch you," he said, repeating the motion again and again, until her mouth followed his, pleading for more. "All I have to do is touch you, and I start aching like a boy of fifteen. I want you, Kenna, I want to lay you down in the grass and open that dress and bare your body to the sun and my eyes and my mouth...!"

Even as he spoke he was pressing her lips apart with his, so that she could feel every warm, smoky curve of his mouth meeting hers exactly. He opened her mouth with a whispering pressure, his tongue teasing, his lips brushing, cherishing in a perfect orgy of foreplay that made her moan and clutch at his broad shoulders.

"Kiss me," she ground out, aching for it, for completion, perfection. "Kiss me, kiss me hard, and don't stop, don't ever stop!" she moaned against his seeking mouth.

She trembled at the sudden rough crush of it, grinding her mouth into his, loving the intimacy of it, the feel of his tongue, the taste.

He groaned something she couldn't hear, and his big arm tightened, dragging her breasts against the fabric that separated them from his hard chest.

Only Pooch's sudden fierce bark kept the kiss from going much further than its wild beginning. Regan drew back from her mouth with eyes blacker than midnight, his body trembling as he held her.

He dragged his eyes away from the sight of her hungry, soft eyes and looked over her body at Denny and Margo.

"We've got company," he said tautly. He set her back on her feet, and drew in a long, shuddering breath. "We've got to stop this," he reminded her.

She searched his face with quick, possessive eyes and wondered at her wild reaction to him. "Yes," she agreed.

He wasn't even trying to look away. "You trembled," he breathed.

"So did you."

He dragged a hand through his hair and glowered down at her. "I am not taking you to bed," he ground out.

"Wait until you're asked," she flashed back, her eyes sparkling, her face radiant, so that she held his appreciative gaze against his will.

"The point behind teaching you to be seductive was not to teach you how to seduce me," he said shortly. "I am not going to get sexually involved with a virgin."

"So you keep saying," she returned. "Then why don't you stop kissing me and saying outrageously suggestive things to me?"

"Why don't you stop begging to be kissed?" he fired at her.

"Can I help it if God gave you unbelievable talents in lovemaking to compensate for your lack of looks?" she asked.

He scowled. "Kenna..."

"All right, all right," she sighed. "If that's how you appreciate my quite understandable weakness, then just don't expect me to take my dress off for you, so there."

He was fighting a chuckle. He lost. "Damn you, stop flirting with me."

"Me, flirting?" she asked, her eyebrows going straight up in mock innocence. "I wouldn't dream of it. You men are all alike, flaunting your gorgeous bodies at us poor women and then getting all insulted when we try to show our appreciation of them."

He burst out laughing. "I've created a monster," he observed, glancing toward Margo and Denny, who were coming along the path toward them. "Whatever happened to that blushing little virgin who used to hide in the records room to avoid me?"

"You'll have to ask my fairy godfather," she told him. "I haven't the foggiest idea where the poor frumpy thing went."

"I called you that, didn't I?" he murmured, watching her with quiet, dark eyes. "I think I even meant it, at the time." He sighed. "What a transformation."

"I'm glad you appreciate your own handiwork. I hope Denny

does," she added, just to spite him, and turned a beaming smile toward his stepbrother.

Margo was glaring at her, but she pretended not to notice. "Hi, Denny, Regan brought me down for the day."

"How nice," Denny said, and he seemed to mean it. He stepped forward, and bent to brush his mouth over Kenna's cheek. She felt a pleasant tingle, but nothing like the electric charge she felt in Regan's presence. Two years of patient waiting had been rewarded, but too late. Now Denny seemed strangely unthreatening. Pleasant, fun to be around, very nice. But not stormy and physically dangerous like Regan. She stared at the shorter man and all at once knew why she felt that way.

Regan was handing her Denny on a silver platter. And quite suddenly she knew that she didn't want Denny, because she was hopelessly in love with Regan. Regan, who didn't want involvement, who was going to be her friend from now on, because he only desired her. But he didn't seduce virgins and he was through with love. The irony of it almost made her cry.

"We are glad that you were free to join us," Margo said with cold courtesy, clinging to Denny's arm with the tenacity of flypaper.

"We thought we'd sprawl under the trees and watch the lake for a while," Regan said, moving close to Kenna. He caught her hand in his and smiled down at her with every part of his face except his eyes. "I'd planned to spend some time with Dad, but we passed him on his way out, and Abbie's hunting worms with a spade. On the Sabbath too."

Margo looked puzzled, but Denny laughed and squeezed her hand. She was wearing a red silk blouse with white slacks and shoes, and against her dark coloring, the combination was devastating. Even in her new finery, Kenna felt dowdy by comparison and envied Margo her perfect sight. Glasses were the pits.

She pushed the frames up over her hair with a flourish. "I love your blouse," she told Margo. "I wish I could wear red, but I look washed out in it."

Margo started, as if the compliment were unexpected. "Oh," she murmured. "Thank you."

"We could go and sit with you, but Margo has to catch a plane at eight," Denny said apologetically, and his eyes kept going back to Kenna and her wispy, sexy dress. "I have to drive her to the airport."

"Going home for a visit?" Regan asked politely.

Margo smiled. "A necessary one," she agreed. "Some European breeders are coming to see our bloodstock. Papa insists that I help him decide which of the Thoroughbreds to sell. It will be a difficult choice," she sighed. "I love them every one."

"Thoroughbreds?" Regan murmured, glancing toward Denny with a frown.

"Margo's family breeds champion racing horses," the younger man replied. "Among their other interests. They also own several hundred thousand acres of land, herds of cattle, international real estate..."

"Please, you embarrass me," Margo said quickly, touching Denny's arm. "It is not proper to speak of such things. It is like, how you say, blowing one's pipe?"

"Horn," Denny corrected. He threw an arm around Margo. "Care to have coffee with us before we leave?" he asked his stepbrother. "The lake will still be there later."

"I think we would," Regan replied. "Honey?" he added, glancing down at Kenna.

"I'm pretty thirsty," she confided.

He nodded, tugging at her hand. "Then let's sit down and rescue the worms from Abbie."

Kenna walked quietly at his side, puzzling over Margo's confession. So the foreign woman wasn't a mercenary poverty case. She wondered how that tidbit of information was going to affect Regan's point of view. Not that it mattered to her anymore. She was in enough mental turmoil as it was.

They spent an hour inside, drinking coffee and talking. Regan was obviously impressed by Margo's intelligence, and the South American woman warmed to his interest. She even managed a kind word for Kenna, although she kept darting concerned glances in Denny's direction. The younger man's fascination with Kenna was becoming more obvious by the minute. Great, Kenna thought miserably, staring down into her coffee. She'd spent two years mooning over Denny, and *now* he was interested, when it was too late, when her heart had been taken over by a man she had thought she hated, and there was no hope of her ever getting it back whole.

"I like your new look, Kenna," Denny told her while Margo was saying her good-byes to Abbie in the kitchen. "So different..."

She avoided his eyes and tried not to look at Regan, because she didn't want to see the contempt in his face. "I had help," she murmured with a smile.

"Yes, I know," Denny said curtly, glancing toward Regan, who was idly thumbing through a book over by the bookcase. "Are you getting involved with him?" he asked, moving closer and lowering his voice.

Kenna looked startled. "What do you mean?"

"I mean," he said shortly, glancing apprehensively at Regan, "there's no future in it."

"Isn't there?" Kenna asked. "Why?"

"Because he was married once," he said flatly, meeting her level gaze. "She died, and he's never gotten over it. I should have told you that before..."

"Regan told me," she interrupted. "Everything."

He blinked. "He doesn't talk about it to anyone, he never has," he said on a frown.

"I'm not just anyone, Denny," she said with a smug grin.

He sighed angrily and rammed his hands in his pockets. "How about having lunch with me tomorrow? I need to talk to you."

"All right, boss," she agreed.

"Don't call me that," he said uncomfortably. He glanced past her and saw Margo and Abbie coming out of the kitchen. "We'll talk later. Watch yourself."

"Oh, I let other people do that," Kenna said demurely, avoiding his gaze. She smiled at Margo. "I hope you have a good trip," she said.

Margo glanced uncomfortably from Kenna to Denny and frowned. "I'm sure I shall," she said. "However, it will only be for a week."

"I thought you said two weeks," Denny remarked.

Margo smiled sweetly. "Perhaps you didn't listen, darling," she said, her dark eyes flashing.

Denny scowled. "Perhaps you didn't tell me you'd changed your mind...darling," he returned.

"I think we should go," Margo said curtly. "Thank you for your hospitality, Mrs. Cole. I hope to spend more time with you when I return. Regan, Miss Dean," she added, nodding at each in turn. She glanced toward Denny and swept out the door.

"See you tomorrow," Denny told Kenna and Regan. "Bye, Mom," he added, pausing to hug his mother. "See you. Thanks for the coffee."

"Any time, son," Abbie murmured absently, watching him hurry out the door with a frown. "Now, what's going on?" she grumbled, glaring toward Regan.

He arched both eyebrows innocently. "How should I know?"

"You know everything," Abbie returned. "Especially where Denny's concerned. Spill it, Regan, what's going on? Is it something to do with you and Kenna? Is he jealous? Is he going to marry Miss de la Vera?"

"No, I don't know, yes, probably, your guess is as good as mine,"

Regan rattled off, catching Kenna's arm. "That answers your barrage of questions, Abbie, and you can spend the rest of the afternoon fitting it all together. Kenna and I have to go. Thanks for the coffee. *Ciao.*"

Kenna barely had time to call good-bye and add her thanks to his before he dragged her out the door and shoved her into the car.

"Do you mind?" she gasped, rubbing her arm.

"Sorry, honey, but if we'd stayed a minute longer, the Spanish Inquisition would have been in session," he grinned, starting the Porsche. "You know Abbie by now, don't you? She smells a scoop."

"That's right, she met your father when she was working as a newspaperwoman, didn't she?" She grinned. "I'd forgotten."

"She never does. And she could pry information out of a clam with a plastic dipstick." He pulled out of the driveway, tooting his horn just as his father had, in the old family tradition. "What was Denny whispering in your ear?"

"He's taking me to lunch tomorrow to warn me off you," she said with a wicked grin. "He's afraid you're going to corrupt me and lead me into a life of sin."

"I'd love to," he said, with a wistful glance in her direction. "Your place or mine?"

"You just got through saying that you don't seduce virgins," she said.

"Damn," he grumbled. "I forgot."

"I'll keep reminding you, so that you don't have lapses," she promised.

He laughed softly as he lit a cigarette and smoked it quietly. "Where do you want to go?"

"I like riding around," she confessed, settling comfortably in her seat.

"So do I. We'll ride, then." He turned on the radio. "Classical, soft rock, hard rock, easy listening?" he asked.

"Soft rock," she said immediately.

He pushed one of the preset buttons and laughed at her expression. "I'm only thirty-five," he reminded her.

She blinked. She hadn't really thought of him in terms of age until now, but come to think of it, he didn't look old. Mature, yes, masculine, yes, but not old.

"Ten years older than me," she murmured.

"And Denny," he added, smiling. "Though he gets mistaken for twenty-two."

"Why did you want to be a lawyer?" she asked, curious.

"I don't know," he said honestly. "I suppose it had something to do with a library full of Perry Mason novels. I like details, I like finding hidden things." He shrugged his broad shoulders. "I like the challenge, I suppose."

"Why criminal law?" she persisted.

"Because it's the most challenging field," he said immediately. "Life and death."

"Yes, it's that," she agreed, recalling cases she'd typed for him, transcripts she'd copied, all the bits and pieces of information that filled a plea, and that might save a man's life or keep him out of prison.

He glanced at her. "Why did you want to be a legal secretary?"

"I needed a job, and I was tired of working for a bank," she replied with a smile. "Numbers aren't really my forte. But I liked law, and Denny had a one-girl office where I'd mostly be my own boss."

"And then he took in a partner..." he murmured drily.

"You were horrible to me!" she said, glaring toward him. "Absolutely horrible. I don't know how I managed to get through those months without writing out my resignation on your desk top in red lipstick."

"I hoped you would," he said quietly. "You bothered me. Frumpy outfits and all, you really got to me."

"Denny said the secretary you had in New York was a real dish," she murmured, glancing sideways.

"She was. And if she'd stood in the middle of the floor naked, I'd have walked past her on my way to court without blinking an eye." He crushed out the cigarette. "I've been more involved with work than women since Jessica died."

None of it was making sense, and she stared at him pointedly, trying to make the pieces fit.

"You have a delicious young body," he said matter-of-factly. "And I didn't need a program to tell that it hadn't been out on loan to anyone who asked." He sighed deeply as they wound down a picturesque country road, his eyes dark and curious as they swept toward her and away again. "I was curious about you, about why you deliberately downplayed your looks."

"You were just plain hostile," she corrected. "I felt the same way about you, and I wasn't curious about your looks, either."

He chuckled softly. "What looks?"

"There was an actor when I was a kid, who played in a Western TV series," she told him. "He was uglier than sin, but he had a way with women that made him the hottest property going." She smiled in his direction. "Of course, he didn't have big feet."

"My curse," he admitted. "I was always falling over them when I was a boy."

"Now other people fall over them," she murmured, and reminded him about the client who tripped over Regan's large feet and fell headfirst into a potted palm.

He laughed with her. "I thought the leaves suited him, at the time." The smile faded as the music began to change to a slow, sensuous tune that set a new mood. He glanced at her. "Denny's interested."

"Yes, I know," she said.

"Margo knows too. She doesn't like it."

"And you thought she was mercenary," she murmured.

"Nobody's perfect. An heiress, no less. A very possessive heiress, and unless I miss my guess, she's going to try to add my stepbrother to her acquisitions."

"Would you really mind, knowing what you do about her?" she asked curiously.

He didn't answer that. His fingers went to his pocket, produced another cigarette and lit it. "Don't jump at anything Denny offers, will you?" he asked quietly. "You'll throw the game if you give in too soon."

"God forbid," she said. She leaned back in the seat and glanced at his set features. "How soon is too soon?"

"Let him sweat for a week," he suggested.

"Margo will be back in a week."

He took a long draw from the cigarette. "So she will." He turned up the radio. "Do what you please, Kenna. I've set the scene. The rest is up to you." His jaw was set and he looked grim. "You could do worse than Denny, if he's what you really want."

Her eyes narrowed as they studied his profile and she felt a cold, dull emptiness inside. He'd already said that he had nothing to offer her except an affair. And she wasn't stupid enough to think she could survive one with him. She wouldn't be able to let go. Never having was better than letting go, she supposed. It looked as if it would have to be.

He'd admitted being interested in her physically, but why had that made him so hostile? And what had he meant about being more involved with work than women—that he didn't have affairs? And was that why he was antagonistic toward Kenna? Her mind felt as if it were on a merry-go-round trying to find answers.

She turned her face toward the window, feeling lost. She'd felt so close to him. She'd learned things about him, she'd begun to like him, genuinely like him. Now it was all over, and he'd done his improvement bit, and he was going on to bigger and better things. And Kenna was to go after Denny and take him away from Margo and live happily ever after. The end. Except that this wasn't the right fairy tale, either.

She closed her eyes and let herself drift with the music. The laughing camaraderie they'd shared earlier seemed to have died completely, leaving a grudging truce in its place. The taciturn man at her side looked like a man who'd never smiled in his life. And what frightened her was that he might be setting a pattern for the future. At least be my friend, she pleaded silently. Be my friend, Regan, don't walk out of my life. Before they reached the city, tears were threatening behind her closed eyelids.

Chapter Seven

The office felt different when Kenna walked in the next morning. She was wearing the tailored navy suit Regan had bought for her with a white V-necked blouse and a navy and white scarf to set it off. She looked jaunty and young and on top of the world, despite her sleepless night.

Denny was pacing the floor when she walked in. He turned and stared at her, running his eyes up and down her slender body.

"I just can't get over the change," he remarked as she walked slowly, gracefully, to hang up her coat, using all the tricks Regan had gone to such pains to teach her.

She smiled at him. "You'll get used to it," she assured him. Her eyes went to the closed door of Regan's office, and her heart jumped at the thought of seeing him this morning.

"He's gone," Denny said flatly, watching her curious gaze.

"Gone?" she echoed. Her eyes widened, and she felt cold all of a sudden.

"To New York for the week," he informed her with a smile. "One of those spur of the moment decisions he makes. No warning, no nothing, I found a note on my desk."

She searched his eyes. "Did he leave one for me?" she asked.

He shook his head. "Nope, I figured he'd already told you. How odd that he didn't."

She avoided his suspicious appraisal and sat down at her desk. "Did Margo get off all right?"

"Margo?" He grimaced. "Yes," he said darkly, "she took off in a cloud of smoke."

She lifted her eyes, surprised at the venom in his tone. Denny was never sarcastic. "That sounds strange."

He looked down at her broodingly, his arms folded over his chest, his blond hair gleaming in the sunlight that streamed through the open curtains. "We had a knock-down, drag-out fight, if you want to know," he told her. "Over you."

Her eyes widened. "Me?"

"She thought I was paying you too much attention." He smiled at her, a new kind of smile, teasing and flirtatious and interested. "And I suppose she was right."

Her eyebrows arched. She lifted her eyes to his and lowered them quickly. "I'm flattered," she replied. That was all she was, unfortunately, not thrilled half to death as she would have been a month, even a week, ago.

"I'd never have known you were the same woman," he continued. "Everything about you has changed all of a sudden. Regan's influence?"

She smiled. "He has a way with him," she murmured demurely.

His face clouded. "Yes, I know. And a way with women, period," he added coldly. "I could never keep track of them until he married Jessica. He draws them like honey."

That hurt. She wondered if he meant it to, or realized how successful the remark was. Now she'd spend the whole week thinking about Regan with other women in New York, and she'd never sleep a wink tonight.

"He's rich," she remarked.

"Yes, he's that," he agreed. "And macho. Regan's always had everything he wanted."

She read the hurt in that cold statement, and she felt a surge of compassion for him. "Growing up in his shadow wasn't easy, was it?" she asked.

He laughed shortly. "That's an understatement. No matter what I ever did, Regan did it better. His grades were higher, his athletic prowess put me in the shade, he could make Dad sit up and take notice if he made a suggestion about the corporation...." He shrugged. "I'm jealous of him, you know. Men like Regan make up their own rules as they go along. He's one of a kind."

She agreed with that in her heart. He was one of a kind, and she didn't think she'd ever stop wanting him. But Regan had nothing to offer her.

She glanced up at him. "Does that lunch invitation still stand?"

"Of course." He grinned. "I'll take you to Tonie's for spaghetti."

"I love spaghetti," she sighed.

"I know, that's why I suggested it. I hate to mention mundane subjects, but how about getting the mail and let's answer it? I've got a case at ten."

"Sure thing, counselor," she murmured sweetly, and got up to go get it. His eyes followed her all the way out the door.

The morning went by quickly, especially with Denny and Regan both out and the phones ringing constantly. Kenna finally got a minute to put Regan's mail on his desk, and she found herself standing by it for a long time, just staring at the huge swivel chair that barely contained his massive bulk. She missed him. The color had gone out of the world for her, and she wondered absently if this was going to set the pace for the rest of her life? Surely she could forget him. After all, what she'd felt for Denny had already begun to fade quietly away to leave affection in its place. Perhaps it would be that way when she finally got over Regan. When she was 106 years old or so.

Denny was back right at noon, and she rode down to Tonie's with him in his blue Mercedes.

The restaurant was crowded, but they were seated in a tiny alcove, where they ate spaghetti and garlic bread and drank a pot of coffee between them.

Denny talked about the office and his father's corporation. And it seemed that Regan wasn't the only one worrying about what would happen when Angus retired.

"Regan would never be satisfied running the corporation," Denny said. "He likes what he does too much. On the other hand," he added with a bitter laugh, "Dad doesn't think I could handle it."

"Have you ever considered asking him to let you into the administration for a while, on probation?" she asked. She smiled at him impishly. "And show him what you can do?"

He brightened. "What a thought. No, I hadn't." He pursed his lips. "It would mean giving up the practice, of course, and Regan would probably go back to New York and take up his own again. I've always had the feeling he threw in with me to give me a head start, anyway."

Kenna could have bitten her tongue out. Now she'd just put her job in jeopardy. If Regan went back to New York, she surely wouldn't be asked to go with him, and it would be the end of seeing him every day.

"You're white as a sheet," Denny observed, frowning. "What is it, are you sick?"

She swallowed down a sip of hot coffee. "Just indigestion," she countered. "That sauce was spicy!"

"I know what you mean." He studied her. "Of course, you're upset," he said quickly. "I didn't mean to imply that you wouldn't have a job, Kenna. You could always come to the corporation with me.'' He grinned boyishly. ''You'd love it; it's full of potted plants and light. You're always complaining that my office looks dark and dead.''

She managed a wan smile for him and tugged at her scarf with restless fingers. ''I suppose I could,'' she murmured, hurting as she thought of Regan moving out of her life forever. Even though it might be the best thing that could happen, the thought brought a pain like nothing she'd ever felt.

''How involved have you gotten with my stepbrother?'' he asked gently, and looked genuinely concerned.

Her eyes lifted. ''Well...''

''Don't let him cut you up,'' he said softly. ''He's a sausage grinder. Nothing and no one means a damned thing to him since Jessica was killed. He only goes through the motions of living.'' He set his cup down. ''They had to drag him away from the graveyard,'' he added, remembering. ''I've never seen anything like it. I didn't know people could grieve that much...'' He put down his napkin, unaware of the pain in Kenna's eyes. ''We'd better get back. Want to stroll through the park on the way? I think there's some kind of folk concert going on.''

''I'd like that,'' she agreed. Anything to get her mind off Regan. She smiled at him. ''I'd really like that.''

They wandered hand in hand through the wooded park, where a group of folk musicians were playing to an audience of young people seated on the grass. It was a balmy spring day, and Kenna was holding Denny's hand and should have been on top of the world. But her mind was on that big, dark, lonely man who'd lived so long with his grief that he'd forgotten how bright and beautiful the world could be. She wanted to soothe the lines of pain in his face and give him peace. She wanted to sit and listen to him and love him all her life.

Tears misted her eyes and she bit her lip to stifle them. She missed him so. And he was probably out consoling himself with some woman, she thought suddenly with a flare of violent, unreasonable jealousy. She could picture him with a blonde, someone who'd remind him of his beautiful Jessica—his dark skin and curling body hair pressing down on smooth, pink flesh.

She gasped, and Denny stopped to stare at her. ''What's wrong?'' he asked.

''Nothing,'' she said quickly. ''Let's go closer.''

They stood just outside the circle of spectators and listened to a bluesy folk song about lost love, while Kenna tried her best to forget the embarrassing picture that had painted itself boldly behind her eyes. Why should she care what Regan was doing? He had told her that he wasn't going to involve himself with anyone ever again, except physically, so why should she care if he did it with some other woman? Some sophisticated woman on the pill who wouldn't complicate his life by getting pregnant or clinging to him. Tears burned her eyes. He had to numb the ache, of course, from time to time. She shouldn't begrudge him what little peace he could find. But she did, she did, and she wanted him!

Denny clasped her hand, and grinned down at her. She smiled back. This was nice. Pleasant. Just a friendly kind of camaraderie that would have put her on top of a cloud once. Now all it did was remind her of what she could never have. Regan had spoiled her for any other man.

They finished their work for the day and Denny took her home. She invited him in and cooked supper for him. As the week went on they spent a lot of time together, and Thursday night after he'd taken her to see a science-fiction movie, he kissed her at her front door.

It wasn't bad. Very nice, in fact. But his lips were cool and gentlemanly and very tender. Nothing as fierce and demanding as Regan's. The insistent intimacy of his kisses could make her blush even in memory. Denny was nothing like his stepbrother.

He moved back, smiling at her strange expression, because he thought he was responsible for it.

"You shouldn't do that," she said softly. "Margo..."

His brows drew together. "What would Margo care?" he asked harshly. "She's off in Argentina with that ever-so-suave neighbor of hers, probably having a ball every night. So what would it matter to her if I kissed you?"

So that was it. They'd had a fight and Margo had taunted him with another man, and he was jealous and hurt and wanted to get even. She almost smiled, but caught herself in time to spare his pride. Let him think he was succeeding in catching his secretary's eye; let him salve his ego. Thank goodness she was over her crush on him, or it would have cut her to ribbons, being used as he was unintentionally using her.

"Suave neighbor, huh?" she murmured, peeking up at him through her lashes.

He shrugged. "Some guy she's known since she was a kid."

"Oh, those are dangerous, all right. But she's supposed to be back tomorrow, isn't she?" she added.

He seemed to brighten. "Supposed to," he agreed. "Well, I'll say good night. See you in the morning."

She smiled. "Of course."

He started down the hall and looked back over his shoulder. "Heard from Regan?"

Her own eyes clouded. "No," she said gently, turning back into her apartment. "Good night."

She hadn't heard from Regan for the whole week, nor had she expected to. Apparently he'd decided to give Denny a clear field and let her do what she pleased. That hurt, too, that he didn't care enough to fight for her. But why should he, when he didn't want her, except briefly and physically?

"Do you want to ride up to Gainesville with Margo and me in the morning?" Denny asked on Friday afternoon, just before Margo was due to return. Now he seemed to feel guilty that he'd been courting Kenna, and didn't know what to do about it.

"No," she told him. "I'll wait for Regan. I'm sure he'll be back in time for the anniversary get-together."

"He promised Dad he would," he agreed, "and Regan never breaks promises. Don't forget to pack an overnight bag, Mom's got a room ready for you. The four of us will find something to do." He looked hunted. "Kenna, about this week..."

She touched his arm lightly. "It's been great fun. But only fun," she said. "I know you've missed Margo. I was glad to fill in for her."

He flushed wildly and averted his eyes to her desk. "God, I'm sorry," he ground out. "I didn't realize until this morning that you might have gotten the wrong idea."

"I didn't," she assured him with a genuine smile. "I know how it feels to miss someone until you ache."

His eyes came up to probe hers. "Regan," he said.

She covered up her typewriter. "Time to go home, counselor. Margo will be waiting."

"Kenna, don't let him hurt you," he said suddenly.

She laughed bitterly. "Now you tell me," she sighed.

His hands gestured helplessly. "You're such a babe in the woods, and he's an old fox. I don't know how to put this..."

"He doesn't prey on lambs," she told him gently. "He told me so himself, and he's stuck to it. The problems are all on my side, not his. He's been perfectly honest. We're...friends," she said, almost choking on the word. "Because that's all he has to offer, and he won't take any more than that. And yes, I've offered," she said harshly. Tears moistened her long lashes. "On my knees...!" Her voice broke, and Denny grimaced.

"You poor kid," he said with genuine sympathy, and pulled her gently into his arms. He held her while she cried, his face in her hair, his whole posture comforting. Nothing but that, only comfort.

But to the big, dark man who opened the door and stared into the office, it looked like far more than comfort. His face contorted and he hesitated uncharacteristically before he suddenly set his lips in a thin line and slammed the door behind him.

Kenna and Denny burst apart. Her heart seemed to shake wildly as she saw Regan standing there, staring at them. She knew instinctively what he was thinking, and there was nothing she could say.

"Welcome home," Denny said brightly. "Have a good trip?"

Regan nodded. His eyes went to Kenna. "Don't let me interrupt anything. I just came in to pick up my mail."

He went into his office and slammed that door too. Denny raised his eyebrows and looked down at Kenna with a speculative smile.

"Well, well," he murmured. "Someone's in a snit."

She giggled at the wording, despite the fact that her heart was breaking. Well, he'd told her to go after Denny, hadn't he? What was he so angry about?

"Think it's safe to ask if he wants any dictation taken before I leave?" she asked, dabbing at her eyes.

"Let me get out the door before you ask him, if you don't mind," he said, glancing toward Regan's office. "My insurance has lapsed, and I don't want to get caught in the crossfire."

"Rat, deserting the sinking ship," she accused. "Go ahead, leave me here alone with the dragon."

"Regan keeps ice in the bar behind his bookcase if there are any bruises," he advised. "See you tomorrow. I hope," he added.

She stuck out her tongue at him. He left, and the office became deadly quiet.

Gathering her wits, she knocked briefly at Regan's door and opened it.

He was standing by the window, one hand in his pocket, the other holding a cigarette. The beige suit he wore made him look bigger, and she hesitated in the open doorway. He didn't seem approachable anymore.

"How was your trip?" she asked after a minute, feeling his coldness like an Arctic breeze.

"Fine, thanks."

She glared at his broad back, picturing him with dazzling women dripping diamonds and sensuality. "I'm leaving," she said shortly. "Do you need anything before I go?"

He turned, his dark eyes blazing, narrowed, as they searched over her like hands feeling for breaks. "I'd have thought you'd go with him."

"He's going to pick up Margo at the airport," she began.

He laughed shortly. "Tough luck, honey. What happened, didn't you measure up?"

So that was how it was going to be, she thought miserably. The truce was over, the friendship was dead. They were going back to earlier days and hostility. Well, if that was how he wanted it, it was fine with her!

"Wouldn't you like to know?" she asked with a cold smile. "How about writing out my paycheck, counselor, so that I can cover my bills? Denny forgot."

"Why didn't you pick his pocket?" he asked with a mocking smile. "You were close enough."

"Yes," she agreed with a wistful smile and a sigh. "I certainly was. I can't tell you how much I appreciate all your help, Mr. Cole, it sure did the trick."

He moved closer, his face hardening. "Have you slept with him?"

Her eyes popped. "That's none of your business!"

"The hell it isn't; have you slept with him?" He took her by the shoulders and actually shook her, his face frightening. "Well?"

She swallowed. "No!" she said quickly, intimidated by the tone as well as the bruising grasp.

He let her go abruptly and moved to his desk. "Make sure he's through with Margo before you tangle up your life, will you?" he asked as he pulled out the big office checkbook.

"Is that actually concern for my welfare I hear?" she asked in a quavering tone.

"No," he returned, busy writing the check. "I don't want to have to pull Denny out of a paternity suit."

She couldn't remember ever wanting to hit anyone so much—not even Regan. Her body shook with rage, but she suppressed it. She had a feeling he'd enjoy it if she attacked him.

He handed her the check and she took it with trembling fingers, her face white as a sheet. She didn't even try to thank him; she couldn't manage it.

She turned and walked back out. It only took a minute to clear her desk and put on her sweater and get her purse out of the drawer. But she was aware of him the whole time, watching her.

When she started to leave he stepped in front of her, blocking her path.

She wouldn't look up. "Will you let me by, please?" she asked as calmly as she could.

He took a deep breath, and it sighed out like an ode to weariness. "I'm sorry."

The apology was unexpected. It surprised her into looking up, and at close range his face was startling. It had new lines, deeper lines, and it was drawn. He looked as if he hadn't slept or rested since he'd been gone. That made her even madder, because she imagined him carousing till dawn in New York.

"You look horrible," she said bluntly. "Too many late nights on the town, counselor?"

"Jealous?" he taunted.

She flushed, averting her gaze to his vest. "I don't have the right to be jealous. Our relationship is all play-acting, remember? To fool Denny. To make him jealous. To take him away from Margo so that I can marry him and live happily ever after. And what the hell does it matter to you who I sleep with?" she added in a temper, glaring up at him.

Her face was extraordinarily lovely in anger, bright as a penny, radiant, animated. He looked at her as if he were starving for the sight of her.

"I don't think this is a good time to go into why it matters," he said. "Are you coming home with me tomorrow?"

She swallowed. "Denny said I could ride down with him and Margo."

"You'll ride down with me. I'll pick you up about nine. That will give us time to take the boat out on the lake, if you like."

She nodded.

He tilted her chin up. "You look lovely today," he said.

She searched his dark eyes and smiled faintly. "I wish I could lie and say you looked the same. You should have rested instead of painting the town red."

His thumb caressed her chin idly. "I haven't had a woman since Jessica died, Kenna," he said quietly.

She felt the color leave her face. "But those women in the paper, and Denny said..."

"What did Denny say, that I had a line at my door?" he laughed bitterly. "Denny knows even less about my private life than you do. I don't have affairs. Not since the day I met Jessica, and not since her death. Sex for its own sake appeals to me about as much as working in the nude." He let go of her chin and moved back toward his office. "I've been trying to help find enough evidence to convict a client's wife of attempted murder. It seems that since he wouldn't agree to her terms, she decided to get rid of him without the formality of a divorce. And in a much more final manner."

"My God," she breathed. "People do the craziest things to each other."

"Yes, they do," he replied harshly. "The woman's going to face some hefty criminal charges too. My client is an old friend. He asked for help, and I couldn't refuse him. That," he added curtly, "is why I look dragged out, not because I've been sleeping around."

She drew in a slow, steady breath. "I was jealous," she admitted softly, avoiding his eyes. "I'm sorry."

She opened the door to leave, but he came up behind her and his hand covered hers on the doorknob. She didn't turn, although she could feel the length of him, warm and powerful against her back.

"I won't let it happen," he said in a strained tone. "We agreed at the beginning that we'd doll you up for Denny's benefit, and that's what we've done. I won't let it happen, Kenna, I won't...!"

She was trembling, and he felt it. She knew he felt it, because all at once he caught her arms and whirled her against him. The hold he had on her was crushing, but she didn't protest. It was all of heaven to be in his arms again, to feel the strength and warmth of them, while she drowned in the scent and sight of him.

There was a tremor in his arms as they molded her against him, and she slid her own arms under his jacket, taking pleasure in the warmth of the muscles barely concealed by his shirt and vest. Her breasts were crushed softly against him, and she loved the hard brush of his thighs on her own. She loved everything about him, every single thing.

His breath sighed out unsteadily at her throat, but he didn't kiss her, or make any effort to increase the intimacy of the embrace. He simply held her against him, and that seemed to be enough.

"No more," he said finally, relaxing his hold a little. "We've got to let the bomb defuse itself. I can't live like this."

She knew instinctively what he was talking about. Her cheek nuzzled against his chest. "Why don't you just take me to bed?" she asked quietly. "There has to be a first time...."

"Yours isn't going to be with me," he said. He let her go with a hard sigh, and his eyes were weary. "I can't offer you anything except a temporary liaison. An occasional weekend. That's not my style, and to hell with what Denny thinks."

She searched his dark eyes. "Regan, is it because of Jessica?" she asked gently. "Is that why you...why you don't sleep around?"

"Look who's asking that question," he remarked curtly. "Why don't you sleep around?"

She laughed at the irony of it. "I'm a woman. You can't get pregnant, you know."

"That isn't the only reason you've kept your chastity," he murmured with a knowing smile.

She grimaced. "Men are supposed to be different."

He laughed softly. "I sowed my wild oats years ago, Kenna. I know what it's all about, the mystery's all gone."

Her eyes searched his quietly. "It isn't for me," she said. "Books and reality are worlds apart."

His chest rose and fell heavily as he studied her face. "That will give you something to look forward to, when you marry," he said finally. His eyes clouded. "With Denny, perhaps."

She lifted her chin proudly. "Perhaps," she agreed coldly. "I have to go."

His fingers held her upper arms tightly for a minute, and something dangerous lingered in his eyes. "I can't take the risk again," he said enigmatically.

"Oh, be safe, by all means," she agreed. "Never walk in the rain, you might catch pneumonia. Never go on a trip, the plane might crash. Never love, she might die!"

His face contorted. "What the hell do you know about love?" he asked harshly.

Her eyes fell and she pulled away from him. "I know more than you think," she said with enormous dignity. "I know how it hurts." She turned away and walked out of the office, leaving him standing there alone.

Chapter Eight

Kenna had looked forward to a beautiful day for the Coles' anniversary party, but she woke up to a driving rain outside her apartment window. It wasn't the best possible omen and she had to force down a feeling of utter dread. There was one bright spot, and that was the thought of spending a few precious hours with Regan outside the office. If only it hadn't rained. In the speedboat they could have been alone.

She dressed in navy blue slacks and a blue and white striped blouse, carrying the sea-colored gown that Regan liked so much to put on that night for the party. She felt dreamy as she packed her small overnight bag. Perhaps Regan would dance with her, at least.

At nine the doorbell rang and she rushed to let Regan in. He lifted an eyebrow at her hurry, but there was no welcoming smile on his face. A curtain had been dropped between them.

"I'm almost ready," she said, turning away. She couldn't bear to look at him. In that open-throated wine colored shirt and gray slacks, he looked good enough to wrestle down on a couch.

"There's been a change of plan," he said.

She turned, dreading what he might say. They'd canceled the party, that was it—or Denny had eloped—or...

"We're still going," he said, anticipating her nervous outburst. "But Denny and I have to fly up to Greenville about one o'clock for a quick meeting with some of Dad's colleagues about a possible merger."

"But it's Saturday," she said. "And the party..."

"We'll be back well in time for it, don't get overheated," he said with mild sarcasm.

She sighed. "Well, I guess business doesn't take holidays, does it?"

"No, it doesn't. I'll have Denny back in plenty of time," he said shortly.

She glanced at him, but he turned away to light a cigarette. He did that a lot when he was with her, but his ashtray was hardly used during the day when he was alone. She sighed. She was definitely a threat to his health.

"How are you going, on a charter flight?" she asked as she closed her overnight bag and checked to make sure everything in her apartment was turned off.

"No. We're flying up in the corporation's airplane."

She felt a twinge of fear, and gripped the small bag close as she turned. "The one your father almost crashed in a month ago?" she asked, recalling the day it had happened with vivid unease.

"It's been completely overhauled," he said curtly. "For God's sake, Denny's a big boy. What do you want to do, carry him up to South Carolina on your back?"

She couldn't tell him that her fear was all for him, that she didn't think she could go on living if anything happened to him. So she kept her mouth shut and followed him out the door. Anyway, she told herself, it would be all right. For goodness sake, planes were safer than cars, weren't they?

As soon as they arrived at the house Regan went straight to the study, where his father and Denny were talking quietly. After the initial greetings were exchanged, Kenna turned to Denny. "Where's Margo?" she asked, noting the other woman's absence.

Denny smiled grimly. "She wasn't on the flight yesterday. I got a call from her last night. Long distance. She's decided to spend the extra week at home after all. I told her that was just as well, since I'd been spending a lot of time with you," Denny concluded with a wicked light in his eye. "We've had a great time together this week, haven't we, Kenna?"

Kenna groaned inwardly and made a face at Denny, knowing the effect his words would have on Regan.

But Regan wasn't looking at her expression, and he turned into the study. "I need to take another look at those contracts, Dad," he told his father.

Angus glanced from one of his sons to the other and shrugged. "All right. Denny?"

"I think I'll keep Kenna company," the younger man said.

"Have your mother bring us some coffee, will you?" Angus asked. He winked at Kenna and walked into the study. Regan glared at his stepbrother and Kenna before he slammed the door behind him.

"He's making a habit of that lately," Denny observed, grimacing.

"Oh, you should have stuck around yesterday afternoon," she told him as they walked into the kitchen, where Abbie was taking a tray of homemade cookies out of the oven.

"Why?" Abbie asked immediately, glancing toward Kenna with a wide-eyed grin. "What happened?"

"Mom, you're impossible," Denny told her, laughingly perching himself on the kitchen sink to watch her work.

"I always was, that's why your father married me. Come on, Kenna, spill the beans. Something very fishy is going on around here."

Kenna lifted both eyebrows. "Maybe you only smell your worms," she murmured.

"Stop that," Abbie admonished. She piled cookies on a platter with a spatula. "Regan drags Angus off into the study when they've already discussed those contracts six times. Denny looks like the end of the world. You," she stared pointedly at Kenna's flushed face, "look as if you'd like to take a bite out of something or somebody. And Margo," she glanced toward her youngest son, "mysteriously lengthens her stay at home. And you tell me nothing is going on?"

"Why don't you write whodunnits?" Denny suggested. "You always have such suspicions...."

"I only want to know one thing," Abbie persisted. "Is it you and you," she glanced from one of them to the other, "or is it another combination?"

"It's Denny and Margo," Kenna said with a smile. "Or at least, they're hoping it is."

"And where do you fit in?" Abbie asked.

"I lost the glass slipper," came the wistful reply.

"Huh?" the older woman said blankly.

"For your birthday, I'll tell you the whole story," Kenna promised. "It's awfully complicated."

"So I gathered."

"Why do I get this feeling that I'm as much in the dark as you are?" Denny asked Abbie with a frown.

"Probably because you are. Okay, honey, we'll stop ganging up on you," Abbie told Kenna and hugged her quickly. "But on my birthday, I'll expect you here with all your facts on the tip of your tongue."

"Yes, ma'am," Kenna said politely.

"Am I invited, too?" Denny asked.

"Ask your mother. Oh, Regan asked if he and his father could have some coffee in the study," Kenna added, just remembering.

"Asked?" Abbie scoffed. "The last time Regan asked for anything was when he had his appendix removed, and that courtesy only lasted until he got out from under the anesthetic. Here, Kenna, you take it to them."

Kenna looked hunted. Denny noticed her reluctance and stepped in.

"I'll do it," he said, lifting the tray. He winked at his mother. "It's too heavy for a mere woman."

"I'll sue," Kenna called after him. "But thanks."

"Anytime."

"Now," Abbie said, seeing her opportunity. "He's part of the problem, isn't he? You're head over heels in love with Regan, or I'm a white mouse."

Kenna sank down in a chair, looking utterly miserable. "You see, Regan was going to help me get Denny's attention—which I thought I wanted. So he took me shopping and got me this haircut," she indicated the short, flattering style, "and makeup and showed me what clothes to buy. Then he taught me how to walk and talk and flirt and act seductive. Then he sent me after Denny."

"The fairy godmother." Abbie grinned wickedly.

Kenna laughed despite her misery. "Fairy godfather," she corrected. "Anyway, now Denny's about to lose Margo because Regan was throwing me at him, and Regan walks around smoldering and looking purely hostile."

"I know that. But why?"

"He doesn't want to get involved, he says," Kenna sighed. She glanced up at Abbie, saw an ally, and decided to tell the whole truth. "He wants me, but he won't do anything about it because I'm still a virgin. And he doesn't want anything else, so..." She shrugged and hung her clasped hands between her knees. "Oh, damn it, Abbie. I hate men."

"So do I," the older woman agreed with a grimace. "I imagine he's afraid, Kenna. He did love Jessica obsessively. He's like that. He can't give a part of himself, he gives everything."

Kenna studied her fingernails. "She was lucky to be loved so much. I can't imagine a man caring about me that way."

"You might be very surprised. Here, honey, help me get these cookies into the fridge. Denny will be back any minute, and I don't think he needs any more ammunition to use against Regan. He's violently jealous of him, you know," Abbie sighed.

"Yes, I know, but he shouldn't be. He's quite a man himself," she said with a kind smile. "Why won't your husband give him a chance?"

"My husband," the older woman growled, "is a haughty, arrogant type who thinks he knows everything there is to know about personalities. But I'm working on him. So is Regan. We'll change his mind about Denny yet."

"I'd gladly put in my two cents' worth if I could," Kenna said on a sigh.

"Don't look so depressed, love," she said soothingly. "This is going to be a great party, even if I say so myself, and we'll dance and drink champagne and let the future take care of itself. Just take it one hour at a time."

"I hope you're right, Abbie."

"I hope you brought something eye-catching to use on Regan," Abbie grinned.

Kenna lifted her eyebrows and smiled back. "I certainly did. Want to see it?"

"Yes, as a matter of fact, I do." She took off her apron and tossed it over the back of a chair. "The caterers can take care of everything else. Come on, show me yours and I'll show you mine."

"How long have you and Mr. Cole been married?" Kenna asked as they mounted the carpeted staircase.

"Twenty-six years today," the shorter woman sighed. "How time flies. And I still think Angus is the sexiest man I've ever known."

Kenna couldn't imagine anyone thinking Angus Cole sexy. But probably Abbie still did. She wondered how she'd feel if she and Regan were celebrating their twenty-sixth wedding anniversary, and tingled all over at the thought. She knew she'd think he was sexy twenty-six years from now.

When she and Abbie came back downstairs, Denny and his father were in the study with the door open, and Regan was nowhere in sight.

"Where did he go?" Abbie asked, her voice lowered conspiratorially as the women joined the men.

"He's gone to get dressed," Angus offered, raising an eyebrow in Kenna's direction. "In a hurry to get away, it looks like. We've got another hour before we have to leave for the airport."

Denny was watching Kenna, too, and he drew her to one side while Angus and Abbie discussed the party arrangements.

"Regan gave me his blessing," he told Kenna with a sly grin. "Not generously, but he gave it to me, then he poured himself a slug of Dad's gin and went up to dress."

"Oh," Kenna said miserably, staring at her shoes.

"You don't understand," he persisted. "He hates gin. I don't think he knew what he was drinking. Why don't you go up and tell him I'm on the verge of proposing and see what happens?" He grinned. "I dare you."

"I've got bad vibrations about doing that," she said nervously.

"You never know until you try."

"That's true."

"Go on," he challenged. "What have you got to lose?"

"My pride, my self-respect, my..."

"Go, girl," he told her, turning her around. "I'm going to call Margo and see if she'll give up her neighbor and come home and marry me. We're both going to get it together before we quit. Now get in there and fight, troops!" he said with his old familiar enthusiasm.

She laughed helplessly. "He won't like it."

"Good. It will make him see what he's giving up."

She sighed. "All or nothing, huh?" She straightened the hem of her blouse and pursed her lips. "Wish me luck."

"Will you need it, looking the way you do?" Denny asked.

"That reminds me. Here." She tugged off her glasses and handed them to him, and smoothed her hair. "Point me toward the staircase, please."

"Right there. Up the stairs and first door to the right."

"Thanks, partner."

She marched up the long staircase with her heart hammering in her throat. Please, let it work, she prayed silently. Let him care. Let him be insanely jealous and tell me not to go near Denny again!

She walked up to his door and hesitated. Well, Denny was right, what did she have to lose? And she was the one who'd been lecturing Regan about daring to live....

She knocked firmly on his door.

"What is it?" he growled.

"Could I talk to you for a minute?" she called through the heavy wood.

There was a pregnant pause, and she stood nervously outside in the hall, wondering what she'd do if he said no. But after a minute she heard heavy footsteps, and then the door swung open.

She wasn't prepared at all for the sight that met her shocked eyes. She'd seen Regan in his shirt sleeves, but that was as disheveled as he'd ever been in her company. Until now. He was stripped to the waist, and Kenna wondered if it was acceptable for a modern woman to faint at such sights. He was the most gorgeous-looking thing she'd ever seen. The pickiest connoisseur of men's bare chests couldn't have found a flaw in him. He was heavily muscled, bronzed and fit, and there was a wedge of thick black hair curling from his collarbone down to his belt, and probably far below that. Kenna had to clench her hands at her sides to keep them from making a grab for him.

"Well?" he asked curtly.

She dragged her eyes up to meet his and forgot everything she'd come upstairs to say.

He had a towel in one hand, apparently having just come from a shower, because his dark, shaggy hair was still damp. But if he was irritated because she'd interrupted him, it didn't show.

Wordlessly, he caught her clenched hand and dragged her into the room, closing the door quietly behind them. His eyes searched hers for a long, static moment before he abruptly tossed the towel into a nearby chair and brought both her hands to his broad chest.

"Well?" he asked quietly.

It was all she could do to answer him. She could think of nothing but the feel of that thick, cool mass of hair under her fingers. She had to force her hands not to start anything by caressing him as they ached to.

"Denny's asked me...to marry him," she said, giving the lie straightforwardly as Denny had suggested.

His chest rose and fell heavily under her hands. She closed her eyes and wished with all her heart that he loved her as much as she loved him, that he'd tell her so and carry her the few feet to the brown-patterned bedspread and lay her down on it....

Her heart throbbed wildly when he suddenly lifted her clear of the floor and did almost that. He carried her to the bed and dropped her into its softness, throwing himself down with her. His arms supported him as he poised himself above her.

"Is this what you want?" he asked coldly. "One last fling with me before you give him an answer? Why not? Maybe we can get each other out of our systems before you start wearing his ring..." Before he finished the sentence, his mouth was crushing down against hers.

She stiffened, but only for a minute. She'd waited too long, wanted him too long, to protest. Burying her pride, she reached up and touched him, feeling the smooth texture of his bronzed skin, tugging at the thick hair over his chest, exploring every hard muscle with fingers that trembled with hunger. Her mouth opened without any coaxing, her tongue answered the hard thrust of his. Her body seemed to curl up with pleasure at the sweet, wild intimacy they were sharing.

"Is this what you want?" he asked against her mouth, and his voice was unsteady.

"Yes," she whispered unashamedly. Her arms reached up to bring him even closer. "Oh, yes, this is what I want, Regan."

His mouth brushed against hers softly, feeling its silky texture, while his fingers went down to the front of her blouse and began to methodically unfasten the buttons one by one.

She knew what he was doing, but she didn't make a sound or try to stop him. Her body belonged to him, as it could never belong to any other man. If he wanted it now, he was welcome to it. She wasn't going to fight.

"No fuss, Cinderella?" he asked when he freed the last button and eased the edges apart, baring the lacy little bra she wore under the blouse.

"No fuss," she whispered, watching his face as he reached under her to unclasp the bra and tug it loose.

He lifted her, deftly sliding the blouse down one arm and then the other. The straps of the bra followed, and when he lowered her back to the bed, there was nothing between his dark, quiet eyes and her body.

She tried to breathe normally, but her heart was beating madly. She caressed his dark face with her eyes, fascinated by the expression that had claimed it as he looked down at her small, taut breasts.

"Are you disappointed?" she asked softly.

"No." He brushed his fingers over her collarbone and lifted his eyes to meet hers. "No, I'm not disappointed." he watched her as his hand moved, lightly stroking her smooth flesh. He caught the hard peak between his fingers and tugged gently at it, and she arched and caught her breath at the aching pleasure.

Her fingers clung to his hard arms and she stared at him like a tiny wounded thing, helpless in the hands of its captor. But it wasn't a wound she felt, it was a kind of pleasure she'd only heard about until now.

"Lift up, darling," he whispered, moving his hands around her to bring her body up against his bare chest. "Let me show you how it feels," he breathed, watching her softness disappear into the tangle of hair over his warm chest. "Oh, God, I never dreamed anything could be so sweet!"

She caught her breath and pressed close, shutting her eyes to savor the wild magic of this new intimacy. She slid her arms around his neck and burrowed her face into his throat, while he eased onto his side and brought her completely against his powerful body. Her legs brushed his, feeling their strength, her hips arched against him and felt the immediate response of his body to the soft contact.

"Regan," she whispered drowsily, her voice hungry and soft with love.

"I could take you now," he whispered roughly. His hands slid down her sides, brushing her breasts, and still further down until they found the base of her spine.

His leg edged between hers and his mouth sought hers again, taking it with a lazy, insistent pressure that dragged a moan from her throat. His hands were smoothing her skin, finding the gentle rise of her body with reverence in their touch.

He bit at her mouth softly and drew away. "I want to kiss you here," he murmured, emphasizing the whisper with his hands. "You're like velvet, so soft to touch." He eased her onto her back and looked down at her body, his face unreadable, his eyes blazing.

She arched her back like a cat being stroked, faintly shocked at her own abandon. She wasn't embarrassed with him or shy or even self-conscious. She loved the feel of his eyes, his hands. It was so beautiful with him.

His fingers caught her waist, pressing into it to test its taut perfection. They moved over her flat stomach, around to her back and lifted her to his mouth.

She trembled, and an odd little sound surfaced as she felt for the first time the magic of a man's warm mouth on her soft flesh.

"I could make a meal of you," he whispered quietly. "Every time I touch you, I go a little mad."

Her fingers stroked his dark, cool hair and her eyes closed on wave after wave of sweet pleasure. "So do I," she whispered back. She arched, forcing her body closer to his seeking lips. "This is beautiful," she managed unsteadily. "So...very beautiful."

"Come closer, Kenna," he whispered. His mouth slid up to cover hers, and he folded her into the curve of his body, so that they were closer than they'd ever been.

She answered the soft hunger of his mouth with a response that dragged a groan from his taut body. His hands at her back trembled slightly, and his hips moved against hers with a strange rhythm.

"No," he ground out suddenly. His body stilled and he crushed her for an instant before he let her go and rolled away. He sat up, swinging his legs off the bed, and bent his head into his hands. "No, Kenna."

She lay against the pillows, dazed with delightful sensations, staring at him. Her breath trembled into her throat. "Regan?" she whispered.

He drew in a harsh breath. "I can't," he bit off. "Don't you understand, damn it? I can't!"

Her lips trembled. The rejection was so complete that it hurt. She forced herself to sit up, to tug her bra and top back on without saying anything.

He got to his feet and pulled a cigarette from the pack on the chest of drawers, lighting it with hands that could hardly hold the flame steady. Then he went to the window and stared down at the rose garden it overlooked with blank eyes.

"It's because I'm not Jessica, isn't it?" she asked, getting unsteadily to her feet. "Because nobody can ever take her place with you."

He turned, scowling at her. "What the hell are you talking about?" he demanded harshly. "Don't start trying to shift the blame, honey, you're the one who came in here after me."

"Yes, I did," she admitted, "but you're the one who carried me to bed!"

"Were you protesting?" he asked. "I didn't notice any maidenly reservations. Just don't get the idea that once you're married I'll be willing to supply what Denny apparently can't," he added coldly.

Her face flamed. "I hope you can type, counselor, because after that crack, you'll be doing you own damned petitions from now on!"

"Quitting, are you?" he asked.

"Yes," she returned recklessly. "Denny's going to ask his father to let him work at the corporation, and I'm going, too! You can have the office all to yourself!"

"I won't need it," he said, turning back to the window. "I'm going back to New York next week. Denny and Dad and I settled it a few minutes ago."

She wanted to sit down in the middle of the floor and cry. Just for an instant, she considered it, if only to see what he'd do. He'd probably walk over her, she thought miserably.

With her heart around her ankles, along with her pride, she turned to open the door.

"I'm sorry I caused you to compromise your principles," she said bitterly. "I won't throw myself at you again."

"The blame isn't all yours," he said wearily. "I can't seem to keep my hands away from you lately. I didn't mean for that to happen."

"I know." Tears were welling up in her eyes. "When will you leave?"

"Monday," he said firmly. "That attempted murder case I told you about comes up on the calendar the following week, and I need that time. I don't intend to lose.''

"When have you ever lost a case?" she asked with bitter humor. "I hope you get a conviction, counselor."

"You and Denny," he said, "remember to invite me to the wedding."

"Sure," she choked, careful to keep her back to him. "Thanks again for all the help. I'll pay you back for the clothes just as soon..."

"Consider them a wedding gift," he said curtly. "I hope Denny will make you happy."

I'm not going to marry Denny, and he'll never make me happy. I'll grieve all my life for love of you, she thought in anguish. But she only nodded, and kept the damning words to herself.

"We won't talk again," he said as she opened the door. "Not like this. I hope we'll part as friends, Kenna."

She couldn't look at him. "You'll always be my friend," she said quietly. "As long as I'm alive."

"Are you crying?" he asked suddenly.

"No, of course not." She walked through the doorway. "I think I'd like to go home after the party. I'll get Denny to drive me, you won't have to."

"You don't have to go that far to avoid me," he said roughly. "Stay. I'll go back to Atlanta myself."

Tears burst over the dam of her lower lids and spilled onto her cheeks. "Damn you," she choked, "crawl into the grave with her and see if I care!"

She ran down the hall as if the hounds of hell were after her, ignoring the harsh sound of her name on his lips as he called after her. She went into her own room and slammed the door, locking it. And she stayed there until she was sure Denny and Regan had gone.

Chapter Nine

The day dragged after the two men had gone. Kenna tried to stay out of the way when the caterers arrived to start their own preparations for the evening. The florist delivered the arrangements Abbie had ordered, and Angus busied himself in the study while Kenna helped Abbie with last minute touches in the living room.

The tables were lovely—covered with white linen and Abbie's best silver, dotted with fresh flower arrangements and trays waiting to be filled. The kitchen was alive with the caterers as they began to prepare the evening's canapés and finger foods.

Abbie rushed around trying to get everything together, but as the afternoon wore on she began to look troubled.

She checked her watch as she joined Kenna in the living room for a quick cup of coffee. "They should be calling from the airport by now," she murmured. "Oh, where are they? The guests will be here in just a few hours...Kenna, men have no consideration whatsoever," she grumbled just before she got up and started back to the kitchen. "And they say women are bad about spending hours talking."

Kenna only smiled. "They'll be here soon," she said confidently, trying not to think about the fact that the airplane had already malfunctioned once....

To take her mind off her own worry, Kenna strolled around the grounds with Pooch. He followed her lazily, pausing occasionally to bark at shadows in the woods. She tossed a crust of bread to the swans at the edge of the lake and let her mind drift to more pleasant thoughts. At least she'd have something of Regan to remember when he went back to New York. A scrapbook of sweet dreams and bits of happiness to tuck away in the back of her mind and bring out on lonely winter nights.

If only he could have put away his grief. She would have helped him. Not that she'd want him to forget Jessica entirely. Love came in so many forms, each one subtly different and special. It was possible to love more than once, and she couldn't begrudge Jessica the part of his life she'd shared. He was the kind of man who deserved to be loved deeply and completely. What a pity that he'd decided he could do without love for the rest of his life.

She ruffled Pooch's fur and they started back to the house. Abbie was just coming down the tree-lined path, looking for her, with trouble written on her like a slogan.

"What's wrong?" Kenna asked without preliminaries, already fearing the worst.

"The plane went down," Abbie said hoarsely.

Kenna stood frozen in the middle of the path, while the world seemed to blacken and die around her. No, it couldn't be.

"The plane?" she echoed blankly.

"Yes," Abbie said, going close to hug Kenna to her. "Oh, Kenna, they've crashed in the damned thing," she moaned, breaking down completely. "My sons, my boys...!"

And now Kenna had to believe, because she'd never seen Abbie Cole cry. Numbly, her arms enfolded the shorter woman and she felt a cold ache inside as the full impact hit her. The plane had gone down. It had crashed. With Regan and Denny inside. Regan might be dead.

She couldn't remember ever feeling so full of terror. It came over her like a black sickness, blinding her with tears.

"Oh, no," she whispered, as if words could stop the nightmare before it began. "No."

"Damned plane," Abbie growled in anguish, her voice breaking. "Damned, damned plane! They promised us it was safe...!"

Kenna soothed her with hands that felt numb from cold and shock. "How did it happen?"

"We don't know." Abbie pulled away and wiped at her eyes with a big handkerchief before she handed it to Kenna, who hadn't realized that huge teardrops were rolling down her own pale cheeks. "All we know is that they left Greenville hours ago. When they didn't arrive at the airport, the airport operator called us. He's a close friend, you see. He called the Greenville airport to see when they'd filed their flight plan and when they'd left. The mountains...and it's raining. Oh, my God, why did they have to call that stupid meeting today, of all days? My anniversary...!"

"It will be all right," Kenna said quietly, using the routine words that people said at times like this. Words that didn't mean a damned thing.

"I hope so, Kenna," Abbie groaned. "I hope so! Come on; we're going out to the airport. I can't sit here and wait for telephone calls; I've got to be where I can find out something."

Angus was already pulling his car keys out of his pocket when they got back to the house, his face hard and grim and so much like Regan's that Kenna burst into fresh tears.

"Regan was flying," Angus told the women as they got into his Mercedes and started for the airport. "He's level-headed at the controls; he's flown combat missions. If it was possible to bring that plane down in one piece, he'd have done it."

"Pilot error accounts for most accidents," Abbie agreed, "but equipment failure accounts for its share. And that damned plane's already gone down once," she reminded her husband with trembling lips.

Kenna, sitting in the back seat with fear numbing her body, listened without trying to join in the conversation. Regan, she whispered, oh, God, please let Regan be alive, please don't let him die. Please don't let him die.

"If they walk away from this one, I'll have that machine taken apart piece by piece and melted down," Angus promised curtly.

"Do they have any idea, any at all, where it might have gone down?" Abbie was asking. "Those mountains around Toccoa, or near Robertstown..."

"That would have been off their flight path," Angus murmured.

"Yes, but it's raining; they might have been blown off course. Or if their instruments malfunctioned...Angus, I can't bear to lose them both," she broke down. "Oh, God, I've covered so many plane crashes! I know too much about what happens, things that never get into print because they're too horrible."

"Stop it," Angus said quietly. "Just calm down and stop thinking the worst. Don't borrow trouble, darling."

"I'm sorry." Abbie dabbed at her eyes and turned to look back at Kenna. "Are you all right?"

Kenna nodded. "Will it be a long time, before we know?"

Angus shrugged. "I don't know," he said with suppressed emotion in his deep voice. His hands tightened on the steering wheel. "Maybe we'll get lucky."

"Our anniversary," Abbie murmured miserably, and sniffed back fresh tears. "I told the caterers to take care of the guests if we're not back; it's too late to cancel. And I...I just can't start phoning people now...."

"One step at a time, Abbie," Angus said gently. He reached over and caught his wife's hand in his and held it firmly. "We'll wait and pray and hope for the best."

"Yes, Angus," the tearful woman agreed, returning the pressure with her own fingers.

Kenna, watching them, began to understand what Abbie saw in the older man. He's like Regan, she thought. He's strong and gentle and like a rock when she needs someone to lean on. That brought the tears back, and she dragged a tissue from her purse.

Later, she huddled next to Abbie on the bare wood bench outside the airport office, watching the gray skies with eyes that didn't even see. Despite the fact that the plane was overdue and very likely down somewhere, Abbie couldn't stop herself from looking for it. Greenville was only a little less than a two hour drive from Gainesville; it was hardly any distance at all. How could it have happened? The thunderstorm might have driven them off course, but the airport manager said that they hadn't radioed in. The Atlanta Flight Service had phoned him when the twin-engine plane was overdue, and a telephone search had resulted as they called airport after airport looking for the missing pilot and his passenger.

"We're going to be soaked if we stay out here, I guess," Abbie said, "but I'll be damned if I can go inside and listen...." Her voice broke and she burst into tears again. "I can't bear to lose them," she confessed.

Kenna hugged her close with a sob. "Neither can I," she confessed. Her lower lip trembled and the runway blurred in front of her eyes. "Abbie, if anything happens to him, I don't think I can bear to go on living."

The older woman drew back to look into Kenna's tormented eyes. "Regan?" she asked.

Kenna nodded. "Regan."

"My dear," Abbie said helplessly. She put her arms around the younger woman and they sat there in the rain, comforting each other, while the skies darkened and the mist settled around them.

Angus brought them cups of steaming black coffee. "It will be dark soon," he said. "They won't start searching until tomorrow morning, if it comes to that." He shrugged his broad shoulders as he scanned the skies. "Even if they went down safely, it would probably take time to get to a telephone. There are lots of rural areas between here and Greenville...."

"Yes, that's true," Abbie said numbly. "But there are lots of hilly places—the mountains to the west."

"Come inside, both of you," Angus said gently. "You'll have pneumonia, sitting out here."

"I can't stand it in there," Kenna whispered.

"Neither can I," Abbie agreed. "You'll call us...?"

"Angus!" the airport manager called. "In here!"

Angus paused, as if he would have liked to protect the women from what he might hear, as if he wanted to forbid them to come in with him. But Abbie and Kenna were already on their feet, looking as if they'd fight him if he tried to stop them. He shrugged, and drew them into the office with him.

The manager was laughing. Laughing! "They're fine," he said without preamble, a microphone in one hand. "Regan got the plane down okay, but they've had a cold, wet wait for the rescuers. He landed it in a cow pasture in northeast Georgia."

"What the hell happened?" Angus demanded, fear giving way to anger.

"The instrument panel caught fire and they had to put down. Regan managed to ditch in time, so that the emergency location transmitter remained intact. But their navigation equipment had been damaged and they were way off course. A private plane caught the signal and relayed it to ground rescue units." He grinned. "Would you like me to tell you the odds against landing a twin-engine plane in a cow pasture? Good thing he flew fighters in Nam, wasn't it, Angus?"

Angus was laughing, but there were tears of relief in his eyes. "Good thing," he admitted. He paused to catch his breath. "Where are they now?"

"On their way here," the operator said, grinning. "An old flying buddy of mine's bringing them down in his own plane."

Kenna was crying quietly, along with Abbie, and she offered up a silent prayer of thanks. The light had come back into her life. Despite the rain and gloom of the past few hours, it was beautiful to be alive and in the same world with Regan. Even if she never saw him again, that would be all right now. He was alive. Thank God, he was alive.

The next half an hour seemed to take forever, while Kenna drank black coffee with the others and scanned the dark skies with eyes that were hungry for sight of a beloved face. She was bedraggled and wet through and through. One of the airport people had loaned her his sweater, and Abbie had Angus's jacket, but Kenna didn't even feel the cold.

When the single-engine plane landed and taxied to a stop on the apron, Kenna started running toward it. She didn't care anymore about her stupid pride or keeping secrets. She loved Regan, and she didn't care if it showed, she didn't care who knew it. Nothing mattered now except touching him and holding him, and making sure that he was really alive and not just a figment of her tortured imagination. She was hardly aware of Abbie and Angus behind her, of other people.

Regan and Denny came out of the plane and stood together, watching her run toward them. They looked as wet as she did. Regan's face had some cuts, and his jacket was torn; Denny was holding his arm. But they were alive.

"Regan!" Kenna cried, sounding like someone returning from hell.

She ran straight to him, hardly seeing Denny or the shocked expression in Regan's dark eyes as he opened his arms for her.

Her body hit his with the impact of a blow. Her arms reached up to cling as she held him with every ounce of strength in her trembling body. Her eyes closed on a flood of tears. He was safe. He felt warm and solid and she could feel his breath at her ear. He was safe.

His arms contracted hungrily, painfully at her back, bruising her against his big body. His face nuzzled urgently against hers as he sought her mouth and found it. They kissed hungrily, taking each other's mouths with a hot, wild anguish that took them far away from the drizzle and the curious stares. She clung, feeling him tremble, loving the bruising abandon of his big arms, the devouring pressure of his mouth biting into hers.

She didn't see Denny hugging his parents, she wasn't aware of Angus's hand touching Regan's back, of Abbie's loving stare. Her whole being had concentrated itself into showing Regan how glad she was that he was alive. That he was home.

A long, long minute later he lifted his head. His eyes were glittering with an odd wildness as he looked down at her, and he was trembling from head to toe. So was she, but for a different reason altogether, she imagined. She let her arms slide away from him, but she couldn't drag her eyes from his.

Her fingers touched his face. "You're hurt," she whispered on a sob.

"No," he said in a strangely shaken tone, "it's just a cut."

"We were so worried," Abbie interrupted, taking the opportunity to hug him. "Landing a plane in a cow pasture. That's a new one."

"It was hairy for a few minutes," Denny chuckled, looking from Kenna's white face to Regan's darkly flushed one. "But Regan's combat training came in handy. Uh, Dad, the plane..."

"Damn the plane," Angus grumbled, shaking Regan's hand warmly. "We'll melt down what's left of it and buy a new one."

"Thank God we had those life jackets up front with us," Denny remarked. "We used them to cushion our faces from the impact."

"Is your arm broken?" Angus asked his youngest son.

"I don't think so, but we'd both better stop by the emergency room at the hospital and have ourselves checked," Denny sighed. "We're both a little banged up."

"We'll do that," Angus agreed. "You've got ten days to write a report on this to file with the National Transportation Safety Board."

"I phoned them before we left to fly down here," Regan told his father. "They're mailing me the forms."

He sounded shaken, but Kenna supposed he had a right to be. She was looking at him with eyes so wide with fear and relief and concern that Abbie had to stifle a telling remark.

"We'd better go," Angus murmured. "Fellas, you'll never know how much we appreciate your help," he began, moving into the throng of airport personnel to express his gratitude.

"Are you all right?" Abbie asked Denny, putting a supporting arm around him.

"I'm fine," he said with a grin.

Kenna belatedly moved away from Regan to hug Denny. "I'm sorry you were hurt," she said numbly. "But I'm so glad you're both alive."

"I'll be back in a minute," Regan said quietly and walked into the office where Angus had gone.

"You gave the show away, you know," Denny murmured with a wry smile as he looked down at Kenna. "You can't go around kissing men that way unless you're pretty involved emotionally, and Regan isn't stupid."

She sighed with a weary smile. "Isn't it a good thing he's going back to New York?" she asked miserably. "I won't have him giving me pitying looks."

"If the way he kissed you just now was pity," Abbie murmured, "I'm a duck."

"He didn't have much choice, since I was doing the kissing," Kenna said. She brushed the hair away from her eyes. "It doesn't matter, anyway. I'd rather have the two of you alive than have my pride intact."

"Amen." Abbie grinned. "Come on, let's get you to the emergency room."

"The party," Denny burst out, just remembering.

"I'm sure the guests are having a great time," Abbie said carelessly. "So will we, when we get there. What a nice anniversary present you are, my darling," she added, and reached up to kiss him with a smile.

Denny only laughed and kissed her back.

It was crowded in the Mercedes going home. The emergency room doctor had put an ace bandage around Denny's sprained wrist and treated the cuts on Regan's dark face. After which, he had given them both a clean bill of health. Kenna was sandwiched in between the two men, feeling Regan's hard thigh against her leg and his shoulder brushing hers.

If she'd embarrassed him, it didn't show. But he didn't speak, letting Denny tell the harrowing story of the ditching.

It was enough for Kenna to sit beside him. So little a thing to give so much pleasure. She leaned back against the seat and closed her eyes, while the conversation around her buzzed in her ears without making sense.

The house was full of curious people, none of whom Kenna recognized. They came forward as the Coles walked in the door, and Angus briefly explained what had happened.

"Anyway," he told the guests, "the excitement's over, and if you'll excuse us for just a minute while we change clothes, we'll be right with you. We've sure got something to celebrate now!"

And he led the way upstairs. Kenna quickly changed into her evening gown and ran a brush through her short hair. She put on a light coat of pale lipstick and gave thanks all over again that Regan was alive. That both men were, she corrected silently. Well, he knew the truth now, she thought miserably. Everybody knew it.

With a sinking heart, she went back down to join the others. This would surely be the last time she'd see Regan. That would probably be the best thing for both of them. It would be as much of an embarrassment to him as it would be to her, to have everyone know she was wearing her heart on her sleeve for him.

Abbie was standing apart from Angus in the family room, a glass of champagne in her hand.

"Have some, dear," she said to Kenna, lifting a filled glass from the table. "I poured it for you."

"Thank you." She searched the room. "Where's Denny?"

"On the phone. With Margo," she added with a grin. "She just called, and he's regaling her with tales of his bravery. Isn't it great?"

She laughed. "Oh, yes, it is. I think he's hooked this time, you know."

"Well, she'll be a handful," Abbie observed. "But I like her well enough, and she is easy on the eyes. And we have the satisfaction of knowing she isn't after his money. That bothered all of us, before we found out about her background.''

Kenna nodded, staring into her glass. She tended to forget how wealthy the family was. They didn't flaunt what they had, or act superior to other people.

"That sounded terrible, didn't it?'' Abbie said gruffly, touching Kenna's arm lightly. "I sound as if I'm immediately suspicious of every woman who looks at my sons. Kenna, no one who saw you with Regan this afternoon could ever accuse you of being a gold digger. Do you know, I've never seen people kiss that way—except myself and Angus, years ago. I knew everything you were feeling. And it wasn't a sudden thirst for money.''

"I knew you didn't mean me,'' Kenna said quietly. She glanced up and looked at Regan, filled with love and gratitude for his safety. As if he sensed that searching stare, he looked up into her eyes. And time seemed to stop around them for a space of seconds until he looked back at his father.

"He thought you were going to marry Denny,'' Abbie said abruptly.

"Did he?'' She sipped her drink.

"Was he supposed to think that?''

She nodded. "We, uh, thought it might make him jealous.'' Tears clouded her eyes. "Wasn't that funny?'' She turned away. "I don't think I can stand any more tonight. Would you be terribly offended if I said good night and went to bed?''

"But it's barely ten o'clock, darling,'' Abbie protested gently. "You haven't danced one dance,'' she added, nodding toward the couples moving to the delightful sound of a small combo that had been hired for the occasion.

"I don't really feel like it.'' She put down her half finished glass of champagne and hugged Abbie impulsively. "I'm glad they're both safe. See you in the morning, okay?''

"Okay. Sleep well, my dear.''

"You, too. Uh, will you...tell the others?'' she asked nervously, dreading a confrontation if she had to do it herself.

Abbie nodded understandingly. "Of course I will. Want some aspirin?''

"No. Just a warm bath and my bed. Are we all going to church in the morning?'' she added.

Abbie smiled. "You bet. You can borrow a dress from me if you didn't bring one.''

She returned the smile. "I did. 'Night.''

She turned and walked quickly out of the room, oblivious to the dark eyes that followed her path with mingled confusion and hunger.

Chapter Ten

Kenna stretched out in the blue bathtub with a sigh, letting the warm water surround her with the delicate lilac scent she'd added to it. It felt so good to let her aching muscles relax.

She lathered and rinsed and arched her back as she trailed water down it to wash the soap away. And that was when she became aware of someone in the room with her.

She opened her eyes and turned her head toward the door. Shock froze her in place for an instant, and Regan took full advantage of it to look down at her soft, pink bareness with dark, possessive eyes.

Apparently, he'd given up on the party, too, because his white frilled shirt was open all the way down the front and all he had on with it was his slacks.

"I'm taking a bath," Kenna managed in a high-pitched, breathless tone as she tried to decide what to do. The washcloth would hardly be of any use at all, and he was standing next to her towel.

"Yes, I can see that," he said gently. He smiled at her, the first genuine smile she could remember on his hard face in a long time. "My God, you're a delight to the eyes."

She flushed at the compliment and waited there, sitting up, in a flurry of confusion.

"Stand up," he said quietly. "I'll dry you."

He pulled the towel from the rack and she tried to decide between diving under the water or making a run for it.

That indecision must have shown, because he laughed softly. "There's nothing to be embarrassed about, darling," he said, moving closer with the towel raised. "You're beautiful, and I love looking at you. Now stand up. You can't stay in there."

He made it seem so natural. Her own reaction startled her, because she got gracefully to her feet and stepped out onto the bath mat, searching his quiet face with wide, curious eyes.

"You see," he said quietly, wrapping her in the towel, "there's nothing to be ashamed of. Nudity is beautiful. It's the distortions people make of it that bring shame."

Her eyes searched his face, lingering on the deep cut beside his jaw. She reached up and touched it gently where the antiseptic stopped. "I'd never been so afraid in my life as I was when Abbie told me the plane was lost," she said involuntarily. Tears sprang to her eyes with remembered terror.

"I could see that for myself, Kenna," he murmured. He dried her slowly, gently, and tossed the towel aside to swing her up in his big arms. "I can't tell you how I felt when you ran to me instead of Denny at the airport. My God, I almost cried...."

She buried her face in his throat, feeling the warmth and strength of him like a brand against her bareness. Involuntarily, she pulled his opened shirt aside to press her body against the hair-matted muscle and gasped at the sweet contact.

"I love you," she breathed, dragging her breasts against him slowly, with an aching hunger. "I love you, and I don't care if the whole world knows it...!"

"I imagine most of it does, if they saw the way you kissed me at the airport," he murmured huskily. "Don't be so aggressive, baby, you'll make me lose control."

"I want you to lose control," she whispered in his ear. "I want you to make love to me. I want to belong to you. I don't care if all I can ever have is tonight," she added, clinging, as her voice broke. "I love you...!"

His mouth slid across her cheek and onto her lips, stopping the words, taking possession with a slow, sweet intimacy that made her moan under its expertness.

"Be quiet," he whispered tenderly. He carried her into the adjoining bedroom and laid her down on the bed. He watched her closely as he drew his shirt off and tossed it onto a nearby chair. His slacks followed, and she averted her eyes as he joined her on the bed.

He turned her face back to his with a slow smile. "I doubt you can see this far, anyway, without your glasses," he remarked affectionately. "Not that it matters. You'd better get used to looking at me. I don't think people need to hide lovemaking in the darkness, like a guilty secret."

"It isn't that," she said breathlessly. "It's just that it's new territory for me."

"For me, too," he sighed, and looked down the length of her with a long, possessive appraisal. "You're going to be my first virgin."

That was shocking, and the look on her face told him so.

"Jessica had been married before," he said quietly. "And before we go any further, I want you to understand something. She was a part of my life that no longer exists. I loved her. But she's dead and I'm not and life goes on." He touched her face with a lightly caressing movement of his fingers, and his eyes glowed with some deep emotion. "You don't know beans about taking precautions, do you?" he asked suddenly, and grinned at the flaming blush on her face. "Never mind. If you get pregnant, it won't be the end of the world."

Her face was deep red, but she didn't look away. "You won't have to feel guilty about it...."

"Don't be absurd," he interrupted. He ran his hand down her body and watched her tremble with reaction. "We're going to be very good together. I knew that the day I walked into Denny's office for the first time and sparks flew between us. I fought you hard, honey. I was even willing to throw you at Denny's innocent head to save myself. But it all misfired." His face clouded. "When you came in here this morning and told me he'd proposed, I think I went a little crazy. It was all I could do not to throw a punch at him when we left for the airport. I gave him hell all day, and he just sat there and grinned at me. When you came flying into my arms at the airport, I began to understand what was going on."

She arched close to him, gasping as she felt the impact of his skin against every inch of hers. She nuzzled her face into his throat and let him feel the trembling of her body.

"I didn't have any pride left by then," she whispered shakily. "I was scared silly. I still am."

"Is that why you're trembling?" he murmured wickedly. He let his hands run down her back to press her even closer. "It's contagious, too," he added as his own body began to answer that wild shudder.

"I won't ask you for anything," she whispered. "I...I have to be independent."

He folded her close and kissed her flushed face, light, tender kisses that belied the hunger she could feel growing in his big, taut body.

"You can be independent to a certain point," he agreed. "But I'll want you with me when I travel. I don't want to spend nights away from you."

She found it increasingly hard to think as his hands began to move in strange, sweet patterns on her body, exploring her with an expertise that was at once embarrassing and wildly sensuous.

"You...you want us to be together more than just...on weekends?" she asked, tingling all over at the thought of being with him every night. Even if it only lasted for a few weeks, it would be all of heaven.

"Um-hmmm," he agreed, bending his head to drag his lips over her breasts, lingering on the taut peaks until she moaned wildly.

"For how long, though?" she managed. Her body was getting out of control, going its own way with a reckless abandon that startled her.

"Oh, fifty years or so," he murmured against her warm, flat stomach. "Maybe a few more than that...."

"Fifty years?" she burst out.

He lifted his head and arched an eyebrow at her. "Well, that's a pretty conservative guess, of course," he told her. "What with all these damned wonder drugs... Will you lie down and stop interrupting me? I thought you wanted to make love."

"I do...but...?"

"It's going to be love, too, Kenna," he said, and all the humor was gone out of his face, leaving it quiet and tender. He moved over her, resting his weight on his forearms to study her face while he shifted his warm, abrasive chest across her softness and smiled shamelessly at her helpless response. "It's going to be the sweetest, wildest expression of love you've ever imagined."

Her eyes were wide with love and passion and she was just barely hearing him. She felt an ache that had nothing to do with sore muscles.

"I love you, didn't you know?" he asked, holding her eyes. "Never more than when I thought I'd lost you to Denny, and I walked out the door hurting in so many ways that I didn't know how I was going to live. You will marry me, won't you?"

Tears sprang to her eyes. "Yes. Oh yes! I'd follow you barefooted through the snow," she whispered brokenly, "if you wanted me to."

"I know that," he said roughly. "I'd do the same for you. My God, I love you!"

Her arms reached up to bring him down to her. "Show me," she whispered tearfully. "And teach me how to show you."

He bent slowly to touch his open mouth to hers. "What a sweet thought," he whispered ardently. "Don't be nervous. I'm going to treat you like three-hundred-year-old china."

She tangled her trembling hands in his thick, dark hair. "I only want to please you," she whispered against the increasing intimacy of his lips.

"You will," he whispered. "And I'll please you, if it takes all night."

His hands touched her gently, in new ways, in wildly pleasing ways, until the flames burned high and bright and beautiful. And he watched her the whole time, his dark eyes tender and loving as he took her with him on a roller coaster. All the books Kenna had read hadn't prepared her for the sensations she learned as he eased her again and again into a perfect frenzy of pleasure only to calm her and soothe her and start over again. Time dissolved into a kaleidoscope of movement and urgent whispers and a pleasure that bordered on agony, until his incredible control finally gave out. She learned the mystery of total possession in such a storm of hunger that she didn't even notice whether there was pain.

Later, lying spent, her face wet with her own tears, she snuggled against his damp, pulsating chest, and could barely believe where she'd been. He was propped up on the pillows, looking down at her, and finally she was able to slide her head down his arm far enough to see his face.

"You liar," she whispered, shaken. "Only a few wild oats, my foot! Where did you learn how to do that? Never mind," she added quickly, touching his lips to keep the words back, "I don't want to know."

He arched an eyebrow. "Well, you said yourself that God compensated me for being ugly, didn't you?"

She laughed wearily, delightedly, smoothing the dark hair away from his broad forehead. "Oh, my darling, you'll never be ugly. Not to me. I love every break in your nose, and your big feet, and your ferocious scowl, and your temper...."

"You could have stopped at loving me, you know," he murmured lazily, "without enumerating my bad points."

"And I haven't even gotten to the best part," she grinned, blushing wildly as she realized how that sounded.

He laughed delightedly, and folded her against his side. "Imp. Delightful imp. Did I hurt you very much?"

"That's what I've been trying to tell you," she confessed, nuzzling her face against his. "I don't know. I really don't know, I was so out of my mind...Regan, will it always be like this for us, even when we're old and wrinkled?"

"Speak for yourself, I don't plan to get old. Just better. I'll improve with age." He kissed her softly. "So will you. We'll just better away together."

She laughed softly. "Or love away. I adore you."

"I adore you."

She sighed and stretched. "I'm so sleepy...do you suppose it will shock the household if you stay all night?"

"Dad will give us amused looks, Denny will grin, and Abbie will ask when I expect to make an honest woman of you. But no one will be shocked. They already know how it is with us. I think they knew before we did." He crushed out the cigarette in the ashtray by the bed and turned off the light. "You'd better sleep while you can. I have plans for you around dawn."

She giggled delightedly and snuggled close as he pulled the covers over them. She drank in the fragrance of his big body and drowned in love and the glory of sharing it. Her eyes opened, seeking him in the dim light from the moon outside the window.

"Regan?" she asked softly.

"What, darling?" he murmured sleepily.

"I'll give you a child."

"Yes." He drew her closer, like the most precious kind of treasure. Neither of them said "to replace the one you lost," but it was between them, all the same. She smiled, thinking about how it would be, the two of them and a little boy or a little girl to share their love with. Tears came to her eyes. I'll take care of him for you, Jessica, she said silently. And outside in the cool darkness, a nightbird began to sing.

This Matter of Marriage
by Debbie Macomber

For Paula and Dianne
You know why

One

Starting Now

January 1

A new year generally starts out with me writing a few in-spiring lines about how I'm going to lose five pounds—let's be honest, it's ten—and pay off all my credit cards and other high expectations like that. It's the same every January. But <u>this</u> year's going to be different. Oh, I still want to lose those extra pounds, more than ever, but for a different reason.

I want a husband. And eventually a family.

And that means I need a plan. Being a goal-oriented person, I usually begin by identifying what I'm after (MAR-RIAGE!!) and then I work out a logical procedure for get-ting it. Which, in this case, includes <u>looking good</u>. (Not that I look bad now, if I do say so myself. But I'm talking <u>really</u> good. Are you listening, thighs?) Because, as I've learned in advertising, <u>packaging counts.</u>

Putting all this into words is something of an eye-opener for me. I've come a long way from those college days when I refused to give in to what I called the "female es-cape route," like some of my friends. Cassie, Jamie, Rita and Jane all got married within six months of graduation, and as far as I could see, the only reason they did was because they found the real world more of a challenge than they'd anticipated, and used marriage as a cop-out.

Not me. Oh, no, marriage was much too conventional for me. I wanted to kick some butt in the business world first. Make a name for myself with my very own graphic arts firm. And I've done it! Now I feel like I've come full circle. I've accomplished a <u>lot</u>, and I won't minimize my achievements, but this Christmas I realized there's more to life than getting the Woman of the Year award from the Chamber of Commerce.

So, last week I made <u>the</u> decision: <u>Marriage!</u>

It's time to let a man into my life. Until now I've viewed relationships like...dessert. Nice occasionally, but not with every meal. My friends have been tossing potential husbands in my direction for years, and I've frustrated them again and again.

I'm too picky, that's what Rita says. Not true. I have my standards; every woman does. But my work's the reason I haven't married. I've poured my heart into making a success of Artistic License. For the past six years my focus, my talent and all my energy have been with the business. It's filled every waking minute.

Then, this Christmas it hit me. <u>I want more</u>. I suspect this has something to do with losing Dad last June. Mom's still struggling, but then so are Julie and I. The holidays were really hard without him. Somehow, the celebration seemed empty and sad, and we were all kind of weepy thinking about the Christmas things he used to do—getting the tree every year and making a big deal out of hanging the decorations Julie and I made when we were kids. Reading the Nativity story on Christmas Eve. Putting on his Santa apron to carve the turkey. Things like that.

I'm so sorry Dad missed his granddaughter's first Christmas. I knew Julie's baby would help Mom through the grieving process, but I didn't expect little Ellen to have such a profound effect on me.

I've always thought of myself as the strong independent type. I haven't wanted a man around for fear I might be forced to admit I <u>need</u> someone. I don't know why I'm like this. (Then again, I'm not sure I want to know, either.) The point is, I feel differently now.

It started when Julie gave me the baby to rock. I swear my heart melted when I held her. In that moment I felt something I can only describe as maternal instinct, and I realized <u>this</u> is what I want. This is what's been missing from my life. A husband, a family.

With the right husband, I know I can have it all. Home, family and career. Plenty of women do it, and I can, too. Funny how a little thing like holding a baby can change a person's attitude. I'm ready. Past ready. Starting now, my life's taken an abrupt turn. What was vital a month ago has shifted to the back burner.

So, yes, I admit it.

I want a husband and children. Obviously, what I need first is the man. (I plan to do things in the right order!)

Mom always says that once I make up my mind I don't let anything stand in my way. I've set my goal, made my plans, and I figure I should find a husband in two, three months, tops. This time next year, I expect to be a married woman. (Maybe even a pregnant one!)

Just how difficult can it be?

Sweat rolled down Hallie McCarthy's forehead, dripping in her eyes and momentarily blurring her vision. Using the towel draped around her neck, she wiped her brow. Although she'd promised herself she wouldn't, Hallie glanced at the timer on the treadmill.

One minute left.

Sixty short seconds. She could endure that. With a renewed sense of purpose, she picked up her pace and waited impatiently for the buzzer.

The treadmill had all the bells and whistles, as it should, considering what she'd paid for it (plus the three designer running suits, color-coordinated with the treadmill). At the end of her workout a digital message would flash across the four-inch computer screen, complimenting her on a job well-done.

Donnalee had suggested she join a gym to meet men, and she would, Hallie told herself, once she was at her goal weight. But not now. She wasn't about to go prancing around a gym with thighs that resembled ham hocks. Which, she supposed, was something like cleaning her house before the cleaning lady arrived—but she'd done that, too.

Huffing, her heart feeling ready to explode, Hallie gripped the sides of the treadmill as the timer counted down those final seconds. This last minute was proving to be the longest of her life.

Needing a distraction to take her mind off the physical agony while she raced toward an imaginary finish line, Hallie turned to look out her living-room window at the luxury condominium next door.

Hey, she was getting a new neighbor. A moving van was parked in front and a crew of able-bodied men—*very* able-bodied, she noted appreciatively—unloaded its contents. A big truck that probably required a step stool to climb into was parked behind it. The license-plate frame was one of those customized ones. Squinting, she was able to make out the words: BIG TRUCK. BIG TOOLS. Hallie groaned aloud and rolled her eyes. Men and their egos! Two muscular guys wandered into her line of vision, and she wondered if one of those good-looking hunks might be her neighbor.

Willow Woods, the condominium complex where she'd moved six months earlier, had all but sold out. She'd speculated it wouldn't take long for the place next to hers to sell. Especially since it was a three-bedroom unit, the most spacious design available. Must be a family moving in. She was definitely cheered by the thought of having neighbors.

The timer went off, and the treadmill ground to a halt. Hallie heaved a sigh of relief and rubbed her sweat-drenched face with the towel. Her cheeks felt red and hot and her short curly hair was matted against her temples. Her old gray sweats—she didn't feel comfortable sweating in her new color-coordinated ones—were loose around the waist. A promising sign. The temptation to run into the bathroom and leap on the scale was strong, but she'd made that mistake too often and vowed she'd only weigh herself once a week. Monday morning, bright and early—that was when she'd do it.

She'd lost five pounds in twenty-one days. The first two had fallen away easily, but the last three had been like chiseling at a concrete block with a tablespoon. She'd starved herself, exercised faithfully. She'd counted fat grams, carbohydrates, calories and chocolate chips to little avail.

Her best friend, Donnalee Cooper, claimed Hallie was putting too much stock in the physical, but Hallie believed otherwise. It was that packaging thing again. The men she knew based their reactions to women—at least their initial reactions—on looks. It didn't matter if the woman had a brain in her head as long as her waist was tiny...and her other assets weren't. Of course, attracting a man wasn't Hallie's *only* incentive for becoming physically fit. She didn't exercise nearly enough, had taken to skipping breakfast and was downing fast food on the run. Not a healthy life-style. Donnalee seemed unconvinced when Hallie explained this, though, pointing out that she hadn't worried about her health *before*.

Donnalee was single, although she'd had a brief disastrous marriage in her early twenties. To Hallie's delight, when she'd shared her goal of finding a man and marrying within the next twelve months, Donnalee had decided to join forces with her. She said that she'd never meant to wait this long to remarry, and like Hallie, she wanted children. But Donnalee brought a different strategy to their marriage campaign.

"Just be yourself," she'd advised.

"Being myself hasn't attracted a whole lot of attention so far," Hallie complained. That, at least, shut her friend up. Dating opportunities had dwindled to a trickle in the last few years, but she was determined to improve the situation.

Hallie showered and changed clothes, then phoned her mother who lived across Puget Sound in Bremerton, on the Kitsap Peninsula. Hallie and her father had been close, both in personality and in appearance, but it was from her mother that she'd inherited her artistic talent. Despite her ability, Lucille McCarthy had never worked outside the home. It had always troubled Hallie that a woman so genuinely talented would be content to do little more than keep house. Not until she was an adult living on her own did she recognize her mother's contribution to the family. Over the months since her father's sudden death, Hallie had come to appreciate her mother's quiet strength. At Christmas, she'd encouraged her to take up oil painting, and Lucille had recently begun a class.

The conversation went well, with Lucille cheerfully describing the portrait she'd started to paint of a sleeping Ellen. Afterward, Hallie wrote her weekly grocery list, threw on a jacket and hurried out the door, eager to finish her Saturday-morning chores. It was when she climbed into her car that she saw her new neighbor. At least, she thought he was the one. He was tall and not as brawny as she'd thought at first glance. Solid, she decided. All shoulders, with good upper-body strength. Handsome, too, in an unobtrusive way. In other words, seeing him didn't make her heart beat faster—which was just as well, since he was obviously married with children.

He did have an interesting face, a lived-in face, and seemed the type of person she'd like to know. Not romantically, of course, but maybe as a friend. She turned her attention from him to the two kids at his side. A girl and boy, who were probably about eleven and nine. Great-looking kids. The girl waved, her smile wide and friendly.

Hallie waved back, inserted the key into the ignition and drove off.

The moving van was gone by the time she returned an hour or so later. The two kids were riding their bicycles when she pulled into her driveway.

The girl headed her way, long coltish legs pumping the bicycle pedals.

"Hi," she called. "My dad just moved next door." She stopped abruptly and hopped off the polished chrome bike.

"So I saw," Hallie said, leaning across the front seat and removing her bags of groceries.

"I'm Meagan. That's my brother, Kenny." She nodded toward the younger boy, and as if on cue, Kenny joined his sister.

"You got any kids?" Kenny asked hopefully.

"Sorry, no." She balanced both grocery bags in her arms.

Some of the enthusiasm left the boy's eyes. "Do you know anyone around here who does?"

"Unfortunately, I don't think there are any kids your age on this block." Most of the couples who'd moved into the complex were just starting out. Hallie suspected there'd be any number of children in the neighborhood within a few years, but not now.

"Here," Meagan said, tilting her bike onto the grass. "I can help you carry those in." She took one bag out of Hallie's hands.

"Thanks." Hallie was touched by her thoughtfulness and said so.

The girl beamed at the praise. "Mom says I'm a big help to her now that she and Dad are divorced."

Meagan's expression grew sad when she mentioned the divorce. Hallie's heart immediately went out to her—but she couldn't help musing that her new neighbor was available, after all. It was an automatic reaction, triggered by her newly activated husband-seeking instincts.

Hallie briefly recalled her first impressions of him and decided then and there that she wanted someone with a bit more...finesse. A guy who drove a truck with a license-plate holder advertising his big tools didn't overly impress her. It wasn't only that, either; she'd seen what the movers had carted into his house. Sports equipment. Boxes and boxes of it. There didn't seem to be anything this guy hadn't tried. From mountain climbing to kayaking to scuba diving.

Hallie led the way into the kitchen, where she dumped her sack on the countertop. Meagan carefully put hers beside it. "Thanks again, Meagan."

"Are you married?" the girl asked.

"Not yet." But there were visions of entwined wedding rings dancing around in her head. She had a prospect, too. A man she'd just met yesterday, as a matter of fact.

"Well, gotta go have lunch. See you next weekend," Meagan said, rushing for the front door.

As Hallie started to put the groceries away, she saw that the message light on her answering machine was blinking. Probably her mother again, or her sister, Julie, calling to report on baby Ellen's latest adorable exploit. But what if it was *him? Him* being the new loans officer at Keystone Bank. Hallie had gone in on Friday afternoon to make her deposits and been introduced to John Franklin.

The minute she'd laid eyes on him she realized he was everything she sought in a husband. Tall, dark and handsome. Friendly, polite and clearly intelligent. He met all the basic criteria, including availability; she'd noticed the absence of a wedding ring. He was close to forty, she estimated, but that didn't disturb her. An eleven-year gap didn't make much difference, not at her age. She'd be thirty in April, three months from now. Surely she'd be engaged by then.

Unfortunately the message wasn't from John. It was from Donnalee, who sounded excited and asked Hallie to phone the minute she walked in the door.

Hallie rang her back. "You called?"

"I've found the answer," Donnalee blurted.

"What's the question?" Hallie grumbled in response; she hadn't had lunch and was never at her best on an empty stomach.

"Where do we meet the men of our dreams?"

"Hmm." Her friend certainly had her attention now. "Where?"

"The answer's a bit complicated, so stay with me."

"Donnalee..."

"All I ask is that you hear me out. All right?"

Hallie muttered a reply. This dating thing had been much easier in high school and college. Apparently she'd lost the knack. Oh, there'd been a few romances in the years since, most of them what you'd call short-term. One had lasted the better part of six months, until it, too, fizzled out. The fault, Hallie admitted, had been her own. Gregg had complained about her long hours and her total commitment to Artistic License, and she'd told him that wasn't likely to change.

"I found an ad in the *Seattle Weekly* for a dating service," Donnalee announced.

Hallie groaned. As far as she was concerned, only people who were desperate resorted to dating services. She didn't even want to *think* about the kind of men who applied to meet women that way. "You're joking, right?"

"You promised you'd hear me out."

Hallie closed her eyes and prayed for patience. "Okay, okay. Tell me all about it and *then* I'll tell you I'm not interested."

"This is different."

"They use videos, right?"

"No," Donnalee said indignantly. "Would you kindly listen?"

"Sorry."

"You and I are successful businesswomen. Most men are intimidated by women like us."

Hallie wasn't convinced *that* was true, but didn't say so.

"In my case, I've been married once and it was a disaster."

"That was over thirteen years ago."

"Soon it'll be fifteen and then twenty, and my whole life will have passed me by. All because I made a stupid mistake when I was barely out of my teens. Hallie, I want a man in my life."

"The whole nine yards," Hallie added.

"Children, the house in the suburbs with a white picket fence. Cat, dog, family vacations. I can't believe I've put it off this long! I'd probably still be putting it off if you hadn't come up with your plan."

"You're saying you want me to contact a dating service, too?"

"Would you *listen,* darn it? First you have to apply and if you're accepted, you pay a hefty fee and they'll arrange for you to meet a suitable match. One on the same financial level as you, whose personality fits yours. The woman I talked to claims they're very selective and only take on a certain number of clients. If you're accepted, the company is committed to finding you a match."

"How hefty is the fee?" Hallie had recently forked over fifteen hundred bucks on exercise equipment. So much for paying off her credit cards.

Donnalee hesitated a moment. "Two grand."

"Two thousand dollars!"

"Yup."

"I damn well better get a date with Brad Pitt for that."

Donnalee laughed. "Brad wouldn't date someone as old as either of us."

Her friend's words were of little comfort. "You aren't serious, are you?" For that kind of money Hallie figured she could have liposuction and forget the treadmill and the dieting.

"Yup," Donnalee said with a hint of defiance. "I'm thirty-three. I don't have as much time as you. If this agency can help me find a decent man, then I'd consider the money well spent."

"You *are* serious."

"Just think of it as a shortcut."

Hallie still wasn't sold. "I haven't actually started looking yet." Using a dating service felt like waving a white flag before she'd even stepped onto the battlefield. Surrendering without so much as a token effort.

"What are you going to do, wear a sandwich board that says AVAILABLE in big black letters?" Donnalee asked.

"Don't be ridiculous."

"You've had your entire life to find a husband, and you haven't. What makes you think it's going to be different now?"

"Because I'm ready." This probably wasn't the time to remind her friend that she'd had relationships over the years, the most promising one with Gregg. While it was true that those relationships had grown fewer and fewer, and her social life had become rather dull, she'd barely noticed, working the hours she did. However, since the first of the year, she'd taken measures to correct that, delegating more responsibility to Bonnie Ellis, her assistant.

"And your being ready for marriage changes everything?" Donnalee sounded skeptical. She sounded skeptical a little too often, in Hallie's opinion.

"There's a man I'm interested in right now," Hallie confessed, thinking of John Franklin.

"Really? Who?"

She should've guessed Donnalee would demand details.

"A banker," she answered with some reluctance. "He's the new loans officer at the Kent branch of Keystone Bank. He transferred this week from the downtown Seattle branch. We met Friday, if you must know. I liked him immediately and he liked me. He's really good-looking. Sensitive, too."

"Good-looking and sensitive," Donnalee repeated.

"Single good-looking men are hard to find," Hallie insisted, wondering at her friend's slightly sarcastic tone.

"That's because the majority of them have boyfriends."

Hallie paused. John? Was it possible? "Do you know John Franklin?" Since Donnalee managed a mortgage company, she was familiar with many bankers in the area.

"I know *of* him."

Hallie's suspicions mounted. "What do you mean?"

"John Franklin's the perfect reason you need the services of Date-line."

"Oh?" Her confidence was shaken.

"You're right," Donnalee continued. "John's sensitive, friendly, personable and handsome as sin. He also happens to be gay."

Hallie's spirits sank to the level of bedrock. John Franklin. Hmm. With some men it was obvious and with others...well, with others, it wasn't.

"So, are you going to join Dateline?" Donnalee asked.

"Two thousand dollars?"

"Consider it cheap since the men are screened."

"If Brad Pitt's out, then for that kind of money they'd better come up with royalty."

"If they do, kid, I've got first dibs," Donnalee said with a laugh.

"I'll look into Dateline, but I'm not making any promises."

"Just call and they'll mail you a brochure. Phone me once you've read it over. Promise?"

"Okay, okay," Hallie mumbled, and wrote down the number. She replaced the telephone receiver and shook her head. Who'd ever have thought this matter of marriage could be so complicated?

Two

Breaking Up Is Hard To Do

Steve Marris's day wasn't going well. A parts shipment was lost somewhere in the Midwest, his secretary had quit without notice, and he suspected his ex-wife was dating again. The parts shipment would eventually be found and he could hire another secretary, but the news about Mary Lynn was harder to take.

He poured himself a cup of coffee and noted that it'd been at least a month since anyone had bothered to clean the glass pot. He'd make damn sure his next secretary didn't come with an attitude. This last one had refused to make coffee, claiming she'd been hired for her secretarial skills—not that they'd been so impressive. And she'd never understood that in *his* shop, everybody pitched in. No, he was well rid of her.

He sipped the hot liquid and grimaced. Todd Stafford must have put on this pot. His production manager made the world's worst coffee. Steve dumped it and rinsed his mug, then sat down at his desk, sorting through the papers amassed there until he found the invoice he needed.

Todd opened the door. "You going to sit in here all day and fume about Danielle quitting?"

Todd was talking about their recently departed secretary. "Naw, we're better off without her."

Todd came into the office, reached for a coffee mug and filled it. He pulled out Danielle's chair and plopped himself down, propping his feet on the desk. "If it isn't Danielle walking out, then my guess is you're sulking about Mary Lynn."

His friend knew him too well. "I heard she's dating again."

"Heard? Who from?"

"Kenny," Steve admitted reluctantly.

"You're grilling your kids for information about your ex-wife?"

"I know better than that." Steve experienced a twinge of guilt. He hadn't *intentionally* asked his nine-year-old if his mother was dating. Kenny had been talking about joining a softball team in the spring, all excited about playing shortstop. He'd wanted his mother to toss him a few balls, he'd told Steve, but she couldn't because she was getting ready for a date. The kid had Steve's full attention at that point. It hadn't taken much to get Kenny to tell him Mary Lynn was seeing Kip somebody or other.

What the hell kind of name was Kip, anyway? Sounded like a guy who traipsed around in ballet slippers.

"So, what'd you find out?"

Steve ignored the question. He didn't like *thinking* about Mary Lynn dating another man, let alone talking about it. What had happened between them was painful even now, a full year after their divorce. An idea struck him suddenly, and he marveled at the genius of it. "I wonder if Mary Lynn might consider filling in here at the office until I can hire another secretary."

"She hates it here," Todd muttered. He sipped his coffee, seeming to savor every drop. "You know that."

What his friend said was true, but Steve welcomed the opportunity to spend time with her. She might even tell him about Kip. "It couldn't hurt to ask," he returned, sorry now that he'd said anything to Todd.

"You're divorced."

"Thanks, I guess I must've forgotten." Steve glared at him, hoping his sarcasm hit its mark.

"It's time to move on, old buddy. Mary Lynn has."

Steve rose abruptly from his chair. "Shouldn't you get to work?"

"All right, so I touched a raw nerve. No reason to bite my head off." Todd hurried back to the shop, and Steve swallowed his irritation. Damn it, he still loved Mary Lynn. No one had told him how painful this divorce business would be.

They'd been married twelve years and fool that he was, Steve had assumed they were happy. Then, one day out of the blue, Mary Lynn had started crying. When he'd tried to find out what was wrong, she couldn't say—except that she was unhappy. They'd married too young, she'd missed out on all the fun, all the carefree years, and now here she was, stuck with a husband, kids, responsibilities. Steve tried to understand her concerns, but everything he said and did only made matters worse. The thing that really got him was her claim that she'd never had her own bedroom. As it turned out, that was more important than he'd realized, because she asked him to move out of theirs shortly afterward.

Steve had called her bluff, firmly believing it *was* a bluff. He'd voluntarily moved out of the house, thinking that would help her "find herself," something she apparently couldn't do with him there. She needed to make contact with her "inner child," become "empowered" or some other such garbage. Okay, maybe he wasn't the most sensitive man in the world. She became incensed when he suggested she was watching too many of those daytime talk shows. Then, a month or so after he'd left, Mary Lynn shocked him by asking for a divorce. Before he could fully comprehend what was happening, they'd each hired lawyers and were soon standing in front of a judge.

By that time, with attorneys involved, things had gotten heated, and he and Mary Lynn were more at odds than ever. It'd taken over a year to even start repairing the damage the attorneys and courts had done. He was sick of living apart from his family. He wanted his wife back.

Never mind what Todd had said—he *would* ask Mary Lynn to fill in for Danielle. Just until he could hire another secretary. Just until he could convince her that being apart was pure insanity.

Feeling pleased with himself, he reached for the phone. Mary Lynn answered on the third ring. "Hello," she murmured groggily.

She never had been much of a morning person. "Hi. It's Steve."

"Steve. Good grief, what time is it?"

"Nine."

"Already?"

He could hear her rustling the sheets in an effort to sit up. During their marriage, he'd loved waking her, having her cuddle against him all soft and warm and feminine, smelling of some exotic flower. Their best loving had been in the mornings.

"What's wrong?" she asked, and yawned loudly.

"Nothing. Well, my secretary quit."

She went very quiet, and he could almost hear her resentment over the telephone line. "I don't type, Steve, you know that."

After all those years together, Mary Lynn could read him like a book. He took a certain perverse pride in that. "I need someone to fill in for a few days until I can hire a new secretary."

"What about getting a temporary?"

"Sure, I could call an agency and they'd send someone out, but I'd rather give you the money."

"I've got school. It isn't easy for me attending classes all afternoon plus keeping up with the kids and the house, you know."

"I realize that, but it'd help me out considerably if you came in for a couple of days, just in the mornings. That's all I'm asking."

Since paying for her education had been part of the settlement, he was well aware of her schedule.

"You always say that!" she snapped.

"What?" This conversation was quickly taking on the same tone as their arguments before the divorce. He'd say or do something that irritated her, and for the life of him, he wouldn't understand what he'd done.

"You *say* you realize how difficult my schedule is. You don't."

"I do, honest."

"If you did, you'd never ask me to pitch in while you take your own sweet time finding a new secretary. I know you, Steve Marris. Two days'll become two weeks and I won't be able to keep up with my classes. That's what you really want, whether you know it or not. You're trying to sabotage my schoolwork."

Steve choked back an argument. "I understand how important your classes are," he said. And he did. What he failed to understand was why her getting an education precluded being married to him. Not only that, he wondered what she intended to do with a major in art history. Get a job in some museum, he supposed—if there were any jobs to be had. But he certainly couldn't say that to her.

"Do you really, Steve?"

"Yes," he said, still struggling to show his respect for her efforts. "It's just that I thought since your classes don't start until one, you might be willing to help out, but if you can't, you can't."

She hesitated and he closed in for the kill.

"All I need is a couple of hours in the morning. And like I said, if you can't do it, that's fine. No hard feelings."

"Do you realize how much reading I have, how many assignments?"

"You're right, I never should have asked. I guess that's been the problem all along, hasn't it?"

"Yes," she agreed sharply. Then there was a pause. And a sigh. "I guess I could fill in for a couple of days, but no longer. I want to make that perfectly clear. Two days and not a minute longer, understand?"

"Perfectly." Steve wanted to leap up and click his heels in the air. Calling Mary Lynn had been one of his better ideas. He was confident it wouldn't take long to make her forget all about this other guy.

"I hope you don't want me there before eight?"

He let the question slide. "You're wearing the pink nightie, aren't you?"

"Steve!"

"Aren't you?" His voice grew husky despite his attempts to keep it even. Some of their best sex had come after the divorce. It was so crazy. Mary Lynn wanted him out of the house but continued to welcome him in her bed. Not that he was complaining.

"Yes, I'm wearing your favorite nightie," she whispered, her voice low and sexy.

Slowly his eyes drifted shut. "I'm coming over."

"Steve, no. I can't. We can't."

"Why not?"

"Well, because we shouldn't."

Steve was instantly suspicious, convinced her decision had something to do with what Kenny had told him. "Why?"

"We're divorced, remember?"

"It hasn't stopped us before. I could be at the house in fifteen minutes. You want me there, otherwise you'd never have told me about the pink nightie."

Mary Lynn giggled, then altered her tone. "Steve, no, I mean it," she said solemnly. "We've been divorced for a year now. We shouldn't be sleeping together anymore."

His jaw tightened. "When did you make that decision?"

"Since the last time."

He exhaled, his patience fading fast. He did a quick review of their last rendezvous. It'd been late morning, before her classes and while the kids were in school. He'd invented some excuse to stop over. Mary Lynn knew what he wanted, and from the gleam in her eye and the eager way she'd led him into the bedroom, she'd wanted the same thing.

He couldn't imagine what had changed, other than her dating this Kip character. Unfortunately he couldn't ask her about it or let on that he knew. The last thing he wanted was to put his children in the middle, between two squabbling parents, something he'd seen other divorced couples do all too often. The divorce had been hard enough on Meagan and Kenny without complicating the situation. So their private lives, his and Mary Lynn's, would stay that way—private. At least as far as the kids were concerned.

"What happened to change your mind about us sleeping together?" he asked, instead.

Mary Lynn sighed. "Nothing. Everything. We have to break this off. It's over for us, Steve."

Steve didn't say anything. He knew his wife—ex-wife—well

enough not to argue. Something else he knew about Mary Lynn—she possessed a healthy sexual appetite. As strong as his own.

"You'll be here in the morning, then?" he said, just to be sure.

"I suppose. But remember I agreed to two days, and two days only."

"Bring along the pink nightie."

"Steve!"

"Sorry," he murmured, but he wasn't.

He hung up the phone a few moments later, his mood greatly improved.

The rest of his day was relatively smooth. The transport company located the lost shipment in Albuquerque. The parts were guaranteed to be delivered within the next forty-eight hours. The majority of his orders came from a major aircraft builder in the area, for whom he supplied engine mounts, but he also did lathe work, blanchard grinding and other steel-fabrication work for a number of customers. His company was growing, taking on larger and larger orders, and he employed almost a dozen people now.

On the drive home that afternoon, Steve's gaze fell on his hands—clean hands—gripping the steering wheel. He used to have grease under his fingernails, and that had always bothered Mary Lynn. The irony didn't escape him. The last year and a half, he'd spent the majority of his time in the office and rarely dirtied his hands. She'd always wanted him to have a white-collar job; when he was finally able to grant her wish, she wanted him out of her life. Damn it all, the machine shop had been good to them—it had bought her house, supported the kids, paid for her education. A little grime around his fingernails seemed a small inconvenience.

The January drizzle grew heavier, and the truck's windshield wipers beat against the glass, slapping the rain from side to side with annoying regularity. He exited the freeway and headed down the west hill toward Kent. He hadn't been keen to buy the condominium. If he'd had a choice, he'd be moving back in with his family, but it was going to take longer than he'd first thought for that to happen.

He probably wouldn't have moved into this complex if he hadn't grown tired of apartment living. A small apartment was no place for kids, and Meagan and Kenny spent almost every weekend with him.

He would have preferred a real house but living on his own, he didn't want the bother that went along with it. The condo was a decent compromise. A friend who sold real estate had convinced him it was a good investment. In addition, the builders were offering an attractive buyer-incentive program. The condo was just as nice as the house Mary Lynn and the kids lived in. Not quite as big, but that was okay. The kids liked it, and they'd managed to make friends with his next-door neighbor in short order too, he mused, as he switched off his windshield wipers. The rain had tapered off to almost nothing.

Steve hadn't met Hallie yet—Meagan had told him her name. From what he'd seen of her, she was an exercise freak. His kitchen window overlooked her living room, and she had a treadmill set up there, alongside one of those stair-stepping machines. Every time he caught a glimpse of her she was working out. She didn't seem to be enjoying herself, either.

Steve turned into the Willow Woods complex and stopped in front of the two rows of mailboxes aligned at the entrance. It wasn't until he climbed out of the truck that he saw her. Hallie stood in front of her mailbox studying a large envelope as if she wasn't sure what to do with it.

"Howdy, neighbor," he greeted her, inserting the key into his mailbox.

Startled, she looked up. "Hello."

"Steve Marris." He thrust out his hand. "I moved in next door this past weekend."

She blinked a couple of times. "You're Meagan and Kenny's dad."

"That's me."

"Hallie McCarthy." She placed her hand in his. "Nice to meet you."

"Same here."

"You've got two terrific kids."

"Thanks," he said, and smiled. He felt that way, too.

With a nervous motion, Hallie glanced down at the envelope she still held, then shoved it into her purse. "Well, uh, Steve, I have to go. I'm sure we'll be seeing each other again."

Steve had caught the logo on the envelope. Dateline. He'd heard plenty about the pricey exclusive dating service. Shortly after the divorce, a well-meaning friend had tried to talk him into signing up, but he'd recoiled at the idea of paying two thousand bucks for a date. He'd have to be a whole lot more desperate than he was now before he'd even consider it.

Hallie raised her head just then. "I... A friend suggested I write for information," she blurted. Her cheeks had turned a bright shade of pink. "I'd never..." She paused, squared her shoulders and gave him a smile that was decidedly forced. "I want you to know I don't need any help finding a man.'' Head high, with a dignity Princess Diana would have envied, Hallie McCarthy walked to her car. However, the speed with which she drove off kind of spoiled the effect.

Watching her leave, Steve slowly shook his head. Maybe he should steer the kids away from her. She seemed nice enough, but a little on the weird side.

Three

Seven Down, Three To Go

A rare burst of February sunshine showered Puget Sound, and after weeks of being cooped up inside for her daily exercise routine, Hallie decided to take advantage of this respite from the rain. She donned one of the three coordinated running outfits she'd purchased; it was a lovely teal green with a hot pink racing stripe up the outside of the legs and a geometrical design decorating the zippered jacket. If nothing else, Hallie knew she looked great—and she felt great. Seven of those ten unwanted pounds had vanished. Not without considerable effort, however.

She wasn't entirely confident that those pounds were gone for good. Were they hiding around the corner, waiting for her to lower her guard? One day away from the treadmill or succumbing to the temptation of a chocolate-chip cookie and they'd be back. Which was why she'd been so rigorous about her diet and exercise regimen. Three pounds to go, and she'd weigh the same as she had at her high-school graduation, more years ago than she cared to remember.

Goal weight. What perfectly lovely words they were.

She hoped she'd manage to achieve it before Valentine's Day. She'd set the target date back in January, giving herself ample time to reach her physical best. Already she'd let a few select friends— the ones who'd wanted to line her up with their single brothers, unattached male acquaintances and recently divorced colleagues— know she was in the market for a meaningful long-term relationship. She hadn't heard back yet, but it was still early.

She opened the front door and stepped into the welcome sunshine. It didn't take long to realize she wasn't the only one outside enjoying the warmth.

Her next-door neighbor and his son were playing catch in the front yard. She was afraid she'd started off on the wrong foot with Steve Marris, but wasn't sure how to correct that. Of all the rotten luck for him to see the envelope from Dateline! Her mistake had been not keeping her mouth shut. Oh, no, that would have been too easy. *She* had to go and blurt out some stupid, embarrassing remark. She wanted to groan every time she thought of it.

"Hi, Hallie."

Steve's daughter raced over to her. With no other kids around her age, Hallie thought, Meagan must get restless spending weekends with her father.

"Howdy, kiddo. What're you up to?"

"Nothing," she said in a bored voice. "Dad's teaching Kenny how to be a great shortstop. I don't like baseball much."

"Me, neither," Hallie said. It wasn't that she disliked sports; she just didn't understand the big attraction. A bunch of guys racing around a field or across some ice, all chasing a ball or whatever—what was the point?

Hallie raised her hands above her head and slowly exhaled before bending forward and touching her fingertips to the walkway. She wasn't sure of the reason for this, but she'd seen runners do it before a race, and she supposed they knew what they were doing. Warming up or something.

After a month on the treadmill, averaging two miles a day on a preset course that simulated a run on hilly terrain, Hallie thought she was ready for one real-life mile. From her car speedometer, she knew it was exactly half a mile to the entrance of Willow Woods. She figured she should be able to run there and back without a problem. Actually she hoped she wouldn't work up too much of a sweat, fearing it would leave marks on her new running suit.

"What are you doing now?" Meagan asked, watching her go through a series of bends and stretches.

"Getting ready to run."

"You run?" The kid seemed downright impressed.

"Sure."

"How far?"

"A mile." That was as much as she wanted to tackle her first time out. If it went well, she might consider longer distances later.

"Can I come, too?"

"If it's all right with your dad." Hallie shook her arms, then placed her hands on her hips while she rotated her head.

Meagan quickly ditched her bike on Hallie's lawn and raced toward her brother and father.

Hallie felt almost smug. Watching "Wild World of Sports" with Gregg had taught her something, after all. Or was that "Wide World of Sports"? She heard Meagan hurriedly ask permission and felt Steve's scrutiny before he agreed.

"Dad said I can," Meagan shouted, racing back.

In deference to Meagan, Hallie set a slow rhythmic pace as she started down the road. Meagan picked up the tempo as they rounded the first corner. Within minutes, Hallie became winded. That was understandable, she told herself, since they were running uphill. By the end of the third block, she felt the strain.

"It isn't a race," Hallie gasped when she found the oxygen to speak.

"Oh, am I going too fast for you? Sorry." Meagan immediately slowed down.

An eternity passed before the brick-walled entrance came into view. "I...think I'm...wearing the wrong...kind...of shoes," Hallie panted. She stopped, braced her hands on her knees and greedily sucked in as much air as her aching lungs would allow.

There wasn't a damn thing wrong with her shoes, and Hallie knew it.

"You okay?" Meagan looked worried.

"Fine...I feel great."

"Can you make it back? Do you want me to run and get my dad?"

Hallie wasn't about to let Steve Marris see her like this. She straightened and, with effort, managed to smile and act as if nothing was amiss. The burning sensation in her lungs made it nearly impossible to breathe normally. The good news was that the trek back was downhill. The bad news was that she was half a mile from home with an eleven-year-old kid who could run circles around her.

"I'm sure my dad wouldn't mind. He's real understanding."

Hallie lied through her teeth. "I'll be fine, no problem."

"You're sure?"

"Positive." Leave it to a kid to humiliate her. As for not sweating, that was a lost cause. Perspiration poured out of her, soaking her hair, beading her upper lip and forehead.

She made a respectable showing on the way back, jogging past her neighbor and his son toward her front porch. She collapsed on the top step and tried to look as if she'd been enjoying herself, which was something of a trick considering she felt like a candidate for CPR.

"Aren't you going to cool down?" Meagan asked.

"I thought I'd take a shower."

"Dad says you're supposed to walk after a run and give your body a chance to catch up with itself." Meagan strolled about, and Hallie joined her, soon discovering that, yes, this part of her workout she could handle. A cool breeze refreshed her, and after a couple of minutes her heart settled back into place.

After thanking Meagan for the company, Hallie turned to enter the house and saw a familiar car round the corner. Donnalee. Pleased to see her, Hallie waved. Both women led busy lives, and although they talked on the phone practically every day, they weren't able to get together nearly as often as they would have liked.

Donnalee was tall and svelte, a striking woman with thick shoulder-length auburn hair. She unfolded her long legs from the car and stood, wearing her elegance naturally, as much a part of her as her soft Southern drawl. They'd met through a mutual friend five years earlier and quickly become friends themselves. Their friendship had grown close; Hallie had much more in common with Donnalee—especially when it came to attitudes and values—than with her college friends. Most of them had married, and some were already on second husbands—while Hallie had yet to find a first. And she wanted her husband to be her first *and* last. She wanted a marriage like her parents'.

As professional businesswomen, Donnalee and Hallie shared a great many similar experiences. Over the past couple of years they'd become a support system for each other. If Hallie was having trouble with an employee or a customer or just about anything else, it was Donnalee she talked to. If Donnalee had a problem, it was Hallie she phoned. That they should both feel a need, at the same time, to change the focus of their lives didn't surprise Hallie. Their thoughts often followed the same paths. They read the same books, enjoyed the same movies, had many of the same tastes. In fact, two years earlier they'd gone shopping separately and purchased the same pair of shoes. The only difference was the color.

Hallie was a personable sort, and she'd had a lot of friends from the time she was in kindergarten, but she laughed more with Donnalee than she ever had with anyone. Laughed and cried. Donnalee was that kind of soul friend. That kind of real friend.

"Did you call them?" Donnalee asked.

"You know I did." Hallie opened her front door and led the way into the kitchen. She might have lacked culinary skills—she was the first to admit it—but she compensated for that with her artistic flair. The room was bright and cheery, decorated in yellow and white with ivy stenciled along the top of the walls. Hallie removed a plastic bottle of springwater from the refrigerator and poured herself a glass. Her throat felt parched.

Donnalee pulled out a stool at the kitchen counter and declined

Hallie's offer of water with a quick shake of her head. "What'd you think?"

"About the brochure?" Hallie decided to break the news quickly, before Donnalee could talk her into signing up. "I'm not going with Dateline."

Donnalee didn't bother to hide her disappointment. "You haven't talked to them, have you? Because if you had, you'd realize that this is the only practical way to break into the marriage market these days. It isn't like when we were in college, with eligible men in every direction."

"I know that, but I want to try it by myself first." Two thousand bucks wasn't anything to sneeze at, and Hallie figured the least she could do was try to meet someone on her own before resorting to spending big bucks. Besides, Donnalee made more money than she did; she could afford Dateline. Hallie's plan was to give it her best shot and wait to see what happened before maxing out her American Express card.

"I called Rita," Hallie confessed. Rita was the mutual friend who'd introduced Hallie to Donnalee. She had a reputation for being both unpredictable and romantic, and she wasn't above arranging dates for her friends.

Looking mildly worried, Donnalee leaned forward. "You didn't tell her I went to Dateline, did you?"

"No, don't worry. That's our little secret. All I said was that I had sort of an awakening this Christmas and decided it's time I committed myself to a long-term relationship." She smiled at the memory of their colleague's reaction. "Rita has this theory about my sudden desire to meet a man. She thinks it has to do with losing my dad, so she says I might end up in a situation I'll regret." Hallie shrugged comically. "After all these years of her pushing me to date one man or another, I would've figured she'd be pleased to know I was serious about getting married." Hallie paused, remembering the conversation. "When I told her I was ready for a family, she suggested I find myself a guy with good genes, get myself pregnant and dump him."

"Rita said that?"

Hallie nodded. "Awful, huh?" She liked Rita, made an effort to keep in touch, but they were basically very different kinds of people. For instance, Rita prided herself on saying the most outrageous things.

"I guess that's an idea if all you want is to have a child," Donnalee said hesitantly.

"Which I'm not. I'd also like a husband. I'm no fool—I watched my sister with Ellen and I don't know how she managed. A newborn demanded every minute of her time, even with Jason and Mom and me all helping. Fortunately for her, Jason's one of those really involved fathers. I don't know how *any* woman can manage alone. It's more than I want to attempt.''

"Me, too," Donnalee agreed, her drawl more noticeable than usual. Donnalee had moved from Georgia when she was thirteen, but had never quite lost the accent. Unexpectedly she grinned. "Can you imagine us as mothers?"

"Yes," Hallie said, although it seemed a stretch. She wondered if other women their age went through this. If so, it wasn't a subject her single friends discussed often or frankly. Many were like Donnalee, divorced and gun-shy. Hallie didn't have that excuse.

"Guess what? Dateline called me yesterday," Donnalee said, avoiding eye contact. She fiddled with the leather strap of her purse, opening and closing the zipper, a sure sign she was nervous. "They came up with a match for me." She darted a look in Hallie's direction.

"Already?" Hallie hated to say it, but she was impressed.

"They faxed over the pertinent information and asked me to review it and call back. So I did. Then Sanford phoned me an hour later and I'm meeting him for dinner this evening."

"Sanford?"

"I know. The picture of a stuffy conservative type immediately comes to mind, doesn't it, but then we spoke and..."

"And?" Hallie prodded when her friend didn't continue.

"He seems, I don't know, ideal."

"Ideal?" Dateline was beginning to sound better every minute.

"I'm frightened, Hallie. I felt the same way about Larry when I first met him, but what the hell did I know? I was nineteen and away from my family for the first time. I probably would've welcomed attention from a serial killer."

Donnalee didn't mention her ex very often. He'd dumped her for another woman after their first year of marriage. Donnalee's self-esteem had been shattered and her ego left in shreds. It'd taken a decade to regroup, and even then Hallie wasn't sure some of the damage wasn't permanent. She could appreciate her friend's fears and said so.

"But it's different this time," Hallie assured her. "You're not a kid governed by hormones."

"No, I'm thirty-three and governed by hormones."

They both laughed, and then Donnalee took a deep breath. "Okay.

Sanford's thirty-six and an insurance company executive. No priors."

"You mean he doesn't have a police record?" Hallie certainly hoped not!

"Means he's never been married. It's Dateline lingo."

"Oh." So the outfit even had a specialized vocabulary. Interesting. Or maybe not.

"We couldn't stop talking," Donnalee went on. "Sanford felt the way I did. We both signed up for Dateline the same week. He was just as nervous as I was about doing it. We were at work and we talked for more than half an hour. You know, he put me at ease right off and he said I did the same for him. It was as if we'd known each other all our lives. He loves Tex-Mex food, the same as me. He lives on a houseboat, which I've always thought of as wildly romantic. He'll watch anything Emma Thompson's in and reads Steve Martini novels. Can you believe it? I know this is all surface stuff, but it helps to know we're compatible. And at least we have lots of things to discuss." She broke into a radiant smile. "He was just as surprised and pleased after talking to me. We had trouble saying goodbye."

"He lives on a houseboat?" This guy was beginning to appeal to Hallie, too. Maybe if it didn't work out, Donnalee would consider introducing her.

"Now do you see why I'm a nervous wreck?"

Hallie nodded. She wouldn't be any less nervous herself.

"He sounds too good to be true," Donnalee moaned. "The minute I meet him, it'll be over."

"You don't know that." Hallie tried to sound confident, but she shared her friend's fears. There had to be a flaw in this guy somewhere. People weren't always what they seemed, and it was often the small undetectable-to-the-naked-eye character defects that threw her.

"At first I wondered why someone this successful and charming hadn't been married," she continued, as if thinking out loud, "but his letter explains all that." At Hallie's questioning look, she added, "Dateline enclosed a letter he'd written to introduce himself. He's been waiting to marry because he wanted to pay off his college loans. Financial security is important to him. I respect that. Dateline makes it a policy to check their clients' credit records. It's part of the agreement before your application's accepted."

Hallie knew immediately that the minute Dateline got hold of her credit card statements, she was headed for the reject pile.

She was about to say as much when the phone rang. Hallie reached for the receiver and through her kitchen window caught a glimpse of Steve Marris with his son. He was showing Kenny how to hold a softball.

"Hello."

"I hope you appreciate this," Rita said without preamble.

"Appreciate what?"

"I found you a potential husband," Rita announced. "Are you interested in meeting him?"

Four

First There Was Paul, Then George...

Steve glanced at his watch again, although he knew it'd been maybe five minutes since the last time he'd looked. He was wrong. It was three minutes. Almost five o'clock Sunday afternoon and Mary Lynn was late picking up the kids, which could mean only one thing.

She was with this faceless, spineless Kip character.

Steve had gotten his ex-wife to admit she was dating again. That was the reason she'd cut him off physically, although she'd been reluctant to admit it. Probably wouldn't have, if he hadn't cornered her. It left him wondering whether she was sleeping with Kip, but for reasons having to do with his sanity, he didn't pursue the thought. If she was, he didn't want to know.

As for his idea about using Mary Lynn as a replacement secretary, it didn't turn out to be so brilliant, after all. Mary Lynn was ten times worse in the office than Danielle had ever been. He knew she wasn't much good around a computer terminal, but he hadn't realized she didn't know how to answer a phone. Another few days with her and he'd be out of business. She'd filed invoices, instead of mailing them, and managed to insult one of his biggest accounts. It didn't take Steve long to recognize his mistake. He quickly hired a new secretary, wrote Mary Lynn a generous check for her trouble and took her to lunch. While still in her good graces, he followed her home, thinking—despite her telling him the sex had to stop—that they'd head for the bedroom the way they normally did when he dropped by in the middle of the day.

But she'd meant it when she'd said no sex. And she'd also told him she was seeing Kip.

Once he'd persuaded her to confess she was dating again, he couldn't shut her up. She'd met Kip in a bookstore, she told him, smiling at the memory. Steve knew his ex, and she'd never been a reader, which was probably a detriment when it came to school. He couldn't imagine her buying books for pleasure, something she considered a waste of money. It was clear that her sudden interest in them had nothing to do with enjoyment. Mary Lynn had been looking to meet eligible men. Steve had heard that the singles scene had moved out of the bars and into the bookstores; he supposed this proved it.

Although she'd been more than willing to tell him about meeting the new love of her life, Mary Lynn had kept quiet about what they did together. Curious he might be, but Steve refused to grill his children about their mother's activities. His gaze shifted to the two kids. Meagan and Kenny were curled up in front of the television watching a Disney video. Neither seemed to notice or care that their mother was late.

He stared out his living-room window. His neighbor was outside vacuuming her car, and he smiled, remembering her embarrassment when she realized he knew she'd been talking to Dateline. So Hallie McCarthy was on the prowl. He wished her well. As far as he could see, she shouldn't have much of a problem finding a husband. She was actually kinda cute. Petite with dark brown hair that she wore in short curls. She had a nice face, and she seemed friendly, approachable. Certainly Meagan had taken to her right away. Hallie was just fine in the figure department, too.

He wasn't sure where she worked, but it must be in an office. They'd crossed paths a couple of times in the mornings, and she always maintained a professional appearance. He guessed her to be in her mid to late twenties. Possibly thirty, but he doubted it.

If he had any interest in dating, which he didn't, Steve would be more attracted to her friend. Now *there* was a looker. He'd been outside, horsing around with Kenny, when she'd arrived, and he'd practically dropped the ball. The woman was all legs. They went on and on. Shapely legs with a body to match. But Mary Lynn was beautiful, too. With his thoughts back on his ex-wife, Steve moved away from the window.

"Your mother's late," he said, hoping he sounded casual and unconcerned.

"Kip's taking her to a wine-tasting party," Meagan murmured. Her eyes grew huge, as if she'd said something she shouldn't.

"It's okay. Your mother told me she was dating Kip." Steve didn't want his children worrying about what they did or didn't say.

"She told you about Kip?" This seemed to surprise his daughter.

"Yeah." He sat down between the two kids on the couch and draped his arms around their shoulders. "I bet it's a little weird to have your mother dating again, isn't it?" If he was upset about Kip, then it made sense his kids would be, too. He wanted to reassure them that, no matter what happened, they could always count on him.

"Not really," Kenny said, not taking his eyes from the television screen. "She's gone out lots before."

She has? This was news to Steve.

"First there was Paul, then George."

What about Ringo? Steve scowled.

"None of them lasted very long," Meagan supplied.

"And Kip?" Steve wanted to jerk the words away the moment he uttered them.

"Mom really likes Kip," Kenny said.

"How do *you* feel about him?" Again this was a question that bordered on the forbidden, but Steve couldn't keep himself from asking. This was his wife's—all right, ex-wife's—boyfriend they were talking about, and ultimately that involved his children.

"Kip's okay," Kenny responded with a shrug. "But he doesn't know much about baseball."

That bit of information cheered Steve considerably. Kip had taken Mary Lynn to a wine-tasting party. Steve liked wine, too, but he preferred drinking it to spitting it out—wasn't that what they did at wine-tastings? Not once in their twelve-year marriage had he thought of taking Mary Lynn to something like that. On the other hand, she'd never told him such affairs interested her. One thing was certain, he'd spit wine if it'd help win back his ex-wife.

Steve heard a car door slam and leapt up, racing toward the front door. Mary Lynn was climbing out of her van, and it struck him how happy she looked. Some of that joy faded when she saw him. The words to inform her that she was late died on the tip of his tongue. Mary Lynn could tell time as well as he could. She knew she was late, and reminding her would only serve to widen the rift between them. He wanted to build bridges, not tear them down.

"Did you have a nice afternoon?" he asked, pretending he didn't know she'd been with Kip.

"Wonderful. How about you?"

"Great. Kenny's going to make a helluva shortstop."

Mary Lynn grinned. "Like father, like son." She glanced past him to the condo. Kenny and Meagan were at the door. "You ready, kids?"

"Why don't you come inside?" Steve invited. "You haven't seen the place since I decorated, have you?"

Mary Lynn snickered. "I don't call moving the dirty-clothes hamper out of the living room decorating."

"Hey, I've got a real sofa and chair now. And a dining-room set."

"I heard, and I applaud you for replacing the patio furniture and the card table. That's progress." She motioned for Meagan and Kenny, who trudged past him, carting their overnight bags.

Steve gave them each a quick kiss.

"Bye, Dad."

"Bye, Dad."

Soon his family was inside the van. Steve remained on the sidewalk, waving when they pulled away. He buried his hands in his pants pockets and watched the vehicle disappear.

After a moment he returned to the empty house.

Donnalee was definitely, undeniably nervous. She'd arrived at the restaurant half an hour early for the simple reason that she didn't want to be the one to search out and identify Sanford. This way, she hoped to have a few moments to appraise him without his knowing.

After thirteen years, Donnalee was finally ready to marry again. But that meant meeting men, going through the whole process of acquaintance and courtship—maybe more than once. Apart from some casual and ultimately meaningless dates, she hadn't been involved with a man since her marriage. If she wanted to fall in love again, she had to lower her defenses, make herself vulnerable.

That was the terrifying part. She should have gone into counseling following her divorce. Intensive counseling. Any smart woman would have done that. Well, it'd taken Donnalee far longer to get smart than it should have, but she was there now. Savvy. Worldly. Mature.

Those were the very qualities that appealed to Sanford. He'd told her so during their telephone conversation. She sat at the table, facing the door, eyeing everyone who entered. His picture had shown him to be an attractive dark-haired man with strong classical features— but, as Donnalee knew, studio portraits were often deceiving.

A restaurant was neutral territory. Sanford was the one who'd chosen this upscale Mexican restaurant, located in the heart of downtown Seattle. Judging by the succulent scents drifting from the kitchen, he'd chosen well, although Donnalee wondered how she'd manage to swallow a single bite.

A tall distinguished-looking gentleman entered the restaurant and hesitated. Donnalee quickly lifted a pair of glasses from her lap and slipped them on, then peered toward the door Like an idiot, she'd lost the last of her disposable contact lenses down the bathroom drain and had to resort to her old glasses. But Sanford had seen her picture, too, and he wouldn't recognize her wearing glasses, so she donned them only when absolutely necessary.

He spoke briefly with the hostess and darted a glance in her direction.

Donnalee lowered the glasses to her lap again and squinted hard. Unbelievable. He even looked good blurred. It was him. It had to be him. If she'd been nervous earlier, it was nothing compared to the way she felt now. As for all her self-talk about being worldly and mature, she felt no evidence of *those* qualities at the moment.

He approached her table. "Donnalee?"

"Sanford?"

His slow easy smile relaxed her. "Your photo doesn't do you justice."

"Yours doesn't either," she murmured, meaning it.

Grinning, he pulled out his chair and sat down.

That was the start of the most fascinating night of her life. Hours later, when she phoned Hallie, Donnalee was still in a dreamy swoon. "He's fabulous. Just fabulous. We talked and talked and talked. We were at the restaurant until midnight. They had to boot us out, so we found someplace else for coffee and talked some more."

"What time is it?" Hallie asked, with a loud yawn.

Donnalee would never have phoned this late if Hallie hadn't left three urgent messages, demanding she call the minute she got home. "Two o'clock."

Hallie gasped. "You mean to say you just got in? But this was just your first date."

"I know." Try as she might, Donnalee couldn't keep the wistful tone out of her voice.

"He's not there with you, is he?" Hallie's voice dropped to a whisper.

"No. Good grief, what kind of woman do you take me for?"

"A woman who's been too long without a man! Was he everything you hoped?"

"More. Hallie, I can't believe it! He's warm and gracious, romantic and so much fun. I could have talked to him all night. We walked along the waterfront and held hands."

"Did he kiss you?"

"Yes...and I even told him about Larry." The subject of her divorce wasn't something Donnalee discussed freely or often, and certainly nothing she'd intended to talk about on her first date. When she'd mentioned it to Sanford, she'd made light of it. The marriage was a mistake, she was too young to know what she was doing, that sort of thing. It amazed her how easily he'd read between the lines. His hand had tightened around hers and he'd stopped. With the breeze off Puget Sound ruffling her hair and the ferry gliding across the dark waters, its lights a glittering contrast to the night, he'd placed his hand under her chin and raised her eyes to his. Then, ever so gently, he'd kissed her.

Donnalee didn't elaborate on the kiss. Hallie was her best friend, but some things you kept private.

"Are you seeing him again?"

"Tomorrow. Today," Donnalee amended. She'd planned to play this cautiously, and she still would but...she *liked* this man, liked him so much it frightened her. It was all happening too soon.

"You're really crazy about him, aren't you?" Hallie sounded almost disappointed. Surprisingly, Donnalee understood. She knew her friend didn't begrudge her happiness; Hallie just hadn't expected her to find the right man this effortlessly. Frankly, neither had Donnalee. So far, Sanford was...perfect. She realized it was too early to say he was the person she should marry—but marriage was a distinct possibility.

"What about you?" Donnalee asked. The last time she'd talked to Hallie, she'd agreed to meet with Rita's husband's friend. The one Rita had declared the ideal match for Hallie. "Did Marv phone?"

"Precisely at seven."

"Isn't that when Rita suggested he call?"

"Yes, and that worries me. He seems to carry this punctuality thing to extremes."

"He's an accountant, so what do you expect? How'd he sound?"

Hallie giggled. "Like an accountant. He couldn't squeeze in a date with me until next Thursday night."

"It's tax season," Donnalee reminded her. "What do you expect?" she said again.

"I don't know. Going out with a guy named Marv doesn't exactly thrill me."

"You might be surprised. I had a preconceived idea about Sanford, remember?"

"Do people actually call him that?"

"Apparently so. He said when he was a kid, his friends called him Sandy, but that just didn't suit him anymore. He said I could call him Sandy if it made me more comfortable. But he doesn't look like a Sandy. He looks like a Sanford. It's a perfectly respectable name, and so is Marv."

"Marv," Hallie repeated slowly. "You're right. It's not a bad name."

"Not at all." Neither of them pointed out that Hallie had gotten a date—without paying two thousand dollars for the privilege.

"How long did you two talk?"

"A minute," Hallie murmured, "two at the most. He's on a schedule."

Donnalee was beginning to understand her friend's qualms. "Don't be too quick to judge him. Who knows, he might turn out to be Mr. Wonderful."

"Why am I having trouble believing that?"

Five

Bachelor #1

February 20

Tonight's the night. I'm meeting Marvin—Marv. It goes without saying that I shouldn't count on this blind date, but I can't help myself. Not after the way I've worked to turn myself into a desirable enticing woman, irresistible to mortal man.

Yes, I'm at goal weight. It would have been easier if I'd blasted away those ten pounds with dynamite, but they're gone, which is reason enough for celebrating. Marv's taking me to the Cliffhanger, a pleasant surprise. The fact that I actually have a dinner date (with someone Rita feels is perfect!) excites me. I have faith in networking. Donnalee is delighted with Dateline, as well she should be for two thousand bucks, but I prefer to tackle this dating thing on my own. So far so good, although I haven't actually <u>met</u> Marvin—Marv. We've talked a couple of times and he sounds…interesting.

It isn't like I've spent the last six years in a vacuum. Dating isn't exactly a new experience. But now, I'm looking at each man as a potential husband and father. Not that I'm going to ask for a sperm count or character references, but there are certain traits I want in a man. Commitment is a biggie to me. I want to do this marriage thing once, and only once, so I plan to do it right.

This date with Marv is the beginning of a journey, though I can't say exactly where this journey will take me. My, oh my, I do get poetic. I'll write tomorrow after I meet Marv. I only hope Rita knows me as well as she thinks.

Hallie was going to annihilate Rita. The instant she opened the door and met Marv, she had her doubts. For starters, he didn't look like she'd expected—or Rita had implied. Not like Sean Connery at all. More like Elmer Fudd. *And* he wore a checkered bow tie.

She wasn't the only one disappointed. Marv seemed dissatisfied, too. So much so that Hallie wondered what Rita had told him about *her.*

"You must be Hallie," Marv said, stepping inside her home. He glanced around like an appraiser, as though tallying the worth of her furniture and personal effects.

He was so short—*that* wasn't his fault, though Rita might've warned her—she was a good two inches taller without wearing her heels. But his brusque unfriendly attitude was another matter. If he'd bothered to greet her with a smile, she would have felt differently. Instead, he scrutinized her the way he had her furnishings, without emotion, without warmth.

"Would you like a glass of wine before we leave?" she asked, hoping her first impressions had been wrong, willing to give the evening a try, if for nothing more than the fact that she'd spent almost a hundred dollars on her dress. Besides, he was taking her to her favorite restaurant, one she could seldom afford on her own. Any man who invited her to dinner at the Cliffhanger was probably redeemable.

He declined her offer of wine, explaining severely, "I'm driving."

"Coffee, then?"

"Decaffeinated, please." He helped himself to a chair while she got their drinks. He pinched his lips in disapproval when she returned with a mug for him and a wineglass for her. If this was how the evening was going to continue, she'd need that wine. Maybe she should bring the bottle with her; a swig now and again was bound to improve her mood—if not his.

"I understand Rita's husband works with you," she said, hoping to cut through the awkwardness and salvage this so-called date.

He nodded. "You're a friend of Rita's, correct?"

"Uh, correct."

"You've known her how long?" he asked, removing a pad and pen from inside his suit jacket.

"Rita?" She frowned, wondering why he felt this information was important enough to warrant documentation. "Oh, for years. Actually we've known each other since college. Nine or ten years, I'd guess."

"I see." He entered the fact on the pad. "You're how old?"

"Twenty-nine." Hallie took a restorative sip of her wine.

"Never been married?"

"No. What about you?" she asked, gritting her teeth. She hadn't agreed to an inquisition, and this was definitely beginning to resemble one.

He ignored her question. "You own a graphic-arts business?"

"That's right." She felt as if she was filling out a credit application. "Look. Is there a reason for all these questions?"

"I prefer to have significant background information on any woman I date."

"I...see." She almost wished he'd asked how much she weighed. For once in her life, she would've been happy to tell someone.

He flipped the book closed and reached for his coffee. "Overall, I rate you at seven and a half."

"You're rating me?" She was furious enough to throttle him, and they hadn't so much as left the house.

"I do every woman I date." He grinned suddenly and the movement of his mouth softened his expression.

"Do that again," Hallie said, waving her finger at him.

He frowned, destroying the effect.

"Smile," she demanded.

He complied, then immediately lowered his gaze, and Hallie realized he was actually shy. He hid behind the questions and his ratings and obnoxious demeanor. Knowing this made her slightly more sympathetic toward him.

He helped her on with her coat and opened the car door for her. Hmm. Good manners were gentlemanly. Things seemed to be improving. They were on the freeway, with Marv driving at a predictably cautious speed, when she first heard the engine rattle.

"What was that?"

Marv scowled and pretended not to hear her or the noise.

"Sounds to me like there's something wrong with your car," Hallie pressed.

He took his eyes off the road long enough to glare at her. "My car is in perfect running order."

Uh-oh, the date was going downhill again. "I'm sure you take good care of your car," she said soothingly. "But I'm telling you I hear something that doesn't sound right." Whatever the problem, it didn't delay them. They arrived five minutes ahead of their reservation time. Hallie figured that if Marv chose to ignore signs of engine trouble, there wasn't anything she could do about it.

The Cliffhanger was perched on the side of a high bluff that overlooked Commencement Bay in Tacoma. Everything about the restaurant was first-class. Hallie smiled with pleasure.

Once they were seated, however, and the waiter had taken their order, Marv removed the pen and pad from his pocket again. He read over his notes, then said, "I have a few more questions for you."

"More?" She didn't bother to disguise her irritation.

"I'll get through the questions as quickly as possible. I hope you don't mind, but it'll help me later when I make my decision."

When he made his decision? Did he think she was applying for the opportunity to marry him? "Decision," she repeated. "*What* decision?"

"Unlike others, I prefer to choose my wife based on facts rather than feelings, which I think are completely unreliable. Since marriage is a long-term contract, I believe it's necessary to gather as much information as I can. I understand that you, too, are in marriage mode, so this evening can be beneficial to us both." He held her gaze for a moment. "I have to tell you, Hallie, you're getting good marks." The tips of his ears turned red and he cleared his throat before saying, "You're quite...attractive, you know."

The compliment mollified her—although she had to admit she was a little shocked by his blatant approach to this date. *And* to the matter of marriage.

"It doesn't hurt that you're in a financially superior position," he added, ruining any advantage he'd gained.

"Financially superior?" Her? Now that was a joke if ever she'd heard one.

"You own your own business. That puts you several points ahead of the others."

"Exactly how many others are there?"

"That's, uh, privileged information." He smiled lamely, unfolding a computer printout. "We've finished with the preliminaries. Let's get into your family background now."

"I beg your pardon?"

"Medical history, things like that." He sounded impatient. "It's important, Hallie."

"All right, all right," she muttered, resigned to the fact that their dinner was going to be one long interview. Thank goodness their appetizers had just arrived. While she had the waiter's attention, she ordered a glass of wine. Marv frowned and wrote a lengthy note. "What do you want to know?"

They'd discussed heart disease, alcoholism and mental illness by the time their salads were served. Surely the entrées couldn't be far behind! But before she tasted a single bite, he was making inquiries about STDs, fertility and childhood illnesses. Hallie had finally reached her limit. This guy wasn't shy, nor was he hiding behind a pad and pen. He calculated everything down to the size of her panty hose.

"Any problems with—"

She held up both hands. "Stop!"

"Stop?"

"I'm finished answering your questions. You aren't going to find a wife by interviewing for one. I thought this was a dinner date so we could get to know each another."

"It is," he argued. "I'm getting to know you by asking questions. What's wrong with that?" He made another notation, writing furiously.

"What was that?" she demanded.

"Attitude. I'm beginning to have my doubts about you in that category."

Hallie pushed aside her half-eaten salad. "*You* have your doubts. Listen, buster, I'm not answering another question. This is ridiculous—a woman wants to be wanted for who she is, not what she has to offer in the way of good genes!"

Her outburst appeared to unsettle him. "But you've rated the highest of anyone."

It was a sad commentary on the state of her ego that she was flattered by this. "Thank you, I appreciate that, but I refuse to spend the entire evening talking about my grandmother's arthritis." Now was as good a time as any to break the news. "I'm sorry, Marv, but I don't think this is going to work."

"I wouldn't be so quick to say that. Although your attitude is a bit problematic, I find myself liking you. Once we know each other better, you'll value the effort I went through to gauge our compatibility."

"I believe I've already gauged it. Unfortunately, we aren't the least bit compatible." She tried to be gentle, to tell him in a way that left him with his pride intact. "I have my own test, so to speak, and I can tell that a relationship between us simply isn't going to work."

"You're sure?"

"Yes." For emphasis she nodded.

Marv didn't blink, didn't even put up a token resistance. Instead, he closed his pad, placing it inside his suit jacket, and refolded his printout. "Well, then," he said, "I'm relieved you recognized it this soon. You've saved us both a considerable amount of time and effort."

Hallie congratulated herself for not rolling her eyes.

Neither spoke, and before long Marv reached for his pad again. Now he seemed to be jotting down numbers—but Hallie didn't ask.

Finally he glanced up. "You might be interested in knowing that out of a possible one hundred points, you scored a seventy-six for the opening interview."

"Really?" She'd be sure and let her next date know that.

"But I have to agree—it wouldn't work."

Their dinner arrived, and Hallie savored the silence as much as she did the blackened salmon. Marv seemed equally engrossed in his meal; in a restaurant noted for its steak and seafood, he'd ordered liver and onions.

After declining dessert, Hallie decided to turn the conversational tables on him. "What about *your* family's medical history?" she asked. It wouldn't surprise her if there was a case or two of mental illness.

"Fit as a fiddle. I have one grandfather who lived to be ninety."

"Longevity runs in the family, then?"

"On my maternal side. It's difficult to say about the paternal." The waiter brought the bill and Marvin grabbed it. "Unfortunately, very little is known about my father's people." He launched into a lengthy dissertation on what he'd managed to learn thus far. Ten minutes into it, Hallie yawned.

Marvin stopped midsentence and pulled out a pocket calculator. "Did you have three or four of the crab-stuffed mushrooms?"

"I beg your pardon?"

"The appetizer," he said, his finger poised above the calculator keypad.

"Three."

"You're sure?"

"Was I supposed to have counted?"

"Why, yes." He appeared surprised that she'd ask.

Hallie stared in shock as he tallied the dinner bill and stated, "Your half comes to forty-five dollars and thirteen cents, including tip."

"*My* half?"

"Why should I pay for your dinner?" he asked. "You said yourself that we're incompatible."

"Yes, but...you asked me out."

"True. Nevertheless, it was with the unspoken agreement that this date was between two people interested in pursuing a relationship. You aren't interested, therefore, your half of the dinner bill comes to..." He appeared to have forgotten and looked down at his calculator.

"Forty-five dollars and thirteen cents," she supplied. "That includes your portion of the tip."

Disgusted, Hallie picked up her purse. It wouldn't do any good to argue. Luckily she had two twenties and, yes, a five, which she kept hidden for emergencies. The thirteen cents practically wiped her out.

With nothing more to say, they left soon afterward.

Hallie heard the car well before the valet drove it into view. She glanced at Marv, wondering if he'd ignore the clanking sound *this* time. He did.

Rather than point it out again, Hallie climbed inside and steeled herself for a long uncomfortable ride home. She wasn't far from wrong. When they reached the interstate the engine noise had intensified until even Marv couldn't miss it.

"What was that?" he demanded, as if she was somehow responsible for the racket.

"Your car?" She was unable to avoid the sarcasm.

"I *know* it's the car."

"There's no need to worry," she said, parroting his words, "your vehicle's in perfect running order, remember?"

"Correct. Nothing could possibly be wrong." Then he cursed and pulled off to the side of the freeway. Smoke rose from underneath the hood, billowing into the night.

"Oh, dear," Hallie murmured. This didn't look good. The way things were going, he'd probably make her pay for half the tow truck, too.

Marv slammed his fist against the steering wheel. "Now look what you've done."

"Me?" Of all the things he'd said, this was the limit. The final insult. "I have a few questions for you," she snapped. "When was the last time this car had an oil change? A tune-up? Did you bother with antifreeze this winter?"

Marv leapt out of the car and slammed his door.

Hallie got out, too, shutting hers just as hard.

He glared at her over the top of the hood. "I don't find your attempts at humor the least bit amusing."

"The biggest joke of the night was my agreeing to go out with you!" The cold wind whipped past her and she tucked her hands into the pockets of her coat. Unfortunately, she'd worn a flimsy coat, more of a wrap, because its jade green went so well with her new dress. Her wool coat hung in the closet. The only thing she had to keep her warm was her anger—and so far, it was working.

"Until I met you, my vehicle *was* in perfect running order."

"Are you suggesting I put a hex on it?"

"Maybe you did," he growled.

Hallie seethed, crossing her arms. "You're the rudest man I've ever met!"

His eyes narrowed and his mouth thinned. It wasn't until then that she realized how deeply she'd insulted him. Marv obviously prided himself on his manners—opening the door, helping her on with her coat, those gestures so few men observed these days. Well, she'd take a normal man who let her open car doors over Marvin anytime!

"If that's how you feel," he said stiffly, "you can find your own way home."

"Fine, I will." She carelessly tossed out the words, slapped her silk scarf around her neck like Isadora Duncan and started walking, high heels and all.

This wasn't the smart thing to do, Hallie soon realized. She was chilled to the bone, blinded by all the headlights flashing by and, dammit, one of her heels chose that moment to break off.

At least it wasn't raining.

Six

The Loan Ranger

The ringing woke Steve out of a sound sleep. He rolled over, thinking the incessant noise was his alarm. He hit the switch, but it did no good. Then he noticed the time. Eleven-thirty. What the hell?

He sat up and realized the irritating sound wasn't his alarm clock but his doorbell. He grabbed his jeans and pulled them on as he hobbled into the living room. He had no idea who was calling on him so late at night—but the last person he expected was his next-door neighbor.

"I'm sorry to wake you," Hallie said, her eyes desperate in the pale porch light. A scruffy-looking fellow hovered behind her, and a taxi stood parked in her driveway. "Could I borrow twenty dollars?" she pleaded. He stared at her. "Just until tomorrow afternoon," she added.

"Sure," he said, and reached in his hip pocket for his wallet, extracting a bill.

"Thank you," she breathed, then whirled around to give the taxi driver his money. "I told you you'd get paid!" she said fiercely.

"You can't blame a guy for doubting. You wouldn't be the first lady who tried to stiff me."

"Well...thanks for bringing me home."

The cabbie handed her a business card. "Sure, lady. Listen, the next time some guy dumps you on the freeway, give me a call and I'll make sure you get home."

"Thanks," she muttered, sending an embarrassed glance in Steve's direction. She waited until the driver had left before explaining. "Really, it's not as bad as it looks." Nervously she pushed a trembling hand through her tangled hair. "I'll get the twenty dollars to you after work tomorrow afternoon. I...I quit carrying my credit cards and didn't have my ATM card with me," she explained, rushing the words. "It took all my cash to pay for my half of dinner."

"Don't worry about it."

"I promise to have the money back by tomorrow. You have my word on that."

He grinned. "I said not to worry about it."

"At this point, it's a matter of pride." She turned away and limped toward her own condo. It took him a moment to realize the heel on one of her shoes had broken off.

"Hallie?" he called out, curiosity getting the better of him. "Do you want to come in for coffee and tell me what happened?"

She paused, and he knew she was tempted to accept. "If you don't mind, I'll take a rain check on the coffee. I'm fine, really. It was just a date gone bad."

"From Dateline?"

"No. I decided against...I didn't sign up with them. This was a date arranged by a friend. A *former* friend." She filled in a few of the details: the questions, the restaurant bill, the car. He listened sympathetically, nodding now and then, marveling at her ability to laugh at her situation.

"Don't let it get you down," he advised.

"I won't," she said, and although she looked disheveled and pitiful, she managed a weak smile. "It'd take more than a pudgy accountant to do that."

"Good girl." He waited until she was all the way inside her house before he closed his own door. Only then, did he allow himself to laugh. He had to hand it to Hallie McCarthy. The lady had grit.

"What's so funny?" Todd asked Steve the following morning.

"What makes you think anything's funny?" Steve leaned over a pile of metal shavings to avoid meeting his friend's gaze. Todd was right; his mood had greatly improved. It was because of Hallie, he suspected. Every time he thought about her and that jerk accountant, he found himself grinning from ear to ear. No wonder he wasn't eager to get back into the dating scene. It made far more sense to win back his ex-wife. He only hoped Mary Lynn met up with a few of Hallie's rejects. Then maybe she'd realize he wasn't so bad, after all.

"You've been wearing this silly grin all day." Obviously Todd wasn't about to let the subject drop.

"Would you rather I stormed around making unreasonable demands?"

"Nope," Todd admitted. Then he shrugged. "You ready for lunch?"

"Sure." Steve packed his own now, same as he had when he was married—which meant he picked up something at the deli on his way into work. He and Todd headed for the small room adjacent to his office, stopping to let Mrs. Applegate, his new secretary, know he was taking his lunch break. She was working out well. He'd found her through a business college. She was older, described as a displaced homemaker, whatever that meant. But Mrs. Applegate appreciated the job and worked hard.

"Would you care for a cup of coffee with your lunch?" she asked.

"Please."

"That woman's going to spoil you," Todd commented as he sat down across from Steve. He pulled a submarine sandwich from his lunch pail and peeled away the wrapper.

"I'm going to let her, too." In comparison to Danielle and Mary Lynn, Mrs. Applegate was a paragon—organized, efficient, cooperative. He wondered how he'd ever managed without her.

"Now tell me what's so damn funny," Todd said after the coffee had been served. "I could use a good laugh."

"My neighbor." Steve could see no reason not to relay the events of the night before. "Apparently she's on the hunt for a husband."

"What's she look like?"

"Why? You interested?"

Todd took a big bite of his sandwich and chewed vigorously as he considered his response. "I might be."

"You? It wasn't so long ago you told me you wanted nothing to do with women."

"*Some* women. Go on, I want to hear what happened to your neighbor."

"She got me out of bed at eleven-thirty last night and asked to borrow twenty bucks. The guy she'd been with acted obnoxious all evening—even made her pay for her own meal. Plus he had car trouble, blamed it on her, then dumped her on the freeway and told her to find her own way home. Which she did."

"Good for her."

"That's what I said." He bit into his pastrami-on-rye and found himself smiling again as he recalled Hallie's story. She'd done a hilarious imitation of this Marv guy demanding his forty-something dollars.

"You like this neighbor of yours, don't you?"

"Like? What do you mean?" Sure he liked Hallie. What wasn't to like? But he had no romantic interest in her, and there was a difference.

"Are you going to ask her out?"

"Naw," he answered, dismissing the suggestion. "She's not my type."

"Exactly what is your type?" Todd pressed.

"Damned if I know." The only woman he'd ever loved had been Mary Lynn. She was all he'd ever wanted, all he'd ever thought about. That wasn't going to change.

His answer appeared to satisfy Todd, who nodded. "Same way I feel. I might date again, and I might not. Sure as hell, the minute I start getting serious about a woman I'll run into problems, just like I did last time. So I figure, if I meet someone, fine. Great. But I'm not going out of my way."

Steve frowned as he listened to Todd. It distressed him that Mary Lynn seemed to be involved with another man, and according to his kids, had been dating for some time.

"You look upset," Todd remarked.

Steve set his sandwich aside, his appetite gone. "Mary Lynn's seeing someone."

"I know, you told me earlier. You've been divorced a year or better—what did you expect?"

"I expected her to see the light," Steve muttered.

"Well, it's not going to happen. She wanted out of the marriage. And as far as I can see, nothing's changed."

"When did you become an expert on my relationship with my ex-wife?" Steve asked irritably. They'd had this discussion before, and it irked him that his friend saw things differently. More than anyone, Todd knew he hadn't wanted the divorce. More than anyone, Todd knew he loved Mary Lynn as much now as he had the day they'd married.

Todd threw up his hands in disgust. "Let's drop it, all right? I butted in where I didn't belong. You want to moon over Mary Lynn, for the rest of your life, then be my guest."

Seven

Make Mine A Double

"Donnalee Cooper's holding for you on line two," Bonnie said. Hallie stared at the blinking phone. It wouldn't help to put it off any longer. Her friend had a right to know—even to gloat.

"Hi, Donnalee," she said with forced cheerfulness.

"You didn't phone," Donnalee accused. "What happened?"

"You don't want to hear."

"I wouldn't have called if I didn't. I haven't got much time, either. I've got clients due in five minutes, so cut to the chase, will you?"

"Okay, then—gloat. This guy was a jerk. Big time. He wanted to investigate my family genes to make sure I was qualified to bear his children. When I told him I didn't think we clicked, he made me pay for my half of the dinner. Then his car broke down on the freeway and I was stuck finding my own way home. To add insult to injury, I had to get my neighbor out of bed and borrow twenty bucks to pay the cabdriver."

A lengthy pause followed her condensed version of the previous night. Hallie suspected Donnalee had covered the receiver with one hand to hide her laughter.

"Well?" she challenged. "Say something."

"Okay," Donnalee replied slowly. "Are you ready to invest in Dateline yet?"

"No." Hallie was determined to pay off her credit cards, not add another two thousand dollars to the balance. "Besides, I have another date."

"Who?" Donnalee—predictably—sounded skeptical.

"Bonnie's uncle Chad." Bonnie had mentioned him early in January, but Hallie had wanted to be at her best before agreeing to a date with him. "You know that old saying about getting back on the horse after you fall off? Well, I accepted a dinner invitation this very morning."

"When are you seeing him?"

Hallie didn't know what to make of Donnalee's tone. It was a mixture of wonder and patent disapproval. "Soon," Hallie said. "Monday night." Actually she wondered how smart this was herself. Monday was only three days away.

Chad Ellis had sounded nice enough over the phone, and Bonnie had said he was her favorite uncle. Someone related to a member of her trusted staff seemed a safe bet—especially after the disastrous Marv.

"Did you go out with Sanford last night?" The change of subject was deliberate.

"Yes—and it was wonderful. He's a dream come true," Donnalee said with the same wistful note she used whenever his name was introduced into the conversation.

"Have you talked to him today?" Hallie didn't know why she insisted on torturing herself.

"He sent me a dozen red roses this morning."

"Roses?" Hallie was almost swooning with envy. While Donnalee was being courted and pampered, she'd been grilled for hours and then abandoned on the freeway.

"I'm falling in love with this guy," Donnalee confessed. "Head over heels."

"So am I, and I haven't even met him."

Her friend chuckled. "I wish you'd reconsider Dateline. Chad might be Bonnie's uncle, but how much do you really know about him?"

"Just what Bonnie told me. He's divorced, has been for five years. He sells medical equipment and is on the road quite a bit, but he'll be back in town after the weekend. For a while, anyway." She wasn't sure if that was luck or fate. Their one all-too-brief conversation had taken place that morning. He sounded...interesting. Which, come to think of it, was the same word she'd used following her telephone chat with Marv.

"If you don't call me Tuesday morning, I'll track you down and torture the information out of you," Donnalee warned.

"I'll phone," Hallie promised. No date could possibly be as awful as the one with Marv. Sheer chance assured Hallie that the odds of Chad's being a decent date were good.

At this point she wasn't even looking for Mr. Right. Mr. Almost Right would satisfy her nicely. If she'd learned anything from the experience with Marv—and she *had*—it was that she needed to lower her expectations. No Mr. Knight-in-shining-armor was going to gallop up to *her* front door.

On her way home that evening, Hallie stopped off at the bank for cash. Her ATM card remained in her bottom dresser drawer, along with her credit cards—safe from temptation.

Wanting to put the task of repaying her neighbor behind her, Hallie headed directly for his condo after she parked her car. His lights were on and she assumed he was home, but it was Meagan who answered the door. "Hi, Hallie!"

"Hi, Meagan. Is your dad there?"

"Yeah. He's in the shower. You can wait, can't you?"

"I don't actually need to talk to him." She pulled the twenty-dollar bill out of her purse. "Would you give this to him?"

"Sure."

"Give me what?" Steve strolled barefoot into the hallway, wearing jeans and an unbuttoned plaid shirt. A damp towel was draped around his neck, and his dark hair glistened with water. "Oh, hi, Hallie."

"Hi." She smiled weakly, embarrassed about their last meeting.

"Hey, Dad," Kenny shouted, leaping off the sofa. "Hallie brought you twenty bucks. Let's go out for pizza, okay?"

"Uh..." Steve hesitated.

Meagan's eyes were as bright as her brother's. "Can Hallie come, too?"

"I...can't. Really." Hallie looked over her shoulder at her empty condo, tempted to suggest she had places to go, people to meet. It would have been a lie. "I just wanted to repay the loan and thank you for coming to my rescue. I don't know what I would've done if you hadn't answered the door." Well, she would have managed— she would've retrieved her bank card from the bottom drawer and... But Steve had saved her time and spared her inconvenience. She'd been in no shape to go driving around with a seriously annoyed cabbie, looking for a bank machine.

"*Can* we go out for pizza, Dad?" Kenny asked again, his hands folded in prayerlike fashion. "Please, please, please?"

"I don't see why not," Steve relented, grinning. He turned to Hallie. "You're welcome to come along. Actually, I wish you would. The kids will desert me for the video games the minute we arrive and I'll be stuck sitting there with no one to talk to."

She wavered. Even if she didn't have any plans, she didn't want to intrude.

"Please come!" Meagan urged.

"Sure," Hallie said before she could change her mind. Although it wasn't the thought of her empty condo or equally empty refrigerator that persuaded her. It wasn't even Meagan's invitation. It was the pizza. Pizza, loaded down with cheese, spicy sausage and olives.

After nearly two months of exercise, after week upon week of eating lettuce and vegetables, skinless chicken and Dover sole, she deserved pizza. She'd walk an extra mile on her treadmill, but heaven help her, she wanted that pizza.

"I'm glad you decided to come," Meagan told her when they arrived at the local pizza parlor, a five-minute drive away. To Hallie's relief, Steve had taken his car—not his truck, which he'd left at work.

The place was filled with Friday-night family business, the noise roughly equal to that of a rock concert. While Steve stood in line at the counter to order their dinner, Hallie steered the kids toward one of the few empty tables.

Steve returned five minutes later with two soft drinks, a couple of beers and a pile of quarters. Kenny's eyes lit up like the video games he loved and he reached forward to grab the coins. "Twelve quarters each," Steve said, gazing sternly at his offspring. "And they have to last you all night. Once they're gone, they're gone. Got it?"

"Got it."

The quarters disappeared along with Meagan and Kenny.

Steve sat down across the picnic-style table from Hallie. She spread one of the red-checkered napkins on her lap, aware that it was taking her an inordinately long time to do so.

"It was kind of you to invite me," she finally said, slightly uneasy at being left alone with Steve. To her surprise she found herself revising her earlier estimation of him. He was really quite good-looking. Funny she hadn't realized that earlier. The fact that he'd been willing to help her out only added to the attraction.

"Hey, I appreciate the company. Mary Lynn and I used to bring the kids here once a month. Meagan and Kenny would like to come more often, but I feel stupid sitting by myself."

"What about trying your hand at the videos?"

"Are you kidding? It's an invasion of territory. None of the kids want me there. The one time I tried it I was banished and sentenced to sit out here with the rest of the parents."

Hallie smiled. She'd half expected him to ask her more about her awful date and was grateful he didn't.

They each talked about their jobs, which took all of five minutes. Their discussion of the weather took less than one. A not-uncomfortable silence followed before Steve spoke again.

"Listen, you can tell me to mind my own business, but why was a gal like you going out with a creep like that?"

She sighed. She might as well level with him, seeing that he'd already had her groveling at his front door in the middle of the night, needing a loan. "I guess you've gathered I'm trying to meet a man. I, uh, decided this was the year I'd get married."

His head came up and his eyes narrowed. "Women *decide* this sort of thing?"

"Not all women," she told him. "It's just that I'm turning thirty in April, and—"

"Hey, thirty isn't old."

"I know, but I'm not really sure where my twenties went, if you know what I mean. I was busy, happy, working hard, and then one day I woke up and realized most of my friends were married, some for the second time. My dad recently died, and my younger sister just became a mother." She struggled to explain. "Somehow, things changed for me. My goals. My feelings about what's important in life. For years, I threw all my energy into my work—and now I want...more. I want someone to share it with."

"So you figure marriage is the answer."

"Something like that." Hallie shrugged comically. "I've been dating since I was sixteen, and not once in all that time did I ever meet anyone like Marv. It's appalling how slim the pickings are. You see, Donnalee made it look easy." Maybe Donnalee was right; maybe she *should* reconsider Dateline.

"Is she the friend who stopped by your place a couple of Saturdays ago? The one with the long...the tall one?"

Men rarely had a problem remembering Donnalee. "That's her. She found Prince Charming after *one* date."

"You mean to say she isn't married?"

"Not yet. She's the person who suggested I sign up with Dateline. She plunked down her money, and first time out she met this fabulous guy. From everything she said, he's wonderful." Hallie couldn't hide the wistful longing in her voice. "It wouldn't surprise me if she was married by summer."

"Slim pickings," Steve repeated, and Hallie wondered if he'd heard anything else she'd said. He became aware of the lull in conversation and cast her an apologetic look. "I was just thinking over what you said about available men. My ex-wife is starting to date and frankly—" he paused, grinning broadly "—it wouldn't hurt my feelings any if she was to meet up with the joker you went out with last night. Maybe she'd be more willing to talk about the two of us getting back together."

"You want to patch things up with your ex?"

Steve nodded, and his eyes held hers sternly, as if he anticipated an argument.

"I'm impressed." In Hallie's opinion, too many families were thrown into chaos by divorce. It did her heart good to know there were men like Steve who considered it important to keep the family intact.

Predictably, Meagan and Kenny arrived within seconds of the pizza. The biggest pizza Hallie had ever seen. Pepperoni, sausage, mushroom and black olive. Her favorite. For a while, there was silence as they all helped themselves to huge slices.

When they'd eaten their fill, Steve and Kenny went to find a cardboard container for leftovers. Meagan smiled at Hallie. "I'm glad you came with us," she said again.

"I'm glad you asked."

"Kenny and I like this place, but we don't come often because Dad gets lonely without Mom here."

It wasn't the first time Hallie had noticed Meagan worrying about her father. Her tenderness toward him was touching, and Hallie squeezed the girl's shoulders. "I hope your parents get back together," she said.

"Kenny and I used to talk about it a lot."

"Your father certainly loves your mother."

"I know."

But Hallie noticed that the girl's eyes dimmed as she spoke, and she wondered what that meant.

"Mom's dating Kip," Meagan said. "Dad knows. Kenny and I weren't going to tell him, but he knows. Mom is…I don't know, but I don't think she wants Dad back. She likes Kip and gets upset if we try to talk to her about Dad. She said that sometimes people fall out of love, and that's what happened with her and Dad."

Hallie was a little uncomfortable with these confidences. "Everything will work out the way it's supposed to," she said, wanting to reassure the girl and afraid she was doing a poor job of it. It was clear that Meagan loved both her parents, and like every child, wanted them together.

"I like that," she said, biting her lower lip. "Everything will work out the way it's supposed to." A smile brightened her pretty face. "I'll remember that, Hallie. Thanks."

Eight

Bachelor #2

It was déjà vu all over again, as a baseball great—often quoted by her father—used to say.

Hallie sat across the linen-covered table from a man she normally would've crossed the street to avoid. "Sleazy" was the word that came to mind. Chad Ellis had hair combed from a low side part to disguise his baldness; it contained enough grease to avert an oil shortage that winter. He wore a suit coat with a bright floral-print shirt unbuttoned practically to his navel and no fewer than fifteen gold chains in various lengths. He looked up from the menu and flashed her a smile that said she was lucky to be with him. Hallie had trouble believing that her own assistant, someone who *knew* her and presumably liked her, could possibly believe she'd be compatible with this clown.

Hallie reviewed the menu selections, keeping an eye on price. If she was going to end up paying for her half of dinner, she wanted to be sure she ordered a meal she could afford.

Chad made his selection and set aside the menu. "How about a little something to loosen our inhibitions?" he suggested. The thought of loosening anything with this character terrified her. "Such as a double martini."

Hallie had ordered a martini once, and the only thing worth remembering was the olive. "Uh, I'd like mineral water."

He jiggled his eyebrows a couple of times. "Liquor is quicker."

A blind person could read the writing on the wall with this one. She chanced a look in Chad's direction and her stomach tightened. This creep was Bonnie's uncle? Did her assistant honestly think she was that desperate?

The waiter arrived and Chad ordered a double martini, while Hallie chose a Perrier. They both ordered their meals—seafood pasta for her, steak for him. "You aren't nervous, are you, cupcake?"

She gritted her teeth. "The name's Hallie."

"Women like pet names."

"Not this woman." Hallie was determined not to get into an argument with him until he'd paid the bill, but she wasn't sure she'd last that long.

"Chad said you're—"

"Chad said?" Then understanding dawned. "If you aren't Chad Ellis, who the hell are you?" She was almost shouting.

"All right, all right. Damn, I should've known I couldn't pull this off. Chad had to leave town unexpectedly and he asked me to fill in for him. My name's Tom Chedders."

"I was supposed to have dinner with Chad Ellis!" Her blood heated to the boiling point. That Chad had lacked the decency to tell her he couldn't meet her and sent a stranger in his stead was all she needed to know about him.

"Don't worry, you'll have a good time with me," Tom told her, glancing around to make sure they weren't attracting attention. "Chad will vouch for me. We've been good buddies for a lot of years. We work for the same company."

"Why didn't you tell me right away who you were?"

"I was afraid you wouldn't have dinner with me if I did," he said. "Like I told you before, I'm an all-right kind of guy. No need to get bent out of shape, now, is there?" He flashed her a toothy grin.

Hallie wasn't sure. "I would've preferred it if you'd been honest with me from the beginning."

He did at least look mildly guilty. "You're right, I should've, only...I didn't want to give you an excuse to cancel. All I'm asking is that you give me a chance."

Hallie sighed deeply. "Let's be honest with each other from now on, okay?"

"Scout's honor."

"You were a scout?"

He shook his head. "Nah, they were a bunch of sissies, far as I was concerned."

"I see," she muttered, and gazed yearningly toward the front door. The evening could prove to be a very long one indeed.

"So you're divorced," Tom said, then thanked the cocktail waitress with a wink and a quarter tip. It took him a moment to turn his attention back to Hallie.

"No, Chad must have misunderstood. I've never been married."

She'd say one thing for Tom. He had the most expressive eyebrows she'd ever seen. Right now, they rose all the way to his hairline. "Never married. What's the matter with you?"

"The matter?"

"There's gotta be a reason a pretty gal like you never married. Well, never mind, I'm going to take good care of you, sweetie pie. You and me are gonna have fun."

Hallie sincerely doubted that. "The name is Hallie," she reminded him, feeling the beginnings of a headache. "Not cupcake or sweetie pie or anything else."

He gulped down his double martini and raised his glass in the direction of the bar to signal for another. "Whatever you say, dar-lin'."

Hallie ground her teeth in an effort to maintain her composure. "How long have you been selling medical equipment?" she asked, striving to sound interested.

"I don't. Now before you get all upset again, I didn't lie. I work for the same company as Chad, only on the pharmaceutical side. I sell condoms."

A lump of ice went down her throat whole. "Condoms?" she choked.

"Yep. We've got 'em in all kinds of flavors. Our flavor for February is cotton candy. We've got 'em in all colors, too." He stared at her intently, and Hallie shuddered. "White's the top seller, though. Can you believe it? Why would anyone choose white over candy-apple red?"

"I couldn't tell you." Hallie slid a guarded look in both directions, praying no one could hear their conversation. "Do you mind if we discuss something else?"

"Sure," he responded amiably. "I do a brisk business in laxatives, as well. Won the top salesman award two years running." He laughed as if what he'd said was uproariously funny. "Laxatives...running. Get it?"

Ha. Ha. Ha. "No," she said flatly. Hallie's head was starting to pound in earnest now, and she knew she couldn't go through with this. Even if she ended up paying for a meal she didn't eat, she couldn't stand another minute in this man's company. "Tom, listen, I'm really sorry, but this isn't going to work." She set her napkin on the table and reached for her purse.

He assumed a hurt little-boy look. "Not going to work? What do you mean?"

"I was expecting to meet Chad Ellis, not you."

"Gee, I thought we were getting along just great. What's wrong? Tell me what's wrong and I'll fix it."

"In this instance I think it might be best to leave well enough alone."

"But I thought, you know, that you and I would get together later." He did that jiggling thing with his eyebrows again.

"Get together?"

"You know. In bed."

"Bed?" She said it loudly enough to attract the attention of the maître d'. "Let me assure you right now," she hissed, "that I'm not interested in going to bed with you."

"That's not what Chad said."

"What *did* Chad say?" Bonnie was going to hear about this.

"That you were hot for a real man—and, baby, I'm the one for you. I can teach you things you ain't never gonna see in a textbook. I haven't been in the condom business all these years without learning a few tricks of the trade, if you catch my drift."

His drift came straight off a garbage heap, in Hallie's view. "I don't know what to say, Tom. You've been misinformed. I'm not even mildly lukewarm as far as you're concerned, and I'm not interested in any of your...lessons."

"You mean you were willing to let me wine and dine you—but you weren't gonna give *me* anything? I thought this was a bread-and-bed date."

"What I'll give you is money for my meal." She pulled out her wallet and threw a fifty-dollar bill on the table. Her fingers tightened around her purse strap. "Good night, Tom. I wish you well." She couldn't in good faith tell him it had been a pleasure to meet him. It had been an experience she didn't want to repeat. An experience she wasn't likely to forget. No more blind dates, she swore to herself. It wasn't only discouraging, it was getting too expensive.

"Good riddance. I'll find a real woman, one who knows how to satisfy a man." She noticed that he snatched up the money and shoved it in his pocket.

As Hallie walked out of the restaurant, she felt every eye in the place on her.

"Would you like me to call you a taxi?" the receptionist asked.

Hallie nodded, then with a sinking sensation, she checked to be sure she had enough cash to cover the fare. No, that fifty was all she'd had—and her pride wouldn't allow her to run back to Tom Chedders and demand change. It looked like she was going to need another loan from Steve.

"Your cab will be here in a few minutes," the receptionist told her with a sympathetic smile.

"Thanks." She glanced toward the door, groaning at the thought that Steve might not be home. She'd better phone him first.

Not knowing his phone number, she called directory assistance.

The way her luck was going, she was afraid he'd have an unlisted number. But the operator found it and Hallie released a sigh of relief.

Steve answered on the first ring in a lazy I've-been-sitting-here-waiting-for-your-call voice.

"Hi," she said, deciding to ease into the subject of another loan, rather than blurting out the sorry details and throwing herself on his mercy.

"Hi," he responded.

Hallie suspected he didn't recognize her voice. "It's Hallie, from next door."

"Yeah, I know." He chuckled. "Wouldn't it be easier to stick your head out the kitchen window and yell?"

"I'm not at home. I went out on another blind date."

"Not with that same jerk?"

"No—I found an entirely new jerk. I just walked out on him and I don't have enough cash for the cab fare home. Could I take out another loan?" It humiliated her to ask, but she had no option. "This'll be the last time it ever happens, I promise you."

"Where are you?"

"Some restaurant—I don't know where." Dumb. Next time she'd pay attention. Next time she'd bring her own car.

"I'll come and get you."

"No." That was the last thing she wanted. "I appreciate the offer, but I refuse to let you go to that trouble."

"You're sure?"

"Positive."

The taxi arrived and Hallie rattled off her address, climbed into the back seat and closed her eyes. The urge to give in to tears was almost overwhelming.

Naive and stupid. That was the way men viewed her. Well, no wonder. You'd think she'd have learned something the first time around—but no, all her credit cards and her bank card were still at home. Though who would've guessed this would happen *twice?*

Steve's front door opened the minute the taxi pulled up in front of her place. He loped across the lawn and took out his wallet.

"How much do you need?"

"Eighteen bucks. I'll have it for you tomorrow afternoon."

He paid the driver, who promptly left. "You all right?" Steve asked.

"No," she admitted, "but I will be soon enough. Thanks for the loan. Again."

"Hey, what are neighbors for?" He smiled, patting her gently on the back.

Hallie unlocked her front door and walked into her darkened home. She tossed her purse on the sofa, switched on the lights and headed straight for the phone in her kitchen.

Donnalee answered immediately. "You're right," Hallie said without preamble.

"I love hearing it," Donnalee said, "but I'd like to know what I'm right about."

"Dateline. I'm calling them first thing in the morning."

Her announcement was followed by a short pause. "What happened?"

"You don't want to know and I don't want to tell you. Suffice it to say I'd pay Dateline double their normal fee if they could find me a halfway decent man."

"Oh, Hallie, you poor thing. I'm sure there's someone out there for you."

"I'm sure there is, too, and at this point I'm willing to pay for the privilege of meeting him."

Nine

Bingo!

March 20

They say the third time's the charm. Well, I'm charmed.
Dateline took long enough finding me a match, but Mark
Freelander was worth the wait. We met last night for the
first time. I drove to the restaurant myself—Donnalee advised me to arrive early—only to discover that Mark had,
too. We laughed about that.

I was nervous, but Mark put me at ease. I like him. That
on its own is a scary thought. I know it's too soon to tell,
but I could see myself married to someone like Mark. He's
intelligent, well mannered and just plain nice. The kind of
guy my mother would approve of. Dad, too, if he were
here.

Mark's an engineer, divorced, no kids. The fact that he
was willing to invest two thousand dollars to find the right
woman tells me he's as serious about this matter of marriage as I am. We're seeing each other again soon.

I can hardly wait.

Hallie rolled her grocery cart over to the display of fresh tomatoes
and carefully made her selection. She wanted everything to be perfect for this dinner. She'd been dating Mark for two weeks now, and
he'd teased her into agreeing to cook for him. Granted, her expertise
in the kitchen was severely limited, but she knew how to grill a
decent steak. Her antipasto salad—thick tomato slices, mozzarella
cheese, Greek olives, roasted red pepper and salami—was impressive; even her mother said so. Add baked potatoes and steamed as-
paragus, and she'd come off looking like a younger, slimmer version
of Julia Child.

"Hey, Dad, there's Hallie."

Hearing her name, Hallie turned to find Steve shopping with his kids. His cart was filled with frozen pizza, canned spaghetti and a dozen or so frozen entrées.

"Howdy, neighbor," Steve called out.

"Hi, guys," Hallie replied, pleased to see them. "How's it going?"

"Great," Steve said. "I haven't seen you around lately."

"I've been putting in a lot of extra time on a project at work and—" she beamed as she said it "—I'm seeing someone."

"Seeing someone?" Steve prompted.

She looked around and lowered her voice. "I signed up with Dateline. They put me together with Mark."

"Congratulations. I knew you'd eventually land on your feet."

"Thanks. Mark and I've been seeing each other a couple of weeks now, and so far so good." She held up both hands, fingers crossed.

"Hey, Dad, ask Hallie," Meagan urged, pulling on her father's sleeve. "She'd be perfect."

"Yeah, Dad, you can ask Hallie," Kenny said excitedly.

Steve ignored the pleas and would have moved on if Hallie hadn't stopped him.

"Ask me what?"

He shook his head. "It's nothing."

Clearly he was lying. "Steve!"

"All right, all right." He didn't seem too eager to elaborate. "Would you mind if we talked about this over a cup of coffee?" He gestured at the small round tables set up in front of the grocery-store deli, which sold sandwiches, salads and hot drinks.

"Sure." Hallie had to admit to being curious. She followed the Marris family to the deli; while she made sure their carts weren't blocking the aisle, Steve purchased two cups of coffee, plus hot chocolate for the kids.

His son and daughter sat down with them, Meagan waiting patiently for her father to speak. Kenny, less patient, kicked at the legs of his chair.

With a quelling frown at his son, Steve asked Hallie, "Do you bowl?"

"Bowl? As in ball and pins?" Hallie said. "Yeah, I guess, although it's been a few years." She hadn't been all that adept at bowling, but then she'd never been athletically inclined.

"What was your average?"

"Well, I could generally knock down three or four pins. Why?"

"Dad needs a woman who can bowl," Kenny explained.

Steve darted his son another quelling look. "I prefer to do this myself, all right?" He turned back to Hallie. "I'm part of a couples bowling league, and since my marriage breakup my sister's bowled with me. Unfortunately her husband was transferred to Wichita last month and she had to drop out of the league just before the tournament.''

"Dad needs a female partner for the tournament," Meagan clarified.

"Oh," Hallie muttered, her heart sinking. She was sure she'd be more of a liability to Steve than a benefit. Heaven knew she owed the guy, but she wasn't sure he'd appreciate the kind of help she could give him.

Steve noted her hesitation. "Don't worry about it, Hallie. It's no big deal. I'll find someone."

"It's just that I don't think I'd do you any good. Like I said, I haven't bowled in years."

"It'd just be one afternoon." Again it was Meagan who spoke. "You could bowl one afternoon, couldn't you?"

"Surely there's someone better qualified than me?" she asked hopefully. Maybe she could rope Bonnie into helping him. Her assistant was due a little penance.

"Nope," Kenny said. "Dad's already asked everyone he knows."

"Kenny, Meagan," Steve said gruffly, "Hallie says she can't do it. Let's leave it at that, shall we?"

"But...but we could teach her," Meagan persisted. "She can't be that bad." So said the girl who'd run circles around her.

"Well..." Hallie felt herself weakening. Twice this man had come to her rescue, and not once in the weeks that followed had he reminded her what a fool she'd made of herself. That in itself demanded her consideration.

"I'd be willing to give it a try," she offered, gesturing vaguely. "The kids are right. All I probably need is a refresher course. And, really, one afternoon isn't going to hurt. It's the least I can do after all the help you've given me."

"So you will?" Steve asked, sounding pleased.

"Like I told you, I'm going to need a little coaching first."

"No problem," Steve replied. "How about Friday night? We'll take the kids bowling and then go out for pizza."

"When's the tournament?"

"The next day—Saturday afternoon."

"Okay." Hallie hoped she didn't live to regret this. "I'll mark my calendar."

"I knew Hallie would do it!" Meagan grinned.

"Glad to help," Hallie said, and swallowed tightly. "What are neighbors for?"

* * *

The dinner with Mark went even better than she'd dared hope.

He arrived with a bottle of her favorite wine and a bouquet of spring flowers. He raved about the meal, especially her antipasto salad, and claimed he'd never tasted better. Hallie figured she could get used to having a man tell her how wonderful she was.

They sat in front of the television, sipping the last of the wine from her best crystal goblets. The latest action-movie video played, but neither paid much attention to the actors racing across the screen. Mark relaxed against the sofa, his arm around her shoulder.

"You've been holding out on me," he said in a chiding voice.

Half smiling, she twisted her head to look at him. Not for the first time, she was surprised at how classically handsome he was. Blond, blue-eyed, with a square jaw and perfect masculine features.

"What do you mean?" she asked, linking her fingers with his.

"Not only are you a successful career woman, but you can cook. Do you know how rare that is these days? Most women do whatever they can to keep out of the kitchen."

The last thing Hallie wanted was to mislead him. "Sure, steak and a baked potato. Everything else is a challenge."

He chuckled and kissed the tip of her nose. His eyes grew serious. "Everything feels right with you, Hallie. I can't believe I'm here with you in my arms."

She lowered her gaze, not ready to let Mark know how attractive she found him. "I feel the same way. You're worth every penny I paid for you."

He threw back his head and laughed. "I knew when you arrived at the restaurant a half hour early that we'd get along just fine."

She snuggled closer to him. "I was a nervous wreck."

With deliberate movements, Mark took the wineglass from her fingers and set it aside. Cradling her head between his hands, he slowly lowered his mouth to hers.

Hallie felt the kiss all the way to her toes. She'd been kissed plenty of times before, but not like this. Never like this. His touch, his kiss, reminded her that she was indeed a woman. A desirable woman.

"You taste so damn good," he murmured close to her ear.

"It's the wine."

"It's you," he countered. "You intoxicate me."

She opened her mouth to remind him that they'd shared an entire bottle of wine, which might have explained any intoxication, but he chose that moment to lower his mouth to hers again. The kiss was deep and involved, and when he raised his head they were both breathing hard.

"Oh, my," Hallie whispered, her eyes closed. The taste of his lips lingered on hers.

Mark began to kiss her neck and the underside of her jaw. Hallie leaned her head back as awareness shivered up and down her spine.

"I knew almost from the moment we met that you were the one," Mark whispered.

She'd shared his reaction, his enthusiasm. Meeting Mark had made up for her unhappy experiences with Marv and Tom. He was everything she'd hoped to find in a man—in a husband.

He continued kissing her, and his hands traveled to the front of her sweater, cupping her breasts. "You're so damned beautiful," he whispered.

Hallie bit her lower lip, as he manipulated his thumb over her nipples, which rose instantly to attention.

"Look how responsive they are." His voice was elevated slightly with sexual excitement. "I can't believe how perfect you are."

He slipped his hand under her sweater, his fingers investigating her warm smooth skin. All the effort that had gone into losing those ten pounds had been worth it, Hallie realized. She'd gladly do it all over again just to hear the awe in Mark's voice as his hand stroked her abdomen.

He kissed her once more, his tongue parting her lips, exploring her mouth. His breathing was heavy and labored when the kiss ended. "Hallie, sweet Hallie."

"Oh, Mark..."

"I realize we haven't known each other long."

"Two weeks." It seemed as if he'd been in her life for months.

"Let me spend the night. I know it's soon, but I need you so much."

Her eyes flew open and the warm sensual fog began to clear. She'd known—hoped—that eventually this would happen. She thought of the glorious silk nightgown she'd purchased a couple of months ago with this moment in mind. But it was too early in the relationship.

"I'm crazy about you." He kissed her again, weakening her resolve. The series of kisses that followed left her drowning in a sea of arousal. She searched desperately for a life preserver, a reason, an excuse.

"Hallie, can't you see what you're doing to me?"

"Yes, but..."

"It'll be good, I promise you."

"Mark, I need to think."

"Don't think, Hallie, feel." He removed her bra before she was aware of what he was doing. When she heard her jeans zipper ease open, she pressed her hand over his. Their eyes met in the semi-darkness.

From somewhere deep inside she found the answer. "Not yet."

Disappointment clouded his eyes. "Soon, though, right?"

She smiled and kissed him. "Soon."

Mark accepted her decision with good grace, then helped her adjust her clothes. When her desire had cooled slightly, she went into the kitchen to make a pot of coffee. Mark followed her and agreed they were both in need of something to sober them up.

They sat back down in the living room with their coffee. "I've got a tight travel schedule this week and I'll be gone for a few days," he said regretfully. "I'll call you, though."

She nodded. "I'll be here every night but Friday."

"Friday?" He frowned suddenly and studied her.

Rather than launch into a lengthy explanation, she said, "I'm helping a friend. Saturday afternoon, too, but I'll be home by about four."

"A friend?"

"Yeah." She didn't elaborate.

Again she felt his scrutiny. "Save Saturday night for me."

She smiled, oddly discomfited by his frown and at the same time relieved that he hadn't questioned her further.

Ten

The Lady With The Curve Ball

This wasn't going to work. Steve knew it the moment he saw Hallie grip the bowling ball and step in front of the pins. The first time he watched her throw the ball, he was reminded of an old Fred Flintstone cartoon. It looked, honest to God, as if she'd raced down the alley on tiptoe. And the bowling ball had headed straight for the gutter.

She looked guilty when she turned back. "I don't remember it being this difficult."

"Don't worry. Just relax." He tried to reassure her, a little afraid that if he offered her too much advice she'd change her mind and run.

The bowling ball was returned. Hallie reached for it and approached the line a second time. She made some inexplicable movements with her feet, shuffling a couple of inches to the left, to the right and then back to where she'd started, which was by no means where she should be. Up she went on her toes, glared menacingly at the pins, then raced forward like a ballerina terrorist.

"You might try aiming for the pins," he suggested when her bowling ball slammed into the gutter again. He had to give her credit, though; her ball had gone maybe a foot farther before falling off the lane this time.

"I *am* aiming for the pins," she said righteously. She rotated her arm and shook her hand back and forth, as if all she needed to improve was her wrist action.

"My turn," Meagan said, rushing forward. Both his children had inherited his talent for sports. Meagan walked up the alley like a pro, released the ball just the way he'd shown her, and effortlessly knocked down eight pins.

Steve placed two fingers in his mouth and whistled loudly in appreciation. Meagan had missed the spare, but she hadn't had a chance to warm up yet.

Kenny was next. Steve got a real kick out of watching his son bowl. What he lacked in strength and finesse, Kenny made up for with instinctive skill. He carried the bowling ball up to the foul line, studied the pins, then bent forward and gently let the ball go. It moved as if in slow motion and when it reached the pins, they fell almost gracefully. He knocked down six and then three.

Now it was his turn. Steve threw a strike, his ball exploding against the pins. He was good and had the trophies to prove it.

Hallie waited for the rack to reset the pins. She retrieved her ball, walked up to the starting point, shuffled to either side, then turned back and looked at Meagan.

His daughter shook her head and motioned with her hand for Hallie to move to the left. Hallie did as Meagan advised, but when she released the ball, Steve could see that she was standing in the wrong place. Again. The bowling ball headed straight for the right-hand gutter, just as it had earlier.

Steve closed his eyes. Maybe it wasn't too late to back out of the tournament. He opened his eyes in time to see Hallie's bowling ball balancing precariously on the outer edge of the lane, then unexpectedly taking a sharp turn toward the headpin. It missed that and struck two pins to the left. *The left.* The bizarre thing was that her ball had been slanting toward the right-hand gutter two seconds earlier.

All in all, Hallie managed to strike down six pins. Steve had seen plenty of curve balls in his day, but this was something else. She missed the spare, but returned to her seat, looking pleased with herself. Steve congratulated her.

"It just took me a while to remember what I was supposed to do," she informed him. "This isn't difficult, you know."

"Right."

They bowled three games and Hallie improved with each one. She never did get a strike, but came close a number of times. If for no other reason, her handicap would help him in the tournament, and he'd save face. It'd look bad if he couldn't find a replacement for his *sister.* It was bad enough having Shirley bowl with him, but to show up without a partner on Saturday would be a blow to his image. Hallie would have to do. He realized that seemed grudging; actually, he was grateful she'd agreed to help.

He wondered if anyone tomorrow would mistake Hallie for his girlfriend. Not that it really mattered. At the very least, it might convince his league buddies and their wives to lay off the matchmaking.

Plenty of people knew he was divorced, and more than a few had tried to set him up with women. He'd resisted their attempts for the simple reason that he wasn't interested in dating again. He preferred to keep trying with Mary Lynn, despite the fact that she was still dating that Kip character. They talked frequently, which Steve considered a promising sign, and Mary Lynn had him over for a family dinner every now and again. Less in the past couple of months than he would've liked, but he wasn't complaining.

Mary Lynn's birthday was coming up next week, and he'd ordered her a dozen red roses, plus two white ones. She loved roses, and he wondered if she'd figure out the significance of the two white ones. They'd been married twelve years and apart two. Those two years had been the most confused, difficult, painful years of his life. Damn it all, he wanted to be a full-time family man again. And he wanted Mary Lynn back—not the manipulative woman she'd become, but the loving passionate wife she'd once been. They both had to make some changes; he understood that. He was certainly willing to work on it, but he couldn't do it alone.

"Are you guys ready for pizza?" he asked the kids when they returned from handing in their bowling shoes.

"You bet."

"How many quarters do we get this time?" Kenny demanded.

Steve hid a smile. "Who said anything about quarters?"

"Aw, Dad."

"Don't worry, you'll get quarters." He ruffled Kenny's hair.

Although it was almost nine, the pizza parlor was as busy as it had been their previous visit. There weren't any families at this hour; the place seemed to be inhabited by teenagers. Hallie and the kids located a table while he ordered the pizza and bought a pitcher of root beer for the kids and glasses of dark ale for Hallie and him.

Once he'd brought over the drinks and relinquished the quarters into his children's hot little hands, he sat down with Hallie. "I really appreciate your doing this for me," he said. As for helping *her* out, that had cost him no money and little effort. She'd conscientiously repaid him each time. If anything, she'd added comic relief to his life when he needed it most.

"I'm glad I can return the favor."

She really did have lovely brown eyes, Steve realized. Eye color wasn't something he particularly noticed in a woman and he probably wouldn't have this time if she hadn't looked so happy. Her irises were an unusual color. Sort of like the ale they were drinking. Deep, dark. Striking.

"Do I have a frosty mustache?" she asked, and raised her fingertips to her upper lip. When he shook his head, she said, "I don't? Then why are you staring at me?"

"I was just thinking how happy you look."

The skin around the eyes he'd been studying a moment earlier crinkled with silent laughter. "I *am* happy and for a very good reason. Remember I told you I met a wonderful man through Dateline? Well, I think I'm falling in love with him."

"Really?" Steve didn't mean to sound skeptical, but he thought it all seemed awfully quick. He'd seen the guy who'd come by her house a couple of times. Steve hadn't thought much of him; he wasn't sure why. But he just didn't see this guy as Hallie's type, although if she was to ask him to define her type, he wouldn't be able to do it. But then, what did he know about love and romance? Apparently not much, seeing that his own marriage had been such a failure.

"Uh, I haven't seen him around lately, have I?" Steve added. It'd been a week or so since he'd last caught sight of the guy. The same day, in fact, that he and Hallie had met in the grocery store.

"He's been out of town. The last few days have felt like forever. We've talked long-distance for an hour every night. I hate to think what his telephone bill's going to be."

Steve didn't know what two people could talk about for an entire hour. He'd never been one to chitchat comfortably over the phone. Even face-to-face was something of a strain. He and his good buddy Alex Rochester used to fish for hours without saying so much as a word. Steve always figured they didn't need to talk to communicate. Pretty good basis for friendship, he thought. Well, that and the fishing.

Alex had moved to Texas three years earlier, and Steve still missed him. Come summer, he planned to take a couple of weeks and drive down to visit Alex. But then he'd been saying that every summer since Alex moved. Maybe this year.

"I'm happy for you, Hallie," Steve said, and he meant it. He didn't know his neighbor all that well, but he liked her. Finding a husband had seemed important to her, and he wished her and this Mark fellow the best.

"Thanks." Her hands circled the chilled mug. "Mark's everything I want in a husband. He's friendly and outgoing, smart, responsible, kind. I haven't met too many men like that. He's tender, caring, romantic..."

She had the dreamy look women get when they're crazy about some guy. His former secretary, Danielle, had fallen in and out of love half-a-dozen times in the three years she'd worked for him, so he was familiar with that faraway expression.

It wasn't until they'd all piled into the car for the ride home that

Steve realized he'd actually enjoyed himself. He had the other time, too, when Hallie'd gone out with him and the kids. He was *comfortable* with her. He supposed that was because they weren't romantically involved. They could be themselves without worrying about impressing each other or meeting inflated expectations.

"Can you be ready at eleven-thirty tomorrow?" he asked as they drove through the brick entrance to Willow Woods and onto the well-lit streets.

"Sure, no problem."

"Great."

Hallie inhaled sharply. "That looks like Mark's car!" she exclaimed, excitement raising her voice. "He must've been able to get away sooner than he expected."

Steve pulled into his driveway.

"Have you got a moment to meet him?" she asked.

"Sure," Steve answered, feigning enthusiasm.

Hallie climbed out of the car and waved. "Mark!" she called. "You're back early."

As Steve retrieved his bowling ball from the trunk, he heard Mark say, "Is this the *friend* you were helping out?"

Steve detected the nasty sarcasm in the man's voice, even if Hallie didn't. The kids caught it, too, and they exchanged startled glances.

Steve introduced himself, then stuck out his hand. Mark ignored it.

"You and I need to talk," Mark said to Hallie, his tone glacial. He didn't look at Steve at all.

Eleven

Disappointments

Donnalee should have known. Sanford was too perfect. Too wonderful.

And this evening, she found that out.

He'd cooked her a fabulous dinner aboard his houseboat on Lake Union. The Seattle skyline and the snow-capped Olympic Mountains had served as a romantic backdrop. Afterward, when the sun had set and they'd finished their meal, they sat in front of the fireplace, cuddling. She leaned against the solid strength of his chest and he wrapped his arms about her. Every now and again, he'd bend forward to kiss her neck, taste her, tell her how beautiful she was. How desirable.

But now she understood why he'd never responded whenever she made comments about children or talked about family. Why he'd seemed distant.

He didn't want children. She loved him, yet they wanted different things.

"Surely this doesn't come as a surprise," he prodded gently.

That he would even ask told her how little he knew her. "It does, Sanford. It comes as a shock."

"But if I'd wanted a family I would have married years ago. When I contacted Dateline I was specific about the type of woman I wanted. One who's as career-oriented as I am. One without children."

"But *I* want a family. That's the reason I decided to go ahead with the dating service. I've always wanted children."

Sanford released his breath slowly and leaned forward to rest his forehead on her shoulder. She felt his frustration as keenly as she did her own.

"Oh, Donnalee, I never dreamed this would be a problem."

"I don't know what to say." A heavy sadness weighed on her heart. There could be no compromise for them.

"I've never seen myself as a father," Sanford insisted. "I have no desire to bring children into this world."

"Perhaps in time?"

"No." His voice was adamant, final. "I'm afraid this isn't something I'm willing or able to negotiate. I feel very strongly about it, always have. That's the reason I went ahead and had a vasectomy a few years back."

Donnalee felt as though her heart had gone into a spiraling free fall. A vasectomy. He'd felt so certain about not having children that he'd had a vasectomy?

"I'm crazy about you, Donnalee," he whispered into her hair. "I don't want to lose you."

All these years she'd waited for a man like Sanford. He was everything she'd ever dreamed of finding. It excited her that he seemed to care for her just as deeply. He was a considerate lover, gentle and eager. He'd be a perfect husband.

But not as perfect as she'd once thought.

"Say something," he urged, sounding anxious. His grip on her shoulders tightened. "It worries me when you're this quiet."

"I've...always wanted a family." She knew she was repeating herself, but it was the only thing she could say.

"We won't need children. We'll invest all the energy a family would require in each other. We'll build our dreams around each other and enjoy the freedom other couples our age will never know." He spoke softly, persuasively of the future, painting a glittering picture of what their lives would be.

Donnalee closed her eyes and tried to let his fantasy carry her away. Tried to make herself accept his vision of the future. She tried, she honestly did. But what he described sounded shallow and empty to her.

They'd never argued before, never found themselves in opposing camps. So this, she realized, was a true test of how they would settle their differences.

"What if I said I couldn't continue to see you if you didn't agree to having the vasectomy reversed?"

He stiffened momentarily. "I don't want to think about that."

"I don't, either," she whispered. Then, because she was afraid, she twisted around to face him. "Kiss me, Sanford. Hurry, please, show me how much you love me."

He answered her urgent demand with a hunger of his own, sliding her body down onto the thick carpet and lowering his mouth to hers. Soon they were panting and needy, eager to bridge whatever kept them apart. There had to be a solution. She'd find one, Donnalee vowed, rather than lose Sanford.

They never did make it to the bedroom. Their lovemaking was wild and abandoned, right there on the living-room carpet, with the log fire spitting and hissing beside them. Tears glistened in her eyes when they were finished, but she didn't let Sanford see.

It was in those moments of passion that Donnalee had finally grasped what was wrong. She loved Sanford and he loved her, but he held back a part of himself. While he gave her his body, he held back his heart—his deepest feelings. While his body filled and satisfied hers, he kept her at arm's length emotionally.

Now she knew why. Only when she relinquished her dreams would he commit himself wholly to her.

If then. If ever.

She understood that their relationship would have to be on his terms. Either she accepted them or broke this off now, before it went any further.

Donnalee closed her eyes and breathed in the warm musky scent of the man she loved. Children weren't everything, she told herself. She could pamper and lavish attention on her sister's brood, and eventually Hallie would marry and start a family. She'd love her sister's children and those of her friends; she'd make do. Sanford was right. They didn't need anyone but each other.

"You're quiet again," Sanford whispered, then kissed her gently, stirring the fires he'd so recently quenched. "Tell me what you're thinking?"

"I'm not sure I can."

"I need to know, Donnalee." He took hold of her hands, interlocking their fingers, and pressed them against the carpet. Slowly he positioned himself above her. Their eyes met in the firelight.

"I love you, Sanford."

"I love you."

The urgency in his voice thrilled her. "If you don't want a family, then I have to accept that," she finally whispered.

She saw the relief in his eyes, the gratitude.

"I'll make it up to you," he promised, kissing her over and over. He rolled onto his back, taking her with him. "We don't need children, we never will, not when we have each other."

"Yes," she whispered.

He made love to her again, and this time he gave her everything she wanted—unreservedly gave her all that was in his heart.

Donnalee recognized this.

But she still felt empty inside.

Twelve

Bachelor #3

"Mark?" Hallie had never seen him like this. He was a stranger. Now he grabbed her arm and steered her toward the condo.

"Tell me what's wrong," she demanded.

She felt his hand tighten, as though he resented her questioning his order. "We'll discuss it inside," he snarled.

Hallie tossed Steve an apologetic glance, not knowing what to say. He stood next to his car, his face hard. Was he waiting for her to ask him to intercede? One look at his clenched fists told her he was more than ready to do so. Meagan and Kenny hovered beside him, Kenny clutching his father's bowling bag with both hands. The kids seemed stunned, their eyes wide with shock.

Too numb even to think, Hallie unlocked the front door. Her hand trembled as Mark urged her to hurry, then followed her inside. "I notice you didn't mention that the *friend* you were helping was male."

"Does it matter?" She didn't like his attitude or the way he'd embarrassed her in front of her friends. Mark was behaving like a jealous idiot, but it would do no good for her to get angry, too. One of them had to remain calm. Surely there was an explanation for his behavior.

"Damn right it matters." He punctuated his words by repeatedly stabbing his index finger at her. "I'm not going to have any woman of mine—"

"I'm *your* woman?" This was news to Hallie.

"I paid two thousand dollars to meet you, bitch," he shouted. "You damn well better consider yourself my woman."

Hallie was so outraged she couldn't find the words to speak.

"Let's get something straight right now," he went on. "You don't go out with another man when you're with me. Understood?"

It took her all of two seconds to recover. She met his look, her own anger spilling over. "For your information, I'm not your woman, not your bitch and not your friend. As of here and now, it's over. We're finished. Now leave!'' In case he needed help finding the door, she pointed it out to him.

"I'm staying until you get this straight," Mark insisted.

"Oh, no, you're not. You're going to walk out that door and never darken it again."

"The hell I am!"

She planted her hands on her hips. "No man calls me a bitch. You and I are through. Now get out."

"Just a minute here—"

"What part of 'get out' don't you understand?"

The doorbell chimed and they both ignored it, too intent on staring each other down.

"Hallie?" Steve shouted from the other side. "Answer the door, damn it. Are you all right?"

Mark switched his attention from her to the front door and the sound of Steve's voice. "I suppose you're sleeping with him. That's why you turned me down, isn't it?"

His idea was so ridiculous she almost laughed. "I suggest you leave now before this gets any uglier," she said without emotion. While she might have appeared outwardly calm, her heart raced, thundering wildly in her ears.

"We're going to settle this," Mark said, his voice ominous.

Hallie wanted nothing more to do with him. She walked across the room and threw open the front door. "Leave. Now."

Steve was now pounding on the patio door off the kitchen. "What's going on in there?" he demanded.

"Mark was just about to go, isn't that right?" She waited for him to walk out, but he surprised her by holding his ground.

"Okay, okay," Mark said, sounding calmer, more in control. He raised his hands apologetically. "Okay, so maybe I overreacted."

"Perhaps you didn't hear me," Hallie said, her voice equally calm. "I want you to go. Now."

Mark blinked, just as Steve raced around the house to the front lawn. "I believe the lady asked you to leave," he said. His hands flexed several times, as if he was itching to help Mark out the door.

"All right," Mark growled, pushing past Hallie. "If that's the way you want it, fine."

"Don't come back, either," she said. She stood on the top step, her arms wrapped around her middle as she struggled to ward off the embarrassment and bitter disappointment. She was beginning to doubt herself and her own judgment. Mark had seemed so perfect— until tonight. She shook with fury every time she thought about the way he'd claimed she was "his woman" and the ugly word he'd called her. She would never have guessed he was capable of saying such things.

Steve met Mark on the grass, apparently ready to escort him to his vehicle. With military-style precision Mark walked toward his parked car; halfway there he paused and turned around. "I still think we should talk this out," he said, directing the comment to her and ignoring Steve.

Meagan and Kenny stood on the lawn a few feet away.

"I've heard everything I need to hear," Hallie replied. "You aren't half the man Dateline led me to believe. Goodbye, Mark."

From under the glow of her porch light, Hallie saw his eyes narrow.

"You do have something going with this caveman, don't you?" he accused. "I knew it the minute I saw you with him."

"Get a life," Hallie shouted, wondering what she'd ever seen in him. To think that only a few days earlier they'd been kissing on her couch and she'd actually been tempted to go to bed with him. It made her sick to her stomach, knowing she'd allowed herself to be deceived this badly.

"You aren't any prize yourself, Hallie," he yelled back. "Take a look in the mirror if you don't believe me. No wonder you have to pay a dating service to find a man."

"Belt him, Dad," Kenny shrieked, punching the air a couple of times with his fist.

"Yeah, Dad, teach that creep a lesson," Meagan joined in.

Mark hurriedly climbed into his car, slamming the door loudly. He revved the engine and took off with the tires squealing.

Hallie sank down on the step and closed her eyes, barely able to believe what had happened. Mark had shown up at her place tonight to *spy* on her, see who her friend was. Then when he saw her with Steve and his kids, he'd exploded into a jealous rage.

"You okay?" Steve asked with a gentleness that nearly brought tears to her eyes.

"Fine," she said. "Hunky-dory." But she was shaken to the core.

Kenny flew to her side. "Was that your *boyfriend?*" he wanted to know, sounding incredulous that anyone with half a brain would date a guy like that. Hallie didn't blame him.

"Not anymore," she told him, and managed a frail smile.

"Good thing, 'cause that guy's a real jerk."

Mark had succeeded in fooling her. From the beginning, there'd been signs of his possessiveness, his proprietary attitude, but she'd lacked the ability to interpret them. No, she'd refused to see them.

While he was out of town this past week, he'd called her at the oddest hours, wanting to know where she'd been and who with. She hated to admit it, but his phone calls weren't because he'd missed her. He was simply checking up on her.

Hallie recognized now that because she so badly wanted a man in her life, she'd answered all his questions, spent hours reassuring him. She was ashamed to acknowledge that it wasn't only her desire for a husband that had blinded her to Mark's character flaws, it was also the money she'd invested in Dateline. Seeing that she'd paid top dollar to meet Mark, she'd been determined to make the relationship work, convinced that it should. After all, Donnalee's experience with the dating service had gone so well....

In retrospect, she told herself, if Mark thought *he'd* been short-changed, it couldn't compare with how cheated *she* felt.

"She doesn't look so good," Kenny whispered to his dad.

Hallie opened her eyes to discover Steve and both his children staring at her as if she were about to shatter and break into a million pieces. She was afraid she already had.

"Hallie?" Steve asked.

Hallie realized she was incapable of pulling this off. She'd put on a brave front, but now that Mark was gone, reaction had set in. She started to tremble visibly.

"Come inside. You need to sit down." Steve carefully took Hallie by the arm, then led her back into the house. Meagan and Kenny followed.

Racing ahead, Meagan grabbed the pillow off the sofa and fluffed it up. Kenny got her a glass of cold water.

"Who was the jerk, anyway?" Meagan asked.

"Yeah. He's lucky my dad didn't kick his butt."

"Kenny!"

"You wanted to, Dad."

Steve didn't bother to contradict his children. "Maybe it would be a good idea if you two waited for me at home," he suggested.

Both kids seemed reluctant to leave. "You sure?" Meagan asked in a soft voice.

Steve nodded. "I won't be long."

Rarely had Hallie been more embarrassed. Her face burned. "I can't tell you how sorry I am, Steve," she said when they were alone.

"You? What did you do that was wrong?"

"Dated Mark Freelander." She shuddered as she said his name.

"You didn't know."

Hallie just shook her head. What a fool she'd been. Marrying

Mark would have been the biggest mistake of her life—and had his behavior tonight not forcibly opened her eyes, she might have done it.

"*You* didn't do anything wrong," Steve repeated.

"I wore blinders," she said, unable to forgive her own stupidity. "You know what it was, don't you?" She paused, but he didn't respond. "The money. I figured if I paid two thousand dollars to meet him, he had to be okay. I figured if there was anything wrong, the fault must be with me."

"Don't you think you're being a little too hard on yourself?"

"No!" she countered sharply. Sitting still was nearly impossible. She stood and started pacing the living room. "Apparently I'm not the judge of character I thought I was."

"Hallie, there's no need to blame yourself for this."

"Why not? It's what I deserve."

Steve sat down, reached for the glass of water Kenny had fetched for her earlier and drank it himself.

"Look at me, Steve. Really look." She stood up straight, squaring her shoulders. Her gaze pinned his. She could trust him to tell her the truth; she didn't doubt that for a second. "Answer me this and don't spare my feelings. Is there something wrong with me?"

"Wrong?"

"Am I repugnant? Ugly?"

"Good grief, no."

"Do I look naive or stupid?"

"No." But this he said with less conviction.

"Then what is it about me that attracts major jerks?"

"Hallie, be fair. The first two were blind dates."

"Yes, but Rita's a good friend and she knows me, and she hooked me up with Marv."

"He's the one who made you pay for your dinner and dumped you on the freeway?"

Hallie didn't appreciate being reminded of the details, but nodded.

"The second creep was a colleague of your blind date's, sort of a blind date once removed, right?"

Again she nodded.

"You can't blame yourself for Mark, either. An agency trained in personality assessment set you up with him. He buffaloed them, too."

"It doesn't matter," she muttered miserably. "I'm finished." She waved her arms dramatically, wishing she could obliterate the last three months of her life—except those ten pounds. She didn't want those back.

"Finished?" Steve echoed.

"With men." She had a sudden craving for double-fudge macadamia-nut ice cream. It'd been Christmas since she'd last eaten anything cold and sweet, and if she searched her freezer, she'd be willing to venture she'd find a carton there.

"Don't you think that's a bit drastic?"

"Eating double-fudge macadamia-nut ice cream?"

"No," he said, confused, "cutting yourself out of the dating scene."

"At this point, no." She hurried into her kitchen and opened the freezer door. Standing on her toes, she peered into the deepest recesses. She shoved aside her Weight Watcher frozen entrées and thrust her arm in, feeling around for an ice-cream container. There was none.

She rested her forehead against a stack of vegetarian lasagna. "No. No. No." Oh, the unfairness of life, without even the consolation of ice cream. When she looked up, Steve was standing next to her.

"Maybe I should call a friend for you. I think it's a woman you need just now."

Steve was right. On her way over, Donnalee could stop off at Baskin-Robbins.

Thirteen

Bring On The Ice Cream

As it happened, Hallie didn't have a chance to talk face-to-face with Donnalee until Sunday afternoon, and by that time she'd managed to collect herself. Mark Freelander had taught her a valuable lesson.

"I can't believe a guy would *do* something like that," Donnalee murmured, for the third time, her expression stunned as Hallie relayed the sordid details.

Hallie sat cross-legged on the sofa. She tilted her bowl and scooped up the last of the melted double-fudge macadamia-nut ice cream, then licked the back of her spoon. "Believe it. I don't think I've ever been angrier."

"Did you lose your cool? I can't blame you, but you're usually so calm in a crisis. I've always admired that about you."

"I barely raised my voice," Hallie said. "It wasn't until later that I completely lost it."

"How do you mean?"

"Check out my freezer," Hallie said, motioning with her head to the kitchen.

"Your freezer?" Donnalee's eyes widened.

"Peek inside and you'll know what I mean."

Donnalee went into the other room and opened the upper half of Hallie's refrigerator. A moment later Hallie heard her friend laugh. She knew it was because the entire front was stacked with ice-cream containers, one on top of the other, four across. "What did you do, buy out the store?" Donnalee said, returning to the living room.

"That's exactly what I did. The five-gallon container wouldn't fit in my freezer, so I bought Baskin-Robbins's entire supply of double-fudge macadamia-nut in one-quart containers. And that isn't all." She gestured at the fireplace mantel. "Did you happen to notice my trophy?"

"As a matter of fact, I did. When did you take up bowling?"

"I haven't, but I filled in for Steve's sister, and we took third place in a tournament yesterday."

"You and Steve took third place! That's wonderful!" The admiration was back in Donnalee's voice—or was it amazement? Well, Hallie had to admit she was pretty amazed herself. "I didn't know you bowled that well," Donnalee added.

"I didn't, either," Hallie said, and smiled to herself. Steve had been no less surprised. Friday night when they'd gone out to practice, she hadn't scored more than a hundred points in any of the three games they'd played. But during the tournament she'd averaged more than 160 points a game. If she had to credit anyone with this sudden turnaround, it was Mark Freelander.

Her anger had carried over to the following day, and it seemed as if she couldn't do anything wrong on the alley. She was much more focused than she'd been in her few previous attempts at sports. Maybe it came from imagining Mark's face on every one of those pins. She suspected Steve wasn't pleased with the amount of attention she'd attracted from his friends and competitors, but he didn't say anything. He'd been thrilled, however, when they took third place and was kind enough to let her keep the trophy.

"What's with you and your neighbor?" Donnalee asked, settling down on the big overstuffed chair.

"With us? Nothing. We're friends." Hallie dismissed the question, hard-pressed to put into words her relationship with Steve. "He's a great guy, you know, but he's hung up on his ex-wife."

"You've had a steadier relationship with him in the last couple of months than you have with anyone. And he *is* single."

It was true. She'd gone out with him and his children more consistently than anyone, except maybe Mark. But she wasn't romantically interested in Steve. Knowing how obsessed he was with his ex-wife, Hallie had never really considered her neighbor "available." He was exactly what she'd told Donnalee—a friend.

"Ever thought about getting together with him?" Donnalee suggested in a way that implied the idea should have been obvious. "Friends are supposed to make the best lovers."

"Nope," Hallie answered. "I like Steve, don't get me wrong, but he's not my type."

"Do you have a type?"

"Sure," Hallie answered casually. "Don't we all?"

Donnalee lowered her eyes. "I suppose. Tell me, what's your type?"

Hallie had given this a good deal of thought, mulled over the perfect man in her mind. "Well," she began, "I'm not necessarily

looking for someone tall, dark and handsome—although I wouldn't
rule him out if he was. As long as he met my other qualifications."
She dropped her bare feet to the floor and rubbed her hand down
her jeans. "Looks are nice, but frankly, I've discovered they're not
all that important."

"I agree," Donnalee murmured.

"I want a man who'll love me, who'll appreciate me for the
woman I am," Hallie said thoughtfully. "Someone generous and
honest. A man of integrity, who values family and commitment. I
suppose I'd want him to be a risk-taker, but not foolish enough to
jeopardize what's important."

"Hmm."

"Hmm?" Hallie repeated. "What's that mean?"

Donnalee wore the skeptical look of a banker when the numbers
don't add up. "Does such a man really exist?"

"Of course. There are men like that. Lots of them." Hallie *had*
to believe that, or she'd give up hope of ever getting married. She
stood, taking the empty ice-cream bowl to the kitchen. "It was easy
for you," she said as she returned.

"Easy?"

"To find the perfect man. You met Sanford, and that was that."
She tucked her hands into her back pockets. "I can't help being a
little envious." At one time, she'd assumed it would be that easy
for her, too. It sounded a bit conceited in light of her recent failures,
but she'd viewed herself as, well, something of a prize. She still
did—despite Mark's parting insult.... She was creative, outgoing,
intelligent. She had her own business, was fairly attractive, financially solvent. No emotional baggage from a previous marriage, either.

Donnalee had gone strangely quiet. "How are things with you
two, anyway?" Hallie asked.

"Great. We've decided to shop for an engagement ring next weekend."

Hallie couldn't believe Donnalee hadn't said something sooner—
but then, she hadn't given her friend much of a chance. The moment
Donnalee arrived, Hallie had launched into her sad and sorry tale of
Mark Freelander.

"That's wonderful! Congratulations."

Donnalee smiled, but Hallie noticed that the joy that should have
shone in her eyes was missing. Did Donnalee feel nervous about
making this commitment, or what?

"You *are* happy, aren't you?" Hallie asked.

"Of course. Who wouldn't be?"

"Oh, Donnalee, you're going to be married." Hallie felt almost giddy. "I'm thrilled for you. Sanford's wonderful. I like him a lot." They'd met briefly a few weeks earlier, and she'd definitely been impressed. With good reason. Just looking at him made the backs of her knees sweat. The guy was gorgeous. A hunk. And he obviously adored Donnalee.

Hallie's mood changed swiftly and she flopped down on the sofa. "I'm taking a reprieve from this whole dating thing," she announced solemnly.

"But, Hallie, it's too early to throw in the towel."

"I'm not quitting, exactly. I feel like I need to step back and analyze what I'm doing. Adjust my attitude. Regroup. Maybe I've been going about this the wrong way."

"Don't give up on Dateline," Donnalee said. "And what about having Steve set you up with a friend of his?" she suggested. "Really, it makes sense."

Hallie gave that a moment's thought, then shook her head. It was just too demeaning to ask Steve to scrounge up a date for her. If he'd *offered* to introduce her to a friend, that would be different. But he hadn't, and she wasn't going to ask.

Besides, after meeting Rita's "perfect" man, Hallie had serious reservations about letting her friends arrange blind dates for her. You never knew what type of person they might consider suitable dating material. Although, granted, Rita had been shocked by Marv's behavior and apologized profusely.

"Personally," Donnalee said, "I think you and Steve would make a good couple. You like him, and you're always talking about his kids."

"Forget it," Hallie said, rejecting the idea with a wave of her hand. "It would be like hanging out with my brother. If I had a brother. I can't even *imagine* kissing him. No romance."

"You're sure about that?"

"Pretty sure." Steve's longing for Mary Lynn was unmistakable. Hallie had never seen a guy so much in love with the woman who'd divorced him. "Anyway," she added, "I told you how he feels about his ex."

Donnalee nodded slowly. "Okay, but the least you can do is make him your ally. Steve could be an excellent resource for you, give you a few hints, maybe teach you a little bit about men, what they're looking for and so on."

Now that was good thinking—the kind of thinking that made Donnalee so successful in business. Evaluate the circumstances, identify resources, then use them. Yes. Hallie wondered why it had never occurred to *her.*

She smiled, and Donnalee's eyes brightened. "Great. Talk to him tomorrow—and quit being so hard on yourself."

Hallie wanted insider information from Steve Marris, and she'd come to get it.

After work Monday night she'd given him plenty of time to shower and have his dinner before she'd walked across their connecting yards and rung his doorbell.

He looked mildly surprised to see her. "Come on in," he said, gesturing toward his living room. Hallie had never been in his place before; one glance told her he hadn't put a lot of effort into decorating. The walls were practically bare, although the fireplace mantel was crowded with sports trophies. Not a look she favored.

She noticed the photograph of his wife and kids prominently displayed on the big-screen television. Noticed? She could hardly miss it. The TV was the visual focus of the room, and his furniture, the little she saw, was plain. Utilitarian. Sofa, chair, coffee table, lamp. He seemed to view living here as a temporary thing.

"I need your help," she said, figuring he'd appreciate it if she came right to the point of her visit.

"Another loan?" he asked, smirking. He sat on the chair across from her, one ankle resting on the opposite knee.

"No." She didn't find the question humorous, even if he did. "As you know, I'm hoping to find a husband, settle in suburbia, have a couple of kids. Live happily ever after."

"You haven't exactly made a secret of that."

"Right. Well, after my recent failures—Mark Freelander, most notably—I've been forced to give serious consideration to my...approach."

"And?" He looked wary, suspicious, as if he feared she was going to propose something he wasn't going to like.

"And I realize I've made a fundamental mistake. All along I've looked at a potential husband for what *he* could bring to a partnership. Is he intelligent, kind, financially solvent, a man of integrity—those sorts of things."

"That's wrong?"

"No, not wrong. But in retrospect I see that, as well as looking at what a man can give *me,* I should examine what *I* have to offer a relationship."

"Oh." He settled against the back of the chair. "Like what?"

"Basically the same things. Intelligence, integrity, et cetera. What I need to know is how to present myself in the best light."

"You think being who you are isn't enough?" He frowned.

"I need an edge."

"An edge?"

"You know, a gimmick."

The frown deepened. "This is where I come in?"

"Exactly." She was glad she didn't have to spell it out. "Actually Donnalee was the one who had this idea, and she's right. If I'm going to be open enough to admit I'm looking for a committed relationship, then I need an edge. Something that'll attract the attention of the kind of man I want to meet."

Steve didn't respond.

"Something that'll give me an advantage—that'll tell him who I am and what I want without scaring him off. Men don't like the idea of commitment. It terrifies them." She shook her head. "Fifty-three million men in the world, and only twelve of them are serious about a permanent relationship."

"I hate to admit it, but you're right."

"I feel I have to be up-front because I can't afford to waste time in a dead-end situation with some guy who'd rather play house. I want it all and I want it yesterday."

"What am I supposed to do?" Steve asked.

"It's simple." She noticed that his shoulders relaxed when she said this. "All I need you to do is tell me what a man *really* wants in a woman he intends to marry. The first thing he's going to look for."

"What a man wants in a woman he intends to marry," he repeated slowly.

Hallie could almost see his mind working. "Think about it. There's no need to rush. You don't have to come up with an answer right away." The question was complicated, and she wanted him to give it his full consideration before responding.

"I don't have to think about it. I already know."

Hallie's heart started to pump with excitement. "You don't mind telling me?"

He grinned. "No problem."

Hallie waited.

"Let's start with the physical."

She should've known that would get top priority. "All right."

Steve studied her as if to gauge how honest he could be. "I don't know a man who isn't attracted to a woman with big, uh, boobs—" he glanced at her quickly "—and long legs."

He paused, waiting for her reaction. Hallie refused to give him one, although she had to bite the inside of her mouth to keep quiet.

"It doesn't hurt if she can cook, either," he added, "and these days that's something of a plus. The fact is, I'd marry a woman who could make a roast chicken dinner as good as my grandmother's."

Unable to contain herself any longer, Hallie leapt to her feet. "You mean to say that for a man everything comes down to the physical? And if she can cook? That's disgusting! I'm serious here."

"Hey." He raised both hands in a conciliatory gesture. "So am I. Most men check out the equipment first. You wanted the truth and I'm giving it to you. Don't blame me."

"This isn't a joke?" She stared at him hard, her outrage simmering just below the surface.

"No way."

He might have looked sincere, but she still wasn't sure if she should believe him. "What about integrity and commitment? What about loyalty and honesty?"

"What about 'em?" he asked.

"Don't any of those qualities matter?"

"Well, sure, but that was understood. I thought you wanted something to give you an edge. Well, I'm telling you what it is."

"You mean men really are that superficial?"

"Well...yeah."

Hallie rolled her eyes. As far as she could see, she was a lost cause. She was short, had small breasts, and other than steak and salad, she couldn't cook worth a damn.

Fourteen

Does He Wear Panty Hose?

April 16

Something's wrong with Donnalee. She should be happier than Cinderella, since she's marrying Prince Charming. The woman's sporting the Rock of Gibraltar on her ring finger, yet it seems to be an effort to even smile. Sanford is a dream come true, but every time Donnalee and I chat, I'm left with the feeling that something's wrong. I've tried to talk to her about it, but she keeps dodging me. Says I'm imagining things. But I know Donnalee too well to be fooled. Something is wrong, and come hell or high water, I'm going to find out what it is.

It's been a couple of weeks since my big blowup with Mark Freelander. I couldn't believe it when he phoned the other day as if nothing had happened. The man's got nerve—and little else. I told him not to call me again, and I doubt he will. Dateline called, too, with the name of another man and asked if I was interested in meeting him. Right away the adrenaline started flowing and my imagination kicked in and I saw myself standing behind a colonial house with a white picket fence. I could picture two toddlers and a puppy frolicking on the lawn. The man beside me in this idyllic scene was kind of shadowy, though. That made me realize the odds of being disappointed again were way too high—which says a lot about my state of mind. Like I told Steve and Donnalee, I still need time to regroup, think things over and analyze what's happened. With regret, I told Dateline I'd pass, but to keep me in mind.

My problem is I need a break from all this. I've thought about Steve's so-called advice and I'm still annoyed. But I guess men do like well-endowed women. It's a fact of life;

girly magazines prove that much. It makes me feel sort of disgusted, sort of amused—and a teeny bit envious of women like Rita. (And Donnalee!)

Plus, that cliché about the way to a man's heart being through his stomach obviously has some basis in fact. So I could have saved myself the embarrassment of asking Steve, since he had nothing new—or useful—to tell me.

Speaking of Steve, Mary Lynn has taken to dropping off Meagan and Kenny on Friday afternoons before Steve gets home. I've talked to her a few times, and frankly, I find her shallow. A real airhead, in my opinion. I'm probably prejudiced because I like Steve, but it seems crazy for a woman with a decent husband and two beautiful children to destroy her marriage in order to "find herself." She's easy enough to like, though, and I wish her well. Steve, too, of course.

Meagan has a key to Steve's place and the kids are perfectly capable of staying on their own for an hour or so, but they've been coming over to my house, instead. Actually, I enjoy their company. They're great.

As for dating, I've decided to stop for a while. I'll try again as soon as I've repaired my confidence. That shouldn't take too long. I've got too much invested in this project to quit now. Whenever I'm tempted to give up, I sit down and read through my goal planner.

This is possible. I can do this. I will do this.

The knot in Donnalee's stomach hadn't gone away from the moment Sanford had slipped the two-carat diamond engagement ring on her finger. She'd tried to ignore her discomfort, tried to pretend she was happy and, to her surprise, fooled everyone except Hallie. So far Donnalee had been able to put her off, but she didn't know how much longer her stall tactics would work.

Sanford joined her on the park bench. They'd been selecting china patterns at a downtown department store and had taken a long-overdue break to walk along the Seattle waterfront. Donnalee tried to absorb her surroundings, tried to shut out her thoughts. April winds whistled down the wooden piers, whipping the canvas awnings, and the American flag outside the fire station snapped to attention. The scent of seaweed and deep-fried fish blended with the tang of salt water.

Sanford wrapped his arm around her shoulders. "You've been so quiet lately," he murmured.

Donnalee looked out over the water, and for no reason she could explain, her eyes filled with tears.

"Donnalee?"

She couldn't do it.

Right then and there, she realized she couldn't go through with the wedding, with pretending it didn't matter that this man she loved wanted a different future than she did. He'd made the idea of life without children sound wonderful and exciting—with exotic travel and expensive cars and sophisticated pursuits. She'd tried to believe it. But when she was alone, she found herself thinking that what he'd *really* described was a self-absorbed life-style—empty and devoid of everything that was important to her. Not having a family was the right choice for some people; Donnalee wasn't one of them.

She stood slowly, her legs weak and trembling. "I'm sorry," she said, her words breaking as she struggled to speak.

"Sorry?" Sanford looked confused and Donnalee sympathized. Her friends would call her a fool for letting Sanford go. He was a good man, a loving person, and she loved him, but this one thing came between them. He didn't want children.

For days she'd walked around attempting to convince herself that she'd made the right decision in agreeing to marry him. But no matter how adamantly or how often she said it, she couldn't make herself believe it.

Unable to speak, Donnalee removed the diamond from her finger and handed it to Sanford.

He shook his head in puzzlement. "I don't understand. Don't you like the ring?"

"Very much. It's just that... Oh, I feel so awful about this." She bit her lower lip hard enough to taste blood. "I've decided it would be a mistake for us to marry."

He paled. "You don't mean that."

"I'd give just about anything if it wasn't true. I've tried to tell myself it didn't matter, us not having a family..."

"So that's what this is all about." His face tightened, and she knew he was closing himself off from her.

"I'm not judging you for that," she went on. "It's not right to bring children into the world if they aren't loved and wanted. You recognize that, which says a great deal about the kind of man you are—honest, mature..."

"Then what's the problem?"

"I'm the problem," she whispered, fighting to hold back tears. "Me, not you. Please don't think I blame you in any way."

"You're going to have to explain this a little more clearly, Donnalee."

She wasn't sure she could. "I married when I was young and for all the wrong reasons. I was in love, or so I thought. I had this dream of raising a houseful of happy children, being an at-home mom while they were young, continuing with my own education after they started school. I had this warm wonderful fantasy—and I had a husband who'd married *me* for all the wrong reasons." She took a deep breath. "I thought my dream had died with the divorce. But you woke that dream in me again. You allowed me to believe in the possibility of it. Your love restored what my ex-husband stole from me.

"I do love you, Sanford. But I want children. More than I ever realized. And you don't. It would be wrong to marry you under these circumstances."

He didn't say anything for a long moment. "You're sure of this?"

"Yes," she whispered, her voice cracking under the strain of her anguish.

"Then that says it all, doesn't it?"

"Yes..."

"I hope you get what you want, Donnalee."

"You, too." She saw regret in his eyes, even some pain. But without another word, he pocketed the diamond and walked away. In her heart of hearts, she knew she'd never see him again.

Somehow Donnalee made it home. She didn't remember getting into her car, driving, entering her house—nothing. She sat in her living room, arms wrapped protectively around herself, feeling a numbness that was very like what she'd experienced after her divorce.

Eventually she phoned Hallie. She needed a shoulder to cry on. Someone to talk to. A friend.

Hallie was on her doorstep within the hour.

"I *knew* something was wrong," Hallie said forcefully when Donnalee answered the door.

"I broke off the engagement," Donnalee whispered, sobbing and shaking.

Hallie said nothing. Taking Donnalee by the hand, she led the way into the kitchen and pushed her gently into a chair. Hallie moved about as if it was her own home, opening and closing drawers, putting a kettle of water on to brew tea. "My mother always said nothing's quite as bad over a pot of tea."

Donnalee was content to let her friend do as she pleased.

"All right," Hallie said, carrying two steaming china cups and saucers to the table. "Tell me why."

"You'll call me a fool," Donnalee said, and blew her nose into a crumpled tissue. "Everyone will."

Hallie frowned. "I doubt that. What did Sanford do—wear panty hose to bed?"

Donnalee laughed and wept at the same time. "Hardly." The picture was ludicrous. Sanford in panty hose.

"Are there problems with the family? His mother refused to allow another woman in her son's life, right?"

"No." Again, laughing and crying, Donnalee shook her head. She grabbed a fresh tissue, inhaled deeply, then announced, "Sanford doesn't want children."

Hallie slowly lowered her teacup. "No children?"

"He doesn't like children. He doesn't want them in his life."

"Not even his own?"

Donnalee wearily closed her eyes. "No. He's very certain of how he feels—so certain he's had a vasectomy. It'd be foolish to get married, hoping that in time he'd change his mind. And even if he did, there's no guarantee the procedure could be reversed." She wiped her eyes. "Getting married would be unfair to both of us. Unfair and wrong."

"I agree." Hallie gripped Donnalee's hand and squeezed her fingers.

"I tried to believe we could be happy, just him and me—but, Hallie, I want a family. Every time I see a young mother I find myself longing for the day I'll have a child of my own. I want to feel a baby growing inside me."

"It was holding my sister's baby that woke me up, remember?" Hallie reminded her in a soft voice.

Donnalee smiled tremulously. Her friend had recently framed a photograph of herself and the baby. In it, Hallie sat in a rocking chair cradling Ellen, gazing at her with a raptness and a wide-eyed concentration that revealed the intensity of her desire.

"I know plenty of women are single mothers by choice," Donnalee said, sipping the hot tea, feeling it begin to revive her. "But I want it all. Husband, traditional family, the whole thing. Am I being selfish?"

"No," Hallie said, her voice rising with the strength of her conviction.

They sat in silence for a while. "How did Sanford take it?" Hallie asked at last.

"He didn't argue with me. I know he was hurt, but then so am I. I should never have accepted the engagement ring, but I'd convinced myself I could live with his decision. Not until later did I realize I...just couldn't."

"Oh, Donnalee, I'm so sorry."

"I am, too. I thought I'd be content lavishing love and attention on my sister's two children. But then, a couple of Saturdays ago, I had my niece and nephew over—so Sanford could meet them. In the back of my mind, I was thinking, hoping really, that he'd be so enthralled with them he'd be willing to reconsider."

"Didn't work, huh?"

"Hardly." She raised her eyes to the ceiling. "It was a disaster. Katie and Ben are six and eight, and it didn't take them two minutes to pick up on his attitude. Sanford and the kids did an admirable job of ignoring each other. After we dropped them off at the house, he asked how often I'd be seeing them and—" it was painful to say the words "—he hoped I didn't mind, but in the future, if I wanted them around, he'd prefer that he wasn't."

"Oh, my."

"I understand his feelings. He's never spent any time with children. He's an only child and he feels awkward around kids."

"There'll be someone else for you," Hallie said with such confidence Donnalee was tempted to believe her.

"Yeah, but is it going to take me another thirteen years to find him?"

"I doubt it." She ran the tip of her finger along the edge of the china cup. "Do what I'm doing and take a breather. Give yourself time to get over this, then try again. There's someone else waiting and wondering if the right woman is out there for him. I comfort myself with that whenever I think about giving all this up. Next time you'll find someone who wants the same things you want. I'm sure of it."

"You know what I'm going to do?" Donnalee said, feeling better already.

"Tell me."

"I've got two weeks' vacation scheduled, and I'm going to take one of them, call my mom and book us a trip to Hawaii. I've never been there and we could both use a break."

"That sounds like a great idea." Hallie stood and refilled their cups. "I know how difficult this is for you. I want you to know how much I respect you for refusing to compromise your dreams. You *will* find the right man."

Donnalee wanted with all her heart to believe that. In the beginning Sanford had seemed to be that man. But now... She looked at Hallie, grateful for the friendship they shared.

A good friendship—like this one with Hallie—endured. It sustained you during times of crisis. It was there for you during the good times and the bad.

The same thing, Donnalee reflected, couldn't always be said of romance.

Fifteen

What Friends Are For

"Hey, Dad, do you know what tomorrow is?" Meagan asked Steve as he led the way from the soccer field to the parking lot. He'd played on an adult league for a couple of years, and both kids participated in the children's fall league. Steve enjoyed helping them hone their skills. It was good for killing a Sunday afternoon, like today, when the kids were restless and ready to go back to their mother and their friends. Their weekday lives. It hurt to know they were sometimes eager to leave him, but he swallowed that pain along with everything else the divorce had brought.

"Dad, I asked if you know what tomorrow is," Meagan said impatiently.

Other than the fact that tomorrow was the twenty-eighth of April, Steve had no idea. He'd never been much good at remembering important dates. Valentine's Day had come and gone, St. Patrick's Day, as well as April Fools' Day. Mary Lynn's birthday...no, that couldn't be it. That was last month and he'd actually remembered it. What the hell was so important about April?

"Hallie's birthday," Meagan announced. "She's turning thirty. Her friend sent her flowers, and when I asked her, she said they were for her birthday. She said it was the big three-O."

"Really?" Steve hadn't seen much of his neighbor lately. He got a kick out of her reaction to his husband-hunting advice—he'd heard from the kids that she'd signed up for cooking classes. He knew he'd offended her by mentioning a woman's bustline, but what he'd said was the truth. He wasn't talking about himself, of course. He didn't spend a lot of time looking at a woman's chest. Oh hell, he'd own up to it. He did look now and then. What man didn't?

"She isn't dating anyone," Kenny added, climbing into the car behind his sister. The kids preferred him to take his car rather than his work truck. More room.

"How come?" he asked. His kids saw far more of Hallie than he did.

"She's regrouping," Meagan explained.

"Yeah, she's baking cookies and stuff." Kenny bounced the soccer ball on his knee. "When I asked her why, do you know what she said? She said men needed help knowing they wanted to get married. Is that true, Dad?"

"Ah...I guess so."

"Do you like Hallie?" The question came from his daughter.

"Like her? Sure."

"I mean *like* her."

"You mean romantically?" Steve knew that was exactly what Meagan meant. He could tell by his daughter's tone that his answer was important to her. Wouldn't his kids be more interested in seeing him back with their mother? Most children were. Maybe they knew something he didn't.

"Hallie's a wonderful person," Steve answered carefully. "I like her a lot, but she isn't the woman for me." It didn't seem necessary to remind his children that the only woman he'd ever loved was their mother.

"Why isn't she the woman for you?" Kenny asked.

"Well, because...she just isn't. Don't get me wrong, Hallie's great, but—"

"She isn't Mom," Meagan finished for him, and he thought he heard a note of sadness in her voice.

"Yeah," he said. "She isn't your mother."

"But Mom's dating Kip," Kenny threw in.

The sound of the man's name made Steve clench his teeth. He didn't know where Mary Lynn was going with this relationship or how serious it was. Every time he asked her she got defensive.

"So she's still seeing the ol' Kiperroo," Steve joked, trying to disguise his concern.

"A lot." Kenny sighed deeply.

This was the last thing Steve wanted to hear, but he'd rather know the truth so he could deal with it. Clearly it was time to change tactics if he wanted to win back his ex-wife. This hands-off wait-and-see-what-happens-with-Kip approach hadn't worked. He'd call Mary Lynn, he decided, and talk to her again. Soon.

"I think you should ask Hallie out," Meagan said, studying him intently.

"Hallie and me on a date?" Steve tried to keep it light. "No way."

"But she's a lot of fun, Dad," Kenny insisted. "And her chocolate-chip cookies are real good. She let me take some to the guys last week and everyone liked 'em." He paused. "She's funny, too. She bakes all these cookies and then gives them away. I asked her why she doesn't eat some, and she said it's because she's come to hate her treadmill."

Steve grinned.

"Will you think about going out with Hallie sometime?" Meagan asked.

He should have known his daughter wouldn't let this drop. "I'll think about it," he promised.

"Which means no," Meagan muttered.

Steve felt he had to justify his hesitation. "Not so," he argued. "I will think about it." The last thing he wanted was to disappoint his kids, but he couldn't allow them to dictate his love life.

Steve didn't give his conversation with Meagan and Kenny another thought until the following evening. He'd never been keen on yard work, but the lawn badly needed to be mowed. Monday afternoon he returned home from work and decided he couldn't delay that chore any longer. If he did, the condo association might come pounding on his door.

At least the weather was beautiful, unseasonably warm and summer-bright. Perfect for outdoor tasks.

Steve made sure he had a couple of bottles of cold beer in the refrigerator before he started. It took three tugs to get the old mower going, but it finally kicked in.

Being a generous kind-hearted soul, or so he told himself, he tossed aside his shirt and mowed Hallie's half of the shared yard when he'd finished his own. She'd done more than one favor for him, and he appreciated knowing that Meagan and Kenny could stay at her place if he was late on Friday afternoons.

It was when he turned off the lawn mower that he heard the music. A blues number. The wail of a solitary saxophone that seemed to speak of sadness and trouble. He thought the music was coming from Hallie's place.

He stood quietly, listening to be sure. When he glanced through her sliding glass door, he caught a glimpse of her lying on the living-room carpet, arms spread out. Her eyes were closed and she wore the woeful look of a woman done wrong. He paused and wondered what *that* was all about. Then he remembered what Meagan had told him.

This was the day Hallie turned thirty.

Steve had spent his last two birthdays alone. He'd tried to tell himself he didn't care, that birthday celebrations were for kids. But he remembered the empty feeling in the pit of his stomach when he'd climbed into bed those nights, regretting that there hadn't been anyone around to make a fuss over him.

Was anyone making a fuss over Hallie? Like him, she'd probably heard from her family and a few friends—one of them had sent her flowers. But she was alone now and obviously miserable. Poor thing. His heart went out to her.

Steve showered and changed clothes, but couldn't forget how depressed and lonely Hallie had looked. Hell, he'd been there himself.

Before he could change his mind he stuck a candle in a snack cake, grabbed the two bottles of beer and knocked on her front door.

He listened as the mournful music abruptly ended. A moment later he heard the lock turn as she opened the front door.

"Happy birthday to you," he sang, and handed her the chocolate-flavored cupcake.

"Who told you?" she asked, wide-eyed with surprise and what he hoped was delight.

"The kids. Hey, it isn't every day you celebrate your thirtieth birthday."

"Come on in," she said, leading the way into her living room. "Although I don't know that I'm fit company."

"Because you've turned the dreaded three-O?" He'd heard some women saw thirty as the end of their youth, which struck him as ridiculous. Besides, if the kids hadn't told him, he wouldn't have guessed Hallie was a day over twenty-five. All right, twenty-eight.

"Thirty," she muttered, collapsing onto the sofa, "and not a marriage prospect in sight."

Steve uncapped one of the beers and passed it to her. "Tell Uncle Stevie all about it."

"*Uncle* Stevie?"

"Hey, I'm five years your senior. I've spit in the eye of middle age—spreading middle, weak knees, failing eyesight and everything."

A smile twitched at the corners of her mouth.

"Thirty's not so bad," he assured her, "once you get used to it."

"That isn't all. I have other reasons for being depressed."

"You owe the IRS?" Since they both owned their own businesses, he knew what a killer tax time could be.

"Yes," she said with a groan, as if he'd reminded her of something *else* to be depressed about. "But that's the bad news with the good. I made more money than I did last year, so I can't really complain too much.'' She tipped back the bottle and took a respect-able swig of beer.

Some women sipped beer like they were tasting fine single-malt Scotch. Not Hallie, and he liked her the better for it.

''I gained back five of the ten pounds I lost,'' she said plaintively. ''I suffered to lose those five pounds. One little slip with the double-fudge macadamia-nut ice cream and they're back.''

As far as he could see, those few pounds hadn't hurt her any. He didn't think she had any cause for concern. Despite having reached the big three-O, she looked just fine.

''I don't know what made me decide to step on the scale this morning. I told myself I wouldn't, seeing that it's my birthday and all.'' She downed another swallow of beer. ''And there they were.'' She fell back against the sofa cushion and closed her eyes. ''It wasn't supposed to happen like that.'' Suddenly she gave him a stricken look. ''I can't believe I'm telling you this. Usually I only discuss this kind of stuff with Donnalee. You must be a better friend than I thought.''

''Uh, maybe there's something wrong with your scale,'' he said, trying to be helpful.

''I'm not talking about that,'' she muttered, although she was touched by his attempt to shift the blame for those five pounds to her scale. ''The thing is, according to my goal planner, I should have met him by now.''

She opened one eye and stared at him. He suspected she was asking him to inquire further, which he obligingly did. ''Him?''

''My husband-to-be,'' she said, enunciating just a little too clearly.

''Oh, yeah. Him.''

''This beer tastes really good.'' She finished off the bottle and set it aside.

Steve had barely tasted his. ''Have you had dinner yet?''

Her head lolled against the back of the sofa, both eyes tightly shut. She seemed to find the question amusing and smiled broadly. ''Not breakfast or lunch, either. Too much work.''

That explained why the beer had gone to her head so fast.

''Then listen, this is your lucky day because I was about to order Chinese. There's a new place off Meeker that delivers. It's on me.''

''Happy birthday to me, happy birthday to me.''

''Exactly.'' He walked over to her phone, removed the business card from his wallet and ordered enough to feed them both for two or three meals.

''Donnalee's in Hawaii,'' Hallie said.

He had no idea why she felt the need to tell him that.

"She had flowers delivered."

"That was nice of her."

"Very nice," Hallie agreed.

He noticed that she perked up after the food arrived. The scent of sizzling pepper beef and almond fried chicken wafted enticingly through the compact kitchen. "This is one of the sweetest things anyone's ever done for me," she said, arranging two plates on the table and putting water on to boil for tea.

Steve was impressed that she used chopsticks. He did, too, pleased that she was willing to eat in the traditional Chinese way. Mary Lynn had refused to even try and lost patience with him when he insisted on doing so.

Because they were both hungry, they ate in silence. It no longer surprised him how comfortable he felt with Hallie. As he'd explained to his children, he wasn't romantically interested in her, but he considered her a friend. He'd come to believe that in many ways friendship was of greater value.

"I feel so much better," she said when she'd finished. She pushed her plate aside, placed her hands on her stomach and slowly exhaled. "Both physically and emotionally. Thank you, Steve."

"No problem." He didn't want her getting all sentimental over a little thing like a bottle of beer and some take-out dinner. "You've been a real help to me with the kids on Friday nights. This was the least I could do for your birthday."

"My thirtieth birthday," she said.

Afterward Steve wasn't sure when he'd made the decision to kiss her. It was an impulse, he rationalized later, no doubt prompted by Meagan and Kenny's questions from the day before.

It happened as he was leaving.

"I'm glad you're my neighbor," Hallie said, walking him to the front door.

"I am, too." He opened the door, then turned and gently held her shoulders.

He saw the surprise in her eyes and wondered if it was a reflection of his own. "Happy birthday, Hallie," he whispered before lowering his mouth to hers.

As kisses went, it was good. Unexpectedly good. Her lips were soft and pliable, molding easily to his. She smelled and tasted great. Her mouth parted slightly and he found himself deepening the kiss. The ol' adrenaline started to flow about then, and he drew back abruptly, not wanting things to get out of hand.

She buried her face in his shoulder. He ran his fingers through her hair and kissed the top of her head. "There's someone special just waiting to meet you, Hallie,'' he whispered, and her hair tickled his nose. ''Don't worry, he's out there, wondering why it's taking so long.''

''That's funny,'' she murmured.

''How's that?''

''I recently told Donnalee the same thing. It sounded much more convincing when I was saying it, though.''

Steve chuckled. ''You'll be just fine.''

She broke away with obvious reluctance. ''Thanks again, Steve. For everything.''

He wondered if she was including the kiss.

Sixteen

Not My Type

"Did you have a nice birthday?" Kenny asked, leaning against Hallie's kitchen counter.

"Very nice," she answered, lifting cookies hot from the oven off the baking sheet. She'd mastered chocolate-chip and was moving on to oatmeal-raisin. She intended to create a repertoire of baked goods to entice the most discriminating connoisseur. Kenny was an enthusiastic admirer of her baking, but hardly discriminating. Right now, he waited impatiently for the cookies to cool. "Your dad bought me dinner."

"Dad did?" This bit of news evidently piqued Meagan's interest. She slid off the sofa where she'd been reading and hurried into the kitchen, joining her brother at the counter.

"It was a kind gesture," Hallie said. She'd thought about it a lot since Monday night—thought about the kiss too, more than she should. It was a kiss between friends, nothing more, yet she found herself remembering it at the oddest moments. Like this one. But maybe that was good, because Meagan and Kenny were a reminder of how much Steve hoped to reconcile with Mary Lynn.

Unable to wait any longer, Kenny reached for a cookie and burned his hand. "Ouch," he yelped, sucking on his fingertips.

"Hallie told you they were hot," Meagan chided. "Where did Dad take you?"

"He ordered in Chinese." She didn't tell the kids she'd been so depressed she'd lain on the carpet listening to the saddest blues CD she could find. She'd stacked an entire music menu on her player, including bagpipes, funeral dirges and mournful ballads. Sad troubled music for a sad troubled day.

"Do you like my dad?" Kenny asked, tossing the hot cookie from hand to hand.

"Sure." Hallie absently scooped dough onto the sheet for a new batch of cookies.

"Enough to marry him?"

"Marry him?" Hallie gave her full attention to Steve's kids. Both were studying her with dark unblinking eyes. She remembered the kiss again. Although it had been a *satisfying* kiss, it wasn't a kiss between lovers or even potential lovers. She could embellish it in her mind as much as she wanted, but she knew very well that Steve wasn't interested in a more complex relationship. They were friends and neighbors, and that was all.

"You said you liked him," Kenny said.

Hallie placed the cookie sheet in the oven while she considered how to respond. Something told her the answer was important and she needed to choose her words carefully, a task made more difficult by not knowing the status of Steve's relationship with Mary Lynn or the likelihood of reconciliation.

"I think your dad's great. He works hard and loves you kids. I've been impressed with what a good father he is." She paused, wondering how much she should say. Meagan and Kenny continued to study her as if waiting for more. "I like his sense of humor." Kenny smiled encouragingly. Recalling how Steve had twice lent her money to pay taxi drivers, she added, "He's generous and caring." He hadn't pressured her into the bowling tournament, either. "He's a friend, a good one, but—"

"That's great," Kenny interrupted her, "but do you like him enough to marry him?"

"Don't rush her," Meagan barked, glaring at her younger brother.

Kenny ignored his sister. "You'd make a cool stepmom."

"You would," Meagan agreed, nodding.

They were still watching her so intently. Hallie felt a bit unnerved. "I'm glad you think so," she said slowly, frowning as she glanced from one to the other. "But..."

"But?" Kenny cried. "I hate it when Dad says 'but' because it always means no." His shoulders sagged and he propped his chin on the kitchen counter. "Go on," he said in a resigned voice, as if he already knew what she intended to say.

"I'm just not the right woman for him." Honesty was the best policy, Hallie had determined, even if it disappointed her young friends. "Your dad's a great guy, but he isn't for me. I hope you don't mind too much."

Kenny helped himself to a cooled cookie. "Not too much. That was what I figured you were going to say."

Hallie was relieved.

"Besides, when we asked Dad, he said almost the same thing."

Goose bumps rose on the back of Hallie's neck. "You asked your father about marrying me?"

"Sort of," Meagan answered.

"And what *exactly* did he say?"

"That you have a neat personality and everything," Kenny explained, "but then, like I told you he said almost the same thing you did. You aren't his type, either."

"Not his type!" Hallie couldn't believe her ears. "Well, if that doesn't beat all," she muttered under her breath, not wanting the kids to hear.

The timer rang and she grabbed the last tray of cookies from the oven rack with more force than necessary. "Not his type," she muttered again, her back to the kids. The man's attitude rankled—never mind whether or not *she* was being rational.

She clumsily scraped the cookies off the sheet, mangling more than one. Why, Steve Marris would be the luckiest man in the world to marry a woman like her. Of all the nerve!

"Hallie, are you mad about something?" Meagan asked.

"Mad?" she asked, her voice squeaking. "What do I have to be mad about?" She'd wring Steve's neck, that was what she'd do. How dared he tell his kids he liked her "personality." That was the kind of thing men said about the women eager mothers pushed on unwilling sons. It was the kind of thing men said about women they found sexually unattractive. But then, what did she expect from a man who'd suggested the way to find a husband was to enhance her bust size?

The phone rang and Hallie whipped the receiver off the wall. "Hello," she snapped, suspecting it was Steve. *Hoping* it was, so she could set him straight about a few things.

"Hallie?" Donnalee asked uncertainly. "Is something wrong?"

"Donnalee!" she cried. "You're back! How was Hawaii?"

"Wonderful. I'm relaxed, tanned and feeling more like myself. Have you got plans for tonight?"

Hallie's mood lifted instantly. "I suppose you brought me one of those windup hula dolls?"

"Yes," Donnalee teased, and they both laughed.

Her friend had been gone eight days and it felt like a month to Hallie. "Come on over any time." Friday night, sitting around with a girlfriend—that pretty well summarized the sorry state of her love life, she thought, smothering a giggle.

"I'll be there in an hour," Donnalee promised.

As it happened, Hallie didn't get a chance to talk to Steve, which was just as well all round. Kenny was looking out the window when

Steve pulled up. "Dad's home," he yelled, leaping off the sofa. He grabbed his backpack and headed toward the front door.

"Don't be upset with my dad," Meagan said, staying behind a moment. "He didn't mean anything by what he said."

"I'm not upset," Hallie assured her. Well, she had been at first, sort of, but as the kids had pointed out, she'd said the same thing about him. It was her ego talking, not her reason. In fact, she felt a little embarrassed over the way she'd reacted—like a woman scorned.

Still Meagan lingered.

"You wanted to ask me something?" Hallie asked. Generally Meagan was as eager to see her father on Friday nights as Kenny.

"Next week is Take Your Daughter to Work day," she announced, speaking quickly as though the words were bursting to get out. "Mom's not working 'cause she's in school, so I asked Dad about it, and he said I could go to the office with him, but I don't want to be a machinist. I'm kind of interested in art, though, and I'd like to see what you do, Hallie. Can I spend the day with you?"

The idea appealed to Hallie right away. She recalled herself at Meagan's age, how she would have given anything to see a commercial artist at work. "That would be wonderful. Are you sure your dad won't mind?"

Meagan beamed her a wide carefree smile. "He'll be glad. He'd take me if I really wanted, but it'd be much more fun going with you. Thanks, Hallie." Meagan gave her a quick shy hug and raced outside.

Hallie walked to the door and watched as Meagan excitedly told her father that Hallie had agreed to take her to Artistic License. Steve looked over to find her standing in the doorway. Hallie waved.

"You're sure Meagan won't be a bother?" he called.

"Positive."

Even from this distance, Hallie could see his relief. He pointed his finger in her direction. "I owe you one, neighbor."

Hallie shook her head, laughing. "Don't worry about it. We'll have a good time."

True to her word, Donnalee arrived about half an hour later. She hadn't exaggerated about her tan; she looked bronzed and beautiful. Rested and obviously at peace with herself and her decision.

They hugged and Donnalee presented her with a box of chocolate-covered macadamia nuts. "It's an emergency supply in case you don't have any ice cream handy when the next tragedy strikes," she joked.

Unable to resist, Hallie opened the box, sampled one, gave one to her friend and then promptly stuck them in the freezer and away from temptation.

"Something's different," Donnalee observed, studying her.

"Different?"

"Physically," Donnalee said. "You haven't done anything to your hair, have you? Something's up."

Feeling smug, Hallie threw herself onto the sofa. "That's an interesting turn of phrase, my friend. What's up, quite literally, is my bosom."

"Hallie, you didn't!"

"I did. I succumbed and got myself one of those enhancer bras." She was unwilling to admit that Steve had been the catalyst.

"I can't believe you'd do that," Donnalee said with more than a hint of indignation. "It's ridiculous to think that a push-up bra is going to make you a better person—or even help you meet a man."

"True," Hallie agreed, feeling a little silly. "But it's given me a psychological boost, which, after more failures than I care to admit, is one I badly needed."

"It's sexist. Those bras take the women's movement back ten years. It's degrading." Donnalee sounded stern and unrelenting. She paused, dragged in a deep breath, then asked, "How much did it cost and where can I buy one?"

Both dissolved into giggles. It felt good to laugh again.

"No, seriously," Hallie said. "I thought about this. I don't see it as sexist. It's no different from makeup or hair spray or anything else women use to enhance their appearance. It's fun and it makes me feel good, and if it happens to be attractive to men...well, all the better."

"I know, I know," Donnalee said. "Hey, do I smell cookies?" She wrinkled her nose and sniffed loudly.

"I've been taking cooking classes," Hallie admitted with some reluctance, wondering if her friend was going to comment on that, too.

"The old 'way to a man's heart is through his stomach' routine?"

"Yup." No point in denying it.

"Good thinking," Donnalee said with a grin. "Why not go for the tried and true? Then, once you've lured him and fed him, you can dazzle him with your *real* personality."

In that moment Hallie noticed the sadness in her friend's gaze. She reached for Donnalee's hand. "Second thoughts about Sanford?"

"Every day," she admitted. "I really loved him. It's difficult to turn off my heart. Forgetting him isn't easy."

"He hasn't called or contacted you in any way?"

"No, but then I didn't expect he would. And I really don't want him to." She brushed the hair from her face and inhaled sharply as if struggling to hold back tears. "Hawaii helped. Mom and I had a wonderful time. We slept in every day, lazed on the beach, visited all the tourist places and shopped till we dropped. It was exactly what I needed."

"And now you're home," Hallie said, watching her friend.

"And alone once more. Only..."

"Only now you feel even *more* alone," Hallie finished, certain she knew what Donnalee was experiencing.

"Yes," she murmured.

"Are you going back to Dateline?" Hallie asked. She was preparing to leap back into the dating world herself, with hesitation but resolve. After several weeks' sabbatical, she was ready to try again.

"I'm going to give it a bit of time first," Donnalee said thoughtfully. "Some time for myself. The way you suggested. I'm feeling kind of battered."

"It's a good idea," Hallie said. "Step back, evaluate and then move forward from there."

Donnalee grew quiet. "I remind myself on a daily basis that there's a man out there for me. Someone who'll share my dreams."

"I know there is." Of this Hallie was confident. For her friend. Although she still had some doubts concerning her own prospects.

"What about you?" Donnalee asked, apparently reading Hallie's mind. "Are you ready to go back to Dateline?"

"Yes. Actually I already have." She reviewed the name of the applicant she'd been paired up with this time. Larry McDonald. She'd received the information on him the day before. "They sent me another bio this week."

Donnalee sat up excitedly. "Let me see."

Hallie brought it out, and while Donnalee read over the page of information, Hallie studied her reactions. Nothing. Donnalee didn't reveal so much as a flicker of emotion—which described her own feelings, too. She'd read the file numerous times, and each time she felt completely...untouched, completely dispassionate about the details of this man's life. He seemed nice enough—a science professor was sure to impress her family—but unfortunately he also seemed dull.

"Larry." Donnalee said the name slowly, as if the sound of it would help her decipher his personality.

"It's unfair to judge him without meeting him first, don't you think?"

"Absolutely," Donnalee agreed. "Have you set up a time?"

Hallie nodded. "We're meeting in a bookstore. It's not very original, but we both like to read and, well, it seemed a good idea at the time."

"When?"

"Sunday afternoon."

"You'll call me afterward?"

Hallie agreed, but frankly, she didn't hold out any great hope for Larry McDonald.

But then, she reminded herself, she was certainly willing to be surprised.

"What are you doing?" Meagan asked. The eleven-year-old stood behind Hallie at the drafting table in the large workroom at Artistic License. The front office was staffed by two employees, Liz and Evie, who handled walk-in traffic, took orders and answered the phone. Four copy machines of various sizes hummed, while the largest of the printing presses droned like a snoring troll in the room next door to Hallie.

"You're done helping Bonnie?" Hallie asked. It had taken her a moment to break her concentration.

"Yup. It was fun, too." Meagan maintained a respectful distance from Hallie's drafting table.

"I'm working on a logo design," Hallie told her. She'd been playing with a number of ideas for the better part of an hour. This was often the most difficult aspect of her job. The client had approached her with several ideas, but unfortunately translating those concepts into a viable image was proving difficult.

"Bonnie let me move things around on the computer screen."

Because Hallie was working to deadline with this logo project, she'd had Meagan work with her assistant on the production of a brochure they were creating for the local school district.

"Did you enjoy that?" Hallie asked.

Meagan's eyes lit up. "It was great. I learned a lot."

"She did a good job, too," Bonnie called out from the other side of the room. "Hallie, I've got to go over the layout for the Bergman Hardware ad. The newspaper needs it before three."

"No problem. I'll have Meagan work with me."

Hallie glanced at her watch. It was another hour until lunch, and she'd hoped to have a couple of designs ready for the Prudhommes by that afternoon. "Pull up a chair, kiddo, and I'll explain what I'm doing—after I talk to Hank about one of our print jobs."

Hank Davis took care of all the print orders, which had steadily increased every month since the first of the year. She jumped up to discuss a question of priorities with him, then stayed a minute to chat about their expanding workload. If her business continued to grow at this rate, she'd need new equipment, more staff and either another building or an addition to the existing place. The prospect delighted her. Her reputation for quality had been earned, one customer at a time.

She rejoined Meagan, who'd dragged a chair next to Hallie's. "I don't draw very good," Meagan said, sounding worried, "but I'll try if you want."

"What I'm looking for now are ideas to advertise a French bakery," Hallie told her. "The logo will be printed on the front window, takeout boxes, napkins, letterhead and so on. The logo is an important promotional tool for any business."

"It's going to be on everything then?"

"Just about. Mr. and Mrs. Prudhomme have specific ideas about the kind of image they want—something clever and cute. They serve coffee and pastries, but their specialty is petit fours."

"What're those?"

"Small frosted cakes a little larger than chocolates." Hallie's mind refused to stop spinning and she deftly sketched a picture of the Eiffel Tower. Next she drew a van with the name of the bakery on the side, to show that the Prudhommes also welcomed catering opportunities.

Meagan sat by her side and watched silently.

"Do you want to try?" Hallie asked. She was fresh out of ideas herself. While she understood what the Prudhommes wanted, she hadn't managed to translate it onto paper.

Meagan picked up the pad and sucked on the end of her pencil the same way Hallie did. Hallie smiled, sliding her arm around Meagan's shoulders. The girl smiled back. "Being a graphic artist is fun, isn't it?" Meagan asked.

"Sometimes." Also frustrating, challenging and a few other choice adjectives, Hallie mused.

"It's a lot different than I thought it would be."

"What do you mean?" Hallie asked as she scribbled away at a new concept. She didn't want to lose the idea.

Meagan glanced over her shoulder, drew a deep breath and gestured around her. "It's so big. Dad's going to be surprised when he picks me up this afternoon. When I asked him what your shop was like, he said he wasn't sure, but he thought you sat around and drew pictures all day."

"Really?" That amused Hallie. Poor Steve hadn't a clue how

involved or complicated her business was. She did everything from letterheads, designs and printing to commercial photography. The list was endless. But then, she didn't know all that much about machine shops, either. Hallie suspected if she was to visit *his* workplace, she'd have her eyes opened, too.

"You know what I thought when you said petit fours?" Meagan asked. "I thought of really short numbers." She laughed softly to herself.

"Short 4s?" Hallie asked.

Meagan nodded.

Hallie nimbly drew a series of elongated numbers, each with a face and personality. Their only apparel was a French beret, rakishly tilted. A row of short 4s stood in front of their much taller cousins.

Meagan looked at the drawing and giggled.

Hallie laughed, too. It wasn't bad, although the other numbers distracted from the overall effect. She set the 4s dressed in their berets on top of a linen-covered table. The steam from two smiling cups of coffee circled a base with a single red rosebud. Clever and eye-catching, just the effect Hallie had been trying to capture. She needed to work with it, develop the idea further, but she was on to something. Thanks to Meagan.

Hallie took Meagan to lunch at Lindo's, her favorite neighborhood restaurant, although it'd been at least a month since she'd gone there. Because she was so often working to deadline, she'd gotten into the habit of ordering her lunch to go and having someone stop by for it. She'd designed and printed the menus for the owner, Mrs. Guillermo, several years earlier and had recently updated them.

When Hallie arrived nearly a full hour before the heavy lunchtime rush, Mrs. Guillermo welcomed her enthusiastically. "I don't see you for too long," she said in her heavily accented English.

Hallie introduced Meagan, and Mrs. Guillermo's expressive face broke into a wide smile.

"Today is Take Your Daughter To Work day," Hallie explained.

The older woman nodded. "I read this is special day in newspaper. My granddaughter is here."

"That's wonderful."

"Your daughter is as beautiful as you," she said, and before Hallie could explain that she wasn't Meagan's mother, Mrs. Guillermo handed the menus to a girl about the same age. "Rosita will see you to your table," she said proudly.

Meagan didn't say anything until after they were seated. "I'm glad you didn't tell her I'm not really your daughter," she said, then shook her head sadly. "Sometimes I can't help wishing you *were* Dad's type."

Seventeen

She Bakes

June 2

Larry and I have been seeing each other steadily for a month now. Steadily, but not often. Once a week at the most, which, to be honest, is fine with me. Everything was so intense with Mark. He had to know where I was and who I was with every minute of the day. It felt like we were constantly together.

Larry's on the quiet side, and that makes me all the more talkative. I don't know why I feel this need to fill the silences, but I do. Anyway, I suppose you could say he's your basic nice guy. Once we're more comfortable with each other, I'll be able to judge my feelings more accurately. Right now, our relationship is still a bit awkward.

So far, we've gone to a number of museums. These are all places I've wanted to see, but have never taken the time to visit. If we aren't touring museums, we're in bookstores. The most exciting date so far has been to a Moroccan restaurant. Larry's a mathematics professor, and I don't think he has a lot of discretionary income, but then, I'm not interested in a man for his money. He was serious enough about finding a wife to plunk down the two thousand bucks, which is all I need to know.

He kissed me for the first time last week—on our third date. It was all right. It's come as something of a shock to realize how wildly romantic I am. I want a man panting with desire for me, one who won't be able to remove that silk nightgown fast enough. The nightgown that's lying untouched in my bottom drawer. For reasons I have yet to understand, I can't imagine Larry panting with desire for anything.

Speaking of that nightgown, I take it out occasionally

and wonder how long it'll be before I don this masterpiece of silk and lace. Will it be for Larry? Try as I might, it's difficult to think of Larry getting excited about anything. Nor can I picture him nude. I wonder if he'd wear his glasses to bed.

Mom always said still waters run deep. If that's the case, Larry's deep all right, so deep I wonder if I'll ever touch bottom.

On a brighter note—all isn't wasted. Larry likes my cookies.

It was well past closing time, but Steve had to finish this paperwork. He left as much of the bookkeeping as he could to his secretary and the accountant, but there were some things he had to handle personally.

Todd stuck his head in the door. "You staying late again tonight?"

"I won't be much longer," Steve replied without looking up from his desk. He wondered if it was true. "Go ahead, I'll lock up."

"How about a cold beer? I don't mind waiting. Fact is, I've got some stuff I need to clean up, anyway."

A cold beer sounded good. It'd been a long day, and with a stack of paperwork looming in front of him, it was going to be longer still. "Sure. That'd be great."

Tackling the pile with renewed enthusiasm, Steve finished within an hour. He found Todd and they drove to a local bar, taking their own vehicles. Although Steve considered Todd one of his best friends, they didn't often socialize. No need to, really, since they saw each other five days a week. Todd had been a good confidant during the divorce proceedings and the days that had followed. If Steve had ever needed a friend it was then.

He hadn't heard much from Mary Lynn in a while, and that worried him. Kenny hadn't said anything about Kip lately, but that didn't mean Mary Lynn wasn't seeing the guy—who, he'd recently learned, was a car salesman.

They arrived at the Sure Shooter separately and parked out front. "It's been ages since we were here," Todd said when the waitress, dressed in Western garb, delivered a pitcher of beer and two frosty mugs. Country music blared from the jukebox. A twanging female voice belted out the tale of a man who'd done his woman wrong—and paid the price. A cry-in-your-beer kind of song about a truck-driving, gun-toting, whiskey-guzzling son of a bitch.

Steve filled the mugs and realized that Todd was right; it'd been damn near seven or eight months since they'd sat across from each other in a tavern. It sometimes shocked Steve to notice how fast the time flew by. Without much trouble he could remember changing Meagan's diaper. Now, before he knew it, she'd be a teenager.

Thinking about babies and diapers brought Hallie to mind. He'd gotten a panic call from her the other day. Apparently her six-month-old niece would be in her care for the weekend, and Hallie wanted to make sure Meagan would be around to lend a hand if she needed one. Steve couldn't even begin to imagine the trouble Hallie could get into with an infant. He planned on sticking around himself, just for the hell of it.

A few years back Steve had tried to talk Mary Lynn into having another child. She wasn't interested. It'd been a disappointment at the time, but considering what had happened with them, he was grateful she'd refused.

"So," Todd said, gazing at his beer, "how's it going?"

"Great," Steve replied automatically. "What about you?"

"Good. Damn good. I've been spending most weekends at the lake, working on the cabin, remodeling it. You ought to stop by with the kids one weekend. You'd be surprised at the changes."

"I will." Todd had inherited the summer home from his grandparents. If Steve remembered correctly, it was out near Key Center on Carr Inlet. Every now and again Todd brought him some fresh oysters. Steve had never tasted any finer.

"Everything's going well, then," Todd said.

"Great. Say, did I tell you Meagan wants to take art classes? She spent a day at work with my neighbor a few weeks back and has since decided she wants to be a commercial artist."

"Really?"

"Yeah. Apparently she came up with an idea that Hallie used, and now Meagan's convinced she's found her career path." He grinned every time he thought about it. Not that he didn't believe Meagan could do it. What surprised him was the effect that one day of working with Hallie had had on his daughter. He was genuinely thankful for Hallie's encouragement.

Hallie. He smiled just thinking about her. They'd had a confrontation of sorts a couple of weeks back. He'd been minding his own business, washing his car late one Sunday afternoon, when she'd come out of the house, looking dejected and miserable. It'd taken him a while to ferret out the reason. He'd been sure it had to do with the latest character she was dating, but no, that wasn't it. Seemed she'd stepped on the scale that morning and discovered she'd gained two pounds. Furthermore, she said *he* was to blame, since he was the one who'd talked her into baking all those cookies.

Steve told this story to Todd, then laughed until his throat felt raw. Two pounds, and she'd made it sound like fifty.

"Are you sure you aren't more than friends?" Todd asked.

The question caught Steve unawares. "Of course. What makes you ask something like that when you know how I feel about Mary Lynn?"

"Well..." Todd folded his hands around his mug. "Your eyes light up when you talk about Hallie."

Steve digested that and shrugged. His eyes? Todd must have been watching "Oprah" a few too many times. "Hallie makes me laugh," he said simply. He'd never been friends with a woman the way he was with Hallie.

"She's bright and funny," he continued, "and the thing is, she doesn't realize how funny she is. She paid this agency two thousand bucks to find her a husband, and I'll tell you, she's dated some real screwballs."

"You sure you're not interested in her yourself?"

Steve shook his head. "No way. You should meet this guy she's dating now. He's got 'nerd' written all over him. He comes complete with a slide rule and thick glasses. Hallie tells me he teaches math at Green River Community College. Now I'm sure he's a perfectly okay guy, but him and Hallie? That matchmaking service has got oatmeal for brains if they think Hallie'd be happy with this joker."

Grinning, Todd leaned back and listened.

"My kids love her, and with good reason. She spends more time with them than Mary Lynn ever did. Plus, I've never eaten better since she started those baking classes."

"You mean she bakes more than just cookies?"

"Yeah, homemade bread and cinnamon rolls, for starters. She brought over a huge plate of maple bars last weekend. The kids and I stuffed 'em down before lunch. They were the best I've ever tasted."

"I can't remember the last time I tasted homemade anything," Todd muttered, and it was easy to tell he envied Steve a neighbor who baked. "A man could marry a woman for that alone."

Steve straightened and laughed outright. "That's exactly what I said."

"You offered to marry her?" Todd studied him as if he wasn't sure if this was a joke.

"Don't be silly." The question was ridiculous. "Hallie isn't interested in me, and vice versa. But she *is* looking for a husband, and I helped."

"She got advice from *you?*"

Steve decided not to take offense. "Some time ago Hallie asked my opinion on what a man wants in the woman he marries, and I told her."

"You told her?" Todd sounded even more incredulous.

"Damn straight," Steve announced proudly, although he refrained from repeating his comment about a woman's physical attributes. "I was honest, and Hallie was smart enough to take my advice seriously." She wasn't the only one who'd put on a few pounds since then, either. Steve knew from the way his clothes fit that he'd gained four or five pounds himself, although in his case it didn't really matter. He'd lost at least that much in two and a half years of making his own dinners.

Todd reached for the pitcher and refilled their mugs. "The kids are fine? They've adjusted to the divorce?"

"As far as I can tell. Meagan's turning into quite the young woman. Kenny's sprouting faster than a weed. They spend most weekends with me—I wish it could be more. I miss having them around all the time."

Todd bent forward, resting his elbows on the wooden table. "You haven't mentioned Mary Lynn in quite a while. You two still seeing each other?"

"Sure we see each other," Steve said, knowing he sounded defensive. "Every week when she drops off the kids. She calls once in a while, too." Generally when she was low on cash and needed a loan until the next support check. She'd never mentioned the roses he'd sent on her birthday. When he'd brought up the subject, she'd smiled and thanked him, but her heart wasn't in it. He'd almost felt as if she'd resented his sending her flowers. He'd been disappointed by her reaction and tried not to think about his lack of progress in the past few months.

"I saw her the other day," Todd said casually. Too casually.

His tone instantly sparked suspicions in Steve. He decided to make it easy on his friend. "I suppose she was with some guy."

From the abrupt way Todd inhaled, Steve could tell he'd taken him by surprise.

"As a matter of fact she was."

"Probably Kip," Steve told him, shrugging it off, although it gave him no pleasure to confront what he'd been ignoring for months. Mary Lynn was still involved with this sleazy salesman.

"Is this the same guy she was dating right after the first of the year?" Todd wanted to know.

"Yeah, I guess it is," Steve admitted reluctantly. He'd been waiting for her infatuation with this jerk to run its course; so far it hadn't happened. "What's he look like?" It was the kind of question he couldn't ask his children. One thing he knew for sure: Kip didn't get grease under his fingernails.

"Hell, I don't know," Todd answered. "Polished-looking. He was wearing a suit."

"Like a talk-show host?" That was the way Steve pictured the other man—slick, debonair, just the type of guy who fit Mary Lynn's new taste in men.

"Yeah," Todd said, with a sharp nod. "That pretty much describes him."

"Where were they?" he asked, his lips tightening despite his effort to hide his feelings.

"At Southcenter. I had to run into Sears to replace a wrench, and I happened to catch sight of Mary Lynn. Looked like they'd been there for some time, too. Kip's arms were full of packages."

Steve snorted softly. "So she finally found a man who likes to shop. More power to him. I last ten, fifteen minutes tops in any mall. I don't care how many discount stores there are. You take that SuperMall in Auburn. The kids were after me for weeks to take them there. It was a madhouse. I'd rather tear apart and rebuild a car engine anytime." He hoped the change in subject wasn't too obvious. He didn't want to talk about Mary Lynn, and he sure wasn't interested in hearing about Kip.

Apparently his effort to change the subject wasn't obvious enough, because Todd said, "You seem to have dealt with Mary Lynn dating again."

Steve sighed. "The hell I have." Continuing with this charade was turning out to be more than he could handle. Every time he thought about his ex-wife with another man, he had to grit his teeth. When he'd learned she was dating Kip, he hadn't pressured her, suspecting that if he did, he'd drive her straight into the other man's arms. So he'd bided his time, confident that it wouldn't take her long to lose interest. Clearly he'd made a tactical error. Well, he could still reverse his strategy. Starting now.

Steve stood and slapped a ten-dollar bill on the table.

Frowning slightly, Todd looked up. "You're leaving?"

"Yeah." He reached for and drained his mug.

"Where you headed?"

"Where else? To talk to Mary Lynn." As he turned away, he

thought he heard Todd groan. He left the tavern to the accompaniment of Garth Brooks belting out something about friends in low places. Kind of fit Mary Lynn's image of him, he told himself sourly.

The tires on his truck churned up gravel as he sped out of the parking lot. He drove around for an hour or so, clearing his head. Then he stopped for some take-out food and spent a while figuring out exactly what he wanted to say to Mary Lynn. But he waited until he knew the kids would be down for the night before he approached the house. No need to involve them.

He never could get used to knocking on the door of the place he'd bought and paid for himself. Legally it was Mary Lynn's house now, but still...

Mary Lynn answered the door, obviously surprised to see him. "Steve. What are you doing here?"

"Have you got a few minutes?" he asked. He was struck again by her beauty, her delicate features and dark glossy hair. He'd missed her in so many ways; perhaps what he missed most of all, what he most wanted to recover, was the companionship of their early years together. He'd made a lot of mistakes in his marriage, but then so had she. It was time for them to admit that and try again. He couldn't understand why Mary Lynn seemed so unwilling to agree.

She hesitated, then joined him on the porch, quietly closing the door behind her. They used to sit on this very porch and gaze at the stars, but that had been years ago. The porch light was off and the stars smiled down from the heavens, the same way they had back then, on fine summer nights. To Steve it was a good sign. He needed one.

Mary Lynn sat on the top step, and he sat beside her. He was glad he'd followed his instincts, instead of waiting until Mary Lynn came to her senses. This conversation was already long overdue.

"What's on your mind?" she asked.

"Everything's okay with the kids, isn't it? They aren't having any problems in school, right?"

"No, of course not. What makes you ask?"

"Nothing," he assured her. "You're doing a good job with them, Mary Lynn."

"Thanks, but I'm sure you didn't come all this way to compliment me."

He hesitated. "You did a fine job being my wife, too."

She lowered her head so she wouldn't have to look at him. "That was a long time ago."

"Not that long ago. I remember everything about us, especially how good you felt in my arms and how we used to—"

"Steve," she said abruptly, cutting him off. "Don't say any more."

"Why not?" He'd thought very seriously about what he wanted to tell her. He'd planned to remind her of good times in the past, talk about how the kids needed an intact family, promise to be the kind of husband she wanted. She had to know he'd do damn near anything to get his family back.

"It's over, Steve. It has been for years."

"Not for me it hasn't."

"Then maybe it's time you faced facts." She stood and he reached for her wrist, stopping her.

"Don't go," he asked gently, and because this was important, he added, "Please."

Sighing, she sat back down on the step. He placed his arm around her shoulders. She held herself stiff and unyielding against him, but gradually she relaxed as he nuzzled her neck, stroked her hair. "Remember how we used to sit out here and watch the stars?"

"That was years ago."

"You sure? Seems like yesterday." She smelled so good it was all he could do to keep from burying his face in her hair and inhaling her sweet perfumed scent. He planted soft moist kisses along the side of her neck, working his way toward her ear. He felt some of her resistance melt away when he caught her lobe gently between his teeth.

It'd been so damn long since they'd last made love that he was already hard. His hands fumbled with the opening of her blouse.

"I don't think this is a good idea," she whispered, but he noticed she wasn't actually stopping him.

"On the contrary I think it's one of the best ideas I've had in months."

Her hand closed tightly over his. "Don't."

He dropped his hand, but continued kissing her neck, knowing if she allowed this, his chances of getting her in bed would increase a hundredfold. That was where he wanted her, soft and pliant beneath him, reaching up to him with her arms, drawing him down. Loving him, taking away the ache of his loneliness. Afterward they would talk....

"Let me kiss you," he said, his voice husky with need. He wasn't someone who pleaded often, but he did now, feeling like a man who was about to let something of great value slip out of his grasp. He loved Mary Lynn. Needed her and their family.

"I...have to get back inside."

"We'll both go in," he whispered. Taking her face between his hands, he directed her mouth to his. Her resistance was weak, a token effort, and that gave him hope. She might not say it, but she damn well wanted him as much as he wanted her.

The kiss was almost brutal with sexual energy. Soon he had his tongue entwined with hers and she was crawling all over him. The only reason they ended the kiss was to breathe, and even then it was with reluctance.

"Don't you remember how good it is with us?" Steve whispered. "Let's go inside," he urged with a groan.

Mary Lynn buried her face in his shoulder, breathing hard.

Steve got to his feet, pulling her with him. He was halfway to the door when she stopped him.

"We can't go in there."

"Why not?" If the kids were awake, they'd hurry them off to bed and then head in that direction themselves.

Mary Lynn didn't answer.

Steve advanced another step.

"No," she cried, breaking away from him.

"Why not?"

She squared her shoulders and whispered, "Kip's here. He fell asleep in front of the television. I had him over for dinner."

Steve couldn't believe his ears. Mary Lynn had sat on the porch making love with him while another man waited for her inside the house?

"You shouldn't have come," she whispered angrily. "Don't do it again, Steve. We're divorced. I wish to God you'd remember that."

Eighteen

Aunt Hallie

She was insane, Hallie told herself. Because only an insane woman would have agreed to look after a six-month-old infant for two days while her sister and brother-in-law spent the weekend camping on the Oregon coast. Lucille McCarthy had originally agreed to watch Ellen, but she'd come down with a bad cold she was afraid of passing on to the baby.

Julie had phoned Hallie in tears, distraught because she'd have to cancel this long-awaited retreat with Jason. Caught off guard, Hallie had offered to take Ellen for the weekend. Just how much trouble could a six-month-old baby be? she asked herself with bravado. Infants that age slept twenty hours out of twenty-four. Didn't they?

Hallie's first doubts had surfaced the moment she'd hung up the phone. Though she loved kids, she hadn't done much baby-sitting as a teenager. Well, maybe as an adult she'd do all right. And this time with Ellen would be a bonding experience. Two minutes later she called Steve to make sure Meagan was going to be around.

The next day, when Julie arrived with enough paraphernalia to fill a moving van—including a portable crib, a mammoth diaper bag, a miniature plastic bathtub, and more—Hallie was once again gripped by the anxiety of those who know they're in way, way over their heads.

"Ellen's a good baby," Julie assured her. "You've got nothing to worry about."

"All right." Besides, her mother lived little more than an hour away. Not so far that Hallie couldn't leap in the car and drive to the Kitsap Peninsula if she got desperate. "And," she told her sister cheerfully, "there's always Mom. She must be getting over her cold by now."

Julie and Jason glanced at each other as if silently debating which one should tell her.

"Mom's gone away for the weekend," Julie finally said.

"Away?" Hallie said, her throat closing up on her.

"She felt a lot better yesterday, and then this morning a friend invited her to Vegas for the weekend. Jason and I told her she should go."

Jeez, no one had asked *her,* Hallie thought. And her mother's defection left her without parental support—her ace in the hole, if things went wrong. Now that Lucille was hanging out with Wayne Newton and Hallie had no way of contacting Julie and Jason—except through Smokey the Bear—she was on her own. With maybe a bit of help from next door.

Hallie's fears exploded to life even before the fumes from Jason's car had disappeared.

Ten minutes later Ellen woke up.

The kid, even at six months, was no fool. She knew immediately that the woman holding her wasn't her mother or grandmother. She took one look at Hallie and let out a scream a horror-movie starlet might envy.

Hallie cuddled the baby. "It's Auntie Hallie," she said, a little desperately. "Remember me?" Apparently not, but really, who could blame Ellen? She'd only seen Hallie a handful of times, and then it had been at family gatherings when she was surrounded by familiar faces. Now there were only the two of them, and Ellen didn't like it.

"Hey, McCarthy, you said you wanted to be a mother." Hallie tried again, this time with a bit of self-talk. If she couldn't comfort Ellen, she'd work on reassuring herself. "This is where the rubber meets the road."

Motherhood wouldn't be all baby powder and gurgles. What she was experiencing was the real nitty-gritty of being a parent. This was what she wanted for herself, so she might as well practice now.

Hallie continued to hold and rock Ellen until the screams gradually eased to pitiful sobs.

When Meagan appeared at the kitchen door, Hallie could have kissed her.

"This is your niece?" Meagan asked.

"She isn't all that familiar with me yet." Hallie felt she had to explain Ellen's discontent.

"Is her diaper wet?"

Her diaper. Hallie hadn't given it a thought. "Poor, poor baby," she cooed, reaching for the diaper bag Julie had left behind. The *big* diaper bag. Hallie extracted baby food jars, bottles, blankets, rattles, teething rings, a squeezable yellow duck, a pacifier, comb, brush, socks, three different pairs of shoes. But no diapers.

"I think they might be in the side," Meagan said.

Sure enough, there was the storehouse of disposable diapers. Plenty of those, along with wipes, powder, diaper-rash ointment and a furry blue bear. No instruction manual, though.

Ready to prove she was capable of such an undertaking, Hallie spread a flannel blanket on the carpet and placed a squirming Ellen in the center. She smiled proudly over at Meagan. "This isn't so bad."

She promptly revised her opinion when it became apparent Ellen wasn't going to make this easy. The only other diapers Hallie could remember changing had been on childhood dolls. The ones she'd owned had talked and cried and wet their pants. But none had kicked and fussed, twisted and turned, making the task damn near impossible.

By the time she'd finished, Hallie was exhausted.

"You did great," Meagan congratulated her.

A glance at her watch showed that Julie and Jason had been gone less than an hour. Only thirty-five more to go. Piece of cake, Hallie mumbled under her breath.

"Dad's taking Kenny to softball practice, but I can stay and help you, if you want."

If you want... Hallie all but grabbed the girl's shoulders and hugged her, she was that grateful.

With Meagan's help, Hallie made it through the rest of the morning and well into the afternoon. When Ellen went down for a nap, Hallie did, too. No one had bothered to tell her about the energy required to entertain a six-month-old.

The afternoon passed quickly, and at suppertime she said goodbye to Meagan, feeling confident now that she could manage. It seemed that Ellen had become accustomed to her. Hallie felt ecstatic; she wasn't as inadequate at this motherhood business as she'd feared. Yes! She could do this.

She changed her mind shortly after midnight. Ellen woke her out of a sound sleep, screaming so loudly that Hallie hurled herself out of bed and stubbed her toe while madly searching for the light switch. She'd completely forgotten about the lamp on her nightstand.

If Ellen had felt comfortable with Hallie earlier, she wanted nothing to do with her now. In fact, the infant had taken a sudden and apparently irreversible dislike to her aunt.

Babe in arms, Hallie walked until one of her slippers formed a blister on her big toe. It did no good; Ellen was in no mood to be comforted. Even a rerun of "The Andy Griffith Show" didn't interest the kid.

"You're a hard sell," she muttered.

After two hours, Hallie was at her wits' end. She'd done everything she could think of. Ellen's forehead was warm to the touch, but Hallie couldn't be sure if that was due to hours of nonstop screaming or a raging fever.

Maybe Ellen was seriously ill and needed a doctor. Maybe she'd eaten or swallowed something while Hallie wasn't looking. Maybe Hallie had done something wrong.

Just as the thought of calling 911 entered her mind, she happened to notice a light on in Steve's kitchen. Hallie raced to the phone.

"What's wrong?" Steve asked groggily.

"If I knew that, I wouldn't be phoning you," Hallie snapped. "What are you doing up at this time of night, anyway?" Whatever the reason, Hallie felt only gratitude. Steve was a father; he'd been through all this and survived. He'd know what to do.

He made all the practical suggestions.

"Do you take me for an idiot?" Hallie cried, close to breaking into sobs herself. "Of course I changed her diaper! Ten times or more."

"How long has she been crying?"

"Three lifetimes," Hallie said. "Listen, big boy, I'll give you a thousand dollars if you can get her back to sleep."

That shut him up. "You're kidding."

"Do I sound like this is a joke?" She was forced to yell as Ellen increased the volume of her cries.

"Give me five minutes."

It took him three. "Come on," he said, standing in the doorway, dressed in wrinkled gray sweats.

"We're going somewhere?" So he felt Ellen needed to go to the emergency room, too. Relieved, Hallie reached for a thigh-length sweater and slipped it over her pajamas.

While she wrapped Ellen in an extra blanket, Steve carried the car seat out to his truck, positioning it in the middle of the seat. At the last minute Hallie remembered her purse and grabbed that, locking the front door on her way out to Steve's monster truck.

He skillfully took the baby out of her arms and placed Ellen in the car seat, then helped Hallie climb inside. "What hospital are we going to?" she asked, locking her seat belt. Luckily Julie had given her a signed permission slip before she left, in the event of something like this.

"We aren't." He had to speak loudly to be heard over Ellen's fevered cries. Hallie had to give the kid credit; Ellen had one fine pair of lungs.

They hadn't gone more than two blocks before silence reigned. At first, Hallie waited, tense, expecting the noise to start again any second. Gradually she relaxed as the silence continued. She'd never heard anything more blissful in her life.

"My guess is she's teething," Steve said.

"So soon?" Hallie assumed kids didn't get teeth until much later. Not that she'd really thought about it.

"Sure." He glanced over at her and nodded for emphasis.

Well, Steve should know.

"My kids fell asleep the minute I turned the engine on. My car's in the shop so I've got the truck tonight, but I figured it'd work just as well. Based on experience, I'd say that if there's nothing seriously wrong, Ellen should fall asleep within six blocks. How're you holding up, Aunt Hallie?"

"Good," she said, lying through her teeth.

He drove along the Green River where there were few streetlights, and the rumble of the engine and the twisting road lulled Ellen into a deep slumber. But it wasn't only Ellen who fell asleep. Hallie discovered her own eyes drifting shut, and she struggled to stay awake.

She must have dozed off because the next thing she knew they were parked outside her condo. She jerked her head up and discovered Steve lifting Ellen, car seat and all, out of the truck. "Sorry to wake you, Sleeping Beauty," he whispered.

Hallie opened the passenger door and climbed awkwardly out of the truck. Turning around, she slid off the seat on her stomach, inching her feet toward the ground.

Her house was dark and still when she unlatched the dead bolt.

Gently Steve removed Ellen from the car seat and placed her in her little crib. They both waited, fearing the worst. After a few minutes it became apparent that Ellen wasn't going to stir, and they tiptoed out of the room.

"Thank you," she whispered.

"Think nothing of it," Steve returned. "Just don't forget you owe me a thousand bucks."

Hallie opened her mouth, then closed it with a groan. She'd forgotten their ridiculous bargain.

Steve grinned. "Hey, not to worry. I take VISA." Having said that, he kissed her on the forehead and let himself out.

Hallie had decided long ago that shopping was therapeutic, and the weekend after playing the role of Aunt Hallie she decided to treat herself. Donnalee agreed to come with her. They were both in need of a little self-indulgence, and the solution was a shopping spree. Not the normal half-off sale in some local department store, either. Oh, no, Donnalee declared that their current depressed state called for a full-fledged bout of conspicuous consumption. Something that included a passport, a facial and cheesecake.

"I'll have you know I emptied my entire Christmas savings account for this," Hallie grumbled as they neared the Canadian border.

"Not to worry," Donnalee said as she eased her vehicle into the long line of cars waiting to clear customs. "By Christmas you'll be married and your rich husband will foot the bills."

Husband. So many of her thoughts and plans in the past few months had focused on that word. *Husband. Marriage. Family.* Recently Hallie had come to a deeper understanding of what had brought her to this stage in her life.

"Hey," Donnalee said, taking her eyes from the road long enough to glance at Hallie. "You look awfully serious all of a sudden."

Hallie forced a smile, then decided that if she couldn't tell Donnalee about the emotional crisis she'd endured all week, she'd never be able to tell anyone.

"What's up?" Donnalee prodded gently.

"It's been a year now since my dad died, and I don't think I've ever missed him more." Her voice broke and tears filled her eyes, embarrassing her. She ran the back of her hand under her nose and, with tears streaming down her cheeks, she laughed. "I apologize. I didn't realize I was going to do this."

"Hallie, it's me—Donnalee, your best friend—remember?"

Hallie reached for her purse and rooted around for a tissue. "Besides Dad, I've been thinking about Gregg. I should have married him. In the back of my mind I knew it then, but I was too...stubborn to realize that I *wanted* what he was offering."

"Gregg Honeycutt? But I thought the two of you broke up years ago."

"We did. He wanted to get married and I didn't." She paused long enough to blow her nose. "Quite a switch, isn't it? The guy being the one who wants to marry. I'd taken out a huge loan to get Artistic License up and operating, and I refused to allow my personal life to get in the way of business."

"You think you should've married Gregg?" Donnalee asked, sounding skeptical.

"Oh, I don't know." Hallie sighed deeply. "My hindsight isn't as clear as I'd like it to be. He was so wonderful and I loved him, I really did." She paused and added, "But apparently not enough."

"What makes you think about Gregg now?"

Hallie wasn't sure. At Christmas she'd received a photo card of Gregg, his wife and their two small children. He looked happy, really happy, and so did his wife. After her weekend with Ellen, Hallie's feelings about wanting a family of her own had grown even stronger and more certain. It was because of this, she supposed, that Gregg's family photo had come to mind. She'd even mentally replaced his wife's image with her own—but only for a moment.

"It's like this huge hole opened up inside me," she confessed, twisting the damp tissue around her index finger. "I first noticed it after my dad died, and that hole has gotten bigger and bigger ever since."

"Is that why you decided to marry?"

The tissue around her finger grew tighter and tighter. "Yes. Last weekend with Ellen was crazy, but you know what? I loved it. By the time Julie and Jason arrived, I was hooked on motherhood and I didn't want to let her go."

"You didn't?"

"Oh, I made it sound like it was one disaster after another, but it wasn't. On Sunday Steve brought over some ointment to numb her gums, and after that, Ellen was a jewel. I know now that I could deal with the sleepless nights and hard times—because I know it's worth it." She drew a shaky breath. "Rita's been telling me for a long time that when it comes to finding a husband I'm too picky. I laughed her off, but you know what? I'm beginning to think she's right."

This appeared to surprise Donnalee.

"Not that I wouldn't still be discriminating. I mean, a few years back I might have married someone like Mark. I wouldn't have had the maturity to know otherwise. But I do now." Drawing another shaky breath, she added, "And now there's Larry. I really don't know how I feel about him. He's sweet, but...oh, I can't imagine being married to him."

"Come on, Hallie, stop fretting and let's enjoy our weekend."

"You're right." Hallie said, determined to take Donnalee's advice. While she was plagued with doubts about the status of her relationship with Larry, it didn't compare to what Donnalee was going through.

Word had gotten back to her that Sanford was dating again. Some so-called friend had taken delight in filling her in on the particulars. Shortly afterward, Hallie and Donnalee had arranged this getaway, and Hallie figured Donnalee needed it even more than she did.

Hallie had been a bit concerned about the cost, but on reflection realized she had very little to worry about. Her taxes were paid, her head was above water, she had plenty of work coming in. If she had to shop at Wal-Mart for Christmas, her family would understand.

The hotel deserved every one of those tiny stars listed in the tourist guide. It came complete with little chocolates on the pillow at night, plush bathrobes, perfumed lotion, plus a sauna and exercise room. Not that either one of them needed exercise after three hours of shopping.

Hallie's shoulders ached from hauling packages around, but they soon found a cure for that—the hotel masseuse. Never having experienced the delights of a massage, Hallie was apprehensive, but the woman put her at ease immediately. An hour later Hallie felt as relaxed as a wet noodle, not sure whether she wanted to crawl into bed or bound out to face the world. A facial followed, and then a manicure.

They dressed for dinner in short skirts with dark hose and ate in the revolving restaurant atop the hotel. Anything they'd saved shopping with a thirty-five percent discount, thanks to the Canadian dollar, they splurged on a bottle of Dom Pérignon—certainly the most expensive champagne Hallie'd ever had.

The night was lovely. Vancouver spread out before them, a panoply of twinkling lights. Hallie didn't know if it was the beauty of their surroundings or the shopping or the effect of having her body deliciously pummeled, but she felt rejuvenated—and surprisingly happy.

"It's like we're celebrating," she said. Although there was little evidence that she was any closer to achieving her goal now than when she'd started, she felt a sense of anticipation, of renewed energy.

"We *are* celebrating," Donnalee said, holding up the crystal flute. "To us. And to our future husbands, whoever they may be."

"To our future husbands," Hallie returned as they touched glasses. Husband. It meant a man who would be her lover, her partner, her friend. Her companion in life.

"I feel good," Donnalee said, leaning back in her chair. "Not just physically, either."

"I do, too," Hallie said.

"Funny—losing Sanford doesn't hurt as much as it did this morning." She smiled. "I guess that's what a day of total self-indulgence will do." Donnalee gazed at the view below them for a minute. "I knew it would be painful when I broke the engagement, but I wasn't prepared for how...lonely I'd feel afterward. How empty."

Hallie admired her friend for being unwilling to accept less than her dream in such an important matter as family. For trusting that eventually there would be someone else, a man who shared her goals and who wanted children as much as she did. A man worth waiting for.

They slept late the next morning, ate breakfast at the hotel and with reluctance began the drive back to Seattle early in the afternoon. This weekend had been an escape from their real lives, and now they were returning to those lives, refreshed and optimistic. Hallie was determined to hang on to her positive feelings.

It started to rain shortly after they crossed the border, but she tried not to read any significance into that.

"You're the one who told me there'd be another man for me after Sanford," Donnalee said. She smiled softly. "I feel ready to look for him now."

"That's great." Hallie pressed her head against the seat, pleased with Donnalee's decision. "Then you're going back to Dateline?"

Donnalee took a long time to respond. "I don't think so."

"Why not?" Donnalee couldn't have surprised her more had she announced that she'd already met the man she planned to marry.

"I can't give you a logical explanation. But I have the feeling I won't meet him through any dating service."

It was on the tip of her tongue to remind Donnalee that *she* was the person who'd convinced her to sign up with the service. She supposed she had no real reason to complain, though; Dateline had already sent her a number of potential dates. Two of them she'd dated extensively. Mark and Larry. But Mark had been a serious—even frightening—disappointment. And Larry...well, Larry was probably as indifferent to her as she was to him.

Hallie was mulling all this over when she noticed that Donnalee had exited the freeway. She was only minutes away from home. Once they arrived, she felt a rush of pleasure and satisfaction; her condo, with its neatly planted shrubs, its hanging basket of ferns, its bright door and attractive curtains, looked so welcoming, so dear and familiar. She unloaded her suitcase and all her accumulated treasures from the trunk of Donnalee's car, then waved a fond farewell as Donnalee drove off.

When she was inside out of the rain, Hallie glanced at her phone. She should call Larry and let him know she was home safe and sound. Hesitating, she wondered if Larry really cared—and knew the answer.

Before she could talk herself out of it, she walked to her wall phone and lifted the receiver. Her purse was still draped over her shoulder. Her suitcase and assorted packages sat in the middle of the living room.

"Hello," Larry answered without enthusiasm, as if he resented the phone's intrusion on his day.

"It's Hallie."

"How was Canada?" he continued in the same dry tone, devoid of any hint of enthusiasm or energy. Hallie often wondered how his students were able to sit through his lectures and not fall asleep.

"Canada," she repeated when she realized he was waiting for her answer. "Spectacular. Wonderful."

"Good."

Silence.

"Larry...this time away has given me an opportunity to do some thinking." She was a coward, Hallie decided, to be doing this over the phone. A living breathing coward. "I haven't made any secret of how much I admire you," she said, focusing her eyes on the ceiling, praying God would forgive her for this lie. She wanted to spare his feelings as she delivered the message that she no longer wished to date him.

"I imagine that a man of my education and background is impressive to someone like you."

She took exception to the "someone like you" and under normal circumstances would have questioned him. Doing so now would only prolong the inevitable.

"This time apart has been good for us both," she began. "It's given me the opportunity to, uh, clear my head."

"A person needs that occasionally. Eliminate the frivolous and concentrate on what's important."

"Exactly." Now all she had to do was find a way of explaining that she no longer considered *him* important. Unsure how to accomplish that, she asked, "Did you miss me while I was away?"

"Miss you?" He sounded surprised. "I suppose I did...but you weren't away more than thirty-two hours. We haven't known each other long, Hallie, and it's really not a question of missing you. The significance of someone's absence is relative to the amount of time two people have been exposed to each other, which in our case has only been a matter of weeks."

"Six," she muttered, cursing herself for doing such a miserable job of this.

"My point exactly."

"If you don't know how you feel about me now..."

"Feel about you," Larry said. "I hardly know you! Are you pressuring me to propose, Hallie? Because if so, I think you should know that I refuse to bend to pressure."

Propose. He thought she wanted him to propose!

"I wasn't expecting a marriage proposal," she told him, wondering how their conversation could have gone so far off course. "Actually I was looking for a diplomatic way to say that I think it would be best for us both to move on and date others." In case there was room for misunderstanding, she added, "Not each other."

Her announcement was followed by a stiff silence. "You mean to say you want to break up with me?" He sounded aghast. Shocked.

"Yes," she replied meekly, then hurried to say, "I don't want to hurt your feelings. I'm sure there's someone perfectly wonderful waiting to meet you."

"That's what the last woman told me," he said gruffly.

"I'm sorry, but there just isn't any...spark between us."

The line grew quiet. Then, "If you're looking for sparks, I suggest you snuggle up with an electric fence." With that, he hung up on her.

Hallie allowed herself a little sarcasm. "Goodbye, Larry. I wish you well, too." Shaking her head, she replaced the receiver.

Nineteen

Take It Like A Man

Meagan glanced guardedly over her shoulders, as if she expected her brother or father to show up at any second. She'd appeared at the kitchen door minutes after Hallie—or rather, Larry—ended the phone call.

"What's wrong?" Hallie asked, anxious to know what was troubling the girl. She'd rarely seen Meagan agitated or upset—unless it was at her younger brother. For the most part, Hallie found Steve's daughter to be good-natured, congenial and easygoing.

Meagan's nervous gaze returned to her father's house. "Can I come in?"

"Of course."

She helped Hallie pick up her packages from the living-room floor and carry them into the bedroom. Then, as if she'd been holding them in all weekend, Meagan's words came out in a rush. "Oh, Hallie, I'm real worried about my dad."

Hallie frowned; surely Steve wasn't sick or injured? "What's wrong with him?"

The half-wild look was back in the girl's eyes, and it seemed Steve wasn't the only distressed one. "Mom's decided to marry Kip."

Hallie felt her heart sink. It went without saying that the news would devastate Steve. "I take it your father doesn't know?"

"Not yet," Meagan said. "Mom said she was going to tell him tonight when she comes to get Kenny and me."

"Oh, boy," Hallie whispered, dropping onto her bed. Steve had always made clear that he was working hard toward a reconciliation. He'd based his entire future on their remarrying.

"My dad still loves my mom," Meagan said, her voice slowly fading. Hallie watched as the girl's eyes filled with tears. Like any kid, Meagan wanted her parents together. Even when Meagan and Kenny had asked her if she'd be willing to marry their dad, Hallie hadn't taken them seriously. She suspected that all along they'd been more aware of Mary Lynn's intentions than Steve had, but now that their mother was actually getting married, they weren't ready to face this new reality. Steve's children, like Steve himself, wanted a reconciliation.

Hallie held out her arms and Meagan walked into them, hiding her face in Hallie's sweater. "Will you talk to my dad?" she asked after a moment.

Hallie's gut instinct was to stay out of it, and she would have, if it wasn't for two things. Steve had been there for her. He'd seen her through the heartache of celebrating her thirtieth birthday alone. And only last weekend, he'd saved her sanity by helping her with Ellen. In many ways he was as good a friend as Donnalee.

"I'll do what I can," Hallie promised, but she didn't know what she could say, or if Steve would want to hear it. She stroked Meagan's hair, murmuring, "Don't worry, honey, your dad's an adult. He can handle this."

It wasn't as if the news would come as any great shock. Steve knew his ex-wife was dating again, although he'd chosen to ignore what that meant.

Meagan lifted her tear-streaked face to Hallie's. "I've been waiting for you all weekend."

"Oh, honey, I'm sorry I wasn't here when you needed to talk."

Meagan shrugged. "That's all right. It's more important that you be here for my dad. He's going to need a friend and he won't call Todd."

"Todd?"

"His best friend. You haven't met Todd?"

"Not yet." Other than the bowling tournament and a few pizzas with him and the kids, Hallie hadn't socialized with Steve. Come to think of it, he'd never formally met Donnalee, either.

Hallie heard a car pull up out front.

"I gotta go. It sounds like Mom's here." Meagan wiped her face with her sleeve and slid off the bed. "Bye!"

Because she knew what was coming, Hallie stood and watched out her living-room window, hidden behind her drapes so Steve and his family wouldn't be able to see her. She felt like a voyeur but told herself she'd now become part of this scenario; if she was going to be any comfort to Steve, she needed to understand his reaction. Looking dejected, Meagan and Kenny climbed into their mother's car, dragging their overnight cases. Both slumped in the back seat, heads lowered.

Steve followed the kids across the lawn to the car. Mary Lynn waited outside the vehicle, with the open door on the driver's side between her and Steve. As a barrier, it couldn't have been more obvious.

Hallie watched as Meagan put on earphones, as if she needed to drown out the conversation between her parents. Steve's ex-wife had her back to Hallie, and Steve was smiling at the woman. Hallie knew he looked forward to these Sunday afternoons when Mary Lynn stopped by for the kids.

After a few moments Hallie noted that his mood changed dramatically. He repeatedly shook his head, in denial, and he made a confused helpless motion with his hand. Next his face tightened and he slammed his fist against the hood of the car.

Hallie grimaced, sure he must have injured his hand. He and Mary Lynn were now exchanging comments—insults?—in low voices. Unable to watch any longer, Hallie turned away, angry with herself for intruding on what should have been private. She felt sick to her stomach at what she'd seen.

Knowing that Steve was probably in no mood for company, Hallie waited an hour. Daylight filtered weakly through a dark and threatening sky—but she managed to see into Steve's condo. It took her a moment to realize he was lying on the carpet, listening to the stereo at full blast. Hallie didn't know whether to laugh or cry; it was exactly what she'd been doing that night in April. Her birthday. She had to listen carefully before she recognized the song: "Send in the Clowns."

She searched the back of her cupboard until she found the bottle of rich Tennessee bourbon a grateful client had given her last Christmas. She didn't often drink hard liquor, but if ever an occasion called for booze, this was it. She scrounged up a shot glass, souvenir of a trip to Las Vegas for her twenty-first birthday, and headed for Steve's.

Standing in the rain at his front door, she repeatedly rang the bell, but to no avail. Wasn't he going to answer?

"Steve," she shouted, pounding on the door. "Would you open up before I drown?"

He threw open the door a moment later—having turned down the music—and didn't look any too pleased to see her. "What are you doing here?"

She held up the bottle and the shot glass. "I thought you might need medication."

He frowned in puzzlement. "You know?"

"Meagan told me."

He stepped aside and let her in. "I can't believe it." He looked like a man walking around in a daze, like an accident victim left to deal with the aftermath of tragedy. He collapsed onto the sofa and leaned forward, wiping a hand down his face.

Hallie made her way into the kitchen and found a couple of clean glasses. She filled them both with ice and poured him a double with no mixer. Her own, she watered down considerably.

He glanced up and offered her a feeble smile when she handed him the drink. He held on to it for several minutes, gazing blankly ahead of him, until Hallie suspected he'd forgotten she was there. She figured if he wanted to talk he would; she had no intention of pushing him.

Sitting down in the chair across from him, she tentatively tasted the drink and blinked rapidly as it seared a path down her throat. Her eyes filled with tears and she pounded her chest in an effort to keep from coughing.

"You all right?" Steve asked.

She nodded, blinking furiously, wondering what her reaction would have been had she taken the bourbon straight.

Their eyes met, and Hallie could barely look at the misery in his. "I'm so sorry, Steve. I know how much you wanted to get back together with Mary Lynn."

His shoulders heaved in a deep sigh. "She's actually going to marry that creep."

This didn't seem the time to point out that Steve didn't know Kip well enough to judge his character. All he cared about was that this other man was stepping in, taking *his* place within the family. He didn't need to say it for Hallie to know what he was thinking.

"We met in high school," Steve said after a while.

"You and Mary Lynn?" she asked, not sure she wanted to hear him talk about the other woman or how much he loved her. She was tempted to ask him to stop, to say that stirring up the memories would only hurt him, but she didn't have the heart. If he wanted to vent his pain with her, the least she could do was listen. She owed him that much.

"Mary Lynn was new that year and so damn pretty my heart would stop every time I saw her. She used to come by every day to watch the football team practice...."

"I imagine you were the star player." Athletic as he was, Hallie couldn't imagine Steve being anything else.

"Quarterback. How'd you know?"

"Lucky guess," she returned with a grin.

Steve downed the undiluted drink in one giant swallow. He closed his eyes and shook his head like a dog stepping out of a lake. He cursed under his breath, then set the glass aside. "Damn, but that's good bourbon."

"Only the best for my friends."

Steve leaned back against the sofa cushion. The music continued to play softly in the background and Hallie recognized Paul Simon singing "Still Crazy After All These Years."

"I loved her from the moment I saw her," Steve said. "That's never changed, not once in all that time."

Hallie remembered her own high-school sweetheart and the intensity of their relationship. They'd broken up during her senior year and he'd taken someone else to the prom. Hallie had ended up attending the dance with her best friend's out-of-town cousin, whom she'd met the summer before. He was a nice guy, but he wasn't Les.

It'd killed her to watch Les dance with another girl, but for pride's sake, she'd been forced to pretend she didn't care.

Steve laughed once, sharply. "I asked her to marry me on our first date." Steve let his head fall back against the sofa and closed his eyes. "I knew the first time I kissed her that I was going to love her. Later, my dad told me the same thing happened to him when he met my mother. He asked her to dance at a USO party. One spin around the floor was all it took."

How romantic. Hallie wished it could be so easy for her. Instead, she was stuck dating a cast of misfits, one after another, in her search for a man to love. She almost giggled as the CD player picked Tina Turner next, singing "What's Love Got to Do with It?" Then she sighed. Here was Steve, her friend and neighbor, and he'd found the woman he loved when he was a teenager. Now Mary Lynn didn't want him. A broken marriage, a betrayed love, might be an everyday tragedy, but it was a tragedy nonetheless.

"I gave her a ring the very next week," Steve said, his voice low and mellow, presumably from the bourbon. "Naturally we didn't tell anyone it was an engagement ring. Our parents would've hit the roof if we'd been talking about marriage on such short acquaintance."

Hallie would never have guessed that Steve possessed such a romantic soul. This was the kind of thing women dreamed about, this consuming once-in-a-lifetime love. And Mary Lynn had thrown it all away. It was so terribly sad. Her throat tightened; the kind of love Steve felt was exactly what she'd hoped would happen to her. But no man had ever loved her like that, or wanted her so much.

"I married her in my heart the night of our first date. That was when we found each other. That was when our hearts connected and I knew I wanted to spend the rest of my life loving Mary Lynn."

The lump in Hallie's throat thickened painfully, and she tried unsuccessfully to stifle a sob.

Steve's eyes fluttered open. "Hallie?"

She bit her lower lip and searched in her pocket for a tissue. "It's nothing."

"You're crying?"

"I'm not." The lie was ludicrous since it was patently obvious that she was.

Steve disappeared and returned with a box of tissues. He studied her as if he didn't know what to say.

"Thanks," she said, reaching for a tissue. This was more than a little embarrassing. She blew her nose and tucked the tissue in her pocket. Steve sat down next to her.

"I'm sorry," she wailed, and reached for a fresh tissue. She clutched it tightly, trying to ignore Eric Clapton's plaintive "Tears in Heaven."

"Sorry for what?" Steve asked gently.

It didn't look as if she was going to be able to stop crying. Her shoulders trembled and she grabbed a handful of tissues, jerking them out of the box two and three at a time. "I'm supposed to be the one—" she sobbed openly "—comforting you."

He placed his arm around her shoulders, and she pressed her head against his, soaking up the solace, even though *she'd* intended to be the one offering it. She couldn't begin to explain the tears.

"I never understood why Mary Lynn wanted the divorce," Steve whispered.

"I don't know why, either," she said, sniffing hard in an effort to stop crying.

It'd been the grief, the pain and absolute desolation in Steve's eyes, she decided. He was about to lose the family he cherished, and his life would never be the same. He'd lost the woman he loved.

Steve had gone to the kitchen. Just as she thought she should leave, he was back. "Here," he said, handing her a fresh drink.

"Alcohol creates more problems than it solves," she said, forgetting that she was the one who'd hand-delivered the bottle.

"Trust me, I know. The day the judge declared the divorce final, I got rip-roaring drunk. It was the sorriest day of my life, and the night didn't improve. Next morning, I had the mother of all hangovers. I haven't gotten drunk since and don't plan to."

"I'm glad to hear it," she said, then gulped down the drink. Choked, gasped and had trouble breathing.

Steve patted her on the back. "You're a good friend, Hallie McCarthy," he said.

"You, too, Steve Marris."

His arm came around her and they hugged for a long time. It amazed her how good it felt to be in Steve's arms. To feel his heart pounding against hers, his breath against her neck. Peaceful. Friendly.

His kiss didn't come as a surprise. He lifted his head, and she gazed into his eyes before he lowered his mouth to hers. His lips were undemanding and tender, restrained. It was a kiss like the one they'd exchanged on her birthday. A kiss free of promises, free of claims. A kiss between friends.

He pulled away and asked, "Want me to walk you home?"

"No. I can make it across the lawn just fine." She swiped at the moisture on her cheeks. "Are you going to be all right now?" she asked.

"Sure."

Although he sounded confident, Hallie didn't know if she should believe him. Mary Lynn's announcement had come as a blow. But he'd taken it like a man.

Dionne Warwick's "I'll Never Love This Way Again" followed Hallie out the door.

Twenty

Chicken Soup For The Heart

Steve stepped up to home plate and swung the bat around a couple of times to loosen the stiffness in his shoulders. He assumed the batter's stance and waited for the pitcher's first throw. A fastball zoomed toward him. It wasn't a baseball Steve saw, but Kip Logan's face.

The unmistakable cracking sound as the bat slammed against the ball and shattered echoed across the field. Steve dropped the piece he still held on the ground and raced toward first base. He kept his eye on the ball and was satisfied to see it fly over the fence. Another home run.

He was out of breath when he returned to the dugout. His fellow team members slapped him jovially on the back and congratulated him.

"What's with you tonight?" Todd asked, shifting seats to sit next to him. "This is your third home run."

"Really?" Steve said, pretending he hadn't noticed. He leaned forward on the hardwood bench and braced his elbows on his knees. "I'm having a good night, is all."

"True, but this is the second bat you've busted all to hell. Something's eating you."

"You're imagining things." Steve's gaze didn't waver from the field. The problem with friends like Todd was that it was difficult to hide things. Removing his hat, Steve slapped it against his thigh, aware of Todd's scrutiny. He supposed he might as well let Todd know. "Mary Lynn's decided to remarry," he said with forced nonchalance. Billy Roth stole second base and Steve leapt to his feet and cheered wildly.

Todd remained seated. "When did you find out about this?"

Steve sat back down, keeping his attention on the game. "Sunday night."

"I wish you'd said something sooner." Todd sounded as if the news about Mary Lynn affected him personally.

Steve told himself he should have taken drastic steps as soon as he'd learned she was dating again. Instead, he'd assumed her relationship with that vulture of a car salesman would die on its own, without any help from him. What he'd hoped for was that Mary Lynn would date some of Hallie's rejects. Or similar losers. He was convinced that once his ex had gotten a look at some of the weirdos out there she'd come running back to him.

Steve had spent hours daydreaming about her asking him to move back in with the family. Welcoming him back into her bed. The bubble of his fantasy world had burst on Sunday afternoon, when Mary Lynn broke the news about her engagement.

"Are you okay with this?" Todd asked next.

"Yeah, I'm jumping up and down for joy," Steve said dryly.

Todd shook his head. "I was afraid something like this would happen."

The comment earned a glare from Steve. What he didn't need was his best friend saying he'd told him so.

Todd took immediate offense. "I told you I saw her shopping with Kip, remember?"

Steve wished Todd would quit while he was ahead. Every time he opened his mouth, he only made it worse.

"I could tell then that she was serious about this guy," Todd continued, undeterred. "It isn't the kind of news you want to tell a friend. I said what I could and hoped you'd read between the lines."

Unfortunately, Steve hadn't seen what in retrospect should have been obvious. He had no one to blame but himself. Kenny had hit him with the news that his mother had a boyfriend shortly after the first of the year. Meagan, too, had dropped a number of hints. He should have recognized that something was going on when Mary Lynn cut him off physically. But then, Steve figured he always did have trouble seeing the obvious; it was what had led to the divorce in the first place.

"You're up to bat next," Steve said, grateful Todd was leaving the dugout. He didn't want to talk about Mary Lynn. Didn't want to think about her, either. Every time he did, his head pounded and his gut twisted. He had to let go of her, of their lives together. A dozen people had said the same thing: it was time to move on. That was also what the relationship experts recommended—and he should know, because he often listened to talk radio. He'd learned their jargon, about "taking ownership" of his past and his problems, and "affirming his validity" and "forgiving" himself and Mary Lynn for the failure of their marriage. He'd even started to believe this stuff. Recently he'd happened upon a program with a phone-in psychologist, and he'd actually sat in his car and listened until the program was over. It'd helped.

Dr. Brenda wasn't the only one who'd come to his emotional rescue. Hallie had been there for him, as well. In a week filled with pain and sadness, thinking about Hallie made everything seem more bearable. She'd come to him, bottle of bourbon in hand, offering comfort—and ended up blubbering her way through an entire box of tissues.

In some strange way her crying had been a release for *him*. When she'd first arrived, he'd wanted to send her back to her own place. He'd been in no mood for company. What man would be? His heart felt like it had been ripped from his chest...and yet Hallie had managed to bring a smile to his face.

Steve felt fortunate to have a neighbor like Hallie McCarthy. When he counted his blessings, she was among them. He sure hoped she found a man worthy of her.

Todd struck out at bat. He'd been in a hitting slump during their recent practice sessions, and now he returned to the dugout muttering curses.

"Don't worry about it," Steve said. "This is only the first game of the season."

Todd looked as if he wanted to say something, but instead, he found himself a quiet corner and sat there scowling. If it had been one of his kids, Steve would have called it pouting.

After the game several of the team members, including Todd, decided to stop off at the local watering hole for a few cold beers. Steve declined, not wanting to answer uncomfortable questions about Mary Lynn. He'd said everything there was to say and didn't care to elaborate.

It was still daylight when he arrived home. He noted that Hallie's car had been parked in the same spot for the past two days. It wasn't the kind of thing he normally paid much attention to, but she was just shy of being ticketed for parking too close to a fire hydrant.

He glanced at her condo as he started walking toward his own. It probably wouldn't hurt to check on her, he decided. Yeah, that was the neighborly thing to do.

She responded to his knock by calling faintly for him to come inside. Steve opened the front door to discover her sprawled on the sofa amid a conglomeration of pillows and blankets. Dressed in an old robe, she lay facedown, her arm dangling over the edge, knuckles brushing the carpet. A variety of medicines lined the coffee table, along with three or four dirty cups, a box of tissues and a thermometer. An empty wash bucket was positioned close by.

"You look like hell," he said. "Are you sick or something?"

"You don't miss much, do you?" She didn't lift her head.

"My, my, are we a little testy? And what, by the way, is your front door doing open? This isn't 'Little House on the Prairie,' you know."

"Don't come any closer," she called, raising her arm to stop him. "Believe me, you don't want whatever brand of flu I've got." She frowned. "Oh, the door. Donnalee's supposed to come over later, and I wasn't sure I'd have the energy to get up and let her in."

"Have you seen a doctor?" he asked.

"I'm too sick to see a doctor. Do I look like I'm in any condition to drive?" she returned crankily.

"No," Steve admitted. "Do you need someone to take you?"

She appeared to consider his question. "Thanks, but no thanks. The worst of it's passed." Then she added, "I appreciate the offer, though."

He walked into her kitchen, which was, to put it mildly, a mess. Used mugs and glasses littered every surface. An empty orange-juice container had toppled and the last dregs of juice had dried on the counter. A package of soda crackers lay open, crumbs scattered about.

"When was the last time you ate?" he asked, poking his head around the living-room corner.

"Please," she whispered miserably, "don't talk about food. I haven't been able to keep anything down for two days."

"I hope you're drinking plenty of liquids."

"I must be, otherwise there wouldn't be anything to vomit."

She had his sympathy there; he knew what it was like to be sick and alone. He stuck the dirty dishes in the dishwasher and wiped off the counter.

"Thank you," she said when he brought her a cup of tea.

"Anything else I can do for you?"

"Would you mind helping me into the bathroom?" she asked weakly. "I tried to get up earlier, but I felt light-headed."

"Of course."

She sat up, and he saw that her skin was pale, her hair on one side had gone completely flat, and the upholstery of her sofa had left a floral imprint on her cheek. She wrapped the housecoat around her and tied the sash.

She swayed when she stood upright, and he slid his arm around her waist to steady her. Once he was confident that she could maintain her balance, he guided her down the hallway. He turned on the bathroom light.

"Would you move the scale away from the wall for me?" she asked in the same weak voice.

"The scale?" he asked incredulously.

"I want to weigh myself."

Steve was certain he'd misunderstood. "Why in the name of heaven would you want to do that?"

She gave him a look that suggested the answer couldn't be more obvious. "To see how much weight I've lost," she explained, enunciating each word with painstaking clarity. "I haven't had anything but juice and crackers for two days."

It made no sense to him, but Steve knew better than to argue. He crouched down to pull the scale away from the wall.

"There," he said, patiently waiting for her to step forward.

She hesitated. "You can't look."

"I beg your pardon?"

"Turn around."

"For the love of…" But Steve did as she requested and turned his back. He heard Hallie step on the scale, and then a pathetically feeble cry of triumph.

"I take it you've lost?"

"Yes," she answered in a whisper. "Isn't that wonderful?"

"If you say so." He'd never understood why Hallie was so obsessed about her weight. He thought she looked just fine. Yet the entire time he'd known her, she'd analyzed everything she put in her mouth. Well, other than that one episode with the double-fudge macadamia-nut ice cream.

He helped her back to the living room and fluffed up the pillows. "Where's Nerdman when you need him?" It seemed to Steve that professor friend of hers should be the one checking up on her.

"We decided not to see each other anymore," she replied. Steve couldn't detect any deep regret.

"Oh."

"I couldn't imagine him naked."

Steve did a poor job of hiding a grin. "Do you do that often? Imagine men naked?" He made a show of clutching the neck of his uniform in a false display of modesty.

"Hardly. Just some men. You don't qualify."

"Glad to hear it."

"The only thing I ever saw him get excited about was a program on the public channel about mold."

If there was a hidden message in that statement, Steve wasn't sure he wanted to dig for it. "So you called it quits?"

"I'm back to square one—again."

"There's a man for you out there, Hallie. Don't lose heart."

"That's what Donnalee keeps saying. I don't understand it. I thrive on challenges. I write out my goals and plan to succeed, and so far all I've done is fall flat on my face."

"Don't be so hard on yourself."

Hallie sighed dramatically. "I never thought I'd be this thin and without a man in my life."

Steve didn't know how to respond to that.

"Thanks for coming by."

"No problem. You sure I can't get you anything else?"

"I'm fine now. Thanks for asking."

Steve left, and as he crossed the lawn to his own condo he realized he was smiling. He did that a lot when he thought about Hallie. She seemed to find the humor in life; at any rate, *he* tended to find it when he was with her.

He showered, changed clothes and checked out the contents of his kitchen cupboards. He found a can of chicken-noodle soup and heated it. Pouring it into two bowls, he left one on the table for himself and brought the other to Hallie.

She looked surprised to see him again.

"Here," he said, setting it down on the coffee table for her and grabbing the soda crackers from the kitchen. "Eat this and you'll feel better."

"You're so thoughtful," she told him, her dark eyes wide with gratitude.

"That's what friends are for," he said, and leaning over, kissed the top of her head.

Twenty-One

Back In The Saddle Again

June 22

Well, Larry's out of my life, not that I'm gnashing my teeth or anything. But I do admit to being disappointed. It seems I take one step forward, stumble back and fall into a ravine. Tom Chedders and Mark Freelander disgusted me, but Larry McDonald discouraged me. Is he the best I can do? How depressing.

On a brighter note. Donnalee accepted a date with a real-estate broker she's known for a number of years. It'd be a hoot if Donnalee ended up marrying someone she's known and worked with for years. But even if she doesn't, I don't imagine it'll take her long to find the right man. She's smart, attractive and, according to Steve, she's got what it takes. Physically, for sure. And she's a wonderful, loving, compassionate person. If she wasn't my best friend, I might even hate her!

Speaking of Steve, he's been really great, dropping by when I was sick, cleaning up for me—even moving my car. I sometimes toy with the idea of the two of us, but I'm afraid he's still hooked on his ex-wife. He claims otherwise, but I can't help wondering.

I talked to the people at Dateline and they're reviewing their files. The woman I spoke to said they'd have another name for me by the end of the week. I told them to take their time. I'm in no hurry to meet someone new just yet. I want to take a week or two to revive my enthusiasm. Maybe I should do what Donnalee's doing (and what I started out doing!) and be willing to date someone I haven't met through the agency. The new man from the office-supply store is cute. I wonder how old he is, or if he's married.

I'm feeling ambitious now that I'm over the flu and bought myself some Martha Washington geraniums, lovely deep red ones. I'm going to plant them this afternoon.

Steve was washing his company truck when Hallie went outside to plant the geraniums. She'd never known a man who took having a clean truck so seriously. He was wielding the long green garden hose, which snaked across the lawn, but he paused when he saw her.

"You seem a lot better," he said.

He looked darn good, Hallie noted, with his shirt unbuttoned all the way down, revealing a strong muscular chest. The bronze sheen of his skin invited investigation—not hers of course, she was quick to add. After living next door to him all these months, she found herself oddly *surprised* to realize how physically attractive Steve was.

"I'm feeling much better," she told him. She adjusted her large straw hat and wished she'd applied sunscreen to her bare arms. Kneeling on the soft moist grass, she cleared a space between the tulips and daffodils that had bloomed earlier in the spring.

"What are you planting now?" he asked.

She replied in far more detail than he'd wanted to know, Hallie suspected; she'd even explained about leaving the stalk and leaves of her tulips and daffodils so the bulbs could absorb the nutrients. She'd seen his eyes glaze over, but he'd listened politely. Hallie wasn't sure why she was being so talkative. It probably had to do with the weather, which was glorious, and the fact that she'd spent the week cooped up inside, sick as a dog. Then, too, it might have to do with his open shirt.

When she'd finished transplanting the geraniums from the plastic containers to the flower bed, she strung her hose across the yard.

"I've never understood what a woman sees in flowers," Steve said. "If it was up to me, I'd stick a couple of plastic tulips in the ground and let it go at that."

Hallie rolled her eyes. "Well, it's men and their he-man trucks that get me."

"Women and their romance novels."

Hallie wasn't going to stand still for that. "Men and their remote controls."

Later Hallie couldn't remember if she'd *intentionally* doused Steve. She'd laughed while holding the hose, which had jerked and splashed water on the legs of his jeans.

When it happened, Steve's eyes slowly met hers. She opened her mouth to apologize, but then realized she wasn't sorry. Not at all. He was so smug and self-righteous.

"Do you have anything to say for yourself?" he asked, advancing toward her, a menacing look on his face.

Hallie retreated one small step for each giant step he took. The water dribbling out of her hose was no match for the power sprayer he'd been using on the truck.

"I stand by my convictions," she announced with melodramatic fervor.

"Do you, now?" He sprayed the legs of her jeans the same way she'd sprayed his, only the water pressure in his hose was much stronger and she was soaked to her knees.

"I'd like to remind you that I've been ill. I probably shouldn't be outside at all." She feigned a cough.

"You should've thought about that before you started this water war."

"Water war?" she repeated. "You wouldn't, would you? Seeing that I've been so terribly ill." She coughed again for effect.

He turned away as if the guilt factor had worked, giving her ample time to cross to the outdoor faucet and increase the water pressure. If she'd stopped to think about what she was initiating, Hallie might have resisted—but the temptation was too strong. Without giving him any warning, she liberally sprayed his backside.

Steve's reaction was quick as lightning. Soon an all-out water fight had erupted, complete with threats and shouts of retribution. In seconds they were both drenched to the skin. Wet tendrils of hair dripped onto Hallie's neck and shoulders. Her hat had long since disappeared, and her blouse was plastered to her front.

"You're a wicked, wicked man," she declared after being forced to plead for mercy.

"And you're not to be trusted," he returned.

She laughed, enjoying their exchange. "I just lost control," she said—which was true enough. His attitude had certainly inflamed her, not to mention his open shirt...well, no man had the right to look that sexy.

"You better get inside and change clothes before you catch your death of cold," he said.

"You, too." He might not be as wet as she was, but Hallie had done womanhood proud. Water dripped from Steve—just not as much of it.

"Do you have any plans for later?" he called unexpectedly just as she was about to enter the house.

"Apart from remaining dry? No, not really."

He smiled. "I thought I'd ride my bike along the Green River. Want to join me?"

Hallie smiled back. The idea was appealing; she'd seen lots of folks on the trail and had always thought it seemed a great way to enjoy a sunny afternoon, biking along the paved road. Exercising, but with scenery. Minus the boredom.

"I'd love to, but I can't," she said regretfully. "I don't have a bike." She didn't mention that it'd been at least ten years since she'd ridden one.

"You could use Meagan's. I'm sure she wouldn't mind."

Hallie's spirits lifted. She knew Steve was at loose ends this weekend. Meagan and Kenny were at their mother's parents for some family function. He didn't seem to know what to do with himself without the kids there.

"This shouldn't be such a difficult decision, Hallie."

"I...don't know if I remember how to ride a bike," she admitted, a little embarrassed.

"Sure you do." He sounded very definite. "Haven't you heard the expression 'It's like riding a bike'? Once you learn, you never forget. It's like sex."

She tossed him a perturbed look. "Very funny, Marris."

"I'll give you a refresher course. On the bike-riding, I mean." He grinned. "It'll take you ten minutes, I promise."

She didn't hesitate. "You've got yourself a deal. I'll change clothes and be right out."

She changed in short order and met Steve in front of his garage.

"I'll probably need to raise the seat a bit," he said, looking at her legs and then the bike pedals. "Here, climb on and I'll see how much I should adjust it."

"But..."

"Don't worry, I'll hold on to the bike. You aren't going to fall."

Doing as she was instructed, Hallie perched on the seat and placed her feet on the pedals. Since Meagan was considerably shorter than she was, her knees thrust up toward her face. Conscious of making a comical sight, she glanced at Steve to discover that his attention had left her and was riveted on a car down the street.

Hallie's gaze followed his to the dark blue vehicle.

"It's Mary Lynn," he said. His voice had a breathless quality that spoke of surprise and delight. His ex-wife pulled to a stop and parked.

Completely forgetting about Hallie, Steve released the handlebars and started walking toward Mary Lynn. Before Hallie could free her feet from the pedals, the bicycle toppled sideways onto the grass.

Steve didn't notice. Hallie lay sprawled on the wet grass, and for all intents and purposes she might have been invisible. Her backside was completely drenched before Steve looked back at her. He might not have even then if Mary Lynn hadn't said something.

"Are you all right?" Mary Lynn asked when Hallie awkwardly lifted the bike away from her and stood. They'd met briefly a few times, including the day Meagan had gone to work with Hallie. The conversations had always been a bit awkward. They'd waved to each other a couple of times since, when Mary Lynn was either dropping the kids off or picking them up.

Hallie brushed the grass from her pants and noticed a trickle of blood on her elbow, where her arm had struck the concrete. She twisted her arm around to evaluate the damage. It wasn't much, just a little scraped skin, but it fired her anger.

She stared at Steve who was gazing longingly at Mary Lynn. It was pathetically obvious that he was hoping his ex-wife had come to announce she'd had a change of heart and wanted him back.

"Can we talk for a moment?" Mary Lynn asked Steve in a voice that couldn't have been sweeter.

"Of course." He nearly fell all over himself leading the way into the house.

Mary Lynn had the grace to glance guiltily toward Hallie. "If now's convenient?"

"Why wouldn't it be?" Steve asked.

When Mary Lynn continued to look at Hallie, Steve finally seemed to realize she was there. "Hallie, sorry. You okay?"

"Just peachy."

Either he missed the sarcasm or he chose to ignore it. "We'll go cycling another time, all right?" He didn't wait for a response.

Apparently she was of such little consequence, he could leave her without a thought. How dared he treat her like this, dismiss her with no regard for her feelings—as if she was nothing.

She stood in the driveway, hands on her hips. Steve Marris wasn't any different from the other losers she'd met. He was rude, inconsiderate and thoughtless. Good thing she had no romantic illusions about him!

Angry, Hallie returned to the house and doctored the cut. The small scrape didn't really require a bandage, but she applied the largest one she could find. She'd actually been looking forward to cycling with Steve, but there'd be frost in the tropics before she'd consent to do anything with that man again.

Twenty minutes later the doorbell chimed. It was Steve.

"I can't believe it," he muttered in disgust.

"Neither can I," she said coolly.

Apparently he didn't notice her remark. "Wait'll you hear what Mary Lynn wanted."

Hallie supposed he was going to tell her whether she was interested or not. She crossed her arms and blocked the doorway.

"She left the big family get-together to come and ask me in person if I'd be willing to take the kids for two weeks while she's on her honeymoon with Lard Butt."

He seemed to be waiting for her to respond. Hallie didn't.

"Doesn't that beat all?" He shook his head as if this was the most unreasonable thing he'd ever heard.

Hallie would wager a month's income that he'd agreed to do it, too. Anything for his precious Mary Lynn.

"Are you going to?"

"Well, yeah, but that's beside the point."

"Uh-huh. That's what I thought."

He squinted at her. "Is something wrong?"

"Should there be?" she replied, wondering how long it would take him to realize how badly he'd insulted her.

He stepped off her porch as if to get a better view of her. "Mary Lynn used to do that," he said, wagging his index finger. "If you've got a beef with me, spell it out. Don't expect me to play guessing games."

"Beef?" she repeated, highly amused by the term. "What you did to me just now was..." She couldn't find a word bad enough. "Despicable," she decided, spitting it out. "Mary Lynn drives up and not only do you completely forget I exist, you let me fall off that stupid bike right in front of her. I was mortified."

"Oh, come on, Hallie..."

"You embarrassed me. You discounted me. All so you could jump through hoops to satisfy your ex-wife." Hallie had wanted to remain calm and disdainful; instead, her voice shook with anger.

His eyes widened with surprise.

"Friends don't treat each other that way," she explained pointedly, forcing herself to calm down.

He waited a moment after she'd finished. "Okay, I apologize, but frankly, I don't think it was that big a deal."

"It was to me."

He briefly closed his eyes, as if to suggest she'd stretched the incident out of all proportion. "Get over it and let's go bike-riding."

"*Get over it?*" she gasped. "You left me to fall flat on my face! I told you—friends don't do that to friends. Now you want me to get over it, pretend it didn't happen?'' Her hands tightened into fists. ''Well, I don't need friends like you.''

''Fine,'' he returned. ''I don't need any grief from you, either. I get all I can handle from one woman. I don't need another one messing with my life.'' He turned and stalked toward his house.

''It'd help if you accepted the fact that your marriage is over,'' she shouted after him, too angry to censor her words. ''In case you haven't noticed, Mary Lynn's engaged to someone else.''

Steve whirled around, his eyes hard and cold as they raked her. ''I suggest you mind your own damn business,'' he flared. ''You can offer me all the marital advice you want once you've found yourself a husband.''

His words felt like a slap in the face. She held her breath against the unexpected stab of pain and retreated into her house.

Twenty-Two

The Girl Next Door

Damn, but he missed Hallie. He'd really blown it with her. He'd recognized his mistake the moment his eyes met hers and she'd escaped into her house. He'd seen neither hide nor hair of her since, which was quite a feat considering how often they ran into each other most of the time. They usually met at the mailboxes at the end of the day or walking out to their vehicles in the morning. Hallie must be avoiding him, and Steve found that thought damned depressing.

Even the kids had noticed. "Is something wrong between you and Hallie?" Meagan asked the weekend before Mary Lynn's wedding.

"Wrong? What makes you ask that?" He pretended ignorance rather than admit he'd insulted Hallie. It didn't help that she'd attacked him just after he'd been sucker-punched by his ex-wife.

Mary Lynn had come to him just the way he'd dreamed she would. Only that was as far as his romantic scenario matched what had actually happened. She'd come begging, all right, but not to ask him back into her life. She'd needed a favor, a rather large one as it turned out. Instead of rejoining his family, he would act as guardian while his ex-wife honeymooned with her new husband. He adored his kids; it wasn't that. His feelings had nothing to do with them and everything to do with Mary Lynn. Her remarriage was real to him now, and it meant that hope was truly over. He'd become just a convenience to his ex-wife.

Hallie's lecture afterward had felt like a kick when he was already down. Nevertheless, he shouldn't have said what he did. It was all too easy to recall the hurt and disappointment in her expressive brown eyes.

"Dad?" Meagan waved a hand in front of his face. "I was talking to you about Hallie."

No use trying to hide it any longer. "We had a, uh, minor falling-out."

"That's what Hallie said."

Steve brightened. "Hallie mentioned it?"

Meagan shrugged. "Not really. I asked her if she wanted to come to Kenny's baseball game. It's boring there without someone to talk to, and I thought maybe Hallie could come. I think she might've too, if it wasn't for what you said."

"She told you that?"

"No." Meagan shook her head emphatically. "Just that you were angry with each other."

Kenny walked into the house and slammed the front door. He threw his baseball mitt on the floor. "It's raining," he said, sounding thoroughly disgusted. "How am I supposed to play ball when the weather's like this?" He fell onto the sofa, not bothering to pull off his muddy shoes.

Steve sat down next to his son. Everyone had been short-tempered this weekend, and he suspected it had little to do with the weather.

"We need to talk," he announced. "You, too, Meagan."

"Yeah, Meagan," Kenny taunted.

"About what?" She ignored her brother and sat in the chair crossing her arms defensively, just the way Hallie had the last time they talked.

"We've all been in a bad mood," he began. "And—"

"Not me," Meagan insisted.

To be fair, she'd been the most even-tempered of anyone, including him.

"You think you're perfect." Kenny glared at his sister and probably would have stuck out his tongue if Steve hadn't been watching.

The corners of Meagan's mouth edged upward. "That's because I *am* perfect."

"I think I know what's wrong," Steve said, unwilling to wade into an argument between his children.

"It's the rain," Kenny said. "It rained last week during the game and I played terrible."

"You *are* terrible," Meagan muttered.

"I'm a lot better than you!"

"Kids, please," Steve said, waving his arms in referee fashion. "I think all this has to do with your mother marrying Kip." He dove into the conversation headfirst. At least he had the children's attention.

"I know how you feel," Steve told them, putting his arm around Kenny's shoulders. "But I want you both to know that nothing's going to change with the three of us. It doesn't matter who your mother marries. I'll always be your dad."

"I don't like Kip," Kenny said sullenly. "He doesn't know how to throw a ball and he can't catch worth beans."

A perverse part of Steve was thrilled to hear it. "But he was willing to try, and that's all that counts, isn't it?"

Kenny lowered his eyes rather than answer.

"How can you say nice things about Kip?" Meagan cried, and to his shock, his daughter's eyes filled with tears. "Mom's marrying him when she should still be married to you."

That more or less summed up what Steve felt, but he couldn't say as much. Mary Lynn had her own life to live and she'd chosen to live it without him.

"Your mother has a mind of her own and she's in love with Kip, so much in love that she's decided to marry him. Now it's up to the three of us to accept her decision and be happy for her."

The words stuck in his craw, but he managed to say them with enough conviction to sound as if he meant it.

"But I don't *like* Kip," Kenny said for the second time.

"Give him a chance," Steve urged. His children had to live with Mary Lynn's new husband, and it would behoove them to make their peace with him. "I'm sure he isn't so bad once you get to know him," Steve added.

"He isn't you," Meagan said, getting to the heart of the matter.

It hurt to let go of the dream of getting back together with Mary Lynn. It hurt like hell. That was one thing, but having Kip step into the role of stepfather to his kids was another.

"I love you both," Steve whispered and held out his arms. Meagan and Kenny crowded next to him on the sofa. He wrapped an arm around each one, loving them with an intensity that made his heart ache.

"Nothing's going to change between us," he promised, struggling to find the words to reassure them. "I'm still your dad. I'll always be here for you, no matter what happens."

"I wish Mom—"

"Shh," Steve said, and pressed Kenny's head against his shoulder.

"You'll always be my dad, no matter what?" Kenny repeated. "Do you promise?"

"You can count on it, son."

"Even if *you* get married again?"

Steve couldn't see the likelihood of that happening. "Even if I get married again," he vowed. Nothing on earth was strong enough to keep him from his children.

"Feel better now?" he asked after a few moments.

"I do," Meagan confessed.

"Me, too," Kenny said.

Mary Lynn stopped by to pick up the kids an hour later. Steve didn't walk outside to chat with her the way he did most Sundays. Frankly, he couldn't see the point of it. Why torture himself?

School was out for the summer, and the kids were at the stage where they weren't sure what to do with themselves yet. He'd make a point of seeing more of them and concentrating on being a good father. Actually he was looking forward to having his children with him the two weeks Mary Lynn and Kip were away. It might help ease the loneliness—his, anyway.

The silence that followed their leaving seemed to echo in Steve's mind. He turned on the television, hoping to fill the place with noise, but that depressed him even more than the quiet had.

He decided what he needed was a workout, so he donned his running shoes and sweats. Every once in a while the urge to jog hit him. And right now, pounding out his frustrations on the pavement suited his mood perfectly.

He left the house just as a car pulled up in front of Hallie's—one of those new BMWs he'd admired from afar. The Z3, the one from that James Bond movie.

It took Steve a couple of minutes to realize that the well-dressed man who'd stepped out was Hallie's date. Steve did a number of warm-up exercises, which were little more than an excuse to stick around long enough to get a good look at the guy she was dating this time.

He had to admit this character was better-looking than the others had been. Successful, too, judging by the car he drove.

Steve hoped things worked out for Hallie. And he hoped he and Hallie could be friends again. He missed the laughter she brought to his life and the companionable hours she'd spent with him and his kids.

Yeah, he should've kept his damn mouth shut. He wished he knew how to repair the damage, but he was at a distinct loss when it came to letting a woman know he was sorry. His marriage was a good example of that.

He set off on his run, getting his heart rate up to aerobic level in a few minutes. He soon discovered that his mind was filled with thoughts of Hallie. Not Mary Lynn. Hallie.

He wasn't sure if he should be grateful or infuriated.

On impulse, Steve left a one-word note on her windshield the next morning.

SORRY.

Nothing happened. He was convinced she hadn't noticed. And

then, the following morning, he found a piece of paper tucked under his windshield wiper. He unfolded it.

YOU'RE FORGIVEN.

Smiling, Steve stuck it in his pants pocket and headed for work. Todd noticed his improved mood right away.

"You're in good spirits this morning," he commented.

Steve poured himself a cup of coffee. "What do you think is appropriate for a man to give a woman when he wants to apologize. Flowers or candy?"

"What woman?"

"Never mind. Flowers or candy?" Steve repeated.

Todd frowned. "Does this have something to do with that neighbor of yours? Sally? Hattie? No, Hallie, that's it. Hallie."

"How'd you know?"

"Come on, Steve, you talk about her practically every conversation we have. She must be a comedian because you're constantly going on about something funny she's done. I expect to hear you two are hot and heavy under the covers any time now."

"Me and Hallie?"

"Yeah, you and Hallie."

Lovers? The two of them? He thought about it a moment, then shook his head. "Nah. It wouldn't work." It was kind of unfortunate, because he liked her. And because he knew instinctively that they were well matched in ways that mattered.

"Why not?"

"Well…" A long list of excuses crowded his mind. So many that he found it difficult to sort through them all and spit out just one. "Mainly because she's seriously looking for a husband."

"So?"

"Been there, done that, bought a T-shirt," Steve returned flippantly. "I like her as a friend, but I don't want to complicate our relationship with anything physical."

"That sounds like a pretty weak excuse if you want my opinion."

"I don't," Steve said. Then he shook his head. "You see, I don't know if the friendship would hold up if we mixed the two." Why ruin a good thing with sex?

"That's not the way I see it," Todd said. "Friends often make the best lovers. The sexual aspect of the relationship is enhanced by familiarity."

"Maybe." Steve was willing to concede that much. "You never did answer my question. Flowers or candy?" He wanted to divert Todd from the subject of sex, which only served to remind him how long he'd gone without it. Months. Many months. Longer than any other period in his adult life.

"Flowers," Todd said, adding a tablespoon of sugar to his coffee mug. "Definitely flowers."

Steve was leaning toward candy, thinking Hallie would want to share. He'd had a craving for chocolate truffles lately. Todd was right, though; flowers would be for Hallie, but he would've been the one eating the candy.

On his way home from work Steve stopped at an upscale grocery store and bought a single red rose, a small box of chocolates and, to be on the safe side, a bottle of chilled white wine. That way he'd covered all the bases.

He showered, changed clothes and waited until he was certain Hallie was home. Grabbing the wine and chocolates and placing the long-stemmed rose between his teeth, he rang her doorbell.

Hallie answered, took one look at him and laughed. Her smile was like sunshine, and Steve basked in its warmth. "Friends?" he asked.

"Friends," she answered softly, and let him inside.

Even though they'd only been on the outs a week, it felt like a month. He was lighthearted with relief now that the friendship had been rescued. But a rose between his teeth was one thing; a heartfelt apology another.

"What I said about getting yourself a husband before offering me marital advice," he started, then cleared his throat. "I regretted it as soon as the words left my mouth. I'm sorry, Hallie."

It seemed to him that her bottom lip quivered ever so slightly, but he might have been wrong.

"What you said was true," she told him, her voice impassive. "I spoke out of turn."

"Not really. Besides, letting you fall off the bike when Mary Lynn arrived wasn't one of my finer moments. You had every right to be upset."

"Let's put it behind us."

"Fair enough." He handed her the wine, the chocolates and the rose.

"Thank you," she said, and stepped forward to kiss his lips. It was a feathery kiss, a light kiss, a kiss without passion.

It was just like the other times they'd kissed.

Which made the heat soaring through his blood difficult to explain. He resisted the urge to reach for her shoulders and pull her back into his arms. Resisted the urge to kiss her again. He longed to feel the pressure of her mouth on his, and the soft and feminine imprint of her body.

Something was definitely very wrong.

Steve could feel his pulse pounding in his temple and was grateful when she suggested they drink the wine on her patio. The evening was lovely, with a cloudless blue sky and the gentlest of breezes.

Hallie sat back on her folding chair gazing up at the sky, her legs stretched out in front of her.

Steve relaxed, too. "You dating Bill Gates these days?" he asked, thinking about the man with the fancy car.

"Bill Gates is married."

Clearly she wasn't going to be forthcoming with the information he wanted. "Who drives the Z3, then?"

"Oh, you mean Arnold. Arnold Vance, Dateline's latest offering." She glanced at him. "You two met?"

"No, I went out for a jog a couple of nights ago and saw him parked outside your house." He hated to reveal how curious he'd been, but there wasn't much point in hiding it now. "He looked like the perfect candidate for a husband."

"You think so?" She sounded surprised. "Arnold's polite and sensitive, a very nineties kind of man, but I didn't feel we hit it off the way we should have."

"Are you seeing him again?"

She nodded but without a lot of enthusiasm. "Next Wednesday. You know what irritates me? This guy is everything a woman could ask for, and all I can manage is token interest. He leaves me yawning."

Steve put a concerned expression on his face, but inside he was grinning widely. So, the car didn't make the man.

"Donnalee's experiencing the same thing," Hallie was saying. "She's dating this real-estate broker she's known for years. A catch with a capital *C,* and for the life of her she can't dredge up any excitement."

"Why?" Steve asked.

"If I knew that, I wouldn't be sitting here drinking wine with you." He smiled, remembering a similar smart-ass remark the night she'd looked after her baby niece.

This felt good, sitting out on a warm summer evening with his friend. "So," he said, "did you miss me?"

"I did," she said without elaborating. "It surprised me, too. You worked hard at avoiding me all week, I noticed."

"I didn't. I thought you were avoiding me."

"No, but my schedule was crazy," she said. "I left early and got home late." The smile was back in place, and Steve noticed, not for the first time, how pretty she was when she smiled. "In case you're interested, I not only missed you, I felt miserable and guilty. I hope you're satisfied.''

"So did I," he said, figuring that if she was willing to be open and honest, he wouldn't be anything less.

They sat in companionable silence for a few minutes, then chatted about this and that—the kids, the neighborhood, movies they'd seen. Eventually the subject of vacations arose.

"I'll be gone a couple of days at the beginning of next week," she told him. "Would it be too much trouble for you to pick up my mail?"

"I'd be happy to." He'd get her mail, water her plants and miss her, too. Sipping his wine, Steve found himself studying Hallie with fresh eyes. He remembered what Todd had said earlier in the day.

Lovers? He and Hallie?

She *was* attractive. Tonight she wore shorts and a blouse with a V neckline. By lifting his head just a bit, he could see the swell of her breasts. His gaze lingered there far longer than it should have. He caught himself thinking about her breasts and how he'd like to see them and—

For heaven's sake, this was Hallie! Steve frowned as he reminded himself. His friend and neighbor. He resisted the impulse to shake his head to clear it.

She continued chatting, and Steve listened with half an ear while she told him about the short business trip she'd planned—to attend a trade fair in San Francisco. He noticed small things about her that he hadn't paid attention to in the past.

Her mouth was incredible; her lips were perhaps the most perfectly shaped he'd ever seen. He studied them as she spoke, noticing the way she moistened them with the tip of her tongue. It was a purely innocent movement, not intended to be seductive at all. Furthermore, he'd seen her do it a thousand times and it'd never affected him like this.

"Mary Lynn's getting married this weekend." Steve wasn't sure what prompted his sudden statement.

"You okay?" she asked with a gentleness that was like salve to his battered soul.

He shrugged. "I don't have any choice but to accept it."

"What about the kids?"

"They aren't happy, but they're young and they'll adjust. I told them to give Lard Butt a chance to prove himself."

"Steve!"

"What?"

"You didn't actually call Kip Lard Butt, did you?"

He chuckled. "Not out loud."

"I should hope not." She threw him a schoolmarm's disapproving glare.

He sighed and gazed up at the heavens. "So Mary Lynn's getting married." He said it again. "Can you imagine her and Lard Butt in the sack together?"

"Steve!"

"I hate to tell you how long I've been without sex," he muttered, downing the last of his wine in one gulp.

Hallie glanced his way. "I'd hate to tell you how long it's been for me."

"Really?" That surprised him, seeing that she'd been dating a long line of men practically from the moment he'd met her.

"Don't act so shocked."

"What about Mark and Larry and the others?"

She pressed her lips together in annoyance, and Steve decided she'd missed her calling. Hallie really should've been in a class room; she had looks some teachers couldn't imitate.

"I don't sleep with every man I date."

"Don't get all bent out of shape. How was I supposed to know that? A lot of women do."

"That's the most ridiculous thing you've ever said to me, Steve Marris."

"Sorry," he said, meaning it. He reached for the wine bottle and replenished their glasses. "I certainly didn't want to offend you."

"I'm not offended...just, I don't know. You sometimes say stupid things."

The wine was affecting her, he observed. Her cheeks were flushed with color and a sheen of perspiration had moistened her brow. He could see the outline of her breasts and her nipples, pearl-hard, through her thin cotton blouse. She probably wasn't wearing a bra, which was a thought he'd rather not entertain in his present deprived—or was that depraved?—state of mind.

"Well, how about this?" He paused, grinning. "Are you interested?" Hell, it didn't do any harm to ask, and she might surprise him.

"Interested in what?"

"Sex, the two of us," he suggested nonchalantly. Maybe it was time to test Todd's theory about friends making the best lovers.

"You're joking!"

"Am I?" His brows rose.

If her face was flushed earlier, it bloomed a deep shade of scarlet now.

He gave a lazy indulgent sigh. "Hey, I didn't think it'd do any harm to ask."

"That's not exactly a turn-on, you know." She wrinkled her face and gave him a goofy look. "'Duh, come on, baby, let's do it'? No wonder you haven't had sex since God knows when."

Since he'd only been joking, Steve didn't take offense. "How else does a guy ask a woman to go to bed?"

"Not like that!"

"If I got down on one knee and said pretty please, would you reconsider?"

"No!"

He laughed. "Yeah," he said. "That's what I thought."

Twenty-Three

Back In The Game

Steve Marris hadn't the foggiest idea how to seduce a woman, Hallie decided, sitting at her desk. Furthermore he had no interest in making love to her. His invitation, if one could use that term for something so crude, was based wholly on his insecurities. His ex-wife had remarried, and Steve was feeling needy and unloved. He longed for a warm body beside him to ease the ache in his heart. Any warm body would do.

Hallie tore the pages—for Monday and Tuesday—off her calendar, since she'd been in San Francisco attending the trade fair those two days. She was about to toss them in the garbage when she paused. Mary Lynn was married to Kip now and Steve would have his hands full with the kids for the next two weeks. Maybe she—

That thought was interrupted by her phone ringing. It was Arnold Vance, calling to break tonight's date. He was going out of town on business. Hallie couldn't scrape up any feelings of regret. On paper Arnold was a perfect match; she should be thrilled to be dating him.

Only she wasn't.

She couldn't even claim he was dull. Arnold was thoughtful, successful and generous, with one prior marriage and no kids. Like her, he was looking for someone special to settle down with and raise a family. Yet they didn't *click,* and she was sick to death of analyzing why he bored her and, she thought fatalistically, why *she* seemed to bore him. What distressed her most was the feeling that she was the one at fault.

By the time Hallie arrived home from work, she was tired and irritable. Her mood lightened when she saw Steve with his kids on the patio. Apparently he'd decided to barbecue hamburgers. Kenny wore a chef's apron that hung to the tops of his tennis shoes. The sliding glass door off the kitchen was open, and Meagan was traipsing back and forth, carting their dinner out to the small picnic table set up on the grass.

"Care to join us?" Steve called out when he saw her. "Kenny's cooking."

"Kenny?" Hallie tried to sound delighted.

The nine-year-old grinned from ear to ear and held up a spatula with an extra-long handle.

"I wouldn't be so eager if I were you," Meagan warned. "Kenny doesn't know how to cook meat any way but well-done. *Real* well-done."

"Meagan made the salad," Steve boasted, patting his daughter on the head. "It looks fabulous."

Meagan shrugged one shoulder as if to say it wasn't any big deal, but Hallie could see she was pleased by her father's praise.

"I'll just get changed and come right over," Hallie promised. Actually she was glad Arnold had canceled their dinner date. She'd much rather spend time with Steve and the kids than in some fancy restaurant making small talk. An evening with Arnold would be spent trying to dredge up enthusiasm for a perfectly acceptable marriage candidate, and wondering why she couldn't.

Meagan followed her into the house. "Mom's married to Kip now," she announced as Hallie sorted through her mail and tossed the majority of it in the garbage.

"So I understand."

The girl lounged on the end of Hallie's bed while Hallie changed into a comfortable pair of jeans and a red-checkered sleeveless blouse.

"The wedding was nice. Lots of people came."

Steve had mysteriously disappeared over the weekend. Hallie had later learned that he'd made a trek to the mountains and gone camping with a good friend from work. It was just as well he hadn't been home. He'd have moped around and been miserable the entire weekend.

"Mom and Kip are in Hawaii," Meagan continued. "She hasn't phoned, not even once."

Hallie heard the hurt in the girl's voice. "That doesn't mean she isn't thinking of you, sweetheart. You're with your father, and there's really nothing for her to worry about, is there?"

Meagan shook her head. "I guess not."

Hallie placed an arm around the girl's shoulders, and they went out to join Steve and Kenny. It soon became obvious that the two males were desperately in need of help. One burger had fallen into the fire, and a frazzled Kenny was trying to lift it out with the spatula, dumping the remaining hamburgers directly into the fire. In his attempt to help, Steve burned two fingers. While Meagan got ice for Steve, Hallie rescued the burgers.

They laughed at the incident as they ate; in fact, the entire meal was spent laughing, teasing and talking. Hallie realized again that this was much more fun than any dinner date with Arnold would have been.

"Will you come to my baseball game tonight?" Kenny asked when they'd finished their food, which surprisingly had been delicious, charred burgers and all.

"Please, please come," Meagan added, folding her hands prayerlike.

Steve's gaze caught hers. "You're welcome if you don't have other plans."

"Arnold canceled."

"Then come. You'll be surprised how much fun it is."

"Don't believe him," Meagan muttered.

Kids' baseball couldn't possibly be more entertaining than watching Steve and his son barbecue, but she left that unsaid.

Cleanup following dinner was a snap. Paper plates went into the garbage and leftovers were stuffed in Steve's refrigerator. While Hallie and Meagan wiped down the counters and Steve cleaned the grill, Kenny changed into his team uniform.

"You're coming, aren't you, Hallie?" Meagan asked again, her eyes expectant, hopeful.

"I sure am."

"Yippee!"

The Little League baseball field was across the street from Kent Commons, the community center where Hallie had taken her cooking classes. They parked there and crossed the busy intersection to the enormous grassy field. Eight baseball diamonds were located on several acres, all with portable bleachers.

Steve seemed to be assisting the coach, because he promptly positioned himself at home plate and hit fly balls to the boys. Meagan and Hallie were left to their own devices.

"Your dad's a coach?" Hallie asked, watching Steve interact with the youngsters and admiring his knack with them. She could tell that Kenny's friends liked Steve.

"Not officially, but Dad always attends Kenny's games and started helping out. Now Coach Hawley relies on him," Meagan explained.

Hallie got the impression that her presence had generated a number of curious stares. In the beginning she'd assumed it was because she was an unfamiliar face, but then she realized that the people staring at her were whispering back and forth.

Meagan gestured surreptitiously at one of them. "That's Mrs. Larson," she whispered. "She's got the hots for Dad."

"The lady in the short pink pants?"

"Yup. She introduced herself as divorced and available."

One look assured Hallie that Mrs. Larson more than fulfilled Steve's criteria for the perfect woman. Her breasts threatened to spill out of her top, and she wore tight shorts and high heels. Hallie couldn't help wondering if Mrs. Larson had managed to pique Steve's interest—but somehow she couldn't imagine Steve interested in someone so...obvious.

It didn't take long for the bleachers to fill up with family and friends. A couple of women quizzed Meagan about her mother's wedding; while she answered their questions, the women studied Hallie.

"I'm Steve's next-door neighbor," she told them. "Kenny asked me along to watch him play."

"How nice of you to come," one woman cooed.

"Pleased to meet you," Mrs. Larson said, sounding anything but. The woman had daggers for eyes and they were aimed directly at Hallie, shamelessly assessing her and finding her lacking. Hallie wished she'd thought to wear her enhancer bra.

"This is the first time Dad's brought anyone with him to Kenny's games," Meagan whispered now. "Everyone must think you're dating."

"Oh, so *that's* it." Hallie pretended to be enlightened.

The game started and Steve joined them in the bleachers. Soon everyone's attention—even Mrs. Larson's—was riveted on the playing field.

When it was Kenny's turn at bat, Hallie bit her lip tensely, wanting him to do well. He swung at the first pitch, connected and raced headlong toward first base. The player on second base tried to throw him out, but the umpire raised both arms, declaring him safe. Only then did Kenny glance at the bleachers; Steve who was watching closely, gave his son a thumbs-up.

Hallie whistled and cheered and, in her excitement, stumbled and nearly fell off the bleachers. Would have, in fact, if Steve hadn't caught her. His laughing eyes met hers, and he slipped an arm around her waist. For protection, Hallie told herself. To keep her from losing her balance again.

The next time Kenny was up at bat, Hallie persuaded Meagan and Steve to form their own family cheering wave In rapid succession they took turns standing with their arms above their heads, moving them slowly back and forth to create the effect of a cresting wave. Soon the entire section was involved in the cheer.

Kenny's team won the game, with a final score of six to three. He raced off the field, beaming. "We're in first place now," he shouted, holding his index finger high above his head.

"Congratulations, sport," Steve said, grabbing the bill of Kenny's cap and pulling it down over the boy's face. He momentarily left them to congratulate the coach and help assemble the equipment.

Another team member strolled over to Kenny's side. "Is this your dad's girlfriend?" the boy asked, looking at Hallie with unabashed curiosity.

"Sort of," Kenny answered. "But I don't think he's going to marry her."

Hallie noticed how the Larson woman's eyes lit up at this tidbit of news.

"You played a good game, Ronnie," Steve said, mussing the other boy's hair when he returned.

"Thanks, Mr. Marris." Ronnie grinned, then glanced over his shoulder at his mother, who'd moved back toward the bleachers. "My mom wants to know about your lady friend. Kenny said you aren't going to marry her."

"Ronnie." His name was faintly heard from the other side of the bleachers. "It's time to go."

"Does Ronnie belong to Mrs. Hot and Pink?" Hallie asked Meagan under her breath.

"You got it."

"Tell your mother, Ronnie, that Hallie and I are very *close* friends." Steve sidled over to Hallie and wrapped his arm around her shoulders, squeezing hard. He gazed down at her, looking lovelorn and deeply infatuated.

"Steve," she hissed, and elbowed him in the ribs.

Steve's infatuated gaze didn't waver. "I'm crazy about this woman."

"You're overdoing it, Marris," she muttered. But she smiled benignly and went along with his stunt. What troubled her, though, was the excited way her body reacted to having Steve this close.

"Head over heels crazy," he elaborated.

If he didn't cut it out soon, Hallie was going to do him physical harm.

Ronnie took off running and Steve dropped his arm.

"What was that all about?" Hallie demanded.

"Loretta Larson," he admitted. "She always considered me fair game, but now that Mary Lynn's remarried, it's open season. Frankly, I'm not interested.''

Now that Mary Lynn's remarried. Of course! She didn't know why she hadn't realized it earlier. She had an idea, one that made perfect sense. With his ex-wife out of the picture, Steve had no choice but to move forward in his life. Date again, possibly even marry. That meant meeting someone new—and Hallie thought she knew just the right woman.

"We need to talk," she said as the four of them walked toward the parking lot. "Privately."

"We do?" They stood at the curb waiting for the light to change. "About what?"

"Dad, are we going for ice cream?" Kenny interrupted, tugging at his father's sleeve.

"You bet, sport."

"Great." Kenny tucked his mitt under his arm and, when the light changed, raced across the intersection toward the car.

"You can't say what you want with the kids around?"

"I'd rather not."

"All right, all right." But he didn't sound too happy.

It was dark by the time they arrived home. While the kids flopped down in front of the television, Hallie and Steve sat in her patio chairs and gazed up at the stars. "What's so important you have to drag me out in the middle of the night?"

"Donnalee!" Hallie said excitedly.

"What about her?"

"She's my best friend and I want you to meet her."

"Why?" he asked, sounding suspicious.

"Why?" she repeated. "Isn't it obvious?"

"No."

The man was dense, but then she had been, too. "I can't believe I didn't think of this earlier."

"Of what?" he asked impatiently.

"You and Donnalee. She's perfect for you."

"Me?"

"It's time you started dating again," she said. "Otherwise women like Loretta Larson are going to drive you crazy."

"Since when did you become my social secretary?"

"Since tonight. Now don't argue with me, because it won't do any good. I'm going to arrange a date for you and my best friend."

Steve was silent for a moment. "There's always Todd."

"Who's Todd?" She couldn't understand why he was throwing a stranger's name at her.

"*My* best friend. He's perfect for you."

"Really?" Funny, he hadn't mentioned Todd earlier.

"Friday night," he said, "the four of us. Agreed?" He held out his hand.

Hallie placed her palm in his. "Agreed."

Twenty-Four

Four Blind Mice

"You didn't *tell* Steve, did you?" Donnalee cried, furious with Hallie. "You didn't tell him I don't want to do this...this date thing." She sighed; it was difficult to remain angry with your best friend for long. Still, after everything Hallie had been through with blind dates, you'd think she wouldn't be inclined to arrange them for others.

"I didn't have the heart to disappoint him," Hallie said solemnly, as if breaking this ridiculous dinner date would send him over the edge. "You don't know how much he's looking forward to meeting you."

"Yeah, I'll bet," Donnalee muttered. Hallie had just announced yesterday morning that they were going out on this double blind date. Despite Donnalee's loud protests—she wasn't interested in Steve Marris, or any other man at the moment—her friend had apparently gone full steam ahead.

"Come on, one date with Steve Marris."

"No, Hallie. No, no, no." But Donnalee should have known Hallie wouldn't give up so easily. She'd listed her neighbor's virtues— kind, considerate, responsible, blah, blah, blah. According to Hallie, the guy was too good to be true, which in Donnalee's limited experience generally proved to be exactly right.

"Just one date," Hallie pleaded. "That's all I'm asking."

"No," Donnalee insisted. "Hallie, I'm not interested."

Refusing to be deterred, Hallie glared at her friend. "You two are so right for each other!"

"I don't see it that way." Donnalee refused to budge. Really this was useless and a waste of time. For a whole bunch of good reasons: she couldn't handle another disappointment, he was probably still in love with his ex, she had her doubts about getting involved with the friend of a friend. Besides, she wasn't the one for Steve. Hallie was. Steve was the topic of every conversation—Steve said this, Steve did that. If Hallie wasn't talking about him. it was his kids, whom she adored. Donnalee had trouble understanding how a smart, perceptive woman could be so obtuse. Anyone who listened to Hallie would know she was close to falling in love with Steve. If she hadn't already. Donnalee had seen it weeks ago.

"But he's wonderful with kids. He's patient and good-hearted and more fun than just about anyone. I can't understand why you won't go out with him. Come on, Donnalee, what would it hurt?"

"I can't."

"You can't or you won't?" Hallie's mouth fell open. "Don't you realize how embarrassing this is going to be? Steve's going to arrive in a couple of hours with Todd, just the way we planned, and you won't be anywhere in sight."

Donnalee paraded out her first major objection. "You told me he's divorced and—"

"So are you."

"True," Donnalee concurred, "but from everything you've said, he's still in love with his ex-wife."

"She's remarried now," Hallie argued, "and you're going to make him forget all about Mary Lynn."

Donnalee nibbled on her lower lip. If anyone was going to make Steve Marris forget his ex-wife, it would be Hallie, not her. "Let me ask you something. Why aren't you dating Steve yourself?"

That brought Hallie up short. "Well, because..." she faltered.

"It's a fair question," Donnalee pressed, hoping her friend would stop long enough to examine what was really happening.

"Well, Steve and I are friends. Neighbors. And even if I was interested in him, I'm not the sort of woman he needs right now. There's nothing romantic or mysterious about me. Not like you. I'm just plain old Hallie McCarthy from next door. We do stuff with his kids and go out for a pizza now and then, and..."

As Hallie prattled on, Donnalee felt her resolve cracking. One date. One lousy dinner date wouldn't be so terrible. Perhaps she should reconsider; after all, Hallie was her best friend, and she'd be going along tonight, as the unknown Todd's date.

"If you don't come, the whole evening'll be ruined," Hallie wailed. "I was looking forward to meeting Todd, too." She sounded almost convinced, but Donnalee remained skeptical. Hallie wasn't interested in Todd any more than Donnalee was in Steve. To Hallie's credit, though, she actually seemed to believe she was doing them all a great favor.

"I knew a Todd once," Donnalee said slowly. She'd moved to the Pacific Northwest from Georgia while in junior high. Because of her soft drawl, she'd stood out and been teased unmercifully. She still remembered the interminable Scarlett O'Hara jokes with a shudder. By the time she was in high school, she'd grown quiet and introspective. Much too shy to let a good-looking boy know how she felt about him.

"I've known two or three myself," Hallie said. "Big deal. Now are you going to make me look like a fool, or will you do this one small thing?"

"All right, all right," Donnalee groaned. "Why not?"

"Thank God." Hallie closed her eyes and threw back her head in exaggerated relief.

"But in the future," Donnalee said sternly, "I expect you to confer with me before you commit me to a date."

Hallie folded her hands as if making a vow. "I will. I promise I will."

"Good." Donnalee hoped Steve liked what she was wearing, because she wasn't about to change. What he saw was what he got. "I thought you said his kids were with him this week?"

"They are, but his parents are taking them for tonight." Hallie grinned suddenly. "It's going to be perfect. I don't know what I would've *done* if you'd refused."

"It'd serve you right, best friend!" Hallie was going to be paying her back a long time for this one.

"They're picking us up at eight." Hallie studied her watch. "Which gives us plenty of time to get ready."

"No, thanks," Donnalee said. "This'll have to do." She was wearing black leggings and a long jersey top, black and sprinkled with gold stars. Hallie looked her over appraisingly, then nodded and ran off to her bedroom to change. Not pushing her luck, Donnalee figured.

She settled down to wait for her friend. Hallie had succeeded in wearing down her defenses, not only because she was persistent and persuasive, but for another reason. Sanford was engaged.

He'd had the courtesy to call her himself. The news had come as a shock, so soon after their breakup, but it wasn't unexpected—or especially painful. He'd found the right woman, and Donnalee was pleased for him. It wasn't regret that she suffered, not anymore. Just... She was afraid of not finding someone to love, not living the life she wanted. Not having a family of her own.

Hallie's doorbell chimed precisely at eight. Donnalee'd say one thing for Steve: the man was prompt. Hallie tossed her a look of encouragement mingled with hope as she answered the door. Donnalee recognized Steve Marris from glimpses she'd caught of him during visits to Hallie's place. He entered the condo with a tall attractive man at his side. She could tell by the other man's stance that he wasn't any keener about this double blind date than she was. It was when she saw his face that her heart stopped. Todd Stafford. The Todd from high school.

Somehow Donnalee managed to smile politely while Hallie introduced her to Steve, but she had trouble taking her eyes off Todd. He didn't seem to recognize her, and she wasn't sure she should say anything.

"Hallie, this is Todd Stafford." He shook hands with Hallie, but his gaze returned to her. "Donnalee Norman?" His question was more breath than voice.

"It's Cooper now. I married when I was young." She realized she couldn't leave it there. "Unfortunately, it didn't last."

"Me, too." With apparent reluctance, Todd dragged his eyes from Donnalee and turned his attention to Hallie.

"You two know each other?" Hallie asked, looking from one to the other.

"We attended the same high school," Todd answered for them.

Hallie's gaze questioned Donnalee, as if to ask whether this was the Todd she'd mentioned earlier. Donnalee nodded. Talk about a fluke. Talk about fate. Talk about coincidence. It was just as it had been all those years ago—he was with someone else. *Hallie.* Her very best friend. All she could do was smile and pretend it didn't matter.

The years had been good to him, Donnalee noted. He looked exactly as she remembered...only better. There was an unmistakable maturity about him that had been lacking at eighteen. The lines on his face revealed depth and character, and his lanky boyish body had matured into hard-muscled masculinity.

"I thought we'd take my car," Steve said, interrupting her reverie.

"Sure." Donnalee had to make an effort to stop staring at Todd. It was even more of an effort to remember that Steve was her date, and Hallie—judging by her expression—was trying to remind her.

Soon they were outside and in the car. Donnalee sat in front with Steve, and Hallie and Todd were in the back. No one seemed inclined to speak. It could have been her imagination, but Donnalee was sure she felt Todd's gaze on her. The way her thoughts were on him.

Steve did try to engage her in conversation, but Donnalee doubted that her one-word replies made sense. She'd assumed she'd outgrown her shyness, but her tongue felt as if it were glued to her teeth, and all because a boy she once knew was in the back seat with her best friend. One thing was certain, she thought with a silent laugh, she needn't worry about Steve wanting to date her after tonight. He'd be glad to be rid of her.

Involuntarily she remembered the Todd of years past. The closest she'd ever come to actually speaking to him had been in the cafeteria a few weeks before he graduated. They stood next to one another in the food line, and afterward, hating herself for being too shy to murmur so much as a greeting, Donnalee had left a note on his car.

It read: *I think you're wonderful.* She hadn't been brave enough to sign her name, something she'd always regretted.

And then there was no more time for memories; they'd arrived at the waterfront Mexican restaurant. The place was filled with wonderful exotic scents—cilantro and chilies—and festive mariachi music played in the background. Donnalee and Todd sat side by side, opposite their "dates." Donnalee noticed that Steve and Hallie did most of the talking. When the waitress came to take their drink order, everyone asked for margaritas.

Donnalee focused her attention on the menu. Hallie and Steve helped themselves to salsa and chips, but Donnalee restrained herself, preferring her tortillas whole and warm from the grill, not deep-fried.

"Could I have an order of soft tortillas?" Todd asked their waitress when she returned with their drinks.

"Me, too," she found herself adding.

Todd glanced at her and smiled, his gaze lingering. She felt indescribably foolish, blushing as if she were sixteen all over again.

When the friendly waitress returned for their order, Donnalee chose one of the specials—two cheese enchiladas and a chili relleno. Todd's choice echoed her own.

"Did you two plan this?" Hallie joked.

"No," Donnalee whispered. It was only a similarity in food preferences, she told herself. *Don't make too much of it.* But she knew, she *knew* that something special was beginning.

Steve asked Hallie a question, and soon the two were deep in conversation. The space between Donnalee and Todd seemed to evaporate. She kept her gaze straight ahead, not knowing what to say, almost frightened by the way her heart behaved at seeing him again. There was so much she wanted to ask him, but she couldn't find the courage. The shy teenager she'd once been had returned to possess her.

Todd seemed equally uneasy. Finally he said, "You won't believe who I ran into recently. Mrs. O'Leary from senior English. Did you ever have her?"

She'd been Donnalee's favorite teacher back then—and she was a safe topic of conversation right now. "Yes! How is she? I haven't heard about her in years."

"She's the same. I don't think time will ever change her. Oh, her hair's a little grayer, but her eyes still twinkle when she talks. I was happy to see her," he said simply. "I always wanted her to know she was my favorite teacher."

"Me, too." Donnalee nodded vigorously. "She was so passionate about literature. She turned Shakespeare's plays into experiences that I lived and breathed." Donnalee's thinking was coherent once again, and she warmed to the topic. "And Jane Austen... Mrs. O'Leary taught me how to look at her books and see not only the past she described, but the way her comments about men and women are still relevant. I reread *Pride and Prejudice* every few years." She paused. "I'll always be grateful to Mrs. O."

"So will I."

By now they were both relaxed, laughing and reminiscing. Soon Donnalee noticed that Hallie and Steve had stopped talking and were watching them with renewed interest. Her best friend seemed none too pleased with her. Hallie pulled her chair in, closer to Todd.

Steve pulled his closer to Donnalee.

Donnalee got the hint. Steve was *her* date and Hallie was Todd's. Donnalee didn't blame her; it must be disconcerting to find your friend being so friendly with your date!

Steve appeared to be having much the same thought about Todd, because he was frowning darkly.

All of a sudden this wasn't going well, and Donnalee didn't know how to improve the situation.

Somehow she made it through dinner, although she didn't remember tasting a single bite. When the waitress came for her plate, she was surprised to see that half her meal was missing and could only assume she'd eaten it.

Steve suggested a walk along the waterfront and everyone seemed agreeable, but as they left the restaurant, Donnalee saw Todd pulling Steve aside. They conducted a low-voiced conversation, with frequent glances at the two women.

Donnalee could guess what they were discussing, but her immediate reaction was gratitude for the opportunity to speak privately to Hallie.

"Don't hate me," she whispered, not knowing how to explain what was happening between her and Todd.

"You mean because you've stolen my date?"

Donnalee had rarely felt so wretched. She couldn't spit out an apology fast enough, but Hallie stopped her before she uttered a word. The irritation in her eyes was replaced with a gentle chagrined look.

"Don't worry about it. I could see the lay of the land the minute you two recognized each other."

"I was crazy about him, Hallie." Donnalee reflected that it hadn't taken long for those feelings to rekindle. Being with Todd was like peeling back the years and uncovering that vulnerable, yearning girl again. What terrified her, though, was the knowledge that she could easily fall in love with him—really in love. Not an adolescent infatuation this time but adult emotions with all their power and complexity.

A minute later she watched as Todd made his way to her side. "I squared it with Steve," he said, and reached for her hand, his fingers closing tightly around hers.

"Do you mind if we go our own way, just the two of us?" he added.

Her heart pounded hard. "What about Hallie?"

"Steve's talking to her now."

Donnalee looked over her shoulder in time to see Hallie grin and wave. "Have fun, you two," she called out cheerfully. Then Steve and Hallie turned and walked in the opposite direction.

She swung back and found herself staring into Todd's unbelievably intense eyes.

"This is the way it should've been from the first," he said, almost daring her to contradict him with what surely would have been a lie. "Hallie and Steve should be the ones dating. Not you and Steve or me and Hallie."

"I think she's half in love with him already," she said.

"Steve's already in love with her."

Donnalee wanted to believe that. "But I thought Steve was in love with his ex-wife."

Todd hesitated before he answered, as if carefully weighing his response. "Yeah, I guess he is. I've never understood it. Mary Lynn's selfish and self-centered. I won't say any more because it isn't fair for me to judge someone else's actions or motives."

Donnalee smiled to herself. "I always admired that about you."

Todd glanced at her. "Admired what?"

"How fair you are. And how generous."

Her answer left him suspiciously quiet. "I saw you leave the note on my car."

Donnalee felt the color explode in her cheeks, and yet she didn't fear the truth. "I meant what I said then and I mean it now."

"I was always sorry I didn't talk to you in the cafeteria that day," he said quietly. "I always had a difficult time talking to girls. Still do," he admitted on a sheepish note. "I wanted you to know that I thought you were nice. The other sophomore girls seemed immature, but not you."

"You were my first crush," she whispered. "I dreamed about you every night that entire year."

They stopped outside the ferry terminal, the cooler evening wind dancing around them. "I dreamed of you, too, Donnalee."

Unexplained tears crowded her eyes. She wasn't a woman prone to open displays of emotion; mortified, she turned away, not wanting him to witness the effect of his words.

"Donnalee." Todd placed his hand on her shoulder. "I said the wrong thing, didn't I?"

She shook her head. "No, it's not you. I'm...I'm sorry." Fumbling for a tissue in her purse, she blotted her eyes. "Something...strange is happening."

He repositioned himself so that he stood directly in front of her. With one finger he raised her chin so their eyes could meet. "You're trembling."

"It must be a chill from the wind." She offered the first sane excuse that presented itself.

His tattered breath struck her face, as if he'd been unconsciously holding it inside and released it all at once. "You're right. Something very strange is happening. I feel it, too, and damn it all, it frightens me."

"I was married and...the divorce nearly killed me," she said.

"My marriage didn't last a year. I vowed I'd never get involved again. I don't think I could take the pain if something went wrong."

"And now?" she dared to ask.

"And now..." His expression seemed to say he was as shocked, as wary, as she was, and his breathing was ragged.

"I have a cabin," he said, his eyes burning into hers. "Come with me tomorrow—we'll spend the rest of the weekend there."

It didn't take Donnalee two seconds to decide. "Yes."

Twenty-Five

When Todd Met Donnalee

"Doesn't that beat all," Hallie said wonderingly. She walked down the waterfront at a good clip, easily outpacing Steve. "I wouldn't have believed it if I hadn't seen it with my own eyes." She paused and waited for him to catch up. "What is this, *When Harry Met Sally?*"

"When who met who?" Steve asked, pretending to be out of breath.

"That movie—it was out a few years back. Two people arrange dates for each other with their best friends and then the *friends* fall in love and marry."

Steve feigned a look of shock. "Are you saying Todd's going to marry Donnalee? On such short acquaintance?"

"Don't get cute with me, Steve Marris. All I know is that my best friend just stole my blind date."

"In case you hadn't noticed, you aren't exactly building up my self-esteem here," Steve remarked pointedly. "First, I lost *my* blind date to my best friend and then *you* complain about getting stuck with me."

"I'm not complaining." Steve was taking this all wrong.

"Well, you don't look happy."

She slid her arm through his and pressed her head to his shoulder. "Oh, you aren't so bad."

Steve snorted. "Your enthusiasm is underwhelming."

"It's just that I'm disappointed."

"Rubbing salt in the wound?"

Hallie giggled. "I'm disappointed for *you.* I was so sure you and Donnalee would hit it off. She's exactly the type of woman you need, and you're perfect for her. Who would've guessed she'd known Todd in another life?"

"What makes you say Donnalee's perfect for me?"

Hallie sighed loudly. Like every other man she'd ever known,

Steve needed help seeing the obvious. "For starters, Donnalee's beautiful *and* intelligent. Plus, she's been through a painful divorce, so she understands what you've been through with Mary Lynn. Donnalee's great with kids, too. I'm sure Meagan and Kenny would like her once they met her. Of course, she's also got what you said a man's looking for."

"What I said?"

"You know—her physical...endowments."

"I hadn't noticed."

Hallie'd just bet! "And your personalities complement each other." She gave another dramatic sigh, this time of regret. "Now it's too late."

"Too late?"

"For you and Donnalee. Because of Todd. I've never seen a man fluster Donnalee that way. Not even Sanford, and he was one in a million." It occurred to Hallie, not for the first time, that she wouldn't have minded dating Sanford herself. Except for his unwillingness to have children, he was every woman's dream. A dream Donnalee had walked away from, refusing to sacrifice something as important to her as family. She hadn't done it lightly. Hallie wasn't sure what she herself would have done in similar circumstances and was grateful she didn't have to make the decision.

They paused near the waterfront fire station and the large bronze statue honoring Ivar Haglund, a local restaurateur and philanthropist. Suddenly tired, Hallie slumped down on a park bench, as if waiting for a bus.

She looked over at the waterfront concessions. "I wonder if any of them sell double-fudge macadamia-nut ice cream." It was that kind of evening.

"Wouldn't vanilla do just as well?" Steve asked.

"I guess. In a pinch."

"Be right back." He disappeared and returned a couple of minutes later with two hand-dipped chocolate-and-nut-covered ice-cream bars. "It was the best I could do."

Hallie gladly accepted the treat. "I've underestimated you, Marris."

"Hey, I've been telling you that for weeks."

"You don't seem very upset about all this." He wasn't revealing the slightest regret, while her own ego was scraping bedrock. Hard not to feel that way when your date abandons you without a backward glance—although she certainly didn't begrudge Donnalee any happiness.

"Todd going off with Donnalee works for the best as far as I'm concerned," he muttered, unwrapping his ice-cream bar.

"Your best friend walks off with your date and you don't care?"

Steve shrugged. "Nothing would've come of it, anyway."

"How can you be so sure?"

"Easy. Donnalee's looking for a husband, and frankly, I'm not interested. I tried to tell you that earlier. I've been married, and believe me, once was enough."

"In other words, the entire evening was a waste of...of my match-making efforts." Irritated, Hallie bit into the ice-cream bar, the cold almost painful against her teeth. Apparently Steve intended to spend the rest of his life mooning after his first and only love. It made Hallie so angry she took another bite of ice cream. A big tooth-chilling bite.

"Why is it we can never have a conversation without talking about Mary Lynn?" she asked, once her teeth had recovered from the shock.

"Mary Lynn? Who's talking about her?" He tossed his half-eaten ice-cream bar into a nearby garbage container.

Hallie sighed. "Look. If you're never going to get married again, why'd you let me set you up with Donnalee?"

His expression was the picture of self-sacrifice. "I did it for you."

Yeah, right.

He must have read the skepticism in her eyes. "I thought you and Todd might hit it off. Todd's a good guy and I wanted to steer you toward somebody decent, instead of those losers you've been dating."

He sounded sincere, and Hallie felt contrite. Then he said, "If things do work out between her and Todd—great. He needs someone."

Hallie couldn't stop the thought of poor Steve, all alone for the rest of his life. "Are you telling me you plan to live like a hermit?" she asked bluntly.

"Hardly. The way I figure it, Mary Lynn's married now and it isn't likely we'll get back together. I can accept that. So I don't see why I can't start dating again. I may not be interested in marriage, but I do want a...social life."

Social life. Uh-huh. The truth was out—his actions hadn't been entirely altruistic. "Then that's the real reason you let me set you up with Donnalee?"

He chuckled. "Bull's-eye."

"Are there any other potential dates lurking close by?" she asked, mildly curious. All right, very curious. She remembered Mrs. Hot and Pink from Kenny's softball game, and suspected there were others. After all, Steve was a virile, handsome guy. Successful, good-natured, in the prime of life.

"A couple."

This came as no surprise. "Who?" Mrs. Hot and Pink and probably someone from the bowling alley, Hallie guessed.

"A friend from bowling."

She nearly laughed out loud. She was right. Too bad his friend, whoever she was, hadn't been around when he needed a partner for the tournament last spring. It would have saved Hallie a lot of grief. Well, not grief; she'd had a good time, reluctant though she was to admit it.

"As it happens," he said, "we're stuck with each other's company for tonight, and you know what? I'm glad."

Hallie sat up a bit taller. "Thanks, I needed that." Was he going to say anything else and ruin the compliment? She braced herself for the insult she was sure would follow. None came. "But..." she prodded, gesturing with her hand for him to finish the thought.

He cast her an amused glance. "No buts. I meant it."

Hallie ate the rest of the ice cream, taking small careful bites. She and Steve were quiet for a while, watching the steady stream of tourists and local visitors. The smells of fresh seafood, the colorful souvenir shops, the trolley cars and street merchants hawking their wares made for a carnival atmosphere.

"Feel like riding the ferry?" Steve asked. The *Walla Walla,* a three-deck car and passenger ferry was docked at the terminal.

"Where to?" It sounded like a good idea, especially if the ferry would take her someplace exotic and wonderful. Like maybe Alaska, which had lots of eligible men and a shortage of women. Or so she'd heard.

"Bainbridge Island. It's only a half-hour crossing. We can walk off, have a cup of coffee and walk back on again."

It wasn't Alaska, but what the heck. "Let's do it." She placed her hand in his and they walked toward the terminal.

Steve purchased the tickets, then led the way onto the ferry. As they stood on the outside deck looking out at the water, they listened to the distinctive sound of car after car crossing the metal gangplanks.

Steve draped one arm casually around her shoulders. Hallie felt comforted; although she'd put on a brave front, she was feeling low. All these months, and she was nowhere near her goal.

She turned to face Steve, prepared to thank him for his company and cry on his shoulder, but instead, found herself incapable of speaking. The words stopped abruptly in her throat as she realized that Donnalee was the one who'd missed out. Steve was a wonderful man.

For some reason she found herself remembering the day she'd seen him washing his truck with his shirt unbuttoned—and the almost unwilling attraction she'd felt. She'd been assailed by a host of contradictory feelings, many of which still confused her. She hadn't wanted to consider him as anything but her friend, her neighbor. And yet...

"Yes?" he asked, gazing down at her.

There could be no denying that she enjoyed the warmth of his body close to hers, the sensation of his arm against her back, his hand on her shoulder. "I was...just thinking."

"It's that difficult?"

"Sometimes." All at once it was impossible to swallow. She turned to face the water, but was blind to the beauty spread before her.

She felt the ferry pull away from the dock and heard the horn blast that followed.

"Excuse me," Steve said, pounding his fist against his chest as if the sound had come from him.

She laughed at his childish joke and shook her head. It was best to leave their relationship as it was. Friends. She could laugh at his jokes, freely tease him. They would continue to help each other. He'd start her lawn mower and she'd watch his kids. It was a fair exchange, she'd always thought. Neighborly. Everything would change if they became lovers. The terms of their relationship would shift and they might risk losing what they had now—an uncomplicated, mutually supportive friendship. Not only that, a romantic and even sexual involvement with Steve wouldn't lead to marriage, given his feelings for Mary Lynn. And marriage was what Hallie wanted.

With the wind beating against her upturned face, she forced herself to think of Arnold. Dear, sweet, perfect Arnold. No. She couldn't do it. She'd rather swallow cod-liver oil. Hmm, maybe *that* was what she needed. Medicine.

What made being with Steve different from being with any of the men she'd recently dated was a lack of tension, Hallie reflected. An ability to find pleasure in each other's company, regardless of the circumstances. She'd discovered that she and Steve didn't need to talk in order to have fun together. Right now seemed to be one of those easy, silent times. They stood side by side, gazing out at the beautiful green waters of Puget Sound.

When the ferry docked at Winslow, they walked off and found an outdoor café, where Hallie ordered an espresso and Steve a latte.

"Did Todd remember that you drove?" It occurred to Hallie that Todd and Donnalee were stuck downtown without a car.

"He remembered."

"Then how's he going to get home?"

"I gave him the keys to my car."

"You what?"

"We can take the bus easily enough."

"The bus."

"If you're worried abut it, I'll get us a taxi."

"Are you nuts, Steve? First you let Todd steal your date and then you give him your car." She shook her head in mock disgust. Really, though, she was impressed—once again—by Steve's generosity.

It was dark by the time they boarded the ferry for the return trip to Seattle. The city lights blazed in the distance, and the stars shone in the clear night sky above. The sight was breathtakingly lovely, and just as she had earlier, Hallie made her way to the front of the ferry, with Steve following. The wind, chillier now, buffeted her.

Closing her eyes, she gripped the boat's railing, her hands wide apart. Steve moved behind her and stretched his arms out on either side of hers. His warmth seeped through her clothes and deeper, much deeper. A small tremor ran through her.

"You're cold." He folded his arms around her middle. Resting her head against his shoulder, she could feel Steve's heart beating in rhythm with hers. Their chests rose and fell as if each drew the same breath. How long had it been like this, she wondered, this closeness they shared?

They might have remained just as they were forever. Despite the wind, Hallie had no inclination to move, and apparently Steve didn't, either. She was utterly content to stand there, staring at the approaching harbor, wrapped in the protective warmth of his embrace.

All too soon the ferry had docked and they were filing out. Hallie felt a little awkward and wondered if Steve did, too. Their intimate companionable mood had vanished.

"I had a wonderful time," she confessed as they strolled toward the bus tunnel.

"Even if you were stuck with me for the evening."

"That's just fine, since Todd dumped *me* on you."

"You aren't so bad, McCarthy." He reached for her hand, intertwining their fingers.

"Neither are you, Marris. Neither are you."

Twenty-Six

Second Chance At Love

Donnalee awoke to the scent of sizzling bacon. A slow easy smile crossed her face as she rolled onto her back, stretching her arms high above her head.

A glance at the clock told her it was after ten. That couldn't be right. Tossing aside the covers, she climbed out of the narrow bed, reached for her robe and looked over the balcony of the A-frame loft.

Todd stood in front of the stove, humming softly while he turned the bacon, looking masculine and wonderful. Her heart swelled at the sight of him. They'd spent Saturday trout-fishing from the canoe. He'd insisted on cooking dinner, treating her like company. She'd never known fish could taste so good. Later they'd sat under the stars, talking, and there was no subject they didn't discuss. Donnalee had never spent a day she'd enjoyed more. She'd loved every single second.

"Good morning," she called down to him now.

Todd looked up and grinned. "I wondered when you were going to get up."

From the look of him, he'd been awake for hours. "Is it really ten?" she asked, tying the sash of her robe.

"Yup. Hungry?"

"Starved. I'll be down in two shakes." Her overnight bag sat next to the bed, and she quickly found a fresh T-shirt. Pulling on her jeans, she raced down the stairs barefoot.

She arrived just as Todd was dishing up the fried eggs. "I can't remember when I've slept better," she told him, smiling.

"There's something about the country air," he said, his gaze approving as she sat down at the table. "I sleep like the dead out here at the cabin. It's one of the great mysteries of the universe."

He carried two glasses of orange juice to the table, and Donnalee found herself watching him. Watching him and loving him. The realization caught her unawares. *Love.* She was falling in love.

As a teenager she'd been infatuated with him. When they'd met again over dinner on Friday, the flame had sparked back to life. But spending all day Saturday together had set it ablaze.

"My grandparents always talked about how coming here restored them," Todd said, looking at her. "They were the ones who bought this place nearly fifty years ago. It was their private getaway. When the pressures of job and family became too much, they stole away for a weekend."

"It's kind of romantic, isn't it?"

He seemed not to have heard her. "After my divorce, Gramps sent me here and said I should stay a week. I stayed two months. The first month I worked on the place and was up until all hours of the night. I did hard physical work, anything that would keep me from thinking."

"And the second month?"

"I read and slept and healed as much as I could. When I returned to my family, I'd made some basic decisions about my life. First and foremost, I announced I wasn't returning to college—which really disappointed my father."

"You're good with your hands. It makes perfect sense for you to work with them."

"I'm content, but to my parents, having a son choose a blue-collar trade was a step backward. They had big dreams for me as an attorney. It's taken them a long time to accept that I love what I do and I'm good at it."

"It was a wise choice for you."

"I believe so." He stared down at his food. "For the first time in fifteen years I'm questioning the second decision I made that summer," he said. "After the failure of my marriage I decided I'd never love any woman again. I know it sounds pretty melodramatic, but I meant it, and not once in all the years since have I been tempted to change my mind." He paused, his eyes on her. "Until now."

The words were spoken without any telltale inflection, as if he were discussing something as mundane as television listings or the weather.

Donnalee hadn't taken even one bite of her breakfast and realized she couldn't eat to save her life. Emotion clogged her throat. She set the fork aside and pushed herself away from the table, then walked outside. She stood on the porch, head bent, staring at the cedar planks.

"Donnalee." He'd followed her out. His voice was rough, almost sorrowful. "I apologize. I should never have said that."

"Did you mean it?" she asked, her own voice barely above a whisper.

"Yes."

They'd spent an entire day together and he hadn't so much as kissed her. When they'd headed into the house for bed, he'd escorted her to the loft, wished her good-night and promptly left.

"Does that bother you?" he asked. "What I said?"

"No. It makes my heart...glad."

Todd slid his arms around her and brought her close. For the longest time they did nothing but stand in the sun, locked in each other's embrace. Then Donnalee kissed him.

That first kiss was soft, tentative, yet full of raw hungry need. Her whole body began to tremble. She gripped his collar, crushing the material, holding on to it as if this was all that kept her from being swept away in a raging storm. Her moan was wanton. She hardly recognized the sound of her own voice.

Todd bunched the material of her T-shirt at the small of her back. "Do you know what you're starting?" he asked. Then, not giving her time to respond, he asked another question. "Are you sure this is what you want?" She felt his muscles tense with restraint.

"Yes...I know. I'm sure."

His tongue stroked her lips before dipping into her mouth, creating an electricity that arced through her, heating her blood. When he did fully claim her lips, she nearly fainted.

One kiss, one deep kiss, and she was hot and restless. So very restless.

She wasn't alone. Donnalee could feel his need. It shuddered through his body and hers. This urgency was far too potent so early in their relationship. Things were moving too fast. She'd never been a woman who leapt from bed to bed. She'd watched others, friends, moving from one partner to another, from one desperate relationship to the next, without thought, without regret. Without their hearts ever being involved.

Well, if anyone's heart was involved, it was hers.

They kissed until Donnalee felt she'd die if he didn't make love to her. When he wrenched his mouth from hers, she whimpered, begging him without words to go on.

"Either we stop now," he whispered, his voice heavy with need, "or...or we continue."

She pulled back until her eyes found his. What he was really asking was permission to make love to her. He could have carried her into his bedroom, her head clouded with passion, and taken her right then and there. Instead, he'd stopped, giving her the opportunity to end their passion now if she had any hesitations. Making sure she wanted him as badly as he wanted her.

She smiled and kissed him softly and slowly. Thoroughly. "Don't stop. I want you. So very much..."

That was apparently all the reassurance he needed. He swung her into his arms, carried her into the house and made straight for his bedroom, where he gently placed her on the mattress.

They spent the day there. All day. When they weren't making love, they napped or shared desultory conversation. Donnalee woke late in the afternoon and knew it was time to return to the city. She had to be at her office early Monday morning to meet with clients. For two glorious days, she'd escaped from her world into one that was simpler. Happier. And incredibly sensual.

Todd lay on his back, his hands behind his head. "Now that I think about it, I'll bet this is how my grandparents spent their time here."

"Making love?"

"I wouldn't put it past Gramps. They were married more than sixty years, and to the best of my memory, I never heard them say a cross word to each other."

"What a wonderful legacy."

"My divorce was the first in the family," he said.

Even now, years later, Donnalee could hear his guilt. She pressed her head to his shoulder and slipped her arm around his neck. "I don't want to leave," she whispered. She feared that once they were back in the city, everything they'd discovered this weekend would be lost. Todd would return to his life; she'd return to hers. She was afraid these brief hours shared in each other's arms would be forgotten, reduced to a pleasant interlude without any further meaning.

Silently they dressed and loaded his car. On the long drive back to Seattle, they exchanged snippets of conversation, but no subject held their attention long.

By the time Todd pulled up in front of her house, Donnalee was convinced he'd experienced a change of heart and regretted everything he'd said and done—the confidences, the lovemaking, the implied promises.

"I had a wonderful weekend," she said, unable to meet his gaze. "I can't thank you enough."

Todd carried in her suitcase and left shortly afterward. He didn't even kiss her before he walked out the door.

Hardly aware of what she was doing, Donnalee unpacked, then

sat on the sofa and started to sob. Soon she was crying so hard she could barely breathe. When she'd managed to control her breathing enough to speak, she reached for the phone and punched in her best friend's number.

"Hello," Hallie said cheerfully.

"I did something so stupid!" Donnalee wailed.

"Donnalee? Is that you? What's wrong? Do you need me to come over?"

This was what Donnalee loved about Hallie. Close friend and staunch ally, she was always ready to drop whatever she was doing and rush to her aid. "No. I'll be fine in a little bit." Another lifetime was more accurate, but there was no reason to alarm her friend.

"What happened?"

"Nothing," Donnalee said. Then, with a sob, she added, "Everything."

Hallie was suspiciously quiet. "What do you mean, everything? You went away for the weekend with Todd to his family's summer cabin and..." She hesitated. "You didn't...?"

"We did."

Donnalee could hear Hallie's soft gasp. "You and Todd slept together?"

"We went to bed, but let me assure you, there was very little sleeping."

Hallie gave a snort of disgust. "If you're calling for sympathy, you're plumb out of luck. I'm so jealous I could scream. Why is everyone in the world having sex but me?"

"It was so beautiful," Donnalee whispered, and started crying again. She'd practically emptied the box of tissues, and still the tears showed no sign of letting up.

"Why in the name of heaven are you crying?"

Hallie's question was perfectly logical, but Donnalee didn't have an answer. "I don't know. Because it was good—more than good. Oh, Hallie, I can't even *begin* to tell you how good it was."

"My sympathy level is sinking fast."

Donnalee laughed and wept at the same time. "It's just that I'm so afraid."

"Of what?"

She took a deep shuddering breath. "I love him. Don't laugh, Hallie, please. I couldn't bear it if my best friend told me what a fool I am."

"I wouldn't laugh at you, Donnalee."

"I guess I knew that." She didn't say anything for a moment; Hallie didn't speak, either. "I love him," she said again. "It makes no sense that I'd be so sure of it when we've spent hardly any time together—but I am. Now I think I've ruined everything.''

"By sleeping with him?"

"Yes. I've never done anything like this before, and I'm afraid I'm going to lose him.''

"Why would you think that?''

"He hardly spoke to me on the drive back.'' They'd both made an effort to avoid the one subject they should have discussed—how they felt about each other. Donnalee had no idea where their relationship would go from this point. If it was going anywhere at all. Thinking about it terrified her.

"You've got absolutely no reason to worry,'' Hallie said.

"How can you say that?'' Donnalee challenged. She wanted to believe it so badly but didn't dare.

"I saw the way he looked at you during dinner,'' Hallie muttered "Him being *my* date and all.''

"Oh, Hallie, I'm so sorry.''

"Don't be. I was joking—I'm not interested in Todd. Just calm down. Things have a way of working out for the best.''

"You sound so sure.''

"I am sure.''

"Now I know why I didn't marry Sanford...'' Donnalee said, clenching the damp tissue in her fist. The pain of that separation crept into her consciousness like a bad dream, one she struggled to forget.

Hallie completed the thought for her. "You didn't marry Sanford because of Todd. Your heart must have known there was someone else for you. Someone who wants the same things you do. And what's even better,'' Hallie went on excitedly, "it was someone you already knew!''

"That's what I want to think, but I can't be sure—especially now.'' Donnalee could only imagine what Todd thought of her, falling into bed with him like that. Until Todd, she never would've believed herself capable of such a thing.

"Well, my friend, marriage and family are about to be yours.'' Hallie sounded downright gleeful. "One look at Todd, and I could tell he's got a high sperm count.''

"Hallie!''

"You want children, don't you?'' Hallie's voice had become serious again.

"Yes, but—''

"Oh, Donnalee, don't worry. Everything's going to be fine.''

Donnalee found herself smiling for the first time since she'd arrived home. She did feel better. They chatted for a few more minutes and then rang off.

Keeping busy would help, Donnalee felt certain. If she just kept moving, kept doing routine tasks, sooner or later everything would fall back into place and she could get on with living. She put a load of clothes in the wash. She reorganized her refrigerator. She was plugging in the vacuum when she looked out the window—and her heart stopped. Todd's car was parked in front of her condo. Paralyzed, she watched as he climbed out, walked halfway to her front door, paused and then turned back.

The paralysis snapped. She rushed to the door and threw it open to find him standing on her doorstep, hand raised to knock.

Speechless they stared at each other.

Todd shoved his hands in his back pockets and refused to meet her eyes.

It was over, Donnalee told herself bleakly. He'd come to tell her he didn't want to see her again. A darkness had descended on her when her marriage ended, and it had taken her years to fight her way back into the light. Donnalee thought it might kill her if Todd walked away from her now.

"Walk away from you?" he said.

Good heavens, she'd said it aloud! Mortified to the very marrow of her bones, Donnalee wanted to bury her face in her hands.

"I didn't come back to tell you I don't want to see you again," he said. "I was trying to figure out a way to ask if you'd be willing to see *me* again after what happened this weekend. I didn't mean for things to get so intense so quickly. I was afraid I'd rushed you and ruined any chance I had with you."

"You didn't ruin your chances with me. If anything... Oh, Todd, I'm so glad you're here!" She leapt off the step and into his embrace.

Todd locked his arms around her. She didn't let him speak, but spread kisses, one after another, all over his face. "I want to see you again. I need to see you again and again and again."

"I'm not sure I'm any real bargain," Todd murmured between kisses.

"*I'm* sure." She directed his mouth to hers and kissed him with a thoroughness that left them both breathless.

"The first thing you'll need to learn is that it's useless to argue with me," she told him, knowing he could see the happiness radiating from her eyes.

"But maybe it's too soon..." He continued to hold her, continued to stroke her hair.

"As far as I'm concerned, it's about fourteen years too late."

"Oh, Donnalee, this is all so crazy." He released her and took two steps away from her, as if he wanted to turn tail and run.

"But it's a wonderful kind of crazy! I found you again and I'm not about to let you go. Let's both accept that we were meant to be together and leave it at that." She reached for his hand and led him into her home. Without pausing she closed the door and pushed him down on the sofa, then promptly sat on his lap and wrapped her arms around his neck. "It looks like you need to be convinced. How long do you think it'll take?" she asked.

Todd grinned. "How about forty or fifty years?"

Twenty-Seven

Large Women Wearing Helmets With Horns

Steve was astonished how quiet the house was after the kids returned to Mary Lynn. He'd moped around yesterday—Sunday—fighting off a sense of loneliness, but that passed soon enough.

He loved his children to distraction, and he'd enjoyed the two weeks they'd spent with him, yet in the past year he'd learned to appreciate solitude, too. He was comfortable with silence now. In the early days of his separation, it had damn near driven him crazy. But over time he'd managed to accept the traumatic changes in his life; he'd adjusted to strange new schedules, such as seeing his kids only on weekends.

He was grateful Meagan and Kenny had adapted so well to their new circumstances, and grateful that he and Mary Lynn had been able to maintain civility in their dealings.

If he was making a list of things to be grateful for, Steve figured he should include Hallie. She'd come to his aid more times than he could count, especially during the past couple of weeks. Thinking back, he realized that Meagan and Kenny had spent nearly as much time at her place as they had at his.

The blind dinner date they'd arranged for each other hadn't gone as planned, but these things happened, and he didn't take it personally. Hallie had seemed a little upset in the beginning, but she'd been a good sport about it since. And she seemed genuinely pleased that the date had worked out so well for her friend.

Standing in front of his refrigerator, Steve surveyed the contents, wondering what he could rustle up for dinner. Cooking for one didn't excite him. Briefly he wondered what Hallie was eating. More often than not these past two weeks she'd either cooked or joined him and the kids for dinner, and he'd come to rely on her suggestions.

Steve glanced out the window to see if she was home. He strained to catch a glimpse of her car, and his spirits lifted when he saw it. So far, so good. Then, feeling a bit like a Peeping Tom, he focused on her kitchen window. Ah, yes, there she was, talking on the phone. She had the cord wrapped about her wrist, and from the way she leaned against the wall, he could tell she was annoyed about something. After a moment she hung up, then immediately reached for the phone again.

His own phone rang and he jerked around. "Hello, Hallie," he answered, thinking himself rather clever.

"Guess what?" she said furiously. "Arnold just called to break our date tonight. That's the third time he's canceled out on me at the last minute, the low-down dirty rat."

Steve didn't understand why Hallie continued to see the guy. She'd never been keen on him, yet she insisted on beating the relationship to death. Although Steve had never been introduced to Arnold, he could tell it was a lost cause just from the few glimpses he'd caught when he was out jogging or—*let's be honest, Marris*—watching him through the window.

"I bought theater tickets through the Chamber of Commerce for this wonderful production I'd been looking forward to seeing." Hallie sounded exasperated and angry. "Arnold had agreed to come and now..." She sighed. "The thing is, I've got two perfectly good tickets, which I refuse to waste."

"Maybe you can exchange the tickets for another night and go with Arnold then."

"I don't ever plan to see Arnold again. I told him so, and what annoyed me even more than being stood up is his attitude. He *expected* me to break it off, and he even seemed relieved when I told him." She paused long enough to catch her breath. "Anyway, I can't exchange them and I don't want to waste them."

He didn't bother to suggest she go by herself. If she'd considered that an option, she wouldn't have called. He was afraid she planned to ask him and groaned inwardly at the thought. Frankly, it'd been a long hard day and he wasn't interested in sitting through a play, no matter how good it was reported to be. "What about Donnalee and Todd?" he tried.

"Donnalee and Todd? You're joking, right?"

"I guess I am." Well, Hallie was right. Those two were in their own little world. Every morning of the past week, Todd had arrived at the office wearing a silly grin. Silly, perhaps, but also...satisfied. Steve had never seen a man so much in love.

"Can you go with me?" Hallie pleaded. "Oh, shoot. Monday's your bowling night, isn't it?"

"No," he was sorry to report. "The league takes a break during the summer."

"Then please, please come with me."

It was one of the rare times she'd requested anything of him. In that moment Steve realized he didn't have the heart to refuse her.

"How formal is it?"

She hesitated, a sure sign he wasn't going to like her response. "You'll need to wear a suit," she informed him. "Dark, if you have one."

He cursed silently. "I do."

He hated that suit. Hated it more every time he was forced to wear it. He kept the thing around primarily for weddings and funerals, so he hadn't worn it in some time, since most of his friends were married and no one he knew had died recently. What he particularly loathed was wearing a tie, which felt like a noose around his neck.

"Does that mean you'll go?"

Steve paused and reminded himself of all the times Hallie had come to his rescue. "I guess," he muttered.

"A little enthusiasm would go a long way, Marris," she muttered back.

Steve grinned. "I'm beginning to think Arnold might have had the right idea."

"I think not. These tickets were fifty bucks. Each."

A hundred bucks was nothing to sneeze at. "What time do you need me to be ready?"

"Seven-thirty." He could hear the relief in her voice and was pleased that he was the one responsible for it.

"Are you throwing in dinner with this invitation?" If he was going to strangle himself with a suit and tie, he might as well get as much out of it as he could.

"You expect me to buy you dinner, too?"

She had a point there, but the kids had cleaned out his checking account. "I'll bring a can of chili," he said.

"I've got..." He turned to the window and watched as she stretched the phone cord as far as her refrigerator door and bent over while she sorted through its contents. Actually, he appreciated the view of her cute little butt. "There's a head of lettuce here and some cheddar cheese. We could make a taco salad. Do you have any chips?"

"If Kenny didn't find them, I do."

"Okay, you're on."

It was a pleasant surprise to discover what culinary magic Hallie could make with a can of chili and a few leaves of lettuce. And he had to admit dinner was a lot more enjoyable with her company.

For fear of dribbling salad dressing on his one tie, knotted for him years ago by Todd, Steve changed into his suit after dinner. He suddenly recalled the last time he'd worn it—the day he stood before the judge when his divorce was finalized. He discovered his attorney's business card in the jacket pocket and quickly tossed it in the garbage.

As he looped the tie over his head and tightened it, he reflected on that devastating day. He'd been divorced more than a year and a half now, separated even longer. It didn't seem possible. The familiar pain threatened to darken his mood, but he managed to ignore its pull. Mary Lynn had remarried and life had gone on. Not the way he'd wanted, but he'd survived. He was even experiencing some of his old pleasures again and finding new ones.

When he arrived to pick up Hallie, he did a double take. The deep blue dress, slinky, silky and body-hugging, did incredible things for her figure. This was Hallie? Damn, he'd never noticed how well proportioned she was. Everything was right where it was supposed to be. And how.

His first thought when he saw her—other than how good she looked—was to wonder if a dress like that required a bra. Not that it was any of his business, but he couldn't help being curious. The sleeveless gown stretched tightly across her chest and hooked behind the neck. Yup, he was almost certain she was braless.

He released a low whistle.

"You like it?" Hallie held her hands stiffly out at her sides—a bit like a penguin, she thought—as she turned in a slow circle to give him the full effect.

"Wow." He'd have whistled a second time if he'd found the breath to do so, but she'd stolen it. Telling her she looked good was an understatement. A gross understatement. Arnold was more of a fool than Steve had realized.

"You look..." All descriptive words and phrases deserted him.

"Fat," she supplied. She pouched out her stomach, what there was of it, which to his mind wasn't much.

"No!" He'd never been a flatterer, and he'd always struggled with compliments. It was a talent, Steve decided, and unfortunately one he lacked. Hallie waited expectantly. It was the same look Mary Lynn used to get when she needed him to say just the right thing to reassure her. The pressure was building and he was afraid he'd fail Hallie the same way he'd too often failed Mary Lynn.

"You look wonderful." It was the best he could do. He paused and waited for some sign of reaction.

She closed her eyes and exhaled.

"Really wonderful," he added, hoping that would help.

"Thank you." She smiled softly. "I won't tell you what this dress cost, but I fell in love with it the minute I tried it on. Let me just say that I'll be packing my own lunch for the next ten years."

"Whatever the price, it was worth it."

"You can be a real charmer when you want to be, Marris."

Him? A charmer? Not likely, but if Hallie wanted to think so, he wasn't going to correct her.

The play was at the Fifth Avenue Theater in downtown Seattle. Their aisle seats were in the first row of the balcony. Steve stopped counting the number of times he had to stand in order to allow other ticket holders into their seats.

Hallie acknowledged several people. A number of names were tossed his way, and he soon quit trying to remember them all. He was a member of the local Chamber of Commerce himself, but he did little more than pay his dues. He'd only attended two meetings in all the years he'd owned his business. From the looks of it, Hallie was an outgoing and popular member, which didn't surprise him.

The theater darkened and the play began. It didn't take Steve long to realize it wasn't a play at all. It was an opera. All the lines were sung. He opened his program and read it for the first time. He didn't recognize the opera's title, but it was clearly German.

While he was no aficionado, Steve liked classical music as much as the next guy, but this was no Mozart. The composer wasn't one he knew or cared to.

Hallie's rapt attention was focused on the stage. As far as Steve could figure, the opera was some tragedy that had people running back and forth across the stage. There were frequent deaths, too— but not frequent enough.

By the end of the first scene, Steve's attention began wandering. He studied the lovely crystal light fixtures suspended from the ceiling, craning his head back as far as possible to get a better view. The theater had recently been renovated and he was impressed with the improvements.

"Steve?" Hallie was frowning at him. "Is something wrong?"

"Nah, just checking out the new fixtures," he whispered loudly. "I wonder if they're real crystal. You wouldn't happen to know, would you?"

"I wouldn't know."

"The seats are new, too."

"Uh-huh."

He rotated his shoulders, testing out the cushions for comfort and gave a thumbs-up.

Hallie rolled her eyes and reverted her attention to the stage.

Quickly bored, Steve asked her for a pen.

Hallie leaned forward for her handbag, and Steve was given a momentary peek at her front. He'd been right. No bra.

Once she'd retrieved her pen, she placed it in his hand with just a hint of impatience. Steve doodled geometric designs across the front page of the program and then found himself drawing what resembled—he hated to admit it—a series of female breasts. Actually, he was surprised by how good he was.

Years earlier he'd visited an art museum, where he'd seen a painting by one of the century's more revered artists. The painting was on loan, part of a highly touted exhibit, and Steve had studied it for several minutes. All he'd seen was a clothes hanger with two misshapen boobs. The breasts weren't even properly aligned, and yet the artist had made millions.

Steve toyed with the idea of sending his doodles to the artist's agent. Perhaps this was his life's calling and he'd make a fortune drawing breasts. He kind of liked the idea. Hiring women to pose for him, that sort of thing.

With that thought in mind he sketched a couple of ideas. He drew a torso and gave the woman four breasts with multiple nipples. He was just warming to his subject when Hallie glanced over at what he was doing, gasped and grabbed the program away from him. Giving him a pinched-lip look, she promptly crumpled it up.

Okay, okay, he got the hint. Steve tried to pay attention to the actors, he really did, but he'd rarely seen anything this boring. Opera had never appealed to him. Large women who wore helmets with horns and stormed across a stage holding spears and pretending to be warriors were of questionable sexual persuasion as far as he was concerned.

After a while, sure that Hallie was absorbed in the acting, he stole her program and folded it into a paper airplane. He had no intention of flying it, but apparently Hallie assumed otherwise. Her expression would have cracked concrete.

"What?" he asked under his breath.

"You have to ask?" she hissed.

Hands lightly folded in his lap, he focused his attention on the stage again, determined to be a model member of the audience. His eyes drifted closed and he found himself falling asleep, only to jerk awake a second or two later. He yawned loudly, twice. Then swallowed a third yawn when Hallie glared at him. His cheeks puffed out with the effort.

Next he checked the time and attempted to calculate just how much more of this he'd have to endure. Another hour he could take, but two hours was out of the question.

The curtain fell and the lights went up. Intermission. Free at last, he all but leapt out of his seat. "I'll get us something to drink," he said, and was halfway into the aisle when Hallie thrust out an arm and stopped him.

"What's the matter with you?" she demanded.

He knew he was in trouble because she spoke through clenched teeth. "Nothing," he insisted brightly.

"This work is masterful, brilliant..."

"Boring," he said.

"For you, perhaps, but not everyone agrees. Kenny would do a better job of paying attention. You're worse than a five-year-old. Furthermore, what was that you were drawing?"

Steve was convinced she didn't really want to know. He buried his hands in his pockets and shrugged. "I don't know. I was doodling. I do that sometimes. It doesn't mean anything."

"Have you ever shown your doodles to a psychiatrist?"

"I'll be better the second half. I promise."

"Never mind, let's go."

"Go?" His heart raced at the thought of escape. Surely she wouldn't tease about something like that. "Where do you want to go?"

"Home." She didn't elaborate.

His heart filled with gratitude. But once they'd walked down the large curved stairway and outside into the cool evening, he realized this reprieve might well have come at a price.

"You aren't angry, are you?" he asked. Hallie was a good friend, and if keeping the peace meant enduring the rest of this opera, then he'd do it.

"I'm not angry," she replied, but the way she said it suggested she wasn't pleased with him, either.

"We can stay," he offered, all the while praying she wouldn't change her mind.

Not until they reached the parking garage did Steve recognize the truth. Hallie had been as bored as he was, only she was too polite to let it show.

"You didn't like that opera, either." His step lightened and he cast her a smug look.

"That's not true. The music was—"

"Don't lie, Hallie, or your nose will start to grow."

He watched as a smile quivered at the corners of her mouth, struggling to break free.

"Be honest."

She was suspiciously quiet for a moment, then took one glance at him and burst out laughing. The mirth virtually exploded from her. She wrapped her arms around her middle and bent nearly double. Still laughing, she positioned herself in front of him on the sidewalk, strolling backward as she spoke. "I wish you could've seen yourself!"

"Glad I'm such a source of amusement." A smile threatened to overtake him, too. He took her hand, gripping it firmly in his own. It felt *right* to be walking hand in hand with Hallie.

Both of them thought it seemed a shame to head back home immediately, so Steve suggested coffee. They were a bit overdressed for an all-night diner, but that was where they ended up. Although they attracted plenty of curious stares, neither paid much attention.

When their coffee was served, Hallie doctored hers with cream and sugar, then stared at him as if she was shocked by what she'd done. "I only add cream when I'm depressed," she told him, her shoulders sagging. "I bet this has something to do with Donnalee."

Steve had trouble following her thought process—cream in her coffee, depression and Donnalee. Apparently there was a connection. Whatever it was would take him a while to work out.

"It wouldn't surprise me if those two got married," Hallie said next.

"It wouldn't surprise me to learn they're already living together," Steve muttered. He'd never seen Todd like this. Todd, his closest friend. The guy he worked with every day. The guy who'd shared the secret password to reach level ten of the video game King Kong. He'd fished with Todd, camped with him, even taken a weekend trip to Vegas with Todd.

Yet in all the years they'd been friends, he'd never seen Todd in love. It was almost frightening what love could do to a levelheaded man. He told Hallie exactly that.

"I agree with you completely!" she declared, leaning closer to him. Her hands cupped the coffee mug. "If you think Todd's acting strange, you should see Donnalee. It's...nauseating." Barely pausing, she added, "I'm so jealous I could scream. Can you tell?"

Jealous, Steve repeated mentally, and wondered if that was his problem with Todd. His friend arrived promptly for work, accomplished each task satisfactorily and left at the end of the day. Steve had no right to ask more of him, yet he found himself tallying a list of complaints at the end of the day. Trivial stuff. He *was* jealous. Damn it all, he really was.

"Donnalee has had more sex in the past week than I've had in my entire life," Hallie said, glancing down at her coffee. "That explains it."

"Explains what?"

"Why I'm putting cream in my coffee."

"Oh." Well, okay, he supposed that made some sense, now that he understood the connection. "Same with Todd," he grumbled. "It's like he's walking around in this bubble, breathing in happy gas."

"Exactly," Hallie moaned. "Nothing can burst their bubble. It's...it's disgusting." She raised the mug to her lips, paused halfway there and set it down on the table with a loud clatter. "Are we being petty?"

"No way." He dismissed the question without thought, then reconsidered. "On the other hand, I don't know if I'd be complaining nearly as loud if it was me."

"That's my point," Hallie said, gesturing with both hands.

"What gets me is that I practically had to bribe Todd into going out on this blind date in the first place. He wasn't interested in meeting you. Not even when I mentioned how attractive you are and how much the kids like you."

Hallie glared at him. "If you're telling me all this to make me feel better, I suggest you stop."

Steve grinned. "From what you said, Donnalee wasn't any more interested in meeting me."

She sighed expressively. "True."

"So Todd and Donnalee found great sex together. You had your chance, McCarthy. You turned down the best offer you're likely to get," Steve reminded her. "I was willing to take you to bed, remember?"

"Right!" She rolled her eyes. "How could I refuse a romantic invitation like 'Wanna do it?'"

Steve chuckled, amused as he often was by Hallie. He'd lacked finesse on that particular occasion, he'd admit it. He'd been feeling low at the time. What he'd really needed was someone to listen, and Hallie had provided a sympathetic ear, for which he'd been grateful.

"They're going to wear themselves out," Hallie said. "They'll end up dying of exhaustion."

Steve could only assume she'd returned to the subject of Donnalee and Todd. "Yeah, but what a way to go."

The gleam of pure unadulterated envy was back in her eyes. "If it's like this before the wedding, can you imagine what it'll be like afterward?"

"Yeah," Steve said, then frowned. "My advice to Todd is to get it while he can."

"Steve!"

"You think I'm joking?"

Hallie stared at him as if to ask exactly what kind of wife Mary Lynn had been. But he didn't want to talk about his ex, especially now that she was married to another man. Sleeping with another man. He couldn't dwell on that, otherwise he'd go crazy. So he avoided the subject entirely.

"Seriously, I think Todd and Donnalee will do fine," Hallie said.

"Yeah, I'm sure you're right."

She reached for the small cream pitcher and added more to her coffee, stirring it slowly around and around.

"There's someone for you, Hallie."

She raised her eyes sadly to his. "But when am I ever going to meet him?"

Steve didn't have the answer to that any more than she did.

Twenty-Eight

The Movies

Hallie arrived home late that Friday afternoon, after a long tiring workweek. Meagan and Kenny raced toward her the moment she'd parked.

"Dad's taking us to the drive-in!" Kenny said excitedly.

This was a perfect night for it, Hallie mused. August and the weather was flawless, as it can be in only Puget Sound.

"Wanna come?" Meagan asked.

"I don't think so, sweetheart. Thanks, anyway." It'd been one of those frustrating weeks when little had gone right. It had started with one of her key staff members suddenly up and leaving because her husband had been transferred to the East Coast. And it ended this afternoon with a canceled order, followed by a visit from Donnalee. She'd arrived at Artistic License unannounced wearing a lovely diamond engagement ring. Hallie had hugged and congratulated her, thrilled for her friend. But she was also aware that Donnalee had managed to acquire *two* engagement rings this year, while she hadn't even scrounged up a piece of Cracker Jack jewelry. It wasn't the rings, of course, it was the thought that two men had fallen in love with Donnalee. *Two* men. And during the same period, Hallie had met a selection of losers, cheapskates and creeps.

No wonder she felt depressed.

"Please, please, please, come," said a voice from behind.

She swung around to find Steve gazing at her with an exaggerated expression of woe.

"I'm exhausted," she said. It was a legitimate excuse and true. She was looking forward to a half-hour soak in a bubble bath, and then a lengthy vegetation in front of the television watching reruns of "Mary Tyler Moore." It seemed that she, like Mary Richards, was destined to live the single life.

"I'm tired, too," Steve told her. "But I promised the kids last week that I'd take them, and they invited ten or fifteen of their closest friends along.''

"Two," Meagan corrected, rolling her eyes. "We each invited one friend.''

"I've got it all figured out," Steve said, squeezing Hallie's shoulders. "We can take both cars and park next to each other. The kids can stay in my car and I'll come over and join you in yours. Does that sound like a plan or what?''

He had obviously given some thought to this, and it was easy to see what would happen to his escape strategy if she refused. He'd be trapped in a vehicle filled with four shrieking kids.

Still, she *might* have refused him if not for one thing. Steve had agreed to accompany her to that ridiculous operatic extravaganza. Not willingly, maybe, but he *had* gone.

"Oh, all right," she mumbled.

"A little enthusiasm will go a long way, McCarthy," he said, echoing the remark she'd made herself earlier in the week.

She grumbled under her breath, but if the truth be known, she wasn't all that opposed. Yes, she felt exhausted, but being with Steve and his children had a way of reviving her. If she didn't go, she was likely to drown her sorrows in a bowl of double-fudge macadamia-nut ice cream—something to be avoided at all costs.

Besides, Steve had kissed her when he'd walked her to her door on Monday night. A quick, friendly kiss, very much like the others they'd exchanged. Warm and comforting. But for the first time Hallie had felt *more* than comfort and friendship. She'd felt that kiss all the way to her toes. A nice friendly good-night between neighbors shouldn't curl a woman's toes.

So she agreed to this drive-in idea of his for the elementary reason that she wanted him to kiss her again. Just to check things out.

"Dad's going to make popcorn," Kenny said breathlessly, as if that qualified his father for some major cooking award, "and not use the microwave." There was real awe in the boy's voice. "Dad explained that when he was a kid you used a *stove*."

Hallie remembered making popcorn that way, too. She felt about a hundred years old. "That should be interesting."

"He said we could watch."

"I don't suppose you'd care to help?" This from Steve, who didn't even attempt to disguise his plea for assistance.

"Oh, all right." Although she made it sound like a sacrifice, Hallie found herself grinning. "I'll change out of my work clothes and be right over."

Meagan followed her into the house and helped her choose a pair of shorts and a summer top. "I'm glad you're coming," she said, hopping onto the end of Hallie's bed.

Hallie noticed that the girl looked unhappy, but didn't want to pry. From experience she knew that if something was troubling Meagan, she'd tell Hallie in her own way and her own time.

"I'm glad I'm coming, too."

"Dad let me invite Angie. She's my best friend. Everyone needs a best friend." She paused. "I think you're Dad's."

Hallie was touched. "Your dad's one of my best friends, too."

The girl was quiet for several moments while Hallie changed out of her business garb and donned what she thought of as real-people clothes. She removed her jewelry and makeup and tossed her panty hose and heels aside for canvas slip-ons.

"I don't think Mom and Kip are happy."

The softly spoken statement came out of the blue. Hallie paused, wondering how or if she should comment. "Sometimes when people first marry they have difficulty adjusting to each other. Give them time, Meagan."

"I don't think time's gonna help. Mom found out that Kip's been married before. Twice. She only knew about one ex-wife."

"Oh, dear." Hallie immediately sympathized with Steve's ex.

"He's paying child support to two children, and my mom only knew about the one."

If Kip had misled Mary Lynn in a matter of this importance, Hallie had to wonder if he was trustworthy in other areas.

"Dad doesn't know," Meagan added.

"Don't worry, sweetheart, I won't tell him."

"I don't really like Kip. I don't know why Mom married him. He tells Kenny and me that we're going to do something fun and we get all excited. But when the time comes he has all these excuses why he can't do it."

"Some people are like that," Hallie said, and sat down next to Meagan. "I had a friend like that once. It got so I never put much faith in what she said. It wasn't that she was a bad person. She just couldn't possibly do all the things she planned or keep all the promises she made. I'm sure Kip's intentions are good, but not everything he promises will happen. Try not to be disappointed when it doesn't, and pleasantly surprised when it does."

"Are a lot of people like Kip?" Meagan asked.

"I don't know, but I don't think so."

"I hope not," the girl said, then she smiled. "You know what? I'm glad you're my friend, too."

"So am I, Meagan." The girl gave her a fierce hug.

As soon as Hallie and Meagan walked into Steve's kitchen, father and son mysteriously disappeared, leaving the women to the serious work of popping the corn in an old kettle. Hallie quickly assembled "goodie bags" for everyone. And she had a great time, laughing and teasing with Meagan.

Because Meagan and Kenny's friends lived in other neighborhoods, they left an hour early, stopping at a McDonald's for takeout burgers and drinks. Meagan and her friend rode with Hallie, while Steve led the way with the two boys. As planned, they parked at the drive-in theater side by side.

Hallie hadn't been to a drive-in since she was a child. She remembered her mother and father sitting close together in the front, she and Julie, wearing pajamas, in the back. It had been an occasional summer-night treat. She couldn't recall any movies they'd watched—just that wonderful childhood feeling of being loved and protected.

The first feature scheduled tonight was an action thriller with Bruce Willis. The kind that was sure to be an edge-of-the-seat fast-paced movie. The second feature was more or less the same kind of show, but without the big-name star.

Once the cars were situated and the radios fine-tuned, Steve left his vehicle and climbed into the front seat of Hallie's. It looked like a perfect plan—until Kenny and his friend started fighting with the girls.

Meagan rolled down her window and shouted, "Kenny ate all his popcorn and he's trying to steal mine."

"And mine," Angie chimed in furiously.

In an effort to keep the peace, Steve sent the boys off to the refreshment stand. "I can't believe I allowed the kids to talk me into this. I asked them how much it would cost me to buy my way out, but they wouldn't hear of it."

Steve, Hallie thought, had no idea how crucial it was to his kids that he follow through on his promises. It told them far more than he'd ever know. "I'm proud of you," she said without thinking.

"Proud?"

"You kept your word."

"I didn't have a choice," he said, protesting her compliment. He leaned back in the passenger seat and closed his eyes. "It isn't just the drive-in movie, either," Steve grumbled. "Tomorrow is Kenny's Cub Scout camp-out. I can't believe I actually volunteered to spend the night in the woods with ten nine-year-old boys."

"Better you than me," Hallie told him.

The movie started just as Kenny and his friend made it back to the car. They climbed in and all was blissfully quiet as they gazed at the huge screen.

"What I'd really like to know," Steve said in a conversational tone, "is how I got talked into this slumber-party business. Meagan asked if Angie could come to the drive-in, then the next thing I know, Kenny's got a friend and they're both spending the night."

"Don't look at me," Hallie said, eating her popcorn. "I'm an innocent bystander."

He chuckled and helped himself to a handful from her bag. With the console between them, it was difficult to get too cozy—not that the Bruce Willis movie encouraged coziness in any form. Although Hallie had already seen it, she covered her face during a couple of the more gruesome scenes.

"You talked to Todd recently?" she asked as the credits scrolled down the screen.

"Yeah. He told me he asked Donnalee to marry him, but I have to say it didn't come as any surprise."

"Donnalee's hoping to get pregnant right away," Hallie said wistfully. At the rate things were progressing, Donnalee would be a grandmother before Hallie even found herself a husband.

"I figure it'll be a miracle if she isn't already pregnant. Todd's so tired he can barely stay awake. What's Donnalee do—keep him up all night?"

"My guess is they're keeping each other up."

"It's downright sickening, that's what it is," Steve muttered.

"Couldn't agree with you more." Hallie put down her popcorn, her appetite gone. "You know what? We're both so damn jealous we can barely stand it."

"Amen," Steve said. They glanced at each other and broke into peals of laughter. When they looked at the screen again, the second movie had started.

Hallie's seat was as far back as it would go. She was enjoying herself—and it had very little to do with the movies. Reviewing her conversation with his daughter, she felt good that Meagan had described her as Steve's best friend. It was refreshing, she told herself solemnly, when a man and woman could be friends.

She turned to Steve. "Thank you for being my friend," she whispered.

"Thank you for being mine." And then he leaned over and kissed her. His mouth grazed hers and lingered. Hallie kissed him back, increasing the pressure.

She felt the sexual energy of the kiss immediately and so, apparently, did Steve. He bolted upright and looked at her long and hard.

She studied him, too. It was as if all the oxygen in the car was suddenly gone.

Neither seemed capable of breathing, let alone talking. The only illumination came from the screen and a solitary light by the refreshment stand, but it was enough for Hallie to see Steve's face. His eyes were wary, as if to say he wasn't sure about any of this. For that matter, Hallie wasn't sure how *she* felt, either.

At last he spoke. "Hallie?"

"Yes." She suspected she didn't sound like herself at all. Her voice seemed distant.

"What just happened?"

"You're asking me?" She tried to make a joke of it and found she couldn't. "We kissed and—"

"And, hell, it was good. Damn good." As if he needed to test this new discovery, he placed his hands on the curve of her shoulders and leaned forward to press his mouth to hers. Hallie closed her eyes, but her mind and her heart were wide open, eagerly anticipating a repeat performance.

At first he was gentle, almost tentative. Her lips parted, welcoming him. The nature of the kiss shifted almost immediately. His mouth grew fierce, demanding. He angled his lips over hers, urgently dragging her as close as the confines of the car would allow.

Her hip was being bruised by the console, but Hallie didn't care. She wanted—no, needed—his kiss. She forgot who she was, where she was. Nothing mattered but Steve. She could feel the beat of his heart throbbing beneath her palm.

She slid her hands from his chest and clenched his shirt collar in a feeble attempt to anchor herself against the oncoming sensual storm. His tongue deepened the level of intimacy.

She whimpered at the erotic play as he sought out every part of her mouth. Her own tongue responded to his, curling and coiling in a passionate game that left them both panting and breathless.

He moaned.

She whimpered.

Abruptly he broke it off and braced his forehead against hers. His breath hissed raggedly through his teeth.

Hallie's breath fled entirely.

When he kissed her again, it was slow and gentle, the way their first experimental kisses had been months earlier. Mmm. A series of nibbling kisses followed that. He tasted of buttered popcorn. He tasted incredible. Long, deep, slow kisses came next.

When he stopped, breathing hard, Hallie fell against the back of the seat, her eyes closed. "Tell me this isn't real."

"It's real."

"Tell me we're all wrong for each other."

"You know better."

She tried again. "Tell me this is just our reaction to what's happening between Donnalee and Todd."

"It isn't. This is real, Hallie. You and me—as real as it's likely to get."

"How can we have been so blind?" This was fantastic. Steve. Steve Marris! For months she'd been conducting this fruitless search to find a man, and Steve had been there all along. Right next door.

It was crazy. No, *she* was. She wanted to kick herself.

Throwing her arms around his neck, she whispered, "I might be a slow learner, but I'm ready to make up for lost time."

He laughed. Then he kissed her cheek, her nose, nuzzled her neck, explored the scented hollow of her neck with his tongue, moistening her skin as he slowly, methodically, worked his way back to her lips. By the time he caught her lower lip between his teeth, Hallie was whimpering anew. She'd waited and waited for the right man. What a fool she'd been not to realize all along that he lived next door.

"I can't believe this is happening," she said in a low voice.

"Believe it, Hallie, believe it." He eased his hand under her top, cupping her breast. It filled his palm, overfilled it.

She bit her lip as he traced his finger around the outline of her erect nipple.

"Uh-oh," Steve murmured, his voice weighted with frustration. He slipped his hand downward, past the smooth skin of her abdomen. "I'm afraid we have an audience."

"What?"

He tipped his head toward the car with the kids. Hallie casually glanced in that direction and found four pairs of eyes staring at them out the side windows. Apparently she and Steve were putting on a much better show than the one on the screen. When Kenny saw that he had their attention, he waved. Hallie and Steve waved back. She could feel the heat rise in her cheeks.

Steve lowered the window, which had steamed up considerably, something for which Hallie was grateful. "Are you kids ready to go home?"

This question was followed by a long chorus of nos.

"Then you'd better watch the movie."

"Dad, were you kissing Hallie?" Kenny sounded genuinely distressed. "On the *lips?*" He cringed as if he couldn't imagine anything more revolting.

"She's not so bad," Steve said casually.

Hallie elbowed him in the ribs; he greatly exaggerated his reaction, and everyone, including Hallie, laughed. Once they were sure the kids had returned their attention to the movie, Steve raised the window.

He gripped her hand tightly in his, lacing their fingers. He stared straight ahead, but she knew he wasn't watching the screen. "Okay, tell me, where do we go from here?"

She knew exactly what he was asking. "Where?" she repeated, giving herself time to think. "Are you asking me to go to bed with you, Steve?"

"Yes."

She swallowed. "We need a dose of what Donnalee and Todd have been experiencing, right?"

"No!" She was taken aback by the vehemence of his response. "This has nothing to do with Donnalee and Todd, and everything to do with you and me. I knew something was happening between us long ago—at least I suspected it—and it scared the living daylights out of me."

"I'm scared, too."

He looked at her, and as their eyes met, Hallie saw the hunger in his, realizing it was a reflection of her own. She wanted him. Needed him. Steve lowered his mouth to hers and kissed her with unconcealed desire.

"Does that tell you anything?" he asked.

"Yes." Her heart refused to slow down. She felt she was about to dissolve into hysterical tears—or laughter. She didn't know which. The pendulum could swing either way.

Steve stroked the side of her face, his eyes full of wonder. "I love you, Hallie."

Tears. The pendulum swung to tears. They instantly filled her eyes and spilled down her cheeks. "Oh, Steve, I love you, too," she sobbed, her shoulders shaking with emotion.

"Then why are you crying?"

"Because it took me so long to see the truth. Because I'm so happy. Because...I don't know. No wonder I found Arnold such a dud. I was in love with *you*."

He raised her hand to his lips and kissed her palm. "Like you said earlier, we're going to make up for lost time. Tonight, Hallie, I'm not waiting a moment longer."

"Tonight?"

"As soon as this movie's over, we'll drive home. I'll get everyone to bed and the minute they're asleep, I'll sneak over to your house."

"This is beginning to sound better and better."

"You have no idea how good it's going to be."

Hallie closed her eyes and sighed deeply. "Promises, promises."

"Even though Meagan and Kenny have friends over, it shouldn't take them long to crash." He sounded so eager, just as eager as she was. Her heart pounded with anticipation.

"Last January I bought myself a sexy silk nightgown," she whispered. "I never dreamed I'd be wearing it for you."

Steve groaned as she described the outfit. "Hallie, if you want me to make love to you right here and now, just go on. Otherwise, kindly be quiet."

"I don't think I *can* be quiet. I'm too excited."

He kissed her again and again, and she knew he would have continued if not for the carload of kids parked next to them.

The movie seemed to last forever. The instant the credits began Steve kissed her and leapt out of her car and into his own. He broke the speed limit all the way home. It was a minor miracle neither one of them got a ticket.

When they arrived, Steve ushered the kids into the house. "What's the hurry, Dad?" Meagan complained.

He didn't answer her. "Don't take time to clean out the car now," he ordered. "We'll do that in the morning."

"But you always say we shouldn't put something off we can do now," Kenny whined.

"I lied," Steve said, propelling his son forward by the shoulders. "To bed, everyone. It's late and we've got a big day tomorrow."

Once he'd herded the kids into the house, he raced outside where Hallie was waiting. "Give me twenty minutes, half an hour tops, all right?"

"Half an hour?" It sounded like an eternity.

"I'll sing them lullabies, read them stories. The second their eyes are closed, I'm out of there." He kissed her, then rushed back into the house.

If she had that much time, Hallie was determined to make use of every minute. She'd been waiting months for this; she'd planned it out, detail by exquisite detail.

First she filled the bathtub with hot water and poured in an exotic mixture of scented oils. Then she stripped out of her clothes and sank neck-deep into the water. Closing her eyes, she dreamed of Steve.

Steve. She loved him, really loved him. It astonished her that she hadn't recognized it earlier. All at once everything that had happened in the past few months added up, and the sum total made perfect sense. She loved Steve with an intensity that made her heart ache.

Drying herself with a thick soft towel, she pulled on the slinky silk nightgown, then checked her reflection in the mirror. She liked what she saw—and knew Steve would, too. Tonight she was a beautiful alluring woman. Tonight she would give Steve her body, as well as her heart.

Time to set the scene. First she bundled all the bed linens into her laundry hamper, remaking the bed with fresh sheets and her best quilt. Next she liberally squirted her favorite cologne around the bedroom, then spread her arms and walked gracefully through the aromatic droplets as they fell. Finally she scattered dried rose petals on the antique white quilt. She envisioned Steve carrying her into the bedroom and gently placing her on the bed before he made wild passionate love to her.

Glancing at the digital clock on her nightstand, she realized he'd arrive any minute. Once she'd settled herself on the bed, she decided to pose for him like a tigress on the prowl, the way she'd seen women pictured on calendars. She attempted a number of positions, but felt most comfortable with her hands and one leg outstretched, balancing her weight on one knee. She made a small growling noise deep in her throat.

She held that position for all of three minutes before her knee gave out. Thirty-five minutes had passed. She was ready. More than ready, but Steve had yet to arrive.

She paced.

She stewed.

She peeked.

One look at his place showed that the lights were still on. Hallie thought she saw Kenny race out of the kitchen, and she definitely heard Steve yell after him.

So he'd take a few extra minutes; that was all right by her. Their first time together would be perfect. Steve wanted it as much as she did. She yawned and decided to lie down on the sofa to wait for him. When she heard him opening the door, she'd leap up and race into the bedroom, assume the role of tigress and let him find her on the bed, hungry for her mate.

Sleepy, she leaned her head against the back of the sofa. It'd been such a long day. Soon her eyes were drifting shut. She struggled to keep them open, but to no avail.

She'd hear Steve, she told herself, and if she did fall asleep, he'd wake her.

He didn't.

Hallie woke at first light shivering, still on the sofa, with a decorator pillow bunched under her head.

Steve Marris had stood her up.

Twenty-Nine

Love Is Better Than Chocolate

August 17

If I wasn't so damn much in love with Steve Marris, I'd be
furious. But I'm not. Oh, I was in the beginning. It isn't
every day a woman's left waiting, wearing a silk nightgown—but I found the sweetest note taped to my front
door this morning. Poor Steve. If I was frustrated and disappointed, he was—possibly—even more so. The kids
outlasted him. What's really killing him is that he promised
to go on Kenny's camp-out. The fact that he'd keep his
word makes me love him even more.

I'm in love!! Really, truly in love. I can't believe it's with
Steve Marris. I'm shocked that it took me this long to recognize what should have been obvious. It was practically
staring me in the face!

I never expected love to feel like this. I get teary-eyed
just thinking about Steve, and at the same time I want to
throw out my arms and sing, sort of like Julie Andrews in
the opening scene from "The Sound of Music." How easy
it is to envision myself spending the rest of my life with
him! He's fun and witty and irreverent—and <u>exactly</u> the
kind of man I've always dreamed I'd marry. (How come I
didn't see it sooner??) Heaven knows, I've dated my share
of potential husbands (read: mostly losers) this year. I've
run the gauntlet, paid my dues and—finally—found the
man of my dreams.

I've decided that since Steve won't be back from the
camping trip until Sunday afternoon, I'll cook a veritable
feast for him. I'll serve it wearing my enhancer bra and a
low-cut blouse—let matters develop from there. I know exactly where they'll lead, too. Ah, well, I still have enough
scented rose petals to leave a trail into the bedroom, al-

though if his note was anything to go by, he isn't going to need any help finding the way.

I hope he enjoys spending time with Kenny and the other boys out in the woods, but I pray he isn't too tired to enjoy what's waiting for him right here at home.

Steve lifted his son's sleeping bag out of the trunk of his car, which stood at the curb outside Mary Lynn's. His back hurt, he'd gotten a grand total of maybe three hours' sleep the entire night and he was half-starved. Not only that, he was so damn eager to get back to Hallie he almost hopped back in the car and drove off without saying goodbye to Kenny.

Glancing at the house, he saw Meagan waving through her upstairs bedroom window, telephone receiver attached to her ear. She'd spent the weekend with Mary Lynn—and had probably been on the phone most of that time. He waved back, then turned to his son.

Kenny hugged him close, his skinny arms squeezing Steve about the neck. "Thanks, Dad. I had a great time."

"I did, too, partner." Not so great he'd leap up and volunteer the next time, but good enough to help him forget how miserable he'd been.

"Hello, Steve." Mary Lynn stood on the front porch, looking oddly lost. Her arms were folded protectively around her middle and her mouth was drawn down. He recognized the look. It was the one that usually said she was out of money and needed a small loan to see her through until the first of the month. Well, she had another husband now and she could go to Kip for money. He strengthened his resolve, refusing to allow her to manipulate him.

"Hello, Mary Lynn." He stood next to his car and slid his hands into the hip pockets of his jeans.

Kenny raced toward his mother. "We had a great time! We stayed up real late telling ghost stories and then we all crowded into one tent. In the middle of the night Jimmy McPherson had to pee, but he was too afraid of ghosts to go outside and so he peed in the tent on Johnny Adams's sleeping bag."

Mary Lynn glanced at Steve to verify the story. "It's true," he said. "It'll probably take poor Jimmy McPherson thirty years to live it down. Johnny Adams wasn't too pleased about it, either." Although Steve was anxious to leave, he'd treasured this time with his son—especially now that he had only weekends to build memories with his children.

"I'm glad you two enjoyed yourselves." Even from this distance, Steve could see that Mary Lynn's smile was forced.

"Well, I'm off," he said, as Kenny carried his camping gear into the house.

"Can't you come in for a few minutes?" Mary Lynn asked. "You look like you could use a cup of coffee."

He toyed with the idea of accepting but didn't want to take the time. Instead, he tightened his jaw and reached in his back pocket for his checkbook. "How much?" He'd rather pay her and be done with it than be forced to listen to a long litany of reasons she had to have the child-support check early.

She cast him a hurt look as if he'd deeply insulted her. "I'm not asking for money."

"Fine." He started back toward the car. He needed a shower, shave and Hallie, in that order. Damn, but he was crazy about her. His stomach growled and he amended his list. Shower, shave, food and *then* Hallie.

"You always do this to me," Mary Lynn accused, stopping him dead in his tracks. The woman knew which buttons to push and didn't hesitate to push them, either.

"Do what?" he asked out of sheer habit.

"That. I have something I need to talk to you about. Something I consider important, but you brush me off without a thought and go running to some stupid ball game or bowling or something else that takes you away from your family."

"All right, Mary Lynn," he said, his patience on a short string. "What do you want this time?"

"I hate it when you use that tone of voice with me."

He closed his eyes in an effort to compose himself. "If there's a problem, perhaps we should schedule a time to discuss it." Not now, in other words. Definitely not now.

"Do you have to stand all the way over there? It's ridiculous for us to shout at each other with half the neighborhood listening in."

Steve knew that the minute he stepped into the house he'd be trapped for hours. Mary Lynn always did that to him—and at one time he'd actually welcomed it—but he wasn't up to her games and schemes this afternoon.

He walked across the lawn and noticed that it was long overdue to be mowed. If Kip was going to be living in "his" house, then Lard Butt had damn well better keep up the yard.

He paused at the bottom step. "Better?" he asked.

"Not really."

"Listen, Mary Lynn, I don't have a lot of time. Just say what it is you want."

"You're using that tone with me again."

He felt like he was talking to his aunt Hester. "Is this important or isn't it?" he demanded.

"I already said it was, but it's clear that you're not willing to help either me or your children. I never thought I'd say this about you, Steve Marris, but you've got a cold unfeeling heart." With those words she burst into tears and stormed into the house.

Any other time, Steve would have raced after her. Not now. Mary Lynn had a husband to deal with her moods. He wasn't responsible anymore. His obligation was to his children and to them alone.

Keeping that in mind, he returned to the car and drove off. But despite his intentions, despite his decision about her place in his life, he couldn't stop thinking about Mary Lynn. Must be habit, he thought, or residual guilt. He shook his head, determined to put it behind him. He had another life now, one that excluded Mary Lynn. One that included Hallie.

What he'd told Hallie about loving her was true. Even truer than he'd realized when he said it. He felt like he was seventeen all over again. He wondered at what precise moment he'd fallen for her. Or had their love developed more gradually, based as it was on friendship? It didn't matter, he decided. It had happened and he was head over heels crazy about her.

For the first time since Mary Lynn had asked him to move out, he felt alive and happy. The kind of happy that went clear through him and didn't get bogged down in regrets and what-ifs. The kind of happy that caused a man to smile from his heart outward. A happiness that wouldn't easily be taken away.

His mind raced as he neared home. He parked the car and headed directly for Hallie's, pounding on her front door. He smelled of camp-fire smoke, sweat, Jimmy McPherson's pee and God knew what else, but he didn't care. He needed to kiss her. Tell her he was home. Hold her, if only for a moment.

At last she swung open the door.

"Am I forgiven?" he asked, barely giving her time to let the fact that he was standing there register.

The screen door was still between them. "That depends."

"On what?"

"On how long it takes you to kiss me, you fool."

He almost tore the screen door off its hinges in his haste. Hallie gave a soft cry of welcome and threw herself into his embrace. He locked both arms around her waist and hauled her against him, savoring her warmth, breathing in her feminine scent.

He'd dreamed of this moment, anticipated it every second he'd been tramping through the woods with ten Cub Scouts. Generally he liked the outdoors, but this time his mind and heart had been with Hallie.

Their kiss was long and slow, filled with the wonder of their newly discovered love. He wanted her to know the depth of his frustration, his profound need for her. His blood quickly fired to life, and it demanded every ounce of restraint he possessed not to make love to her right then and there.

He buried his face in the curve of her shoulder, thinking her love was the closest thing to heaven he was likely to find. Already it was healing him; already he'd felt its effects. Her love was a gift he wouldn't abuse or accept lightly.

"I cooked you dinner. Roast chicken." She said this as if it had some significance.

"I'm hungry enough to eat it, too," he said, and kissed the tip of her nose.

"Hey, I'll have you know I've taken cooking classes."

"Then feed me, woman."

They kissed again with an intensity that all but consumed them. When they drew apart, Steve noticed that his beard had chafed her face. "I'll be right back," he promised, setting her on her feet.

"That's what you said the last time."

"Not to worry. Nothing's going to keep me away again."

"I'm glad to hear it." She smiled, a smile he could get lost in. Maybe it wasn't such a good idea to come here first, because leaving her even for ten or fifteen minutes was proving damned difficult.

He was halfway between their houses when she called out, "In case you've forgotten, you told me you'd marry a woman who could cook you a decent roast chicken dinner."

He froze. "Marry you?"

She planted her hands on her hips and narrowed her eyes. "You're going to marry me, Steve Marris, if I have to hog-tie you and drag you down the aisle myself."

He forced a short laugh and hurried into the house, his heart in his throat. Hallie wanted a husband; he'd always known it. And now she wanted *him* for a husband. Marriage. He shouldn't be shocked, but he was.

Marriage was serious stuff. *Real* serious. He'd been through it once, fathered two children. The next thing he knew, Hallie would be talking about having kids of her own. The financial responsibility for Meagan and Kenny already weighed heavily on him, and the thought of taking on that kind of obligation for more children—well, it scared him.

He walked into the bathroom, stripped off his clothes and stepped into the shower. The minute the warm spray hit his skin he felt worlds better. They had a lot to discuss, he and Hallie. He loved her, that much he knew, but their entire relationship didn't need to be defined within the next thirty minutes. Not every decision had to be made right now.

Out of the shower, he stood in front of the bathroom mirror with a towel around his waist and shaved a two-day growth of beard from his face. He cut himself once thinking about Hallie, which made him smile. What he should've been doing was paying attention to the blade.

Now that he thought about it, he *had* mentioned roast chicken to Hallie. He remembered their conversation—how his grandmother used to roast a chicken for the family every Sunday, after church. They'd been memorable, those chicken dinners. In all the years he'd been married to Mary Lynn she'd never attempted it. He loved Hallie's willingness to please him.

He slapped some cologne on his face, dressed, grabbed a bottle of white wine from the fridge and hurried back to her house. He entered without knocking.

Hallie stood by the table, smiling when he walked inside. She glowed with happiness, and he felt it as keenly as he did the warmth of the sun.

"Welcome back," she said, sounding almost shy. Damn, but she looked good. She wore a scoop-necked full-length summer dress and sandals. Her dark curly hair was pinned back from her face with two daisy pins.

It was plain to see she'd gone to a lot of trouble with this dinner. A floral centerpiece sat in the middle of the table; there were crystal wineglasses and linen napkins. It was a nice feeling, knowing she'd done all this for him.

Steve frowned, however, when he looked into the kitchen. The chaos was daunting. Judging by the stack of pots and pans, she'd used every cooking dish she owned.

"There's dessert, too," she promised in a low sexy voice that made his blood percolate in his veins.

"I have a feeling it isn't apple pie."

"Time will tell, won't it?" she teased.

As he opened the wine, he noticed a trail of rose petals leading out of the dining room and down the hallway. "What's that?" he asked, pointing.

"Dessert," she answered, smiling coyly.

He followed the fragrant dried flowers as far as her bedroom. Pausing in the doorway, he saw that the top of her bed was covered with a whole slew of petals. Smack-dab in the middle was the sexiest cream-colored silk nightgown he'd ever laid eyes on.

"Do you actually think you're going to have time to put that on?"

"No, but I wanted you to at least see it."

He brought her into his arms and debated making love to her right then. But considering the effort involved in preparing this dinner, he didn't want anything to spoil it. "You aren't going to need that gown or anything else, Hallie," he whispered before he kissed her. "I want you so damn much now that I'm about to bust out of these jeans."

"You might not be one of the most romantic men I've ever met, but you sure know how to get a girl's heart pounding."

He left the bedroom reluctantly, glancing over his shoulder more than once as he walked down the hallway. Hoping to speed matters along, he tried to help her get dinner on the table, but she wouldn't let him. She took a green salad out of the refrigerator, tossing it with oil and vinegar, then removed the chicken and baked potatoes from the oven. The scent of rosemary and sage bread dressing drifted through the house.

He replaced the handful of cookies he'd stolen from the cookie jar.

"Weren't you the one who told me the old saying's true—that the way to a man's heart is through his stomach?" she asked.

"You already have my heart, Hallie." Surely she knew that.

She held out her hand, inviting him to her table. "Come and sit down."

As if in a trance, he walked over to where she stood. He poured the wine and remembered to pull out her chair before he seated himself. Hallie served him, complimented him on his choice of wine and then spread the napkin across her lap.

She waited for him to take the first bite, watching him carefully. It seemed to Steve that she was holding her breath. He saw her teeth worry her lower lip. As far as he was concerned, the food could taste like monkey vomit and he wouldn't care.

It didn't. The chicken was every bit as good as those his grandmother used to make. For effect, he closed his eyes and kissed his fingertips. "Perfect," he said. "The best I've ever tasted."

"You're sure? It isn't too crisp?"

"No. Taste for yourself."

She did, sampling a tiny cautious bite. Her eyes met his. "It *is* good," she said, sounding bewildered. "It's really good."

Steve took another bite and then another.

"You'll notice this tastes nothing like the chicken from those fast-food places," she said. "I did everything myself, including the stuffing. I had to phone my mother three times for help, but I managed."

"I'm proud of you." And he was.

He ate two huge servings, then helped her clear the table. Try as he might, he couldn't keep his hands off her while she attempted to pour them each a cup of coffee. She stood with her back to him, facing the kitchen counter.

He moved directly behind her, his hands cupping her breasts while he nuzzled her neck. She smelled faintly of roses and a variety of herbs and spices. The mixture wasn't one he'd find at a perfume counter, but it had an immediate effect on him. He rubbed against her, leaving her in no doubt about his state of arousal.

"Steve!"

"I can't help myself. I'm crazy about you."

"Crazy to go to bed with me, you mean."

He couldn't see any need to deny it. "Guilty. Are you sure we need this coffee?"

She hesitated. "It's a special blend..." She hesitated, then turned around to face him. "No, I don't need this coffee. All I need is you."

A frenzy of deep kisses followed, mingled with moans, whimpers and a sense of breathless wonder. Steve was about to lift her into his arms and carry her into the bedroom when the phone rang.

They stopped and stared at each other.

"Don't answer it," he said.

"It's my mother," Hallie whispered, pressing her forehead against his shoulder. "She wants to know how the chicken turned out. If I don't answer it now, she'll phone back later. Like in ten minutes."

Steve wasn't sure how he knew that phone call meant trouble, but he did. The instant she reached for the telephone, he had to bite back the urge to beg her—again—to let it ring.

"Hello." Hallie's eyes zeroed in on his. "It's Meagan," she said, handing him the phone. "She needs to talk to you right away."

Steve took the receiver. "Meagan, is something wrong?"

"I'm sorry to bother you, Dad, but there wasn't any answer at your place, and I thought Hallie might know where you were."

"It's all right, honey, just tell me what's wrong." He turned away so he wouldn't have to face Hallie.

"It's Mom."

Steve heard the worry and fear in his daughter's voice. "What's the matter with her?"

"I don't know, she won't tell me, but she can't seem to stop crying. I don't know what to do anymore—she said she won't talk to anyone but you."

Steve swallowed a groan.

"Dad, what should I do?"

"Nothing, honey. I'll be right over."

Thirty

Mr. Nice Guy

"What do you mean you're leaving?" Hallie couldn't believe her ears. For the second time in as many days, Steve was walking out on her. Her chest tightened with a growing sense of frustration and anger.

"Hallie, it isn't like I *want* to go." It helped to hear the regret in his voice. But not enough.

"Why? What is it this time?" Although she'd heard his half of the conversation, it hadn't told her much. Hallie guessed this supposed crisis had something to do with his ex-wife. Steve had made his feelings for her no secret, and it seemed he'd be forever at the woman's beck and call.

"There's trouble at Mary Lynn's," he explained.

"With one of the kids?"

He hesitated, and in that instant she knew. Whatever the problem, it did indeed involve Mary Lynn. Her knees felt as if they were about to buckle, and she lowered herself onto a kitchen chair. "It's Mary Lynn, isn't it?"

He paused and with reluctance answered, "Yes."

At least she should be grateful he hadn't lied. "I see."

"Hallie, trust me, walking out on you now is the last thing I want."

"Then don't go." Her voice was high-pitched and mildly hysterical.

"I have to. Meagan sounded near panic. It isn't like this is a common occurrence. In fact, it's never happened before." He knelt in front of her and gripped her hands tightly in his. "I'll be back, I promise, and then we can talk. Just remember it's you I love."

Hallie desperately wanted to believe him, but she'd been a fool before and was determined not to repeat the same mistakes. "I don't want to argue about this. If...you feel it's necessary to go, then you should."

His relief was evident.

Steve started to get up, started to walk away, but before he left she had to ask him one last thing. Hastily she got to her feet. "Steve."

He turned to look at her.

It wasn't the time to ask him this. Wasn't even fair, but right now, that didn't matter to her. She'd seen his expression when she'd brought up the subject earlier. Viewed the stricken look in his eyes and laughed it off. She wasn't laughing now. She had to know where they stood before he went to Mary Lynn. "Are you going to ask me to marry you?" she said.

He couldn't disguise the dread in his eyes. "Do we have to discuss this now?"

How odd that she'd smile just then. Perhaps it was because she'd guessed his response long before he spoke. His eagerness to delay the discussion was an answer in itself. "No," she said, putting on a brave front, "we can talk about that later—that and everything else."

"I'll be back before you know I'm gone."

That wasn't possible. She felt his absence immediately, felt it like a knife in her gut. Caught on a gust of wind, the door closed hard. Hallie sat down again after he'd left and shut her eyes. Breathing in deeply, she was surprised to discover she was trembling.

Steve was furious by the time he arrived at Mary Lynn's. He had to hand it to his ex-wife; her timing was incredible. The very last thing he'd wanted to do was walk out on Hallie just then. She'd gone to so much trouble, cooking dinner, preparing a homecoming for him. She'd been trying to prove how much she loved him, and his response had been to walk out on her.

He slammed the car door and marched up the front walk, taking the steps two at a time. He almost walked in without ringing the doorbell—something he was prone to forget since he'd once lived in this house.

As soon as Meagan opened the door, she hugged him tight, obviously relieved to have him there. "I'm so glad you came, Daddy.., I didn't know what to do."

"It's all right, sweetheart. It wasn't any problem." So, he lied. He had the feeling Hallie wasn't going to forget and forgive as easily this time, and he didn't blame her. He'd deal with whatever was bothering Mary Lynn and be on his way, hoping he could make amends to Hallie. "Where's your mother?" he asked Meagan.

"In the bedroom." She pointed toward it as if he needed directions. He didn't.

"Where's Kip?"

"I don't know. I haven't seen him since this morning. I...I don't think they're getting along."

"What about Kenny?"

"Asleep. He went to bed soon after you dropped him off."

Bed was exactly where Steve longed to be, and he didn't plan on cuddling up with a stuffed animal, either. He ran his hand through his hair and exhaled sharply. He was tired, impatient and in no condition to deal with one of Mary Lynn's moods.

He walked through the kitchen on the way to the master bedroom. Meagan had apparently made a peanut-butter-and-jelly sandwich for dinner; the peanut butter was still out and so was the jelly, along with an open loaf of bread.

"I didn't do that," she said, her gaze following his. "Kenny did."

"Have you had dinner?"

"Not yet," she said with a shrug. "I'm too worried about Mom."

"Hey, sweetie, I'm sure everything will work out. You eat something now and I'll go talk to your mom." He left Meagan rummaging in the refrigerator and hurried to the bedroom. He knocked once, then entered.

Mary Lynn was lying facedown on the bed, sobbing steadily. She raised her head to see who it was. When she saw him, she cried out, flung herself from the bed and ran into his arms.

"I'm so glad you came," she wailed. "Oh, Steve, I don't know what to do." In all the years he'd been married to Mary Lynn he'd never seen her this distraught. Meagan was right to be concerned.

He wrapped his arms around her and they both sat on the edge of the bed. "What's wrong?"

Her crying subsided to soft sniffles. "I...I'm such a fool. Oh, Steve, how could I have been so incredibly stupid?"

"You're not stupid," he assured her, gently rubbing her back. "Now tell me what's upsetting you so much."

"It's Kip—he lied to me."

Steve forced himself to relax. He was concerned about his children, and the effect Kip's lie, whatever it was, might have on them.

"I learned he's been married twice before—he didn't tell me about his second wife. I found out by accident. I...I opened some mail. From his ex—his *second* ex. He has a little girl by that marriage. She's barely two years old."

Steve continued patting her back. Okay, Kip had been married one time more than Mary Lynn realized, but she made it sound like the end of the world. "I'm sure this is a shock, but—"

"That's not all," she cut him off. "There's something else..."

Steve's shirt was damp with her tears. She lifted her eyes to his and bit her lower lip, as if to gauge how much she should say. "You can tell me anything, Mary Lynn, you know that."

"I...I'm afraid I might be in trouble with the law."

"The *law?*"

"I married a man...who's already married."

It took a moment for the meaning of her words to sink in. "You mean to say Kip never divorced his second wife?"

"No, he didn't. I talked to her myself, and she told me. I didn't want to believe her, and when I asked Kip he was so convincing. He said she was a shrew and a bitch who'd say or do anything she could to ruin our happiness."

"Maybe she *is* lying."

Mary Lynn shook her head violently. "I asked Kip if I could see his divorce decree and he couldn't find it, and then...then I had a friend—you remember Kelly, don't you?—check at the courthouse for me. There's nothing there. Nothing." Her shoulders shook with the force of her tears.

"Did you ask Kip about that?"

"Yes. He...he was furious I'd gone behind his back and had Kelly check the court records. He tried to tell me he'd gotten a divorce in Vegas. I said if that was true, he should be able to produce the documents and...he couldn't."

"Oh, Mary Lynn, I'm sorry."

"We had a terrible argument and he walked out. I don't think he'll be back—I'm not even sure I want him back. Oh, Steve, how am I ever going to face my friends? What will I tell my family? I feel like such a fool."

"When did you find all this out?"

"I talked to Kelly Friday afternoon, but Kip was away at a sales conference and I hadn't had a chance to hear his side of it. It's been eating away at me all weekend...you can't *know* how dreadful this week has been. He...he hadn't mentioned the second marriage, but I assumed he was divorced until Linda told me otherwise. Then Kip arrived and we had this terrible fight—and then he...he drove off in a huff."

"He'll be back," Steve said, looking toward the closet—formerly his closet—filled with Kip's clothes.

His ex-wife gazed up at him with wide appealing eyes. "You'd never have done anything like this to me. You were always a good husband."

If that was the case, he wondered why she'd been so quick to divorce him. He continued to hold her because that was what she seemed to need. Really, there was nothing else he could do. Nothing he could say.

Kneeling on the bed, Mary Lynn placed her arms around his neck and pressed her head to his shoulder. "Hold me, Steve, please, for just a little longer."

His ex-wife had never been a clinging violet. "Everything will work out," he reassured her, repeating the words he'd said to Meagan. "Kip will be back and you two can sort all this out. You loved him enough to marry him, didn't you?"

"I...I've been so foolish."

He wanted to agree with her, but resisted the impulse.

Mary Lynn lay back down, and the pressure of her arms still circling his neck pulled him down with her. "Make love to me, Steve. I need you."

He groaned. Not with desire, but with anger and frustration. She could have had him anytime, anyplace, a few months earlier. Instead, she'd left him high and dry and turned her loving attention to Kip. Now she was back. He'd gone through several of the longest and most sexually frustrating months of his life, and in the space of a single day he had two women wanting him. If it wasn't so ironic, he might have laughed.

"I don't think that's such a good idea," he said gently, trying not to distress her any more than she already was.

Mary Lynn raised her head from the pillow and kissed him, using every bit of knowledge, every advantage, that their years of marriage had taught her.

Steve broke off the kiss.

"No, Mary Lynn," he said sternly. "It isn't going to work for us any longer. You're feeling low and miserable. You don't really want me."

"I do, Steve. I want you so much." She squirmed and bucked beneath him, grinding her pelvis against his. "Don't reject me now. Please. Not when I feel like the whole world's caved in on me."

It wasn't him she wanted, Steve recognized, but the security his love had always offered her.

"Come on, Mary Lynn, you're involved with someone else." He nearly made the mistake of saying she was *married* to someone else when in all likelihood, she wasn't.

Steve struggled to a sitting position. She sobbed louder and clung to him, refusing to release him. "Lie down with me. Please. Is that so much to ask? I can't even remember the last time I slept."

He let her direct him downward, back onto the bed. She snuggled close, still sniffling. Steve kept his arm around her, thinking she'd soon drift off to sleep. The minute she did, he'd slip away.

"I don't know why I ever fell for Kip," she said, apparently needing to talk.

"He seems all right," Steve muttered.

"He's deceitful and stubborn," Mary Lynn countered.

Steve didn't feel obliged to list Kip's good points; besides, he didn't know the man. But as long as Kip was a decent stepfather, Steve didn't really care.

"I don't think he'll be back," Mary Lynn said bleakly.

Now Steve understood: *This* was what truly bothered her. "He'll need to pack his clothes, won't he?" he asked. "You can talk to him then."

She raised herself up on one elbow and reached for a tissue to blow her nose. "I don't know. He might have someone else come for his things. I told him I never wanted to see him again, and I don't think he'll want to see me, either. I really don't."

"Let's not borrow trouble."

"How could Kip *do* this to me?" she asked, sounding more and more like a frightened little girl.

"Shh." Steve cradled her head against his shoulder. "Go to sleep." The sooner she did, the sooner he'd be free to leave. It wasn't Mary Lynn he wanted to hold, but Hallie. Although his ex-wife was in his arms, the woman he loved was in his thoughts. Her rose-petal-littered bed, the promise of her smile. The joy he felt just thinking about Hallie made him impatient to return to her.

"I'm so tired."

So was he, Steve realized with a yawn. After spending a whole night in one huge tent with ten Cub Scouts, he was exhausted. The nine-year-olds had been up and down until well after two. Steve was convinced he didn't get more than a couple of hours' sleep, if that. His son had already crashed.

Mary Lynn sobbed quietly.

"Everything will work out," he whispered again. "Everything does sooner or later." He wouldn't have believed it a few months ago, but he did now. Mary Lynn's decision to file for divorce had drastically changed the course of his life. For a time, a long time, he felt it had all been a terrible mistake. His pride, his ego, his sense of who and what he was had suffered one hell of a beating. It'd taken damn near a year to fight his way back, to rise above the shock and the rejection.

A year, and things hadn't seemed to get any better. And then he'd learned Mary Lynn was dating Kip. That had hurt, and it'd hurt even more when she remarried. But her marriage, above anything else, had helped him face the truth. It was over for them.

He loved her, yes; a part of him always would. His being with her now was evidence of the depth of his feeling for her. She was the mother of his children, his first love—but their marriage was over. Dead and buried.

Accepting that had probably taken much longer than it should have, but he'd felt like he was fighting for his family, for the dream of what it could have been. He didn't blame Mary Lynn for the failure of their marriage, nor did he accept full responsibility himself. Despite his best efforts to keep his family intact, the divorce had happened and he couldn't turn back the clock.

Steve loved Hallie now. He wasn't sure about leaping into another marriage, but he knew her well enough to realize she wouldn't take anything less. The two of them could discuss that later.

Mary Lynn released a long wobbly sigh. Her shoulders trembled and her grip about him tightened, as though she feared he was about to leave her.

He would eventually, but only after she fell asleep. He battled back his own fatigue and decided to rest his eyes. But only for a minute. One minute.

The next thing he knew, Kenny was standing over him. "Dad?"

Steve's eyes flew open.

"What are you doing here?" Kenny whispered. "Where's Kip?"

Steve glanced to the other side of the bed to discover Mary Lynn curled up with a loose blanket tucked around her shoulders.

"I can't find my shoes," Kenny said, again in a whisper. "Are you and Mom getting back together?"

"Your shoes?" Steve sat up and tried to focus on his wristwatch. "What time is it?"

"Six."

"In the morning?"

Kenny nodded, and Steve cursed under his breath and bolted off the bed. He was going to have one hell of a time explaining this to Hallie.

Thirty-One

Goodbye, My Heart

Hallie didn't think she'd ever spent such a miserable night. Every hour or so she leapt out of bed, convinced she'd heard Steve's car. Not until after three did she finally acknowledge that he wasn't coming. That he'd spent the night with Mary Lynn.

His ex-wife had claimed she needed him and he'd rushed to her side, deserting Hallie. It didn't take a rocket scientist to realize this wasn't going to change. If she and Steve were to become involved, she'd better accept his feelings for the other woman now. But it stuck like a fish bone in her throat. Hallie doubted she could ever swallow Mary Lynn's presence in her life.

After three o'clock she didn't get out of bed whenever she thought she heard a car, but she didn't sleep, either. She tried. Heaven knew, she tried, and as the clock ticked on and the minutes rolled by, she fumed. The remaining hours of the night were spent tossing and turning. And trembling. She trembled like someone who'd almost made one of the biggest mistakes of her life.

At five she gave up the effort, threw aside the sheets and got up. She showered, changed into her work clothes and brewed herself a pot of coffee. She was going to need it.

Sitting at her kitchen table, she wrote in her journal, spilling out her grief and anger, when a loud knock sounded at her front door. She didn't need anyone to tell her it was Steve.

It amazed her how calm she was. Whatever emotion was left in her had burned itself out during the endless night.

Steve's eyes widened with what appeared to be surprise when he saw her. "You're up. I wasn't sure if I'd get you out of bed or not."

It was all too apparent that he'd recently come from one, Hallie noted.

"Hallie, I'm so sorry." He held out his hand in a gesture of hope, a request for understanding. "You have every reason to be furious, but if you'll let me explain—"

"I'm not angry," she said, interrupting him.

"You're not?" He paused and sniffed the air. "Is that coffee? Damn, I could use a cup."

"Help yourself." She motioned toward the kitchen.

He walked past her and took down a mug from her cupboard. After he'd finished pouring, he turned and leaned back against the counter. His eyes held hers. "I can imagine what you're thinking."

"I doubt that." She folded her arms and stood on the other side of the room, distancing herself from him physically and emotionally.

"Mary Lynn found out some distressing news about Kip," Steve went on. "I've never seen her this distraught."

"And so you spent the night with her." Hallie could see no need for them to tiptoe around the obvious. "You slept with her." He'd practically admitted as much.

"No!" He said it with such vehemence that for one tiny instant she almost believed him.

"Yes, I slept with her," he corrected, "but I didn't *sleep* with her." He stopped abruptly and shook his head in unmistakable anger. "All right, we were in the same bed, but—"

"Please, spare me the details." Her stomach was already in knots, and she wasn't up to listening to a lengthy explanation, however plausible it might sound. He'd spent the night with his ex-wife. The reasons didn't matter. He'd been with Mary Lynn and not her, and damn it all, that hurt.

"It isn't as bad as it looks," Steve said, his gaze holding hers and refusing to let go.

"Perhaps not," she said, forcing a smile. She wasn't sure how well she'd succeeded. "But as far as I'm concerned, we were given a reprieve from making a major mistake."

"Mistake?" His echo was a demand for an explanation.

She sipped her coffee and prayed she could pull this off. "Yeah. You've heard what they say about friends and lovers—how sex ruins friendship. It wouldn't work with us, Steve. You know me too well, and—"

"Why wouldn't it work?" His eyes narrowed. She saw that his hands tightened around the coffee mug until his knuckles paled with the strength of his grip.

"You love Mary Lynn. You've never tried to hide that from me—"

"I love *you*."

It didn't slip her notice that he made no attempt to deny his feelings for his ex-wife. "I know," she said with an air of frivolity. "I love you, too. That's the way it is between friends. Good friends."

"We're more than friends," he declared.

Maintaining her forced smile had become impossible. "Perhaps at one point we might have been, but not now."

Steve slammed the mug down on the counter, and coffee sloshed over the rim, spilling onto the floor. "Are you telling me you don't want me?" His eyes dared her to contradict him.

Hallie had never been a good liar. "Don't misunderstand me, Steve. I'm grateful to Mary Lynn. She saved us from progressing into an area that would have been a disaster for us both."

"The hell she did."

"I can see the writing on the wall. You love her—"

"I was married to her for a long time. I can't turn feelings off like a faucet. She was frantic and frightened. All I did was hold her! If you want to crucify me for that, then be done with it."

"I know how you feel about Mary Lynn." Hallie countered his anger with a calm serenity. "She was your first love, your high-school sweetheart, your former wife. It's only natural that she'd continue to have a special place in your heart."

His eyes pierced hers. "I love you."

A lump formed in her throat. How convincing he sounded, how sincere and forthright. "But it's clear now that Mary Lynn comes first in your thoughts...and in your heart."

"If you'd give me a chance—"

She spoke quickly, not allowing him to finish. "She'll *always* be first with you, Steve—no matter what's happening between us."

"What was I supposed to do?" he shouted. "Meagan phoned, not knowing what to do. She's just a kid. She didn't know how to help her mother. Mary Lynn was hysterical."

Hallie's point exactly. "And so you hurried to her side." It was hard not to suspect Mary Lynn of manipulating him—and hard not to resent Steve for buying it. She bit the corner of her lip at the deep rush of anger. She loved Steve and Meagan and Kenny, and hated the emotion that surfaced whenever Mary Lynn's name was mentioned. Hallie had never seen herself as jealous and petty, but that was how she felt, how she acted.

It made her uncomfortable with herself. Hallie couldn't deal with the negative feelings his first marriage brought out in her. "It won't work, Steve," she insisted. "I'm just as sorry as you are, but it isn't meant to be."

"Why the hell not?"

"I want a husband, not—"

He interrupted her. "So that's what this is all about."

She ignored his comment and finished, "—an ex-husband."

That stopped him. His head reared back as if to assimilate what she'd said. "An ex-husband? What do you mean?"

"I only plan to marry once in my life—"

"You know that saying about the best-laid plans. I didn't even want that stupid divorce. It was Mary Lynn who was unhappy, Mary Lynn who claimed she'd missed out on life because she'd never lived on her own, never attended college, never made love with other men." His words became more heated, more angry. When he stopped, the silence seemed louder than his outburst.

Hallie waited before she spoke again, letting the silence surround them both. "I saw the look in your eyes when I mentioned marriage, Steve. You've been badly burned. I understand that, and I know why the thought of marrying again isn't exactly appealing."

He stood tight-lipped and Hallie was grateful he didn't deny his feelings.

"I guess what I'm trying to say, obviously not very well, is that I want a man who'll make a wholehearted commitment to me. A man—"

"Who'll come to you without a load of emotional garbage from his divorce and two emotionally needy kids."

She hesitated, and then because this seemed the easiest way to put an end to it, she nodded.

"Fine." He opened and closed his fist. "Be warned, this Mr. Perfect you're looking for may not exist. Let me know when you're ready for a real man and not some ideal." Without a further glance, he marched past her and out the front door.

Hallie tried to pretend it didn't matter. That they could still be friends, still rely on each other. Her hope was that if they couldn't be lovers, at least they could salvage the friendship. She had to admit that, to their credit, they both tried. And yet…they didn't succeed.

She'd met Steve on her way to work the morning after their confrontation. When she'd recovered from the unexpected encounter, she'd smiled cheerfully. "Beautiful morning, isn't it?"

"Lovely," he'd answered, making the one word sound anything but. Then he'd climbed in his truck and promptly driven away.

Hallie had sat in her car, hands gripping the steering wheel as she battled wave upon wave of sadness.

She didn't see Steve again until Thursday. Her week had been limping along as well as could be expected and then—wham, she ran into Steve at the local grocery. They chatted, but the camaraderie was gone. Their conversation was forced, their enthusiasm false. Afterward, it seemed to her that the hole in her heart had grown larger, more ragged. It would always be like this, she realized. Seeing him would always be a reminder of what might have been. And she was reasonably certain from Steve's reactions that he felt the same way.

Something had to be done.

Friday afternoon, Meagan and Kenny stopped by her place. Apparently Steve wasn't home from work yet. "Hi, Hallie," the girl said, coming in and collapsing onto the sofa. Kenny helped himself to the television remote control.

"You two look like you're ready to go back to school," Hallie remarked. Both seemed bored, uninterested, lacking in energy. Meagan was half on and half off the sofa, and Kenny flipped through television channels as if he were counting them, instead of watching them.

"Mom and Kip made up," Meagan told her.

Hallie was pleased to hear it, particularly for the children's sake. She sat down on the sofa between them. "I have something to tell you both."

"What?" The kids perked up immediately.

"I bet you're marrying Dad," Kenny said, and stuck out his tongue at his sister.

"No."

"Hasn't Dad asked you yet?" This came from Meagan, and she sounded disappointed. "Don't worry, he will."

"No." Hallie folded her hands together. "I listed my condo with a real-estate agent." At their blank look she continued, "It's up for sale."

"Are you moving in with Dad?"

"No—I'm moving." It had been a difficult decision, one she'd debated all week. Then, when she'd almost made up her mind, she'd talked it over with a friend in real estate—the same one who'd found her this condo. Gabby convinced her the market was right to sell. That cinched it for Hallie.

This horrible tension between Steve and her wasn't going away. It would only get more awkward, and their friendship would become more and more forced. If she was ever going to find a man to marry, it wouldn't be while she lived next door to the man she already loved.

Nor was Hallie sure she could keep her feelings about his ex-wife to herself. It would hurt too damn much to watch him run to Mary Lynn every time the woman had a problem. Every time she felt like yanking the leash. It was useless to fight a losing battle.

"You're moving?" Meagan asked, her voice filled with shock.

"Eventually. Not right away. I have to sell my place first."

"But why?" Kenny wailed.

She ruffled his hair.

This was the question she wasn't sure she could answer. Hallie could think of no way to explain that she was leaving in order to protect her heart. She was still struggling with a response when Kenny asked another question. "Does Dad know?"

"Not yet." Hallie hadn't gathered the courage to tell Steve. Nor had she wanted a For Sale sign posted in her front yard.

"When are you moving?" This time the question was Meagan's.

"I don't know, but it probably won't be soon. It'll take several months to sell and a couple more to handle all the paperwork. I'll be around for a long time yet." She would miss Steve's children, almost as much as she'd miss him. "It doesn't mean you won't see me again." She could tell that neither one believed her, but she meant what she said. She'd come to care deeply for Meagan and Kenny and would make every effort to keep them in her life.

"It won't be the same around here with you gone," Kenny said morosely.

They didn't get a chance to finish the conversation. Steve arrived home as she was trying to reassure the kids; with quick goodbyes, they rushed out the door to join their father. Just as she suspected, it didn't take them long to deliver her news. He was pounding at her front door a minute later.

"Is it true?" he demanded brusquely when she opened the door.

She nodded. "Yes. I put my place on the market."

His eyes widened momentarily and then a slow sad smile touched his mouth. "I guess you were right, after all." He retreated a couple of steps, backing away from her.

"I generally am," she said, hoping humor would help. "How am I right this time?"

"What you said about the two of us. It'd never work. You recognized that before I did."

His words felt like a slap in the face. Hallie had no response, and even if she had, she doubted she could have spoken right then. Her heart actually hurt.

He buried his hands in his pockets. "I wish you well, Hallie McCarthy."

"You, too, Steve Marris." Her voice sounded weak and almost unrecognizable to her own ears.

He nodded once, then turned and walked away.

Thirty-Two

Wide Awake And Dreaming

September 7

I can't believe this summer is almost over.

I was reading over my goal planner and it struck me that here it is, nine months into the year, and I don't have even a single prospect for a husband. What's sad is that I don't care anymore. I suspect this is my ego making excuses for me.

Again and again I'm reminded of what happened with Donnalee. Sanford seemed wonderful, perfect for her. I can still hear some of her so-called friends when they learned she'd broken the engagement. But she was right, because now I'd say I've never seen her happier (or me more miserable). It was a painful time for Donnalee, but in the end she found the man she can love for the rest of her life. A man who shares her vision of the future. If she'd married Sanford, every time she saw a mother and child, she would've longed for a child of her own. In time that desire would almost certainly have destroyed their relationship.

I feel like I'm doing the same thing with Steve. Saving myself a lot of unnecessary grief. He loves Mary Lynn, and he's never bothered to claim otherwise. I don't have a chance competing against his first love.

Damn, this is so hard, especially right now when we see each other practically every day.

The most embarrassing thing happened yesterday afternoon. I was standing in line at the bank—not one of my favorite pastimes—and out of the blue, for no reason I can determine, tears appeared in my eyes and I just couldn't make them go away. I was mortified. I thought at first it might have something to do with missing my dad, but I don't think so. I do miss him—not a day passes when he doesn't come to mind for one reason or another—but I believe I've adjusted to his death. So has Mom. My gut feeling is these tears have more to do with Steve. It isn't easy to stop loving someone—which gives me a bit of insight into his continued involvement with his first wife.

It'll be better once I've moved. I was so surprised and grateful when my condo sold. Gabby had told me it could take as long as six months. I was in shock when I received a respectable offer the first week it was listed. I'm anxious to leave. Anxious to get on with my life. The deal should close in another week, now that the new owner's financing is approved.

I guess I can last another week living next door to Steve. What worries me more is standing next to him at Donnalee's wedding in October. I'm her maid of honor and Steve is best man. I just pray I don't repeat the scene from the bank.

A trickle of sweat rolled down Donnalee's bared abdomen as she sat in the rocking chair in front of Todd's summer home. A-frame cabins didn't traditionally have large front porches, but he'd added one several years before, building it himself. Donnalee loved sitting there in the afternoon shade, looking out over the water. Often she relaxed with a good book while Todd fished or worked about the property.

She wore shorts, and hoping it would cool her off, she'd unfastened her blouse and tied the loose ends together. Closing her eyes, she draped one leg over the side arm of the rocker, dangling her bare foot.

No one from the office would recognize her. Not without an expensive business suit and makeup. Not with her midriff exposed and her hair in pigtails.

Donnalee was happy, happier than she'd been since she was a child. Happy because she was deeply in love.

Hard as it was to believe, their wedding was less than a month away. Todd had wanted her to move in with him, and in reality, she might as well be living at his place now, but she continued to hang on to her own apartment. Every weekend they spent here, at the lake.

As a lazy afternoon breeze blew off the water, she continued to rock slowly back and forth. She dreamed of the future, the years to come, the family they would have.

Donnalee was immeasurably grateful to Hallie. It was because of her friend that she'd found Todd. But thinking about Hallie made her frown. Donnalee was worried about her. Worried about Steve, too. What a pair they were, both headstrong and stubborn.

She heard the porch creak and opened her eyes to find Todd approaching. She smiled and held her hand out to him. How good he looked, so tanned and handsome, so strong in mind and body. Often just seeing him produced a physical ache in her. One that was even deeper than sexual need—although they'd done their share of expressing *that,* too. The ache she experienced went beyond physical longing. It was a heartfelt sense of joy.

Todd clasped her hand in his and raised it to his lips. "You frowned just now. Are you worried about something?" He claimed the rocker next to hers, still holding her hand.

"I was thinking about Hallie."

Todd didn't respond right away. "I'd like to shake those two."

"So would I," Donnalee said. Although she didn't say so, her sympathies were with Hallie, but she'd heard both sides—and she knew her friend well enough to recognize that Hallie was equally at fault.

"Steve's been in a foul mood for weeks," Todd grumbled. "I had the audacity to suggest he patch things up with Hallie and he damn near bit my head off. That's not like Steve." Todd paused. "He apologized later, and we went out for a beer. The sad part is, he loves Hallie. He told me so himself."

This was news to Donnalee. "If he loves her, then why's he letting her move? I don't know that Hallie would admit it, but I think she was waiting for him to ask her not to go."

"He wouldn't."

"Why not?" Donnalee wanted to understand why two people who so obviously loved each other would allow this to happen.

"Well, Mary Lynn manipulated him for years. He's had enough of it. Steve refuses to play those games anymore."

"But Hallie's not like that! And no one knows it better than Steve."

"Another reason—he doesn't want a woman who'll walk out on him at the first sign of a disagreement. If Hallie loves him as much as you think, she should've been willing to work out whatever was wrong."

"That's not how Hallie sees it. She believes Steve will always put Mary Lynn's needs above hers. She decided long ago that if she got married she wanted a man who's as committed to the relationship as she is. Hallie couldn't see Steve committing himself to her alone. I don't blame her, after the way he's behaved."

"Just because he went to help Mary Lynn doesn't mean he doesn't love Hallie."

"You know, I don't think Steve was keen on marrying Hallie." Now it was Todd's turn to frown. "Did she tell you that?"

"Yes...sort of." She sighed. "And now Hallie hasn't mentioned Steve in some time. I hate to pry, but I can see she's miserable. She's deluded herself into thinking this move will be a solution."

"Everything else aside, isn't that running away from him, instead of settling all this?" Todd asked.

"No." The force of Donnalee's feelings drove her out of the rocking chair and to the porch steps, where she sank down, arms resting on her knees. "She doesn't know what else to do. She's in love with Steve, but she's afraid."

"Afraid of what?"

"Steve's feelings for Mary Lynn, and her own for him. She's afraid she's always going to play second fiddle. You have to admit Steve's given her plenty of reason to assume so."

"Mary Lynn's remarried."

"Does that change Steve's feelings for her?"

"I don't know," Todd said reluctantly. "I'd like to think so, but who's to say?"

"Steve?" Donnalee suggested.

"All I can tell you is that he's grieving for Hallie as much as he ever grieved over the end of his marriage."

Donnalee felt an overpowering sadness for Hallie and Steve. "We can't ever let this happen to us," she said, emotion thickening her voice.

"We won't," Todd promised. He moved from the rocker to sit next to her on the step and placed his arm around her shoulders.

"They won't be able to avoid each other at the wedding." She twisted about and leaned against him, absorbing his strength.

"I'd like to think we might be responsible for getting them back together," he murmured into her hair.

"It would be fitting, since it's because of them that *we're* together."

Todd's hand reached inside the opening of her blouse. His fingertips slid close to her breast.

"Todd," she whispered in warning, "you're flirting with temptation."

"Oh, I'm more than flirting with it, Donnalee."

She smiled at him. They slept together every night and joked that they'd be all worn out before the honeymoon. "Will it always be this good with us?" she asked in a whisper.

Todd smiled, as if giving serious consideration to her question. "I certainly hope so. Sometimes after we've made love, I have to stop and pinch myself to believe I've found you."

She shut her eyes and bit her lip when his hand closed firmly around her bare breast. Her body quickly responded; every part of her seemed to release a collective sigh. Taking advantage of her weakness for him, Todd quickly eased his hand between her thighs.

"I went a hell of a long time without a woman in my life and never gave it a thought. But I don't know that I can last ten minutes longer without making love to you." His voice was rough with need.

She moaned stiffly and rolled her head back. "I haven't made the bed yet."

"Good, then we won't need to worry about messing it up."

"Don't you think we should use a bit more restraint?" she asked halfheartedly.

"No." He unfastened the zipper on his jeans. "You're driving me crazy," he said huskily in her ear. He had her blouse completely open now and was molding her breasts with his hands. His kisses left her breathless, his tongue probing her lips and seeking entry.

Donnalee was grateful the property was secluded, seeing that they couldn't keep their hands off each other. She suspected that in time this powerful need of theirs would wane, but it hadn't happened yet and showed no signs of doing so anytime soon.

Todd urged her toward the cabin.

Looping her arms around his neck, Donnalee whispered in his ear. "It's such a beautiful sunny afternoon. Are you *sure* you want to go inside?"

"I'm sure." Without giving her time to argue, he hoisted her over his shoulder and advanced into the cabin.

Donnalee couldn't help laughing, the happiness spilling out of her. "Put me down this instant."

"I have every intention of doing so." He carried her directly into the bedroom and set her on the mattress.

Donnalee smiled up at Todd and was humbled by the love she saw in him. She could search the rest of her life and never find a man she would love more. Slowly she raised her arms to him in open invitation.

"Oh, Todd. I love you so much." Her words were closer to a sigh.

Todd groaned and joined her on the bed, kissing her with a passion that left her head spinning and her thoughts incoherent.

Their lovemaking was wild, wanton and wonderful. Exhausted, they napped afterward. Donnalee awoke to find Todd gently cradling her in his arms.

He kissed the side of her neck. "You're thoughtful again."

"I wish we could do something for Hallie and Steve," she whispered. "I'm tossing her my bridal bouquet," she went on.

"You think that'll help, do you?"

She could hear the smile in Todd's voice. "It certainly won't hurt."

"Is she dating again?" he asked unexpectedly.

"No. What about Steve?"

Todd's shoulders shook with amusement. "You're kidding, right?"

"No. He dates, doesn't he?"

"No. Hallie was the exception."

"She often is the exception," Donnalee murmured, wishing with all her heart that her best friend would experience the kind of happiness she'd found with Todd.

Thirty-Three

The Wedding

Panting and cursing, Hallie dragged the last box out of the bedroom and into the living room. She'd forgotten how much she hated moving, and this time was the most difficult yet. Physically and emotionally exhausted, she slumped onto the sofa. All she had to do now was wait for the movers.

All she had to do now was say goodbye.

It was the task she dreaded most. She knew she was going to miss Steve; she missed him already. She'd taken their friendship for granted and during the past few weeks without him—teasing her, helping her, laughing with her—the world had become a bleak, lonely place.

In an effort to ease the ache in her heart, she'd often stood at her kitchen window and gazed longingly toward his condo. Did he think of her as often as she thought of him? Did he stare out at her place, too? Did he wonder if he'd ever stop feeling so lost and lonely, the way she did?

Moving was supposed to be the answer, the only one she could come up with.

Out of sight, out of mind.

Would it be true?

Unable to stop herself, she glanced through the window at Steve's place. One last time. Just her luck to fall in love with a man who had bowling shoes for brains! She wasn't sure if that thought made her want to laugh or cry—or both.

Out of the corner of her eye, she saw a flash of color; the moving van had arrived. She opened her front door and secured the screen in the open position. The only thing left to do was step aside and let the brawny young men get to work.

Hallie did that, hurrying outside and out of their way. She shuffled aimlessly through the bright leaves that carpeted the lawn. She'd been there for barely a minute when Kenny appeared. He took one look at the movers and charged full speed toward Hallie, arms wide open.

She caught the boy in a hug. Kenny wrapped his thin arms around her neck and held on tight. "Do you *have* to move, Hallie?" he pleaded.

"Yes," she said, hoping he couldn't hear the tears in her voice. "I've got an apartment now." With her condo selling so quickly, she hadn't bought a new place yet. Nothing suited her. She found fault with every home she viewed, exasperating even someone as tolerant as Gabby, her real-estate agent and friend. Time had run out, and Hallie was forced to rent a place, for the next few months, at least, until she came across something she was interested in buying.

"Hallie?" Meagan raced across the yard and threw her arms around Hallie, too. "You're moving already?"

"Looks that way." No one was amused by her feeble joke, least of all herself.

"I don't want you to go," Kenny said, squeezing her neck harder.

Hallie hugged the boy, fighting back the emotion, wanting this to be over quickly because she wasn't sure she could bear much more. After a few moments she loosened Kenny's arms from around her neck. Straightening, she put an arm around his shoulder and held him close to her side. Meagan didn't seem to want to let go of her, either.

"We'll never see you again, will we?" Meagan's question was softly spoken.

"Of course you will!"

"When?" the girl demanded, challenging Hallie to give her a time and a place. "Where?"

"Whenever you want. Wherever you want. Just say the word and I'll find a way to be there." Hallie meant that. No matter how painful it was, she wouldn't abandon Meagan and Kenny. "Here," she said, handing them each a folded piece of paper. "This is my new address and phone number. I'll be on Federal Way—it's not too far. You can call me anytime, and visit, too."

Meagan read the information, but it didn't appear to satisfy her. "It won't be the same."

Hallie couldn't argue with that. "No, it won't be the same."

In what seemed like only minutes, the movers had everything she owned loaded in their truck. She checked the condo one last time to be sure they hadn't missed anything, Meagan and Kenny trailing along behind her. When she'd finished, Hallie discovered Steve standing outside.

They stared at each other, she on the top step and he on the grass.

"Meagan and Kenny are with me," she said, thinking he'd come looking for his children.

"I know. I thought I'd come and tell you goodbye myself."

"Oh." She couldn't think of a single sensible comment. As it was, she had to restrain herself from running into his arms. She ached for him, for his comfort. Her throat hurt from the effort it cost to hold back her tears. Her whole body shook with suppressed longing.

This was hell, she decided. Saying goodbye to Steve and his children, walking away, not knowing if she'd see him again after Donnalee and Todd's wedding. Hoping, wishing, praying things could be different—and knowing they couldn't.

"We're ready now, miss," one of the movers shouted from the cab of the truck.

Hallie briefly turned her attention from Steve. "I'll be right there."

"Don't worry, lady," the second man shouted back. "We're getting paid by the hour. Take as long as you need." The two men laughed.

Steve's hands were buried deep in his pants pockets. "You'd better go."

She nodded. Kenny and Meagan crowded around her.

"Hallie says we can come visit her new place anytime. Can we Dad?"

His gaze continued to hold hers. "If it's okay with Hallie."

"I'd like that, Steve. I'm going to miss...all of you." Her original intention had been to say only the children's names, but that would have been a lie. She'd miss him more. She'd mourn him, yearn for him, cry over him.

"Goodbye, Hallie."

"Goodbye, Steve."

While she still had the courage, she deliberately turned her back to him and locked the front door. Then she dropped a kiss on each child's head and raced past Steve to her car.

The dress Donnalee had chosen for Hallie to wear as maid of honor was one of the most beautiful she'd ever owned. It was simple and elegant, a pale rose that did wonders for her skin. She felt beautiful in it. And thin. Every time she studied her reflection, all she could think of was Steve's reaction when he saw her. But then, thinking about Steve had become something of a pasttime. No, an obsession. Every night she went to bed thinking about him; every morning she woke up to those same thoughts of him.

"He'll go out of his mind," Donnalee whispered.

It took Hallie a moment to realize her best friend was talking about Todd when he saw his wife-to-be in her wedding dress.

"Yes, he will," Hallie confirmed.

The wedding itself was going to be a brief simple ceremony, with only Steve and Hallie as attendants. The guests were family and a few select friends. Not so for the reception; Donnalee and Todd had built strong friendships through the years and wanted to invite as many of their friends as possible to share in their joy. There would be dinner, dancing, drinks.

Hallie hadn't seen Steve in two weeks. Fourteen days. That didn't seem so long, but it felt like fourteen years. She'd eagerly looked forward to the wedding...and yet she'd dreaded it more each day.

She longed to see him, yet was afraid to see him. She was afraid of reviving, strengthening, her love for Steve, afraid of suffering the loneliness, the sense of loss all over again. She wasn't sure she could go through it a second time.

Her gaze automatically sought him out as the four of them crowded around Pastor Channing in the small chapel. Steve's eyes met hers, and with effort she managed to offer him a smile. One that wasn't returned. She quickly looked away.

The ceremony, short though it was, moved Hallie to tears. Donnalee and Todd gazed at each other, wrapped up in their love. For Hallie, their happiness was almost painful to see, and yet she was thrilled for her friends.

Steve stood there stiffly throughout the ceremony. Other than those first few moments, he completely ignored her. When they all signed the wedding certificate, Hallie's hand trembled. Steve showed no sign of emotion, his signature strong and bold.

Donnalee and Todd had hired a vintage 1928 Ford to drive them from the church to the reception at a nearby hotel.

Once they'd climbed into the car amid clapping and cheers, Meagan hurried to Hallie's side. "Hallie, Hallie!" She clamped her arms around Hallie's waist. "You look so pretty. Doesn't she, Dad?" she called to Steve, who was standing a few feet away.

"Lovely," he responded, and lowered his mask long enough to let his appreciation show in his eyes.

His brief admiring look greatly boosted Hallie's sagging spirits.

"Dad's new neighbors moved in and they don't have kids." This disgruntled remark came from Kenny. The boy wore an obviously new suit, complete with tie. Hallie would wager it had taken a good deal of talking and bribing before Kenny agreed to the outfit.

"The new neighbors are okay," Meagan said.

Hallie had met the young couple and thought they were extremely nice. "I'm sure they'll have children soon enough."

"What bothers the kids most is that the new neighbors aren't you," Steve explained with a shrug. "But that's life. People come and people go. They'll adjust, just like I have." He seemed to be going out of his way to tell her he didn't miss her, didn't need her. That whatever he'd felt for her was gone.

"We all miss you, Hallie," Meagan said, as if to counter her father's cruel words. "It doesn't seem right without you there."

It didn't feel right to her, either, but she certainly couldn't say so.

The hotel where the reception was being held was filled with guests by the time they arrived. Applause broke out when Donnalee and Todd stepped inside the gaily decorated room. Hallie stood in the reception line between Donnalee and her parents. Todd stood next to Steve, and Steve next to Todd's mother and father.

Hallie gave up counting the number of hands she shook and the number of names she heard. Remembering everyone was a lost cause, so she just smiled and shook hands.

The reception line was followed by dinner. Hallie and Steve were assigned to the head table with Donnalee and Todd. She found him staring at her once, and she smiled, hoping to lessen the tension between them. She wasn't sure if it was the baked salmon or the champagne that went with it, but Steve finally began to relax. She did, too.

Once the staff had removed the dishes and the wedding cake was served, the music started. Donnalee and Todd danced the first dance, holding each other close. As was tradition, Steve escorted Hallie onto the floor next, but from the loose way he held her, she might as well have been his sister.

They'd never danced together before. What amazed her was how coordinated their movements were, almost as if they'd been partners for years. Almost as if her body sensed and followed his body's movements.

When the music ended, she thought she heard Steve sigh with relief.

"Come on, Steve, it wasn't so bad, was it?"

He stared at her blankly.

"Dancing with me," she elaborated.

He reached for a fresh glass of champagne. "Bad enough."

"I didn't step on your toes, did I?"

"No," he muttered, "just my heart."

"What about *my* heart?" she asked, angered by his response.

"I must say it looks mighty fine in that dress you're wearing. Let me guess who picked it out. Donnalee, right?'' He didn't wait for her to answer. ''The woman's too smart for her own good.''

''What's that supposed to mean?''

''It means it's time for me to shut up and sit down before I make an even bigger ass of myself.'' He strode off the dance floor.

Hallie wasn't about to let him stop now, so she ran after him. If he realized she was right behind him, he didn't show it. Steve sat down at the table where Meagan and Kenny awaited him. A balding middle-aged man, Todd's uncle by marriage if Hallie remembered correctly, caught her by the arm.

''How come a pretty little gal like you doesn't have a dance partner?'' He slid his arm securely about her waist and Hallie could see that Todd's uncle had had a few drinks too many.

''I'm so sorry, Harry,'' she said. ''I've already promised this dance to my friend.''

''Your friend?''

Hallie winked at Kenny and held out her hand. ''I believe you wanted this dance?''

Kenny leapt to his feet and, taking her hand, led Hallie toward the dance floor. The music was fast-paced and lighthearted. Kenny solemnly clenched her hands in his as they stepped onto the polished oak floor.

''Dad needs another bowling partner,'' Kenny announced. ''I told him he should ask you.''

''Really?'' Hallie didn't know how to respond.

''He said you wouldn't be interested.''

''He did?''

''Are you?'' Kenny pressed.

''I...I'm not sure.''

''Is it 'cause you have a new boyfriend?''

Hallie smiled and shook her head. ''No.''

Kenny was silent for a couple of minutes. ''Did you know Kip's back?''

''Yes—Meagan told me.'' Although Hallie wasn't sure of the details.

''He's divorced. Mom thought he might be a big-mist, but he's not.''

''I'm glad to hear that.'' Hallie could appreciate the worry Mary Lynn had suffered while that mess got itself sorted out. It explained, too, what the big crisis had been when Steve disappeared overnight. Not for the first time, she felt guilty of overreaction that miserable Monday morning.

"I asked Dad if he was going to marry again. You wanna know what he said?"

"No."

Kenny acted as if he hadn't heard her. "He said that if he couldn't marry you, there wasn't anyone else he was interested in. He decided to join a men's bowling league this year."

Hallie wasn't sure of the significance of the men's bowling league, but she did understand the first part of what Kenny had told her. Her heart felt weak with excitement.

"Excuse me." She heard Steve's familiar voice behind her. "I'd like to cut in."

"Sure, Dad." Kenny beamed his father a huge smile and walked off the dance floor.

Thirty-Four

The Wedding Bouquet

Steve couldn't figure out what had prompted him to ask Hallie to dance. One thing was sure: the minute she walked into his embrace he was sorry he'd asked her. Her body, all soft and feminine, gently gliding into his arms, was the purest form of torture he'd ever experienced.

Steve closed his eyes. This was heaven. No, it was hell. He didn't want to feel the things he did for this woman, but had found himself incapable of *not* feeling them. Of forgetting. She haunted his dreams, and seemingly dissatisfied with that, she haunted every waking minute, as well.

As luck would have it, the music was slow and sultry. He noticed that neither of them felt compelled to speak. Steve suspected he couldn't have gotten a word out, even if he'd known what to say. Hallie in his arms again was enough. It felt incredibly good—too damn good. He scowled. She was the one who'd slammed the door in his face. She was the one who'd put her house on the market and moved. Talk about cutting her losses! With little more than a backward glance, she'd cast him out of her life. Well, a man had his pride, and although it had been mighty cold comfort, he wasn't crawling back to her. No, siree. Not him.

Nor was he interested in a woman who hightailed it out at the first sign of trouble. What irked him most was that their entire argument had centered on Mary Lynn. She'd called him in great relief a few days after her panic attack and told him Kip *had* gotten the divorce and had shown her the papers to prove it. While he was pleased Mary Lynn wasn't involved with a bigamist, her news had come too late to help him. He'd already lost Hallie.

The music ended and they parted, and both of their own accord moved off the dance floor and in different directions, Steve to his table where the kids were waiting, and Hallie to another. Over the next couple of hours Steve noticed that Hallie danced with a number of other partners. He stopped counting how many after six. When he couldn't stand to watch any longer, he turned his back to the dance floor. He had another glass of champagne, danced with Meagan and then with someone's great-aunt.

"Aren't you going to dance with Hallie again?" Kenny asked.

"No." He downed the last of his champagne in one big gulp, then snared a fresh glass from a passing waiter. He drank enough to dull the ache in his heart and increase the one in his groin. That he'd never gone to bed with Hallie was a blessing in disguise. He wanted her even now. He couldn't, wouldn't, lie to himself about that. But he feared that if they *had* made love, he'd never have found the strength to let her walk out of his life.

"Did you ask her to be your bowling partner?" Meagan demanded.

Steve shook his head. He could tell he was a big disappointment to his children. They loved Hallie. Well, they weren't alone, but a man had his limits.

"Hallie's not dating anyone," Kenny told him. "I asked her."

"Let's talk about something else, all right?"

"Mom's remarried," Meagan reminded him, tugging at his sleeve.

His daughter's assessment caught him off guard. He didn't need anyone to remind him that Mary Lynn was out of his life. It was Hallie he wanted, Hallie he longed for. Hallie who owned his heart.

Without questioning the right or wrong of it, he set the champagne glass aside and strolled across the room to where she was standing. The music had started again. Another slow ballad.

Wordlessly he offered her his hand. She hesitated before giving him hers. Then he led the way to the dance floor.

"We already danced," she whispered, sounding nervous. "Twice."

"I know. The first two times were for appearance's sake. This time it's for me." He brought her close, close enough to feel her breasts against his chest. Close enough to tell her without words the powerful effect she had on him.

She held herself stiff and unyielding. "For you? I don't understand."

"You seem to forget I was denied the pleasure of making love to you."

Her chin shot up to a lofty angle. "Not for lack of opportunity."

"I'll admit the fault was my own."

This seemed to appease her. "It seems this may well be my last chance," he said.

"You're not making any sense. Maybe we should stop now."

"Not on your life." He moistened the side of her neck with the tip of his tongue and was gratified to feel reaction ripple through her.

"Steve...I don't think this is a good idea." Her protest was weak. He saw she'd closed her eyes and seemed to have trouble holding up her head.

While his options were limited, especially with his children looking on, Steve didn't let the mere fact that two hundred people were watching stand in his way. His imagination would work just fine. With his mouth close to her ear, he told her in scintillating detail how he'd planned to love her. How he'd dreamed of it every night since, thought of little else but having her in his bed—and in his life.

While their bodies swayed gently to the music, he held her mesmerized with a whispered account of how he'd intended to satiate their need for each other. Sparing nothing, he told her all they'd missed, all that their pride had cost them.

He didn't know that his words were having the desired effect until he heard her soft gasp against his throat.

The music ended, but they didn't leave the dance floor. Didn't move out of each other's embrace. His arms tightened as he realized that if he lost Hallie this time, he'd forever regret it.

He'd assumed, he'd hoped, that the music would start again. It didn't. Instead, there was an announcement that Donnalee was about to throw the bridal bouquet.

Hallie eased herself out of Steve's arms, keeping her gaze lowered.

Steve glanced over his shoulder to discover that a group of eager young women had gathered around Donnalee, jockeying for position.

Donnalee stood on tiptoe. "Hallie, where are you?"

"I...have to go."

"So I see," he muttered, more than a little disgruntled.

She moved away from him, joining the entourage crowding the bride. Hallie made her way to the back and raised her arms. Once she saw her best friend, Donnalee turned and blithely tossed the bouquet over her shoulder.

It seemed to Steve that she aimed for Hallie, but it wasn't Hallie who captured the prize. A girl, hardly older than Meagan, leapt a good three feet off the ground and grabbed the bouquet in midair. Grumbles and murmurs followed as the teenager displayed the prize, waving it exuberantly over her head. Steve smiled at her display of joy, but when he went to look for Hallie again, he discovered she was gone.

Gone.

The best Steve could figure, she'd disappeared with Donnalee, who had changed out of her wedding dress and into a pretty pink suit before leaving with Todd for the airport.

She'd be back, he reassured himself. He could be patient; considering how long he'd waited already, a few extra minutes wouldn't hurt.

Hallie never did return to the reception.

Defeated, Steve sat with Meagan and Kenny. It was for the best, he tried to convince himself. It was over. That was the way she wanted it. From this point on, there'd be no need to see each other again.

Steve didn't believe any of it.

As soon as he could leave without seeming impolite, Steve took his kids home. They both seemed tired and out of sorts, and his own mood wasn't much better. But despite his misgivings about being with Hallie again, he'd enjoyed the wedding. He'd certainly enjoyed dancing with her.

Today had brought back all the memories and all the hopes, the recollections of what could have been. Todd's happiness pleased him and at the same time made him conscious of his own loneliness. It also emboldened him. Maybe it wasn't too late for him and Hallie....

"I'm going to bed," Kenny said as soon as they got home. He'd already removed the suit coat and was working on the tie.

"I am, too," Meagan chimed, yanking off her party shoes.

"I'm going out," Steve announced.

Meagan and Kenny stopped what they were doing and stared.

"Where are you going?"

The decision made, Steve didn't hesitate. "To talk to Hallie."

Kenny inserted two fingers in his mouth and let out a whistle loud enough to shatter crystal. Then he and Meagan exchanged high tens, slapping hands with their arms raised above their heads.

"Go for it, Dad."

"Yeah!" Kenny had finally managed to pull off his tie, and now he twirled it around like a New Year's streamer. "We want you to marry her."

"A lot has to be decided before we talk about marriage." Unsure how this meeting would go, Steve didn't want to build up his children's expectations.

"I knew she was the one for you ages ago," Meagan said, sounding very much like the teenager she was soon to become. It wouldn't be long now before she was convinced she was far wiser than any of the adults in her life.

"I said so first," Kenny argued.

"No, *I* did," Meagan returned with an air of superiority. "I told you I thought Hallie would be a good wife for Dad the very first time we met her. Remember?"

Whether or not he did, Kenny wasn't about to admit it.

"I don't know how long I'll be," Steve said.

"Take your time," Meagan told him.

"All the time you need," his son added.

Steve hurried out to his car, and as he started the engine, he saw Meagan and Kenny standing in the window, watching him. He waved and they excitedly waved back.

On the short drive to Federal Way, Steve mulled over his approach. After a quick stop at the grocery, he pulled into the guest parking lot at her new complex. It took him another ten minutes to find her apartment. After checking the number against the one listed on the folded sheet of notebook paper, he stepped onto the porch. If the lights were any indication, she was home.

His head was spinning, his skin was clammy, and his heart was dangling precariously from his sleeve when he pushed her doorbell. The door opened and his carefully thought-out greeting stuck in his throat.

A man answered. "Yes?" He was tall and young, too young for Hallie.

"I must have the wrong number." Frowning, Steve glanced down at his paper a second time, wondering if he'd copied the information incorrectly.

"Are you looking for Hallie McCarthy?"

Steve's face shot up. "Yes."

"Then come on in. She's in the bedroom with the baby."

Steve realized he was frowning again.

"I'm Jason, Julie's husband."

"Ah, yes." As Steve told him who he was and the two exchanged handshakes, Steve remembered that Julie was Hallie's little sister. Baby Ellen's mother. Come to think of it, Hallie owed him major bucks for his help in getting the baby to sleep that night last spring.

"Julie and I are on our way to Hawaii, and we're spending the night with Hallie before we catch a flight in the morning."

"I see," Steve muttered. His timing couldn't have been worse. "Perhaps I should talk to Hallie later." Not knowing what else to do with the bouquet of yellow roses he'd bought, he set them on top of the television.

He was halfway to the parking lot when he heard Hallie shout his name. He turned, shoulders squared, back rigid.

"If you walk away from me now, Steve Marris, there'll be hell to pay."

Hallie stood there, arms akimbo. "Is there a reason you brought me flowers?"

"Yes," he said, playing it cool. "It's a wedding bouquet. You were cheated back there and I wanted to give you another chance to catch it."

"Are you going to provide the groom to go with those flowers?" she asked, not missing a beat.

"That all depends," he called back. It seemed silly to be standing half a football field apart shouting at each other. He took several steps in her direction. She did likewise. They stopped with about five feet still between them.

"Why are you here?" she asked softly, her beautiful eyes pleading with him to say what she wanted to hear. "And if you tell me it's because you need a bowling partner, you go straight to jail."

"If I told you I loved you, would that get me past Go so I can collect my two hundred dollars?"

"It's a step in the right direction."

He grinned.

"Why do you love me?" she asked.

"Why?" Of all the things he'd expected her to say, this wasn't it. He rubbed his hand along the back of his neck, giving her a puzzled look. "No one told me there'd be a test."

"Is it so difficult?"

"No." But he had to get the answer right; he didn't want there to be any room for doubt.

"Because of Meagan and Kenny?"

"No." He smiled as he said it. "Do you want me to count the ways?"

"It might help."

"I love you, Hallie, for who you are. For the way you love my children. For the way your eyes light up when you're excited. I love the crazy way you throw a bowling ball and still manage to knock down pins. I think you bake the best chocolate-chip cookies I've ever tasted."

"What about my chicken dinner?"

"It's wonderful, and so are you."

It seemed to him that her eyes were especially bright. He said, "You're zany and stubborn and strong-willed and wonderful. I'm crazy about you."

"IIow crazy?"

"Crazy enough to know I'm going to love you the rest of my

life—and to know you're the best friend I'm ever going to find. Crazy enough to ask you to marry me."

"Marry you?"

He nodded. "That's why I brought a bridal bouquet."

"Bingo."

Steve laughed out loud. "Wrong game. All I want is to get past Go, collect what's due me and spend the rest of my life making love to you."

Hurrying forward, Hallie stumbled into his arms. He caught her and lifted her from the pavement, his arms tight around her waist. If he didn't kiss her soon, he'd go mad.

As if reading his thoughts, her mouth haphazardly searched for his. The kiss was hungry, even rough, a kiss without subtlety or gentleness. It took several more such kisses to appease the pent-up longing. Then, and only then, was he capable of truly appreciating the woman in his arms. He set her back down on the pavement and his hands were in her hair. Her ragged breath was warm against his skin. He inhaled her clean distinctive scent.

"That was the lowest, dirtiest trick anyone ever played on me," she told him, her hands clasped behind his neck.

"What was?"

"Making love to me on the dance floor. Do you have a clue what you were doing to me?"

"I was experiencing the same thing myself. Do you forgive me?"

She nodded, but her thoughts seemed a thousand miles away. "We're going to be married, and if you so much as *think* of sleeping with Mary Lynn again, I'll claw your eyes out."

He lowered his head enough so she'd see and hear the truth in his words. "I didn't sleep with her."

"Fine. If you ever lie down in the same bed with her, then."

"Agreed."

"It's all or nothing with me, Steve Marris."

"Hey, I wasn't the one who packed up and moved out at the first sign of trouble."

Hallie shook her head as if she regretted that. "I was trying to protect myself. I love you too much to lose you, and hell, I didn't know my condo was going to sell that fast."

"Lose me?"

"To Mary Lynn."

"Not hardly. It's true I didn't want the divorce, but it happened and there's no way to go back now. Mary Lynn has apparently found what she wants, and she's welcome to it. By the same token, I've found you."

"I...I didn't think you wanted to marry me."

"I don't take that kind of commitment lightly, Hallie. It's all or nothing with me, too."

She cupped his jaw and spread a dozen kisses over his face, her aim less than perfect; nevertheless, they had the desired effect—as she discovered when he pulled her close against him.

Suddenly she raised her eyes to his. He saw they'd gone dark and serious. "What about children?"

He'd given fair consideration to that question himself. Hallie wanted a family, and he wanted to be the one to father her children. "I got pretty good at the diapering business. I imagine I can dust off those skills for a new baby."

She let out a small happy cry.

"Right now I'm far more interested in making that baby," he said with a lascivious wink.

Pure happiness radiated from her entire being. Giggling, Hallie tossed back her head. "Me, too. Oh, Steve, I love you—and I want you so much—but..." She glanced over her shoulder. "We have to go to your place. My sister and her husband are in town for the night."

He groaned in frustration. "I've got Meagan and Kenny."

Hallie banged her forehead repeatedly against his shoulder.

"Can you believe it?" he said. "We're finally ready to make love and we can't find anyplace to do it."

Snuggling in his arms, Hallie kissed the underside of his jaw. "Let's be patient. We've got an entire lifetime."

Steve closed his eyes and wondered if a single lifetime was long enough to love Hallie properly—in bed and out of it.

Then again, he'd soon find out.

Epilogue

January 1—two years later

Unlike the past few years, I won't take time to be poetic and inspired. I'm a married woman now, and much too tired and happy. Steve is thrilled that Travis decided to make his debut a week early—for the simple reason that we can deduct him on our income tax! For my part, I could have used an extra week's sleep.

Our baby is so beautiful. Steve made me promise I wouldn't say that. Baby boys aren't supposed to be beautiful, but the only other word that suits him is *perfect.* Steve's delighted to have another son to share guy things with. He's such a wonderful, natural father, but, of course, I knew that!

Every time I remember the afternoon I went into labor, I start to laugh. Steve was so calm about everything. He'd assured me again and again that he knew what to do, that I didn't have a thing to worry about. He got so involved in the breathing techniques, he had everyone in his bowling league trained. He must have read ten books and quoted them so often, it was all I could do to listen.

Finally it happened. D-day (*D* for delivery). I'd been to the doctor the day before and he'd assured me labor could start at any time. Steve had his beeper with him. Meagan and Kenny had theirs, too. I think everyone was thoroughly disappointed that they were all at the house when my water broke. They'd been looking forward to getting beeped!

Then my levelheaded, oh-so-prepared husband lost it. When he saw me in pain, when he realized his new child was about to be born, he couldn't remember a thing. I wasn't much help. What surprised me was the intensity of the labor pains. I'd read and heard a lot about labor, but this wasn't like anything I'd anticipated. It hurt, right away. No gradual increase for me. Travis wanted to make his debut as quickly as possible.

With the first contraction—which was like a kick in the stomach—I doubled over and groaned. Steve immediately started barking orders like a drill sergeant. He had Meagan, Kenny and my suitcase in the car and was halfway down the driveway before he realized he'd forgotten something. Me. That flustered him even more, and he ran a stop sign. Meagan was shouting at him and Kenny, whose job it was to time the contractions, miscounted and said they were only thirty seconds apart. Convinced he'd never make it to the hospital in time, Steve pulled over to the side of the road and announced he'd have to deliver the baby himself. Before I could persuade him otherwise, he'd slapped on a pair of latex gloves and donned a surgical gown. Where he got it I'll never know.

Meagan took one look at me and rolled her eyes. Thank heaven she remained sane during all of this! By the time we arrived at the hospital, I was at the wheel. Kenny was in the back seat with his father, fanning him with the instructions for an emergency delivery. Meagan was in the front with me, and the two of us panted together.

All's well that ends well, as they say. Things moved quickly once we got to the hospital, and the birth was textbook perfect. Travis was born five hours later, and it was a contest to see who cried loudest, father or son.

Meagan and Kenny are thrilled with their little brother. Kenny's so pleased to have another boy in the family, and Meagan has to fight her father for the privilege of changing the baby's diaper!

I love being a mother. The other morning as I held Travis to my breast I felt tears in my eyes at the sheer wonder and joy of this little one in my arms. To think he's actually a part of me and Steve, that he came from my body. I thought about Dad, too. I'm sorry he wasn't here to welcome his first grandson. He'd be so proud to know we named Travis after him. Travis Douglas is a pretty big name for such a little boy.

I feel whole now, complete. The emotional void that opened up in me after Dad died doesn't seem as deep anymore. I have Steve now, and our family.

Two years ago when I first decided I wanted a husband and family, I had no idea how far this adventure would take me. But I'm actually glad I delayed it, because otherwise I wouldn't be married to Steve and I wouldn't be a stepmom to Meagan and Kenny—and we wouldn't have Travis. I can't imagine what my life would be like without them.

I sat down this morning with a cup of Seattle's finest coffee—

brought to me by my husband—and my goal planner. Just as I do every January 1. It didn't take me long to realize that my goals have shifted from my business to my home life. For now, anyway.

And that's just fine. This matter of marriage—and motherhood—couldn't have worked out better!

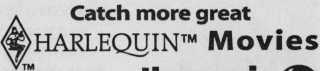
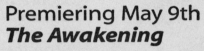

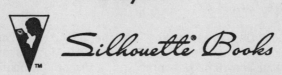

In **July 1998** comes

THE MACKENZIE FAMILY

by *New York Times* bestselling author

LINDA HOWARD

The dynasty continues with:

Mackenzie's Pleasure: Rescuing a pampered ambassador's daughter from her terrorist kidnappers was a piece of cake for navy SEAL Zane Mackenzie. It was only afterward, when they were alone together, that the real danger began....

Mackenzie's Magic: Talented trainer Maris Mackenzie was wanted for horse theft, but with no memory, she had little chance of proving her innocence or eluding the real villains. Her only hope for salvation? The stranger in her bed.

Available this July for the first time ever in a two-in-one trade-size edition. Fall in love with the Mackenzies for the first time—or all over again!

Available at your favorite retail outlet.

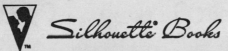

HERE COME THE
Virgin Brides!

Celebrate the joys of first love with more unforgettable stories from Romance's brightest stars:

SWEET BRIDE OF REVENGE
by Suzanne Carey—June 1998 (SR #1300)

Reader favorite Suzanne Carey weaves a sensuously powerful tale about a man who forces the daughter of his enemy to be his bride of revenge. But what happens when this hardhearted husband falls head over heels...for his wife?

THE BOUNTY HUNTER'S BRIDE
by Sandra Steffen—July 1998 (SR #1306)

In this provocative page-turner by beloved author Sandra Steffen, a shotgun wedding is only the beginning when an injured bounty hunter and the sweet seductress who'd nursed him to health are discovered in a remote mountain cabin by her gun-toting dad and *four* brothers!

SUDDENLY...MARRIAGE!
by Marie Ferrarella—August 1998 (SR #1312)

RITA Award-winning author Marie Ferrarella weaves a magical story set in sultry New Orleans about two people determined to remain single who exchange vows in a mock ceremony during Mardi Gras, only to learn their bogus marriage is the real thing....

And look for more VIRGIN BRIDES in future months, only in—

♥ *Silhouette* ROMANCE™

Available at your favorite retail outlet.

Look us up on-line at: http://www.romance.net   SRVBJ-A-T

Watch for this title by
New York Times
bestselling phenomenon

JAYNE
ANN
KRENTZ

Katherine Inskip's life is at a standstill: she is completely overworked, stressed out and indifferent to love—not a great situation for a romance writer to find herself in. She desperately needs some "R & R." A South Seas vacation—complete with sun and surf—sounds perfect. But relaxation is the last thing on Katherine's mind when she meets Jared, the dashing owner of the island resort…and descendant of a famous and ruthless South Seas pirate.

MJAK437-T

THE PIRATE

Available in May 1998
wherever books are sold.

MIRA